INTRODUCTION
Stephen Baxter

The Book of the River (1984), now happily reissued with its two sequels *The Book of the Stars* (1984) and *The Book of Being* (1986) in this new omnibus edition, was not the first Ian Watson novel I read. But it has always remained one of my favourites.

Watson is a master storyteller: that's what first grabs you as you enter *Yaleen's* complex river-country. This is a tale of people doing things, such as making boats and pots and little Jules Verne diving kits to cross the dangerous river that cuts through their fascinating world. And Yaleen herself is one of science fiction's great heroines.

But as the story opens out you start to realise that a new myth is being created here.

A river called the Black Current divides Yaleen's world in two, separating not just one bank from another, but rational from irrational, men from women (Watson says this work is a "feminist utopia, but nobody noticed") and, in the end, Yaleen's past from her future. This kind of dialectic, opposites built into the structure of the imagined universe, is a pattern that runs right through Watson's work, but rarely is it realised so clearly as here.

And then of course this is a river, a key mythic element for a species like us who probably evolved along coasts and water-courses. Watson says his river-beast may have been subconsciously influenced by another great river of the genre, the one in Philip Jose Farmer's Riverworld series. And as this new edition is published our troops are once again on the banks of the Euphrates, perhaps mankind's archetypal river, which Watson visited in his later work *Whores of Babylon* (1988).

All this adds up to a new myth of startling clarity. Watson, digging into our minds as well as our universes, has always been a myth-maker, and in his major *Books of Mana* sequence (from 1991) he explored Finnish myths. What makes Watson's myths so interesting is that unlike, say, Tolkien, he does not draw on rather tired analyses of existing bodies of myth but goes deeper, taking the myths apart to see how they work, and how they reflect what makes us human in the first place. In the dialectical structure of his river-world, for instance, Watson has said he drew on the work of the anthropologist Lévi-Strauss, who analyses structures of human behaviour in terms of binary alternatives.

So the story begins with Yaleen and her river. But it soon opens out further, as the deeper structure of Watson's universe is revealed. A Godmind dominates this reality, a numinous monster with a megalomaniac intention to exploit the consciousnesses of humanity for its own ends. Yaleen must ultimately confront this deranged deity, and to do so she must endure transcendence—and "endure" is the right word, for this transformation, which is thrust on her rather than chosen (another characteristic of Watson's books), is as painful as any birth. Thus in this way as in others *Yaleen* gives you a flavour of many of Watson's novels, which springboard from tight central concerns to much larger scales. The notion of transcendence is also visited in books like *The Jonah Kit* (1975). But rarely have such immense perspectives have been developed from such small-scale beginnings as in the story of Yaleen.

And then there is language. One of the most intriguing passages for me is an introspective meditation by Yaleen, stranded in solitude on the "wrong" side of the river:

> I tried to count the number of conversations I could remember in detail from the previous few months compared with the happier days of yore. It wasn't a rewarding pursuit. There weren't all that many. If I could put it this way, what I had been living all that

time was narrative rather than dialogue. I'd made myself into something of a third person so that what happened to her didn't fully affect me. . . . People, how I yearned for them now that there were none.

So Yaleen, alone, is forced to analyse her own consciousness, and she does so in terms of story, of language.

A central concern in much of Watson's fiction has been the interplay of communication, language and perception: how language affects our sense of self. This finds expression in Watson's very first novel, *The Embedding* (1973), which, in an exploration of competing hypotheses about how grammar may be innate, but language shapes our perception of reality, toys with the notion of alien languages and a general grammar of the universe. Later, in *Alien Embassy* (1977), Watson wrote about powers who attempt to control us through the manipulation of language and perception— prescient in these days of spin, embedded reporting and the rest. Moreover, the passage quoted above actually prefigures Watson's later exposure to the ideas of Daniel Dennett and others on the nature of consciousness, and how a story told to the self is at the heart of our sense of being.

Before becoming a full-time writer in 1976, Ian Watson studied English at Oxford University. He worked as a lecturer in literature in Tanzania and Tokyo; he would say these experiences exposed him to an alien culture and the future respectively, a good idea for a writer of science fiction. In Birmingham he taught one of the first academic courses in science fiction in the UK, under the guise of "Complementary Studies." But, remarkably for a writer who has explored the subjects so deeply in his fiction, he is self-taught in such matters as linguistics and the nature of consciousness. Watson's intellectual fiction has often earned him comparison with HG Wells (such as in the

Encyclopaedia of Science Fiction edited by John Clute and Peter Nicholls, 1993)—and their interests overlap too; interestingly, Watson recently discovered a doctoral thesis written by Wells in 1942 on the nature of consciousness, again prefiguring the work of Dennett and others.

Yaleen was Ian Watson's major project of the 1980s, and it encapsulates many of the themes which have dominated his work before and since. In the end, though, the story is the thing, and what carries you through these pages is the tough, loveable, enduring figure of Yaleen herself, as she struggles through rites of passage, river-crossings and finally transcendence—a whole series of rebirths. The effect is expansive and uplifting. The universe is a bigger and more complicated place than we realise, Watson seems to be telling us, and we can only ever apprehend it partially anyhow. And yet we can endure; and yet there is hope.

In recent years Ian Watson's name has become more widely known for his vigorous novels set in a popular games-based universe (beginning with *Inquisitor,* 1990), and his involvement with the Kubrick-Spielberg movie *AI.* But he has been a well-respected and much-loved figure in science fiction for more than thirty years, and I am proud to say a good personal friend to me and my wife. I am delighted that BenBella's new omnibus edition has brought Yaleen and her remarkable universe back into my life.

Stephen Baxter is the author of eleven science fiction novels. He is a 1999 recipient of the Philip K. Dick award for his work Vacuum Diagrams *and received the 2001 British Science Fiction Award for his short story "First to the Moon!" He is also vice president of the British Science Fiction Association.*

THE BOOK

OF THE

RIVER

CONTENTS

*F*ROM time immemorial no boat had crossed the river on account of the black current. Yet of course that did not stop us from plying our trade up and down the eastern shoreline all the way from Ajelobo in the south down to Umdala in the north where the river fattens out vastly, becoming salt not fresh, and storm-tossed. And it had always been my ambition as a little girl in dusty Pecawar—almost midway along the axis of our navigation—to join the boating guild and be a riverwoman.

And why not? reasoned my parents. At least that's the brave face they put on my decision (or so I thought at the time). I wouldn't remain on the river forever, but would be bound to find myself a man sooner or later somewhere along those seven hundred leagues of shore between north and south and bring him home to Pecawar to settle him there to raise our family, and probably settle with him —just as other girls took passage in the spring and returned in the autumn with a newly claimed husband. In my case it might simply take a little longer, but surely I would tire of wanderlust. The river, though richly varied from the southern jungles to the cold northern marshes, is hardly infinite. So after five or six years of sailing up and down it I ought to be all too familiar with change for its own sake.

My twin brother, Capsi, as though perversely determined to play west to my north and south, had set his heart on joining the tiny monkish fraternity of observers down in the town of Verrino fifty leagues to the north; about whom we knew little enough in Pecawar, apart from the mere fact of their existence—but this was enough for Capsi. From an early age he had peered through a succession of home-made spyglasses over the league-and-a-half of river—beyond the black current that streams midway—at the western shore, even though this is quite blank and barren opposite Pecawar.

I myself had no interest at all in the western shore. Nor did anyone else that I knew of, apart from brother Capsi and those obsessives in Verrino. Why should we be interested in what was unattainable and incommunicative, and which had no effect whatever on our lives, nor had for as far back as records went?

But all this changed subtly when, at seventeen, the very minimum age, I applied for membership of the River Guild, and so learned their first guarded secret, the very existence of which I was sworn, upon *The Book of the River,* to keep secret. Namely, that one did not merely sign on, but must be initiated.

"But what *sort* of initiation is it?" I asked the quaymistress in her clapboard office down on the waterfront, after I had sworn and been told. For I associated the word initiation with strange painful rituals up in the Ajelobo tropics.

"Child, do you wish to travel as passenger, or crew?"

"Crew, of course."

"Then you must be initiated, whatever form this takes." The quaymistress laughed, and tossed her sun-bleached hair. She was a handsome, weather-beaten woman of late middle age. She held up her hands, palms out. "See, we don't chop off fingers. Nor do we keelhaul you, or toss you to the stingers, or anything savage like that! We don't really even haze you, or terrify you. I assure you my hair didn't go white from fear."

I nodded, and she rightly took my silence for consent.

"There's a lateen-rig due in tomorrow afternoon. Be here at sunset." With that she dismissed me, and delved back into her manifests.

So the following evening I duly presented myself and was taken by the quaymistress on board the *Ruby Piglet,* and down below deck to the boatmistress's poky cabin, lit by a single oil lantern; and by now I wasn't so much worried as to the nature of the initiation—which in this setting, it seemed to me, could hardly be spectacular or exotic—as that I might somehow be committing myself to sail the river on board *this* cramped tub. I'd had grander visions in mind, of two masts or three. A brig or a schooner.

When we knocked and entered, the boatmistress was wearing a fish-mask, such as we see at the regatta once a year; nothing particularly daunting in that, even if the lantern light did lend more credence to the illusion of a woman with a piscine head, than whenever I'd seen such a mask by daylight. On a little table before her lay a much-thumbed copy of *The Book of the River*, with a smaller chapbook perched upon it. The boatmistress opened this smaller volume and flicked through it in a desultory way as though to refresh her memory; then she suddenly snapped out at me, giving me quite a start.

"Candidate rivergirl, say what the black current is!"

I suppose I gaped.

"Say!"

"It's, well, it's the current that stops us from crossing the river."

"What is its nature?"

"Black?" I suggested.

"Is it water? Is it oil? Is it thin, is it thick? Is it fast, is it slow? Is it living, is it dead?"

"Anyone who tries to cross it dies," said I boldly. "But first they go mad. They're swept away, they're dragged down, swallowed. . . ."

The boatmistress read out of her chapbook. "It isn't water, and it isn't oil. It is more like blood, but not our red blood. It is more like a nerve, but not our nerves. It is more like a spinal column, but not our bony spines. It is all of these, and none.

"The body of the river lives its life from south to north, and the black current is its secret soul; but not like our souls, if we have souls. The black current is its mind; but not like our minds.

"For the river is a creature, and an entity. We are parasites upon her flesh, and the black current is the life-vein of that flesh. Enter it, and she drinks us, drowns us. But first she makes us mad.

"For all the water on this world is alive; it is all one whole, joined to itself. The river is the flexing tail of the dreaming ocean, ever rippling downstream, ever replacing itself."

Suddenly I was terrified, for to us in Pecawar, ever since I had learned to lisp and point and ask questions, the river had simply been the river: a body of water, something to gaze up and down as boats sailed by (though not to swim in because of the stingers), a supply route, a signpost both ways to different cities, different landscapes.

Certainly we blessed the river as provider of irrigation (the stingers never surviving in still water), of trade and mobility, and of rain and thus of our habitable zone itself—for the baking deserts commenced quite soon inland, even up south in jungled Ajelobo. But *The Book of the River* was no more, really, than a gazetteer and guidebook to everything that lay along the eastern shore: a manual for living in our world. Nowhere did it claim that the river was alive, and maybe malevolent; that it cared about us approximately as a dog cares for the fleas on its back—which seemed to be the implication here, with the added rider "let sleeping dogs lie."

The black current, in so far as I'd ever bothered about it, was simply an obstacle equivalent to whirlpools, though much worse; and what it was an obstacle to—namely the western shore and whoever might live there—was uninteresting except to monkish oddities, since there was no way of reaching it. And what's more, whoever was over there, if there was anyone at all, was as uninterested in us as we were in them.

But if the river was alive . . . Well, we all drank the water, didn't we? And human bodies are almost entirely made up of water. So we were built of river: heart and lungs, blood and brains.

"Women are of the river," I quoted; and the boatmistress snapped back at me:

"But she is not of us!"

Surely this was all some masquerade, precisely equivalent to hazing me or making me walk a plank, blindfolded, to tumble into the midst of stingers: something to bind me emotionally to the sorority of the river and the guild. So that perhaps I might remain loyal to river life and never choose to settle down with my imported husband? There were a few such shore-husbands, though not very many, living in Pecawar—but naturally I had hardly ever even seen their wives, who remained afloat, only returning for holidays. But just then the fortunes of husbands were hardly very much on my mind.

Still, if this was all just an emotional bonding thing, I was convinced! Though it was a warm evening, particularly in the stuffy cabin, I shivered.

"Yaleen," the boatmistress said to me. "If something isn't to notice that you're foreign to it, then it must think that you're part of itself. That's how a parasite survives in the flesh of its host. Every New Year's Eve, from Tambimatu in the south. . . ." She paused.

"Where the river rises, beyond Ajelobo."

"The river doesn't rise, Yaleen. It doesn't come from a little spring or bubbling fountain."

"I know. It flows out from under the Far Precipices. So it must come through an underground channel from beyond."

"And it has the same girth at its Tambimatu source as it does at Umdala, where it spreads into the wild ocean. It emerges from under the Precipices the same way as a worm emerges from the earth, oozing solidly out."

"It has to come through a channel."

"But what is behind the Precipices? We don't know. They're unscalable. They rise into air too thin to breathe, in any case. Maybe they're ten leagues thick, or a hundred; or maybe they're as thin as a sheet of paper. Filter paper. They filter the salts from the sea as it squeezes through to become the river—drawn along by the muscle of the river. And maybe if they filter salt water into fresh, the way our kidneys filter our blood, then deposits of salt are massed up and up within and behind the Precipices. Salt islands like iceberg slabs may calve vertically from time to time and crash back into the hidden ocean, to float away, break up and dissolve somewhere far away. Maybe in time you'll see far Tambimatu, where the jungles reek around the base of the Precipices, and where the whole river oozes out at once into the open; then you can guess, as well as anyone. But, Yaleen. . . ."

"Ah yes. Every New Year's Eve?"

"Right. At midnight when the world sleeps, a guild boat sets sail from Tambimatu across the river to the edge of the black current."

"To try to cross over between one year and the next—as though it mightn't be noticed? As though the river is midway between breathing one year in, and the next out?"

The fish-mask shook in denial. "No, to bring back several buckets full of the blackness. Presumably, since it has always been this way, midnight at year's end is something like the metabolic low point of awareness of the river. Still, that journey out to midstream isn't without its risks to the volunteers so honoured. Occasionally it happens that a crew-woman loses her sanity and throws herself overboard."

"You bring samples of the black current back to analyse?" I asked, perplexed.

The woman shook as though laughing silently; naturally I couldn't see her expression.

"What apothecary has the tools to analyse anything as alien as that? No, that isn't why. But *this* is." And from a shelf the boatmistress snatched a stoppered phial with wet darkness inside it. "Do you still wish to be a riverwoman?"

I hardly faltered, reasoning that the contents of that phial were surely simply ink-stained water. Or something similar.

"Yes, boatmistress. I do."

She unstoppered the phial and held it out to me.

"Then drink. Drink of the black current."

"And what will happen?" For maybe, after all, the liquid wasn't simple and innocuous. Maybe it was exactly what she said it was.

"Why, I'm still alive and of sound mind, aren't I, child?" murmured the quaymistress, at my shoulder.

"What will it do to me?"

"It will make you a riverwoman. Drink it quickly—all in one gulp."

Accepting the phial in my hand, I sniffed it, detecting hardly anything at all: a smell of . . . dankness, perhaps—and I drank.

The sensation wasn't so much that of liquid flowing down my throat, as of swallowing a fat garden slug whole. Or a blob of jelly. One moment it was blocking my throat entirely; the next, and it was gone.

I held the phial up to the lantern light. The glass looked perfectly clean, with no dregs or droplets clinging inside.

Laying the empty phial down on the table before me I awaited . . . I knew not what. A sudden sunburst of light and understanding? A plunge into terror or ecstasy? Creeping clammy cold? Delirium? Menstrual cramps? I sat and waited; and my two witnesses— or assessors?—waited too.

Finally the boatmistress nodded. "You're safe. The black current doesn't heed you. You don't offend it."

"What if I had?"

"Then you would have run up on deck, leapt over the side and done your best to swim oblivious of stingers all the way to the current to join it. In other words you would be dead."

"I've never heard of anyone doing such a thing."

"It doesn't happen to female applicants very often. Once in a thousand times, if that. And then we have to put it about that they signed on and sailed away without telling friends or family, and had an accident, or else that they stowed away and jumped the boat in a distant port."

"So I wasn't very worried," put in the quaymistress mildly.

I laughed nervously. "You said 'female applicants', as though there could be such a thing as a *male* applicant!"

"Poor choice of words. Men may only sail once in their lives, with their wife-to-be; thus our genes are mixed."

I knew this, of course; it was laid down in the preface to *The Book of the River* (though I'm sure this boatmistress had no more notion than I, exactly what "genes" were). "But what if men *do* sail twice? Or try to?"

"Ah, there we have it. The black current calls them, and drowns them. The river is a jealous female entity, I suppose. Once, she permits a man to sail, so that we may thrive. Twice, and she kills."

"I thought," said I, "that she simply ignored us?"

The fish-mask dipped, as if in prayer. "Strange are the ways of the river. But one thing's for sure: if you're a woman who's really a man, she'll cull you out."

"A woman who's really a man?"

"You know! Well, you're young yet, so perhaps you don't. . . ."

I was sure (or at least halfway sure) that all this rigmarole was simply guild lore that had bloomed in the misty dark age after our arrival on this world, as a way of authenticating social patterns that had proved so stable and self-perpetuating: with women being the travellers and traders, with men marrying into their woman's household. Matrilineal descent, and so on and so forth. It was really all gloss on the privileges of the guild; and I reminded myself that any man who was so inclined, and sufficiently energetic, could walk all the way back to his home town away from a wife he had grown to hate, or anywhere else for that matter. But obviously out of self-interest in the status quo no boat would ease his passage.

The boatmistress lifted her mask; she was a sharp-faced freckled redhead, perhaps forty years old.

"That's all over," she said. "Not a word, mind. Now you can forget about it." She reached for a flask from the shelf containing a different kind of liquid—ginger spirit—and brought down three glasses, too. "So: welcome to the river and the guild, apprentice boatwoman." She poured. "Here's to faraway places, and unfamiliar shores."

The spirit was strong, and rushed to my inexperienced head.

"The most unfamiliar shore," I heard myself saying presently, "is just a league and a half away, right over there." Nudging the glass westward.

The boatmistress looked angry, and I hastened to add, "I only

mention it on account of my twin brother. He wants to watch from
Verrino."

"Verrino, eh? That's a long walk, for a young fellow." In the
boatmistress's voice I caught a hint of vindictiveness, as though
Verrino was some bastion of rebellion against the rightful way, the
way of the river. If Capsi wished to get to Verrino he would have to
hike the fifty leagues; unless by some wild chance a husband-hunting girl from Verrino decided to visit us in Pecawar, fell madly in
love with young Capsi and carried him back home with her to wed.
I didn't think that Capsi quite qualified yet as a noteworthy catch.
Maybe in another couple of years he would. But equally, why
should some girl marry him just to provide him with an easy journey downstream to that watchful fraternity of his?

"When do I join a boat?" I asked, in more practical vein. Wishing,
a moment later, that I hadn't—since I had no particular wish to
bunk down on the *Ruby Piglet* (named, perhaps, in sardonic honour of
its red-headed boatmistress?). But I needn't have worried.

Said the quaymistress, "There's a brig due in, day after tomorrow,
with two empty berths; bound for Gangee, carrying grain. They
heliographed ahead, wanting crew. Then they're running back all
the way down to Umdala. Far enough for you, first-timer?"

I got home at nine o'clock, quite tipsy, and went up to Capsi's room;
he was in, playing around with his latest reconstruction of the original spyglass, adding an extra lens or something. For all the good that
would do. Perhaps my face was flushed: Capsi gave me much more
than a second glance.

"I've joined the guild," I said proudly.

"Which guild?" he asked with mock innocence, as though there
was any other guild for me.

"I'm sailing out. Thursday. Bound for Gangee, then Umdala. On
the brig the *Sally Argent.*" As though the name of the brig would
mean anything to him. *He* hadn't spent years hanging about the
quayside, sniffing around the ropes and bollards, and getting in the
way of the gangers unloading.

"Well, Sis, if you're going to Gangee, you'll be back here in about
three weeks."

I advanced on him. "That's the last time you're to call me Sis! I'm
older than you, anyway."

"By two minutes. Fancy some rough and tumble, eh?"

I halted. "Not especially."

"Some sublimated eroticism? Grope and squeeze?"

"How dare you!"

"Well, what do they get up to when you join the guild? Strip you naked and prod you with a windlass handle? Splice your mainbrace, whatever that means?"

"What makes you think they get up to anything? Well, they don't. So there."

"And pigs can fly." Had he slunk down to the quayside, and spied on me? Or had he just happened to notice that the *Ruby Piglet* was in town? Or neither—since it's often said that twins are empathic? Well, there was precious little empathy going on right now! At first I couldn't understand it.

He pointed his spyglass at me. "Seriously, Sis, you need a tumble. You'll probably have to learn to fight with knives, if you're going on a boat."

"Oh, I see. I *see.* You're bloody jealous—because after I've been to Gangee and back, in another week or two I'll be sailing smoothly into Verrino, while you'll still be stuck here burning your eyes out staring at sweet all. Don't worry, Capsi: when I'm home, from Umdala, in six months or so, I'll tell you what your darling Verrino's all about."

His lips whitened. "Don't *you* worry. I'll be there by then."

"In that case," and I peeled off one shoe, then the other, "you'll be needing these, and more!"

The first shoe missed him, bouncing off the wall where he had his pen-and-ink panorama of nowhereland, the opposite shore, tacked up. But the second crashed into his spyglass, spinning it from his hand, with a subsequent tinkle of glass. Curiously, he disregarded its fate. At first, anyway; what happened after, I don't know, for I was already fleeing from the room. No, I wasn't fleeing. I was withdrawing in haughty dudgeon.

During my hastily organized going-away party the following evening Capsi hardly spoke to me at all. Then, when I was on the point of leaving the house the morning after, with my duffle bag over my shoulder—which wasn't too traumatic a parting, from Mother and Father's point of view, since the run to Gangee and back was short— he winked at me, and whispered, "See you in Verrino."

"I'm sailing upstream first," I reminded him. "See you back here in three weeks."

"Don't be too sure of that, Sis." And he dealt me a playful punch on the shoulder.

*   *   *

Learning the ropes on the *Sally Argent* was no less—and no more—strenuous, muscle-forming, et cetera, than I'd expected; and of course there were no knife fights among the crew, or any other such garbage. Being a riverwoman was just work, with free time sandwiched in between.

The spring winds were blowing leisurely downstream, so our course—allowing for the long slow curves of the river one way, then the other—was basically west of south away from shore for a stretch till we were just over a third of a league out, then east of south back inshore again; repeat *ad infinitum*. Downstream river traffic at this season kept to a narrower sailing corridor nearer midstream, though always shunning by at least a sixth of a league the vicinity of the black current.

The dusty complexion of the country did not change markedly till we were almost at Gangee itself; then quite suddenly green hills bunched up, and foliage proliferated, and the semi-arid land disappeared—not to be seen again should we sail on as far as Ajelobo. For the Pecawar section marks the closest approach to civilization of the eastern deserts that parallel the whole course of the river from tropics to cooler north, generally at from ten to fifteen leagues' distance.

What was beyond the eastern deserts, further to the east? There was no way of knowing. Some expeditions had gone into the deep desert, in the past. One or two disappeared; one or two returned with the hard-won but unexciting news that the desert just went on and on.

Gangee, anyway, is on the very edge of the southern tropics, and is rather a fly-blown town, of sandstone buildings and rank weeds. It has neither the scoured dry neatness of Pecawar—with its shady arcades and secluded retreats of courtyards and fountains—nor the luxuriant bloom-bright tangle of cities further south. It's neither one nor the other; so it's weedy rather than lush, and stony without bothering to beautify. Still, I visited the bazaar, and the rather clammy river-aquarium with all its exotic southern species—frills and teeth and blobs of paint—next to its collection of dourer northern specimens.

Then it was time to sail back down midchannel to Pecawar again.

The *Sally Argent* carried a complement of twenty, with one berth still empty; and on the whole my riversisters treated this apprentice in a brisk and friendly way. The boatswain, Zolanda, was a bit of a sod at times, usually in the mornings, as though she always woke up with a headache (and perhaps she did); but my special friend was a rigger, Hali, a dumpy but energetic twenty-year-old with curly black hair and milky opal eyes: depending upon the light these either looked enchanting, or else slightly diseased with incipient cataracts.

The voyage downstream was straighter sailing than all the tacking upstream had been, and swifter with the tail wind. And less than a third of a league to port flowed the black current—which was the closest I had ever seen it, though it wasn't close enough for it to seem anything other than a thin strip of crêpe ribbon laid along the entire midriff of the water. Actually, the current was about a hundred spans wide.

Remarkably, now that I thought of it—for it wasn't something that one generally wondered about in Pecawar, with only one sample of barren shore opposite—there was no river traffic at all discernible across the water to the west, not even the smallest inshore fishing craft, so far as I could see. What's more, there seemed to be no villages on that other bank—let alone towns—yet the land was obviously inhabited, judging by the occasional wisp of smoke and, once, a tower on a hilltop way inland. Didn't they know what boats were, over there? Or that there were tasty fish in the river? (And who *were* "they", anyway?)

I was relaxing on deck, soaking up the spring sunshine with Hali during a slack time two days out of Gangee, and staring vaguely at the black current—which was so much a natural part of the river that it was hard to remember that it meant: *madness,* and *death*—when the events of my secret initiation popped back into my mind, prompting a question that I hoped was discreetly phrased, so that it didn't violate my oath on *The Book.*

"Did you ever eat a black slug, Hali, before you joined the guild?" I asked quite lazily and casually.

And no sooner had I asked the question than I felt as sick as though I had indeed just crammed a garden slug, fresh from a bed of lettuce, into my mouth and was trying to swallow the slimy thing. I had to scramble up, rush to the rail and vomit over the side.

Hali was behind me, steadying my shoulders. "All of us," she whispered, "ask the question once. I was wondering when you would, Yaleen. You see, we are of the river now; and we obey its rules—we break them at our peril."

The convulsions in my guts were easing.

"Riversick?" asked a familiarly abrasive voice. It was Zolanda, of course. "What, on this titchy little swell?"

She stared at me coolly, as I wiped my mouth; and I realized that she was offering me an excuse—because she must have known.

"I'm all right," I mumbled.

"Too much basking in the sun, that's your trouble. Get some work done." And she set me a whole heap of tasks.

Of course, my vomiting was probably all psychological. To violate an oath, or try to circumvent one—particularly one taken on *The Book of the River*, which is our whole life, and all there is for us—is a pretty slimy thing; and essentially in such situations one punished oneself, and sharpish too. So that night in my bunk, as we rode at anchor, I experienced an awful dream in which the black current reared up high out of the river like a serpent, developed a gaping mouth, full of void, and descended on me blindly.

I woke up with a cry, convinced that I'd been about to die. Soon a scantily-clad Hali was comforting me; and presently she was doing so a little too intimately for my taste—or for my depths of inexperience—so that I cooled off from her somewhat for a few days, though we still remained friends. And the dream did not recur; because it didn't need to. I worked at being a good boatwoman.

And so back to Pecawar, to pick up a load of spices.

And home for one night. I even invited Hali home, reasoning that if she liked me, she might like my twin brother too.

And Capsi had gone. Quit the nest. Trekked off northward, leaving his panorama of the further shore and his home-made spyglass behind as though they were but childish toys.

I had to spend some time consoling and reassuring Mother and Father—not so much because Capsi had absconded (a man eventually ought to leave home), nor even because he had departed unwed, as because of the double desertion within such a short span of time. True, *I* would be returning home, but the voyage down to Umdala and back was a matter of months, not weeks. And who knew whether I would be returning on the *Sally Argent* at all? Or if I did stay with the boat, whether it would be sailing as far upriver as Pecawar the next time?

I told Father that I would try to look out for Capsi in Verrino, though this was a fairly vain undertaking since we would be sailing into and out of Verrino before Capsi could possibly have reached the town on foot. I was careful not to *promise* to find him, even on the return trip.

So the overnight stay was a rather muted affair, even though Hali did her best to sparkle. I was only too glad to say goodbye the next morning.

You can spot Verrino from a long way upriver on account of its Spire, the natural rocky column rising from a particularly steep hill behind the town. On top of the Spire, up hundreds of steps with only a guiderope to stop you falling off, was where the little band of observers lived in presumably spartan circumstances, staring across at the further shore through telescopes till their eyes grew dim. From the town itself one couldn't see anything of their activities, and the steep steps were quite a disincentive to further investigation. I did climb up as far as the base of the Spire itself, then gave up, feeling obscurely that I had done my duty. In any case it was quite impossible that Capsi could be up there yet.

So I turned my attention, instead, to exploring the town proper: a pleasant bustling twisty up-and-down place, with sudden arbours and piazzas, wooden footbridges hung with clemato and cisca-vine crossing over alleys, which in turn tunnelled through rock or under buildings, themselves to emerge unexpectedly at rooftop height: rooftops crammed with terracotta urns of fuchsias. After the flatness of Pecawar, I adored Verrino, though the place made my calves and ankles ache. The people scampered everywhere, chattering like monkeys, many of the men with laden baskets balanced on their heads, the further to defy gravity—though no one that I saw ever went so far as to shin down vines as a short cut from one level to the next.

Yet scamper about though they might, it certainly wasn't fast enough for boatmistress Karil, who by the second day was grumbling about demurrage charges, and by the third was inveighing that we would have to spend the whole damn week here, the way things were going.

What was holding us up was a large consignment of spectacle lenses from the glassworks and grindery inland—another reason, by the by, in addition to the towering vantage point of the Spire, why the observers congregated above Verrino—and since lenses are such a costly item compared with their size, and since they were bound all the way to Umdala, Karil was loth to sail off and leave the freighting to a subsequent boat, thus losing a handsome percentage.

So the crew were free to roam—one or two to go looking, speculatively, for possible husbands; those older women such as Zolanda, who were already married with a husband ensconced in some far port, to go hunting discreetly for a spot of carnal appeasement and amorous intrigue with married men; and some of the younger women with whoever took their fancy.

Naturally, married men whose wives were absent were bound to be the husbands of other riverwomen; and you might have thought it was rather poor form for one riverwoman to have fun with another riversister's man while she was away. But actually this was something of a game and generally winked at; and when I came to think of it, it made sense. Some women might be away for months, even as long as a year, and during this time obviously they nursed desires—as did their spouses back home. Better, much better, that there should be a kind of covert swap arrangement, all within the embrace of the guild, even if nobody admitted it publicly.

But besides these stranded husbands, there were always a number of adventurous and available young men—who could hardly look to the girls of their own town to marry; and this firm custom cast a risky pall over seducing those girls, or even flirting too boisterously.

So the next secret of the guild that I learned—from Hali, who else?—was how to avoid getting pregnant in foreign ports, a skill without which these shore-leave adventures could have proved bothersome. A drug, which in river argot was simply called "Safe" —thus keeping it our own preserve, should shore ears be wagging— could be extracted by boiling up the entrails of the barbel-fish.

Not that it was any crime to become pregnant, though given the exertions of our work this could end up by "beaching" a riversister for quite a while; and you would sometimes see girl children on passing boats, though generally all kids were left at home in the husband's care.

Girl children: that was the real problem. Boy children could no more sail the river repeatedly than could youths or grown men— which would mean that boys born or wombed on the river would, when they grew up, have to walk all the way to a future wife's town, should she care to put up with this inconvenience for the sake of love; and sometimes the river might even take exception to a male foetus well before its term, making the mother miscarry; and who was to know whether a foetus was male or female? So a riverwoman contemplating pregnancy generally arranged this with some care, and beached herself for the full term. Many riverwomen played it

Safe permanently; and would only consider adopting a family. And many never bothered marrying at all.

So, on what was to be our penultimate evening in Verrino, Hali winked at me. "Let's try the night life out," she said, and handed me a little blue phial of fish juice.

I accepted it laughingly, only partly out of bravado. "Why not?" I winked back, and drank it down.

A couple of hours later we were in a busy wine-arbour lit by fairy candles, bantering with a pair of slim handsome brothers with coppery skin, lambent eyes and pert turned-up noses—with the banter gradually becoming more serious, though of course destined to remain a game; whatever happened, a game. I was a little tipsy, and my partner, with whom I danced a few turns, said that he was called Hasso—and maybe he really was called that. I kissed him, and when I next paid attention, Hali had vanished from the arbour along with her new friend.

Hasso murmured sweetly, "I know somewhere."

"I know lots of places," I said, rather wickedly. "Pecawar, Gangee. . . ."

But he took my repartee in good part; as indeed he would, since he was anxious to please me.

And not so many hours later we were at that somewhere, the two of us—it was an attic room, window choked with nightscented clemato, reached by a long thin bridge—and I was discovering that I didn't know everything, though I was quick to learn.

Nor did he know everything; though the gaps in his knowledge were other than mine.

"Must be marvellous, river travel," he nuzzled in my ear. Or something to that effect; I was on the point of swinging round to approach him by another route.

"Must see all sorts of things on the far bank, while sailing." He was leaving out the personal pronouns, perhaps without realizing he was doing so. As I surmised presently, he thus drew back from actual spoken breach of faith.

"Cities and such—"

At this stage I wasn't offended; I simply thought that since the aura of the river was about me, this was turning him on as much as my young charms.

"Ah, beyond the black current—"

I thought, capriciously, of telling him what that current *tasted* like, but I had no particular desire to test whether I would vomit as readily on shore as I had on the boat. Besides, I already had my mouth full, being otherwise occupied.

He relaxed with a groan.

"Tell me *something* that's seen over there, eh? Something wild and wonderful. Anything at all."

I broke off abruptly, squirmed aside and found my clothes. I *knew* now. It was no coincidence that Hali and I had fallen in with these two personable brothers at the wine-arbour. They'd been looking for such as us. Or rather, for such as me: someone new and naive, freshly filled with all the wonders of the river and its sights, and probably boastful. No doubt the other brother was simply keeping the more experienced Hali suitably occupied, while Hasso set out to pump me on behalf of the observers up there on the Spire. . . .

I didn't cry or make a fuss or accuse him, consoling myself with the thought that *I* had pumped him. Dry.

"Have to get back," I lied. "I'm on nightwatch."

Why any boatmistress should order nightwatch kept in a harbour, I had no idea; but it was the first thing I thought of.

Hasso propped himself on his elbow, grinning. "Are you *sure* you have to get back to your ship, little Yaleen?"

"My *boat*," I corrected him hotly. "Shorelubber!"

And in another moment I fled past the veils of clemato, whose smell seemed cloying now, and over the high slim wooden bridge, alone.

I'd wondered whether or not to tell Hali of my suspicions; however it was the wee hours before she returned on board and by then it had occurred to me that she might imagine I was rationalizing some sort of sexual disaster; which I was not, by any means. So in the end I pretended to be asleep, and said nothing at all.

And early in the morning the padded boxes of spectacle lenses arrived. Almost immediately afterwards we cast off and set sail downstream, for all points north to furthest Umdala.

I didn't return to up-and-down Verrino for a whole year, by which time I was no longer just an apprentice but newly held my guild ticket; nor was I on the *Sally Argent* any more.

In their first year or two, young riverwomen are encouraged to work a variety of craft, and I was no exception. Besides, I think that subconsciously I chose to hop boats in the way I did so as to delay my return to Verrino (and Pecawar) for quite a while. What I told myself was that I ought to see as much of downriver as I could, while I was still freshly impressionable.

So I had sailed with that first boat of mine all the way down to cool, misty Umdala, calling *en route* at Sarjoy, Aladalia, Port Firsthome, Melonby and Firelight. At Umdala I'd skiffed across the marshes, and I'd wandered the geometrical streets of blockhouses with their steeply pitched roofs, like rows of wedges set to cut whatever weight of snow might settle from the sky in deep winter; and I'd seen the enormous widening of the river where fresh water became salt, a prelude to the angry ocean—with the black current ribboning out and out. And I had wondered whether Umdala was built as it was entirely to defeat white winters, or whether there might not have been another hidden thought in the ancient builders' minds—for this was an outpost city: outpost, not against human enemies, but against what the river became as it broadened out, the unnavigable dire sea.

I returned on the *Sally Argent,* still with Hali, as far upstream as the soft green grazing hills of Port Firsthome, where I wondered at the time-worn Obelisk of the Ship—a "ship", as all but shorelubbers know, being something quite distinct from a boat, which plies water and not the star-void.

At Port Firsthome I hopped off, with a good endorsement on my papers from boatmistress Karil, and signed on the three-mast schooner *Speedy Snail,* a lumbering heavy-duty boat which only cruised from Aladalia to Firelight and back; and through the summer and autumn I stayed with her till I'd won my ticket. Then, as the winds blowing from the north became quite chilly, it was goodbye to the *Speedy Snail* and hullo to the caravel *Abracadabra* and local hauls in the Aladalia region, which distanced me from the worst excesses of deep winter. Not that I was scared of catching cold! Still, I did hail from Pecawar where the desert keeps us dry and where the winter only brings a few ground frosts before dawn. Somehow I didn't yet feel like sailing further south, up Verrino way.

So for a while artistic Aladalia was my home, with its weavers and jewellers and potters and its orchestra, almost as much as the *Abracadabra* herself; and I even got involved in something of a relationship (casual but warm: I needed to keep warm) with one Tam; and because this was a sweet experience I think I'll say less about it than about my first time, with Hasso. Just in case I find any little flaws in this affair, too? No. It remained quite innocent of any reference to what went on or didn't go on over the water.

But came spring, and a letter from my mother, and a concerned note from my father; so from the caravel I hopped to the brig *Blue Sunlight* bound for Sarjoy and Verrino; and who should be waiting on the quayside as the *Blue Sunlight* tied up at its destination, but Capsi.

I waved and waved, and as soon as I was free of my duties I rushed ashore and hugged him.

"How did you *know?*"

He laughed delightedly. "Well, I knew you'd have to pass this way sometime. After all, there aren't two rivers! I simply paid the quaymistress a little retainer to keep an eye on the Guild Register for me."

"You're lucky, then. I only just joined *Blue Sunlight* in Aladalia."

"Lucky, indeed! Fine thing to say about your own guild, Sis. Oops, apologies, Yaleen. But surely you mean 'efficient'? One boat got here ahead of you, with the latest crewlists *ex* Aladalia. And before *Blue Sunlight* it was *Abracadabra;* and before that—"

"You seem quite efficient too. Obviously you know everything about me." (But he didn't know *all,* I added inwardly. I was a girl when last we met; but now I was a woman, and a riverwoman too.)

Arm in arm we strolled up the steep cobbled street to the nearest wine-arbour, to toast our re-encounter.

"So how's it with you?" I asked him, as we sat on a bench beneath familiar garlands of clemato.

"Oh, I sits up the Spire, and I stares," said he jocularly.

"Seen anything amusing?"

His voice quietened. "There's a little town about two leagues inland over there. Just a little one, but we have Big Eye trained on it. That's our newest telescope, with lenses right at the limits of the grinders' art. You must come up and visit me at work."

"Must I?"

"You'd be interested—who wouldn't be?"

"Maybe I wouldn't. I've seen Aladalia and Port Firsthome and Umdala. Why should I want to squint at a nameless *little* town? I bet what you see's all wavery and blurred—and so far away."

"It isn't as blurred as you'd think. We're high up."

"So what do you see?"

"People."

"Surprise, surprise. I expected dragons."

"Very tiny people, of course."

"What, dwarfs?"

"Cut the sarcasm, Sis. This is important."

"More important than our first meeting in a year?"

With a perceptible effort he untensed, and chuckled. " 'Course not. Let's drown that year, eh?" And he drained his glass. "I know a marvellous little spot to eat. Afterwards. When we need something to soak it all up. Fancy some spiced sweet-rice and kebabs?"

And he punched me softly on the shoulder. Somehow though, that particular patch of my flesh seemed sore, from way way back.

After his first over-anxious little outburst, which had been like a premature ejaculation of something long pent up, Capsi played me carefully; I'll give him all credit for that. He kept off the subject and showed me the town, which I already knew, but hardly as well as he knew it. I'd signed off the *Blue Sunlight* and taken a small rooftop room for a while, after writing ahead to Mother and Father to announce that I'd be arriving soonish, a letter which I left with the quaymistress to forward by the next upriver boat.

Credit, yes . . . though there was the genuine happiness to see me, too, and brotherly affection; which rather confused the matter for me emotionally, otherwise I might never have fallen for his suggestions. But my actions seemed correct and brave at the time; and in defence of my own sex, even.

Indeed, Capsi managed to keep off the topic of his own obsession so well that after a couple of days I relented, and asked him, "Well, what about the tiny people over there?"

"Tiny, because they're at the range of the Big Eye's powers of resolution."

"Oh, I *know* that."

He frowned. "But on a clear day, when the atmosphere's still, you can tell the men from the women. They're dressed differently: the women all wear black."

"How can you tell they're women?"

"Babies. Sometimes they take babies with them, into the fields."

"Could as easily be the menfolk."

"*Feeding* a baby? That's how it looked to our keenest-eyed watcher." He hesitated before naming him: "Hasso."

"Ah," I said; I was *almost* prepared for this.

"He sends you his affectionate apologies, Yaleen."

I flushed; did my brother know all about that first night? I was angry, ready to walk away; but instead I shrugged, and said, "It seems to me that you people base a whole lot of inference on one man's voyeuring of something leagues away!"

He waved his hand dismissively. "Maybe, maybe not. The people over there don't go anywhere near the river. They don't sail so much as a plank on it. They don't net any fish. They don't even have a single shack that we know of, anywhere near the water. Why?"

"Because . . . only women can sail the river—"

"And no woman is allowed within a league of it. As I said, it's only a little town—so where are their cities, if they have them? Presumably they do. They're inland; right inland, as far away into the habitable zone as they can get."

"Assuming there are deserts beyond. Same as this side."

"Fair assumption."

"So they don't like the river; that was always obvious. What else is new?"

"What else is new, Yaleen, is that they *burn* women over there."

". . . What?"

"About six months ago, when Big Eye was first commissioned—"

"Only boats are commissioned, brother dear."

"Well, whatever word. Through Big Eye we saw a crowd gather outside the town. Then a little cart was pulled through the crowd, to what looked like a pile of wood. One of the tiny black figures—we couldn't be sure they were women then—was dragged off the cart . . . and soon the flames crackled and the smoke curled up."

"Is this true?"

"I swear on *The Book* it is."

"But why should they do anything so cruel?"

"Because they hate and fear the river. And woman is of the river. And fire is the foe of water."

I gripped Capsi's wrist. "Water," I said, "*quenches* fire."

And this was the beginning of my undoing. Well, perhaps not of *my* undoing personally; but certainly the start of a fateful sequence of events for my brave if wayward brother.

The very next day I was toiling up that damned never-ending stone staircase. Capsi climbed behind me; thus at least I could set the pace.

The stairs wound round the Spire at least thrice before we finally entered an upward tunnel with subsidiary stairways and chambers leading off it, cut in the naked rock; and thus arrived at last back in the open air up on the top stone platform. This was wider than I'd expected from down below: about seventy spans across, with a safety rail around the exposed parts of the rim. On the eastern side a stone wall acted as a windbreak—not that the wind would blow from the east for more than thirty days in the whole year (unless high wind was different from river wind), but up on this exposed eminence a windbreak of any kind was probably better than none. Set on the western edge of the platform, blocking my immediate view of the far shore, was a low observatory building of brick, roofed in slate.

The platform was an austere, breezy place, strangely blank and untenanted—yet at the same time worn smooth by habitation.

"Where is everyone? Where do you live?"

Capsi jerked his thumb below. "Underneath in the rock. There are lots of rooms."

How weird and contrary to my expectations that Capsi, so high up in the air, should be leading what amounted to a troglodyte life!

High, yes: far higher than any mast I had ever shinned up. Walking over to the guard-rail I stared downriver, away and away in the direction of Sarjoy, though even so Sarjoy itself must have been quite some distance beyond the horizon. I picked out familiar landmarks on the eastern shore, and at least half a dozen boats which might almost have been motionless (but weren't); and I missed something. My whole body missed it, so that I gripped the rail for balance. It was movement that was absent: the slight rocking to and fro that I'd known any other time I had been up a height, upon the river, the gentle tilt back and forth of a masthead.

Yet the clouds above looked to be as high in the sky as ever; and the river, strangely, seemed wider rather than narrower now that I was seeing its span entire from bank to bank, the way a bird sees it. The river—with the band of the black current dividing it midway like the loading line along a beached hull. . . .

I scanned the far shore for Capsi's reputed town, somewhere inland amidst the rolling, wooded hills and little valleys, but couldn't pick it out unaided—nor any other landmarks but those of nature. Highways? No, I could see none . . . Unless . . . was that one, far far off, winding inland?

And directly below me was bustling, hither and thither Verrino: half a league of activity and variety, with its orchards and vineyards beyond, and off to the east some sandy hills hiding the glassworks.

"What a sad life up here, Capsi!"

"Sad? What's that got to do with it? Come on, I'll show you Big Eye." He pulled me away from the railing and all its grand vistas, towards the brick building; and it seemed to me that none of the sights were quite real to him unless he spied at them from out of the dark indoors, through a glass like a voyeur.

A wooden door, studded with rusty iron bolts: he pushed it open, and I was prepared to find myself in gloom reminiscent of the river-aquarium in Gangee.

But no: it was light and airy. A whole strip of exposed scenery cut a welcome swathe several spans high through the whole length of the westerly wall; for the midriff of this wall was all hinged windows, with most of the panes hoisted up and out to form a canopy, ventilating the observatory and sheltering the instruments from rain, unless a shower was scudding from due west.

Several ancient telescopes were retired to corners, but three principal instruments poked their barrels through different windows, two of these in use—the westward gazers seated on wooden chairs with straight backs, and cushions as a concession to comfort. There was no doubt at all which of the instruments was Big Eye: it was fully nine spans long, and my arm would hardly have gone around the tube.

The northern wall was shelved, with what I took to be logbooks filed on it, and sketching material: while the whole south wall was taken up by a huge panorama which quite dwarfed the one that Capsi had made for his bedroom wall back home. Quite what use the panorama was, with the reality in plain view, I thought I would forbear to ask—though doubtless it was easier to examine details (such as individual trees?) upon that great scroll of paper, and measure the distances from place to place. (And doubtless too, trees grew . . . so that the panorama must always be inaccurate.)

The man seated at the smaller instrument glanced round. Dressed in worn brown trousers and a tight jerkin, with his shirtsleeves rolled up for business, he was white-haired with a wrinkled impish face. He simply registered our presence, nodded, then got back to his observations—which struck me as something of a waste of time, since surely his aged eyes were feebler than the young man's next to him, and the telescope he was using was less powerful too.

The young man next to him . . . Wearing jauntier attire: boots, flared trousers tucked in, and an unforgettable shirt, striped scarlet and black.

"Hasso," said Capsi; and as though the watcher at Big Eye had awaited this signal, he looked round; and sprang up. Hasso was just as handsome as I remembered.

"See all sorts of things on the far bank," he remarked merrily and unselfconsciously. "Welcome back, Yaleen."

"And sometimes," said I, "you have to go fishing for hints. How's your brother?"

"Oh, he's a townsman at heart. Never comes up here. We just go around together . . . on occasion."

"Okay, okay, I don't mind." (But I did mind, quite a bit.) "That's so much water down the river."

Fortunately he did not attempt anything as crass as to advance and peck me on the cheek; he simply motioned me politely to his chair, and the vacant eye-piece of Big Eye. I sat down, and shut one eye to stare.

The telescope was trained on the little town—no more than a large village, really, nestling in the gradients of the land; and for me the weirdest thing of all in looking upon it was that the place was nameless. Nowhere in *The Book of the River* was its name inscribed; which meant that it did not exist—and yet it did.

Compared with Verrino, or even the smallest settlement on our shore, even to my unpractised eye it looked impoverished and primitive. Straw thatch? Apparently. Walls of dried mud? Some, perhaps, of wood. There was nothing of architecture or adornment about the settlement, except for one central building of stone, with an onion dome at one end. I felt not so much that I was gazing across a few leagues of space, as back hundreds or even thousands of years through time. Perhaps Capsi was right in his obsession, after all, and here was a more curious sight than any to be seen from Ajelobo to Umdala . . . I found myself itching to peel away the hills, step up the power of the telescope and discover what *did* lie further to the west; yet this wasn't a particularly pleasant sort of itch, not the kind that it's satisfying to scratch.

"Do you see a black patch, on the green outside the town?" Hasso whispered in my ear, as though the folk I was spying upon might hear him if he spoke too loudly. "That's where they burned her. Alive. In flames."

I broke off my viewing, not desiring this kind of covert closeness.

"How do you get all this stuff up here, and your food and water and everything?" I directed my question at Capsi, though he was hanging back as if he had arranged for Hasso to be here especially to please me; which it didn't. "Up all those wretched stairs?"

"We hoist heavy supplies. Winch 'em up in buckets."

"And how do you pay for them?"

"Oh, donations," he said vaguely. "And some of us work part-time down in Verrino."

"How many of you are there, anyway?"

"About twenty. Some young, some old. Come and see—we've nothing to hide. It's that lot over there who are hiding. They're hiding from the river. And they make women wear black. And they burn them."

"But you're all *men* up here, aren't you?"

Hasso chuckled. "We aren't misogynists exactly. . . ." He had the good grace not to add: *As you surely noticed.* "I hope Capsi passed on my affectionate apologies?"

"He did. Verbatim. It seems to me that the men over there must be the kingpins, who decide what women do—and *you* aren't above using women, if it suits you! Could there perhaps be a certain element of envy in your activities up here?"

"There could be, but there isn't." It was the old imp who spoke up; so he must have been listening, instead of looking. "Sister Yaleen, knowledge is our goal; that's all. The knowledge of what on earth is going on over there, with the whole other half of our human community. They who share this world with us."

So he already knew my name. Which meant that they had all discussed my coming. I was as much part of a plan now as ever I had been—in a more casual, extempore way—when Hasso lovingly deflowered me that evening a year ago.

"You feel . . . threatened, perhaps?" said the old fellow gently. "Please don't. It's the women over there who are under threat. Your sisters, not you."

Yes. But the observers hadn't known of this threat till recently, when they had acquired Big Eye. And yet maybe they had guessed for a long time that the west bank was opposed to everything that our river society stood for. . . .

"Well, that's Big Eye," said Capsi lightly. "Come on and we'll show you around, below."

"*You* can show me around, brother dear. I'm sure Hasso has lots more peeping to attend to."

Hasso pursed his lips; he seemed more amused than offended.

So Capsi proceeded to give me the guided tour of their eyrie and citadel—carved into cell rooms, kitchen, refectory, store rooms and such, and culminating in the "map room" where was filed or displayed every iota of information, supposition or hearsay that they had ever gleaned about the west bank all the way from Ajelobo to Umdala, a labour of goodness knows how many years. A hundred? Two hundred? More? I saw panoramas and sketches and even maps of the immediate hinter-land, though the maps themselves must have been beset with flaws due to foreshortening, given the perspectives they were drawn from.

Such dusty patience. Such dedicated . . . waiting. Capsi confessed to me offhandedly that he, and they, rather regretted that he had not brought his own pen-and-ink panorama of the shore opposite Pecawar with him from home. But when I offered to collect it from our house and drop it in at Verrino next time I was passing by, he didn't seem quite as glad of my offer as I should have expected. Perhaps he had already promised his colleagues something better?

Then, the tour at an end (if I had indeed seen everything: the place was a bit of a maze), Capsi escorted me back down those ankle-aching stairs to real life and bustle, and a bottle of wine and spicy lamb couscous with minted yoghurt.

If he had further schemes in mind for me, he didn't go into them. Though what they might be, I was hard put to imagine—so much so that I was almost on the point of asking him outright.

Two days later, in the afternoon, just after I'd come back to my little rooftop room after a visit to the quaymistress's office enquiring of a boat with an empty berth to carry me back to Pecawar in another week or so, Capsi burst in upon me, panting with exertion, his face flushed.

"They're at it again," he panted. "Crowd outside the town. Bonfire piled up. Come on!" Strangely, he seemed glad. Almost radiant.

I wondered briefly if this was a trick; but obviously something that happened six months ago can always repeat itself six months later. I raced with him.

It only took us about twenty minutes—with Capsi ducking up and down short-cuts that would have lost me—to snake through the town and out to the Spire, and spiral our way up till, almost heart-burst, we emerged on to the platform.

As soon as we entered the observatory, which was crowded, a path opened for me to Big Eye, where Hasso jumped out of his seat to make room. I was shaking and panting so much from the sprint that I let him steady my shoulders as I sat there.

I peered: at a tiny crowd on a greensward, half of the people robed in black; and an empty cart, and a bonfire burning. With a stake set in the centre of the flames, and something fastened to the stake.

I watched a long while, till the crowd began to troop back towards the wretched village, dragging the cart along with them, leaving a smoking ruin behind.

Then I ran out, around to the guard-rail. Sure enough, away to the west hung a tiny faint smudge.

I returned; the observers, young and old, all watched me expectantly.

"What do you want me to do?" I asked them.

Capsi answered quietly, "We want to send an observer over. To find out."

"Over there? But that's impossible. The black current's in the way. You haven't learnt to fly, by any chance?"

"Our ancestors must have known how to fly," remarked the old imp, whose name I knew now as Yosef. "A lost skill, eh? Perhaps deliberately so. Still, I've had a few ideas on the subject. . . ."

I quoted the preface to *The Book of the River* at him. "Man is of the shore, woman is of the water, only birds are of the sky. . . ."

He stared at me fixedly. "Yes, precisely. So there's no point in my entertaining such thoughts, is there, boatwoman? Or we would threaten the balance of the applecart. Something that no self-respecting guild would ever allow. . . ."

"River society *works*," said I. "And nicely, too. Obviously things don't work very well over there."

"Oh, I wasn't suggesting that this particular applecart is in any danger of overturning. None whatever! I've ruled out any fancy, speculative notions of flying. It's a somewhat visible thing to attempt. Meanwhile, girls like you are burning over there. Twice now, in that one miserable little town."

What I'd seen had been far away, tiny and silent; yet just for a moment I felt an intuition of the fear, the awful fear, and the agony, and was nearly sick from it. Flames licking round my feet, crisping my skin to pig's crackling then burning through to the bone, while I screamed and screamed. . . .

"Somebody has to cross the river and report back," said Capsi. "You do see that, don't you?"

"Men can only sail the river once. Cross, and report back? That's twice. You aren't suggesting that *I* make the crossing? It's ridiculous: the current's in the way, in any case."

"No, Yaleen, I wasn't suggesting you. Obviously a man is safer over there than a woman. It's *me* who'll go. Just once. One way. And I'll report back by heliograph."

"But how could you get through the current? It's madness—and death. That isn't just some rumour that we women put around!"

"Oh, it's true, and no denying," said old Yosef. "The river has a mind of its own, and senses things, and reacts to them. Or rather, let's say that the black current acts this way. So it's a creature: a very long creature that lives in the river, anchored to the Precipice Mountains at one end like a tapeworm, floating all the way along it and spilling out into the sea at its other end. And it can smell what happens in the water. It can scent one man's odour and remember it, and distinguish it from half a million others; and it can put thoughts into his brain, of despair and death, if it smells him twice. Whereas women it favours. No doubt because they pose no threat to it."

His speculations seemed dangerously close to some of the secrets of my initiation ceremony; though plainly the black current couldn't be a creature such as he envisaged—not if it was possible to scoop out parts of it and bottle these in phials. It had to be of a different nature, and much larger than their concept of it: larger than our whole country, and perhaps much more powerful, in its apparently quiescent, unrevealing way, than any of them supposed.

I said nothing at all to confirm or deny to what extent the guild might have reached the same conclusions—which of course had precious little to do with the business of everyday life.

"So," I said simply, "there's no way through. However crazy you are."

"Not through," replied Capsi. "Under."

"Under?"

Old Yosef stuck his oar in again. "Based on the reasonable presumption that the black current doesn't extend all the way to the bottom. Why should it, when it floats? There must be clear water beneath. Maybe the current is only a few spans thick."

"Ah, I *see*. And it's only a hundred spans wide. So Capsi is just going to hold his breath for five or ten minutes, plunge into water infested with stingers, and . . . It's preposterous. Since when, Capsi, could you swim like a fish?"

"I've been practising," he said defensively. "Down at the Verrino baths."

"And is that also where you've been practising holding your breath, till you turn blue?"

"You misunderstand," said Yosef. "Come, and we'll show you how."

Down below, we entered a stone chamber with mullion windows cut in the rock wall facing east. I'd certainly not been admitted here two days before, during Capsi's guided tour.

A long wooden table was piled with curious gear: a large glass globe, a leather suit, boots with lead weights attached and flipper-like protuberances, various flexible tubes sewn out of river-snake skin, bladders, thick glass bottles, satchels—and unmistakably, a dismantled heliograph. So these Observers had mastered our river code, presumably.

"That," announced Capsi proudly, "is my diving suit. Enough air can be bottled under pressure to let me breathe inside the glass helmet for nearly twenty minutes. The helmet and other glass parts are by a special commission from the grindery. The weights and the gear I'm carrying slung about me will counteract the buoyancy of all the air. And here," and he picked up what was plainly a lamp, though of curious design, "is my underwater light supply, if I have to dive deep and need light, fuelled with magnesium."

"It'll explode."

"No, it won't," Yosef assured me. "Been tested."

"Then I float up, discard the bowl, and my head is protected from stingers by this leather cap and wire mask."

I turned to Yosef, who had obviously dreamed up all this apparatus. "You seem to have thought of everything—except for one little detail: what Capsi is going to *do* for the whole of the rest of his life over there."

My brother grinned at me wolfishly. "Explore, that's what. I'd say that there's quite enough *terra incognita* to occupy a lifetime. And I'll report back, of course. At intervals."

"So where do I come into all this?" As though I hadn't already guessed.

"You have access to boats, sister dear. You know the ropes and the routines. We only need a very small craft. Sufficient for me and one other helper, who'll surrender his once-in-a-lifetime chance on the river to assist."

"And I suppose that brave volunteer is Hasso?"

Capsi nodded, unabashed.

"I'm not sure if I can handle even a cutter or a sloop on my own.

. . ." But I thought that I could. *Whether* I should was quite another matter.

"We were on the verge of appealing to your better nature," explained Yosef, in an old wise way. "But now—you have seen what you have seen."

Yes. The bonfire. The burning woman. The smoke rising up. Unsure whether I was championing my sex, or betraying it, I too nodded.

After this, events achieved a momentum of their own. The very next midnight, starlit and clear, saw me—or rather failed to see me, since I had "borrowed" the little cutter discreetly, though with my heart in my mouth—rocking far out upon the river on dark water, within a stone's throw of the deeper darkness of the current.

Masked and helmeted in his preposterous fishbowl, his suit hung with gear, Capsi was assisted over the side by Hasso. And my brother sank.

We didn't hang around; we were drifting closer to the current. I set sail, grabbed the tiller and we fled back to the shore, where I let Hasso off somewhere upstream of the quay before sneaking the cutter back to its berth. Without being noticed. Though I expected at any moment that somebody would stroll up on deck for a breath of air, or reel back from a very late night on the town.

Returning to my room, I tried to sleep but couldn't. By earliest dawn I was toiling up the hundreds of steps of the Spire.

Almost all of the observers were up on the platform, spread out along the guard-rail, keeping silent vigil upon the western shore—with two men even watching the southerly stretch, though it seemed unlikely that Capsi could have forged upstream against the flow. With the exception of Big Eye, all of the telescopes, even the ancient ones, had been pressed into service—brought out into the open, mounted on swivel tripods; though no one was using these to scan just at the moment. One's ordinary field of view, including peripheral vision, was more likely to catch the tiny blink of reflected light when it came; if indeed it ever came. Hasso and Yosef were inside the observatory; so I stayed outdoors.

An hour went by—and meanwhile the sun rose behind us.

Then suddenly, when I was really beginning to fret, a man cried out and pointed—quite far to the north.

Other observers hastily swung telescopes about and clapped an eye to them; but even at that distance I could spell out the winks of the helio-mirror.

"S-A-F-E. *Safe,*" I called out.

The rest of the brief message was: *Tired. Must sleep, then move south.* "Tired" was no doubt a considerable understatement.

No sun-signal was sent in acknowledgement, not merely because the sun was at our backs, but in case anyone on the opposite shore might see it, and be able to interpret. However a smoky billowing fire was lit briefly in a brazier; and after a couple of minutes, quenched.

Since it seemed ridiculous, after that, to keep returning to my room down in the town I accepted Yosef's offer of a little bedchamber in the Spire; and by midday I had stored some of my gear at the quaymistress's office and humped the bare essentials aloft, declining Hasso's assistance.

Yet once ensconced up top, I had nothing to do, and within a few hours I was feeling bored and restless.

And anxious? Where was the use of anxiety for someone whom I could never see again—except maybe briefly through Big Eye?

I ought to have been feeling intensely curious about what Capsi would report, as pre-arranged, at dawn the next day. Yet when it was a question of why women were being burned alive, "curiosity" hardly seemed the right description of my feelings. I . . . dreaded to know the answer. And as to the facts of life on the west bank, well of course I felt some superficial curiosity—but how much of it could Capsi satisfy effectively within the first few days? I was leaving. Soon. And I had no wish to sail away and yet remain in mental thrall to these observers forever more, impelled to dash back constantly to hear the latest. If I acted in that style, why, Capsi would have made me a slave of his for life, on a chain as long as the river!

Selfish little Yaleen? No, not really. Only sensible, I'd have said. . . .

Sensible? Hardly! I soon began fretting that by taking up temporary residence on the Spire I might have identified myself too visibly with the observer men, prompting some busybody in Verrino to ask the question: why?

I realize now that I was in a very confused emotional state, about what I'd done and what Capsi had undertaken. I wished to flee, but had to stay—and *vice versa!* By six o'clock I found myself hesitating at the top of the stairs, craving a drink in town and ordinary chatter around me. I had to pull myself up sharpish and retrace my steps to my room, because actually I was almost ready to keel over in exhaustion and tumble all the way down into town.

So back to my chamber I crept. Then, without my quite knowing how it happened, Hasso was standing by my bedside—where I lay fully dressed.

"No!" I cried, blinking at him.

And he chuckled, indicating the faint grey light beyond the mullion.

"Dawn's breaking, Yaleen."

"What?"

"I thought I'd best come and fetch you—just in case you slept right through. I'm sure you'd never have forgiven me for *that.*"

When the light of the heliograph blinked out, half an hour later, it came from almost opposite Verrino. But we could be fairly sure that no one else would see it. It was very low, and we were high; and besides, who else would be looking out for a signal light from that direction?

Today's message was longer.

Went inland. Avoided contact. Hid near town. All females wear black, confirmed. Town is shabby, poor, dirt-agric. Plus pigs, chickens, goats. Mining activity south side hills, thus reason for location. Male and female workers. Overheard passers-by on track. Same language, few strange words, accent thick but imitable. Diving suit worked a dream. Black current fifteen spans deep approx. Same time tomorrow. End.

So there was nothing to do till then. Unless I wished to pore over panoramas and grub through records of past observations and hearsay from Ajelobo to Umdala; which I did not.

I could just as easily have stayed in town, and climbed up every day before dawn!

Perhaps. Perhaps that mightn't have been quite so easy in poor light. . . .

After a breakfast of black bread, raw fish and pickles in the refectory I decided that I should certainly spend the day in town, and slipped quietly away.

Not quietly enough, however. Hasso caught up with me halfway down the spiralling steps.

"Yaleen, would you let me treat you to lunch? Please."

"Lunch," I pointed out, "is four or five hours away."

"Well, I don't mind waiting, if you don't."

"Did they send you along to keep an eye on me?"

"Of course not. What possible harm could you intend us? And what harm could you possibly do, without harming yourself into the bargain?"

"You've lost me my brother," said I. "You've lost him for my parents. Forever."

"I think, Yaleen, that you and they lost him a long time ago. But don't think of him as vanished. Don't count on his not being hailed as a hero, one of these days."

"A hero—of what?"

"Of the knowledge of why things are as they are."

"And of how to alter them?"

Hasso remained silent.

"He'll be so alone," I went on. "Utter strangers, different customs, always having to sneak around and pretend. . . ."

"Not necessarily. He *is* a man, after all. Who's to say that they won't welcome him over there? Just as soon as he's checked out the lie of the land. And as to loneliness, maybe he was always alienated . . . But you know, where one man can cross, another man can cross too."

"Is that what it's really all about, then? Emigration?"

"Oh, come off it! Diving suits don't exactly come cheap or easily. Will you stop pulling such gloomy faces? We should be celebrating. For the first time in history something new has happened. We even know the depth of the black current now. I'll bet that's something your own guild doesn't know."

"No comment, Hasso."

"No comment asked for, either. Let's stop fencing, shall we? I *like* you, Yaleen. Those few little queries I raised a year ago were very much the second thing on my mind then. If not the tenth! And it was *you*, I'll remind you, who came looking. . . ."

"Hmm."

And presently we did continue on down the stairs together. Though both down in the town itself and later on when we returned up the Spire, I was careful not to seem to be sailing in the direction of *his* personal harbour. However, by then the real truth was that I hadn't drunk any Safe recently.

The next day again dawned bright, as usual at this time of the year; though perhaps it would cloud over later.

And the light winked from the same location.

The message went:

Made contact. Woman alone gathering wood. Pretended am traveller from afar. Asked reason for black patch outside town. River worshippers burnt recently. Mother caught bathing nude in river. Burnt. Later daughter went mad. Questioned. Burnt too. Who by? Brotherhood. Query? Sons of Adam. Why? Incomprehension. Repeated query. River quote Satan unquote. Satan query? Woman alarmed. Tried to flee. Overtook. Tell her am Son of Adam. On mission. Keep mouth shut. Same time tomorrow. End.

"So what's Satan?" asked Hasso, expressing the general puzzlement. "And who's Adam?"

"Maybe Satan is 'sanity', mixed up?" I suggested. "Because the black current drives men mad. . . ."

Yosef nodded. "Possibly. And possibly the word Adam has a negative prefix, as in words like 'abort' and 'apathy'—and dam is a female parent? Thus: 'sons without a mother'."

"There are quite a few of those on this side of the river," commented Hasso, somewhat acidly.

"Were you one of those?" I asked him sharply. "Was your mother a riverwoman?"

"Uh? Oh no. Not at all. Please don't leap to so many conclusions about me, will you not? I thought we'd made it all up yesterday. Well, maybe not *all*. . . ."

"Okay, okay. Sorry. So where does this Satan and Adam business leave us?"

"The answer to that," said Yosef, "is: considerably more knowledgeable than ever before. Plus, we know that some women over there worship the river, as though it's a God."

"Out of despair at their lot, presumably."

"Maybe," he went on, "it *is* a God. In the sense of a very powerful, though rather torpid being. Or perhaps a being which has other, more interesting things to think about than us. . . ." He leaned against the guard-rail, surveying the landscape around Verrino. "Fertile place, isn't it, our habitable zone? With a desert barrier bordering all of it, and precipices to seal off one end, and the wild ocean the other end. Rather like," and he smiled, "an ant colony in a very long trough. How illuminating it might be to watch how two separate ant colonies developed, supposing they were separated by a glass wall midway . . . Granting, of course, the vast difference between ants and humans."

"What are you getting at?" I asked him.

"Just that, if there's a God—or Goddess—around, she doesn't seem particularly worried whether her worshippers are burned alive . . . But maybe if she interfered, that would break the rules of her game?" Yosef hesitated. "And of course, if there were a higher being involved, humans could hardly hope to understand it—or perhaps even to prove that it *was* a higher being. No more than an ant can hope to understand a man, however much time it spends crawling along him from head to foot. In which case, our particular tragedy would be to *suspect* that this was so—because an ant could never suspect anything of the sort in a million years."

Hasso looked impatient, and tried to interrupt.

Yosef simply raised his voice. "Yes, we would be conscious of the existence of a mystery—whenever we bothered to pay attention to it—without ever being able to solve it. Rather like the mystery of the whole universe of space and stars, itself. *Why* is it? *How* is it? We're in it, and of it; and so we've no idea. Perhaps if we could solve the mystery of the river, the mystery of existence might well come next?"

"One thing at a time, for goodness sake!" broke in Hasso. "It's the other shore we're exploring."

"And why is there another shore, so very separated from us? I do sometimes wonder whether there can be men, who act as Gods to other men—without scruple?"

"You mean those Sons of Adam? That Brotherhood?"

"No, not at all. I was wondering: is the black current entirely natural?"

I just had to laugh. None of these men had any concept of the sheer scope of the river. It might well be a creature, or at least part of one, a tendril—its spine or bloodstream or whatever—but that it could be a *made* thing? Oh no.

The old imp smiled at me, unoffended, and bobbed his head. "Quite!" he cried. "Quite! You're right to be amused. Far, far better that the river is an alien goddess, than the handiwork of men like Gods. Or of *women* like Gods."

And so we went below to the refectory, for a breakfast of boiled eggs, bread and hot spiced milk.

"Perhaps Yosef's right," said Hasso, intercepting me on my way to the head of the stairs. "I'm going out to the glassworks and grindery today. Want to come?"

"Why there?"

"The first helmet worked a treat, didn't it? So it's only sensible to have another one on hand. Just in case."

"Maybe Yosef was right about what?" I asked him.

"About women like Gods . . . Supposing that was so, mightn't some wise old guildmistress have an inkling of the truth?"

So she might. If. And supposing. But recalling my initiation on board the *Ruby Piglet,* I suspected not. Unless the boatmistress of the *Ruby Piglet* knew little and cared less. . . .

"Why ask me?" said I, lightly. "I'm hardly a guildmistress."

"Who knows? Some day, Yaleen, some day. . . ."

Rain showered down on our way to the glassworks, settling all the dust which had been oozing out of the cracks of the world, and soaking us both; however this hardly mattered once we arrived at the sand pits with their sheds housing tank furnaces. Before long we were both dried as crisp as biscuits. While Hasso conducted the business of ordering a new diving helmet to specifications—with no particular appearance of furtiveness on his part—I wandered about the sheds, peering at the furnace pots and moulds, the drawing hearths, and the bare-chested glassblowers playing their tubes like fanfare trumpets, arriving eventually at the grindery where much more delicate work was carried on. The time passed quickly.

We returned to town by one o'clock under a clear sky, for the rain clouds had passed away upriver and the sun come out again; and slaked our thirst and filled our bellies with savoury pancakes at a wine-arbour new to me.

Later, as drowsy and replete as if we had made love, we toiled back up the spiralling stairs, pausing every fifty steps or so. I didn't know what was on Hasso's mind, but personally my heart was set on a siesta.

And as we rounded the Spire for the second time, already high above the roofs of Verrino, I saw the tiny winks of light from the far side of the river. Even as I pointed, the signal ceased.

"Something's wrong. Come on!"

We ran all the rest of the way; and I arrived with a stitch in my side.

The platform was buzzing.

Immediately Yosef saw us he hurried over, brandishing the copied message, his face grave. He thrust the sheet of paper into my hand.

"That's all there is. He broke off in mid-word."

I read:

Men hunting me. Surrounded. Wom—

Without thinking, I crumpled up the sheet as though the message would go away. Gently Yosef retrieved the paper from my fist, smoothed it out and handed it to someone else for safe keeping. To be filed in the archives, of course. Then he put his arm around my shoulder.

Three days passed, and they were days of silly hope for me: hope that another message would soon blink, boasting how well in Capsi was—as thick as thieves—with the men over there.

And on the evening of the third day, on that twice-burnt sward outside the settlement, a crowd of tiny figures gathered once more, and a cart was hauled through their midst, and something black was dragged from the back of the tumbril as though it had no more bones or volition than a sack of corn; and presently a bonfire blazed, and smoke rose greasily.

It *could* have been a woman; could have been. . . .

But I knew that it wasn't.

And what could they have been doing during the three previous days, those Sons of Adam, but tormenting Capsi terribly, for information?

The very next evening I signed on a brig, the *Darling Dog,* bound for Pecawar and home. I had no idea at all what I was going to tell Mother and Father. And I still hadn't decided this as I walked up the familiar dusty lane to our door. Contrary to expectation, in spite of all my travels this lane seemed no shorter or narrower or even dustier than it ever had before. Pecawar was just as it had always been. The world no more changes than the river changes; it flows on, and yet stays the same.

I banged the door knocker instead of just pushing on in and calling out, "I'm back." And by this choice I made myself a stranger.

Mother opened the door, and I stared at her in bewilderment, for she was a stranger too. Her body had changed shape: she was visibly pregnant.

My first fleeting thought was: so she's replaced Capsi already! And my second thought: she's replaced *both* of us. My third sad, frightened thought was: she's forty, she'll die, it's too late to have another baby!

But there she stood, young and glowing, with the false bloom of pregnancy about her . . .

How could anybody turn back the clock like this? Way back nearly twenty years to another bout with infancy and toddlerhood and school days? But the truth about a clock is that its hour hand moves on and on inexorably—until suddenly it's back at the very same hour it was, once in the past.

"Hullo, Mother." I embraced her cautiously, though she seemed to have no such reservation about squeezing me, almost to death. (Had the Sons of Adam crushed Capsi with heavy weights? Had they used red-hot pincers, and ropes to rack his bones out of joint?)

And I had my answer to the problem of how to tell her. Was it a coward's answer—or a brave one, because it left me with all the weight to bear myself?

Now that she was pregnant I couldn't possibly tell her that Capsi had just been burnt alive over on the other shore. Not now. The shock would make her miscarry; then there would be two deaths on my conscience, double grief for them. I *would* tell Mother, of course; but not just yet—not till my next visit home, which I would make sure I timed well after the baby was born. Nor could I load this weight upon Father alone.

And one part of me was asking, all this while: how much *had* Capsi and Yaleen ever really meant to her, or even to both of them? Or did Mother only really care about herself?

How strange, this second late motherhood of hers. I felt lost and alone because of it.

"I visited Capsi in Verrino," I said brightly. "I've just spent a week with him."

"Really? You must tell me all his news." Mother laughed. "Young rascal, running off like that! Almost as bad as you . . . So what are we standing here at the door for, like a pair of strangers?"

Thus after a year away I entered my home, which wasn't *my* home any longer but the home of a child unborn who would never regard me as a sister but only as another adult member of the family, a sort of aunt or third parent mostly absent.

I left after less than a week spent brooding around Pecawar, and signed on to sail south upon the schooner *Spry Goose,* determined to remain with this same boat for at least a year or two, as though its crew were my real family; and determined also to become an impeccable riverwoman upon it, thus somehow to compensate for my dereliction at Verrino.

And I suppose I must have succeeded in my aim, all too soon, for by the end of that same year, far to the south in the steamy tropics I was invited by my guild to volunteer for the New Year's Eve journey out to the black current.

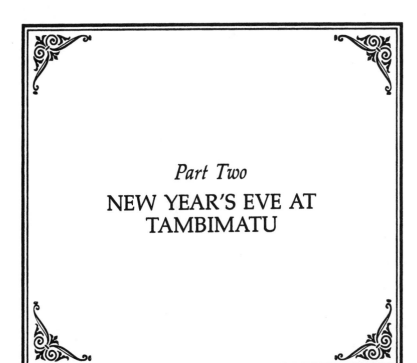

Part Two

NEW YEAR'S EVE AT TAMBIMATU

*W*AS I glad when the *Spry Goose* got to Jangali! Boatmistress Marcialla was actually going to allow her crew a few days' holiday. Imagine that. A rest.

Of course, nothing is ever as simple as it seems. By the time we were to resume our voyage again, a few score hours later, I would feel distinctly relieved to be back on board. When we arrived on that sultry late autumn afternoon, however, I wasn't to know this. A somewhat weary Yaleen was just looking forward innocently to the Junglejack Festival.

The problem with the *Spry Goose* wasn't that Marcialla was a martinet, a disciplinarian. Nor her boatswain Credence, either. It was simply that Marcialla was boat-proud; and the *Spry Goose* being a three-mast schooner, there was quite a lot of boat to be proud of. So when we picked up a load of paint at Guineamoy, and Marcialla had said casually, "Let's give the *Goose* a lick of paint," I didn't know what we were in for.

I soon found that painting isn't a matter of slapping on a fresh coat, then sitting back to admire it. First there's the rubbing down of the old paint, often to the wood. Next, any knots in the exposed timber have to be sealed with knotting juice, and any cracks filled with resin-gum. After that there's priming, and then there's undercoating . . . and a long, long time later you actually get to doing the painting itself—twice over.

The less said the better, I think, about all the laborious hours that

I and several others spent while we sailed south with the autumn winds behind us! Three times over we plied from Guineamoy to Spanglestream and back again. Then from Spanglestream to Croakers' Bayou four times there and back. Rubbing, knotting, priming, painting. And on each of the return trips, as we tacked against the prevailing wind, I had rope and canvas to occupy my idle hands. I think Marcialla deliberately timetabled the loading and delivery of cargoes just so as to build in optimum drying times.

Yet at least this kept my body and mind occupied. Thus it was *almost* "innocently" that I arrived eventually in Jangali, anticipating a little holiday.

Innocent, though, I was not. Not deep in my heart. For had I not helped my own brother to go to a horrible death on the far side of the river, where they burn women alive? Had I not watched through a telescope, while they burned him?

And I had not dared tell my mother or my father, rationalizing this failure of courage on my part as a responsible decision—since anguish at the news of Capsi's fate might make my mother miscarry. (Though what she imagined she was up to by having another baby, was beyond my comprehension!)

All the labour of painting seemed to have laid a coat of paint over these scars in my soul. Yet it hadn't really done so. I hadn't knotted and gummed and primed those scars. When the paint dried, they would soon show through again as dark shadows. The fresh skin of paint would crack and peel.

Also, while busy painting—and reefing and luffing, belaying and shinning up rigging—I had kept my eyes fixed on the tasks in hand. Even so, the black current was always there. No amount of paint, no spread of sails, was going to hide it or erase it.

Was it really a living creature six hundred leagues long and more? A powerful, sensitive yet generally comatose being which for its own purposes allowed women to ply the river, but not men? Was it some kind of alien goddess? Or was it, as old Yosef had implied, something artificially created to separate us from the "Sons of Adam" on the west bank, that mysterious brotherhood of men who turned their backs superstitiously and savagely upon the river; about whom almost all we knew was the little that Capsi had been able to heliograph back before they caught him?

I had drunk of the current, and it knew me; but it I did not know. Maybe it was impossible ever to know what the black current really was. In which case how much more sensible it was to ignore it, and get on painting a boat, and enjoy the journey as much as possible.

And really—hard labour and scars of the heart apart—there were so many new sights for me to soak in. Even when seen twice and thrice over they still remained quite exciting, by and large.

South of Gangee, that scruffy town which I'd visited on my first voyage aboard the *Sally Argent*, was Gate of the South.

The tropics put in their first hesitant appearance there—with the townsfolk doing their best to encourage the show. Butterblooms cascaded from balconies, and biscus trees were kept well watered by a network of tiny cobbled streams, although the red trumpet flowers were smaller than those I was to see further south.

Just as my own home town of Pecawar made a virtue of being on the verge of the desert, so did Gate of the South rejoice in its own position—more so than some towns of the deep south which were tropical through and through. At Gate of the South it was still possible to "garden" the vegetation. There was even a ceremonial stone arch which spanned the road from north to south, with a signpost by it listing all the distances to furthest Tambimatu 280 leagues away. What practical use this was I couldn't say, except perhaps as a disincentive to the local men to set out on foot! My new friend Jambi, with whom I went ashore for a few hours, was a six-year veteran of these southern reaches, and she pointed out in high amusement that no road actually ran all the way from Gate of the South to Tambimatu. The swamps around Croakers' Bayou were obstacle number one. Further south than that, the jungle increasingly had its own way with roads.

Jambi was dark-skinned and jolly, with long black hair which she generally wore in a bun so as not to get tangled, thus hoisting her up the main mast inadvertently. She hailed from Spanglestream, and the only time I mentioned the black current to her she merely glanced and wrinkled her nose, and that was the whole of her interest in it. This made me suppose that she was rather a good choice as a friend. She wouldn't remind me of anything painful. Jambi had a shore-husband and a baby boy at Spanglestream, though she didn't seem to bother about them unduly, except to the extent that she stayed in southern waters.

After leaving Gate of the South, we called at Guineamoy—source of that wretched load of paint. At Guineamoy you could also have gardened the tropics. But the people didn't bother, perhaps because Gate of the South had stolen their thunder. Guineamoy preferred to wear an ugly face and hide everything in grime. The people seemed to make a virtue of this, as though foul air and the stink of chemicals were their way of dealing with the burgeoning extravagance of nature. Smoke and steam belched out of lots of little workshops. There were kilns and smelters and smithies. There were warehouses and rubbish dumps; and outside of the town, half a league inland, was an artificial lake of filth. Inland, yes. Whatever stenches they pumped into the air, obviously they had no desire to risk polluting the river itself. If they had, I suppose the river guild might have banned their cargoes. What the black current itself would have done about such pollution, if anything, I had no idea. Just then, I didn't wish to wonder.

I suppose grime is comparative. If Guineamoy seemed a filthy place to me, maybe to its inhabitants it seemed a paragon of virtue and energy, and everywhere else excessively rustic. Maybe I was unduly sensitive to it, like a green leaf vulnerable to blight—because I was already a little blighted in my soul.

After Guineamoy came Spanglestream, which was renowned for its tasty fish and its dozens of lug-sailed fishing smacks decorated with painted eyes on hulls and sails. It was equally famous for the phosphorescent streamers which snaked across the river at night in bright silver, transforming the river into one of stars. These streamers only occurred for a couple of leagues to the north and south of the town, and looked like bubbly exhalations of breath from the midstream current. I suppose they must have been made up of myriads of tiny organisms which fed on minerals or whatever was abundant in the water there—providing in their turn a non-stop meal for the shoals of larger fish.

I stayed ashore overnight at Jambi's house. Her husband I found obliging and amiable. Obviously he adored Jambi—which relieved her of the need to adore him unduly in return. But otherwise he was just a little bit of a zero. I foresaw trouble if Jambi ever had to quit the river; and I could only wonder quite how she had put up with being beached during the course of her pregnancy. I played with her little boy, too. Alas, this reminded me of the infant stranger my own mother was cooking up. . . .

Jambi, husband and myself visited a raw fish restaurant that evening, where we filled ourselves with thin slices of madder-coloured hoke and yellow pollfish and velvety ajil dipped in mild mustard sauce. And we drank ginger spirit. Afterwards we strolled down to the promenade to view the spangling phosphorescence, which put on a particularly fine display for my benefit; which was the only time that I mentioned the current to Jambi.

"Maybe," I said, "all the tiny silver things feed on something the black current jettisons here? A sort of excrement from it?" I'd asked earlier, and it turned out that no one really knew. The glassmaker's art, *à la* Verrino, had never produced any lenses powerful enough to plumb the really microscopic.

That was when she glanced, and wrinkled her nose. Perhaps this wasn't surprising—in view of the fact that she had just treated me to wonderful fish. Here was I suggesting that the black current used the neighbourhood as a toilet! This may have seemed an unholy slur on her native town.

More likely my remark seemed like tipsy nonsense. Jambi was a bustling, practical person who probably dismissed her own Guild initiation quite soon after it occurred as merely a metaphorical masquerade—as something mystical, in which she had no interest.

As soon as I asked her this, to my alarm I felt a queasiness in my guts. Was this because of the presence of a male, her husband? Pleasantly fired by all the ginger spirit, I might have been on the verge of saying too much. Remembering how sick I had been when I was indiscreet about a Guild secret that one time on board the *Sally Argent,* I promptly shut up and enjoyed the silvery show.

Jambi couldn't have minded my comment, since she invited me back to her home on our subsequent calls at Spanglestream during the next few weeks. I accepted her invitation the second time. That night she was throwing a party for some local fisherwomen she had been at school with—at Spanglestream the call of the river did not necessarily call you very far from home. Yet on the third occasion I made an excuse. These invitations, kind as they were, reminded me of how I myself had invited a friend, Hali, home to Pecawar, only to discover that brother Capsi had decamped. To his doom. And then there was the presence of the little boy. The child seemed, by proxy, to dispossess me of all possible homes except those afloat.

After Spanglestream we came to Croakers' Bayou where the river spilled slackly inland into a maze of hot dank swamps. Here stilt-trees meandered in long winding colonnades, forming vaults and corridors and tunnels. Mudbanks emerged and submerged at whim. Puffballs and great white fungus domes studded the exposed mud. The big froggy croakers squatted and hopped and played their ventriloquists' tricks, voices echoing off the water and the arched tree trunks.

And I thought fancifully that if the anus of the black current was located off Spanglestream, then here at Croakers' Bayou was the mouldy decaying appendix of the river. The grating croaks were a sort of flatulence, a shifting of gases in the bowels.

Once out of Croakers' Bayou forests cloaked the shore. The western bank, far away, was likewise a ribbon of green. It occurred to me that the Sons of Adam might not rule the roost everywhere along the far side. How could they, when they denied themselves the advantages of river transport? Maybe *their* southern reaches were uninhabited. Or perhaps those who dwelled there were savages, without even the dubious level of culture of the Sons.

Savages! Ah, yet gentler perhaps than the Sons in their treatment of women. . . .

And maybe they were even worse than the Sons. I spotted no canoes; no smoke plumes from campfires near the shore. If anyone lived over there, they too shunned the river.

But this was the least of my worries, compared with the unending paint-job. Whenever it rained, which it did with a vengeance now and then, we had to rig tarpaulins.

Gradually the forest knotted and tangled itself with vines and moss-mats, epiphytes and parasites, moving towards true jungle. Which, by the time we reached Jangali, it was.

We carried two young lovers as passengers on our journey to Jangali: Lalo and Kish. Kish was a boy from Spanglestream who was a friend of Jambi's family on her mother's side. Lalo had decided that she loved him and was now escorting him back home to Jangali, on the one river trip of his life, to wed him.

It struck me as a slight shame that Kish's horizons should thus be limited to the small stretch of land between two nearly adjacent towns. Well, granted that Spanglestream and Jangali were 80 leagues apart! But a riverwoman usually thinks big, and I imagined in a rather snobbish way that it was a teeny bit unenterprising of Lalo to seek her husband from a town which was comparatively close to home, rather than from far Sarjoy (say) or Melonby.

We were chatting below decks one day, the four of us, getting better acquainted. Lalo was holding hands with Kish, while I was trying to pumice some paint off my fingers.

Like Jambi, Lalo was dark-skinned, though her hair was short and curly. She had an unusually loud voice and always spoke with particular emphasis. At one point she happened to mention that some trees deep in the Jangali jungles were "quite as high as the Spire at Verrino". She just mentioned this in passing, but so assertively did she voice it that I almost tore a nail off on the pumice stone.

"Ouch!" That Spire, and its observatory, were all too fresh in my memory.

"Oh, so you got as far as Verrino?" asked Jambi innocently. This was indeed a singularly innocent question coming from a riverwoman, since there are half a dozen major towns further north than that. But Jambi, as I say, was a devoted Southerner.

"Why yes," said Lalo. "I didn't waste my time. I just didn't find anybody suitable. Not till Spanglestream on the way back." And she squeezed Kish's hand affectionately.

"It's often that way." Jambi sounded smug.

I couldn't help wondering whether Lalo had not been growing anxious by the time she got as close to home as Spanglestream. But maybe she had been especially choosy on her travels; which meant that she had made a sensible choice. The marriage would last, and last well.

I guess from Kish's point of view there was a whole world of difference between Spanglestream and Jangali. Judging from his questions it was plain that Kish was a little apprehensive at the prospect of becoming a junglejack—if indeed he *would* become one. Lalo teased him with this prospect intermittently. Just about as often, she corrected his misapprehensions. . . .

"It seems to me," I said, and I suppose I spoke thoughtlessly in the circumstances, "that a woman could find her ideal partner in almost any town chosen at random. It's all a bit of an accident, isn't it? I mean, which street you happen to walk down. Which winehouse you pop into. Who you sit next to at a concert. You turn left here, rather than right, and it's this fellow who'll spend the rest of his life with you, while another fellow walks on by. It could so easily have been the other one instead."

"Oh no!" Lalo protested. "A feeling guides you. A kind of extra sense that you only use once. You *know* you should turn left instead of right. You *know* you ought to carry on to the next town, because the scent's gone dead in this one. You're operating by a sort of special instinct during your wander-weeks. Honestly, Yaleen, you'll know this if it happens to you. It's a heightened, thrilling feeling."

"You're a romantic," said Jambi. "Kish is lucky. I tend to agree

with Yaleen myself. Anyone can settle down with anyone else."
(That wasn't quite what I'd said.) "But then," she added, "I also
have the river as my first love."

And lovers in different ports as well, I wondered? Jambi hadn't
spoken of this to me. One didn't gossip about one's harmless amorous adventures. For one thing, it would be demeaning to the men.

"So you turned right instead of left," I said, "but guided by your
nose."

"And now I'll be a junglejack forever." Kish grinned ruefully. He
had a whimsical, expressive face, with twinkling blue eyes, and already a few smile-wrinkles to accompany them. I liked him, and
rather wished that I myself had met him—the way that I had first
met Hasso in Verrino, before I found out why Hasso had been hoping to meet someone like me.

"Phooey!" said Lalo. "A junglejack? Why, that's nothing. I tell
you, in the jungle you're usually better off *up* a tree. It's the creepy-
crawlies down below that bug us. You'll need some good strong
boots. And a stomach to go with them." She couldn't keep a straight
face, though. She giggled. "Oh, I'm just kidding. Jangali's a decent,
civilized place. Not like Port Barbra. That's where the really weird
and queasy things happen, out in the interior. The fungus cult, for
instance. Completely wrecks your sense of time and decency. Us, we
just get smashed on junglejack like decent mortals."

"Tell me more," said Kish. "I like getting smashed, too. Preferably
not by falling off a tree."

"You wouldn't, not with safety lines."

So we began to natter on about junglejack, the drink. Apparently
this was distilled from the berries of some high vine. It went off
quite quickly and didn't travel—alas for the export economy of Jangali, perhaps fortunately for the economy of everywhere else. And
we nattered about junglejacks in general: the people who felled the
hardwood trees and also harvested the tangled heights, picking
fruit, tapping juice, scraping resin, collecting medicinal parasite
plants.

I became quite enthused about the impending festival of acrobatics, vine-swinging and sky-walking, and also about getting smashed
on junglejack, the drink.

As did Kish; which was of course why Lalo had timed her return
for that particular week, to coincide. After a while she even had to
remind him gently that not *everyone* in Jangali was a junglejack. There

were also butchers and bakers and furniture makers, just like any-where else.

And she went on more emotionally, now, about the beauties of the jungle, brushing aside the creepy-crawlies as of little conse-quence.

How I wish she had dampened my enthusiasm about Jangali rather than igniting it! Little did I know then that excesses of enthu-siasm would result in my saving Marcialla's life—bringing me in turn a singularly horrible reward.

Saving Marcialla's life? Well, maybe I exaggerate. Let's change that to: rescuing her from an awkward and potentially lethal situa-tion.

I was looking forward to arriving at Jangali—which was so de-cently distant from Verrino. I was looking forward to really enjoying the events. I even imagined that I was, in a sense, successfully run-ning away. All the while in truth I was running—or sailing—*towards.*

"Sun's shining! Paint detail on deck!" came Credence's call from the top of the companion way. Why I had bothered cleaning my fingers, goodness knows. Except that if I hadn't, it would have been harder later on. Perhaps there's a moral in this: it's almost always harder later on. Everything is.

Jangali rejoiced in massive stone quays fronting the river, quarried and cut with steps and timber-slides. The town itself was founded upon that same great slab of rock, which ran back into the jungle before dipping under, submerging itself in humus and vegetation. In the original old town the architecture was of stone, with wooden upper storeys. The new town behind—which I was to see presently —was wholly of timber, and fused with the jungle itself. Some houses there incorporated living trees. Others were built on to them and around them. Some even slung from them cantilever-style. The entire effect of Jangali was of some strange metamorphosing crea-ture which was living wood at one end and fossil rock at the other— or perhaps of dead rock coming gradually to life the further inland you went.

The locals reminded me of those of Verrino. Indeed, this might have been why Lalo had followed her nose to Verrino in the first place—though with no result. Jangali folk weren't as quicksilver-nimble and chattery, always scurrying every which where. Yet there was an elastic spring to their steps, a bounciness, as if they regarded the stone floor of the town more as a trampoline, ever about to toss them up into the treetops beyond. Its inert rigidity amused them and made them prance, just as a riverwoman sometimes feels about dry land after a long time afloat; they intended never to let themselves be bruised by it.

As I say, the locals weren't chattery. But they did address one another in tones pitched to carry through tangles of vegetation in competition with the other chatterers of the beast variety; in voices intended to penetrate up to the very roof of the jungle. Conversations generally took place a few paces further apart than they did elsewhere, much more noisily, more publicly. Jangali would have been the ideal place for a deaf person to take up residence.

Thus the locals reinforced their sense of community. Otherwise, once you were in the jungle, the jungle could swallow you up, stifle you, isolate you, make you mute. I gathered from loud-voiced Lalo that people around Port Barbra behaved more furtively.

Before Lalo and Kish disembarked, they invited Jambi and me to visit them at their parents' home. Or more truthfully, Kish expressed this desire, so that Jambi (old family friend) could see him in his new abode; Lalo invited Jambi and included me in the invitation too. I suppose Kish was trying to keep a kind of psychological lifeline open to Spanglestream. No doubt he hoped that Jambi would continue to pay the occasional visit whenever she was in Jangali. Personally, I didn't think this was entirely wise—not at this early stage in their relationship. For "a man shall leave his mother and father, and sister and brother, and embrace the family of his wife". That's what it says in *The Book of the River*. In at the deep end, say I! Just so long as there aren't any stingers in the water (or at least in the hope that there aren't).

Yet maybe Kish was right. This established him from the start, in a strange town, as on an equal footing with his wife.

At any rate, it was their own business, and I soon abandoned any minor scruples I might have felt about us getting in the way when I learned that Lalo's parents lived in the new town, in a hanging home high up a tree. This I had to see.

And that's what we set out to do, the very next day. But before that, an odd thing happened.

We'd arrived in Jangali in mid-afternoon. There was the furling of the sails to see to, and the gangers to supervise as they unloaded our cargo: crans of fish from Spanglestream, barrels of salt trans-shipped all the way from Umdala, and pickles from Croakers' Bayou and such. By the time everything was boatshape, we only had time to go ashore for a brisk walk round the monumental old town, culminating in a not so brief visit to Jambi's favourite bar—where I made my first acquaintance with the fiery junglejack.

The bar in question—the whole town, for that matter—was a-buzz in expectation of the festival. The normal population must have increased by half again, what with people trekking in from up-country and from smaller jungle settlements along the shore, not to mention outside visitors. Lalo pointed out women from Croakers' Bayou, and from Port Barbra. The former she identified by a more sallow look to them, and the latter by the hooded cloaks and scarves they wore—to cope, Jambi said, with occasional pesky clouds of insects in their area; besides Port Barbrans spoke much more softly. By contrast the Jangali locals seemed even noisier than I supposed they usually were. The Jingle-Jangle Bar lived up to its name; and I ended up later on with quite a headache—quite independent, of course, of the junglejack spirit.

The motif of the Jingle-Jangle wasn't trees, but carved stone. The bar was an artificial cavern of nooks and crannies and stalagmite-like columns, with fat chunky nude statues holding oil lamps. Around their squat necks hung strings of medallions, and around their loins brief girdles of the same. Presumably these medallions would jingle and jangle if you shook them. To my mind the whole mood of the bar was primitive and subterranean, with a hint of secrets and conspiracy, an odour of dark mystery.

The place was also very hot. There we were in the reeking petrified bowels of a jungle so dense that it had become a cave. I must say that the place had atmosphere: compounded of perfume and oil-fumes, sweat and mustiness, and partly of sheer hot air from all the babbling voices. I wouldn't have been surprised if savage drums had begun to beat; I noticed that there was a stone dais for entertainers, currently unoccupied.

And in the Jingle-Jangle I happened to notice Marcialla and Credence sitting over a drink. This wasn't in itself unusual. What was odd was that they seemed to be arguing. Credence was insisting on something; Marcialla kept on shaking her head.

Every so often Credence glanced in the direction of a small, hooded group of women from Port Barbra; and Marcialla particularly shook her head then.

I should explain that Marcialla was quite a short woman, though in no way squat even if she must have been in her early fifties. She was wiry, and carried no spare flesh. Credence was big and busty and blonde, and at least fifteen years her junior. Marcialla wore her greying hair swept back in short shingled waves; Credence had hers in chopped off pigtails. All in all Credence looked like an inflated, coarsened girl.

"I'm peckish. Let's have a bite to eat," I suggested. So we carried our drinks over to the buffet bar—this was supported by carved stone female dwarfs, pygmy caryatids holding up the food table. On Jambi's say-so we bought spiced snakemeat rolls.

On the way back I ducked into an empty nook just round the corner from our boatmistress and her boatswain. This was just on impulse. Besides, our previous seats had already been taken in our absence.

I admit that I was curious and a little tipsy, therefore bold. But with all the racket going on around us I didn't really expect to hear anything. However, there must have been something of a whispering gallery effect in that nook. Also, the din was so incoherent that paradoxically this made it easier rather than harder to pick out snatches of two familiar voices—the way that a mother can hear her own particular offspring cry out amidst fifty other bawling babies.

Snatches was all that I did hear, but they were interesting enough.

"But suppose you doped the black current with enough of the time-drug. . . ." That was Credence.

A mumble from Marcialla.

". . . slow down its response, wouldn't it?"

"That fungus is a poison of the mind. . . ."

". . . test it by mixing some in a phial of the black current. . . ."

". . . and who'll drink it? You?"

". . . might do."

". . . to prove what?"

". . . achieve more *rapport*, Marcialla! Somehow to be able to speak to it, and it to us. Maybe our time-scales are too different."

". . . contradicting yourself. Slow *it* down? Slow us down, you mean. Anyway, it reacts fast enough when it's rejecting someone."

"Reflexes and thoughts are two different things. If I stuck my hand in a fire. . . ."

"Your trouble is, you're a true believer. Like your Mother; and so she named you Credence. You believe in the godly spirit of the river . . ." A surge in the level of the din cut off the rest of this.

"Besides," was the next thing I heard, from Marcialla, "take this notion one stage further. It's all very well to talk blithely of doping

one phial with this wretched fungus powder. But suppose somebody then thought of dumping a few barrels of the stuff into the
midstream, eh? Slow down its, ah, reflexes long enough to take a
boat through, perhaps? Over to the other side . . . Where does that
lead to in the long run? I'll tell you where: it leads to poisoning the
current. It leads to making the river safe for men. What price your
goddess, then? The whole thing falls apart. A whole, good way of
life goes with it. Always assuming that the black current didn't react
horrendously to being poisoned! What you're saying is sheer madness."

"Sorry, *Guildmistress,*" said Credence unctuously.

"You know those people, don't you?"

"Which people?"

"The Port Barbra ones over there. Do you think I'm blind? You've
arranged something. Now you want a phial of the black current. Or
is it a bucketful? They want it. In exchange. Do they appreciate the
dangers? Any more of this, and we'll be having to flash word to
every boatmistress on the river to keep the stuff under double lock.
Don't you think that would be sad? Is there no trust? No sense any
more?"

Then the noise really did get out of hand. Some musicians had
arrived, to do terrible things to my head—although they played
pipes and flutes and banjos rather than bashing on drums. Jambi
was growing restive about my noncommittal grunts and yes-noes as
I sat with my head cocked, intent on other things.

"You in a trance or something?" she shouted.

"Hmm . . . ? No. Sorry! Cheers."

After a long lie-in the next morning, I was up and leaning against
the rail at the head of the gangplank waiting for Jambi to join me—
when along came Marcialla.

"Yaleen," she said thoughtfully, "saw you in the Jingle-Jangle last
night." She waited for me to volunteer something.

"Quite a place," I said. "Oof. My head." I rubbed my tender skull.

"You meet all sorts in a place like that."

"All sorts are in town for the festival, I suppose."

"Even women from Port Barbra."

"Oh yes, Jambi pointed some out to me. They wear hoods and
scarves."

And so we continued to fence for a while (or at least that's what I thought), and I was feeling fairly pleased with myself, though also praying that Jambi would hurry along and break it up.

"Weird place, Port Barbra," said Marcialla. "Odd people there, some of them."

"So I've heard. Strange jungly rites."

"People sometimes get attracted by strange things." When I said nothing, Marcialla went on, "Of course, you can't judge a place by its oddballs. Its extremists. After all, look at Verrino."

Did she know? Had word got out of what I had done, and passed along the river? I was talking—I remembered—to a guildmistress, no less. I'd heard that much last night.

"And equally," she mused, "people can get mixed up in queer things quite innocently, even the best of them." My heart was thumping. But then, so was my head. That was when Marcialla glanced up at the rigging and furled sails, her boatswain's special province, and sighed; and I realized that she had been thinking all along in a sad and lonely way of Credence, and simply associating me with her because I too had been in the Jingle-Jangle.

"Maybe," I said—I was trying to be helpful, without at the same time betraying myself as an eavesdropper—"maybe people who believe deeply in things are all innocents, but it's a dangerous kind of innocence. . . ." And maybe I only said this to impress, in the hope that Marcialla would be amazed at my youthful perspicacity. What I'd said certainly wasn't true of the Observers at Verrino. Hasso hadn't been an innocent. On the contrary! Nor Yosef, either. Nor Capsi. Dedicated men, but by no means naive. If I had overheard that conversation aright the previous night, though, Credence was both dedicated *and* naive, deep down.

Marcialla obviously regarded me as the innocent, here. She smiled in a kindly way.

"You've done good painting work. Quite commendable. And if I hadn't kept you at it back then, there wouldn't have been time for a holiday now, would there? Don't let me keep you from enjoying yourself."

"I'm just waiting for Jambi." (Where was she, damn it?)

"Take care ashore," Marcialla added softly. More to herself than to me.

"Care, Boatmistress?" And I realized that I was echoing Credence's suave tone, of not so many hours earlier.

Marcialla stared at me, puzzled. "The booze, I mean, girl. Watch the booze; it's lethal." And she patted me on the arm.

"Don't I know it!"

Which was when Jambi turned up at long last.

So we sought out Lalo's home in the new town. We followed her directions scrupulously; but, as directions have a way of being, these ones were perfect so long as you had already been there once. As we walked, the stone of the old town transmuted itself into the timber of the new. Homes were nuzzling against living trees, or were arranged around them in conical skirts so that the tree itself seemed like a huge, out-of-proportion chimney. Other houses climbed the largest giants in cantilevered or buttressed tiers—stepping around the great trunks like flights of steps by which some wood spirit could descend at night from the leafy crowns. Sometimes a walkway ran from one tree to the next, along a branch.

As yet, this was all jungle which had been thinned out and tamed. In the old town the sun was aggressively hot and glary; further inland the unbroken umbrella of foliage would surely blank it off except for vagrant shafts like spears of molten metal. Here then, in the new town, was the ideal compromise: the sunlight dappled down. Unfamiliar flower bushes hugged the roadways and paths, but there was no riot of undergrowth as such. Vegetable gardens were planted here and there, plump with tomatoes, courgettes, cucumbers, sweetgourds, meatmelons, pumpkins. Familiar fruits mostly, though their size was something else.

And of course we got lost. Or more exactly, we arrived just where we wanted to be not that day, but a couple of days later: at the festival site. I suppose this was because quite a number of people involved in the preparations were heading that way too. Like two stray fish caught up in a school of busier fish, unconsciously we went with them.

We came to a very large clearing, on one side of which workers were hammering, fixing and strengthening the terraces of a grandstand.

And at once I felt at home, for the area before the grandstand was like the deck of an enormous boat. Sparred masts soared up to the sky from the flat, stripped ground. Rope ladders ran up some of these; single knotted ropes up others. I spied trapezes, aerial platforms and crow's nests—with more ropes stretched taut from each to the other; while behind this array stood a dead, though still mighty tree. All the minor and lower branches had been lopped, but the surviving high arms were hung with more acrobatic gear. A few junglejacks dressed in tough baggy trousers, scarlet jerkins and flexible fork-toed boots hung from harnesses, checking belays and loops, wood-pitons and snaplinks; one man was abseiling down a rope.

After watching all this activity for a while, we made enquiries and were on our way again—this time in the right direction. My hangover had died away nicely by now.

As promised, the Lalo family home was a tree-house—one of those which "stepped up" around a jungle giant. We reached it by way of a covered stairway bolted to the trunk which mounted the roofs of the houses below.

Yet scarcely had we arrived at the door, let alone met any parents, than Lalo declared that a picnic was in order "out in the *real* jungle". Kish popped out in her wake, bearing a hamper, and within what seemed like seconds we were descending the stairs again.

Perhaps Lalo's parents had hinted strongly that it wasn't good form to invite a friend from Spanglestream so very soon after Kish had left the place. Next thing, all his female relatives and friends might be descending on Jangali, to snap the house right off its moorings!

Or maybe it was Lalo, restored to her home and habits after her long wander-weeks, who had decided of her own accord that she had committed a *faux pas* by casually inviting two boating acquaintances. Kish himself seemed perfectly happy and at ease.

Whatever the reason, off we went into the jungle along a trail of perhaps half a league, which grew increasingly wild and noisy with hidden wildlife.

A jungle seen from afar, from the deck of a boat, can be utterly monotonous. At close quarters the same jungle becomes magical. There seemed to be a hundred shades of green: a whole spectrum composed entirely of that colour, as though the sun shed green light, not a bluish white. And in competition with this first, green spectrum was a second one consisting of flowers and flutterbyes radiating reds and oranges and azures, shocking pink and sapphire, like coloured lamps, the better to be noticed. Wings and petals seemed crystalline, glassy, iridescent, with an inner light of their own.

"Why, the flowers are shining!" I exclaimed. "Aren't they? And that flutterbye there!"

"They are—and you should see them after dusk," said Lalo.

Apparently when all the green leaves grew dim there lingered for an hour or two a parade of floral and insect firelight.

Lalo pointed out the occasional dangerous spinetree, and a squat "boiler" out of which a burning liquid could gush, and oozing gum-sponges. She flushed out a whistle-snake which would shriek to scare you if you trod on it; but it wasn't dangerous except perhaps to your ear-drums. She sent a couple of land-crabs scuttling. These could take your finger off, though only if you stuck it in the wrong place.

She named for us the mammoths of the jungle: the jacktrees, hogannies and teakwoods. She showed us where honeygourds and blue-pears hung up high almost out of sight. We passed a miniature forest of white antlered fungi crowding on a fallen, rotten trunk. These, she said, were edible; whereas the tiny crimson buttons sprouting beneath were instant poison. They looked it. I'm glad I paid attention. I little knew it at the time, but this guided tour was a lesson in survival which I would be very glad of during the early weeks of the next year . . .

Vines dangled down as if to loop and strangle you. Indeed there was one variety known as stranglevine; but you had to allow it a good half-hour to tie itself round you. Moss-mats hung in greenly dripping masses, as though secreting some slime-venom—yet these could staunch blood and disinfect wounds. And webvines wove what looked suspiciously like enormous webs where surely something fat and hairy with lots of legs and eyes lurked; but didn't.

We finally came to Lalo's chosen picnic spot. Deep rock erupted upwards here in the form of a ziggurat rising a hundred spans above the jungle floor. As we neared this stone mass, it took on the appearance of an abandoned, overgrown temple. Briefly I imagined that Lalo was about to reveal an ancient secret to us: the work of some long-dead race, dating from before human beings ever came to this world, from somewhere else.

But no; it was a natural formation. Crude steps, now mossed over, had been cut up one side of it; though perhaps the steps were natural too, due to fracturing and crumbling. We climbed up these to the top, which was flat and almost bald of vegetation except for a cushion of moss. Lalo uprooted a few plants and a shrub which had established themselves, and tossed them over the side—just as hill climbers elsewhere add an extra stone to a cairn. So, high above the jungle floor in this gap squeezed open by the ziggurat, we sat down. Kish unpacked a bottle of wine wrapped in wet leaves to keep it cool; and blue-pears, spiced rolls, smoked snake and a jar of pickled purple fungi.

We chatted idly, and ate and drank and admired the view, mainly of aerial webs and mats of moss—the brighter aspects of the jungle were below these middle levels, mostly. After a while I picked up the half-empty pickle jar and peered at the remaining contents.

"I was meaning to ask you, Lalo. You were saying that people at Port Barbra use some fungus or other as a drug to mix their minds up."

Lalo laughed. "And here in Jangali we always poison visitors with purple mushrooms. To keep them in our thrall for a hundred years."

"No, seriously."

"Why?"

"No special reason. It just seems weird. Interesting, you know?"

"And poor Jangali has nothing half as interesting on offer, alas."

"Oh, I didn't mean to imply . . . ! Why, this is fabulous." I swept my hand around. "I feel like a real junglejack perched up here."

Kish grinned. "I don't think junglejacks enjoy quite as much support as this."

"Anyhow," I persisted, "what *is* the story?"

Lalo considered, while she bit into a blue-pear.

"I don't know all that much about it. We hear bits of gossip now and then. About orgies in the interior. They use this fungus powder to make sex last a long time. To spin out the, um, sensations, so that they seem to last for hours and hours."

"So it's a drug which slows time down?"

"The trouble is, time gets its own back. So I've heard. You speed up afterwards. You run all over the place like a loony. You talk too fast for anyone to understand you. You gobble down heaps of food because you're burning it all up. If you go on using the stuff, you age before your time. You're old at thirty. Worn out, I suppose."

This business about rushing around and chattering nineteen to the dozen didn't quite seem to square with what I'd heard of the "furtive" conduct of people in Port Barbra and environs. But maybe the members of the drug cult kept themselves apart in secret places while they were liable to race about and gabble on. In any case this might just be a tall tale which the drug users fostered, to frighten people off.

"So it's mainly a sex thing with them? It's all just to make sex more thrilling?"

"I don't know that it makes it any more thrilling," said Lalo. "It certainly makes it last longer."

In her emphatic voice, this sounded like some ultimate statement. Kish blinked several times and shook his head as though he hadn't heard correctly. Jambi convulsed with silent laughter.

Lalo pulled a doleful face. "Oh dear! I think I said the wrong thing." And we all began to laugh; after which I couldn't reasonably get back to the topic without seeming obsessed. As if I wanted some of the fungus drug for myself.

Two days later Jambi and I were part of a huge crowd out at the festival ground. Lalo and Kish had promised to see us there, but of course we didn't meet up. There must have been ten thousand people. The grandstand was packed to bursting and the sides of the clearing were thronged. Certainly there were more people than I had ever seen in one place before. It struck me immediately that anything could happen in such a crowd while the acrobatic displays were in progress, and nobody would be any the wiser. Alas, despite the presence of at least a score of jungle-guild marshals patrolling and supposedly keeping an eye on things, I was right.

The clearing had been transformed with banners and bunting, with bright little tents and stalls beneath awnings selling snacks and drinks. There were side shows for the children; giant flutterbyes in twig cages to be won; wrestlers, clowns, conjurors, even a fortune teller.

A fortune teller. I had never had my fortune told. The tent was decorated with golden stars and comets; and when we came upon it there was no one waiting outside.

"Shall we?"

"No thanks," said Jambi. A conjuror was tossing a stream of shiny silver balls nearby. By some sleight of hand he seemed to be making them travel in figure-eights. "I'll watch him. You go ahead."

A fortune teller. Would the person read my palm? Or slit open a fish and examine its guts for auspices? How ancient, how quaint.

Inside, the tent was dim. So until I was already inside and committed, I didn't realize that the fortune teller was a Port Barbra woman. Her hood was pulled well over her head, and her scarf covered her nose and mouth so that of her face there were only two eyes staring out intently—observing the whole of me, while I saw precious little of her.

She spoke softly. "Please sit." On a stool, before a little table.

Which I did. By now I was wishing to flee from the tent, instead. But I was determined to be polite. Or was I too cowardly to rush out? Sometimes rudeness is the better part of courage. . . .

However, I placed upon the table a coin of the value stipulated on the notice outside, 50 scales, or half a fin. Not much, though not entirely negligible.

Cards: it was cards. She was a cartomancer—though maybe she could also turn a trick with fish-guts or palm-lines. Cards were probably faster and took fewer powers of invention.

She handed me a pack, face down. "Don't look. Cut and shuffle three times. Each time you cut, turn half the pack around." I did so, and gave it back.

She fanned the pack on the table, still face-down. There must have been a hundred well-thumbed cards in all.

"Choose nine."

I did so, quite at random. I had no special instinct for this one rather than that. She stacked the rest of the pack to one side then began to turn up the cards I had selected.

The first showed waves on water, with a schooner riding in the distance. The picture was in sepia tones, and pink and dirty white— as were they all to be.

"This is the River. This is you." Her voice was a dull monotone. I nodded, though I shouldn't have done.

The second showed a spyglass. "This lies behind you. You are observant. You watch, though you don't always understand. But since this is behind you, you will understand more in future."

The third was of a babe in arms, but it was facing away from me. "This is your family. Reversed, it suggests negative feelings. You sail on the river to escape this." ("Oh no I don't," I said to myself.) "Or perhaps," she added, "by sailing the river you create these negative feelings." Obviously I had given her some facial cue. I decided to keep my features frozen.

Next was a signal-mirror, hand-held against a backdrop of rolling clouds with the sun just breaking through. Again the card faced away from me.

"These are your hopes or fears. The light of illumination. If reversed, you fear a message. Or a message has filled you with fear. The clouds are your anxieties, which cloud insight."

She turned up the fifth card; and I saw a handsome, laughing man, smartly attired. He reminded me of Hasso (of the dandyish flared trousers and striped shirts), though he was differently attired; but he was just as jaunty. Once again the card lay turned away.

"This is the influence at work: a husband to be sought, a lover. Yet he isn't really for you. Or else he is far away in time or space."

Number six was a cockerel crowing on a dunghill.

"Pride," she interpreted. "Indiscretion."

Indeed? Perhaps it made sense, at that!

Seven was a bonfire, with another cockerel rising in flames from it, flapping fiery wings. An arrow pierced the bird's chest. I had begun to sweat coldly, because his bonfire stirred hideous memories; but she said:

"This is the soul. Also, striving—which is betrayed or disappointed. Or else transfiguration which pierces the heart. The meaning is ambiguous." The bonfire certainly wasn't! "That card shows the *potential* outcome."

Number eight: three men with staffs sprouting green leaves were fighting with three women similarly armed. A fourth man strode away from the fight, his staff over his shoulder supporting a bundle. A house blazed, behind.

"Conflict. A husband walking home. Warfare. Alternatively: resolute bravery, success. This is the *probable* outcome. Again, it's ambiguous."

She turned the last card over, placing it in the centre of the cross-shape she had made with the others. I beheld a river with a black band snaking along it midway. Several fishes gaped out of the water as though to gulp flies.

"The Black Current, what else? This crosses you, obstructs you. Or maybe . . . *you* will cross *it.*" Abruptly the fortune-teller reached out and grasped my wrist. "What do you know of any of this?" she whispered fiercely. Her grip was tight. Outside, drums were beating, and I thought that they were beating in my heart.

"Nothing! Let go of me!" With my free hand I quickly forced her fingers open. After months of working boats this wasn't difficult. And this time I did flee, out through the flap of the tent.

"Hey!" cried Jambi, who was hovering impatiently. "You're missing the show! It's started. Come on."

Those drums beat louder now, unmuffled by the canvas; and pipes were skirling. Jambi had no time to ask me how I had got on in the tent; neither then—nor later.

* * *

If you want to commit a crime, the best place to do so is in public: in a place so public that dozens of other distractions are on hand.

How Marcialla actually got into the predicament she did get into, I never saw. Nor did Jambi. If anyone else noticed they must have taken it entirely for granted, as nothing unusual on festival day. When Jambi did spot what was going on, even she didn't at first register anything amiss. But she wasn't privy to the conversation I'd overheard in the Jingle-Jangle—nor had she heard Marcialla's veiled warning as we two chatted at the head of the gangplank.

It was a good three hours later. The main display was already over: the acrobatics, the climbing and abseiling, the ropewalking and trapezing by professional junglejacks male and female who had been practising for a week and more. That evening would see a fireworks display upon the great masts—the fireworks imported, naturally, from smelly Guineamoy. But the period from now until dusk provided full opportunity for those who weren't part of the official performance to show off their own antics. So when the last professional team had swung down sweating to the ground, a whistle blew. Teenagers, and men and women too, swarmed across the field to the tall masts and began to scramble aloft. Some went high up, some not so high.

"Accidents? Of course there are accidents," Jambi was saying to me as we watched these novices displaying their skill, or lack of it. "Lalo says that someone broke his neck a couple of years back. There are always sprains and fractures."

"It seems silly."

"Isn't it better if it happens here than out in the deep jungle?"

"I don't follow you."

She gestured. "There's a first aid tent. Bandages, bonesetters."

"Why should amateurs do it at all?"

"Oh, Yaleen! If somebody takes a tumble here, obviously they aren't ever going to make it as a real junglejack. The guild won't accept them."

"Oh, I *see*. *We* don't need competitions in mastclimbing, to become riverwomen. We just do it."

"The river's softer than the ground."

"Decks aren't. And don't forget the stingers!"

"Well, that's how they do things here. See: the jungle-guild marshals are watching what goes on, but they won't interfere."

"It seems a bit barbaric." Was it any more of a peculiar ordeal than having to drink a slug of the black current? A slug which might drive you mad? Less, perhaps. Less.

We were debating the pros and cons over cups of cool blue perry which we'd bought from a nearby stall, when Jambi broke off. She squinted and shaded her eyes.

"Isn't that Marcialla up the tree?"

I stared across the clearing. Marcialla, indeed. High high up, swinging freely to and fro on a trapeze. No safety nets of webvine were hung beneath.

"Why does she want to show off? Surely she isn't thinking of quitting the water for the woods at her age?"

Marcialla's posture was . . . peculiar. The tiny distant figure sat immobile, with her fists clenched round the ropes. Her legs and her head weren't moving in proper time with the motion of the trapeze.

And when the trapeze finally swung to a standstill, Marcialla would be marooned high over a gulf of nothing.

At that moment I noticed three figures hastening through the crowd over to our left. They were heading away in the direction of the old town. One was blonde and big and very familiar. The other two were hooded. I couldn't distinguish their Port Barbra features, but something about the way one of them moved and clutched briefly at Credence to say something convinced me that she was the fortune-teller. For all I knew she might have been in the Jingle-Jangle too, a few nights earlier! Then the crowd hid the trio.

In a flash I knew exactly what was going on. (Yes indeed, the signal-mirror had just flashed an urgent message in my mind!)

"Jambi, don't ask questions—it's too urgent. You must do this for me: run back to the docks as fast as you can. Round up any crew you see—and secure Marcialla's cabin! Whatever you do, don't let Credence into it. Particularly if she has any strangers with her. Women in hoods."

"Eh? But I can't forbid—"

"Trust me. Do it!" And I set off at a sprint across the clearing.

I climbed that dead tree by rope ladder, as far as a notch where the main trunk forked. Here was the platform from which Marcialla must have been launched, but this was no use to me at all; Marcialla was way out of reach by now. The trapeze came less close to its starting point on each return swing. At least Marcialla hadn't fallen yet: she still sat propped on her seat like a life-sized doll.

A single knotted rope led higher up—thirty or forty spans higher

—to where a lateral branch of considerable girth left the trunk. It was pointing in the right direction, but so many spans above. Craning my neck, I could see more rope lying on the branch, the coils bulging over like a nesting snake. One end appeared to be fastened by snap-link to a wood-piton driven deep into the trunk itself.

Quite how I managed the rest of the ascent I'll never know. It wasn't like climbing up a mast at all. For me there has always been a certain feeling of elasticity about climbing a mast. Because a mast is rooted in a floating boat. There's a sense that your activities up a mast produce a certain slight reaction in the mast itself. No doubt this is perfectly illusory! Otherwise boats would tip over as soon as a few women swarmed into the rigging. But this tree felt like rock, rooted in rock.

At last I reached the branch which I was aiming for, and scrambled on to it, legs astride, beside the waiting rope. I was relieved to see other pitons set at intervals along the branch; otherwise I don't know how I could have tied the rope to it, given its girth. Unclipping the snap-link, I hoisted the coils over my head on to my shoulders. All coiled up, that rope was quite some weight.

Shuffling my thighs forward as fast as I dared, I soon arrived at a piton positioned above the midpoint of Marcialla's swing, and attached the snap-link again.

She was only swaying to and fro quite gently by now. The wooden bar of her seat was hardly a very substantial one; and I feared that she was in even more danger. While she had still been swinging fairly vigorously, sheer force of momentum may have adjusted her balance and even lessened her apparent weight. Soon there would only be gravity pulling at her. Pulling down.

Down. Much too far below the hard ground waited. . . .

How *did* one abseil down through mid-air? I'd watched enough junglejacks doing it that very afternoon! One of them had gripped the rope with his feet and had slid down while standing upright. Another had wound it around one thigh; and a third fellow around both thighs, with the free end tossed over his shoulder. Those two had descended as if they were sitting in a chair. The fastest junglejack of all, a woman, had simply slipped the rope through her crotch, under one buttock and up over her neck.

I settled on the double thigh rappel. It had looked reasonably safe, and within my ability. Laying the coil across the branch before me, I let out spare rope and looped this around my thighs and over my shoulder.

I realized that I couldn't just toss the rest of the coil overboard. I might knock Marcialla off her perch, and so undo everything. So I paid the rope down; and it was just as well that I did. By the time I had let it all down I knew that the weight of it, tumbling all at once, could easily have yanked me off my branch.

The end of the rope was fairly near the ground; though from as high up as this it was hard to gauge "fairly near". Ten spans short? Fifteen, even?

Then I went over the side.

Almost, I tipped backwards out of the rope; but I recovered myself. And now the rope squeezed me like a tourniquet. It gripped my breeches so tightly that far from tending to slide down like greased lightning, to my surprise I could hardly move at all. But then I recalled how the junglejack using this particular rappel had seemed to hump himself up "in the saddle" when letting out slack, so that he lowered himself jerk by jerk. I did so too. Down I went, bit by bit: dropping, jerked to a halt, dropping again.

It wasn't too far to the trapeze seat. I caught hold as gently as I could, steadied it, transferred my hold to Marcialla.

I was face to face with her, staring right into her eyes. She hardly blinked at all. Her pupils were dilated. Her lips moved slightly but she said no words—she only uttered a long moan. Perhaps this *was* a word, after all. But she was taking too much time over it.

I said slowly, "I'm taking you down. Let go of the ropes. *Let go.*"

For a while she seemed to be holding on as tightly as before.

"They gave you the fungus drug," I said. "The drug that stops time. I know they did. Let go. You'll be safe." No doubt this was a wildly optimistic promise. But there was no alternative.

Not at the time. It did occur to me later on that a better and less adventurous bet might have been to persuade some of the jungleguild marshals that what was going on up the tree was far from ordinary; and so have them send experienced climbers aloft. But at the time I was remembering what Jambi had said about marshals not interfering. Besides, *I* knew what had been said in the Jingle-Jangle; they didn't. And then again, this seemed to me to be a riverguild matter.

Slowly Marcialla's grip did slacken. Maybe she had been sending signals to tell her fingers to unlock ever since I reached her. At last she came away—and thank the River that she wasn't any heavyweight! I hauled her awkwardly across my lap. The rope kept her pressed to my chest and tummy.

Now I had to heave our combined weight up while paying spare rope over my shoulder. When I slid, my right hand had to act as brake and anchor overhead.

It took a long time to descend. And it was a descent into worse and worse pain.

By the time we reached the bottom of the rope I could have screamed. My right arm was almost out of joint. My hand was rubbed raw and bloody; it hurt as if I'd held it in a fire. If Capsi had felt one half of this pain throughout his body . . . I put the thought away.

Even at the bottom of the rope I was still too high. Not too high to stop me from jumping and landing springily—if I'd been on my own. I wasn't. First I would have had to drop Marcialla like a sack of potatoes.

Luckily by now someone had realized that this wasn't just a spectacular display of amateur treetop-rescue. Marshals appeared beneath, stretching out a web-vine net.

"Let go of her! We'll catch!"

I did. And they did too; then they hurried the sagging net aside. I hung slumped in the rappel, letting my agonized right hand relax at last. Quickly they bundled Marcialla out of the net and stretched it again, for me.

"You, now! Drop!"

So I paid the last few spans over my shoulder, and fell. They caught me, lowered me quickly.

They had laid Marcialla on the ground. A marshal was kneeling by her, feeling her pulse. He looked puzzled that she was so obviously wide awake, but didn't move. A whole crowd had gathered round—foremost among whom I now spotted Lalo and Kish.

"Your friend over there," began one of the marshals, nodding in Lalo's direction, "she—"

Lalo ran forward.

"Thanks, Lalo!" I cried. I would have embraced her, except that my palm was running with blood.

"It's one way of making contact in a crowd, I'll say that! Your poor hand, Yaleen. What's it all about?"

"No time to tell! I must take Marcialla back to her boat, right now."

"It's the first aid tent for *you,*" insisted the marshal.

"No!" Then I really looked at my hand. "Yes. I suppose so. Will you two come with me?" I asked Lalo. "Will you help me get her back to the riverfront?"

Naturally enough, there were questions from the officials. But I bluffed my way through these as best I could while they were busy cleaning and anointing and bandaging me. Someone mentioned drug trances, but I pointed out that Marcialla obviously wasn't from Port Barbra. She was given to crippling attacks of vertigo, I said—which explained nothing: neither how she could possibly be a riverwoman, nor how she had got up the tree in the first place. However, they let me get away with my blatant lies. I think they had plenty of other business to attend to.

Briefly Lalo, Kish and I debated the best way to shift Marcialla: borrow a stretcher, carry her between us, or what? I couldn't help much with my bandaged aching hand. Finally Kish hoisted Marcialla and slung her over his shoulder in a fireman's lift.

So, though not as swiftly as I would have liked, we returned to the old town. On the way there I swore Kish and Lalo to secrecy, and satisfied as much of their curiosity as I dared.

When we did at last get back to the *Spry Goose,* about an hour later, we found a strange situation indeed. Jambi had had the wit to pull up the gangplank—something which I hadn't thought of in the heat of the moment. She and two other crew members were guarding the gunwales with belaying pins clutched in their fists; though it did look as though their confidence was waning rapidly, as the prospect loomed of an ignominious beaching for life. For boatswain Credence was berating them from the dockside, as were three other crew-women who had turned up in the meantime. These were innocent of what was really going on; to them it looked like a mutiny. And meanwhile the two Port Barbra women slunk in the background shadows, scarved and hooded. It was growing dark rapidly. Lamps had already been lit along the waterfront.

The situation clarified itself almost as soon as we hove in sight. Kish set Marcialla down, though he still had to balance her. The Port Barbrans whispered to one another, then took to their heels. After some hesitation—teetering between the chance of brazening it out further, and the prospect of what would realistically happen once Marcialla had regained her faculties—Credence shrugged and strode away; though with a show of dignity, I'll give her that.

The gangplank rattled down again on to the stone quay. Jambi and her two stalwarts looked mightily relieved.

We helped Marcialla slowly back on board her command. Shortly after that, the first rocket exploded high above the jungle, showering red and silver stars.

By midnight the distant pyrotechnics were all over, but ours were just commencing. Marcialla had speeded up. She rushed around her cabin, chattering, peering out of the porthole, pulling things out of drawers and stuffing them back in again, unlocking and relocking cupboards, scribbling illegibly on sheet after sheet of paper. We had to take the log-book off her to stop her from defacing it.

She sat down, she leapt up. She demanded hot snacks and more hot snacks, which a groaning cook provided, bleary-eyed, and which Marcialla wolfed down.

At one moment she wanted to run ashore to wake the quaymistress. At another she insisted on setting sail for Port Barbra at once even though it was pitch dark.

We used our initiative. Despite all her strident threats, appeals and protests we kept her confined to her cabin. Finally, around dawn, she flaked out at last. And Jambi and I could at last crawl to our own bunks.

When I woke up hours later I could feel that the *Spry Goose* was out on the river. The light was dying fast, so I must have slept throughout the day. Jambi still lay stretched out, snoring. She only groaned when I shook her. My arms and shoulders ached like hell, and my right hand felt as if it was bandaged in concrete, not linen. I climbed back into the sheets again, and didn't wake until the following dawn. Since the *Spry Goose* had already been under way by evening, Marcialla was evidently made of sterner stuff than me—unless the aftermath of the drug delirium was kinder to the flesh than the after-effect of abseiling from the heights.

It's only in stories that a snip of a deckhand suddenly gets promoted to boatswain; and Marcialla wasn't as foolishly grateful as that, merely because I had saved her life (perhaps), and because Credence had deserted.

By the time I came on deck again, Marcialla had already promoted Sula, from Gate of the South, to the post of boatswain. I couldn't help musing that slim, short Sula wasn't at all the sort of woman who could hoist a paralysed boatmistress all the way up a tree and sit her on a trapeze! ("Let me have those about me that are slight", to parody the ancient fragment *Julius Czar.)*

Of course Marcialla did thank me, and granted me sick leave till my hand healed. No more painting or hauling on ropes for a while for Yaleen! Actually this was a mixed blessing, since it meant that I had nothing to do but bum about the boat like a passenger, and watch the jungle pass by, and get in the hair of the cook by offering to help her one-handed. And all the while bottle up what had happened, like a dose of the black current.

I also had time to think about my fortune, as told by the Port Barbra woman. I had asked a few of the other women what they thought about cartomancy. (I hadn't asked Jambi, perhaps because I didn't want her to ask me in return what the cards had showed.) Only one woman thought anything at all about the matter, and what she thought was rather contradictory. On the one hand, the cards would always tell a story that seemed plausible to the person concerned. But on the other hand this story would be set out quite at random.

I puzzled about this and decided that the pictures on the cards were really so general that somebody other than me could have extracted an entirely different personal saga from the sequence of spyglass, bonfire and such. And I myself could very likely have picked nine other cards, and seen the very same story mirrored in them too.

And yet. . . .

Even in their thumb-marked, washed-out dowdiness there had seemed to be something powerful about the cards, as though they and all their predecessors had been handled for so many centuries that, if there had been no truth in them to begin with, nevertheless by now the images they contained were fraught with generations of uneasy emotion. With each use—here and there, now and then—people put a tiny portion of their own lives and will power into the images on the cards; and this mounted up eventually, so that the cards became, well, genuine.

We weren't sailing under very much canvas, as though now that we had left Jangali safely behind, Marcialla wished to prolong the time till we next made port. Realistically, of course, this allowed Marcialla to keep a leisurely eye on how well Sula was coping with the sudden change in her duties.

Just a couple of hours before we were due to reach Port Barbra, Marcialla called me to her cabin.

* * *

She poured us both a small glass of junglejack from an almost empty bottle.

"Oh dear," I said, regarding it.

"It'll only go off. It doesn't travel." Marcialla smiled. "But you do, Yaleen. You get around. First of all you were in the Jingle-Jangle that night—"

Hastily I raised my glass and gulped half of the stinging spirit down to prompt my cheeks to flush of their own accord.

"—then up you popped at the top of that wretched tree, knowing just what was wrong with me."

"Well you see, Lalo had mentioned the fungus drug, saying how it made time stand still—you remember Lalo and Kish? They were—"

"I remember. They *did* help me back to the boat."

"So when I saw you sitting as still as that in such a dangerous spot—"

"You put ten and ten together and made a hundred. And a hundred was the right answer. I've already thanked you for your prompt and loyal act of bravery, Yaleen. At the time it would have been ungracious to ask you . . . why you eavesdropped on Credence and me." She waved a dismissive hand. "Oh, don't worry about that. I'm not offended. What I'm really interested in, being a guildmistress. . . ." And again she paused but I only stared at her, waiting it out, till she chuckled. "I think you ought to have expressed a degree of surprise there. You should have exclaimed, all wide-eyed innocence, 'Oh, are you?' "

"Word gets round," I mumbled; and I swallowed half of the remaining junglejack.

"As a guildmistress I have a duty to see that, how shall we put it . . . ?"

"The applecart isn't upset?" I oughtn't to have said this. Marcialla had practically forced me to complete her sentence for her, so long did she put off doing so herself.

"I was going to say: the order of things. Maybe you've heard people talking about the balance of our little applecart before. . . ."

This time I certainly did keep my lip buttoned.

"Well, whatever. I won't press you, since I'm grateful. Now I want you to swear that you'll say nothing at all about this particular insanity—this mad idea of doping the current—which is only really just a gleam in someone's eye, as yet." She reached for *The Book of the River* and the guild chapbook, both. "Otherwise people begin to gossip. Other people overhear. Sooner or later some man starts to wonder, *'Shall* we try it?' Before we know where we are, we're deep in the manure."

"I already said something—to Jambi. And Lalo, too."

"Oh, I don't suppose you told *everything,* did you?"

I swallowed. Not junglejack this time. I swallowed saliva—and my heart.

What was "everything"? The drug? The Observers at Verrino? The fact that Capsi had crossed the river without benefit of any crazy fungus drug, but by using a diving suit? The fact that over on the other side they burned women who loved the river, alive?

All these things together made up "everything." Surely even Guildmistress Marcialla had no way of knowing everything!

She peered at me quizzically. "You don't seem like a person who tells . . . all they know."

I took the two books and laid my bandaged palm upon them, wondering vaguely whether this meant there was a cushion between me and my oath. "I swear I won't say anything about what Credence was up to. What she had in mind. May I spew if I do."

"As you have spewed before, I suppose . . . Of course we must remember charitably that Credence was simply acting out of, shall we say, *devotion:* devotion to this river of women, and to the current which is its nervous system. Other people—men in particular—mightn't feel quite so devoted." Apparently satisfied, she took the books back and placed them on a shelf. "You've done well, Yaleen."

"Um, how did it feel when time stopped?" I asked.

Marcialla burst out laughing. "You're *impossible,* dear girl! But since you ask, it was . . . interesting. Though not all *that* interesting, in the circumstances. Imagine wading through molasses for ten days . . . No, I can't really describe it. I suppose you're fascinated by the current too? Yes, I see you are. Most people take it for granted. You can never ignore it, if you're going to be a guildmistress." Her eyes twinkled. "That, incidentally, is *not* a promise."

And she went on to enquire in kindly tones about my hand.

And so to Port Barbra. After all the excitement and the omens in Jangali I approached this town with some misgivings, as if I might at any moment be kidnapped by hooded women, and smuggled off into the depths of the jungle dazed by drugs.

Not so, however. Neither on this first visit, nor on the several return visits which the *Spry Goose* was to pay to Port Barbra during the next ten to twelve weeks. (For we started in on a local run: Jangali to Port Barbra to Ajelobo, and back again.)

Compared with massively stone-hewn and timber-soaring Jangali, Port Barbra seemed something of a foetid shanty town. The main streets were as muddy as the side lanes, though at least the major thoroughfares had wooden walkways along both sides, supported on stilts. Insects were a nuisance, not so much because they bit you, as that every now and then they liked to fly into your nostrils, making you snort like a sick pig on a foggy morning. I took to wearing a scarf, too, when I was in port; and a head scarf as well to keep them out of my hair.

Port Barbra exported precious timbers: the gildenwood, rubyvein, and ivorybone—all of which trees were small and required no heroic junglejack antics. However, the inhabitants only used cheap woods for their own buildings and furnishings. They built as though they intended to abandon the town as soon as they had all made their fortunes. Except that there were no fortunes in evidence. Frankly I wasn't surprised if in such a place a few people took drugs. And perhaps a town which is one large slum either gives up trying—or else it cultivates a certain mysticism and inwardness. Certainly, in their quiet murmurings and hoodedness, and in their apparent contempt for comfort or luxury, the Port Barbrans appeared to have adopted the latter course. Though of mystical extremes I saw nothing. Nor on any visit did I run into that fortune teller—should I have recognized her, if I had!—nor Credence, either, supposing that she had made her way to Port Barbra with the help of her allies.

Naturally, I wondered what *had* happened to Credence. On our first visit to Port Barbra Marcialla spent a long while ashore closeted with the quaymistress. Subsequently I noticed many heliograph signals being flashed up and down stream: signals which I couldn't work out at all. Days later, when we were on the river again, more coded signals reached us, passed on by the boat behind. Later on, I noticed Marcialla observing me with pursed lips when she thought I wasn't looking.

And so to steamy, bloom-bright, aromatic Ajelobo, a paradise compared with Port Barbra.

I could have settled happily in Ajelobo. Jumped boat, like Credence. Signed off. Ajelobo was so neat and . . . yes, so innocent, at least on the surface.

The houses were all of light wood and waxed paper. There were hot springs just outside the town, where the population seemed to migrate *en masse* every weekend. Children, who were all dressed like flowers, flew kites and fought harmless little battles with them in the sky. Old men with little white beards played complicated board games employing hundreds of polished pebbles. There was a puppet theatre, a wrestling stadium—for wrestling was a local passion—and dozens of little cafés where people talked for hours on end over tiny cups of sweet black coffee, one of Ajelobo's prime exports. There were even three daily newspapers turned out on hand presses, filled with fantastic anecdotes, puzzles, serial stories, poetry, recipes and elegant long-standing arguments by letter (about costume, manners, turns of phrase, antiquarian fragments) which no one plunging into midway could hope to follow, but which regular readers savoured with all the avidity of someone reading an adventure story. Of which, in fact, many of the most exotic were written and published in Ajelobo, and exported.

And maybe Ajelobo was all surface, and no depths.

But equally, who needed to settle anywhere—when every town along the river was their home, if they wished it to be?

It was during our fourth call at Ajelobo, as the year was drawing to a close, that Marcialla made her announcement to the boat's company. The *Spry Goose* was going to sail all the way to the source of the river, to the end of the world under the Far Precipices: to Tambimatu, in good time for New Year's Eve. And one of our own boat's company was to be honoured—for good boatwomanship, and for initiative beyond the call of duty. She would be invited to volunteer to sail out to the black current at midnight, between the old year and the new.

Myself. I could have shrunk into my socks.

Not out of modesty, exactly. Let me be clear about that. Everyone loves an honour.

But because of the way it was phrased: "invited to volunteer." Could it be that the best way of keeping the applecart trim, when someone young and irresponsible knew something that they shouldn't know, was to . . . ?

No, it couldn't be that. More likely it was a neat way of making me feel extremely loyal—by putting me through an initiation ceremony, of the second degree.

Everybody on deck was staring at me.

I'd wondered before what a voice sounds like when it's quavering.

If I was quavering when I replied, though, I wouldn't have known since I couldn't hear myself. "I volunteer," I said.

Hands slapped me on the back. Jambi kissed me on both cheeks. Sula pumped my hand; while Marcialla looked genuinely delighted and proud.

I still couldn't forget all those coded signals and wondered whether any searching enquiries had been conducted not only about Credence and her affiliations but also about myself, for instance in Verrino . . . turning up, perhaps, the fact that my brother appeared to have gone missing earlier in the year.

At this point I realized to my amazement that I had been chastely celibate for quite a long while. Whether this was somehow out of respect for my dead brother, or due to horror at the male fraternity across the water, or even from some perverse annoyance at my parents for breeding a new offspring, I had no idea. Maybe I had even been punishing myself by self-denial; and having effectively tortured my right hand on the abseiling rope at Jangali I had had enough of it.

I determined to repair this omission before we set sail again. I must confess, too, that in one little part of me I was wondering whether I really would see the next year in at all. Just in case not, I ought to enjoy some pleasures of the flesh.

So I drank Safe—not with Jambi, who ought to hunt down a languishing shore-husband, a married man, if she felt this way inclined—but with Klare, a jolly brunette from Guineamoy. It was she whom I had asked about the cards; and we went ashore together that night, the last night. As she put it, to celebrate.

I think I can say that we managed very well indeed. But one doesn't wish to boast of one's conquests. One shouldn't degrade men in their absence merely because we have liberty to roam, and they don't. So, like a proper lady of Port Barbra, I shall draw a discreet scarf and hood over a few very pleasant hours.

I was quite unprepared for my first sight of the Far Precipices. Fluffy white clouds with grey sodden hulls had been sailing along all day, occasionally emptying their bilges on us. For hours I'd been scanning the river and jungle horizon ahead for what I presumed would look like an enormous wall. It was sticky and far too hot, even on the river; the heat was soaking wet, unlike the dry heat of my native Pecawar.

Klare happened by, on some errand.

"Where, where, where?" I complained petulantly.

"Lost something, Yaleen?"

"Just the Precipices. Surely we ought to be able to see them by *now!*"

And she looked up into the sky—almost directly at the zenith, it seemed. The clouds had parted there; into that high rift she pointed.

"How about there?"

"Oh. . . goodness me." For that's where the bare peaks of the Precipices were, all right. Up, up, and up above me, scraping against space. I got such a shock. I simply hadn't realized. Of course if it hadn't been cloudy I should have known sooner. As it was, a god suddenly peered down at me from overhead. The tops of the Precipices seemed to be floating free with no possible connexion to the ground.

Though these connexions became evident enough by the time we reached Tambimatu . . .

Not so much a wall across the world—as the end of the world, period! A stone curtain, drawn across the rest of creation: one which hung from the stars themselves at night!

It seemed to be toppling forever upon Tambimatu as though about to squash the town flat. Yet the locals didn't see things quite that way. On the contrary, they hardly seemed to perceive the Precipices at all; any more than I had, when I looked for them in the wrong place. The town of Tambimatu was a tight maze of lanes and yellow brick houses leaning in towards each other with overhanging upper storeys and machiolated attics. The idea seemed to be nudge together and make tunnels of all the routes. It was hardly possible to see those looming Precipices from anywhere in the town itself. Domestically this interruption in the smooth flow of the world did not exist.

By this style of architecture the Tambimatans also excluded the reeking jungle which clung around their town. The dank, festering mass of vegetation was quite unlike the bloom-bright tangles I'd seen elsewhere, quite unlike the noble halls of jungle giants. Spinach purée: that was how I thought of it. A tide of green pulp a hundred spans high.

Naturally, for those who knew, there were ways through it. And there was wealth to find—or there wouldn't have been a town. The wealth consisted of powder-gold and gems and other exotic minerals which turned up in the slime-ponds and mudpools; as if, every now and then, the Precipices nodded and a scurf of riches fell into the purée. Actually this wealth was thought to leach and cascade down through the innards of the Precipices, into the water table, whence it oozed up into the jungle. Bright jewels for mythical magpies—to make them build their nests here! In Tambimatu town were gemsmiths and goldsmiths, cutters and polishers, artificers of sparkling ornaments. Unlike the dowdy shrouded denizens of Port Barbra these locals wore ear-rings and bangles and bijoux to match.

Slime and sharp facets; sparklers and gloomy mud!

Only from the quayside could the diligent eye follow the sweeping planes of stone upwards into the clouds which so often clung to them—picking out precarious trees, at first like green chaff, then like threads. Then dust, then nothing.

Two leagues south of the town, the river emerged. . . .

As a volunteer for the New Year's Eve voyage, first there was an obligatory call to pay on the quaymistress in company with my sponsor, Marcialla. This was soon over. More a matter of checking in, really.

Next there was a civic banquet in honour of all the volunteers.

Besides myself, there were six others. The boat which we would sail to the black current was only, in truth, a little ketch. Perhaps this was to present a smaller profile. The ketch was rigged with a lot of little sails, the better to manoeuvre it when we got in close, and keep us from fouling it in the current. At present it rode at anchor a little way out, conveniently separating it from any male influence along the waterfront. The hull of the ketch was painted black. Its sails also were black. It looked like a fabled boat of death, for freighting corpses, perhaps to be set on fire and scuttled. An extensible boom jutted from one side, to carry the collection bucket.

But I'm digressing from the banquet.

It was there that I met my six new boatsisters for the first time— and took an instant dislike to three of them; which is a very high antipathy score for new acquaintances in my experience! Maybe these particular women were over-proud, or pious, or otherwise screwed up by the honour bestowed on them. Maybe I was too. Screwed up, that is. In any case I was younger than all the others; and thus may have seemed presumptuous. Bumptious, even. Consequently I put them on edge, just as they discomfited me.

Two of the others were all right, I suppose, and fairly relaxed.

And the last one, I actually liked—and felt an instant sense of rapport with. She was called Peli, and hailed from Aladalia, which brought back happy memories. Peli was a burly woman in her thirties with a mop of straw hair and a red weather-beaten face; or perhaps her blood pressure was unusually high. She was urgent, eager, informative, and talked very fast. However, she hastened to add, she was *not* artistic. Even so, she was the only one of us volunteers who had gone shopping in Tambimatu. Now she wore a coiled bangle which had cost her all of ten fish fifty (after bargaining). It must have been the only genuinely hideous gewgaw available in town. I loved her for it.

The banquet was held in the jewellers' guild hall, which doubled as a gem market at other times; however on this occasion there were no men in sight, since this was woman's business.

We mumbled words of introduction to one another; we drank each other's health; we ate grilled fish. Then the quaymistress rose and read out all our citations to the assembled throng. Mine sounded distinctly icky, as though I had won my place simply by swarming around masts like a jackanapes. (No mention, of course, being made of *all* the circumstances.) And won it too for being a dab hand with the paint brush. Since my hand was still visibly scarred, that seemed unlikely. "Someone's little favourite," I heard a voice mutter.

Afterwards we drank more toasts, and generally failed to get to know each other (Peli excepted); or at least that was my impression.

No matter! The quaymistress of Tambimatu, organizer of the New Year's Eve events, announced a leisurely trip to the source of the river the next day so that we could frame up into a working team.

Leisurely, did I say? Well, yes, that's true. It was leisurely. The quaymistress accompanied us aboard the black ketch—which uniquely had no name whatever painted on side or stern, as though whatever was nameless could not be summoned, and compelled to come—and I have rarely sailed more gently before, except perhaps when we were idling away from Jangali after the fateful festival.

But otherwise! Maybe the quaymistress, as a local, could afford to be blasé about our journey. For me it was awesome, almost an ordeal of courage; though fascinating too in a nightmare way. Closer and closer we sailed to that seemingly infinite barrier, to the point where the river which otherwise flowed through our lives unceasingly, was suddenly no more. Where the river ended, vanished. Or rather, where it all *began*—but began as if created out of nothing.

The waters slid forth like tongues out of a thick-lipped mouth. Stanchions of rocky support, like teeth, stood hundreds of spans apart. Surely the action of the water would wear these supports away eventually—and then the whole Precipice would fall on top of us! Perhaps today.

Away to the west the black current emerged through a narrower supporting arch. Yet terms such as arches or stanchions convey the wrong impression. This suggests that the river was flowing from under a kind of bridge. In fact the cliffs extended right down to the surface of the water, and a little below, blocking any possible access or insight into what lay within this long hole in the Precipices. The supports were only visible because of bulges and ripples and what we could see through the dull glass of the water itself. So the river appeared to be oozing out of something solid—like the trail of slime behind a snail (only in reverse). Enormous snail, mighty trail!

I was glad that Peli was on board with me: so bluffly assertive—like the elder sister that I had never had. I was even more glad when we tacked about, almost within touching distance of the Precipice, to drift back towards the town.

The next day a kind of sacred conclave of the river guild was held on board the schooner *Santamaria,* which was also riding at anchor. We lucky seven were invited.

Several guildmistresses were present, besides the quaymistress and Marcialla. (She and I rowed over together from the *Spry Goose,* with myself at the oars.) There followed solemn readings from the private chapbook of the guild; then practical tips, and cautions. I left feeling more chastened than when I had arrived, at the prospect of our holy and dangerous duty. I can't say that I also felt inspired, exactly.

The day after that was New Year's Eve.

So the seven of us set sail in that nameless boat an hour before midnight. It was a clear night. Stars stood gem-bright in one half of the sky. In the other half, nothing: nothing but a wall of darkness. It seemed to me as I hoisted a sail that the black wall was an image of the coming year, containing only the darkness of death. No phosphorescent little beasties silvered the water here. Half-starlight was our only guide; though we did have lanterns, if we chose to light them. We chose not to.

As we sailed out ever so slowly, I brooded much upon the current. Too much, perhaps. The others likewise. Our little ketch was eerily silent, as though we were all holding our breath. Silent, that is, until Peli called out, "How about a song?"

"Be quiet!" hissed someone.

"The current doesn't have ears, dear!" And Peli began to warble one of our river songs out over the lonely deaf waters:

> *"The River*
> *Is the giver*
> *Of life,*
> *Water-wife—!"*

No, Peli definitely was *not* artistic. Tone-deaf, in fact. Though doubtless the tune she was singing sounded fine in her own head.

"Silence!" called the thin woman from Spanglestream who was nominally in command. "The current senses vibrations."

Does it? Did it? I brooded some more.

We finally hove-to within fifty spans of that deeper darkness which clove the dark waters. We dropped a drift-anchor. A lookout watched anxiously lest we glide closer, trailing drogue or not.

"Yaleen," came the thin woman's order, "extend the boom as far as it'll go. Peli, on the winch. Andra, prepare to receive the first bucketful. Salandra. . . ." Something else.

So I guided the first bucket, with its self-sealing lid, out above the edge of the current on the long boom, and waited for the word to dunk the pail in and haul out a portion of the black substance.

"All ready?"

"Aye." "Aye." "Aye."

"Lower away."

And the bucket smacked into the current. . . .

Madness seized me then.

Insanity rushed over me like flames. I still knew what I was doing. But why I was doing it, I had no idea. Nor had I any choice in the matter. It was as though that pack of fortune cards had sucked me into them, and imprisoned me in a picture! I still remember perfectly well how I scrambled up on the gunwale where the base of the boom was secured. I even heard Peli cry out to me, though I couldn't heed her. I even felt the brush of her fingertips as she tried to snatch me back to safety. I even heard the thin woman shout, "No! If it wants one of us, let it!" It made no difference.

Heedless I ran along that slim boom outstretched across the water —like an acrobat. But no acrobat was I. No way could I pause in my rush. No way could I pivot and return, had I wished to. As it was, I had no wishes of my own. Only my mad forward momentum kept me from toppling into the river before I even reached the current. But keep me it did; and I raced all the way to the end of the boom— and beyond. For a moment it even seemed that I was running onward through mid-air. But I fell, of course. And was engulfed.

Questing shapes swam around me, flashes of light dazzled me, soft tentacles slid up my nostrils, down my throat, and elsewhere too— they entered every opening in me. But I did not feel that I was suffocating; or drowning.

Yet my life flashed by me willy-nilly. Scenes of girlhood in dusty Pecawar. My initiation when I drank of the black current. My deflowering by Hasso in his attic bower. Verrino and its Observers. Bonfires on the further bank . . . All my secrets, all.

It was as if I fell asleep. And dreams had come to me. Yet not for my entertainment. They came to examine me, to walk around inside my skull and see what was there.

"Yaleen," sang the dreams. *"Ya-leeeen!"* they wailed.

I was aware of something immense and old and . . . I could not say whether it was wise as well.

It had been watching us, though not with eyes. Rather, with little cells of itself which migrated through us, flavouring us and savouring us before returning whence they came.

It had been feeling us, though not with fingers. Yes, with *vibrations.* But I didn't understand what kind of vibrations these were.

Or was this simply what I had already been told about the current? What I had mused about it? And now it was reading my musings back to me?

How could I separate myself from this strange state I was in—so as to know which was *me,* and which was *it?* I focused, like a dreamer trying to waken in a dream and be aware: not of the ordinary waking world outside, but of the world of the dream itself. I thought fiercely:

What are you?

And stars burned bright, and a world turned round underneath me, seen from so high in the sky that the world was only a ball, a plaything, a toy; and the sky was not blue but black.

What are you? I thought again, twice as fiercely—having no way to cry aloud.

And far away I heard a slurred voice:

"The Worm of the World I am. There is no worm greater. The worm moves not, it flows within itself. On the day when it shall move, the whole world will turn upon its hinges . . .

"Till then, the worm shall watch . . . the flow of things.

"Of Woman and Man. . . ."

Silence.

But why? How? Who—?

Something hidden reared and coiled around me. And within me too it coiled: it coiled around my mind. Crushing, suffocating, erasing. As I sank into oblivion I thought that I felt some other different creature, huge, slippery and scaly, rise beneath me.

To my surprise I woke to light and life.

I was soaking wet. Lying on a shelf of mud.

Raising my head, I saw spinach purée all before me, tangled up with tropic trees. One of my cheeks blazed as if I had been punched. The back of my right hand pulsed from the red weal of a stinger. But that was all there was, in the way of pain.

Pushing my palms into the mud, I doubled up, knelt—and looked behind me. The river flowed, almost lapping the toecaps of my boots.

I rose, to stare out over the waters. Far away—so far that they just had to be beyond the black current—I made out the sails and masts of a boat. A boat which could only be on the eastern side of the waterway.

And shivering in spite of the sticky heat, I knew: I was on the western bank. The sun was halfway up the sky. It was New Year's Day, and I was still alive. And I was all alone.

The black current had taken me and squeezed me through its substance—and its substance likewise through me—and then discarded me. I had been washed up on the far shore. Borne here by some giant fish of the depths, perhaps; a fish commissioned to carry me. . . .

My first irrational thought was to try to swim back to the eastern bank. Ignoring all stingers, since there didn't seem to be many hereabouts. Ignoring the black current. Crashing through it regardless. I would wave and shout, and be picked up by some passing vessel. Alternatively I would swim all the way.

I even went so far as to wade into the water, up to my ankles.

This frantic nonsense soon gave way to reality. I contented myself with quickly washing my hands clean of mud, retreated, and thought about my predicament.

Eventually, I decided that my only hope was to walk to the area opposite Verrino, where Capsi had first signalled to the watchers up the Spire.

I could search for his diving suit and anti-stinger mask. He must have cached them thereabouts. Maybe I could use them. Maybe the suit and mask were still where he had hidden them. No westerners ever willingly strayed near the water. Except for the riverwitches.

And maybe the Sons of Adam had tortured the whereabouts out of him, and burned his equipment too. . . .

If I signalled with a mirror or a piece of broken glass, surely the Observers would see me from Verrino Spire! Only they, along the whole length of the river, would be looking for a signal from this side. Or if not actually expecting one, patient enough and obsessive enough to look out in any case.

Verrino! My only hope lay there: the only hope that I could tease out of this horror.

And here was I, opposite Tambimatu in the spinach jungle. Verrino was four hundred and forty leagues away—a distance rather more than half the length of the river.

Nevertheless, I set out.

Part Three

A WALK TO MANHOME,
AND AWAY

I HAD no idea how far I'd travelled. Or how many days it had taken. Seventy? A hundred? I'd lost count. There was no way to measure the leagues. On this sort of a hell-walk a league seemed an impossibly ambitious unit of measurement. I might have accounted for thirty, or five score. I was hungry, filthy, and fairly crazy.

Inventory for a hell-walk: stout river boots (good for a long journey), a pair of breeches, and a blouse, now tattered. Plus pocket knife and comb and a piece of string. Plus, of course, my wits.

I didn't eat well but at least I did consume enough to fuel me to tramp and thrash my way onward. I ate land-crabs and snakes and grubs, all raw. I ate tubers and fungi and fruit. I suffered stomach aches, and spent one whole day curled up in misery. However, I did remember Lalo's lore of the jungle. This jungle wasn't the same as the Jangali type, at least not at first. Even so, I managed to avoid fatal poisoning. I reminded myself that other creatures happily thrive on a diet of grubs and beetles and live frogs—down on gut level I was an animal too.

The first haul through the spinach purée was the worst; but I still had reserves of fat on me then.

I mentioned my wits as an asset.

In one respect my wits were quite disordered. For wit means knowledge, but what did I know? I knew the east bank from Tambimatu to Umdala. Of the west bank I knew nothing.

Yet the word "nothing" hardly sums up the quality of my ignorance. I hadn't exactly known Jangali or Port Barbra, before I sailed to them. Yet I knew where they were! I knew what *The Book of the River* said about them.

Here on the west bank *The Book of the River* meant nothing at all. It was as if the world had changed into another one entirely. And my map of it was blank.

This sheer blankness was the first shock I had to cope with. For the first time in all my life no reference points existed. My only signpost was the river itself; when I could see it, which wasn't all that often. Once or twice when I was able to "camp" near the water at dusk, I spotted a tiny masthead lantern far away: that was all I ever spied by way of distant nightlights. My only real clue to my whereabouts came from the changing nature of the jungle itself: the decline of purée, the rise of occasional rubyvein and gildenwood, then at last halls of jacktrees and hogannies.

Yet the jungle seemed endless and chaotic. When I thought I had passed beyond one type of vegetation, it would reappear. I would be forced to seek the river to reassure myself that I wasn't simply stumbling back the way I had already come.

While in another respect: I had no *human* reference points. I was utterly alone with myself: more so than any prisoner shut up in a room with no windows, because that at least would imply the existence of people outside. I, on the other hand, could go anywhere I wished; and it seemed there would still be no one to speak to or to hear my voice, ever again.

When you're shoving your way through jungle all day long you don't spend a whole lot of time meditating or soul-searching in any very lucid or logical way. Yet your brain does churn over obsessively for hours on end. And what I was thinking to myself (if you can thus dignify the process whereby the milk of thought gets churned into stiff sticky butter which clogs your head up!), was that in all the time since I'd joined the *Spry Goose* in Pecawar I hadn't really been communicating with people.

Oh, I'd been talking: to Jambi, Klare, Lalo, you name it. I hadn't related, though. I'd been detached. I'd been viewing myself as a character in a tableau.

Here's Yaleen at Spanglestream, admiring the phosphorescent water! Here she is at Croakers' Bayou: behold the swamps and stilt-trees! And here she is shinning up a tree in Jangali. . . .

Even when I rescued Marcialla from that trapeze, I'd been a sort of actor or emblem of a person, like someone pictured on a fortune card.

So it seemed to my churning brain.

I tried to count the number of conversations I could remember in any detail from the previous few months, compared with gabbier days of yore. This might be a more rewarding pursuit than trying to reckon leagues.

It wasn't. There weren't all that many.

If I can put it this way, borrowing from those critics writing in the Ajelobo newspapers, what I'd been living all that time had been narrative rather than dialogue. I'd made myself into something of a third person, so that what happened to *her* didn't fully affect *me*. I hadn't realized this, any more than I'd noticed until Ajelobo that I'd been doing without sex for months.

People! How I yearned for them, now that there were none!

"Oh Hasso, where are you? You who were gentle and witty!" I cried out, silencing the idiot jungle noise; then I stifled my cries in panic lest some savage Son of Adam heard me.

Many were the times I raved and rambled on to myself, and started imaginary dialogues—abortive ones which rarely got far beyond the opening gambits; whilst I ploughed through the purée, and subsequent jungle. Surviving. Surviving!

I guess in such a situation you either go mad, or else you grow up. You become yourself at last, your true self. Because there's no one else available—and "yourself" had better be big enough to bail you out of this scrape!

I grew up—I thought. At other times I wasn't so sure; and regarding this whole period I can't really guarantee the validity of my feelings or supposed discoveries about myself.

Sometimes when I stopped to camp—in the crook of a tree or under a bush—and when I'd been lucky enough to grab a bellyful of crab, worm meat and tubers, I loosened my breeches belt. I masturbated. And I thought hectically: not of insouciant Hasso or of my happy dalliance with sweet Tam in Aladalia in the days of what seemed my youth. But of the wearing of black robes. Of the private lives of humiliated women. Of a great grim Son of Adam who owned me, and was noble, but a brute. Black hateful fantasies, these!

Was this adult behaviour? Perhaps in a perverse way it strengthened my spirit. With my playful, clever fingers I embraced a hateful future. Coming to terms: you could call it that. I think I was sick with loneliness, and this was the only way I could discharge the accumulating poison. I think that to survive such an ordeal—one which just goes on and on remorselessly—you need something to hone you, to enflame you, to make you into a weapon, a mad thing. I could hardly revenge myself on the trees. I could hardly promise myself vengeance against any known individual. So instead I imagined humiliators and enslavers; and thus I advanced to meet them, day by day. I embraced what I most feared, to screw up the courage to continue.

By now I had somewhat discarded the bright idea that I was going to stand opposite Verrino Spire waving my torn blouse till some miraculous rescue party wafted across to me. . . .

My first menstruation of the journey I coped with, using wads of moss. My second flow was thinner; hunger and exhaustion were drying me up.

An heroic slog through wild jungles for weeks on end . . . Do you expect battles against giant reptiles with crystalline eyes (me armed with my pocket knife)—instead of a tale of what I did in my pants?

Well, there *were* incidents. Not many, but some.

There was the day when I stepped on what seemed to be a bed of moss. It was thick green scum, instead. I plunged through into a shaft of water. My flailing left arm was seized by teeth like needles. I never saw what was trying to eat me. Terrified, choking on the scummy water, I battered my free fist against the source of pain. Which let go. I wallowed and thrashed my way back on to dry land.

Blood welled from inflamed stab marks. But I spotted one of those dripping moss-mats which Lalo had assured me would staunch and disinfect. Leaping, I tore handfuls loose, to bind round the wound with my piece of string.

The remedy must have worked. My arm ached, but it didn't swell up or turn purple or throb with pus and poison.

Then there was the day I met a monster. It must have been the great-grandma of all croakers. It squatted in my path like a huge leathery boulder, high as my chest. Its eyes bulged at me unblinkingly. Its throat membrane pulsed.

"Arrk! Arrk!" I heard from directly behind. Naturally I turned to look. At the last moment I recalled the ventriloquist trickery of croakers and hastily converted my turn into a leap aside, and a roll and scramble through undergrowth.

Crash! Where I'd been a few seconds earlier, now the great-grandma croaker sat slumped, a-quiver. Its eyes rotated. It shuffled about.

"*Urrk! Urrk!*"—again from behind. Scrambling up, I fled.

Nor must I forget the day of the piranha-mice.

A sudden hush came over the jungle, stilling the usual modest anarchic racket. In place of this, a moment later, I heard a rustling as of wind-blown autumn leaves down north in Aladalia or Firelight. A surging.

Ahead, undergrowth rippled. A grey living mass was advancing at speed, replacing the green. A million tiny creatures were gobbling everything in their path. Leaping, scuttling, climbing, dropping back —and chewing, always chewing. Leaves, flowers and moss became raggy in a trice, and vanished. Some thrashings and brief squeals marked where more mobile items of dinner took exception to being eaten. Something the size of a cat scrabbled for a tree. I couldn't identify it—it wore a second coat of squirming grey. The unlucky victim clawed bark, then fell back into the mass beneath. It seemed to deflate in an instant as if it had only been filled with air.

This happened very rapidly. In another few seconds I would have become hapless prey myself. The wavefront of hunger was nearly at my feet. I too scrambled up a tree, with a few grey scouts already hanging on to my boots. I crushed the ravenous little bodies against the trunk. I clawed and climbed higher. Obviously the things would eat anything. Even in my half-starved state I was a great prize of meat and guts.

I was terrified. How high would they climb? The grey mass heaped up around the base of my refuge. Parts of it made tentative leaps and forays. Tiny teeth darted. Hanging on precariously, I stamped and punched as best I could, bruising one fist then the other. A thin eager whistling rose from below.

But then—as though clouds had obscured some inner sun which lit up all their vicious little lives—the scouts stopped climbing. The mass subsided. The whole grey carpet ceased its flexing and writhing. It settled. It lay still.

Quickly comatose. Asleep.

The food-run was over. I was of no further interest. Nothing was, but slumberous digestion.

If I slid down the trunk right away, crushing little bodies by the score as I broke out of the cordon, mightn't they rouse again as one creature?

And if I waited . . . Tiny bodies, huge appetites! Mightn't they wake up just as hungry in another hour or so?

I brooded a bit then worked my way up even higher, to where a neighbouring tree tangled with my own sanctuary. I transferred. From there I moved with difficulty to a third tree. After about half an hour of awkward manoeuvres I descended on the far side of the sleeping pack.

For the next league or so I found a convenient roadway through the jungle waiting for me, stripped bare by the beasts. Marking their last few dozen food-sprints and mass snoozes. Presumably the total slumber that overcame the mice fooled other creatures into forgetting their peril. The impromptu road swung this way and that, and latterly vegetation had begun to reassert itself. I had to leave my tunnel when suddenly it veered off at a right angle.

Lalo had said nothing to me about these hungry hordes. Maybe they only lived in western jungles. In which case, what else lurked hereabouts? After quitting the corridor I was nervous and wary for a while, but no further animal prodigies crossed my path. The jungle cackled at me as if planning dirty deeds. Yet I never saw the owners of these voices; they did not follow me.

On the umpteenth day at last I came upon a trail—one which hadn't been made by piranha-mice. This was much narrower and had been hacked, not nibbled. Nor did it run nearly as straight as the rodents' single-minded tunnel spasmodically did. It took the line of least resistance amidst tree-trunks and tangles. Generally it ran east to west. I followed this trail inland, hoping that it would connect with some north-south route.

I could never see very far ahead because of the constant twists and turns. After marching along for a league or so I suddenly heard voices, coming from around the next corner or the one after.

Hastily thrusting aside, I concealed myself behind a mass of dinner-plate-leaves full of peepholes.

Only moments after, three men came along the path. Large boxes were strapped to their shoulders. All of the men sported untidy beards. They were dressed in baggy linen trousers tucked into boots, and coarse cloth shirts. Two wore floppy hats, one a white-spotted bandanna. All were armed, with knives and tarnished machetes. I didn't like the look of them one bit. These were wild men.

And I could have safely gone on not liking their looks—but for where I had chosen to hide.

A burning needle stabbed my hand as it rested on the soil; then another. I didn't cry out. I only gasped involuntarily and snatched my hand away—to tear two insects loose: red things the size of a fingernail. That was enough: the intake of breath, the rustle of leaves.

Boxes were shed. A knife came out. A machete was brandished. Boots crashed towards me; and I was hauled out upon the trail.

"What do we have here?" the hatless one said in wonder. "A girl?" His hair was a wild bush of bright ginger, as was his beard. He said "gairl".

"Obviously!" The black-bearded second man ruffled the tatters of my blouse. "In men's raiment. Mostly."

"Stop it," I squeaked.

"Runaway?" asked the third man, a rangy blond individual. "Witch?" He said "roonaway" and "weetch".

I was released, and Gingerbush put his knife away. "You a witch?"

"No, no." But of course in their eyes I supposed I was. I was a woman of the river.

"Do you think she'd tell?" snapped Rangy Blond. "What are you?" he shouted at me.

"If you don't think I'll tell, why ask me?"

"Ho, spirited!" from Gingerbush.

"Queer accent," remarked Blackbeard. "Audibly."

Rangy Blond gripped me by the shoulders, and I thought he was going to tear off the remains of my blouse. Maybe all my dark fantasies of the past few weeks had come home to roost. He shook me instead. *"What—are—you?"*

I stared into this wild man's eyes, suddenly inspired. "You're *upset.* Scared. *I* shouldn't be here. But neither should you!"

"Perceptive," said Blackbeard.

Rangy Blond seemed incensed. "Shouldn't be here? Why not? Who says? We're prospecting for jemralds." Presumably those were precious stones.

"Why shouldn't *she* be here?" mused Blackbeard. "A deaf man could tell you she ain't one of us. So where's she from? 'Tis obvious. She's from over the river. Ain't you?" He grinned—though not a cruel grin. "Shipwrecked, eh? You all use ships."

"Boats," I corrected him unthinkingly. And he chuckled in triumph. After all those weeks of isolation this was a game too fast for me. Blackbeard might look thuggish, but he was nimble-witted.

He turned to his companions. "Brothers, we've found us treasure."

"Okay," I admitted. "I'm from the other shore. I'm a riverwoman. Do you want to know about it?"

Blackbeard laughed uproariously. "Do we, Brothers? Do we just!" He calmed. "So she came across the Satan-channel . . . Doesn't mean as how she was wrecked, though. . . ." Abruptly he caught hold of my hand and twisted it. "Sting bites, eh? You need ointment." Letting go, he unlatched his box and burrowed. Producing a glass jar, he salved my skin with something that stank. "Nasty buggers, those. So which is it? Boatwreck? Or sacrifice? Tossed overboard into Satan's black lips? Or a *spy?* Found a way over, set up a camp down south?"

Why had they hacked this trail towards the river? Simply to search for jewels? No . . . that was only their cover story—to hide what they were up to, from the eyes of other men. I felt sure of it.

After the comparative monotony of the past week, a lot happened in a little while.

The three men cached their burdens beside the trail and escorted me back to their camp a league to the west, which a couple more men guarded. They gave me a new coarse shirt to replace my blouse, and fed me to bursting point on a stew of meat and veg poured over tapioca; then questioned me.

The camp consisted of a crude log cabin and a pair of tents, in a clearing with a stream nearby. Another narrow trail ran away northwest.

The "Brothers" didn't exactly introduce themselves, but it soon became evident that Blackbeard's name was Andri. Rangy Blond was Harld, and Gingerbush was Jothan. They weren't actual brothers, except perhaps in roguery. The two men who had been left to guard the camp were less savoury specimens: one with teeth missing, the other with a badly scarred left cheek. This pair eyed me but kept their distance, and weren't included in our discussions.

Andri paid intense attention to what I said, questioning me where he didn't understand and demanding the meaning of words he didn't know. I must have been interrogated for two hours. I even told about Capsi and Verrino. Yet Andri never went into unnecessary detail; he blocked in the general picture.

"Right," he said at last. "Yaleen of the River, I believe you. Mainly because no one could be such a thoroughgoing liar, except maybe Jothan here. Lucky you fell in with the likes of us. Saved your life, doubtless. Certainly saved you much pain. Wised up to our ways by those Watchers of yours you may have been. But not enough. Never enough."

"Was it entirely luck?" I asked. "That I fell in with *you?*"

He wagged a finger. "A story for a story, you won't get. Don't expect it."

"Because you're *danger,*" said Harld.

"Potentially," agreed Andri. "S'posing she fell into the wrong hands. S'posing she blabbed her mouth, when those hands started twisting her."

"But I'm treasure to you, aren't I? More precious than jemralds." I'd decided to stop being a lost waif, and to capitalize on my assets.

"Jemralds to one man: dung to most others, only fit for burning. After you'd shat yourself, in the cellars. S'posing you tried to hold back, like a costive. The Brotherhood would always think you was holding back."

"You don't have to try and frighten me."

"Spunky words, girl. But foolish. I simply touch on the truesoil."

"Do you. And which one man might I be jemralds to? The person you work for?"

Andri picked his teeth a bit. "Truesoil is," he said, "you won't be learning no names till you meet their owners. What you know not, you can't babble."

"What's all this 'truesoil' business?"

"Eh, don't know the word? Happen you wouldn't, either! Truesoil is the gritty, the down to earth. It's the permitted land. Near the river is all falsesoil. A lot I'll have to tell you. Evidently."

Which is what he proceeded to do, commencing as night was falling—until I found myself being borne in his arms into one of the tents, lantern-lit by Jothan. I'd flaked out.

Andri slid me into the luxury of a sleeping-bag. That night I dreamed I was in an honest bunk aboard a friendly boat.

My education continued the next morning, after I'd crammed down a huge breakfast. Harld seemed edgy and restless, but Andri insisted on wising me up adequately about life in the west before he would contemplate our setting off (for destination undisclosed).

"She has to know what not to say," he impressed on Harld. "What not to do. We'll get her a robe as soon as we can. Right now we have to robe her *mind.*"

And learn I did: ten-thousandfold what anyone else in the east had ever guessed of the western world. . . .

Men had come to this world, said Andri, from another one called Eeden, a name unknown to me. And when people died here, their minds returned again to Eeden. The westerners were convinced that their physical bodies were artificial dummies or puppets; and these dummies were animated from a distance. This idea seemed a wholly lunatic one, but it did become more plausible—or at least self-consistent—the more Andri explained.

According to their "Deotheorists" real people couldn't live on any world except Eeden, for a hundred reasons which had to do with differences in air and water, foodstuffs, diseases, whatever. Consequently the "God-Mind" had sent forth to a hundred worlds artificial bodies capable of breeding and reproducing. A "psylink" existed between Eeden and our own world, such that babies were born back in Eeden yet they lived out their lives—their mental lives—in puppet flesh here. Meanwhile their original bodies lay entranced in cold caverns underneath Eeden, their growth halted at the infant stage, each to be "revived" when the corresponding puppet body died—as fully-experienced "cherubs" whose "afterlives" in Eeden would enrich the tapestry of that world gloriously, complexly, subtly. The cherubs would bring home to Eeden a hundred different histories, a hundred strange and varied ways of life, from all over the universe.

Yet here on this particular world of ours, Man had encountered the Snake of the River, an evil infiltrating creature intent on subverting the "psycolonists" and invading Eeden, only true Home of Humanity. The Snake worked its wiles especially through women, due to subtle differences in glands and blood and brain—which made all females potential agents of the Snake, Satan. Once infested, people could only be purged by pain and fire; which of course tended to kill them.

Naturally, I was puzzled about the nature of this God-Mind, who had created human life here, and whose all-powerful will could cross the cosmos, only to be thwarted.

It appeared that "God" was a higher intelligence of "an ineffable nature". Inexpressible, beyond the comprehension of mere mortals. One day he would rule the whole universe, and create it. (Which meant that he both did rule, already, and didn't—the Deotheorists' ideas of time were really weird.) The arrival of dummy-people in the demesne of the Snake had awakened that other divine (or devilish) force to similar ambitions. Now there was a second contender for captaincy of the ship of stars.

What's more, the supreme God-Mind, the Lord of Creation, had himself somehow been produced out of the mind of Man; created, given birth to.

So.

This was both crazier, and more rational, than I'd expected. It wasn't simply that the Sons of Adam lorded it over women. They did—with a vengeance. But they actually had a reason. True, as far as I could make out, the average tenor of western life was cruelty, superstition and oppression pure and simple. Self-interest and rabid prejudice—coupled with distinctly backward circumstances. I noted how Jothan and Harld ogled greedily at some of the items I related of life in the east, ordinary items we took for granted. Still, there was a rationale behind their wretched system. The God-Mind, versus the Vile Snake.

I feared it might make me spew to play host to such a hostile concept of the black current; I who had drunk of it. To my surprise, it didn't. I was far from any eastern town or boat, far from the river, far from the community of women. I felt as if a persuasive influence had withdrawn from me; or perhaps it was just lying low, keeping watch.

That afternoon Andri, Jothan and I set off along the trail to the north-west. We left Harld and the other two men to get on with whatever business my arrival had interrupted—business which just had to be intimately connected with the forbidden river. Whose daughter had now fallen into their hands like a ripe peach.

Ripe? Ah well, perhaps "ripe" is an exaggeration! After my many weeks alone on sparse rations I was more like a shrivelled twig. Still, they loaded me up for the journey (I only realized later that they had burdened me lightly compared with the way a woman of the west would ordinarily have been weighed down). Andri and Jothan wore heavier back-packs.

Yet I stepped out relatively lightly. The trek wasn't so bad now that there was a definite path to follow, in the company of guides. That evening we made genuine camp, amidst jungle which seemed far less wild and chaotic.

* * *

Marching in single file allowed few opportunities for chattering. When we sat round a fire that evening Andri and I talked again, whilst Jothan busied himself boiling soup.

"Do you really think you're a puppet?" I pressed Andri. "Or a dummy-body, or whatever?"

He scratched his beard a while. "Look: our forebears weren't born here, for a fact. If you plunge into water, does that turn you into a fish? Likewise, if you plunge into a foreign world, why should you suddenly be at home?"

"We *live* here. We are at home."

He nodded at the cook-pot. "Why should we be able to eat what's here, and live on it?"

"Well, we do."

"That's no answer."

"We must have brought a lot of things with us to eat. Chickens, for instance! Some ancient writings mention chickens."

"Do they? How d'you know they're the same sort of chickens, eh? And why should chickens be able to peck around and live here? Unless, girl, unless we've all of us—chickens *and* people—been made into the sort of bodies as can live here. The Deotheorists say if you just dump a man of Eeden down on a strange world exactly as he is, he'll starve in a few days. He can't digest the local food. Or it poisons him. Same applies to the air and water."

"It couldn't have been *too* different here."

"Happen not. Otherwise maybe we'd have needed scales on our skin, or shells on our backs."

"That's silly."

"No, it ain't. We'd have been made differently. As would the chickens and cucumbers and everything else as came from Eeden. The Deotheorists say that all the kinds of life there are, are spelled out by different words. These aren't like our words, that we speak. They're very long magical words—so long, it would take you ten thousand pages to write but a single one of 'em. These words are written in our flesh. If you change the spelling, you change the shape of life.

"When we arrived here, whatever it was as brought us read all the words of *this* world back to the God-Mind. He thought about them, learned the language of life here, then he changed the spelling of our own words so as we would fit in.

"And on a hundred other worlds elsewhere, other words were read. And other shapes was born.

"Only the God-Mind can understand these words and change our spelling. It only takes Him minutes. Hours at the most. It would take us hundreds of years. I'll warrant He changed our stomachs and our blood quite a bit. Though not our outward looks. We look the same as we would back in Eeden."

If the God-Mind hadn't changed our appearance, why assume that he had changed us in secret, hidden ways? This seemed to be a completely unnecessary theory, in high need of the "razor of logic" to cut it out. I said so.

"Why is the idea handed down, if it's unnecessary?" demanded Andri.

"Because it gives the Brotherhood an excuse to rule the roost."

He grinned broadly. "Ah, you've solved it all in a twinkling! Simplicity itself!" He leaned closer. "Simple as a fellow shoving his squirter in a woman and making a baby pop out nine months later! Would you care to explain just how a baby is made, eh? Or how does a seed make a plant? Come on: tell me the recipe."

"A plant makes itself out of soil and water. A baby makes itself out of its mother and the food she eats."

"How? How does it make itself?"

I knew how to *stop* a baby, with a draught of Safe. But actually I was floundering. It occurred to me that maybe Andri's "long words" were what "genes" were; but "genes" was only a word itself, without much meaning. "It starts out tiny and gets bigger," I said.

"So this here fellow squirts a tiny baby into the woman, does he? Too tiny to see with the eye? How does *he* make it in the first place?"

"No, the woman has a tiny egg in her—"

"How does the egg become a person? What tells it?" Andri guffawed. "Look, girl: *words*—very long words written very small with a million million letters in each word—that's what makes a baby. The word of God. Made flesh." He gazed at me. "Don't have any such notions, do you? Never even give it a thought. Just get on living soft lives—"

"Hey, I resent that! Working a boat isn't any holiday."

"Like beasts, that don't question."

"We're beasts, are we? So now we come to the nub of it. What hatred you must feel for women! What a load of fear! Yes, I said *fear.* Let me tell you something, mister: you're no better than the rest of those Sons. Worse, probably. Whatever it is that *you're* after, you're screwing yourself up twice as bad."

"Maybe it is in Man's nature to torment himself, for truth. To strive."

I snorted. "And not in Woman's nature, I suppose."

"Yourself excluded. Naturally?"

This exchange seemed to be taking rather a vicious turn. Partly my own fault, I admit.

Just then Jothan cut in. "You've failed, girl. You wouldn't last ten minutes. You'd be in the ducking stool. Shrew. Scold. Argumentifier. Heretic. Disobeyer." Placidly he stirred the soup. "Why, you ain't even doing the cooking."

Andri actually winked at me. " 'Tis true, what he says. You'll have to watch that tongue of yours. Or you'll end up pickled or cooked, yourself. The Brotherhood don't brook opinionated females. Us, of course, we're broad-minded. And we're still way out in no-man's-land."

"You'll have to act more appeasing," said Jothan. "Truesoil is, you'd better just stay shut up."

"Okay, point taken," I said. "No one's eavesdropping on us here. So, Andri, do you or don't you believe that you're an artificial person, a dummy? Tell me: I'm fascinated."

"Whatever you start out believing, Yaleen, you'll believe to the end of your days—even if you convince yourself you've changed your mind a dozen times, and turned all your thoughts inside-out. 'Tis true. You can't wash out the dye you're first dipped in. The best you can be is aware of this. Then at least you'll know what stains you always, even when you're going against the grain."

"Dipped in dye, is it?" And I had been dipped in the black current. . . .

How I rejoiced that I'd been born in the east, where people could be happy. Nobody could be happy on this other shore. They must be mad to give themselves up to such misery, when they could have used the river as the highroad to prosperity, variety, civilized lives. As I thought this, something deep in me and far below the surface seemed to agree and flood me with a wry euphoria.

"Soup's ready," Jothan announced.

We walked for the best part of another day till we reached a rough road running north and south. The trail stopped short of this road,

leaving a mask of undergrowth. We must have veered quite a way
inland, far from the river.

Andri jerked his thumb southerly. "Worlzend's that-a-way. We
head north. We'll come to Pleasegod in a couple of hours. You'll stay
out of sight with Jothan, till I find you decent raiment. If we meet
someone beforehand—"

"I know. I'll dive into the nearest bush."

"That might look furtive. Just keep your trap shut. Glance de-
murely at the ground."

We did soon pass a curious contrivance: a cart loaded with packages,
drawn by two huge hairy hounds, the like of which I'd never seen
before. A skinny man trotted behind, clad in doublet and breeches,
cocked hat and wooden clogs, flicking the air with a whip. He paid
us scant heed, beyond a nod and a raking glance across me. Averting
his gaze from my companions' machetes, he stepped up his pace and
lashed the hounds.

"He didn't seem any too curious," I said when he'd passed.

Jothan grunted. "He couldn't be fool enough to fancy we'd rob
him on the high road. I've no wish for a gibbet."

"What's that?"

"Gallows, girl, gallows! Hung up high to rot. God's Peace guards
the high road. Sons of Adam hunt you down, if you transgress it."

"The way they hunt witches down? How many women *do* disobey?"

"Not many. A few. Those as get seduced to the river, as if it sings
'em a song. Enough for entertainment once or twice a year, most
places."

"You call the burning of women *entertainment?*"

"I don't, specially. Mobs do. We're all bloody ignorant savages
compared with you, clever cocky superior Yaleen. 'Cept on certain
matters such as Andri mentioned. Such as why we're here at all; and
how."

An hour later we approached a laden barrow, pushed by a stout,
black-cloaked woman. Her man strolled along with a single parcel
tucked under his jerkined arm. Presumably it had bounced off the
barrow and couldn't be fitted back on. The woman eyed me venom-
ously, no doubt on account of my male attire.

"Ho," said the man, halting. He wore a bronze medal round his
neck, with a circle and arrow design. In his belt was tucked a hollow

tube of metal with a handle, which I assumed must be some sort of cudgel. "God's Peace, save you from Satan!"

"Save you," replied Andri with a smile.

"Who's she? Brotherhood business?"

"No, no. No problem, Brother." Andri made to move on.

"Wait a bit. I asked who."

"Oh, we're prospectors, Brother. We took her with us to cook, carry and comfort. Piranha-mice got her clothes. Had to lend her some." Andri had already told me that's what they called those ravenous little beasts.

"Piranha-mice? Close by?" The man looked dubious.

"Close enough. Better push on. Getting dark soon, isn't it?"

"I'm safe enough."

"Not from mice."

The man scrutinized me. Remembering advice, I glanced briefly at the ground. "What kind of cook is a skinny wretch without an ounce of fat? What comfort's she?"

Andri grinned wickedly. "Thieving cook. Had to teach her a lesson."

"Thieving cooks wax plump."

"Not if they're fasted."

"Doesn't figure. You cook the meals yourself, keep her tethered?"

"Oh, he's a born joker, this one." Jothan nudged Andri aside. Suddenly he looked alarmed, and cocked an ear. "Hark . . . Thought I heard a rustling."

"Mice, this far north?"

"First time for everything, Brother!" Jothan shoved me. "Get along, hussy, while there's still flesh on those bones. God speed," he called over his shoulder. And on we walked; though the man stood watching us till we rounded the next corner.

"Busybody," muttered Andri, once we were out of sight. "At least there ain't nothing like your mirror and lantern signals over here. Though one thing the Sons do have, is pistols."

I repeated, "Pistols?"

He stuck a finger in his belt, where the man had stowed his tube, pulled it out and said, "Bang. Kill you at a hundred paces. Hopefully. Cost a bit, take weeks to craft."

"Oh."

"I'd trust myself to throw a knife first. Pompous things, pistols. As soon explode your hand, as kill your enemy. In my opinion." His eyes narrowed. "Don't know about pistols, hmm? Mentioned none in your account of the east."

"You never asked," said I quickly. "Can't mention everything."

He caught and shook me. "Don't tell any lies, Yaleen! Lies catch you out!"

Soon, at dusk, we arrived on the outskirts of Pleasegod. I stayed in hiding with Jothan while Andri sallied into the town, returning after half an hour with a bundle for me: a ghastly ankle-length frock, with cowl, wrapped around a pair of rope sandals. It was pretty dark by now but I could still tell how hideous the costume was. Surrendering my own well-made serviceable boots and breeches from behind a bush, I watched them disappear into Andri's backpack. I never saw them again.

Being now in disguise as a penitent, slavish female, I attracted no attention in Pleasegod, where we spent that night at the Gladfare Inn. The size of this institution puzzled me at first, till I realized that over here men must be on the hoof constantly. Our own eastern inns were simply places where you caroused. Most eastern travellers had their own floating homes along with them. Those women and girls who hadn't, rented private rooms chosen from the town register.

The Gladfare Inn was boisterous with boozers, in its long hall and out in its colonnaded courtyard. Above the hall rose two storeys of shabby bedchambers equipped with straw mattresses on trestles, ewers of water, soap like chunks of yellow rock. That evening I stayed in my room with the door barred, occasionally peeping down at the lantern-lit courtyard where Andri and Jothan had repaired to amuse themselves. Down below was a jollity in which I could not join. Apparently "a certain type" of woman drank in taverns. Subsequently I heard thumping and crashing on the stairways and corridors, shrieks, and giggles.

In the morning Jothan confessed that there was a more salubrious inn located behind the Donjon, where respectable men with respectable wives would stay. But we weren't seeking the company of pillars of society, were we?

Pleasegod in the morning was a sprawling, tatty, smelly place, with rubbish lying around in the streets, disconcerting nobody but me. Yet from early on it was bustling with barrows, porters, carts, costermongers—all the more bustling, I suppose, because of the low level of technical aids. In other circumstances I might have accounted the enormous marketplace as picturesque, but for me it was overshadowed by two of the buildings flanking it: the great brick prayerhall, and yes, the stern stone Brotherhood Donjon, before which lay a patch of ashes where no one trod.

The heart had quite gone out of travelling, for me. I, who had wanted to see the whole world! Never would I desire to add Pleasegod to the roll-call of other towns I'd visited—blessed names like Aladalia and Ajelobo. Even dirty Guineamoy and neglected Port Barbra seemed paradises by comparison.

I felt the same about the succeeding towns along our route: Dominy, and Adamopolis, each of them spaced apart by half a dozen intervening hovel villages. Life went on there, true; but it wasn't my idea of living.

North of Pleasegod we met an increasing volume of traffic on the high road; and travellers tended to gang up in bands of six to ten folk to while away the trudge convivially with songs and tales. But company was the last thing we wanted. We shrugged off invitations to join a party and attempts to tag along with us.

It had been ages since I had caught sight of the river even distantly. Once we left Adamopolis behind, though, the high road climbed up through hills verging on mountains. The jungle dwindled; and I thought I knew where we were now, for when I'd been sailing north of Spanglestream I had spied peaks inland to the west.

The highest point of our climb afforded a grand view east across leagues of land.

How could anyone enjoy the view? A grisly monument marked it. Boulders were piled together. From their midst rose a pole which supported a rusty cage in the shape of a human body: an iron suit, with a padlock fastening it. Within, a skeleton. This death-cage creaked and grated in the wind. But had the condemned person been dead before their body was locked in—or not? I didn't ask. A group of travellers had stopped to mumble and make signs, and glance furtively at the vast perspective. . . .

Far away, sunlight glinted from a long strip of water, thin and insignificant at such a distance. Even further to the north-east I noted a vague grey fuzz, like a blur in my eye. Could it be the smoke of Guineamoy?

"So here's Lookout Gibbet," Andri muttered sourly. "Don't stare at the river, Yaleen."

We hastened by.

Soon we were descending, somewhat riverwards, into forested terrain where I could see our destination nestling in the foothills.

* * *

Manhome South was a substantial town lying in the cup of a valley, fronting a thin crescent-shaped lake. From above, it almost looked civilized. Broad streets of two- and three-storey timber houses were set out in a grid pattern. These residences petered out into a mass of humbler dwellings built with mudbricks and roofed with reeds— though the grid persisted throughout. By the lakeside rose several large edifices of stone and proper brick.

Jothan pointed. "There's the Tithe Exchequer . . . That's the Brotherhood Donjon, and the Theodral nearby. . . ."

"Theodral?"

"The Deotheorist HQ. And over there's the Academy of Techniques."

Quite a centre of administration and learning! On such matters as how to build death-cages, or bore metal tubes which could kill people from afar. . . .

Once down in the outskirts of Manhome South, we loitered in a scrofulous public park till nightfall. Then we made our way through the blacked-out streets—lit only by whatever glow escaped from houses, plus starlight—till we arrived at a three-storey dwelling surrounded by bushes and a fence.

Jothan and I stayed outside while Andri slipped in through the gate. He was immediately greeted by the savage raving of a hound— which he must have known well, since it shut up quickly. Presently he reappeared, to conduct us round in the darkness to the back stoop where a door stood ajar, spilling dirty amber light. We entered a kitchen. A tall, freckle-faced man awaited us, dressed in a loose grey linen robe. Bunches of gingery hair like thin rusty wire sprouted from the sides and back of an otherwise balding, spotted cranium. On his upper lip grew an incongruously neat little ginger brush of a moustache. Standing there with his big hairy knuckles loosely clenched, he looked as tough as a plank. But he wore spectacles, too, glassy windows behind which his watery eyes were thoughtful.

"Upstairs," he ordered. "Bolt the door, Andri." Picking up an oil lamp, he preceded us.

And so I first made the acquaintance of Doctor Edrick.

I was to spend three weeks in his house being questioned every afternoon and evening while Doctor Edrick made notes in spidery handwriting in a black ledger. At first Andri assisted in the interrogation; and where he had established general outlines, now Edrick filled in the minutest particulars.

I must have spilled out the whole of my life and of all our eastern lives. And why not? Why should I have held back? Was I betraying our way of life, our river-way? Hardly! I felt more like an ambassador of sanity, showing these westerners how life could be conducted more satisfactorily than they obviously conducted it. Was I in any way their enemy? How could I be, when these two had helped and sheltered me? Had there been no Andri and Edrick doubtless I would have spilled out all the same details under much less comfortable circumstances, with a bonfire awaiting what was left of me at the end of it.

Besides, Edrick in particular had a nose for any pussyfooting on my part.

So I told; and told. Trying to put to the back of my mind the fact that I was trading my treasure of information, all for a hope and a song.

It transpired that Edrick was a Doctor of Deotheory: an influential man. He must be leading a double life, it seemed to me, if he was also mucking about with the river and was willing to protect me. Each Firstday that I was there he dressed in white robes, to proclaim in the prayerhouse by the Theodral. Though when I begged to go there, out of curiosity, he flatly refused; I knew none of the responses. Every weekday morning, wearing a less formal version of these same robes, he departed for the Theodral itself. While he was out of the house I browsed through a number of treatises from his small library. That was when I had finished cleaning the house, scrubbing clothes and platters, cooking, and feeding the hound. . . .

For those were my duties. Doctor Edrick had a "housekeeper" apparently devoted to him and thoroughly loyal. But he had sent her away on the morning after my arrival to visit her family in Adamopolis, something which she had been hinting at for many weeks. I was to be her temporary replacement. My presence was more explicable this way.

All in all, this was rather like being aboard the *Spry Goose* again—as an impoverished passenger, who had been set to work cleaning the bilges for my keep!

Edrick's library: it was small mainly because paper was scarce—a fact I had noticed in the night-soil shack out back, where a bundle of rags was spitted on a nail. What books there were, were crudely printed in very small editions—each with the permit of the worthy Brotherhood stamped in them. Maybe that was why paper was scarce, too. The censors restricted the supply.

From Edrick's books I didn't learn much beyond what Andri had already told me on the journey. Or rather, I learned *more*, but I wasn't much more enlightened by all the casuistical hypotheses and dogmas about the motives of the God-Mind, or the nature of the Snake, a topic with which I felt better acquainted than any westerner could possibly be. Nor did I gain an inkling of what Doctor Edrick's private river project was about.

He came back home one day to find me—with some cleaning chore suspended midway—perusing a yellowing old tract entitled *The Truesoil of Manhood.* Taking this from me, he tossed it carelessly on a table.

"You'll wear your eyes out, girl."

I was about to mention that his own peepers could well benefit by replacing those crude spectacles of his with some decent lenses ground in Verrino; however, he frowned as if anticipating some such impertinence. Though actually other matters were on his mind.

"Things are boiling up," he said. "Few know it yet, but it's so. That fine brother of yours set the cat among the chicks a year ago."

"Did he? He was more like a chick among the cats."

"I know, and I'm sorry. That was the decision of the local Sons in Minestead. Understandably."

"Did I hear you—?"

"My dear girl, those folk have to live close to the river, on account of the ore deposits. So they're specially sensitive to river-witchery. When the Theodral at Manhome North heard about the incident, they would far rather have talked to Mr Capsi in a lot more detail."

"Maybe Capsi was lucky they didn't get the chance!"

"At least they had his gear to study, at the Academy. The underwater garment wasn't destroyed. Of course, there's still the problem of men only being able to use the river once. . . ."

So that was where Capsi's diving suit had ended up!

"Manhome North: where's that?"

He looked amused. "Four week's walk and more. It's the other great centre. Anyway, since the Capsi episode there have been two schools of thought . . . I'll rephrase that: two schools have existed for a while. Now events are honing the intellectual conflict between Conservers and Crusaders. The latter being in the minority as yet."

"These Conservers want to keep things as they are?"

"They intend to keep our Truesoil secure and pure."

"Whereas Crusaders want to make contact with the East?"

"Contact?" He smiled grimly. "In a manner of speaking."

"And where do *you* stand, Doctor?"

"What a busybody you are, girl! Still, your family appear to have a history of poking their noses in." He hesitated. "*I* view myself as a sort of mediator between the two schools. The Crusaders, should they prevail, have it in them to provide us with much more exact knowledge of our enemy, the Satan-current, and its minions. All the better to safeguard our human way of life—not by crude fire and torment but by refined skills, by techniques."

"Hence your secret river project in the south?"

"*My* project? Not so! A project on behalf of the Crusaders! One from which I had high hopes of squeezing juicy knowledge. . . ."

"To feed back to the Conservers!" I was guessing, but this seemed unlikely.

"You make me sound . . . cynical. I would rather describe myself as a pragmatic idealist." He debated with himself. "That project was only in its first stages. Maybe now it's stillborn."

"Because I turned up?"

"And maybe it only needs twisting askew of its original aim. One item of great interest stands out from your narrative, Yaleen." Doctor Edrick adjusted his spectacles. "To wit, the existence of a certain fungus drug in the southern jungles."

"Oh no," said I.

"Ah yes," said he. "What a shame you never saw the plant itself!"

"It may not grow on this side of the river."

"You already told me that you survived our southern jungles because of your knowledge of similar jungles on the other bank. Therefore by and large the vegetation corresponds. Most likely that fungus grows in our jungles, too—further south than explorers have ventured recently. Though you have."

"I'm not going back there!"

"Could it be that you're going to Minestead? Opposite Verrino?" Edrick chuckled. "There to stand on the shore and wave a kerchief? In Minestead, where they burn people so impulsively."

"You could tramp around those jungles for ages collecting hordes of different fungi, and none of them the right one!"

"That, Yaleen, rather depends on the effort put into an expedition. The investment, the number of personnel. We'll need rabbits to screen out what's poisonous; and human volunteers to test what isn't."

"I'm not volunteering."

"Goes without saying. You're too valuable as a source of different information. Oh, we'll need lots of other women to cater for such a party, who can act as volunteers."

"So you see women as a superior form of rabbit?"

He wagged his finger astutely. "Point one: you've said that the drug is used in erotic orgies. Presumably involving men and women, though not provenly so. I can imagine many perversions of natural behaviour on your east bank.

"Point two: it's the *women* of your Port Barbra who orchestrate these lecherous rites; and the only time you saw the drug in action was in the case of a woman, your boatmistress.

"Point three: the female brain must have different gland-juices in it than a man's. Hence the woman's vulnerability to the Snake. The effect of the drug on women may be more noticeable than the effect on men. And the effect on the Snake. . . ." He looked pleased at his lucid grasp of the situation.

I could only feel an abject horror. I'd thought I had reached a sort of sanctuary. I'd imagined that somehow this might lead me back to my homeland. I'd fancied that I understood Doctor Edrick—the mediator who stood between me and the cruel Brotherhood.

I hadn't understood a thing. Instead, I was simply a traitor.

"Black current," I whispered silently within me, *"help me.* Help us all." I prayed in the prayerhouse of my skull as a witch might pray to the Satan-snake.

No response. Alas.

Doctor Edrick fiddled pedantically with his glasses. "One adjusts to new circumstances, Yaleen. One adjusts. Have I not adjusted to your arrival here from the land of Satan? I trust I've conveyed *my* position well enough to help you adjust your own—to what must be."

One thing was obvious. I would have to escape from Edrick's house. I would have to get away from Manhome South. To flee, alone, to somewhere else. Probably with Sons and Crusaders hunting for me.

Where could I go?

I believe the black current may have heard my plea for help, across all those leagues of male land. . . .

That night I dreamed. I dreamed I was at Spanglestream with Jambi. We were standing together on the esplanade. Her husband was loitering some way off. Fishing smacks rode on the water, their emblazoned eyes lit by the shimmer of phosphorescence. Streamers snaked across the river like slow lightning flashes—silver arrows pointing the way from west to east. Pointing towards Spanglestream.

And Jambi said to me, in an offhand way, "Whatever the little beauties are, they seem to keep stingers away."

I woke with a start. Her words echoed in me. I repeated them aloud, over and over.

Had she really said that when we were on the waterfront together? Had I forgotten, or not noticed at the time, because I'd been tipsy? Had I not heard consciously—yet some part of my mind heard and recorded what she uttered?

I rose and paced the room in the darkness, thinking hard.

Was this wishful thinking? Dream fantasy? Or was it a sign? A response from the black current? *Which?* Why didn't *The Book of the River* mention that the waters of Spanglestream were free of stingers? If it were true.

Maybe the fisherwomen of Spanglestream—Jambi's old school chums—knew this but didn't make a big deal out of it, except that they felt less leery of sorting their nets by hand without using gauntlets. . . .

Maybe the waters *as such* weren't free of stingers? Maybe it was only the streamers that were safe? These streamers waxed and waned; so the water would indeed be infested sometimes. But not on the most splendid occasions. When the streamers seemed to stretch clear across the river in great swathes, only interrupted by the midway current, would there be a clear path all the way?

If I were to dive into such a silver swathe from *this* shore, and swim with it until I reached the current. . . .

Ah, the current. Problem.

It had let me pass once. Why not twice?

Thence onward to the east bank, safe in another luminous swathe. . . .

A long swim, even so!

Yet if I wasn't threatened with being stung to death, I could take my time. Vary my strokes. Even float awhile to recoup my strength.

I tried to taste and savour my dream again. It had been so vivid, so lucid. But was it *true?*

Maybe Jambi herself hadn't spoken that sentence. Maybe I'd overheard one of her fisherfolk friends say it at the party. And maybe the current itself had spoken to me, through Jambi's dream-lips.

Maybe. Maybe. I could go round like this in circles forever. I decided to treat the dream as true.

I considered. Guineamoy must lie roughly north-east of Man-home South, if that tiny pall of smoke-polluted air I'd spotted from the heights of Lookout Gibbet had indeed been our grimy factory town. So Spanglestream lay to the south-east.

How many leagues away from Manhome South was it? Ten? Twelve? Perhaps no more. I could assume with some confidence that the Sons must shun *that* part of the shore even more fiercely: there where those bright emanations from the Snake coursed across to touch the very bank. All the country opposite Spanglestream ought to be deserted for a long way inland. Once again my dream pointed in the right direction.

I made a mental note to avoid asking Edrick's opinion of the streamers, or show any special interest should he raise the subject. Then I climbed back into bed.

The next morning I began to steal food and store it in my room. Discreetly but busily.

As it turned out, it was lucky that I'd had to feed Edrick's hound. By now the beast thought of me as a friend. Or as something familiar, at any rate.

Otherwise, when I slipped out at midnight a few days later, the wretched creature would have barked everyone awake, in between tearing me to shreds. . . .

In the interim Doctor Edrick had said no more to me about his grand new project. But he had been absent longer than usual each day. On returning he had twice closeted himself in his study for ages with Andri and Jothan. Jothan departed the house a few hours after the second occasion, equipped for the high road. I had no idea whether he was heading back to the south—or northwards, as a courier to the Ka-Theodral in Manhome North. (*Ka*-Theodral was the formal name for the building, "ka" being some old word for the essence of a person, which rode the psylink back to Eeden when he died.) Whichever direction Gingerbush had taken, he was well out of the way. That same night I crept downstairs and unbolted the kitchen door.

I tossed meat to the dog, which appeared as if by magic. Before I had gone half a dozen steps it had bolted all the raw chunks down, and bounded after me. All the way to the gate, I had to soothe it and thump it in the manner which dogs seem to find friendly. When I shut the gate on it, pushing it back, the hound began to whine noisily. I tore a stick off a bush and hurled it far into the dark garden. Away I sprinted on tiptoe, hoping that when the animal came back, slavering on the piece of wood and thrashing its tail, and did not find me, amnesia would overtake it.

It must have forgotten. No barking rent the night.

Onwards through Manhome South I slipped. I'd gathered that a woman out alone at night could only be a "whore" or a witch. But I was conveniently dressed in the colour of darkness, and there was nothing in the way of civic illuminations.

Three hours later, with the town well behind me, I was toiling up a forest trail leading out of the valley.

Getting across town and out through the shanties hadn't been too difficult. The grid layout proved invaluable. Even the fouler, rougher areas were arranged north by south and east by west.

I only had to hide once; and run another time, when I set a dog a-raving—but it must have been chained. I hope it choked. I tripped and filthied myself twice, out in the vegetable fields beyond the shanties.

On the far side of the fields was tangle. Finding a trail through all the bushes and trees took a long time. I had to backtrack. I had to circle to the north. Eventually I found a rutted road heading in the right direction—that direction being eastwards, riverwards.

Just as the sky was starting to grey with imminent light the road reached its destination: a timber camp. Ahead were long huts, felled trees, carts—with yokes and very long traces laid out for teams of men to haul. (Or teams of huge hounds. Or women.)

I debated my chance of racing through the camp, but it was too near dawn to run the risk of being spotted by early risers. And there might be dogs about. Instead I worked my way all around the slope, which had been thinned by felling. By the time the sun did rise, I was beyond.

And a clanging alarm sounded from the camp. My heart stopped for a moment—till I realized that this was the signal to rise and shine; and toil.

I journeyed on for perhaps half a league more till I finally had to stop, exhausted. The undergrowth was thick but not impenetrable. No paths were evident other than minor runs trodden by small creatures unknown. I burrowed into a dense brake, squirmed round several times like a dog to make my bed, and slept.

When I woke in the afternoon, insects were zizzing about me, settling on my scratches and my sweat to feed. I fairly itched with their attentions, but I didn't immediately slap these pests away. Holding quite still, I listened: for any distant shouts, the baying of hounds, whatever. Nothing. I only heard the noises of the forest: a babbling murmur, occasional cackles. So I fed, then I emptied my bowels, burying the evidence with the aid of a stone. I forged onwards. Downhill, now. Away from the heights that lay inland. I navigated by the brightness of the sun.

It took eight days to reach the waters of Spanglestream. I didn't hurry unduly—often I *couldn't*. I avoided easy, exposed routes, though after the first day or so I didn't expect to be overtaken by pursuing Sons. Doctor Edrick must surely decide that I had struck off north in the direction of Verrino. Or perhaps less likely, that I might have fled due east straight towards the enchanted river to have my witch's limbs in it as soon as possible.

Instead I slipped south-east diagonally across the land.

This was no mean journey. Yet with ample food on hand, and compared with those weeks of travel up in the far south, at times it almost seemed a stroll.

At last one evening as the world was darkening I pushed through brush and creepers for the last time, to stand upon the river bank once more. I beheld silver streamers snaking upon the waters, and my heart rejoiced. As night fell, the phosphorescence glowed ever more brightly.

Dream and reality seemed to merge. Once again the myriads of beasties were putting on a show for me, and this was such a show as seemed more allied to my dream than to my memory. As far as I could see in both directions liquid silver floated, hardly broken at all by straits of black water. Even if I drifted downstream I should still be safe.

One tongue of white fire lay particularly close to the shore. It was as wide as could be: three hundred spans, or four. It angled down from the south-east. Faint twinklings of light visible far off in the north-east were perhaps the harbour lanterns of Spanglestream itself.

I slipped off my women's black weeds—they were certainly the worse for wear. I discarded my undershorts. I kicked off my frayed rope sandals. I cleansed myself of the West. I was determined to plunge into the stream quite nude. If any Son of Adam could have seen me, he would have known that a witch was going home, and would have covered his eyes. Or else he would have stared, and lusted for fire.

I plodged out to where the mud fell sharply away—and launched myself upon the luminous highway.

When a light wind stirs even the gentlest of waves, on so wide a river after a while you lose sight of the bank entirely. Stars spread above me in a second river; mainly of silver, with several sapphires and rubies scattered through that setting. I took the constellation of the Axe for my guide, remembering how it would turn about the Pole as time went by.

No stingers attacked. If great shoals of pollfish, ajil and hoke were grazing upon the streamer, I felt no mouths bump or nibble at me. My arms were haloed in a warm white fire. My head, too, I suppose —though I never dunked my face as I swam.

I don't know how many times I varied my stroke—breast, butterfly, crawl—or whether an hour had gone by or longer, when blackness loomed immediately ahead. The ever-splashing silver had begun to blind me to the stars of the Axe; that blackness gave me back my sight.

I didn't tread water or hesitate.

But I did think fiercely in my head: *Worm of the World, it's me: Yaleen! Let me pass!*

If I'd expected it to drink me deep, then spew me out again with a giant fish to bear me senseless to the eastern shore, I was wrong.

I swam through the current sluggishly, breasting what felt like soft butter or congealing lard. And while I swam, it explored me. Dreams rolled around inside my skull, examining the contents once again, laying out the wares. I never sank into the depths, of the current or of unconsciousness. In the midst of my "hallucinations" I remained aware of where I was. Thus I was swimming briefly through the southern jungles—then along the high road in company of Andri and Jothan. Next I was floating in Doctor Edrick's house. Here, the current seemed to shudder, to wobble. . . .

As before, it drained me. It didn't speak, though. Maybe it was too busy with what it was learning from me of the western land to spare time for my immediate problems. For little me, lost in the middle of the river. Maybe it had already communicated enough by sending me that dream. Perhaps I had to be truly unconscious, before it could connect on the personal level.

Or did it communicate? Not in words as such?

Somehow I sensed that it was satisfied with me. Somehow I suspected that I might be able to pass through it in future whenever I wished, or needed to. This was nothing vouchsafed to me directly; no more than an intuition.

Certainly this second passage was far more smoother than my first brain-crunching, suffocating inadvertent one.

Then I was through.

And flailing about in ordinary river water. Phosphorescence dazzled me once more. The invisible shore lay another three-quarters of a league away. I was as far from land as could be. And quite wrung out.

I felt dreadfully, absurdly let down and abandoned. All of a sudden my relief at passing through was replaced by rage. In retrospect I think this was a necessary rage—like my screwed-up emotions on the jungle trek weeks earlier—which gave me the strength to carry on.

"Help me, damn you!" I cried. The current ignored my appeal. I was of no further interest.

"You heap of shit!" I howled.

Then I gathered myself, and struck out again along the quicksilver road, not so quick for me.

Eventually—on the hundredth or thousandth occasion when I craned my neck—I saw lanterns distinctly, tiny pools of light, irregular dark humps of buildings lightly rimed by starlight.

Suddenly: masts spoking the stars, a fishing smack lolling on my left by a moored buoy, another on my right.

Quite unexpectedly I was there.

I stroked along that last lapping shining tongue. I sidled along the base of the wharf. I touched a stone step. I hauled myself out.

Dripping silver, I crawled painfully up the flight. I weighed a ton. Each separate step was unbelievably solid and unmoving.

At the top I slid forward and spread out like a boneless jelly. But before I passed out I decided maybe I was wrong about the imperviousness of stone. Spanglestream quayside suddenly felt more com-

forting, more tenderly cradling, than any other place where I had
lain my head to rest for a very long while.

I'm hazy about the exact sequence of events thereafter—I was discovered presently, still lying there—however the night certainly
ended with me wrapped in a blanket on a spare bunk aboard a brig,
the *Cornucopia.*

Next day was confession day.

After I'd been lent new togs, and had devoured a huge plateful of
good fried river fish, I confessed to the boatmistress of the *Cornucopia.*
That afternoon I repeated my story to an emergency mini-meeting
of the river guild—consisting of the quaymistress, Halassa, and two
guildmistresses who happened to be in port. One of these had been
present at the conclave held on board the *Santamaria* at Tambimatu,
prior to my New Year's Eve departure. She was able to vouch that I
was the person I said I was.

To these three women I told my whole story, Verrino included.
And how I had informed Doctor Edrick about the fungus drug. And
how men of the west believed that all of us on this world were made
of artificial flesh; and when people died, their minds returned to
Eeden—home of the God-Mind which originally sent us forth to
populate strange planets, and multiply. All of it, all.

Many were the urgent coded signals flashing up- and downstream
during the next few days; you can be sure of it!

And me?

I was quartered at the quaymistress's own home in town till a full
guild meeting could be convened. Halassa wavered between regarding me as a miracle, and a miscreant. Or perhaps as somebody who
had contracted a lethal disease and survived it uniquely, to carry its
seeds around henceforth in my veins. I was a prodigy—and a bit of a
pariah. Heroine, and renegade.

The mini-conclave had sworn me to keep mum about the bulk of
my tale. (Though what exactly my oaths were worth when the black
current itself had twice allowed me passage, was another matter.
. . .) The bulk of it; but not all. That was impossible. Word had
spread around the *Cornucopia;* and had leaked ashore, as well as to
other boats. Nor did Halassa try to keep me penned in her house. If
she had tried, she wouldn't have succeeded. Halassa's home wasn't
—*couldn't* be—another Edrick's. After my months of exile, I had to

rub shoulders with real life again: streets, taverns, cafés, waterfront. I was on a leash, but not too short a one.

As I wandered about, I attracted a certain amount of attention. To those in the know, I was a bit of a wonder, to point the finger at. Look: there's the first riverwoman ever to cross the current—and cross it twice! She's the first of us who knows all about the west! Does she not have horns on her head now, or a jet-black tongue, or some other mark of strangeness? Maybe she can read the current's mind and foretell the future! That sort of thing. Some women would try to pump me for information, either back-slappingly or unctuously.

I enjoyed this for a while; then it began to oppress me. Presently —and none too soon—life settled down again. People stopped staring and asking silly questions—or not-so-silly questions, which I dared not answer. Six weeks after I'd swum ashore, a full conclave of eight guildmistresses was held aboard a schooner out of Gate of the South; and I confessed in full all over again.

This conclave spanned four full days. The guildmistresses were not so much sitting in judgement, but more as a tribunal of enquiry: to delve into all available facts about the other half of our world, facts which might cast a new light on what we thought of as the certainties of our existence.

They always conducted their deliberations with me present, and free to contribute. Until near the very end I was never sent out of the elegant cabin, with its silver wall-sconces, gildenwood furniture, and its tapestry of the Obelisk at Port Firsthome. Still, I fancied there was a certain whiff of trial about the proceedings.

On the last day the youngest mistress present—a handsome blonde woman of Sarjoy named Tamath—raised the matter of that obelisk.

The monument rose from a rocky butte overlooking the town. A popular picnic spot, that, commanding a fine view down meadows towards Port Firsthome and the river. Whoever had woven the tapestry had included several family parties. Scarlet and orange rugs were spread, to contrast with the rumpling background grass that rose (in the tapestry at least) to meet the grey conical roofs of Sarjoy, and the blue of river and sky—the heavens wearing a few fluffy clouds for contrast. Some naked children skipped in the foreground, a young couple kissed, and an old man capered curiously, brandishing a flask of wine. The seated mothers and fathers were mostly squat, as though their threads had sagged or the weaver couldn't manage figures at rest. An open hamper spilled fruit and fishes and strings of sausages on to the rug. It looked as though the antic patriarch had kicked the hamper open, in pique of their having forgotten to cook most of the food.

The Obelisk of the Ship was a basalt shaft a hundred spans high, shaped like a sleek fish with tail fins to support it. Really, it ought to have dwarfed the picnickers more than it did. An attempt at perspective had been made—unsuccessfully. The column was leaning, about to topple and crush the people below.

I suppose the tapestry was charming.

Inscribed on one of the black base fins in tiny letters was a simple legend:

**HERE PEOPLE FIRST CAME
INTO THIS WORLD**

Into it they came, with rugs and a hamper, arses like barrels, no clothes on the kids, and a drunken grandad. . . . That was, I recalled from my own visit, the actual inscription carved in time-worn letters on the obelisk. Verbatim.

Tamath rose, crossed to the tapestry, touched the legend.

"Isn't that an odd way of phrasing it?" she asked. "Not 'landed upon' or 'arrived at'—but 'came into'. Almost as though people first *came into* existence on that spot . . ." She eyed Nelliam, a senior guildmistress of Gangee, an ancient wrinkled woman with the face of a prune. She eyed her hopefully. "Doesn't our guild agree?"

"Language changes with time," suggested Nelliam. "The sense of words."

Tamath pressed on. "How do we really imagine we got here? Were thousands of human beings crammed into a ship of space? What would they eat? Consider the cargo problems! Consider, too, what Yaleen has said: a foreign world may not be immediately hospitable."

I looked attentively at Tamath, careful not to grin in gratitude or stupid pride that she valued my report.

"To be sure, it must have air and water and life on it already, or else it's no use whatever. But why should the life be life that people can live with? Why should the air be air they can breathe? Why should the plants and fish be edible at all?"

The more I looked, though, the more I began to suspect that

Tamath was, well, speaking out of fright. As people will babble pointlessly when they don't know the answer; yet they're compelled to speak for the sake of it, to keep up their presence. That sort of fright.

She had raised the matter because she had to raise something—vigorously. The tapestry was on hand to suggest the very thing; as well as providing the pretext for her to parade elegantly across the cabin.

She was only repeating what I had said. She continued repeating it forcefully, as though it was her own idea.

Nelliam shrugged. "Life's life. Air's air."

"Is it? Are they? Maybe we did have to be 'made'—or 'remade'—for this world of ours?" And now Tamath had to conjure something new out of the hat. I could almost see her reaching, straining herself. "If so, then the only place to make us was *right here.*"

Oh well. I supposed some people had to psych themselves up to excel.

But now Sharla, a senior guildmistress, spoke up. She was of late middle age, and if any ultimate secrets were in possession of the guild, surely she should know them. Obviously she didn't; obviously there weren't any. . . .

"You know," drawled Sharla, "that obelisk has always puzzled me on another score. It's a symbol of a ship of space, right? So where's the hulk of the ship itself? Something tough enough to travel between the stars ought to last for lifetimes after it lands—even with rain and rust attacking. Yet there's nothing at all."

Tamath crossed quietly back and resumed her seat. During the next several minutes while Sharla expounded, Tamath nodded sagely, to convince everyone (except perhaps Nelliam) that she had made a valuable contribution by midwifing a truly original idea. . . .

"I wonder about the nature of this ship," mused Sharla. "Need it have been built of metal or anything similar? Imagine for a moment that we could harness a giant fish. Suppose we built a deckhouse on its back and planted masts and dug holes in its body. Imagine that boats were like that—not of wood, with a bit of metal.

"Could this ship of space somehow have been built from living tissue? Could it have manufactured our bodies out of itself, and so consumed itself?"

"You have an over-active imagination," remarked Nelliam.

"Yet the black current is a great living being—of a nature we can't understand. Subtle and immense! Why not the Ship? Imagine that a ship could be a living being, which carried *no* crew or passengers— because it was *its own* crew and passengers. Something godlike, beyond our comprehension." Sharla had whipped up her own enthusiasm now; her voice was awed, ringing with sincerity.

"Yet it was manufactured by people?"

"Maybe people made something greater than themselves—which then produced something even greater: something alive, superbly wise; and it was *this* which built the ship. Or gave birth to it, even. The people who started the process wouldn't be equal to the end result."

"And how could this be, Sharla?"

"A baby grows into a girl—who grows into a woman. The woman is entirely changed from the baby she once was."

Nelliam sniffed. "Whereupon the woman gives birth to another baby. Back we are where we began."

"It's just a comparison."

"Perhaps it's a good one," said Tamath. "Or perhaps: like a leaf-worm changing into a flutterbye?"

"*I* vote we should concentrate on what is sure," Nelliam said. "Such as the likely capers of the Observer-men at Verrino, when Yaleen decides to favour them with an account of her recent travels."

"I wouldn't!" I protested. "Honestly! Why should I? My brother isn't there any longer."

"No, but your lover is. And other acquaintances." Nelliam tutted impatiently. "That's beside the point. I think we should consider enlisting the support of those Observers. If the westerners are so sure that we're the Devil's daughters, maybe they'll try to build bigger pistols to shoot right across the river. Or they may try to take to the air. I suggest an approach in confidence to the Observers, so that they'll report any unusual sightings across the water. I'll go further. We should build observation towers ourselves. Convert the present signal stations. Erect more, and taller. It'll help communications. I can name several blind spots where a message can get held up for hours, if a boat isn't in the right position to relay. A year ago I'd have said no message could be that urgent. . . ." She brooded.

"Yes, but what about the *women* in the west?" I wanted to know. "The vile lives they lead. The burnings."

"Nothing we can do, Yaleen. Not without wrecking our own world."

"But—"

"What would you suggest?"

"We could take to the air!"

"We don't wish to. For reasons which I'm sure even you must appreciate."

"Besides," drawled Sharla, now on the "Conserving" side, "supposing we crossed the river on a wind, how could we be sure of getting back? If we did cross over, what then? Do we land, and make speeches about freedom and happiness? Till they put us on a bonfire. . . ." Sharla, I realized, was one of those who would argue both sides of a case with enough flair to convince you that she was deeply committed . . . to deciding nothing.

Nelliam tapped her finger lightly on the table. "I see a more basic objection against intervening. Something Yaleen appears not to have realized, despite her experiences over there. A vital difference between us and them. One which the Sons should surely work out, given all that Yaleen fed them—if they aren't utterly pigheaded." She looked around the conclave. "Well?"

"The forms of social organization?" It was Marti, the dusky veteran quaymistress of Guineamoy, who answered. Judging by her tone and her raised eyebrows she was telling us, not asking. An ally of Nelliam's, then.

"Exactly," said Nelliam.

"How do you mean?" I asked. "What did I miss?"

It was Marti who told me, briskly. "It's like this, Yaleen. Technically those Sons are more primitive than us. But they possess centralized authority: this 'secular arm', the Brotherhood. That isn't in the least like our own guild system. Their two Manhomes, North and South, are obviously twin capitals, *ruling* towns. Here, no town rules any other. Over there they have what might be called a 'government'."

"Two, surely? If there are two . . . capitals."

"They will need twin capitals because of the slower communications. That doesn't imply two separate countries. On the contrary—judging by the names."

"Oh."

"Our way of ordering society is invisible and unobtrusive. Theirs is visible and brutal. Harsh circumstances lead to harsh solutions. The circumstances of those Sons are tough because they've denied themselves the river—"

"Which itself orders affairs invisibly and unobtrusively?" I hazarded.

"*You* have more knowledge of that than us, girl!"

Nelliam raised her hand, though rather limply. "Whatever mumbo-jumbo's in the Chapbook, our guild isn't founded on mystic wisdom. We're rooted in tradition: *practical* tradition. That Brotherhood is dogmatic. It *is* rooted in mumbo-jumbo—with practicalities playing second fiddle."

"The Chapbook is mumbo-jumbo?" I echoed incredulously. Two or three of the other women, notably Tamath, looked quite shocked.

"Obviously I'm exaggerating. I do so to make my point. We pay lip-service to what's in the Chapbook, because it *works*. If you're to ply the river for your livelihood, the river must accept you. We drink of the current. We obey certain codes. Then basically we forget about it. We don't grovel on our knees on deck every morning and pray to the river-spirit. We don't make a big deal of the black current, always and ever, remorselessly. But they do over there. They're obsessed—with denying it. The current is our background; that's where it belongs. It's *their* foreground, even though they cower away from it."

Silence in the cabin, for a while. If a Tamath had said such things, perhaps there would have been uproar. But then, she wouldn't have.

"Talking of practicalities," said I, "what about Doctor Edrick's scheme for poisoning the current?"

"May it fail," said Nelliam tightly. "May he thrash around for ten years, never finding what he seeks. May he fall between those two stools, of Conserving and Crusading, and get squashed. Really there's nothing we can do about it."

"We could tell everybody, from Umdala to Tambimatu. Put people on their guard. Tell them about the west."

"Why? So that everybody lives in a state of permanent anxiety? So that any malcontents have a lever against us?" Nelliam leaned towards me. "So that your fame spreads far and wide?" Yet her tone was whimsical rather than malicious.

Shortly afterwards the conclave began to wind up. I was left with the odd sense of being high in the councils of the land—yet these councils making little difference. The guild could trim our sails a bit; but could it ever actually alter course? On a long and rather straight river which leads forever from A to B is there even any concept of altering course? Any need to?

After I was dismissed, the 'mistresses must indeed have come up with some last-minute practical conclusions: about the building of better signal stations which could double as spy towers (if equipped with Observer-style telescopes). Some sort of consensus must have gelled, since I was to see the results before too long. Yet basically I felt enormously let down. Once again. First by the current, now by my guild. . . .

When I came to think of it more coolly, what actually could be done? On any scale corresponding to the size of the problem? Reacting prematurely might make it a problem. Once you identify something as a problem, it tends suddenly to get worse.

One of the last things said before I was dismissed came from Tamath:

"Mumbo-jumbo or not," and here she glanced at Nelliam, "may the black current show us our true course." Her look was respectful —but there was a slight edge of, shall we say, ambition in her voice. She was a handsome, engaging woman, as I say. She must have worked hard, and pleased people. And all the while, perhaps, a little frightened of doing the wrong thing—while needing to speak out, proffer her opinion, make decisive choices. She would be admired for it, and she would never quite dare believe it herself.

"To be sure," conceded Nelliam. "Pardon my impieties. Blame them on the crotchets of an old lady. I was just trying to make a point."

'May the current show us our course. . . .' Tamath had no idea how soon and how drastically the current would show us something!

Oh yes. One other final thing was that I was assigned a berth and duties on board Tamath's own command, the *Blue Guitar*, now bound for southern waters.

As so I would continue my life as a riverwoman. Just as we would all continue our lives.

For a while.

And so I did. And so did we all—for the next half year, till New Year's Day came round again, anniversary of my awakening washed up on a strange shore.

This particular new year found me on no strange shore. The *Blue Guitar* was tied up at the stone docks of Jangali. . . .

On New Year's Eve I had walked out through the old town to visit Lalo and Kish, whom I hadn't seen for over a year. The young couple ought to have moved out of the parental home into a place of their own, though it was to that tree-house that I went first, to enquire.

Lalo's mum turned out to be a portly swarthy woman whose hair was a mass of wiry black wool and combs and strings of agate beads.

She directed me in the usual emphatic Jangali style, then added, "If you'll hang on a mo, I'll take you myself. I'm babysitting."

"Baby?" I suppose I gaped. "But how—?"

"Why, in the usual way, dear!" Her laugh boomed out. "How else?"

"I guess it's a while since I saw them."

"Best to get your brood hatched early, I always say! Then all that bother won't wear you out in your prime. They'll have three babies, I think. The first one's a darling little boy, so the next should rightly be a big strapping girl."

I wondered whether Kish would ever learn to raise his voice as loud as hers. . . .

"Has a woman called Jambi visited recently?" I asked on impulse.

"Who?"

So I described Jambi, reminding Mum that she was a friend of Kish's family and that we had both been on the boat which brought Kish and Lalo home.

"Oh, I remember! She did call once. Rootless, gadabout woman! Can't say as I took to her hugely. One shouldn't encourage that kind of thing. It's too unsettling, when a young man's trying to adjust to a new style of life."

Poor Kish. . . .

"I expect you're right," I said.

"Of course I'm right. Now if you'll just wait a mo! There's ever so nice a view from that balcony."

"It really doesn't matter! I was only intending to pop in." I slapped my brow theatrically. "Oh dear, now I've remembered something else I had to do!"

Mum scrutinized me. "Have you really? So what name should I mention to my Lalo?"

"None. Don't bother." I retreated. "Obviously they're busy. Anyway, I'm quite a rootless gadabout myself!"

"What a peculiar whimsical way to behave! Well, *goodbye,*" said Mum, and shut the door.

I left.

As I headed back towards the river, I thought of my own mother and father. I still hadn't been back to see them. Yet that was hardly my fault! Tamath's boat had kept me to southern waters since my return—far from Verrino, so that I wouldn't over-excite the Observers, I suppose. We were scheduled to sail downstream "sometime" but I could be fairly sure I wouldn't be permitted to hop boats to any old vessel I liked, for an earlier passage north. Tamath was keeping an eye on me.

I had written a couple of times to my parents—initially from Spanglestream—and had had two letters back. The second had been awaiting me at the quaymistress's *poste restante* when we docked in Jangali.

Mother's first letter had conveyed a certain air of reproach at my having absented myself for so long without sending word. (Naturally, I hadn't told her that I'd spent some of the time gadding footloose and fancy-free about the western world!)

I detected a degree of anxiety about Capsi, too. *(That* still required a personal explanation face to face. However, any adequate explanation was so intimately bound up with other events on which I shouldn't enlarge that the problem had only got worse with time.)

All in all, both letters from Pecawar were quite complacent. A child had been born, of course. A girl. Her name was Narya. By now she was a year and a quarter old. Things were fine at home. Narya was a joy. Her first word had been "wain". It had rained in dusty Pecawar, impressing her.

Maybe my parents were weeping in private, but I doubted it. The keynote was complacency.

And Lalo's mum was militantly complacent.

And guildmistresses were fairly complacent too. Because in their guts, they couldn't imagine anything ever being very different. For them, the extent of foreignness was somewhere distant like Umdala.

Not, I hasten to add, that I thought there was any inherent virtue in striking up acquaintance with the really foreign, the west. Still, the west existed. And it was pulsing with people, whose souls were sick; some of whom at least were hatching plans which had to do with us.

Such thoughts occupied me while I walked back to the *Blue Guitar.* Then I put them from my mind.

That night a gang of us were planning to hit the Jingle-Jangle for a fine old thrash to celebrate New Year.

Whilst down at Tambimatu a boat with no name would sail out

slowly to the mid-stream. Without (thanks be!) any Yaleen on board. . . .

And a jolly night it was indeed. Music, talk and singsongs—as deafening as ever. A lot of joshing, some kissing (and resort to a certain upstairs room for a six-way tangle), even a bit of a brawl, though a half-hearted one. This time no Port Barbra women were skulking about the premises. I collected a hangover, which I nursed through most of the morning in my bunk; as did many of us.

At last I just had to empty my bowels. So I dragged myself up. I raided the galley for a bite of eel pie then crept on deck, to lean on the rail and recover.

I decided that I, too, felt complacent.

Partly this was a consequence of the hangover: I had no desire to exert myself. Mainly it was due to being there once again on deck at Jangali dock, just as I'd been once before. It seemed as if nothing essential had changed, after all.

So I lazed about. Had lunch with the other walking wounded. Played several hands of cards, winning a few fins and losing them again. There was desultory talk about mounting a return expedition ashore that night, though no one was overly enthusiastic. The air was a hot muggy blanket. The sun boomed down on the river.

At around two o'clock the tall new signal tower to the north of Jangali began to flash. (Oh yes, there *had* been little changes.)

Idly I spelled out the message, which was in plain language.

A moment later I was not so idle.

"Tamath!" I screamed. "Boatmistress! Someone tell her to come!"

Minor commotions occurred on other vessels, too, as more people began to notice the flashing and pay heed.

Tamath was by my side in record time, sprinting from her cabin. She too stared. She had missed the start of the signal, but that didn't matter. It was soon being repeated. Briefly Tamath hesitated between dashing to the lookout station where young Melesina—about the only person actually on duty—was copying the signal down. As the message sank in, she stayed by me . . .

The contents?

Urgent alert. Ex Umdala. Repeat onward. Black current withdraws upriver ex sea. Head of current passes Umdala midday. Speed 17 LH. Wake upsets small craft. Head of current size of small hill. Look of giant croaker. River clear where head has passed. No current remains. Umdala endit.

Two hours since that signal had set out! The black current was withdrawing upstream at a rate of seventeen leagues per hour. Soon the "head" would be passing Firelight. A little over an hour later, Melonby.

Maybe something wild and terrible in the ocean had driven it upstream . . . I doubted this. The current was winding itself back towards the Far Precipices, like some huge rope being winched in. And on the end of that black rope was the living head which had never been seen, or even guessed at, in all our history! A head the size of a hill!

Tamath called to boatswain Hali (no relation to the Hali of the *Sally Argent)* to send someone aloft with a spyglass to observe the midstream; Hali climbed the shrouds herself.

"Nothing can possibly have happened at Tambimatu," Tamath muttered to me. "Last night, I mean. Not to provoke this. Or we'd have heard by now. So has your precious Doctor Edrick doctored the current, after all?"

"How do I know? How can a current flow *up*-river, Tamath?"

"Ah, its substance is curious." She was quoting the Chapbook of the guild, not telling me anything new. Her voice was singsong. Her eyes looked glazed with shock. "It seems a liquid. Yet it flows within itself, and is one. Like an oily sinew, like a tapeworm."

"A worm with a head, so it seems!"

"It doesn't really flow like water. Waves simply pass along it; it remains."

"Till now it did! Incantations aren't going to help us any, Boatmistress!" I spoke as sharply as a slap on the cheek.

She recoiled, then recovered herself. "No, of course not . . . You're right."

"So is there a brain in its head? And eyes that see? And a mouth that feeds? And speaks? Maybe speaks!"

"Speaks," she repeated dully. "What could it say? Now that anybody can cross the river? Now that anyone can sail? The world's turning upside-down. . . ."

"It told me the world would turn on its hinges, on the day when it moved. Now it's happening. Today. Maybe Edrick didn't start this. Maybe the current decided long ago."

"What's going to *happen?"*

From the topgallant Hali called, "I can see ripples rushing all along the midstream water. It's moving, all right!" Hali ordered Zernia aloft to take over the watch, and began to climb down.

"What's going to happen, Tamath, is that it'll pass us here in Jangali. Unless it decides to halt halfway."

"If the head displaces enough water to upset small craft . . . then we'd best slacken our moorings . . . Or even put out, a hundred spans or so. Hali!" she shouted to the descending boatswain.

"Hang on." I interrupted. "It's withdrawing at seventeen leagues per hour. If it keeps on coming, it won't pass here till. . . ." I calculated. "Um, tomorrow, around midnight. Maybe very early, the day after."

"Oh yes, of course . . . Quite right."

"And I want to see it pass," I added. "From close by."

Hali had joined us by now. "Do you just?" Her tone was sarcastic. "We hear and obey. Right, Boatmistress, let's all jump to it and sail the *Blue Guitar* right out so that Yaleen here can get an eyeful!"

Tamath pursed her lips. "Yaleen has a . . . special . . . reason for wanting to be close. It may well be that we all *need* her to see what happens . . . Hmm, yes, we'll probably sail."

Hali stared at us incredulously. She didn't know my past history. By the time the *Blue Guitar* had arrived in Spanglestream for the conclave, six weeks had passed since I'd swum ashore. The waves of gossip had slackened into tiny ripples.

"The crew won't want to get anywhere near *that!*" Hali protested.

"I'll speak to them. Tomorrow. Or tonight. In a nutshell, Yaleen here has crossed the current twice already. It knows her. She spent many weeks on the west bank. And she got back."

"Oh," said Hali. She looked hurt. Because Tamath hadn't taken her into her confidence earlier. "Oh." If I'd been in Hali's boots, that was about all that I could have found to say.

Hali was deeply hurt; and because of this I could see she was very sore at me.

Tamath turned to me. "Isn't the current at its lowest ebb as the year changes? Surely it should have grown *more* sluggish with the drug—not less?"

"Yes, the drug would make it sluggish, at first. Then it would speed up." Just as Marcialla had speeded up, rushing frenetically about her cabin . . . "It would go berserk."

Excluded from this exchange by ignorance, Hali looked even more resentful.

As the afternoon wore on, more signals came our way.

Ex Firelight. Head passing. River clear downstream. . . .

Ex Melonby. . . .

We might have stayed up half the night watching for signals—latterly, lantern flashes—spelling the retreat of the head upstream. However, Tamath ordered us all below quite early. The next night would be a long and risky one. She explained why; and stunned the crew with her explanation.

Going on for ten the following night, we were readying the *Blue Guitar* to sail, working by the light of our own lanterns and those on the dockside.

Dispute had broken out (not least from Hali) as to whether to risk a fine schooner in this enterprise. A little tub would be less of a loss, if loss there was to be. Though equally, a little tub might more easily founder when that living hill rushed by.

Two of our crew had deserted, though Tamath was only willing to consider them as temporarily missing ashore.

And I was in the peculiar ambiguous position of suddenly not being very popular, since I was the reason for this nocturnal jaunt to danger—while at the same time I was something of a miracle. From the way some of my boatsisters spoke, you'd have thought I was personally responsible for the present misconduct of the current.

We cast off. Slowly we sailed out under light canvas, to take up station.

We were about halfway out when, in the darkness to the north, the powerful signal-lantern began to wink. Tamath was loitering near me on the fore-deck. I had been relieved of my ordinary duties; who could say what my extraordinary ones might be?

Urgent alert. Ex Verrino Spire, I spelled.

It was the first time I'd seen such a call-sign. So some accommodation had been reached between the river guild and the Observers. Unless this was a spontaneous message, breaking into the chain of light.

. . . Repeat onward. Explosion in town. Fire. Screaming. Confusion. Quayside appears under attack. Large rafts landing ex river. From West. Alert all towns: arm with any weapons to defend shore. . . .

Tamath clutched my arm savagely, hurting me. She seemed to imagine her fingertips were pressing words into me.

"It's the Sons," said I, wincing. "They've invaded Verrino. . . ."

Sick at heart, I visualized the Sons of Adam rampaging through that lovely town, where in their eyes every woman was a witch.

"Arm with any weapons" indeed! With knives and needles? With pitchforks and mattocks?

Tamath finally found her voice. "The head can only have passed Verrino fifteen hours ago! How could the West have rafts ready? And men, and weapons? Unless Edrick's plan worked! Unless he did poison the current! Damn you, Yaleen, for this thing you've done. *Damn you.* You told them how. And you've destroyed our lives!"

And at Verrino quay were berthed real river-going vessels, for the Sons to seize and press into service. . . .

Of a sudden our world was cut in half.

It all seemed so abominably unfair. Only a while ago the whole river and my life had stretched before me, full of tantalizing distant towns, vistas, bright adventures, friends, lovers, boats, dreams. Anything whatever that was good, within the changelessly rich fabric.

It was all over now, forever, before it had really begun. I felt as though a giant hand had abruptly doused the sun and stars, and drained the river dry.

Because I felt so dry, I wept.

"Don't be such a baby!" sneered Tamath. "What way is this to greet your only friend, who's rushing to visit you? You'll need to see straight, to pat the worm's head."

"Damn it," I gasped. "This is *grief!* Don't you understand? How many of us have ever known such grief before?"

"Congratulations, Yaleen. You're the bringer of grief." How bitter Tamath sounded.

And so the *Blue Guitar* continued onwards towards my tryst with the head of the worm; while three hundred leagues distant, a war had begun.

Part Four

THE WORM'S HEAD

*F*OR a while I'd been hearing a twanging sound. At first it was like singing in my ears. As the hour of our rendezvous drew closer, the noise grew louder; though never so loud that it could have been heard from the shore, I don't suppose, unless you placed your ear directly on the water.

It was the sound of a single enormous chord being strummed; it was the hum of the current winding itself back elastically towards the Far Precipices.

The night sky was two-thirds full of stars; the rest was cloud. With our lanterns doused and our eyes adjusted to the darkness, visibility was about fifteen hundred spans.

Visibility? Ah, that's taking liberties with the word! We would hardly be able to spot details much beyond two hundred spans— and only really when the worm's head sped by at its closest.

I was about to add, "so long as you had the reflexes of a cat". But we used to have a cat back home in Pecawar. Opinion has it that cats can see things that are invisible to human eyes. Well, it isn't true. Half the time cats are simply looking in the wrong direction. . . .

When that head rushed past, we would have about fifteen seconds to see it, but only two or three seconds of clear observation. Unless, of course, the head intended to pause and chat with me. And this I rather doubted.

I was risking lives for a whim—and Tamath was clutching at

straws. I already knew that I was going to disappoint her; and anger her more. I was on the point of swallowing my pride and begging her, "Let's call it off. Let's go back." But this would also be dishonest. What, opt out at the last moment? And thus shift the blame? I could tolerate Tamath's hatred (I thought), but not her contempt. Not hers; she didn't deserve to scorn me.

Ah, my famous self-esteem again! Why should I flay myself for it? But I did. It seemed I couldn't win.

"Here it comes!" cried Hali from the mizzen top. Hali wouldn't allow anyone but herself aloft. I hoped she was lashed securely. I clung to the rail, peering aft.

A huge bow-wave tossed the *Blue Guitar*. Our boat heeled to starboard. Never had a deck sloped so crazily. From amidships came the noise of skidding, crashing and cries.

And in the midst of this: a dark enormity, a minor hill raced by, as if shouldering our schooner from its slopes. A mound of inky jelly, stiff as muscle . . . For an instant in the starlight I saw its face, but an instant was enough.

I'd faced a giant croaker in the jungles: a leathery boulder with bulging eyes and a beaky gash of a mouth. I'd seen gargoyles jutting from the gutters of the Donjon in Pleasegod: twisted faces, perhaps modelled on people burnt alive.

This was worse. The gape of its mouth was a slash through the tissue of the hill, wide enough open to gulp a skiff and crew; a mouth which dripped thick strings of glue. A ledge of a chin scuffed the water below. And above: ridges of bulges and pustules—then two hooded eyes. These eyes were set far apart: long, triangular and white. In them was no expression, no life; as though the salt of the sea had caked them over.

A face sculpted by a lunatic! More awful that it should have such a face, than have no face at all. Surely the worst thing in the world would be to stray anywhere near that mouth, those eyes. The creature was a great grotesque tadpole: simply a head, with a tail hundreds of leagues long. . . .

Already it was gone again into the night.

No sooner had the *Blue Guitar* righted itself than we were heaving down into the gulf to port. The boat jarred shudderingly as it met a wall of water rushing back to fill the trough. Something smashed to the deck from aloft. I feared for Hali. (Or was it myself I feared for, if it was she who had tumbled down?)

* * *

In fact we had snapped our spanker gaff.

Presently our lanterns were re-lit. Just as well they'd been doused, or we might have caught fire. And presently Tamath counted the cost.

"So Zernia broke her ankle. And Challi cracked her skull—let's hope it's only concussion. Then there's the spanker gaff—"

"Maybe the wood was rotten inside." It probably was, but why didn't I keep my big mouth shut?

Tamath rounded on me. "Don't you *dare* speak of anything on my boat being rotten! Unless it's yourself!"

A whimper of pain mounted to a sudden shriek; Zernia's ankle was being set.

"I'm sorry they got hurt," I said. "Truly sorry."

"Are you indeed? That's very small beer when people are being hacked to pieces in Verrino! So what did you learn, Yaleen?"

What had I learned, indeed? Once again the image of a tadpole came to me. The huge head, the inordinately long tail.

"I think . . . maybe it's about to change. Like, yes, like a tadpole. Which has no further use for its tail."

"You think," she mocked. "And of course by sheer coincidence, just when it decides to 'change', those bloody Sons decide to attack us."

To this, I had no answer.

"Well, what wise thoughts did it communicate?"

"None," I had to admit.

"None," she sneered.

"Mind you, last time it spoke I was right inside its body."

"So maybe this time we ought to have tossed you overboard, with a line attached! As bait for the worm's brain." And away she stalked.

We spent the remainder of that night in midstream on deep anchor. This was the first time any boat had anchored quite so far out; but our hooks caught on the riverbed with a link of chain to spare. I lay in my bunk during those dark hours like an unhappy, chilly plank. I was sure that I didn't sleep a wink; though I somehow found myself waking later on to the light of dawn.

When we were hoisting sail that morning, a signal flashed that the worm's head had passed Tambimatu at seven o'clock. . . .

* * *

The *Blue Guitar* headed back to Jangali, where the two crewwomen who had deserted slipped back on board again before the day was out. In time for supper, to be exact. Tamath said nothing to them about their absence, and pretended not to notice.

But neither did she broadcast her opinion that it was I who was responsible for the invasion—otherwise the mood might have turned really ugly. As it was, I only had Boatswain Hali's sullen enmity to contend with. And Tamath's controlled hatred. And some sour looks from other women, who took Zernia's injury personally. Challi had woken up with nothing worse than a headache; and she wasn't the sort to harbour a grudge.

Incidentally, the spanker gaff *had* been a bit rotten at the point where it snapped. It ought to have been replaced, not held together with paint.

Much happened during the next few days, though to begin with little of it happened in Jangali. We learned of events thanks to signals from Tambimatu, and from points north to the Spire at Verrino.

(What *did* occur in Jangali was: anxious crowds gathering on the quay, flurries of panic, rumour rampant, and a besieging of boats every time a signal tower flashed—since shorelubbers couldn't read the signals. The quaymistress soon appointed a herald to proclaim newly-logged messages; and then to pin up the texts on a board in the market place. I don't know that this did a great deal to restore daily business to normal.)

From Tambimatu we learned that the worm's head had ended up jammed in that rocky arch below the Precipices. The head now occupied that point of exit and entry like some ghastly gateway, some portal of black flesh—with its drooling mouth agape, its white eyes staring blindly. The guild had sent the ketch with no name to inspect; thus the crew reported.

Maybe the worm's head had grown in size during the millennia since it first emerged, and now it was too large to slip back inside the mountain. Maybe the bowels of the mountain were already packed solid with its body, leaving no more space within.

Whether it was still alive, or dead and slowly corrupting, who could tell?

From Verrino we learned that the Spire was still in friendly hands. What the Observers saw from their vantage point obviously disinclined them to throw in their lot with the invaders. They signalled that the Spire could withstand an eight-week siege; longer on starvation rations.

On the day after the invasion the signal towers north and south of Verrino had both been burnt to the ground; news which scared us all. Why burn something which could be seized and used? Unless the guild signallers had held out, and been burnt along with their towers. . . .

Yet in the confusion of that first violent night one yawl had somehow evaded capture and set sail. This yawl took up station upriver. After the towers went up in flames, the yawl could still relay signals from the Spire, southwards. No such facility existed to the north of Verrino, thus all contact was lost with the whole stretch of river from Sarjoy to Umdala. Three whole days passed before a brig set sail from Verrino to bear down upon that yawl. The brig was crewed by women, but ineptly so—at least until one of the women was thrown overboard by the men in charge, with her hands and ankles bound. Then the brig's performance improved dramatically. The yawl had to flee upstream; all contact with the Spire was broken.

During those three days the Observers reported rafts being rowed back to the west, then returning with more armed men. Had the Sons been able, obviously they would have pressed real boats into service at once; but it had taken them till the third day to round up a scratch crew for the yawl. So most of the boat crews must have deserted to hide in the town. It might have been even wiser to scatter far inland—though I don't know that this would have been *my* first instinct, or any riverwoman's; and soon, of course, the chance was gone.

From aloft the Observers spied murders, and rapes by the raggy soldiery.

But then men wearing robes arrived from the west; Edrick's colleagues, and maybe the man himself. Vicious incidents tailed off quickly, in full view at least. Corpses were piled and burnt. Looting ceased. Cordons and roadblocks were set up. Patrols prowled the streets, enforcing order. Perhaps the western warleaders deliberately let their soldiers storm around to begin with, to terrorize the town, so that the people of Verrino would feel grateful for the contrast later on. Or maybe the leaders hadn't risked crossing over till the terrain was secure. By the time we lost touch with Verrino, at any rate, an uneasy calm reigned. As yet, the Sons hadn't piled faggots to burn people alive individually. . . .

From Pecawar, dear Pecawar, word continued to flow that all was well. From Gangee and the other towns, likewise. In each a militia was now being hastily raised, though how effective these might prove I could hardly judge by the example of Jangali. Jangali had always boasted an athletic, spirited, tough guild in its junglejacks. Before long, teams of 'jacks were marching about Jangali armed with machetes, axes and bill-hooks. No doubt this was fine for morale— but good for what else? There was only wild jungle opposite, and for long leagues northward.

Meanwhile, leaders of the jungle guild and our own river guild conferred for days on end about what to do. Coded messages were flashed, as well as plain—shorelubbers noticed no difference. I began to worry that Marti had been all too right about the absence of authority.

But then, ten days after the invasion of Verrino, a tight-lipped Tamath instructed me to accompany her to a meeting at the hall of the jungle guild.

The Jay-Jay Hall, as it was known locally, was a massive wooden edifice on the edge of the new town: a real temple of tree-trunks roofed by great beams and naked rafters, with clerestory windows for light and air. Entering the Hall was like boarding a great landship, largely devoted to an empty hold. The principal chamber contained no furniture at all, as though it was an insult to giant trees to trim them into tiny chairs. Instead, everyone sat on tasselled cushions arrayed on the waxed plank floor—and you'd better be sure to leave your boots in the lobby.

I was seated cross-legged beside Tamath. Twenty 'jacks and riverwomen were present in all; and before very long a 'jack dressed in the typical baggy trousers and scarlet jerkin, and sporting braggartly black moustaches, was asking:

"And why should Jangali be invaded *soon?* Tell me that! If I was a westerner, sod his guts, first I'd secure Verrino. Wrap it up tight. Rule the place till the people knew nothing else. After a year or two I'd pick off Sarjoy, then Aladalia, as leisurely as can be. Sew them up too. Where's the hurry? It's us who are in the mess, with our trade routes cut in half. We're wasting our time marching round the town with axes on our shoulders, that should be lopping trees."

A boatmistress said, "Well, *I'd* hurry. Because the current might come back!"

"Come back? Why should your mascot come back? You're crying for the moon."

I'd sometimes wondered what a moon must look like. A ball of rock floating above the clouds? A kind of cold sun? The jibe was insulting.

"I hope you aren't suggesting that women have become like children suddenly. To operate our trade routes you need fully experienced—"

"Persons. Male or female. And s'pose those Sons send boats to raid, like pirates in some Ajelobo romance, who'll be best to fight them off? Those as knows sails and needles? Or those who know axes?"

"Mister, it takes time to learn the ropes."

"And maybe we've got time. Five or ten years."

Another junglejack spoke up. This man was older, with a birthmark—a squashed cherry—on his cheek.

"You riverwomen certainly need to buck your boat crews up with those of the axe, as my friend says. A woman's no match for a hefty man in most fights. But there's danger in hanging back from the fight too long. We might find ourselves stuck in mid-air with no momentum. We simply can't let those Sons pour thousands of soldiers over the river. And I'll tell you why. Judging from what that stupid snitch of a girl said, those westerners are a lot poorer than us materially. Now they'll have heaps of our own goods to use against us. No matter how much they mess up the places they capture, they'll only get richer and stronger."

So the river guild—or Tamath—had already told the jungle guild about my travels. . . .

I was incensed; I spoke without thinking. "That stupid snitch is sitting right here!" I said loudly. I only realized after I'd let this out of the bag that I must have been present for a reason: as a card for our guild to play. But what card could I be?

There were a few intakes of breath. Men's eyes bored holes in me. Women looked embarrassed. Tamath snarled softly, "Shut it!"

"Okay, okay," I muttered.

"Well, well!" declared Moustache. "I'd say the river guild owes us one for that. Why's *she* here? So that we can send her up a jungle giant without a safety line? Or spit her on a spine-tree? Or stick her on a bonfire? Then both guilds shake hands afterwards?" His loud voice sounded more threatening than perhaps he meant it to, I had to remind myself.

Surely this wasn't the card that Tamath hoped to play? To toss me up into the treetops as a way of repairing inter-guild relations?

"We don't *quite* go in for that kind of thing," Moustache went on acidly. "You misunderstand our little annual festival."

"Nothing of the sort was in our minds," protested Tamath. "We can discuss *her* later on." She addressed the man with the birthmark: "Sir, we agree with you that time isn't our friend. And when I say 'our', I include everyone living on the east bank—man or woman, from Jangali to Gangee. So therefore. . . ." And she glanced at the quaymistress of Jangali, a plump silver-haired woman named Poula.

"So therefore," continued Poula smoothly, "we must urge the recapture of Verrino as soon as possible. How may this be accomplished? First, we should restore communications with the towns of the north so that we can co-ordinate efforts. We should build balloons to carry couriers over the occupied zone—and spy on it. This can be done."

A 'jack whistled. "Can it, just?"

"We think so. There'll need to be tests."

"And lightweight couriers! Now I see where the girl fits in."

Poula ignored this. "Next, we need weapons which can match those pistols of the Sons. Guineamoy will have to manufacture these. Therefore Guineamoy must be strongly defended. The Sons might attack Guineamoy next."

"Knowing about its workshops, as they do." Moustache glared at me.

"Oh, a fool could tell from all the smoke!" said Poula.

"Really? Then why didn't the Sons attack Guineamoy to begin with? Why Verrino?"

Maybe the answer to that was that Doctor Edrick had wanted some decent spectacles . . . I suppressed this flippant thought.

"Three reasons. Guineamoy must have seemed our strongest town. They may not have known quite what they were up against."

"Now they do. And the answer is: not much!"

"Next, Verrino is close to Manhome South, where those 'Crusaders' might be more influential. Unless we strike back and win, they'll soon be influential everywhere in the west. Finally, the Sons had a convenient launching place at Minestead. So now Guineamoy must be defended." Poula looked round the meeting. "Defended by whom?" she asked rhetorically. "And who will recapture Verrino with the weapons made in Guineamoy? Success in this enterprise requires a stout team who can lay off their ordinary guild work for weeks without disrupting essential supplies such as foodstuffs. . . .

"In a word, the junglejacks. Women 'jacks can carry on jungle guild business in the meantime, on a trimmed-down basis."

Moustache stared at Poula. "So what you're proposing is that we prune our own guild down to the women members—and turn the other ninety-odd per cent of us into your army!"

"It'll be *everyone's* army: the army of the east. But an army, yes. Meanwhile, riverwomen will be busy ferrying fighters and weapons. Don't worry, we'll be doing our bit."

"Aye, by shipping us off to a foreign town. Men don't go gadding about like your lot, with a lover in every port. Some would say: what's Guineamoy to us that we should quit our homes, leaving Jangali unguarded? Some might say we could survive quite well on our own, from the Bayou down to Tambimatu."

Surely some Jangali men must have come from Verrino originally! Yet it was a truism that new allegiances thrust out old.

"Don't worry about your home town. The jungle protects Jangali adequately from attack."

"Exactly!"

Poula wagged a finger. "Until the day when the Sons come sailing upstream—picking off one town then the next!"

"She's right, you know," said Birthmark.

Moustache subsided somewhat. "So we're to pack our bags, and garrison Guineamoy?"

"Yes," she said.

"While the Guineamoy guild make lots of pistols and things, for us to go to war with?"

"We haven't time to mince words or be diplomatic, Sir. Yes, yes. It's the only way. Guineamoy are prepared to tool up to make swords and pistols. And explosive bombs which you can catapult from a boat deck, or drop from a balloon. And incidentally," she added, "please don't think too harshly of Yaleen. She did tell us about their guns and how the Sons govern the West; that's useful."

But I wondered whether she was defending me personally, or simply the honour of the guild. . . .

"Almost as useful," snapped a 'jack with a vein-smashed drinker's face, "was what she told them about *us!* And about the poison those Barbra weirdos use."

I winced. I did manage to stare back at him, though perhaps my face was as flushed as his.

"We'll need to discuss your proposal," said Moustache. "We'll give you an answer tomorrow."

"Guineamoy already agreed," said Poula.

"Maybe that's because they're closer to the action, and a bit more exposed? And maybe the almighty river guild promised to remit their cargo fees for the next couple of years?"

Poula snorted. "Next you'll be fretting in case we charge you for troop transport!"

She didn't actually answer his question, though. This, I thought, was foolish. If the 'jacks sailed to Guineamoy, sooner or later they would discover whether there was anything in this wild surmise. And who would fight with a stout heart if they even suspected that they were being diddled?

Yet who was I to criticize?

"Tomorrow," repeated Moustache. He stood up, in one smooth scissoring action. Other 'jacks followed suit.

"Wait. One thing more. We haven't discussed the motives of the Sons enough. Their beliefs."

"So? You can turn that one loose on the savants and nitpickers up Ajelobo way."

"We may indeed."

"Marvellous! That'll amuse us while we're on guard duty, and exploding ourselves and dying messily. I wonder how many cords of wood they'll need to print their fantasies?"

Poula remained patiently sitting. Reluctantly a few 'jacks sat down again. Not Moustache, though.

"You have to know what your enemy thinks," she said. "One key to this is, what the black current is."

"What it *was*, you mean."

"Is still! Coiled up as it is, within the Precipices."

"Who cares? Sod all effect it has on the river now."

"Yet it still reaches into all of us, who are of the river," Poula said patiently.

Moustache looked blank.

"I assure you of that, Mister 'Jack. May I vomit if I lie, or betray."

"What on earth are you talking about? What's wrong with you?"

Poula was shivering. Her face had blanched. She bit her lip. Moustache stared hard at her then nodded—as though persuaded, of something at least. Abruptly Poula fainted and keeled over. Her neighbour tended her, tucking a cushion under her head.

"Okay, so I'm impressed," said Moustache. "What conclusions am I meant to draw?"

Tamath took over again. A little too slickly for my taste, as though this incident—genuine though I knew it to be—had been rehearsed beforehand. "And the key to the current," she said, "must be in its head. Where else? Tambimatu tell us that its mouth gapes open." I mistrusted her tone mightily. "An open gateway is an invitation."

"To be swallowed?" Moustache laughed. "Maybe its mouth just stuck in that position. Maybe it's dead."

"In that case, Poula would not have felt so sick and fainted."

"Poo to that," said the florid-faced 'jack. "Some folk believe an idea strong enough, they can make their own hair fall out."

Yet Moustache looked impressed despite himself. "So the thing has a key stuck in its throat. What of it?"

"We will send someone through that open mouth to investigate. We will send the only person who claims to have talked to it. We'll send *her.*"

Me.

I'm sure if Poula had been conscious she would have announced this with less vindictive relish.

Moustache guffawed. "Heh heh! That's one better than sending her up a jacktree without a line."

But the 'jack with broken veins looked troubled. "Hang on a bit! Is it in our interests to have that thing meddled with? I say leave well alone! After a bite to eat, it might revive."

The 'jack with his cherry stain broke in. "Let's face it: what's going on is an invasion. An invasion by barbarians—who'll probably like you and me just as much as they like the ladies here. If jumping into the thing's mouth helps us any, I say we should welcome it."

"Another reason for honouring Yaleen with this special mission," added Tamath, with a nasty smile, "is that she seems to have a certain talent for survival. For popping up again. For being regurgitated."

Which did nothing to diminish the very hollow feeling I had in my tummy. . . .

The next day the 'jacks did give their answer, though I wasn't present myself; and the answer was yes. Yes, they would transform their guild into an army to defend Guineamoy. Yes, they would liberate Verrino. Not try to. They *would* liberate it. When a 'jack decided to fell a tree, that tree fell.

So a day later the *Blue Guitar* set sail for Tambimatu with everyone

on board in relatively cheerful mood. Now that Tamath had won a
victory or two, she was more relaxed. And when she told the crew
the purpose of our trip—that I had volunteered to enter the worm's
head—they eased off in their attitude to me. ("Just so long as we
don't have to pilot her personally," observed Zernia, who was up
and about now and hobbling on a crutch. "No, no," Tamath hastened to assure her. "The black ketch will carry Yaleen.") Even Hali
softened her heart towards me, and became less abrasive.

Ah, my chance to save the guild! To be a heroine, pure and simple.
Or a dead one.

During that voyage I often found myself recalling my glimpses of
the lunatic head: the blind eyes, the mouth dripping glue . . . I
tried not to dwell on this, but I had time on my hands. I was forbidden to undertake any strenuous duties—just in case I broke a leg,
accidentally on purpose.

So I spent my spare hours reading the *Blue Guitar*'s small library of
Ajelobo romances, studying the antics of their heroines and heroes
in disbelief. Nobody ever asked *them* to stuff themselves down a
giant dripping gob. Now that some days had lapsed since the plan
was mooted, it seemed the height of craziness to try to communicate
with the worm by this means. What would *you* think if a bug tried
to make friends with you by leaping into your mouth? The venture
seemed ever more like some primitive rite of human sacrifice; oh
yes, I found a fine example of *that* in one romance—though naturally
the heroine rescued her boyfriend in the nick of time.

We passed Port Barbra without putting into port. Soon we were
approaching Ajelobo, source of those fantasies which had delighted
me once; Ajelobo, whose wiser residents would soon be set the nut
to crack, of whether we were free individuals or puppets. To gnaw
at this nut, while 'jacks died for freedom's sake; I could appreciate
Moustache's sarcasm. No doubt Ajelobo savants would still be debating when a tide of Sons rolled up the river to answer them with
steel and fire. Long after *I'd* been digested as a worm's breakfast.

With Ajelobo half a league ahead, Tamath came to where I was
lounging in a deck-chair; she was rubbing her hands contentedly.

"Signal just came. The first lot of 'jacks are sailing. Isn't that
great?"

"Great," I agreed. "And what happens when they've won Verrino? Will they go back to chopping wood? Will they disband of
their own accord?"

"If the current doesn't return, I suppose we'll need a garrison in every town from the Bayou northwards. For a while, at least."

"For a while—or forever? We'll need a standing army, Guildmistress, and our river guild to serve it. That's quite a change."

"In that case we might have to *invade* the west, and depose those Sons."

"That's no answer, either. What price the rules of marriage afterwards? What of the wander-weeks for girls? What of men staying put? What of *The Book?* All down the drain."

"Yaleen, you're forgetting the economic power of our guild."

"And you're forgetting how that power depends on us having a monopoly! I don't see any way back to where we were before. Paradise is lost, because the worm has gone."

"In that case," said Tamath tightly, "it had damn well better come back. You'll see to that, won't you, dear? Then you'll be promoted to 'mistress, just like me."

"Oh sure, I'll see to it. Dead easy, really! I just pat it on its snout, gaze soulfully into its eyes and ask, 'Is oo sick, Wormy? What medicine makes oo well? Me? Am I oo's medicine, Wormy? Tell-ums, then!'"

Tamath slapped me briskly on the cheek, and strode away. Soon there was cheering on deck, and up aloft, as she shouted out the decoded signal.

With watering eyes I returned to my romance, *The Cabin Girl and the Cannibal.* One by one I tore out pages, folded them into darts and launched them over the rail. Soon we had a little paperchase behind us; though nothing much compared with the expanse of water.

Tambimatu again! The Precipices soaring up through the clouds; spinach purée humping up against a town which couldn't see beyond its own roofs nodding together . . . Jewels and muck.

I blew my accumulated cash, upwards of sixty fish, on a splendid diamond ring. If I was doomed to plunge into foul saliva, I might as well be properly dressed for the occasion—if only on one finger.

The guild had other notions of how I should costume myself for the encounter. Somebody must have had a fine sense of irony: the guild had prepared a sort of diving suit.

"For your protection, Yaleen," explained Maranda, the squat, bland quaymistress; she who had skippered us to the Precipices and back, the year before. On a table in her office rested a glass helmet, a tight pigskin bodice with a brass collar to clamp the helmet to, and lots of straps on the back; and a tough belt with a padlock of a snaplink.

"Why not naked, rubbed with costly oils and unguents?" I'd found the "unguent" in *The Cabin Girl and the Cannibal.* It sounded sexy.

"You might need air, Yaleen. We've considered the way your brother crossed the river. See this valve here, in the glass? You'll carry several compressed air bottles linked in series on your back—enough for two hours. The finest craftsmen in Tambimatu have made them. The bottles are going through final trials right now."

"Are they of gold and silver?"

"And there'll be a long rope fixed to this harness, so we can pull you out."

"Oh, won't I just be the fly on the angler's line! Shouldn't I have a hook in my ribs? So you can winch the whole worm out of its hidey-hole, when it bites? Then the good boat *Nameless* can tug it downstream all the way to Umdala."

"I'm glad to see you've braced your spirit for what may prove something of an ordeal."

"Ordeal? Gosh, I'm used to it! The only thing that mildly worries me is, how will it *hear* me through the helmet?"

"You can set your mind at rest on that score. If there's no result, we'll send you in again without a helmet. Now here's the lamp you'll use. . . ."

At least this time, unlike my first trip to the head of the river, we would be dispensing with any banquets or solemn hoo-hah. Who needed them? For some curious indefinable reason I felt quite off my food—and as for solemnity, whatever flip badinage I might utter, you can believe I felt solemn enough inside. In the pit of my tummy.

I was to transfer to the black ketch immediately. Departure time was set for a day hence.

So out to the moored ketch I was rowed by an apprentice, the oars dabbling like ducks on a pond. As our rowboat neared the ketch, a face peered over the gunwale: a face as ruddy as the sun through morning mist, a red orb topped with straw—and the sun rose a little in my heart.

"Peli! Peli, it's you!" I cried.

A moment later I was scrambling up the ladder, boarding. Peli from Aladalia! The water-wife with the warbling voice!

For five seconds we simply stared at one another. Then Peli cried.

"Why, let me take a look at you!" and did just the opposite, rushing to embrace me and thump me about the shoulders to check that I was solid. I laughed and laughed; so did she.

"Oh, it's so good to see you!" I gasped, when we untangled. "But what are you *doing* here? Surely you haven't been stuck in Tambimatu ever since—"

"What, faithfully dragging the river for your body? No fear! Mind, I gave that skinny bitch what-for. The one who wanted you overboard. Don't know if you heard me. . . ."

"I *was* a bit busy at the time . . . No, but I did hear you cry out. And I felt your fingers trying to save me."

"Bless you, when I saw you leap on this gunwale and scuttle along the boom!"

"Did you sail to the current again, this Eve past?"

"No, I was in Ajelobo. The guild summoned me here. I'd been with you last time, that's why. Thoughtful of them, eh? The crumb of comfort. Some of the other 'sisters who'll be with us, *they* sailed to the head this time. And I can tell you they're definitely a better bunch than that tight-nosed lot *we* had. The only fly in the ointment is old Nothing-Bothers-Me—she's the skipper."

"I know. I've just come from her office. She's been working overtime, welding me a wedding costume. It sure looks tight. That old worm had better not put me in the way of a baby."

Peli laughed, and caught my hand to admire the diamond ring. "Is this the wedding band? Won't the worm have a job slipping it on? He's a bit on the fat side."

"Oh Peli! Same old Peli. I bought the ring to make me feel good. *Something* has to. Well, *you* do. Being here."

"Hmm, not completely the same old Peli. Bit bothered, in fact. About Aladalia. I was down there in the summer, and now what's going on?" She sighed—but then her sun shone brightly again. "Oh, the hell with that. You've got enough worries for six people. And six just happens to be the number of the crew. Come meet your 'sisters!"

They were indeed a much better bunch. Three of them—Delli, Marth and Sal—had just sailed to the head and the midstream. Laudia and Sparki were veterans from way back who had been in Tambimatu when events, also, came to a head.

Laudia was a boatmistress and Sparki her boatswain. These two had been together a long time. Laudia was as blonde and elegant as

Tamath, though with none of Tamath's ambitious insecurity. Sparki was dusky, diminutive and peculiarly boy-like. Peculiar, in the sense that the current hadn't thought so when she drank her slug of it. Sparki looked just the sort of person I thought the current weeded out: like a boy who had run away to the river in girl's clothes—as in one daft romance I once read, written without any knowledge of the actual facts.

Plainly enough this bosom couple were the two individuals on board most trusted by the guild; on account of their love of the river and love of each other, which were intertwined. The way of the river was the bond of their relationship; I could tell that from a dozen touches and tones of voice. Lose one; loosen the other? Perhaps. So Laudia and Sparki could be relied on to do whatever the guild required. At least I felt sure they wouldn't behave like martinets.

Five. And Peli made six. Me, seven.

Only, I wasn't crew; I was something else. I was the bucket to dip in the current's jaws.

After our supper of pork stew and rice that evening, we drank delicious strong green tea: Tambi-maté. In its storage jar Tambi-maté looked like a dollop of the local purée, dried. Generous wads were infused in boiling water in individual glass tumblers with real silver caps. Then you sucked the liquid through a thin metal pipe; and quite hard you had to suck, too. Sal, herself from Tambimatu, did the honours. The drinks set was hers, presented by proud parents when she was chosen for the New Year's Eve trip.

We drank quite a few glasses, getting a queer untea-like buzz from the drink, a buzz quite different from tipsiness. This was a clear-headed bright elation, accompanied by a slight anaesthetizing of the body so that after a time I couldn't tell whether I'd had enough to eat, too much, too little, or nothing; and I didn't care which. If only I'd had a jar of Tambi-maté with me a year earlier! It was perfect for someone lost in a jungle, with only grubs and roots to eat, and keep down. Though I'm not sure quite how I would have heated the water. . . .

"Will you sign your glass?" asked Sal, after the fourth or fifth infusion.

"Eh?"

"Your glass. Sign it with that diamond. Delighted to see you supporting local crafts, by the way!"

"You want me to scratch my moniker on this glass because I bought a jewel in town?"

"No, of course not! I want you to do it because there'll be songs sung about you in future years, and tales told."

"If there are, let's hope *I* get the chance to write them, or else they'll be a pack of lies."

"You will. I know you will! In fact, start scribing now: your name, I mean." Sal giggled. "Please! For luck."

"Go on," urged Delli.

"Well, okay then." Feeling rather peculiar about this—and realizing that I hadn't escaped ceremonies after all—I tucked the glass into my lap and inscribed "Yaleen" as legibly as I could.

Sal held the glass up to the lantern to admire, tilting it about; she had to, to make any sense of the spidery scratches against the sodden leaves within.

"I've spoilt it, haven't I?"

"Oh no! Absolutely not! I'll treasure this."

I felt light and euphoric. "It's my glass gravestone," I joked. "Will you put flowers in it if I die?"

She grinned. "No, but I'll drink Tambi-maté from it. All my days."

A while later, Peli blinked repeatedly as if to bring a bright idea into focus. "Yaleen, I've been meaning to ask: why *did* the current call you, a year ago? It wasn't objecting to you, otherwise you'd be dead. So what was special about *you?* I don't mean that as a put-down—"

"No, no, you're right!" She was, too. It seems astonishing in retrospect, but I had never actually asked myself this. I took it for granted, because it had happened to *me.* Like everyone else I was the heroine of my own life, the centre of the universe *et cetera.* Why shouldn't something extraordinary steer itself my way?

"Maranda wondered about that," volunteered Laudia.

"What, old Nothing-Bothers-Me?"

"That would bother her. She's been presiding over the annual trip for years. So when she heard you'd come back from the West, and hadn't been driven mad and drowned, she started puzzling. And she came up with an answer. You were very young to be honoured, Yaleen. I don't know why! Not quite two years on boats, and there you were sailing to the current—"

"I could tell you why, but it's a long story, full of junglejack festivals and. . . ." (And fungus drugs. Better not tell it after all. . . .)

"Let's just ascribe it to your sterling qualities, eh?"

"Um. Right. Qualities now in demand again . . . But what's the answer?"

"That you'd drunk the current more recently than anyone else who ever made the New Year's Eve trip. So maybe that's why it called you. Because you were more in tune with it."

"More in tune? That doesn't figure. The current can call a girl who fails her initiation, from a whole league away! It can call a man who tries to travel twice—"

"It can't *talk* to them, only craze them and destroy them. That's why Maranda is bringing a fresh slug of the current on board tomorrow: some of the new vintage for you to drink. Plus some left over from last year, in case this year's has something wrong with it."

"Oh, shit! Look, I got through the current again just a bit ago. I probably swallowed dribbles and dribbles of it."

"But did it talk to you? Maybe it couldn't quite reach you."

"Maybe it couldn't be bothered."

"So another slug or so should tune you up nicely."

"Tune me up, indeed!" I swung round. "Peli, dear Peli," I begged, "give us all a real tune."

"Okay." And Peli gave voice.

Now, this might have been unkind if we had just sat and listened, grinning within. But we didn't. We all joined in; and not simply to drown Peli out. For the song was that irresistible one:

> *Under the bright blue sun*
> *River-run, river-run!*
> *Under the stars on high*
> *Sails fly, sails fly!*
> *Under the masts so tall . . .*

Presently Sal held up the signed glass again, canting it to catch the light. "Our boat ought to have a naming, too!"

"Why not?" agreed Marth. "Fat lot of use Old Nameless'll be if the current never comes back."

"What name does the current need to heed?" Delli thumped the bulkhead. "Boat, I name thee *Yaleen!*"

"I'll go one better," promised Sal. "I'll paint *Yaleen* on the prow tomorrow."

We all laughed. I didn't think she would do it.

Next morning Quaymistress Maranda boarded, bringing with her the "diving suit", air-bottles and rope. And when she boarded, Sal was hanging over the side, just finishing daubing my name in yellow paint. Maranda grumbled and growsed at this defacing of her precious ketch, till Laudia exclaimed exasperatedly, "We can always black it out afterwards!" Sensing unified opposition, Maranda conceded.

I drank her slugs of the black current, to no very noticeable effect; and soon we set sail.

All too quickly for me we reached the head of the river—and the worm's head, protruding gargoyle-like from that submerged stone arch with its chin resting on the water.

Was the sight more appalling by daylight? I'd feared it would be. Yet I found I could control my rising hysteria by telling myself that this thing wasn't alive—it was simply a mound of crudely-sculpted mud, or maybe basalt covered with mould.

When I'd last seen the worm's head, it was moving. Now it wasn't. The only movement was of water lapping it. Just so long as it didn't move! Just so long as a white eye didn't blink—why, that eye could be a slash of chalk! Even the drool in the worm's jaws hung motionless, like slimy stalactites.

We manoeuvred the *Yaleen* through some down-beating air turbulence almost up to the lip itself, deep-anchoring in the very lee of the Precipice where there was a pocket of calm.

The Precipice! Ah, better that I hadn't looked upwards! I couldn't believe that what loomed above could be a vertical rockface. It just had to be the real surface of the world. In which case, how come we were floating vertical to it?

The whole world bent abruptly at right-angles here, causing an awesome sense of vertigo. For a moment I imagined this was the effect of the slugs I'd drunk. But no; it was a consequence of the planet being hinged in half. I didn't dare look up again or I would fall, fall upward.

We worked silently most of the time, and spoke in hushed tones if we had to say anything. I don't think this was for fear of alerting the worm. No, it was because any words would be as stray melting snowflakes in that place; they would vanish before they could make their mark.

Sparki and Sal helped me don the diving costume. They strapped the bodice skin-tight, then slotted in the air-bottles behind, which effectively blocked access to the straps themselves. The helmet was clamped to the brass collar, a valve was turned and I breathed bottled air smelling faintly of burnt oil. Maranda locked one end of the thin tough rope to my belt at the base of my spine; the rest of the rope lay in loose coils, with the far end tied to the capstan. She lit my lamp and clipped this to the bracket on my helmet. Then Peli thrust out the gangplank, on to the lip of the worm.

We were ready. I was ready. (And a little voice was gibbering somewhere, "Ready? How can anyone ever be ready for *this?*" I ignored the voice inside my head, since it was my own and I didn't wish it to reach my lips.)

Peli squeezed me in her arms, provoking one of the few sounds: a loud *"tssk"* of disapproval from Maranda, in case any of my fine equipment, product of the best Tambimatu artificers, should get scratched or crumpled before the worm could have its way. . . .

Then I walked the plank, with the rope paying out lightly behind me. I stepped on to the lower lip cautiously in case it was slippery and I skidded off into the water. Which would be an uncomfortable and ignominious beginning. But in fact the surface of the lip felt tacky, like paint which hadn't quite dried; and it yielded to the pressure of my feet, giving lots of grip.

Turning, I saluted the *Yaleen* with my diamond ring upraised. I don't know that the crew recognized the gesture as a salute; maybe they thought I was giving them the finger. I elbowed a dangling rope of drool aside—it didn't snap, just bent. I elbowed another gooey streamer, and shoved my way between them.

The inside walls of the mouth were bulgy and bumpy, and so dark they seemed to drink my lamplight. To see, I had to swing my head from side to side. Shadows ducked and dodged, as if racing round to ambush me from behind. I couldn't flick the beam too fast without dizzying my brains. Above me I saw a dark dome, sprouting warts the size of cushions. . . .

Hard to look down, encumbered as I was with helmet, bodice and bottles . . . but a ridgy floor below. Slicker and firmer than the lip.

As I stepped on in, my legs started to shake. Scared? Of course I was scared.

And of course that wasn't why my legs were wobbling.

To say that the floor split open under me would be too precise by far. It would grossly flatter the chaos of the next few moments. Before I knew it, I was a toddler careering down her first carnival slide, shrieking aloud . . . Rope snaking behind . . . Black jelly curve above . . . Light swirling, head thumping and bumping . . . Then the lamp went out. I only realized I'd been swallowed when I was already half-way down the gullet.

The tube swooped upwards briefly. Impetus carried me over a brink. I sprawled in pitch darkness.

And now I *was* shaking like a leaf. I'd pissed myself too. Hot at first, then clammy-cold. The blackness was absolute. In fact, you couldn't even call it blackness. It was *nothing*. I might as well have gone blind.

I lay very still. Or tried to. Since nothing further happened, I rolled over after a bit and felt about. Soft clammy texture here . . . Slithery and harder over there, like muscle . . . My fingers closed on a tentacle, shied away. Ah, it was the rope! My safety line. Should I jerk it? Give three tugs for "Pull me back, quick"?

But beyond being gulped down, nothing dire had happened. At least I wasn't floundering in acid juice. I continued exploring, very gently. Each new span my fingers touched was so much extra safety, so much breathing space. And so much extra cause for jitters, because the very next grope might bring me up against . . . who knew what?

I thought my blind eyes were playing tricks: I saw a flash, a flicker.

I shuffled about, and focused on a spot of shimmery blue. This brightened to a glowing patch. I held very still, hardly breathing. Perhaps the light was only a few spans from my face. In which case, it was far too close! The glow continued to intensify, but since this had no effect on the darkness near at hand, it must be distant. Then all of a sudden everything adjusted mentally, and I *knew* that I was peering along a tunnel of some kind, which eventually debouched into somewhere far larger that was aglow with blue light. I stood up, stretched tall, and my fingertips brushed the roof above. Shuffling to left then to right, arms outstretched, I discovered curving walls; these were squashy, though interspersed with stiffer "muscle-ribs".

So I began to plod forward in the direction of the light, holding my hands ahead of me. After the first ten paces I stepped out more boldly. And the glow increased in apparent size.

* * *

A few minutes later I stood in the doorway to a cavern that was eerie and enchanting. Curving walls and vaulted roof were ribbed and buttressed with blue bone, or stiffened muscle. All across a misty floor fronds waved like underwater weed. Warts humped up through the low mist and hairy "vegetation" in a line of stepping stones. And all glowed softly in various tones of light or dark blue: the fronds were almost mauve, the warts a brighter turquoise as though to mark the way. The cavern was long, long. Far off, the ground mist seeped upward to become a general dense azure fog. Was this cavern part of the Worm—or was the Worm's substance coating cavern walls?

The stepping stones led straight to a kind of island: a large hump of milky, veiny powder-blue. "Opal Island", I thought, giving it a name.

And here was I, held back in the very doorway by that damned rope! Which Maranda had so thoughtfully locked on to me, in case any meddling little fingers inside the Worm unknotted it. By now the rope had reached its limit.

Retreating a few paces, I gathered slack—and set to work fraying the rope with my diamond. Obviously I had to go on into the womb-cavern—why else had it lit up for me? I sawed away till I thought the stone might part from its setting; but Tambimatu craftsmanship prevailed. As well it should; I'd paid a whole bag of coins for the ring! At last the strands parted.

Pry as I might, I couldn't budge the air bottles; though at least I could unclamp the helmet, which was steaming up. . . .

The cavern air smelled faintly of dead fish and humus; nothing very stomach-churning—no swamp-gas or intestinal stenches. Once the helmet was wrenched free, the bottled air blew an annoying draught against my neck; I would probably end up with a stiff neck or earache. . . .

Still and silent stretched the cavern, save for a slight bubbling or susurrus amidst the misty fronds.

Should I bellow out, "I'm here"? The worm must know that already. I kept quiet.

I trod across the stepping stones—without any bother—and reached Opal Island. Closer up, this took on the proportions of the glazed buttock of a giantess: with veins of milky blue flowing within, and a large vague shape like a huge bone, inside towards the top. A rim ran right round the base. As soon as I set foot on this rim, the whole island quaked. Hastily I hopped back on to the nearest stepping stone.

The trembling quickened; shivers ran up the slope, overtaking one another—then there was a sudden loud "plop". The whole top of the island split open.

Two seams flopped apart, and a human arm emerged. It wagged about as though waving to me. A bald head and bare shoulders followed. Unsteadily, a naked man stood up. His skin was the unhealthy white of someone newly unwrapped from a long spell in bandages. He looked like a big jungle-grub. His groin was as nude of hair as his skull.

The man regarded me out of watery blue eyes—then he took a step, and slipped, and skidded all the way down the side of the island on his buttocks, fetching up with a thump on the rim.

"I—" he croaked. Abruptly he retched up a volume of thin white liquid. Maybe I hadn't too much to worry about from this fellow! Wiping his chin, he tottered erect, and contrived a smile—he pushed at his cheeks with his fingers as though trying on a mask for size.

"Hullo, I'm to be your guide. The current took me . . . some time ago. I tried to stow away, see. The current kept my body intact, so now I'm representing it."

"A *man* is representing it?"

He examined himself in surprise. "Goodness, I haven't been a man for ages. . . ."

"You haven't been . . . Are you *crazy?*"

"Actually, I'm dead . . . It kept my body, see. I've been living other lives, in the *Ka*-store."

"In the *what?*" For "Ka" was the name the Westerners gave to the mind-part of a person. They said the *Ka* flew back to Eeden when the body died. Flew to another world . . . "Are you from the West Bank?" I demanded.

"No . . . Sarjoy, once. . . ."

"You did just say '*Ka*', though?"

He nodded.

"Are the Westerners telling the truth, then? About the God-Mind on Eeden? How can there be a *Ka*-store here? What *is* it? What does—?"

He flapped his hands in distress. "Please!" The dead man gestured at another line of stepping stones continuing along the cavern towards the azure fog. "Could we possibly . . . ? Sooner we go, sooner I get back to my dreams."

"Go where?"

"To the *Ka*-store."

"How can there be a *Ka*-store here? This isn't Eeden. The current isn't the God-Mind—or is it?"

He slumped down and clasped his hands around his knees. Maybe he had difficulty standing up, after being dead for so long. . . .

"I suppose we've time to spare," he conceded.

"Time? You do realize there's a war on? That good people are being butchered? And all because the current withdrew! Was it poisoned?"

"If only you'd stop bombarding me . . . Yes, I realize there's a war on. No, the current wasn't poisoned. Will you listen to me? The black current can store the *Kas* of the dead, so long as people were close to it in life. As it links more *Kas* in its store, so its mind grows in power."

"You mean to tell me that all riverwomen who ever lived are still alive here?"

"Well, they're dead, but yes. They dream each other's lives now. And as they interweave, so the creature who was here before us all seeks . . . seeks the mind-key to the universe."

"Oh." The mind-key to the universe. Tamath had speculated that there was a key stuck down the worm's throat . . . So it was the key to the universe, was it? But apparently the worm, too, was still hunting for it. Just then I remembered what Andri had told me: that people couldn't simply arrive on a foreign world and merrily fit in from the word go. "Did the current *shape* this world for us?" I asked.

"I don't follow you."

I did my best to explain. "Did the current alter this world so we could eat and drink and breathe here?" I ended up.

"Quite the contrary! The world grew of its own accord. So did the current. I don't quite know how its body works, but I do know that it takes energy from water. It splits and burns and changes water . . . Well, aeons ago it floated off down the river. And it made a big mistake. On its own, you see, it has no more brain than a worm in the soil. But it can use *other* minds. It has a thirst for them, it can drink them. And after drinking them it can start to think."

"I sometimes feel that way myself."

The zombi looked irked. "Really? Well, the current sensed dawning minds on the land. So it exerted itself to use these minds. But they were only dawning, and it quenched them instead. They withered and died out. Then for aeons more it just lay inertly, sensing only the slow dim wits of fish and the like. It hoped other creatures might become aware, if it let them alone."

"How could it *hope* for anything, if it hadn't a mind of its own?"

"It sensed. It *felt.* The flow of its being is to *know,* through others. To absorb, to drink. . . ."

"So then I guess the Ship from Eeden arrived at Port Firsthome?"

It had indeed. Yet for aeons the creature had been sluggish. It had simply been existing at the bottom of the river like a vegetable.

Before it could grasp what was happening, the world had half changed. New plants and fish and animals were mingling with the native ones, in some cases pushing the old life aside, in other cases even cross-breeding.

Suddenly as if from nowhere, bright strong minds were present. Young minds, printed with mature purpose, newly dressed in knowledge. This was the first generation of settlers.

Amongst whom, the current dimly detected two varieties of being: those of Flow, and those of Thrust. The one, compatible with it; the other, alien. Excited, confused, it rose from the depths, putting forth its senses—to be dazzled, blinded.

It still couldn't "think" about any of this—which in any case after all those dormant aeons seemed to happen instantaneously. And almost immediately, a vast intelligence from far away shone through these bright new minds as through a window; touched the current, tasted it, tried to extinguish it.

This distant intelligence was a being of Thrust, rejoicing in its grandeur and dominion. So, at any rate, it seemed to the current, when the current tried to analyse events long afterwards. However, this ambitious intelligence had already transformed almost the whole of its local substance to breed plants and animals which would be at home on the new world, and then to build human bodies, and to light their minds with *Kas* from afar.

Instinctively the current lashed out to save itself. And there was madness on the land: a storm of forgetting, a whirlwind of disruption. The worm wasn't quite sure whose fault the mind-disaster was. It suspected that the far intelligence might have tried to extinguish its *own* experiment upon this world, to break the link with the creature it had woken.

Some settlers lost less of themselves, some more. All were deeply confused. Two groups survived: one on the west bank, where the far intelligence was remembered, though chaotically; another on the east bank, where its origin was quite forgotten.

Down succeeding centuries, as the current established a rapport with Those of the Flow, in the east, and drank the spirits of the river-dead, it began at last to *know*.

Thus spoke the zombi. His name, he added in an afterthought, was Raf; though he seemed to attach little significance to it, as if it had been centuries since he last used it.

And now events were on the move.

"Poisoned?" Raf chuckled. By now he behaved more naturally, though he wasn't exactly my notion of convivial. "Not on your sweet life! The current got just the ingredient it needed dumped into it. The rennet, to curdle the milk of its mind. To thicken it, enrich it. It had been trying to influence those cult-women inland from Port Barbra, but they were hard to get hold of. . . ."

"What? Say that again!"

Credence, boatswain of the *Spry Goose*, hadn't been so hard to get hold of! Suddenly that whole episode of the Junglejack Festival took on a startling new perspective—and I found myself pitying Credence. She had been manipulated in her beliefs, used as a tool—to be discarded when she couldn't prise open Marcialla's cabin door. Credence mustn't entirely have known why she was conspiring; otherwise she might have proved more effective. Hell, who was I kidding? With Marcialla unpersuaded and marooned up a tree, it was only by a hair's breadth of bad luck—known as Yaleen—that Credence failed.

Raf looked dreamy. "Ah, I have been one of those cult-women. She fled from her coven to sail the river . . . She could see how young they all died, and looking so old! Oh, I've known the Time-stop, and the Timespeed . . . But never mind about it now."

Never mind? In one sense Credence hadn't failed at all. All unwittingly, she had set *me* up as her successor.

And this, Raf was only too happy to confirm. For the second time within a few seconds my perspective on events swam inside-out.

"You came along just at the right time," he said. "The current read you. *You* proved better. More economical! You solved another problem, besides: how to lure those Sons of the God-Mind closer, so that

the current could drink enough dead *Kas* to really get to know them
—and taste and test the link to that far puissance. . . ."

"Hang on! Do you mean to say the current provoked this war?
Just so that Westerners would get killed, and it could harvest some
of them?"

"That is putting it a bit crudely."

"How can it harvest dead Sons now it has *quit* the battlefield?"

"Never fear! After a while it will return downstream. It can judge
the progress of the war by the *Kas* of newly dead riverwomen. Since
they're in tune, they still die into it."

"And am I supposed to applaud this clever scheme? Which brings
agony and death!" If I'd thought Doctor Edrick was unscrupulous,
then surely here was his match!

"Well, it wants to become a God, you see."

"A . . . *God?*"

Raf glanced around. I did, too . . . and my blood chilled. Surely
the cavern walls had crept closer while we were talking? Surely the
roof was lower than it had been a while before?

"The Sons would have waged war in any case," Raf said reasonably. "Sooner or later they would have found a means. In fifty years
or a hundred. The time isn't important."

"It is, to anybody who's alive!"

This part of the cavern definitely was shrinking. The fronds
sprouting out of the ground-mist were getting agitated.

"No, it *isn't* important! Not when you can live a host of other lives
hereafter. Nobody who is taken into the *Ka*-store regrets it. And
remember, when the current becomes a God, all those *Kas* will be
part of that God too."

"According to you."

"You'll find out soon enough, Yaleen. The current is pregnant
with itself—"

"Uh?"

"I'll rephrase that: soon the current will give birth—to something
greater than itself. And it feels it should be fertilized—"

"For crying out, doesn't it *know?* Who ever heard of getting fertilized *after* getting pregnant?"

"I don't mean literally fertilized. It *senses* that it needs the intimate
presence of a living person during the change. Here is the womb;
you are the man-seed."

The womb. And right now the womb was undergoing a contrac-
tion. . . .

"I'm a woman, you dumb corpse!"

"Please! The current is the Flow; you are the stone that shapes the Flow. You are the agent who helps it change, without changing yourself. It'll keep you in dream-life while it broods around you."

"It brooded round me twice already! And crept and crawled inside me. This is getting to be a habit."

"Ah, but this time—"

"Third time lucky?"

"This time you will be a legend, Yaleen. When you finally walk out of its mouth, salvation will be at hand."

"What if I don't want to be a legend?"

Frankly I didn't think the current had a chicken's idea what it was doing. If it had, I didn't think much of the plan. Not when the worm was content to start a war to get its way. Even if it did immortalize assorted fallen victims.

Those walls!

That roof!

"Look, I don't want to sound abrupt, but the place is caving in. Goodbye!" I turned and quickfooted it over the stepping stones towards the tunnel mouth. Fronds writhed up over the warts ahead to block my way.

"Stop!" cried Raf. "The mouth's closed!"

I did stop. "What?"

"The mouth has shut."

Maybe I shouldn't have paused. Fronds were questing for my ankles now. I kicked at them. Maybe the zombi was lying?

"There are such rewards, Yaleen! Access to all the lives that women have lived!"

And maybe if I did fight my way out, with my mission unaccomplished, Maranda and Sparki and Laudia would toss me back inside . . . While I hesitated, the ceiling slumped a little closer. Obviously the cavern was a hole in the Worm's body, a big bubble it had blown in itself within some vaster subterranean space.

Kindly consider the absurd horror and lunacy of this moment. Outside, the world was in chaos. A giant tadpole wanted to make love to me, or something. And the roof was falling on my head. In such a moment, what could save a girl but a sense of humour? (Or a sense of *rage*—somehow rage didn't seem a useful reaction at this point.) I began to laugh. I doubled up. I creased myself.

"What's wrong?" cried Raf anxiously.

"Oh nothing . . . !" With an effort I controlled myself. "It's so bloody funny, this business of becoming a God! How lucky cats and dogs are, never having to try! Just look at it: this collapsing *Ka*-theodral of a womb . . . a zombi for a guide . . . the spirits of the dead spun in a yarn . . . barrels of minced fungus gotten by devious guile . . . all in the guts of a worm . . . a war thrown in! And at the end of the tunnel, what: power and visions? Life is quite absurd!"

"But the universe itself is paradoxical," called Raf brightly. "Existence is. I mean, why should anything exist at all? So maybe true knowledge and absurdity are twins. Maybe the one is the key to the—"

"Oh, shut up!"

Already the wart-stones beyond had all vanished under writhing fronds; where I stood was similarly infested.

"I'm coming back, damn it!" Swiftly the fronds at my feet shrank away.

We set off promptly for the far end of the cavern. Now that I was on the move in the desired direction, the shrinkage back at the island end appeared to have stopped.

So off I trod to confront my destiny, and the Worm's destiny, and the world's; loaded down with useless bottles of fresh air; sporting a jewelled ring, with the power only of cutting rope; and guided by a hairless animated corpse . . . As I followed Raf's lead along those wart-stones, I decided that Doctor Edrick and his cronies would never get anywhere with *their* quest for knowledge. They were far too serious about it. The real and the true could only be seized in a laugh, a laugh which would rattle the stars.

And the trouble was, at the same time it all *mattered;* mattered intensely.

Still, I was determined not to be too tense. It's no good tensing up for love, eh? And our worm had decided to love me. Somehow.

I was in the midst of finding out how to be mad and sane simultaneously. I hoped the Worm could perform the same balancing trick. Then maybe it *would* graduate into a God. . . .

I hadn't known what to expect. A mound of jelly shot through with sparks? A pool, depth-full of flickering darting starlight: *Kas* held in suspension?

What we arrived at finally, somewhere in the azure fog, was a fountain-basin: a phosphorescent powder-blue bowl some nine or ten spans across, bubbling with denser violet fog like foamy suds.

A coldly boiling cauldron. A chalice of flesh. A bathtub.

Of course all the "architecture" hereabouts had to be a purely temporary affair. This chalice, or bath of suds, had been laid on specially for me. I had no idea what the *Ka*-store might look like the rest of the time. Perhaps like nothing at all.

"You climb in," advised my friendly zombi. "You lie down."

The basin bore a certain resemblance, also, to an enormous sphincter muscle. "It won't close up on me, will it?"

"It won't *eat* you—never fear!"

Why did people say things like "never fear" when that's just what anyone in their right mind ought to be doing?

"Perhaps I could assist you with those things on your back?" Raf offered gallantly. "They look cumbrous to lie on."

"Ah, so comfort *does* come into this! That's nice to know."

With a certain amount of fumbling, Raf managed to detach the air bottles. He had no such luck with the locked belt and tail of rope.

So I climbed aboard that basin. As I did so, a sigh of satisfaction seemed to sough through the cavern. I lay down in the violet fog; at once I felt myself departing, into a different kind of place . . .

And I enter the *Ka*-store. . . .

I'm Lalia, a woman of Gangee, thirty years old, dark and tall and strong.

I'm borne along within her life. A stick floating downstream, I go where the water wills; unlike a fish, which can turn and oppose the stream. . . .

I'm a stowaway in her. I wear her like a glove. I see what she sees, feel what she feels, speak what she says, go where she walks. I regard Gangee not as a dingy hole but as home, a drumskin of familiar beats.

She, the Lalia who is experiencing her life unfolding, remains unaware of me. Yet a later, more complete Lalia seems to know me, and nod in recognition. My life as Lalia isn't continuous. I experience her in spurts, like a gashed artery from which her lifeblood springs. Several days, then a skip forward.

Men of Gangee are planning an expedition to cross the desert. By investing in supplies the river guild has bought me a place on this expedition as their observer. Maybe another river flows somewhere beyond the sands?

Why, this must be hundreds of years ago! Yet equally it's *now:* the urgent present moment, the moment which matters above all others.

Which matters most . . . and least. The present moment, the moment you're living through, is often rushed away impatiently for the benefit of future moments. Or maybe you stand quite still and try to halt time, to savour the present moment to the full; but what you're really saying to yourself is: "Look! Concentrate! I'm here now at this point in space and time. I hereby fix this moment in memory forever—so that I'll understand and treasure the meaning of it . . . in another hour, another week, another year. Not now; but *then.*" Only when a moment lapses and is gone, can it be really known. Thus the moment is everything, and nothing too.

Yet since I, Lalia, am living each present moment ordinarily, but also as part of my whole completed self, this treachery of time is healed now. Each instant becomes radiant and luminous. Every act and word is a dewdrop and a diamond.

This is the joy of the *Ka*-store; it could also be the horror, if the moment was evil and agonizing. But even horror is outshone, when the light emerging from each moment is so bright that pain is blinded.

We march inland from Gangee to the verge of the desert, accompanied by a gang of porters laden with supplies. We set up base camp in the dusty outback beside a tree-fringed pool, the last well. Beyond, there's only a plain of fine gravel horizoned by distant dunes.

We have planned well. Taking turns, we lead teams of porters far out into the Dry to lay down caches of food and waterskins filled from the pool. The first such sortie takes a couple of days, to go one day's march and return. The second sortie penetrates twice as far. And so on. In this way we scout a full week's journey into those far dunes, preparing the way, always returning to base. These preparations occupy several weeks and limber us up marvellously.

Then we dismiss all our porters and set out alone to cross the Dry. Six of us: five men, and myself.

Thanks to our preliminary forays, the first week's journey is easy —even though the ridge-dunes we have to cross are soft underfoot and complexly interlinked. We find all our caches without any fuss. Dunes may creep, but not that quickly; and only gentle breezes blow. It's the calmest time of year, the Lull. The river, of course, is breezier even during the Lull, but we're far away from it. We have six weeks before the winds blow strong again.

A sea of star-dunes succeeds the ridge-dunes; we can thread our way through these at speed. On scattered rocky outcrops, landmarks in the arid ocean, we stash food and drink for our return, further lightening our loads.

And I fall in love with one of the explorers, Josep. Likewise, he with me. But this is wrong. He's a man of my own home town. We could only have fallen in love by being so far removed from the breath of the river. By being so isolated.

Isolated! Yet always we are in such close proximity to four other Gangee men (who mustn't guess; yet do) that we can do nothing at all about our love. This is both a torment and a blessing. We burn with frustration and yearning and dread, as surely as we burn in the heat by day. To me Josep seems uniquely brave and beautiful.

Three weeks inland; and still no change in the dearth and death of the landscape. Only minerals grow here.

Impasse: the other four want to return while there's time. But Josep cannot bear to fail—though this is one of those enterprises where even to have attempted it is a sort of success. Josep wants to journey at least a fraction as far as *I* have travelled, on the river; but in his own direction. Only such a one could I love, who mirrors me.

After a parched conference, it's decided that three will stay here, camped in a jumble of crystal-crusted rocks in a shattered region of shale. Three will scout onward: Josep, me, and Hark.

A day later Hark decides that we're marching to our deaths. And maybe we are. Maybe my bones will lie down locked with Josep's bones upon a bed of sand.

Hark and Josep quarrel; not violently but in a softly hateful way. Hark acts as though Josep is betraying the spirit of our expedition, by pressing on with it. Hark can't bear to be within the aura of our love, which grows fiercer the more it is prevented.

He leaves us early in the morning to retrace his steps to where we left the others. When he reaches them, they will stay two more days, then depart, taking all the food and water with them; that's the threat. The promise.

As soon as Hark has gone, Josep and I set out for the nowhere beyond nowhere. We have just one more day, one night.

How defiantly we spend that night! It seems as though the entire purpose of our expedition, all those weeks of preparation, all the porters and supplies, is simply for us to make love. Will we return and report, "Oh yes, we discovered *something*—we found each other"?

Yet at sunrise, when we stir again in one another's arms, the suspicion dawns on me that Josep is making love not to a woman, but to the desert itself—to this naked emptiness far from the river where no codes of river life apply. My breasts are as star-dunes, my flanks a dune-slope under his sliding fingers. Between my thighs is the well of liquid we have not found. I'm the desert made flesh. Only thus can he master it; he who must master something.

That day we return in silence to the place where we parted from Hark. That night, when we unroll our blankets on the sand, Josep is impotent—because he is withdrawing from the desert now. Although he clutches me cruelly and forcingly, in a way I have never known a man act before, he achieves nothing. At last he turns aside in an agony of shame, so that I have to comfort him; and this is worse, for he weeps like a child.

In the morning when I wake his tears are still falling on my face. It feels that way. Actually stray raindrops are spitting down on my skin from a solitary cloud.

Off to the west, an impossibly dark mass of clouds bunches low, dispensing rain; dirty sheets of water drench down. Within an hour the clouds have fled, the sky is clear.

And when finally we reach the jumble and the shale, first we find one drowned corpse then another then a third. The freak flood has vanished; the desert is parched dry again. Waterskins have been washed away and ripped by shale, so that there's only a slop of liquid left in those we recover. We find a fourth corpse, Hark's, his skin already turning to leather.

"You brought the river here!" Josep screams at me insanely.

Thankfully my life as Lalia jerks forward at this point, lurching towards its close.

A few days later, somewhere further west amidst star-dunes, Josep falls down dying of thirst. As I am dying too. . . .

And for a moment I believe that a miracle has happened, and that actually I *have* commanded the river and it has come to pour down my swollen throat and slake my terrible thirst!

But I'm dead; and the black current has received its daughter into it from afar. As I soon discover. I've come home—to myself at last; and it's this which illuminates all other earlier moments of my life . . .

I'm Charna, a teenager of Melonby, eager to join the riverguild in another year or two.

Right now it's the cruellest winter in memory. The river has frozen over. Boats are locked at their moorings, with ropes and spars crusted by frost just like the decorations on iced nameday cakes. No river traffic moves.

With my best friend Pol I venture on to the ice, skating and skidding, and scuffing up the dust of snow in lines and arcs. (It's so cold, the snow is dusty not moist.) I carve my name upon the river for all to see.

Some of those who see are boys, who begin to dare each other, for it seems as if the river has become as safe and solid as a road. They admire me; resent me. They're scared, and proud. In the bitter calm cold they grow hot-headed, jeering and teasing, us and each other. Presently the boldest and most foolish of the boys steps on to the ice himself, and skids along beside us.

"You'll have to walk for a wife now!" warns Pol. "You've used up your one go."

"Nonsense! I'm not on the river, I'm on ice—on top of it! I bet you could cross all the way to the other side!"

"Oh no, you couldn't. The ice'll be thin in the middle. Maybe no ice at all."

"Wheee!" He runs, and crouches into a skid. He tumbles and pratfalls all along the ice. Scrambling up, he slides back to the bank and hops ashore. "Come on, you lot!"

"No fear!"

"Not likely!"

"Chickens," he sneers, and jumps back to his ice-sport. Leaps on the ice a second time.

"Oh, I'm a river-boy," he sings. (Of course, the real song is about a river-*girl.)* "My boat is quite a toy! She brings me heaps of joy—!" (He's just making up the words, mocking them.)

Suddenly he screams: "Destroy! De-ssss-troy—!"

He windmills his arms wildly. He begins to race. Out, out. . . .

We all watch, numbstruck. Soon he's hundreds, a thousand spans away. In his green coat he's a leaf blowing over the ice. Then he's no more than a sprig of grass. Finally, far away, he vanishes. The faintest twang sings through my feet. The ice has cracked, out there.

And a death has happened, because I wrote my name on the river. I'll *not* feel guilty! Of his death I am innocent!

I'm a boatswain of Firelight, a happy and fiercely passionate woman. How can she be both at once? She is. I know; I'm her. She burns like the dancing jets of flaming gas in the caldera outside the town; yet inside she is sunned by her passions, not consumed or exploded. . . .

I'm a multitude of lives, all linked, reflecting into one another. All those vistas and ventures I ever dreamed of as a little girl—and was robbed of so abruptly—just as suddenly are mine; to overflowing. . . .

I am Nelliam, aged guildmistress. . . .
    Nelliam? Guildmistress from Gangee? But *how—?*
    I'm in Verrino, residing with the quaymistress. I've been here for weeks, engaged in negotiations with the Observers. Perhaps I'm not the best choice of intermediary, since I can't possibly climb that wretched Spire in person . . . But I meet a young man on neutral ground, usually one of the many wine-arbours. He has coppery skin, lustrous eyes and a pert little nose. If I were only forty years younger, and less sadly wise than I am now. . . .
    (My own heart lurches—for of course, the young man is Hasso, my erstwhile one-night lover, he who plucked the first flower of my flesh.)
    From another point of view, that of someone who can look back down many thousands of days of life, maybe I'm the best person for the job. But only maybe.
    So I set my sails to the task, applying gentle persuasion, as though I'm out to seduce this young man; and only occasionally do I lose patience with him.
    Much has been agreed in principle, and even put into practice; but now I want those panoramas of the west bank which the Observers have been collecting and hoarding for a hundred years. I want these sent to Ajelobo, there to be engraved by craftsmen—and printed in a gazetteer which our own signallers can emend by pen.
    All of Yaleen's information will be printed in this gazetteer as well. It will be a second *Book of the River,* a ghost guide to a world hitherto unknown. Or maybe I should describe it as a second Chapbook, since its distribution will be strictly limited. No additional, unofficial copies will sneak out; of that I can be sure. Those Ajelobo publishers depend on us to freight their wares.
    Tonight is the night before New Year's Eve, and the wine-arbour is lit by fairy candles. The arbour isn't heavily patronized this evening; most people are saving themselves up for the morrow. A cou-

ple of riverwomen natter together. A lone old man broods. Two lovers—husband and wife of a few week's vintage, by the look of them—whisper in a nook.

Apart from these, only Hasso and I. Age wooing youth—except that Hasso is a little *too* experienced, suave and cautious. Personally I could do with an early night. No rest for the wicked, though.

"What guarantees can you offer?" he's asking.

"Our word of honour," I repeat. "Your panoramas will be perfectly safe. We just want to borrow them. We'll return them inside a year. It'll take as long as that."

Lights flicker softly around us. There should be music to serenade us. But no; music would lull me to sleep.

"Okay, *I* believe you. I'll consult. . . ."

We agree to meet again in this same arbour on the night after New Year's Day; it should again be quiet, in the aftermath of all the parties and revels.

But come that night in the New Year, the arbour isn't quiet at all. It's packed and noisy. Because the head of the black current has passed Verrino. Now everyone is telling everyone else about it, offering explanations, contradicting each other. Instead of peace and privacy there's pandemonium.

It's a clouded black night, as black as the current which has now abandoned us. All those fairy candles are just petty twinklings lighting up the tiniest part of our fearful darkness. Crowds have sought sanctuary in this and the other arbours, away from the now naked river.

And I know that I, Nelliam, am about to die . . . Soon, and bloodily. I try to make myself stand up, to flee while there's time. But that isn't how it was; Nelliam's legs don't heed Yaleen.

Unsurprisingly Hasso turns up late for our appointment. He chucks down two glasses of wine straight off before whispering to me what the Observers saw of the worm's head through their telescopes. I can hardly make out his mumbling, with all the surrounding din. "Speak up, will you!"

He recoils, brows knit, offended.

"I'm sorry, Hasso, we're all on edge. Pardon my tetchiness."

"That's all right. I understand. So *then*—"

A sudden scream from the direction of the waterfront cuts across the babble. Momentarily the hubbub dies—then it rekindles, doubled. People leap up and crush into the alley.

"Wait here! I'll be back." And off goes Hasso, too.

Before long, bedlam is spreading this way. A murky red light leaps up above the rooftops. Somebody cries, "Fire!" Then a huge crash deafens me, and the fairy candles dip in unison to a hot breeze.

Hasso's soon back, out of breath. "Armed men. Must be the west! Come on: to the Spire!" He seizes my arm.

But I resist. "My dear boy, I couldn't climb that Spire to save my life."

"That's exactly what—! Nelliam, I'll help you. I'll carry you up."

"No, you must go on your own. I'd burden you; rob you of your chance. But promise me something. Promise that you'll be true, up there."

"True?"

"Observe! Stay aloof! Record whatever happens. Now *go*. Go! Or I'll get angry with you."

He dithers. Of course. But ruin and terror are racing closer every moment.

So then he leaves me. Though not before, absurdly, passionately, he kisses my wizened brow.

I refill my glass from the beaker. Such a shame to waste good wine. I sip, and I wait.

Though death, when it comes, is by no means as blithe and quick as I expected.

Nor yet so final, either. . . .

At about this time I begin to detect something. For some reason my attention isn't being distracted by my sojourn in the *Ka*-store, so much as sharpened. Maybe that's because I have just been Nelliam, who is no one's fool. Maybe it's because the real significance of events shows clearly—luminously—through these lives, as never was during life itself.

From the corner of my mind's eye I catch a glimpse of what the Worm is doing with me while the "entertainments" are going on. It's using me as a kind of shuttle in a loom, to weave weft and warp together into a new design, a different and superior pattern.

It occurs to me that this might make me instrumental in what *sort* of God it becomes. I might gain some kind of influence over it.

So, during my next slice of life, as a fisherwoman of Spangle-stream, I do my best to ignore the pageant. This isn't easy. As soon ignore your own life while you're busy living it! The proprietor of the life I'm reliving suspects she's being snubbed. But then she cottons on (I think).

Time and again, I present a certain image to myself. I make this image the fiery centre of my attention.

And this image is . . . But wait; not yet.

One day while I'm out in the fishing smack hauling in nets heavy with hoke, a hand reaches into my life. The hand hangs in mid-air like a fillet of white fish, fading off at the wrist. . . .

When I grasped that hand, sky and stream and fishing smack all dissolved at once into a foamy violet fog.

I sat up in the luminous chalice. It was Raf, my blanched zombi, who held my hand.

He helped me up, though I didn't feel particularly weak. On the contrary: quite perky! Perching on the lip of the basin, I decided that the Worm must have nourished me well and kept my limbs toned up while I'd been resting in the bowl. Unless my period of dreamlife had seemed far longer than it really was.

"How long did I spend in the *Ka*-store, Raf? Hours? Days? Weeks?"

He shrugged. "I've been away dreaming again."

"And is the current a God now?"

"I'm not sure. It's . . . different. Maybe when a God's born, it's only a baby God to start with, and needs to grow up?"

That special image was still rooted in the heart of me. I concentrated intently on it.

Worm, I thought, *how goes the war?*

Faint images flickered before my eyes; I couldn't make much sense of them.

Worm! I presented that special image to it.

With my inward ear I heard a groan of acquiescence. Victory! I *had* succeeded in printing that special pattern in the new fabric, in one corner at least.

I hopped down from the lip. "Okay," I told Raf, "I'll be on my way." I hoisted the bottles.

"What do you want those for?"

"Mustn't leave litter! Especially not in a God!"

"Oh, it can absorb them. Dump them."

Yes, when its body thinned out again . . . He was right. So I dropped the bottles, which would only get in the way. Let the guild dock my pay, if they dared.

* * *

Raf and I parted at Opal Island. The tunnel end of the cavern was still shrunken, but no more so than before. The fronds kept out of my way.

I regained the dark exit. The helmet lay where I had abandoned it, but of the rope there was no sign; and the tunnel was pitch-black. I fiddled with the lamp to no effect, then cursed myself for a fool. The solution was simple.

Worm: light up the tunnel!

And presently the walls glowed faintly blue. Grudgingly; but enough to light my way. That I should be able to reach the mouth was a precondition of that special image I'd fed the Worm. Thirty paces along, I spotted the rope.

Maybe it had been jerked along when the Worm's jaws clamped shut. Or maybe the crew of the *Yaleen* had begun to haul it in . . . I tugged the rope experimentally three times, but nothing happened. *Was the boat still waiting?* I laughed. Because it didn't matter; didn't matter in the slightest.

Before long I reached the end of the tunnel, where the rope led over the ledge and angled down a dark hole.

Worm, light your throat!

Light glowed faintly, and I rather wished it hadn't. Originally I had rushed right through the Worm's gullet in darkness, arriving almost before I knew I'd left. Now that I could see what faced me, claustrophobia loomed. I would have to dive head-first down the hole. Suppose I got stuck, would the Worm obligingly hiccup me out?

No point in brooding. Down I went. Fast, for the sides were slippery. I writhed round the bend, and hauled rope hand over hand.

Up. Up. Above me in the dim light I could see the rope sprouting from the lid of the tube like a tap-root. I couldn't see any sign of a seam. Squirming tight up against the lid, I prised. In vain. And maybe when the lid did split open the rope would run free and I would slide back down again.

An image appeared in my mind: of a trapdoor which only opened one way—and only when a weight bore down on it.

Now you tell me! I hung in despair, punching feebly overhead.

A second image blossomed: of the Worm's chin ducking underwater; its jaw cracking open while one corner of its mouth continued to clench the rope (in an askew grin, which seemed directed at me); then tons of river water pouring in.

If that was the only way. . . .

I braced myself as best I could. Clutching the rope in both hands, I shut my eyes, held my breath. *Okay, do it!*

The tube tipped forward. Squelchings and gluggings, offstage. A few preliminary drops dripped down my face, then suddenly a deluge drenched and battered me. I was nearly swept away.

Somehow, *somehow* I clawed hand over hand up through that waterfall . . . And I was still underwater. Why, oh why, hadn't I brought that bloody helmet? If I didn't get some air soon I was going to explode.

Dizzyingly my world tilted upwards. Higher and higher. I hung on for grim death as the river drained down past my eyes and nose. I spluttered, gulped air, blinked—and I could see a great wedge of daylight.

The throat had closed up tight again, leaving a shallow slop of water on the floor of the mouth. It was lucky for me no stingers were flapping about, but none had entered with the flood. (Maybe the Worm could control them?)

Lying hunched where I was in one corner of its jaws, I spied river. Sky and clouds. A chunk of boat—with one welcoming saffron word: my name.

I jerked my head about a few times to knock the water out of my ears. I heard no familiar voices outside, but this hardly surprised me. Given the muting effect of our anchorage, any cries of alarm would have been quickly stifled.

Okay, Worm. Open wide!

As the jaws unglued, I staggered erect. I tore strands of drool out of my way and stepped forward to the lip. The rope, still dripping from its sudden dunking, sagged over the gap of water to the capstan. Since I had stood here last, the boat had ridden back more than twenty spans, dragging its anchor, and half-turned.

The crew were all lined up, staring at me.

"Hi there!" I shouted. "What date is it?"

After goodness knows how many days of whispers, now at my shout a dam of pent-up noise broke open. Laudia, Delli, Sparki and Sal began to babble questions; but Peli bellowed, "Shut up!" louder than any of them, and answered me.

Seven days had passed since I'd gone inside.

A week of war.

"Right," I called, "I'm going to stop the war! And here's how—"

I told them; and they gasped. But I think Peli and Sal believed me, at least.

"I'd like some food and drink sent over. Just in case I get peckish!"

"How about bedding?" shouted Peli.

Hardly. I'd slept in bushes, up trees, on mud and moss, on Spanglestream quayside, and most recently in a chalice of fog.

"No, but I could use a change of clothes and a towel—I'm drenched! And when you've sent everything over, unhitch this rope. Haul your anchor up. Sail the old *Yaleen* well clear!"

Because the boat was already well out of gangplank reach, some debate ensued as to the best method of supplying me; then a wooden laundry tub was dropped in the water, a canvas bag full of my requirements lowered into this, and a line tossed to me to pull the tub across. After emptying the tub, I cast it adrift.

"Hey!" cried Maranda indignantly.

Ignoring her, I stripped off—all but the bodice, which I had to tolerate. Fortunately it was fairly water-resistant. I towelled myself as dry as I could and donned new boots, breeches and a jacket.

"Oh, and you must signal downstream! Beach any 'jacks who are on the river!"

"Will do!" Peli unhitched the rope. I dragged it through the water and coiled it behind me in the mouth, leaving myself a loop to hang on to. Most of the rope was held tight in the gullet trap, of course. So now I had the Worm harnessed, after a fashion.

The crew soon upped anchor, upped sails, and stood off. Sparki was already signalling downstream. I stood there in the mouth, my chest braced against the rope.

Worm! And I presented that special image to it.

I met unexpected resistance. An image of majesty. Puissance. *But I'm a God,* this seemed to say.

So blast me with lightning! I retorted. *If you don't like it.*

There actually *was* a mild rumble, though it came from deep within the Precipices. I guessed the Worm was readjusting itself internally, since this rumbling went on for a while. The noise was more like flatulence, a grumbling of the guts, than thunder. After a while, it stopped. That cavern where I'd been must have deflated by now.

Nothing else happened, but I stood firm, still insisting on that image. This Worm wasn't going to make a fool of me now! Actually, the Worm was already obeying; that was what the thunder meant.

Yaleen. Its voice came clearly in my head. *I shall help, because you helped me.*

Nonsense, you've no other choice. And anyway it's your duty to help people, if you're a God.

Duty? Is it? My duty is . . . to know what I am. To know what the other God-being is.

Why not leave well alone, Worm? Look after your women and your waterway.

The other God has eyes and ears here, girl! I need to gather the Kas of its servants.

You'll collect enough of those, as we clear up the mess you caused.

Afterwards, we'll be quits? You and I? It was almost an appeal. The Worm was beginning to sound a bit more human. Less of that solemn "Worm of the World I am" business! Was that the secret of its change: that in becoming a God, it had become a bit more human at the same time? Less of a great big sponge for soaking up minds; more of a person in its own right? A person with a hint of me in it?

Well, I'm not one to bully a God; in future I'll just ask politely.

Ask . . . what?

Oh, of Kas and God-Minds and other things. Of stars and worlds and Eeden. I'll be sure to let you know, when I know, myself.

Good. If that's all settled, let's move! I waved a warning to the *Yaleen,* then I jerked the rope.

Presently the Worm's head surged out of the Precipice. Propelling itself, I guess, by sucking water into its underside then jetting it out. Or maybe it used the energy it got from burning water. I glanced aside: old Nothing-Bothers-Me was really gawping. Peli was openly weeping with joy. Sal was cheering. I kissed my diamond ring to the two of them. This was the pattern, this the special image: myself riding downriver in the Worm's jaws.

As we swept past Port Barbra a couple of hours later, we weren't of course close enough to shore for me to spot any crowds lining the bank. Nor were any boats likely to sail out and maybe get in our way. However, I still stood grandly at the helm as though steering. Signals were flashing far off, and no doubt numerous spyglasses were trained on me. There are times when one should enjoy one's moments of glory, not shrug them off modestly.

Another four hours, and it would be night. By then we ought to be between Jangali and Croakers' Bayou, and I might as well get some rest. (I wasn't *actually* steering the current.) By dawn we would be approaching Gangee, and getting near the war zone.

I had a choice to make. A decision before me.

For in my eagerness I'd neglected something fairly basic: namely, how I was going to disembark. Perhaps I ought to have hung on to that laundry tub after all! First the diving helmet, now the tub; I seemed to have developed a habit lately of throwing away things that I might need. If only I'd asked for a mirror, too! And not only to tidy myself. Come to think of it, I could probably use one of those bottles my friends had sent over, to flash a signal. . . .

My choice? It wasn't just a question of how I would disembark; though that little problem did rub home the nub of the matter. And the nub was this: I could halt the Worm at Umdala. I could wait for a boat to put out and take me off. Then I could despatch the Worm's head onward into the wild ocean. By so doing I would have restored the current to the whole length of the river, and our world to itself. By and large. Give or take weeks of warfare to liberate Verrino.

But ought I?

I thought of how "conserver"-minded my own guild was at heart; yet how much freer and finer women's lives were as a consequence compared with life in the west. And on account of the fact that men hadn't been able to sail the river. Surely everyone's life in the east, man and woman, boy and girl, was better as a result?

But then I thought of the frustration and resentment the 'jacks would feel after they had tasted travel to distant ports, and sacrificed lives in the process; unless they were all supremely glad to march home . . . three hundred leagues on foot. (For they certainly couldn't sail the river, with the current back in place.)

I thought of the madness of Josep, who had yearned to journey far, only to see his dreams first drowned then parched to death. And I thought of that boy destroyed for a dare on the ice at Melonby. I thought of Kish caught in a spider-web of domestic bliss in Jangali.

I thought of my own brother, destroyed by restless curiosity— because there was only one outlet for it. I thought of my parents, and Narya. I weighed and I balanced.

The Worm could come just *part way* out of its lair. It could stop near Aladalia, say—leaving a further hundred and eighty leagues of northern water free for men and women voyagers, both. True, that was only one quarter of the river's length. But it might be a start, a promise . . . On the other hand, this would leave a long stretch of river-border open between east and west. The Westerners would be wise to assume we could close it if we wished. Though were they wise? And would they refrain from raiding and piracy? Would the towns from Aladalia to Umdala thank me for leaving their shores unprotected?

Ultimately, the wisdom or otherwise of stopping short did rather depend on what the Worm might learn of that distant power in Eeden which had sent us all here in the first place. It hung, too, on what the Worm might learn of itself (God or not). I didn't think the Worm quite knew what a God was; did anyone? Maybe a God was just an idea, waiting for an embodiment—like any other invention, such as the mysterious vessel which had brought our seeds here long ago. Which brought me back to the puzzle of the Big Intelligence, born of men, which ruled in Eeden.

Basically, had I the right to decide to stop short? Had I won this right by restoring the current? Or had I only redeemed the mess I had provoked? In future years would I be seen as a heroine or a criminal idiot?

How could I know the answer to that, till it was far too late to choose a different option? And did this matter? Maybe no one can be a heroine if they set out to be one. And if someone does set out to be one, *distrust* them.

Questions, questions. At least I had a choice. A free choice, for once. On behalf of everyone living, and quite a few who were dead.

The bow-wave rolled foaming away equally towards east and west. I laid down my harness rope and burrowed in the canvas bag, unpacking dried fish, sweetcakes, fruit, a bottle of water, a bottle of wine.

I drank some water then scoffed a few cakes and chewed on a fish-stick. The wine I would reserve to toast Jangali when we passed. A swig or several would help me get to sleep that night; to sleep upon my little problem.

By the time we reached Verrino next day, I would certainly have made my mind up. That's what choices are for. To savour them while you can, and then to seize one. Or the other.

So here ends *The Book of the River.*

My Book of the River, that's to say! The book that the river guild asked me to write, here in Aladalia, even while the war was being fought and won a hundred leagues away. I guess they felt it necessary to explain to everyone from Umdala to Tambimatu exactly what had happened, even if this meant spilling secrets in the process (and perhaps bruising a few egos!). Otherwise, who knows what scare stories and wild rumours would have been flying about for ever more?

Before this book is printed up Ajelobo way they'll probably change the title, though. And maybe some committee of guildmistresses will go through it first with a pot of black ink . . . And then again, maybe not.

At first I imagined that writing a book might be as daunting a task as swimming the river or walking to Manhome South. But once begun, I found to my relief (then delight) that my story flowed easily enough. My reading of all those Ajelobo romances came in handy at long last! I think I even got better at it as I went along. In fact, I can hardly bear to put down my pen.

What else?

Oh yes: I have nutbrown hair and hazel eyes. I'm slim, rather than skinny (except when on my way to Manhome South); and in bare feet I stand just over five spans tall—or short. I have a chocolate mole on the side of my neck. I forgot those little details. That proves I'm modest. Obviously. (Should I add them in? No. . . .)

But of course there's *more;* which is what these last few private words are really about—for my eyes only.

This part doesn't belong in the book, but I'd better write it down in case I get struck by lightning or something.

For the Worm has kept its promise—just last night. (As if it had watched and waited till I'd finished my whole writing task.) Last night I dreamed I was out alone upon the river in a rowboat; when the grim head (which is actually loitering south of here) rose from the depths. Suddenly I was wide awake in my dream, and in my head I heard these words:

Yaleen, I was made, *aeons ago, to keep this world empty of mature minds. I was put here as a destroyer.*

Recently I brushed against the God-Mind of Eeden and it cried, "Wretch! On six worlds since this one, I found your likeness. Habitable worlds, with no high life on them. You aborted intelligence on them, you kept them lying fallow. You injured my people when they came! What made you, *Demon? Name your Master! War will go on between us till I own you and can use you, to find what made you lie in wait a million years, as a trap and barrier.*

But Yaleen, I think I've found how to enter Eeden. I believe I can send a suitable human agent along the psylink. To fabled Eeden, Yaleen! And back again!

Even in a dream I was able to figure this one out. And retort, *Don't look at me! I* like *it here.*

Come, come, Yaleen, chided the Worm. *One fine day you'll die, then your*

Ka *will be with me to send wherever I wish.* Its long white eyes winked, and its head sank back beneath the water.

Me, travel to Eeden along the psylink? As an agent in a war of the Gods?

In the words of some sensible lads of Melonby: not likely! And, no fear! I've some items of human business to attend to.

I *still* haven't seen my parents, to bring them up to date. Maybe I ought to wait till my book is printed and send them a copy first? But that would be churlish. We've been strangers too long. I still haven't bounced Narya on my knee; Narya my sister, not of the river but of flesh.

I'll certainly go to Verrino to begin with. Not merely because it's on the route to Pecawar—nor to gawp at the damage or the prisoners, or to collect horror stories. I very much want to find out if Hasso is alive. I want him to know how much Nelliam appreciated his final kiss. And maybe repay him in kind.

I might stay in Verrino a while, maybe help a bit with reconstruction. But then I'll head on home for sure; back to Pecawar.

Before leaving home again . . . to go where?

I do fear that there's a big "where" waiting for me. And *that* may well be another tale, just as long as this *Book of the River* (new version, by Yaleen of Pecawar). If there is another tale, it may be longer than the river itself—for maybe it will stretch all the way from here to the stars.

I can always hope I'm wrong.

Right now, I just can't tell.

THE BOOK

OF THE

STARS

CONTENTS

Part One

DOCTOR EDRICK'S REVENGE

*T*HERE are always loose ends. Nothing is ever tied up neatly and completely. At times life seems to be one long loose end after another; and if you've read *The Book of the River* by Yaleen of Pecawar (and who hasn't, I wonder, along the east bank of our river?), then you'll know how many loose ends there were for me personally at the end of that book—not to mention all the loose ends left over by the war with the west.

I still had to visit my parents in Pecawar—and see my little sister for the first time. And on the way there I had to visit Verrino to find out whether Hasso had survived, and repay him a kiss.

Most of all, I had to keep out of the clutches of the black current, which had plans to send me (somehow) to Eeden, that planet of a distant star from which we all originally came, and where the God-mind ruled. Whatever the Godmind really was!

Ironically, it was something which I thought *was* all tied up and done with which proved to be quite a ticklish loose end.

You may recall when I was last in Aladalia how I enjoyed a sweet liaison with a boy named Tam. That was in my innocent youth—which wasn't so very long since!—and back then Tam had seemed quite the young man, though in retrospect I knew he had just been a grown-up boy.

So here was I back in Aladalia once more, busily writing my book whilst lodging in a couple of upper rooms rented to the guild for my use by a weaver called Milian, when who should turn up but Tam?

By then I was well into my writing stint, and was dealing with the Port Barbran fungus drug which would inspire Doctor Edrick to start the war—whilst in the now-world the war itself was really getting under way. (It was Edrick who started it; not I!)

But first, a few words about the progress of the war . . .

Initially I'd taken to calling at the quaymistress's office every two or three days to enquire about the latest developments. This, despite the fact that bulletins were posted regularly in town. I fancied that there might be some extra bit of news, which I uniquely was privileged to know—not that I ever learnt any such thing by bothering the woman, and really the bulletins were quite adequate and up to date.

Since the black current had returned to most of the river, women could sail our boats safely again, unmenaced by the Sons of Adam. Thus north-south communications had been restored, on which I rather prided myself.

Had I thought this through properly, I might have realized that yet again, full of good and bold intentions, I had buggered things up!

When I gaily rode the Worm downriver, only the first detachments of junglejack soldiers had actually reached Guineamoy (to guard the town while the factory guild there turned out weapons for them). Oh, and a small advance party of jacks had sailed on towards Pecawar. The remainder of the army had been delayed in Jangali, awaiting more boats from other southern towns to ferry them. Though it finally set sail, that part of our army had only just cleared Croakers' Bayou.

At least I'd thought to tell the crew of the *Yaleen* to signal ahead to warn our own men off the water, otherwise the situation would have been even more of a mess. It could have been a total disaster. Naively, I'd imagined the sound of applause as I rode the Worm north. In reality there was a mad scramble inshore somewhere between the Bayou and Spanglestream to beach our troops before the current arrived. Rather than cheers I guess there was a barrage of ripe curses from many of the men at the prospect of the long, long walk ahead. And in those parts there wasn't even much of a road.

What happened then, to recover the situation, was a clever tactical stroke. But it required a poignant sacrifice on the part of many young men.

Plainly, if all the beached soldiers had to walk the remaining distance, the transport fleet would have had their work cut out just ferrying victuals to and fro. So our marooned troops were divided, ashore, into those 'jacks who had already sailed the river once before with the "consent" of the current, to marry into Jangali; and 'jacks who were born in Jangali and who hadn't yet been wooed away by any husband-hunting girl on her wanderweeks. The latter group, of men who were fresh to the river, accordingly re-embarked to sail all the way directly to Pecawar, using up their "one-go" in the process. These men would drill in Pecawar, awaiting the transport of weapons from Guineamoy and the arrival, on foot, of their comrades. Meanwhile their comrades, who were somewhat the majority, would all have to walk.

This obviously upset the original war plan, as agreed in Jangali. Still, with the current back in place, Guineamoy was safe from attack, except overland from the north.

But before this division of forces was finalized, one brave 'jack—a settler in Jangali who had sailed once before—volunteered to step back on board a boat. His aim, to see if the Worm might perhaps be with us wholeheartedly. Maybe it would allow passage to all eastern men, irrespective of whether or not they had sailed before?

As if the Worm cared about granting a dispensation to our side!

Of course not. The Worm wanted some dead westerners for its *Ka*-store. Sons would need to die in the right circumstances for it to harvest their *Ka*s; that's to say they would have to die in battle very close to the river. Which meant that many Sons would have to be killed, overall. The last thing the Worm wanted was a hasty surrender by the Sons to our superior forces.

If only I'd thought when I had the chance to plant an image deep in the Worm of immunity for all our men. So that they could sail the river as long as the war lasted! But I hadn't thought. I'd only planted the image of myself, valiantly at the helm.

Perhaps I *couldn't* have planted that other image? Perhaps it was too diffuse, too general? Perhaps the Worm would have resisted? Perhaps.

Anyway, the volunteer 'jack went mad and drowned himself.

After that, a volunteer from among the "river-virgins" (who was perhaps even braver) had to see whether the Worm knew or cared that they weren't really virgins. They had already sailed from Jangali to that area by the Bayou. So would the Worm deal them the same death-card?

No: the river-virgins could sail on.

I'm glad I only learned these details quite a while later. Or I would have had that 'jack's horrid death on my conscience; not to mention half an army of sore feet.

When I *did* cotton on to the sore foot aspect, and to how I must have slowed up the liberation of Verrino, I fled from my writing table to the Aladalia quaymistress, full of qualms. By then I was into the last part of my book; much earlier, while I was still getting into my stride and was paying her frequent officious visits, she had reproved me thus (more gently than in exasperation): "It isn't *your* war, Yaleen. You don't have to worry about what's going on. Everything's under control. Now please do go away, and get on writing that book!" This time she reassured me (quite falsely, as it turned out!) that I hadn't messed up anything in particular. Oh no, the run-up to the war had proceeded fine and dandy. Obviously the guild wanted my book written in a not too troubled state of mind; and the quaymistress plainly had me figured as something of a brattish prima donna. But she didn't betray this. She was a cute psychologist. I must have been a real pain in the ass to the woman; she probably wanted to kick me up the backside.

Which at least goes to explain why no one made me a guildmistress for my heroism in riding the Worm down to Aladalia. . . .

I now humbly apologize to all those who wore their shoes out because of my lack of imagination. And yes, to those families who lost kin unnecessarily. I can only hope they were few. May they forgive me.

And meanwhile the war was gathering momentum, even though forced marches must have been the order of the day; even though the 'jacks would have to wade home afterwards through the swamps around the Bayou; or else detour through the desert, all thanks to me. So much for all the insight I thought I'd gleaned during my travels! At the time I merely thought that whilst I was *undoubtedly* a heroine, some Aladalia folk must feel ambiguous about me—because I hadn't "dared" go the whole hog. Because I'd stopped the Worm far short of Umdala, leaving the northern flanks unprotected. "That's the trouble with people," I remember reflecting at the time. "Never satisfied!" Hadn't I made my choice of where to stop most scrupulously (with the aid of that bottle of wine)? Yet a few locals reacted as though I'd built a fine house all with my own two hands, then left the roof off so that the rain could pour in. But at least no one was offensive, not to my face.

Nevertheless, to some in Aladalia I was a heroine indeed. Which brings me back to Tam. And when *he* turned up, none of the other aspects of my worm-ride had occurred to me. . . .

Tam of the tousled hair; Tam of the knuckles.

Tam had such big hands, with unusually knobbly joints. These, he seemed to be forever barking on walls and door-posts and the like. Thus he had adopted a funny stiff stride that involved walking without swinging the arms. His hands dangled sheepishly slack by his sides, to keep them out of trouble; when he remembered—which wasn't always! On my previous sojourn in Aladalia, when I got to know him well, he had told me that strange bone formations ran in his family. The bones didn't seem to know when to stop growing. According to Tam his granddad had looked like a gnarled, bobbly tree-trunk by the time he died; and Tam's knees were definitely knobbly, whilst down in the shin-bone area there seemed to be altogether too much leg, as if his shanks were turning to wood and about to bud out roots; or as if he wore boots in bed.

An apothecary had advised a non-milk diet for Tam and his kin; and apparently this was the answer. Now that Tam had eschewed milk and cheese and butter, his bone problem was under control, or at least wasn't getting worse. In any case, after our first few meetings Tam's hands had ceased to strike me as coarse or lumpish— they were so gentle and clever. When alone with me, they were never sheepish or awkward.

Tam was an apprentice potter, and sometimes it seemed as though lumps and bumps of clay had dried on him; or as if working with clay had somehow caused wet clay to seep through his skin and harden inside him, baked by the heat of his blood.

So there was I, scribbling away alone in my sitting room, when I heard footsteps on the stairs. Then a muffled thump on the door, as of someone knocking with the flat of their hand. I assumed this was Milian the weaver wanting something, since he tended to pat on my door to call me for meals or whatever, rather than batter on the wood. I didn't look round, just called, "Come on in!"

A discreet cough. Out of the corner of my eye I was aware of somebody standing with arms dangling.

"Remember me, Yaleen?"

"Why . . . Tam!"

Of course I was pleased to see him. Yet I also felt curiously disturbed. I don't mean disturbed in my writing—for I tossed my pen down at once. I was disturbed because here was I writing a book in

which I'd noted down my liaison with sweet Tam in Aladalia—
without going into details. I was writing this in Aladalia; where Tam
lived. Yet till now I had made no attempt emotionally to connect my
last stay in Aladalia with my present stay—any more than I had
made an effort to contact Tam himself. I was acting as if the Aladalia
of my book, and the Aladalia of Tam, were different towns entirely.

I think I did this so that I could tell the truth.

Yet here now was the living Tam: a character stepping out of the
pages of a book where he ought to have stayed.

"Why didn't you come round sooner, Tam? If you knew where I
was! I mean to say. . . ."

I mean to say: why did you come round at all? Why, in all these
weeks, hadn't *I* looked up the person who was once my best friend
in Aladalia? By accusing Tam, I absolved myself. A bit of dishon-
esty commenced.

"Didn't you know I was here, Tam?" I stood up, rather too late to
seem spontaneous. So though we approached one another, we didn't
embrace.

"Not know?" blurted Tam. "You must be joking! Everyone knows
your name and what you did and where you're staying. Even little
toddlers know! I just didn't know that you'd stay on here. I thought
you'd go away again . . ." He peered at my work table. "You're
busy. Writing letters?"

"I'm writing a book. About what happened. For the riverguild:
they'll publish it."

"It must take ages to write a whole book. Months and months,
eh?"

"Yes, it keeps me busy."

We were knee-deep in excuses and evasions by now.

I grinned. "It's thirsty work."

This was simply another little lie. The truth was, I didn't want
Tam to look at the manuscript. Supposing he happened upon mention of our sweet liaison? That could have been embarrassing; embarrassing because it took up such a tiny number of lines. . . .

"Thirst, I can fix," said he. "How about a pot of ale?"

Tam had filled out since the last time I saw him. He'd filled out
with muscle, not with extra knobs and spurs of bone. Now he
looked sleeker, his skeleton more sheathed; though I still got a distinct impression of an ill-stuffed mattress . . . Not that there had
ever been anything lumpy or hard about *sleeping* with Tam, save in

the most important respect. I found myself edging away from the door which stood half-open to my bedroom.

"A pot of ale would be wonderful!"

"Remember the *Golden Bugle?*"

"Oh yes! But shall we try somewhere new? A fresh venue for a fresh encounter?" (Not the old haunts. Please.)

So out we went into Aladalia town, with a haste on my part which I can hardly describe as indecent, given the motive.

We walked along wide cobbled streets. We passed the concert hall with its dome of glazed turquoise tiles which looked like a bowl of sky, but richer and deeper. We crossed the edge of the jewelsmiths' quarter; at which point naturally Tam had to enquire about my fine diamond ring.

"No, it isn't from here," said I. "I bought this in Tambimatu."

"Oh?" He sounded sad, and perhaps a mite puzzled.

Actually, Aladalian artisans didn't go in much for costume jewellery; nor did the locals themselves wear many gems. The jewelsmiths of Aladalia mostly worked with semi-precious stones, and thought a bit bigger than rings. They crafted ornaments, artwork. And that's what the local connoisseurs who bought their products preferred.

Come to think of it, I hadn't noticed many Aladalian ornaments when I'd been hunting round the shops in Tambimatu; nor had I spotted any imports of jewellery from Tambimatu on offer here. There's a lot of trade between our river towns, so the distance could have nothing to do with this (though the war might have contributed). Yes, I think I'd made Tam *sad,* in his Aladalian heart. How many husbands, I wondered, were ever wooed away from Aladalia to Tambimatu? (Or vice versa?)

Tam glanced down a long avenue towards distant rolling meadows and the bushy hills beyond: a scenery of downy green thighs, with curly bunches of hair . . . It was as though he was inviting me to roam there with him—as once we had—and perhaps to penetrate even further inland to the cave-pocked mountains where the semi-precious stones were found. . . .

Perhaps, perhaps. Perhaps he was just wondering whether it would rain. My mind was working overtime with images. I was the writer confronting her subject matter, which had strolled around for a second performance, unscheduled, unannounced. At least we weren't heading towards the potters' part of town where Tam had his lodgings.

Oh it was quite a walk we took. Yet this was nothing special in Aladalia. The town liked to spread itself—as if all artists (of whom there were many) each needed a zone of free space around themselves. As if music required a vault to soar into; and paintings demanded breezes from afar to dry the varnish; and potters, a whole public square each to set out their wares without clutter. Everywhere I looked there was sky and long perspectives, and sights of the distant countryside with its farms and pastures.

How different the spirit of Aladalia was from that of Tambimatu with its tall houses packed tightly together, their beetling brows almost butting one another! Yet at Tambimatu jewels were truly precious. The pressure of houses, and the massive weight of the precipices, the density of jungle and the stifling tropic heat all conspired to squeeze out rubies and diamonds.

In fact, it was the sheer spread of Aladalia which had made it easy for me to leave the real live Tam out of my emotional calculations. It wasn't the case that more people dwelled in Aladalia than in other towns. No, there was simply less chance that you would bump into any particular person. If in danger of doing so, you could usually spy them from afar off and change course in good time, casually and naturally.

Though by the same token a native of Aladalia thought nothing of walking close on a league for a jar of ale and a chat. Till now, Tam hadn't done so. . . .

We eventually turned off the boulevard down a lane. This lane would have been a highway anywhere else; and presently we arrived at the *Tapsters' Delight*. The long ancient yellow-brick building wore a red-shingled roof which sagged and rose and sagged again like canvas supported on poles. Orange and crimson zalea bushes grew all round the low-walled ale garden. The very air was intoxicated with sweet smells of brewing mash mingled with the scent of the flowers.

We sat ourselves on a bench by a rough-hewn table. A fat fellow wearing a chequered apron appeared in the doorway accompanied by another who looked like his twin—or perhaps his son, ripely pickled in ale—whom he directed to amble over for our order.

"That chap's an artist in ale," confided Tam, with a nod at the proprietor.

And it *was* an excellent sup. Delicious also were the herb-speckled, coarse-cut sausages.

After the second nut-sweet foaming jar, Tam confessed why he hadn't looked me up till now.

I wish that he hadn't.

Last time round, Tam and I had been warm and casual in our relationship. We had enjoyed each other's company, and enjoyed each other; but we hadn't exactly branded the affair into our hearts. Yet now Tam was madly in love with me. I use the word "mad" advisedly. I suppose love always is irrational, but this was rather different. My return to Aladalia riding in the Worm's jaws had transfigured me for him. If I'd simply popped into town aboard any old boat, I imagine we could have picked up the threads once again as before. But the manner of my coming! I became his muse, his dream, his star and sun. His inspiration, aspiration. He had hauled out his memories of me from store, rejigged them and gilded them in goldleaf. Now I was his heroine, his living goddess. Also he was afraid that I might depart on the next boat or the one after. Therefore he had stayed away, the better to worship me—and to make things worse for himself meanwhile. Oh, what delirious foolishness.

The wretched thing was that he *knew* this perfectly well. He just couldn't help himself. Previously, our amorous intrigue had been like soft clay, spinning freely on the wheel of those happy weeks, moist and malleable, changing shape, able to flop down afterwards. Now this same clay had been fired by my dramatic arrival, and was a hard pot instead—within which Tam was trapped, as surely as if he had stuck his fist inside and kept it there during the baking. The pot of his passion was strong, yet it was fragile too, liable to break into tragic jagged shards.

I didn't encourage him—either on that day or on various subsequent days when we saw each other, days when I couldn't think of an excuse not to. Certainly we didn't make love again. Tam seemed to find this abstinence logical, preferable. I believe he feared he might disappoint me—I who had tamed the current itself.

But though I didn't encourage him, I fear he encouraged me—in my proud notion that I had saved him and Aladalia and everyone else in the east. He bolstered my self-esteem almightily, when I should have been volunteering to spend my next few years resoling worn-out boots and portering the wounded on my shoulders all the way home to Jangali.

Or did he really?

Maybe it was his dewy eyes fixed adoringly on mine which finally made me wake up from my delusion. Maybe his hands held bunched by his sides—so as not to touch me—at last made me grasp the actual situation.

In which case, thank you, Tam. Though that wasn't quite your intention.

Meanwhile, of course, the war was going on. Our army massed in Pecawar. Riverguild vessels ferried stocks of newly-forged weapons, and made ready to accompany the army in the role of supply boats.

And here we come to another twist of the screw concerning my heroic intervention: one which explains, when I look back, why the guild (in the person of the Aladalia quaymistress) treated me so gently despite my having trashed the original war plan. For what had I done in reality but largely restored the monopoly of the river which our guild enjoyed before the current withdrew? I'd restored the status quo all the way from the Far Precipices to Aladalia.

Once more, women only could sail the major part of the river; and maybe the guild calculated that this easily balanced off any amount of inconvenience to the army; any extra delay, any additional deaths.

Naturally the guild could never admit as much! And I would be the *last* person they would admit it to; especially when I was writing a book destined for publication. If they could have marooned me in the desert to write my book uninfluenced by current events, from their point of view this would have been even neater. Yet as it was I managed to maroon myself in a cocoon of falsely modest heroism. Maybe the one thing that did rankle with the guild was that I hadn't indeed gone the whole hog and ridden the Worm all the way to Umdala and the ocean! Strange to realize (as I finally did) that whatever my own motives may have been, to my guild perhaps I was a secret heroine . . . of conservatism.

Oh yes indeed. I could well imagine some slick guildmistress telling an angry council of the 'jacks: "Look, fellows, let's be reasonable! She did stop the Worm as soon as she could. Well, okay, a hundred leagues past Verrino—just to be on the safe side. But you'll have to agree she cut the Sons' supply route at a stroke! She stopped them spreading out."

There would have been truth in this (imaginary) advocacy. The Sons had indeed been stymied. What could they do thereafter but batten down tight in Verrino and environs?

And so the war proceeded (without any courier or spy balloons coming into play, that I noticed)—and presently the war was won.

How messily, I was to learn before long. (Though perhaps the war wasn't so much messy, as simply a war.)

And so I wrote my book. And finished it; then delivered my manuscript to the quaymistress, minus my private epilogue about the Worm's dream contact with me—that, I kept about my person.

Quaymistress Larsha was a neat, composed woman in her late forties. She was neat in speech and neat in her turn-out, maybe to compensate for a weak eye which wandered if she ever got upset. She wore a pair of Verrino spectacles with gilded wire frames.

"Your manuscript will be off to Ajelobo early next week, on board the schooner *Hot Sauceboat,*" she assured me, having locked my work in her bureau for safety. "And how about yourself, Yaleen?"

"Me? I want to go to Verrino. I'd like to help tidy up, and I have a message for somebody there: a message from a dead woman. When you read my story, you'll understand. After that I want to go home to Pecawar. I haven't seen my parents for years. I'd like to leave as soon as I can."

"The day after tomorrow, if you wish." Larsha hesitated. "Don't you perhaps feel that you need to pay a visit to the head of the current first? If you wish, we could sail you out."

"There? No fear!" But I checked myself. Larsha knew nothing of what the Worm had told me the other night. "Don't worry, it'll stay where I moored it."

Larsha adjusted her spectacles and peered at me primly; the mannerism reminded me strongly and suddenly of Doctor Edrick. "You're sure of that, child?"

"As sure as I am of anything." (Which didn't, come to think of it, amount to very much.)

"Our guild will have to think long and deeply before we advise in favour of any attempt to move the current further downstream. If indeed such a move is possible or desirable."

"I'm sure I don't know if it's possible. The Worm thinks it's a God now."

"Well, at least we don't have to worship it. . . ." Larsha's glasses caught the sunlight streaming through the window, as if winking some message at me.

This prompted me to ask, "Is there a list of prisoners, Quaymistress?" Andri and Jothan would likely not have been with the invasion force. They would have been assigned to the wormpoison project. But Edrick could well have been one of the invaders. If so, I was wondering whether he had been killed or caught.

I do wish I hadn't thought of that man as still alive and kicking. I do wish Larsha hadn't adjusted her glasses, just so. Later on it was to seem to me as if I had recreated Edrick by thinking about him just then—and by setting out for Verrino with him in the background of my mind, hiding behind Hasso who occupied the foreground. As if I had brought him back into existence, out of the chaos of war and death.

"A list? Maybe so. You'll be in Verrino in a few days. Ask there."

"I may. It isn't important."

It was, though. It was deadly important.

Before leaving town, I dithered long about whether to go round to the pottery to say goodbye to Tam; but decided not to. I started a letter and tore it up half a dozen times. Now that I'd finished my book, words seemed to have deserted me. I even fancied, for half an hour, that I might send Tam my diamond ring wrapped up in a little packet by way of farewell. A grand gesture indeed, when I'd worn that ring all the way into the belly of the Worm, and back! However, Tam would never be able to slip my ring on to even his smallest knuckly finger. So I might well be taunting him by such a gift. I might be saying in effect: "You can't slip *me* on, either!"

In the end I sent him a flower in a little box. I chose the "farewell" Fleuradieu which blooms from midsummer almost till winter in the northern towns. The Fleuradieu starts out with light blue summer flowers but these grow deeper in hue and darker through the autumn till the final blooms of the year are violet, nearly black. It's the last flower to bid farewell to warmth and fertility.

With my remaining half-pot of ink I carefully painted the petals black before putting the bloom in its box.

Having thus solved the problem to my satisfaction, I decided to repair to the concert hall that evening. No point in brooding, eh? So directly after sharing dinner with Milian and his wife, I set out.

I'd no notion what sort of performance was billed for the hall. Some orchestral music, I supposed. But when I entered the lamplit lobby amidst a fair crush of other patrons of the arts I discovered posters announcing *"The Birds: an Operetta*, by Dario of Andaji". (Andaji being a large village not far south of Aladalia.)

What could this be? Something legendary? I certainly couldn't imagine any of the birds that I knew inspiring an artist. Tiny dowdy things they were, and rare; far less noteworthy than your average flutterbye. And as for birds singing—which I presumed "operetta" implied—well, that definitely belonged to the land of legend. Yet to judge by the chattering throng in the lobby, Dario's *The Birds* had struck some chord.

I bought a ticket and went into the dim domed hall where I found a vacant aisle seat and parked myself. Presently a slim young man excused himself and sat next to me. He wore a long blond pigtail, bound with cord, which he arranged across his heart and held in one hand for a long while as though this was the tassel of a cap which might blow off. His skin smelled of grated lemon peel. But despite my neighbour I still felt private. The hall was dark; all the illumination of the oil lamps was concentrated on the half-circle of stage.

The musicians took their seats: two guitarists, a harpist, a fiddler, a flautist, a drummer, a xylophonist and a bugler. A canvas backdrop descended, depicting a farmyard with a rainbow arching overhead. Then from out of the wings strode the singers, extravagantly costumed as . . . a giant rooster, and a turkey-cock, and a snow-white goose.

Oh, *that* sort of bird! I giggled, and my neighbour hushed me. The music struck up, the overture sounding eerie, plangent and resentful.

"Man is of the shore," sang the goose. "Woman is of the river. Only birds are of the sky!"

"So, bird brothers," the turkey answered, waddling about the stage, "let us fly!"

Which they attempted, with no success.

The plot of the operetta concerned the plans of this trio—ridiculous, grandiose, and poignant by turns—to reach the rainbow, with ever more melancholy consequences. A farmwife soon put in an appearance, though actually this was a man—a sweet tenor—wearing big false breasts; and on her head "she" wore an enormous starched white hat looking for all the world like the sails of a boat. The wife soliloquized tunefully to herself about how she would kill and cook the birds, and what sort of sauces she would serve them up in. Her arias on the subject of cookery were lovely, but so weird.

The Birds ended on a note of gaily ironic acceptance of circumstances, with the feathered flightless trio singing their own paean of praise about those parts of their bodies which the farmwife's cuisine would transfigure from rude nature into brief-enduring art.

In short, *The Birds* was a fantastical satire, at once absurd and hauntingly melodious. But I had soon decided that the operetta wasn't about the problems of domestic birds at all. It was about men

—penned in the farmyards of our various towns, while women sailed forth freely. The subtitle of the work could well have been: *Frustration.* Gaudy, lyric, manic, celebratory and comical by turns, Dario's work at heart was one of rebellion; and I wondered how many people in the audience saw beneath the surface to the tortured feelings which I thought I sensed.

After the finale the young man next to me burst into wild applause. Several voices chanted out, "Author! Author!"—and soon Dario of Andaji stepped on to the stage.

Dario was short and tubby with little piggy eyes. He tilted his head back while surveying his audience, a mannerism which made his chin emerge more pointedly but also made him seem to squint disdainfully from under half-shut eyelids. He took several bows, resuming the same seemingly arrogant, pretentious posture after each. Maybe the truth was that he was nervous; yet I don't think that, had I seen him beforehand, I would have much wanted to see his work.

I couldn't help wondering, too, whether Dario's satire and lyric pain perhaps sprang from disgruntlement with his own body; whether his own uncomeliness made him resent women. (Had he ever made *love?*) Of course, I sympathized—and I guessed that crusaders in one cause or another must sometimes be inspired at base by personal inadequacies and frustrations. But to be honest the sight of Dario on stage did rather modify my appreciation of *The Birds.*

And maybe I was being utterly impertinent, devaluing his achievement because part of me resented its basic thrust.

Dario also wore a pigtail. His was much shorter than my enthusiastic neighbour's, tied tightly at his nape with a red bow.

As Dario withdrew offstage followed by the performers, my neighbour said to me, "By the way, that's my brother."

"Oh." Apart from the pigtail they didn't seem to have much in common. "Do you mean literally your brother?"

The young man stared at me. "How else can he be my brother?"

"Well . . . maybe in the sense that every man's your brother, if you share his sentiments about men and women. Maybe," I joked, "you wear pigtails as a sign of solidarity?"

The rest of the audience was rising to leave, but the young man reached across me and held the arm of my seat so that I was imprisoned. "Wait," he said. Other people in our row were forced to exit by the far end.

"Okay," he said, "we do just that. A lot of men in Andaji wear pigtails. We have our own little artists' colony."

"I had a brother," I said, rather stupidly.

"Amazing. Does that make you my sister?"

"Dario resents women, doesn't he? What about you? Do you follow his lead, just because he's a good artist? Are you a good artist too?"

The young man shrugged. "I paint."

"Paint what?"

"Goose eggs. I paint nude figures around goose eggs, after first sucking them out and cooking omelettes. Highly erotic they are. Each egg's a world of men and boys. If I don't like them afterwards, I dance on them. The fragility appeals to me. So easy to crush." I didn't know if he was serious. "My eggs appeal to women connoisseurs in town here. They think they're titillating, but oh so clever too, so that's all right. A friend pointed you out to me when I was last in town. You brought the current back, damn it."

"Damn it, indeed? And how many good fellows would rather I'd steered the Worm all the way to the ocean?"

"They're women-men. Not true men."

"Like Dario is a true man?"

"You scorn my brother, don't you?"

"No I don't. I just have mixed feelings about his work, that's all."

"That's because you can't understand it. No woman can; because a woman doesn't share the same circumstances."

"Look, I sympathize."

"We in Andaji don't need your sympathy."

"Sorry."

"Nor your woman's sorrow."

"That doesn't leave me much to offer."

"A person who can *offer* things is an oppressor, lady. We don't want offers from women. Of themselves, least of all. Men can love other men beautifully. Dario and I love other men."

"And plait each other's pigtails? Sorry, that's unworthy." I thought of Tam. "If what you're saying's true, then you're really in a tiny minority, Dario's Brother! Frankly, if the world was a bit different you probably wouldn't feel this way about other men at all."

He shook his head. "You can't understand."

By now the hall was almost empty. I pushed his arm aside and stood up. "In that case I suppose I wasted my ticket money. But honestly, how many people in the hall tonight saw *The Birds* this way?"

"Perhaps not many," he allowed. "Just those of us from Andaji. We who know the signals. The others saw other things. The art. The frolic."

"Then I'd say I *did* understand. Even before you decided to rub my nose in it, friend. Because I'm already aware of the problem."

"But we aren't a 'problem'."

"I think, Dario's Brother, that maybe you're your own worst enemy. What a shame you can't paint gander eggs! What a pity male geese don't lay. I'm not your enemy, though, however much you wish to shock me and alienate me from . . . from a memorable performance, because you recognized me. So goodbye. Try to be happy."

And I left, though there was a sour taste in my mouth as I walked back towards the weaver's house. Andaji sounded such a bitter place—though no doubt the artistic men there, who loved each other, felt that they were pure and free and astringent. Small wonder that Dario and company didn't live in Aladalia proper. Aladalia was too generous a town, too ample.

A week later I arrived in Verrino aboard a caravel.

From the river Verrino looked much the same as ever, superficially. (Already new signal towers replaced those burnt, to north and south.) Once I went ashore, though, I found the wounds of war unhealed everywhere.

The town was *seedy.* A lot of windows were broken and unrepaired. Footbridges had been hacked or burnt down, compelling long detours. Terra-cotta fuchsia urns were smashed into shards. Some buildings had been reduced to piles of rubble or heaps of ash.

Worse still was the spirit of the populace. No longer did Verrino folk scamper about, chattering like monkeys. Now they slunk hither and thither shiftily. Many of them appeared ill-fed, even diseased, while the vine-arbours harboured drunks—not a few of them Jangali soldiers getting smashed on crude liquor. Indeed no one seemed to be drinking wine by choice. So where had the fine vintages of Verrino gone? Into hiding? Looted by the Sons? But perhaps Verrino wines were too subtle for the men of Jangali. Soldiers wanted something fiercer to remind them of junglejack. And perhaps wines were too subtle for everyone, these days? These boozing 'jacks were amiable enough, yet at the same time they seemed lost, like tipsy ghosts drowning their sorrows at having lost contact with their own world. Verrino town was quite crowded, yet despite this the place seemed strangely uninhabited, as though people couldn't quite believe in it any longer, even while they went through the motions.

Injuries were visible: lost fingers, hideous puckered slash-marks and scar-tissue, a missing eye here, broken teeth there, blushing burns. I saw one child running half-naked with a festering blotch on her back. Maybe the fresh air would help it heal; maybe. A good deal of garbage was lying about too: rags, stinking piles of fish bones, even dried knobs of human excrement. Oh, those Sons had transformed Verrino into a fine copy of one of their own side streets! The very town itself had been wounded and was still suffering from delayed shock. I watched a small funeral cortége making its way down one street. The procession was silent, not even humming in mourning. The body lay under a dirty sheet on a litter of crudely-roped poles.

I made my way through Verrino that day with difficulty—where I had skipped before. Twice I lost my way, because the ways had changed. But when I arrived at the base of the Spire, that at least looked unaltered—as monumental and austere as ever.

I climbed, pausing a few times for breath.

On my last such halt I surveyed the view. In the direction of the glassworks off to the east I spied several new "villages". Villages of sorts: higgledy-piggledy shacks and canvas awnings, surrounded by spiked palisades. Each village compound was crowded with tiny dots of people doing nothing. Each compound was hidden from its neighbours by the bulge of sand hills.

Obviously those were the prison-pens. The 'jacks had separated their prisoners into four different sections for security—though from the look of it an uproar in one camp would easily be heard in the others. Out of sight, but not out of earshot.

Maybe that didn't matter. Maybe the prisoners were as stunned by their defeat as the people of Verrino had been by foreign occupation and war. And if Verrino folk looked ill-fed, the prisoners were probably weak with hunger. One could hardly starve Verrino or the army to stuff the stomachs of the Sons. So I was glad I was seeing those pens from afar.

I noticed some dark patches staining the stone steps where I stood. Dried blood? Let it be the lifeblood of the Sons!

I pressed on, through the upward tunnel, and past empty stairways and closed doors—a couple of which I pushed, only to find them locked. No hint of activity. No voices, no challenges.

I should have gone to the quaymistress's office initially and asked how it was with the Observers, instead of just turning up as though it was up to me to relieve their siege in person. I should have done. But I hadn't wanted a stranger to tell me the news. I had to see with my own eyes the outcome of events whose beginnings I had witnessed when I was Nelliam. And taste it with my own lips. Yet now that I was here, the place seemed deserted. Not ravaged, just abandoned.

The top platform was empty, save for a heliograph and signal-lantern erected by the rail. The door to the observatory building stood ajar.

I *knew* that Hasso was in there. He simply had to be. I *made* him be there by thrusting myself into a frame of mind where no other outcome was conceivable.

I walked over. I touched the rusty bolts of the door, called softly, "Hasso!" Then I pushed the door open decisively and stepped inside.

There was nobody in the room. Empty chairs stood behind telescopes. Every window pane was hinged wide open as though to ventilate the air of some lingering foetor.

I stood bewildered. What a weird return this was, to a place where no one was! I imagined that I'd died. I thought I was in a *Ka*-world of my own memories—a world where I could wander forever without meeting a soul because everyone else had faded away. During those few moments I felt more alone even, than when I'd found myself washed up on the west bank.

A noise from outside—a cough—broke this melancholy reverie. I whirled. I jumped to the open door.

"Yaleen!" exclaimed a voice. A familiar voice indeed!

Hasso's looks were not quite so familiar. Before he'd been slim. Now he was emaciated. His skin was sallow. His eyes looked larger, as though they'd swollen in their orbits. His once smart attire was dirty and crumpled. A ring of keys hung from his belt, which was tightened to the final notch, leaving a loose tail of leather hanging down.

I rushed towards him—then halted out of reach, like some anxious flutterbye just about to alight on a flower when it realizes that the flower is a deathbloom.

"Where—? How—?" (Was it his ghost whom I'd summoned to

haunt me on this high and lonely place?) "Come inside and sit down!" I made to take his arm now, but he danced back.

"Hey, I'm not about to flake out! I'm putting on fat again. Or at least," and he grinned ruefully, "I thought I was. The siege has ended, you know."

"Ended. How did it end?"

"We held out. Till the 'jacks arrived. Most of us."

"Most?"

"Two of us died of hunger. Or sickness. Same thing by that stage. Yosef killed himself to spin the groceries out. None of us fancied staggering downstairs with a white flag, not after some of the things we saw."

"I saw dried blood on the stairs. Did Yosef—?"

"Jump? No. He hanged himself. Those stains got there when the Sons made a foray. We dropped stones on them. They didn't risk it again, which is as well, since stones got hard to heave later on. Actually, Yaleen, the worst aspect was being drunk all the time and having a permanent hangover."

"Drunk? You're joking!"

"Well, we had a decent wine cellar, so when we ran out of water . . . A glass of vintage really knocks you out when you're weak with hunger. Yosef was drunk when he hanged himself, though he left a note to say why."

"Where are the others, Hasso?"

"Some are recovering in town. Me and Tork—remember him?— we're out at the Pens, questioning prisoners. We're compiling a real map of the west. I just popped back for an old chart. Saw you climbing up ahead of me." He looked around. "Actually, there ought to be a 'jack guard on duty up here—and a riverguild woman as well. Naughty, they are, naughty. Taking time off duty for private business downstairs, I shouldn't be surprised."

Indeed it transpired that there were two guards and two watchwomen assigned to the Spire. When I turned up, the night shift was down below, legitimately asleep. The day shift were merely sleeping with each other. Tousled and embarrassed, the latter pair soon emerged and got on busily with their duties of patrolling and peering.

Another symptom of disorder in Verrino? I could sympathize. They were bored; they were exiled up a shaft of rock. More important perhaps, there was evidently no friction except of the fleshy

sort between 'jacks and riverguild up here. When I went below with
Hasso, the guard saluted me smartly (though I had to ask what the
funny arm gesture meant).

Down below, Hasso let me into his quarters. He set out dry black
bread and cheese, some pickles and a carafe of water. To decide
which of us should tell our tale first, Hasso flipped a coin. The coin
came down value side up: Hasso's turn to tell.

I said he should at least eat his meal first. He shook his head and
nibbled while he talked. He ate as if he had disciplined himself to
disbelieve in food, and still couldn't credit its continuing existence.
But he sipped water like a connoisseur.

He was laconic concerning the siege itself. Maybe there isn't a lot
that can be said about slow starvation. Maybe he said it all by the
way he ate.

He talked much more about what the Observers had observed
from aloft: the brutalization of Verrino. They'd spied faggots piled
round a stake more than once; they'd seen women dragged shrieking
to be set on fire. Yet the final stages of the war were the worst, for
then the embattled Sons really vented their spleen upon Verrino
town which they were about to lose.

I'd finished my own food long ago. Hasso cleared up the last few
breadcrumbs meticulously upon a dampened fingertip.

"So now we have hundreds of those swine in the Pens," he said.
"And what to do with them? Actually, a few aren't such bad chaps
at heart. They regret what they did. They just didn't dare disobey
their leaders. But Verrino folk aren't ever going to have them living
in town. Some people say throw all the Sons in the river. Another
suggestion is we march them down beyond Aladalia and ferry them
across to their own side. I doubt if the Aladalians would appreciate
us dumping an army opposite them . . . Hey, a fin for them?"

"Um?"

"A fin for your thoughts?"

"Oh, sorry. I'm listening, honest!" But what I was thinking was
that I knew why Hasso had skated over the anguish of the siege, in
favour of faithfully narrating what happened below. It was because
he was fulfilling his promise to dead Nelliam. All the time he'd been
talking he was honouring her memory, by being true. I knew; but he
didn't know I knew.

So I started to tell him.

This had to be by a very roundabout route, via Tambimatu and

Manhome South, Spanglestream and Tambimatu again; and even so I had to leave out heaps of events and skip weeks and leagues.

Hasso stared at me attentively, now and then shaking his head in amazement. "My goodness," he muttered once, as I was recounting my adventures, "you're Capsi's flesh and blood all right, and no mistaking."

Towards the end of my account he exclaimed, "So it was *you* who brought the current back! Damn it, but it came so quickly—without warning. By the time we got Big Eye swung round . . . Well, you saved my life! That's what gave us the courage to hold out: the boats following a week or two afterwards, signalling, telling us we had an army on the way."

This made me feel a bit better about my role. Maybe I'd slowed down the war plan—even tied a whopping great knot in it—but at least I'd given some hope to people.

I'd kept till last my revelation about how I'd *been* Nelliam just before she was killed; and how I had a kiss to repay. . . .

But not now merely on the brow. That kiss prolonged itself. It wandered. Soon we also wandered, to Hasso's spartan bed.

Afterwards he lay like a cat basking beside a fire and sighed contentedly. "That was *good*. I thought I'd dried up completely."

"Nonsense." I winked. "Starvation sharpened you, that's all."

I spent three weeks in Verrino, helping Hasso and Tork to compile their map and gazetteer of the west bank. The riverguild gave me their blessing in this. Who better than I to catch out prisoners if they told lies about the territory from Worlzend to Manhome South? I did catch one or two out, but not many seemed to want to lie.

This new work meant that I had to travel out to the Pens by day. Nights, I spent in town; sometimes with Hasso, sometimes not. By and by Verrino began to seem less seedy and sleazy; though ugliness still simmered beneath the surface, a dark shadow upon the soul of the place.

Conditions in the Pens weren't too disgusting; no one wanted to risk an outbreak of serious disease. But life there was hardly elegant or even innocuous. I might have felt I was performing a useful penance by working there—if the 'jack guards hadn't already been doing this as routine.

The ordinary run of prisoners were just coarse, not actively venomous. The leaders were a different kettle of fish, and interrogating some of the robed ones was the nastiest but most necessary task. We had questions for them about the planning of the war and its ultimate aims.

In my final week one of the leaders sat facing our questioning committee. This committee consisted of Hasso and me, a guildmistress called Jizbel and a 'jack "captain", Martan. We held our sessions in a tent pitched just inside the gateway to this particular pen, with bales of uprooted thornbush on sharpened stakes separating us from the largely lackadaisical mass of prisoners; these spent their time playing pebble or straw games on the sand, gambling up imaginary debts, wandering from side to side, mucking out, squabbling over rations, racing insects. Those who could, read aloud to their fellows from a pile of tatty old romances generously donated by the guild. If anyone tried to tunnel out, they wouldn't succeed; the sand would suffocate them.

The Son in question was a big brute, but now he looked baggy, as though his skin was a size too large for him. As usual the prisoner was being guarded by two 'jacks armed with clubs; they kept their swords sheathed.

"That damned Satan-Snake saved you," the Son sneered. "You never saved yourselves."

"Didn't we just?" retorted Captain Martan. "Let me tell you—"

"How do you suppose the current came back?" Hasso glanced proudly at me. He oughtn't to have done that. Jizbel uttered a soft hiss like water cast on coals to cool them. Both men shut up.

I rapped my knuckles on the trestle table. I had to take this swine by surprise if we were going to get anything of value out of him.

"So what are you, then: a Conserver or a Crusader?" I tried.

The Son's head jerked towards me—and a wattle of loose skin like a turkey cock's flopped with it.

"You!" He stared at me. "I know you. It was you who rode in the jaws of the Snake!"

"Rubbish," I said. "At that distance it could as easily have been your own grandmother."

"Witch! Damned witch—it *was* you. I saw; my eyes are keen. That's why you're here now. You're the tool of the Snake."

"Oh, shut up about snakes. You don't know what you're talking about. I asked if you're a Conserver or a Crusader. Because if you're a Conserver—" I hoped I was being cunning—"then we're that much more likely to send you home to your precious Truesoil to keep it pure and secure, and bore yourself to death reading junk like *The Truesoil of Manhood.''*

This was meant to impress him with how much we already knew about life in the west, so that he wouldn't lie. The effect I produced was unexpected.

"Yal . . . een," he said. "That is who you are! You're Doctor Edrick's waterwitch who ran away. Only she would know the names of our Brotherhood books." He spat, though only at the sandy soil. "The Doctor said it was you as swept by in Satan's lips that morn. Didn't know whether to credit him."

"Drivel. Edrick couldn't spy a night-soil shack at twenty spans— even if he did loot himself a decent pair of glasses! He never was far-sighted about anything."

Neither was I, to shout my mouth off; though why should I care if this character knew who I was? Actually, mine was a cheap jibe. To give the dog his due, Edrick had been a devious schemer. And we'd both been hoodwinked by the Worm, he and I in different ways.

What I heard the Son mutter then, was, "Far-sighted enough to give this bloody town the slip!" Something like that. Immediately, as if realizing that I'd heard and desperate to cover his indiscretion up, the Son blustered on loudly: "How did he know? Well, we took spyglasses off those boats, didn't we? And the Doctor had ears. He could hark the description I gave—of *Yaleen.''*

So saying, the Son launched himself out of his chair, leaping at our table.

He didn't reach it. The 'jack guards bludgeoned him senseless.

"Stop it!" I cried, nearly upsetting the trestle top myself. "Don't hit him again!"

The way he had attacked didn't make sense. Just before he jumped, he had glanced at the 'jacks— and they were not lounging inattentively. They were alert. His glance in effect had cued them. Therefore he wanted to be knocked out. He wanted to be rendered speechless.

"Guard: did you hear what he said *before* that bit about stealing spyglasses?"

"Eh, mistress?" The 'jack guard panted.

I wasn't a "mistress", but I let that pass. "Think, man! The Son muttered something. I know what I heard. What did you hear?"

"Hmm . . . something about slipping . . . on all the blood?"

"No," his colleague said, "slipping out of town: that's what. Just what we all want to do."

"That's enough of that!" said Captain Martan.

"What *I* heard him say," said I, "was that Edrick was far-sighted enough to slip away."

"Guess I heard something of the sort," Martan allowed. "There haven't been any reports of runaways murdering or thieving. None that I've heard."

"If Edrick was lying low, you wouldn't have heard anything."

"If he's lying low, how many others are?" Hasso asked the Captain.

Martan looked more embarrassed than annoyed. "Be reasonable. We have our work cut out here, without combing the countryside when nobody reports anything."

I pointed at the slumped Son. "Bring him round. We'll get some *real* answers."

"How do you propose to go about that?" Martan asked coolly. "Just what do you mean, Yaleen?"

The truth is, I had no clear idea what I did mean. Or rather, I did have—but I recoiled at the idea. Momentarily my head swam with images of Capsi being stretched and twisted, crushed and burnt. "No, no, no, never!" I told myself; and I meant it too.

"We'll threaten him, with the sort of thing *they* do to prisoners," said I.

"And supposing he clams up tight?"

I didn't know what to say.

"Threaten something, then don't do it," Martan went on, "and word gets round. You lose credibility. Mind you, *I* totally agree we shouldn't use—" he hesitated—"torture. Because, well because I wouldn't ever want torture used on me." He gazed at me evenly as if it was all up to me to decide. How, how, *how* had I got into this fix? It had all happened so damn suddenly.

"Can't we bluff him?" I suggested.

"He's probably lying there listening to us right now," said Jizbel, "just pretending to be out cold." She regarded me with interest.

Martan disagreed. "He won't have woken up yet. *I've* had a crack on the head before. But you'll have to decide sharpish. This isn't a debating club on morals."

Decide. *I* would have to decide.

"Hasso," I muttered. Hasso seemed to have curled up inside himself.

"Maybe his information isn't so important," I said.

"And what if it is?" Martan asked me unhelpfully.

Indeed, why else had the Son preferred to be beaten senseless as soon as he realized what he had let slip?

When I first came to work at the Pens, I'd asked if there was a full list of prisoners. There was; but Edrick's name hadn't been on it—and of the dead, unsurprisingly, there was no list at all. Here was the first news I'd had that Edrick might still be active; and there was only one way to follow it up. But that one way was unacceptable.

I did decide, then and there. Irrespective of what happened subsequently I'm still sure I made the right choice; otherwise I would have felt polluted.

"We'll just question him normally."

Everyone seemed to relax. Hasso uncoiled, and stretched his limbs. "Fine," he said, "fine." Martan looked relieved. Jizbel smiled sweetly.

One of the guards dumped a bucket of water over the Son's head, then they hauled him, groaning, back into the chair.

We tried to question him normally about whether Edrick had slipped away, where to, and why. And of course it was still possible that Edrick was dead. "Giving Verrino the slip" could have meant just that: getting himself killed.

We tried. The Son put on a fine show of being brain-scrambled and incapacitated, confused and crippled with amnesia. We had to give up, and he was led away. If the brute *was* play-acting, he contrived to stagger and slump about so convincingly that the guards almost had to drag him.

What should happen then, but a complete volte-face on the part of the good Captain? A few minutes earlier he had quite dismissed the notion of combing the countryside. Now he suddenly leapt in the face of that resolve by announcing that he would lead a small party up-country for a day or so in search of clues.

I think Martan had decided that he simply had to get away from the Pens for a while; maybe the bludgeoning had tipped the balance. A two-day stroll around the immediate hinterland of Verrino would be unlikely to bear fruit except by wild coincidence. On the other hand, a brief working holiday might be no bad idea.

Would I accompany him and his patrol? And would Hasso?

Why yes, we would.

"If we head out Tichini way," suggested Hasso, "we could stop overnight by the vineyards."

"Why not?" agreed Martan lightly. "If any Son's hiding in a wine-cask, we'll swill him out."

So the next morning Hasso and I rendezvoused with Martan and six 'jack soldiers, and we set off inland. All of our spirits lightened as we walked along. It was a hot summer's day but the sky remained hazy so that we weren't baked; and the dust underfoot provided a soft tread. All stones and large pebbles had been regularly raked off this road for years, till both sides were lined with low embankments, twin dry walls. A roadman was specially employed to this end by the village of Tichini. Thus empty bottles, making their way by barrow from Verrino glassworks out to the vineyards and returning full along the same route, would not get tossed around and smashed. So Hasso explained as we travelled.

But we had hardly gone half a league before we reached a long stretch of road where the embankments were broken down, kicked around, scattered all over. Amidst the golden-blooming furze bushes off to one side I spied a boot and trouser leg protruding.

I pointed.

Martan pursed his lips. "Seem to recall a skirmish here."

The corpse wasn't wearing a fork-toed boot, so it couldn't be an unburied 'jack.

"Maybe that's Edrick," I said vaguely.

"Might be anybody. Shouldn't think it's him out here, if he escaped near the very end. Assuming that's so."

"Shouldn't you take a look?"

"But I don't know his face, Yaleen—aside from your description. Only you have his features by heart."

"Oh." I swallowed.

"I'll come with you," offered Hasso; and together we made our way through the furze to inspect the dead body.

The corpse lay on its back, leathery and smelly in weatherstained trousers and shirt. The face had been hacked in half, and insects had feasted. The remains weren't recognizable. They weren't even nauseating any longer. Soft torn flesh is awful, but not bone and leather. We returned to the road. I shrugged, and we carried on.

Soon shrubby cones of hills arose around us, disclosing after a further hour or more the village of Tichini hugging a hilltop. That particular hill and its immediate neighbours were all terraced around their southern slopes and neatly vine-clad. The road climbed gently, taking us up through a vineyard where swelling clusters of mauve grapes hung from the new staked growth above the twisted knobbly stocks. The soil looked quite varied between one hillside and the next. When I remarked on this to Hasso, he told me that the soil constituents—clay, limestone and porous mineral-trapping chalk—were the same, but that there were different mixtures on different hillsides. Originally, long ago, the terraced soils had all been blended by hand, to different recipes; and every winter, depending on the taste of the new wine, the slopes were top-dressed with a little more chalk or lime or clay. This, plus a variety of water sources and different vine-stocks, added up to a notable range of vintages within a comparatively small area. A few people were working on the slopes.

"Isn't it neat?" I said. "You wouldn't think there'd been battles."

"There weren't any out here," said Martan.

As we rounded the flank of the hill, we came upon an old white-haired man standing by the road, leaning on a rake.

"Ho," said Captain Martan. "Roadside's broken down, way back. Did you know?"

The man doodled in the dust. "You come to escort me while I rake it?"

"Why? Are there any stray Sons hiding out, so that you need escorting?"

"Who knows? When world's a pest, home's best."

"That isn't much of an attitude," said Hasso angrily. "Captain Martan, here, is as far from his own home as can be. If he'd thought home was best, you'd still have the Sons on your backs."

"Oh we had them. We had them. You needn't tell me. You can make things perfect for a hundred years—every bit of soil and pebble—then suddenly lunatics decide to hold a war. So where's the use in perfection? People might as well drink vinegar. And what's Verrino come to, these days? They blowing any fresh bottles down there?"

"They will be, after repairs to the works," said Hasso.

"So this year we'll just cask the new wine? Or pour it into old bottles, or sluice it away, eh?"

"Are there or aren't there any Sons running wild hereabouts that you know of?" repeated Martan.

"And if there are, and one's caught here or in Little Rimo over the hills or in Bruz, do we pop him in the soil, same as we're popped in the soil when we die, so the rain can wash his foreign substance down into our vine-roots?"

Martan sighed. "You aren't much help, old fellow."

"Help came too late for me, soldier. Those Sons killed my boy and my boy's boy when they came here a-thieving. There was no need of that."

"I'm sorry to hear it."

"Don't be. I'm feeling mellow now. And I'm in my right place, which you aren't. No one here's telling me to walk to Verrino with my rake."

We left the tetchy old man and climbed the rest of the way to the village, which was dominated by the sprawling vinthouse. A few villagers loitered in doorways, eyeing us silently. A goat stood wetting its beard and chewing on ferns growing in an ornamental basin where water bubbled from a pipe. A small boy with a stick was guarding the goat; at our approach he fled up a crooked alley. We entered a little marketplace. At that moment trade seemed to be brisk, in olives and bread, trussed chickens and oil and cheese; but as soon as the people saw us a lot of goods promptly vanished out of sight into bags and boxes. Three fat women sat outside a café, carding wool and singing; the sight of us shut them up.

I could spy no obvious damage (except in one respect), nor disfigurations, nor even signs of reduced diet, but obviously the flavour of the village had soured; and in Tichini the flavour of soil and water and minerals and air was such a delicate subtle thing—blood spilt down a hillside and the smell of fear could spoil a hundred years of care and love.

The one blatant piece of damage was that the great wooden doors of the vinthouse, leading to a courtyard, hung loose—wrenched off their hinges.

We went in, spied a scurrying apron-clad boy, and asked to see the Master or Mistress Vintner, supposing that he or she was still alive. Hasso assured us that this person would be the "mayor" of Tichini.

A man it was, and his name was Beri. He was short and fat, nearly as wide as he was tall. He welcomed us; he bustled. He quickly arranged overnight quarters: in the vinthouse for me and Hasso and Martan, in village homes for the other 'jacks. He commanded doors to open; he commanded people to step out and smile.

Beri was the sort of fellow whom you could never push over without him rolling right back up again. And, as we soon discovered, he was a repository of all human wisdom whose joy it was to preside over everyone else's foibles and follies, orchestrating popular opinion, pronouncing on anything under the sun. In other circumstances he might have struck you as an intrusive, opinionated bore. Given the current apathetic state of Tichini, though, these traits of his were a distinct plus. It seemed as if the village waited, hushed, upon his assessment of us—of our bouquet—to decide whether to spit us out or swallow us. And Beri went out of his way to give us his blessing.

He also gave us a guided tour of the vinthouse and its vaults, pointing out where the buildings had been vandalized and looted; though really neither damage nor losses would have looked too serious if a bit of mess had just been tidied up.

While guiding us, he held forth on how he had handled the Sons. "So I said to those devils, said I, well if that's your opinion, your Honour, why fair enough; but up in the hills here we aren't dipping our toes in the river all the time, so that we aren't as unlike each other as you might suppose! Indeed, your Honour, are people ever so very different from each other as their opinions make them seem? They were brutes, Captain Martan, and murderous brutes too, but I reckon I handled them as best as could be, though I felt in peril of my life a good few times for speaking out. But I think they respected my bluntness—even if I did feel their fists once or twice. And they stole and messed things around something awful, so that we aren't even cleaned up yet. And they raped three of our women, including my own niece; and what could the women do but endure it? And what could I feel but shame and grief, and just bottle it up?"

That evening Beri arranged a celebration in the vinthouse courtyard, attended by a number of the villagers—mainly those who would host the 'jacks. A bonfire was lit. Several chickens were roasted. Bottles of vintage, which had come through the war intact, were opened. (A lot of bottles seemed to have survived intact.) A stringed bouzouki provided twangy, jangly music. And Beri held forth expertly upon the causes and circumstances of war, amidst 'jacks who had actually fought that war. Discovering that we were on the lookout for runaway Sons and had spent weeks interrogating prisoners, Beri discoursed on the psychology of the men of the west, based on his wealth of observations. Then he offered opinions on the black current and the river guild, and wondered whether the guild ought perhaps to compensate civilian victims of war, such as the people of Tichini. And of Verrino too, of course. He invited our comments; he approved or disproved them.

After a while Martan drew Hasso and me aside. "Would you say," he asked quietly, "that our host actually . . . collaborated with the Sons while they were here?"

"What makes you say that?" asked Hasso.

"Beri's too full of how he handled the situation. And I'm sure he's lying his head off, about how rough it was."

"What about the deaths, Martan? The damage? The broken doors? What about the rapes?"

"And why have those doors been left wrecked for so long? Could it be to show visitors how he resisted? And why does the vinthouse look as though the Sons trashed and robbed it, when actually the damage and loss is—"

"Superficial," said I.

"Isn't it just? Yet it's all still on display. As for his niece and those other two women, how do you prove a woman's been raped? If someone has a sword stuck in them, that's visible enough. And how come the vineyards are in such splendid shape—when the Sons burnt and smashed other places, once they found they were losing the war?"

"Hmm, I see what you mean," said Hasso. "But how could we prove it? And if we could, what then?"

"Just that I wonder whether he would really report any runaways in the area—because if we caught them, they might tell us things about Beri's conduct. And if *he* won't tell us, you can bet nobody else in Tichini will. Not even a niece who's been offered to the Sons. They're all in it together. They take their cue from him."

"We can hardly challenge him," said Hasso.

"No, we can't. I might be totally wrong."

I butted in. "So do you reckon that old fellow with the rake actually lost his boy and his boy's boy? Or does he just stand on the road to waylay travellers with a tall tale about how much everyone suffered here?"

Martan shook his head. "I don't know. It's possible. Maybe we could find out from those other places over the hills, Bruz and Little Rimo. And maybe we'd be wasting our time."

The bouzouki music raced and thrummed. Feet stamped the flagstones of the courtyard. Beri presided over the revels, dispensing wisdom and vintage.

"We're wasting our time," said Martan. "Definitely so. After weeks of asking questions and suspecting lies, suspicion becomes a sickly way of life. Let's drink and sing and pretend that everything's right as rain. Dance with me, will you, Yaleen?"

So I did, because he'd asked. And then I danced with Hasso. But after a while the exertion began to tell on Hasso. He became breathless. He wasn't yet truly recovered from the siege.

Neither, perhaps, had Tichini recovered from what had befallen it during the war—namely, its own suspiciously prosperous survival.

The next day we returned to Verrino. On the way back I asked several 'jacks how they had fared in the homes of the villagers; but all had retired to bed late with a bellyful of wine, and had had the consequences to cloud their perceptions in the morning. Besides, they had all been on their best polite behaviour.

So: enigma unresolved. And perhaps, indeed, Beri had done well by his village; cunningly well. At least he had saved the future of the wine trade, though Tichini was, for the moment, lying low; and their old rakeman hadn't gone to repair the road just yet. Too much haste in that regard might have struck Beri as unwise.

The day after we got back I sailed at last for Pecawar, aboard—guess which brig?—the *Darling Dog*.

We drifted in past pale green cinnamon trees, and as we turned to shore the aroma of cloves greeted my nostrils—this, and the dead scent of dust. Even the water close to the bank wore a faint glaze of dust. I sneezed several times. My nose had grown unused to filtering out motes of desiccated soil and wind-blown desert. Maybe in my absence from Pecawar my nostril hairs had thinned out.

Dockside buildings and spice warehouses were all a dusty yellow, like long low sandcastles.

In town I stopped at a café for a glass of cinnamon coffee, to collect my thoughts. Really there were too many thoughts to gather into any neat bundle; so I watched the world go by instead: porters, dockers, factors, bakers' boys with trays of hot sesame rolls balanced on their heads. A lad selling chilled sherbet lemonade: he was quickly scooted away by a waiter.

And amongst the people passing by I spotted my father striding down the street. Riding high on his shoulders, a little girl.

"Dad!"

He stopped, he stared around.

I waved from the café verandah. "It's me! Over here!"

He came at a run, to the wide steps. The little girl bobbed up and down as she hung on to the crinkly curls on the back of Dad's head, with her bunchy little fists. Dad was more bald than when I'd last seen him. Where before there had been some dark wiry sheep's wool on his crown, now there were just wisps; and I couldn't help wondering if this was Narya's fault. Did he so adore her that he had let her idly pluck and loosen his remaining locks? (It was from my mother that I received my own softer nutbrown hair.) The child seemed unbothered at the way Dad's gait suddenly broke into a gallop. She giggled gleefully, but then as he mounted the steps to my table she fell silent. He set her down on the dusty planking, and she just stood there unmoving, gazing . . . while we both lost interest in her temporarily.

Dad hugged me; I hugged him.

"So, so, *so!*" He laughed. "The prodigal comes home. Or at least within a stone's throw of home. . . ."

"That's where I was heading; never fear."

"Oh, these have been terrible times! We were getting quite anxious. Still, with you safely down south. . . ."

"Down south? Was I?"

"According to your last letter . . . goodness, that was long enough ago! What upheavals: Jangali men pouring into town. Arming themselves to the teeth! You *were* down south during the war?"

"Not really, Dad. Oh, I've such a lot to tell you. It's a blessing I met you here, actually. I was worried how you and Mum—"

"Worried?" He raised an eyebrow. "We'd never have guessed." But his tone was humorous, not harsh.

"That's why I stopped for a coffee. To give me a chance to find the words. I've some bad news."

"About Capsi, is it?"

"You know!"

Dad shook his head. "We guessed. Verrino, the Spire, the war. Well, we'd have been foolish to hope! Besides, Capsi made his own choice long ago, and it doesn't seem to have included us, or remembering us." He sounded sad, but not bitter.

Of course! I could let them assume Capsi had been killed in the war . . . Then, in another half-year, they would read the truth in my book.

I chewed my lip. "I'm afraid it wasn't the war. . . ."

Dad held a finger to my lips. "I'd rather rejoice at your return, yet a while. If there's mourning to be done, we'll tackle it later. Your mother and I have got used to the idea of not . . . seeing Capsi again." Dad held his head high, surveying me. He wasn't a tall man, but he out-topped me by a good half-span. "You look well, daughter."

"Do I?"

"No. Actually, you don't. Not 'well'. You look as though you've suffered. But your heart has won through. You've grown up. You went as a girl, you come home as a woman."

"Oh," said I. "Spare my blushes." As yet Dad had no notion that it was *I* who had ridden the Worm downriver. The event was a matter of universal knowledge, but not the name of the heroine in question. Not yet. The guild was keeping mum till my book was published.

"Talking of girls," said I, "how's my new sister?" For the first time I really looked at Narya. She was hardly knee-high, and skinny, with lots of curly bistre hair like the knots in charcoalwood. In this respect she took after Dad. Her eyes were hazel, just like mine. I'd assumed she would seem a complete stranger to me, yet by virtue of those eyes it was as though, in her, I was inspecting a curious version of myself. She must have been watching me attentively all this while, since she hadn't moved from where Dad had set her down. Now she winked at me.

Some dust in her eye? Even as I thought of dust she started to rub her eye with a knuckle. She quit, grinned impishly and toddled towards the table, to clutch the edge.

"Oh, who's a big healthy girl?" asked Dad, tousling her curls. (She wasn't particularly big.) "And so well behaved. Do you know, Yaleen, I've hardly heard her cry. Actually," he whispered, "I think she's almost too well behaved at times."

"Not like me, eh?"

"Oh, she gets excited, does Narya. And she looks as if she's taking everything in, bright as a spark. But other times she just sits for hours like a broody hen. You'd hardly know she was there. Got a mind of her own, though, she has. She won't be overfed, even if your mother tries to pack it in. Just as well, or your Mum would have turned her into a roly-poly!"

"Hullo, Narya," I said. "My name's Yaleen. I'm your sister."

Narya gazed up at me in silence.

"She's slow at speaking," Dad confided.

"What about 'wain'? When it rained. And all that. I thought you wrote saying—"

"She began speaking. A few words. Then she stopped—like someone who finds a whistle then throws it away again. Frankly, we're a bit bothered."

"Oh, I expect it's that way with some kids. The ones who hold

back are just damming it up. One day it'll all flood forth, then you
won't know where you are for chatter." I didn't know too much
about this, apart from something I remembered Jambi saying about
her own kid. However, it seemed a good idea to say so. What *I* was
thinking to myself was that they oughtn't to have had another
baby, so late on in life.

"Ah, she's my big darling, aren't you?" Dad hoisted Narya aloft.
"Let's step on home, Yaleen."

Narya clung to Dad's scanty rigging as if sailing him from the top
of a mast.

Alas for notions of dandling my little sister on my knee! Alas for the
idea I'd gotten from those eyes of hers that she was some sort of
soul-sister! As soon as Narya saw me take up residence at home, she
did her level best to avoid me. I guess she was jealous. She must
have felt I was butting in, out of nowhere, between her and her
parents. But she didn't fuss or cry. She didn't hang around, or cling.
Quite the opposite! She simply absented herself, in so far as it's
possible for a very young child to do so. I thought this was weird,
till I finally rumbled her game—cunning creature that she was. My
mother and father were bothered because Narya was withdrawn
and broody and couldn't talk. And now here was I intruding. Right!
So Narya would withdraw *twice* as much, to force them to come to
her and quit lavishing attention on this invading stranger.

Her ploy worked fairly well. Obviously she wasn't so much backward as plain devious. She was a little manipulator. She had already
learned what is perhaps the most subtle trick in the game of life: to
win by withholding oneself. To reign, by resigning. To triumph by
taking cover; by not talking. She would only romp as a special gift,
to be carefully rationed out. Since these little gifts of herself were so
special, she'd convinced my parents that she was indeed their treasure, their joy.

That's how I saw it—in so far as I saw anything much of Narya
during my stay.

Well, sod her!

By now I'd told Mum and Dad the tale of my travels—though I
told them far less about my inner feelings during my adventures
than I had written in my book. How odd that I felt free to broadcast
my most intimate sentiments to all and sundry who might read the
book, but couldn't confide these in my own mother and father! On
second thoughts maybe this wasn't so curious. Those things which

I'd experienced were right outside my parents' scope. I'd been in such extreme circumstances that their questions seemed impossibly banal—on the level of asking a starving man, "Would you rather have mutton or fried fish for supper?" So during my account I stuck to the bare bones of events; and even then there were moments when I almost gave up. ("But what is this Godmind that comes from Eegen?" "No, no, the name's *Eeden*. And the Godmind doesn't come from there; it's us who came from there originally." "So why did the Worm—?" "But I just told you that!" And so forth.)

Amongst events to be related was, of course, the fate of brother Capsi; tortured and burnt alive on a bonfire . . . This was the worst part to tell. One of the reasons why it was the worst, was that I was sure I was grinning idiotically as I told it. I simply couldn't find the right expression to wear on my face.

My parents took the news as nobly as could be expected. Afterwards Dad even declared, "We should be grateful to the men of Jangali that there won't be any more horrors like that over here. The war was a good thing, don't you agree?"

No, the war had *not* been a good thing. It had poisoned too many people's lives. I myself had been on the brink of ordering another human being vilely tortured. And what of the west, where the same terrible existence went on as before? Except that now we knew about it. And what of a hundred other things—such as the cosmic war between Godmind and Worm? Loose ends were left hanging everywhere. The world after the war was more like a ball of wool a kitten has been ripping up, than like a garment well repaired! My parents couldn't see any of these loose ends; I could. I nodded and looked at the floor; they took my silence for consent.

And I wondered: who would look at me one day when I was older and would know that I couldn't possibly understand something; and then would lower their eyes, lose interest and give up?

I didn't tell Mum and Dad that I'd written a book. Their off-target comments might have annoyed me.

Maybe it was a reaction on my part to this failure of communication; maybe I thought that I could root out the cause by identifying myself with the mutton and fish of life, the ordinary mundane things. But I found myself wondering whether I ought to marry and settle down and raise a child of my own; a child who would of course, after a few years, be my friend and understand me.

Marry whom: someone who understood me? Or someone who

would simply suck me down into the normal business of everyday life?

Should I return to Verrino and propose to Hasso? Ha! Or onward to Aladalia to propose to Tam (assuming that he could shed his mad infatuation)? Ho.

I dismissed this idea. Instead for a while I nursed fantasies of trekking into the interior to live as a hermit and write poetry; not that I had ever written any poems, but presumably that's true of all poets before they start out.

Probably what I *ought* to do (I decided next) was get back on board a boat and be a proper riverwoman. Ah, but wait! My book would soon be published, and might make me famous. In that case should I change my name and sign on a vessel anonymously, with the riverguild keeping this a close secret? Fat chance of that on our little river! (Our long, long river seemed to have shrunk a lot recently.)

Truth to tell, I was getting a bit scared of my book coming out. When I wrote the book, I hadn't really been thinking in terms of people reading it; so I could afford to tell the truth. But soon the truth would escape into the world on its own two legs—not that this ought to embarrass me, but other people mightn't see things exactly the way I saw them; or see me, exactly as *I* saw me.

In view of what was to happen I could have spared myself all these emotional squirmings in Pecawar. If I had put a single one of my fanciful schemes into action, though, I would have saved my life.

Two weeks after I returned home, my mother's cousin Chataly died unexpectedly. She vomited in her sleep and choked on some food. Chataly had lived on her own in a tiny spice-farming hamlet a couple of leagues out of town. A neighbour brought the news, so then of course my mother had to go to see about the funeral rites and clear up the house, she being the closest female relative. Mum would need to stay away one or two nights.

Dad offered to go along with her to help; and Mum quickly accepted. Then they both looked at me.

It was me who ought to have accompanied Mum. We all knew that perfectly well, and at first I couldn't fathom why my father had volunteered his services so eagerly; or why my mother had accepted. Unless (grotesque thought) my parents wanted to be alone together overnight in Chataly's house for some sort of second or third honeymoon without any nearby toddler to hamper them.

On second thoughts, maybe Dad felt that Mum wouldn't really want me with her? *I* wouldn't be much aid and comfort. That wasn't a very flattering interpretation.

On third thoughts, maybe they hoped that by leaving me alone with Narya this would force the little girl to come to terms with her big sister—something that my parents couldn't engineer by themselves. And then, of course, Narya mustn't be exposed to death, must she now? Shelter the little darling!

Fourth thoughts were rather like the third, with a twist. Mum and Dad wanted to show their love for me by trusting me to care for their treasure in their absence.

Aha, *fifth* thoughts! They wanted me to settle down and raise a family. Here was an ideal opportunity to show me the joys thereof.

But whether first, second or fifth thoughts were behind this, the upshot was that I must needs offer to look after the house for a day or two and nursemaid my little sister.

So Mum and Dad explained to Narya that they had to go away to visit someone for a couple of nights. Narya just stared at them, nodded once or twice and sucked her thumb. By then it was late afternoon, and within the hour they were gone. Nor did their actual departure seem to bother Narya one little bit. She even waved goodbye from the door with a certain panache.

I was left alone with her, well before any possible bedtime. What to do? Read her a story? Or ten stories? Play games? Stick her in a corner to mope? At least I didn't need to check whether she was wetting herself; Mum had said that Narya's bowel and bladder control were excellent.

"Shall we have something yummy to eat?" I suggested; and fled to the kitchen. Narya didn't follow me, so I pottered about inventing a new sort of spice pudding, all the while keeping one ear cocked for noises of breakage, screams or whatever. Silence reigned, except amongst the pots and pans.

After half an hour I got guilty and searched for *her*. Oh yes, that's the way she played her game; didn't I know it? Feeling like a fool I went looking. I hunted through the downstairs first, then checked the back stoop in case she'd slipped out through the screen doors into our little walled garden.

I loitered outside a while, pretending that I was looking for her.

Pecawar gardens tended to be mostly dry; and in ours we had a "mountain range" consisting of shapely black boulders set around a white pebble "lake". Half a dozen large knobbly barrel-gourds oc-

cupied the sandy "plains" on either side of this lake. These gourds
were a glossy green, striped with bright orange and yellow zigzags.
When I was a young girl I used to make believe that the gourds were
bulbous cities banded with rows of windows aglow with light—
cities somewhere out in the desert where nobody from the river-
shore had ever been. The barrel-gourds were desert plants which
grew very slowly; these ones might have been a century old. When I
was even smaller I thought the gourds were the heads of monster-
people buried up to their necks in the garden; and when the sun
went down I was a bit scared of stepping outside. As soon as I
discovered the quayside and the river, of course, our garden became
a totally boring place.

While I stood there pretending to look for Narya, I recalled my
childish fancy, and I half expected to see my sister hunkered down
by one of those monster-heads whispering to it: her only confidant,
sole recipient of words from her. I fantasized how I might greet
Mum and Dad on their return with the glad (or sick) tidings, "She
does talk, you know! She talks to the gourds in the garden." Whereupon Mum and Dad could paint their faces green and orange to try
to communicate with Narya by pretending to be vegetables . . .
However, she wasn't lurking in the garden.

I went back indoors, bolting the screens behind me, and I
mounted the stairs. When I was younger these had been of bare
waxed planks, but now they were thickly carpeted, no doubt in case
Narya took a tumble. I found her sitting on the floor of Capsi's old
bedroom, which was now her room. Her head was cocked, listening
to the breeze tinkle some wind-chimes by the open window. The
night was warm so that there was no point in shutting the window
in case she caught a chill, though the thought did cross my mind
(worry, worry).

Capsi's pen-and-ink panorama of the opposite shore was still
tacked to the wall. Someone (Dad, I presumed) had added lovable
colourful baby animals romping here and there. Giant baby animals,
dwarfing the terrain of that one-time never-never-land over in the
west.

"You okay, Narya?"

Narya deigned to notice me; she nodded.

"Nice eats, soon," I said encouragingly. "Yum-yum." I think it
was myself I was encouraging.

* * *

Presently we ate the pudding, which wasn't too bad at all, and we drank some hot cocoa. Then I hunted out some kiddy tale for Narya to endure. I think "endure" best describes the way in which Narya received this treat: with a mixture of stoic boredom and vague tension as to how soon the story would be finished.

By now it was deep dusk, so I announced, "Off to dreamland with you!" and saw her to bed with a kiss on the brow.

I wondered what to do with myself. I tidied up a bit, then trimmed the oil lamp and settled with a book of poems by Gimmo of Melonby, who lived a few hundred years ago. Gimmo the Tramper, who wandered up and down our river shore singing his ballads for coins or a supper.

I must have dozed off. A noise woke me: creak, bump.

Narya must be up and wandering. . . .

I was about to go and check, when in the doorway to the kitchen . . . stood a man.

A tall man with a freckly face and bald head. A few bunches of gingery hair were sprouting from the sides of it. Spectacles were perched upon his nose. I hoped I *hadn't* woken up at all, and was just dreaming.

Vain hope. Doctor Edrick was dressed in baggy trousers tucked into fork-toed boots, and wearing a scarlet jerkin. These were junglejack clothes, obviously looted from some dead soldier. In one big hairy fist he held a metal tube with a handle: a pistol, pointed at me.

Edrick had let his erstwhile toothbrush moustache sprout out into great drooping ginger horns.

"That's clever of you, Doctor Edrick," I said, as steadily as I could. "You haven't skulked. You haven't crawled. You've swaggered about in stolen clothes. You haven't shaved your moustache off—you've grown a dog's tail on your face, instead."

He kept the pistol pointed at my chest. "It's easier to travel, Yaleen, if you stride along the high road, and pay your way in coin of the country."

His voice sounded altered. He'd shed the accent of the west, their funny broad way of pronouncing words. His accent still wasn't any of *our* accents, but it would serve to fool most people here in the middle reaches who would assume, by his clothes, that he was from Jangali.

"I've been watching this house for a while," he said. "And now you're alone. How timely. How lucky that your parents took a trip."

"You didn't . . . kill Chataly, did you?"

"Ah, so someone died? No, there are certain limits to my energy and ingenuity. Whatever errand your parents went on is none of my doing. 'Lucky for your parents,' is my meaning. Lucky not to be here, during what must come to pass." He moved slowly into the room.

Suppose I hurled the book of Gimmo's poems at the lamp? Aye, and burned the house down with Narya asleep upstairs. . . .

"Don't move," warned Edrick. "Or I'll shoot to cripple you. For a start."

I didn't move.

"My dear Yaleen, I underestimated you once—and I shan't make that mistake twice. You were an agent of the Satan-Snake all along, weren't you?"

"What, me? Certainly not!"

"I suppose it let you ride downstream in its jaws as a favour pure and simple?" He snorted. "Oh yes, you were spotted; and I knew at once. *Then,* how do we explain your oh-so-innocent revelation of a certain snake-poison we could use? Or how conveniently you stumbled upon *my* men—who would bring you to me, and not to some Brotherhood cellar where the truth could really have been squeezed out of you! You fooled me, Yaleen. I don't take kindly to being fooled."

"I didn't! Honest."

How much could I tell him? Without giving him valuable information about the current, the *Ka*-store, the Godmind?

"I'll grant," he went on, "that the Snake may well enter into compacts with its witches. If they serve it well, it will repay them with services in turn. In which case, my main problem would seem to be how to *motivate* the witch in question so that she'll really *beg* the Snake to do something for her, hmm? Beg the Snake, for instance, to quit the river once again? For a while?"

"Long enough for you to escape?"

"Long enough for whatever I have in mind."

"You could have crossed the river easily enough if you'd walked north instead of south."

"How so?"

"The head of the current halted at Aladalia. That's beyond—"

"I know where Aladalia is."

"It didn't go all the way downstream." No harm, surely, in telling him that? "You needn't worry about your captured troops. When we've cleared up the mess they made, they'll be sent north then over to the other side. You could be repatriated too."

"How very considerate. But maybe I want to make the Snake perform a few tricks, just as you did? I require a tool for this purpose; a key to unlock the Snake. *You.*"

"How did you know I'd be here in Pecawar?" I was playing for time. I guess people always play for time, even when it'll make not a scrap of difference.

"You described your home to me; you located it, remember? I decided that part of your tale wasn't a lie, since a dollop of truth always smooths the way. So where does someone head for after a dangerous secret mission and a war? Where but home, to rest? Fair gamble! It paid off. Let's move on to more important matters."

I had to chance my hand. "Look, Doctor, you're quite wrong about me. But I've learnt something about your so-called Satan-Snake that's pretty important. You ought to listen before you do anything rash." (Why ever should I call him "Doctor"? He was only a Doctor of Ignorance!)

"I've no doubt that you could spin me a fascinating yarn till the sun comes up again. We'll have hours and hours for it, later on. Right now you and I are going for a walk, to somewhere more secluded, out of earshot."

Did he have any accomplices? Andri and Jothan would most likely have been involved in organizing the poison plot on the other shore. But Edrick might not have escaped from Verrino alone . . . though it would have been easier for one person to get away. Would Edrick have trusted others to be as clever as himself?

He kept the pistol aimed at me, while with his free hand he pulled a kerchief from his trouser pocket. To use as gag, what else? This he tucked into the neck of his jerkin. Next he drew out a length of cord —to bind my wrists. The cord dragged something else from his pocket, something half the size of a person's hand. This fell heavily to the floor, making a metallic clatter. Hastily Edrick scooped the thing up and stuffed it back in his pocket, though not before I got a look at it.

Part of a pistol? No, the tube was too fat and short. And what was that screw on top? The thing looked designed to be worn, to fit over finger and thumb. For punching with?

He hadn't wished me to see it.

Stick your finger inside the tube, turn the screw; and your finger, commencing with the fingernail, would be squeezed slowly till the flesh burst open like a squashed tomato. . . .

Then another finger. Then another. There were plenty of fingers. Then your toes, one by one. I'd caught a finger in a door once. It hadn't bruised me much, let alone smashed anything, but the pain had been excruciating. Imagine that pain prolonged and multiplied.

When I was over in the west, to scare me Andri and Jothan had mentioned such devices, kept in the cellars of the Brotherhood. Later I'd heard tales in Verrino of the cruelties of the Occupation.

I doubted whether Edrick nursed scruples about torturing people, if he thought the gain was worth it. He wasn't me. He wanted to march me off to a quiet spot . . . where nobody could hear me screaming?

Before he could do that, he had to tie my hands and gag me. That isn't so easy to do one-handed—not unless he planned to knock me unconscious with the pistol butt and carry me.

I heard a faint rustle of noise. Ever so quickly, as if shaking my head, I flicked my gaze.

My bowels chilled. Narya was standing in the shadows outside the hall door. She was watching me. As yet the door jamb hid her from Edrick. If he could manage to tie me and march me away, he could carry Narya along under one arm. And torture her. The better to persuade me.

Go back, I thought at Narya. *Back back back. Hide!* I didn't dare look again.

In between Edrick recovering the fingerscrew and beginning to edge round the room, to get behind me, fifty thoughts seemed to have been packed into a few seconds.

Including: would Edrick actually *use* his pistol? What had Andri said about pistols? "Pompous things. As soon explode in your hand, as harm your enemy." Our army had been equipped with some pistols, crafted at Guineamoy. I gathered these weren't too popular compared with a bow. But Edrick probably had the very best.

I threw myself from my chair, rolled head over heels and bounced through the doorway, aiming to crash into Narya and carry her off. That was the idea. Not that I thought it out in detail. I just went.

It didn't work. I hit the doorway a glancing blow, knocking a good bit of wind out of me—but at least I ended up in the hall. Narya wasn't even there. She'd gone.

Where should *I* go? Out of the front door? Edrick *might* have a companion posted outside. Besides, I mightn't get time to unbolt the door. Upstairs and out through Capsi's open window? Climb up to the flat of the roof if I could manage it, and scream blue murder? Rouse the neighbourhood? I leapt up the stairs with Edrick right on my tail. His hand clutched my ankle. Swirling, I slashed flesh with my diamond ring like a cat clawing a dog behind it. He cursed; I wrenched free, and fairly threw myself the rest of the way upstairs. Narya might have fled to her room. I mustn't lead him to her. And my room had a key, hers didn't.

I slammed my bedroom door just a moment too late. Edrick blocked it from closing completely. For a few moments I held him off with my back to the door and my feet braced against the bedstead. What a weird reprise of childhood years when a teasing Capsi used to chase me to my room, pretending to be a bogeyman. Now there was a real bogeyman loose in our home, with a machine in his pocket to crush my fingers. The key was in the lock but I couldn't for the life of me force the door home. Instead the door was forcing me back slowly but surely.

I couldn't hold it. My legs were packing up. A weapon: I needed a weapon!

Scissors! Sharp scissors of best Guineamoy metal were kept in the bedside cupboard. I could use those to stab in the dark. I could smash Edrick's glasses, blind his eyes! I mustn't be squeamish about where I stabbed him.

I let the door toss me right across the bed. I rolled to the floor beyond, dragged the cupboard door open, scrabbled inside, made a fist around those scissors. Staying low, I squinted over the covers.

Edrick bulked in the doorway as a vague silhouette. I made my breath leak in and out slowly so as not to betray myself by panting.

The silhouette announced quietly, "If you try to get away again, I *will* shoot you."

He would have to spot me first. As yet he wasn't venturing away from the door. He was waiting till his eyes adjusted. Already I could see grey outlines. Stars were bright outside the window; but apart from the leaflet up top the window was closed. The only way out would be to burst through wood, glass and all. The fall could cripple me on those ornamental boulders below.

I balanced, clutching my scissors, making believe I was a bouncy ball. Shutting the door behind him, Edrick took a few paces into the room. He didn't lock the door. Either he was unaware of the key, or he wanted to leave himself a quick exit.

"Though," he whispered, "I mightn't need to hurt you if you co-operate. . . ."

I slithered under the bed and backed up against the wall. In this position he couldn't knock me senseless.

Footsteps; faint shape of feet.

"So: gone to ground, eh?"

He was kneeling down. He wouldn't be able to see me immediately in the deeper darkness where I lay, not if I kept still.

Shoulders . . . head . . . get ready!

Unaccountably the bedroom door began to open.

Edrick saw where I was crouched. "Ah," he said.

And past him I saw Narya faintly in the half-open doorway. The stupid, stupid child!

Edrick laid his pistol down and groped for my legs. He would expect me to kick, and would grip my ankle again.

What was Narya *doing?* She had crept around the door. The key! She was pulling the key from the lock!

Hold the scissors just so . . . Squirm—and stab!

"Aaah!" Edrick stifled a cry of pain. "You filthy damn *witch.*"

Narya was backing out—and I was sure she had the key. Yes, I heard it scrape into the far side of the lock! Then I heard the key turn: the faintest click. That damn conniving brat was locking her unwanted sister in with the bogeyman! This bogeyman had obviously come in response to her secret desires to dispose of the stranger called Yaleen.

Edrick took up his pistol again in his wounded hand.

"This is your very last chance. You toss that knife out, or I'll kill you."

"I really don't think you ought to shoot me," I said. "You've no idea what a mistake it'll be if you kill me."

"Ha ha," said tonelessly. But it was true.

"Just let me explain what'll happen."

"I'll count to five."

"No, *listen.*"

"One."

"It isn't in your own best interests, Doctor Edrick."

"Two. You *hurt* me."

"The Worm—"

"Three."

"That's to say, the Satan-Snake—"

"Four. Nobody hurts me."

"—It told me it would—"

"Five. *Die*, Snake-daughter!"

A blinding crash, a punch in my chest as if I'd been impaled by a mast. . . .

Your body is where the world begins and ends. Your body is the boundary. And when that boundary, of the body, is smashed, when it's stove in like a boat rammed on a rock, oddly it isn't you who sinks, it's the world. It's the world that disappears into the depths down a deep dark well of water.

The whole world sank right then.

I was in a blue void. I was aware of nothing except for that azure light. My body had vanished. So had everything else. Maybe I was spinning? I seemed to have nothing either to spin with or to be still with, but I did wonder whether I was spinning.

Maybe I was spinning so rapidly that nothing else was visible? I tried to slow myself down. I don't know *what* exactly I thought I was slowing, since I didn't have a body. . . .

I seemed to be in this empty sky-space for a long time.

Then:

Welcome back, Yaleen, said the Worm.

Damn it.

Edrick had had his revenge, all right. His revenge for dashed hopes, destroyed ambitions. His revenge for being diddled by a slip of a girl.

But what a hollow revenge this was, to be sure! If only he'd known the truth, how zealously he would have fought to keep me alive!

Yet though he didn't know it, this was the best possible revenge he could have had. Because he had made me the Worm's own creature. I'd thought that event would be years and years in the future. It was soon, so very soon.

I said hullo, Yaleen.

I heard you. Hullo, Worm.

That's better. Maybe you're wondering where you are?

In the Ka-store, I suppose.

Not exactly. Do you recall how I was outlining my scheme to send a human agent back along the psylink to Eeden?

How could I forget? That's always been the great ambition of my life: to travel!

The great ambition of your death, surely?

*Of course, my death. I forgot. How silly of me. Good joke, Worm. You always
were a good sport.*

Only since you became involved in my affairs, Yaleen!

How gallant.

*Not at all. I owe you, my dear. Didn't I promise to inform you of Kas and
Godminds, of stars and Eeden? How could I possibly break my word? I have my
honour to uphold.*

I'd be quite happy to overlook all that, Worm. Consider yourself absolved.

*No, no, I insist. My treat. I shall now display how I intend to tackle this
business. I'll show you what's about to happen, hmm?*

*Couldn't you send somebody else to Eeden? No, I suppose not. We're part of each
other, aren't we? In that case, how awful to separate us!*

*Oh, you'll be back afterwards. I'm fairly sure I can manage that. With our
affinity for each other, how could you doubt it? As you say, it's really quite
touching, our relationship: a bit like Mum and daughter. Heigh-ho, a goddess and
her girl!*

*Okay, so I'm touched. Except that there isn't anything hereabouts to touch. I
don't seem to have any hands. I suppose there's no chance of you changing your
mind?*

None at all.

I sighed. *Shall we get on with it?*

That's my girl!

All of a sudden there were images to see; and if I was spinning
around, as I imagined, then those shapes must be spinning around
too, keeping pace with me. This seemed to be so. Like the pattern on
a child's top which wanders widdershins while the top spins the
opposite way, the display slid slowly round me.

I drank those images greedily. I couldn't help myself. Absolutely
nothing else existed, so those images were everything to me—and I
guess this printed them pretty deep in me, the way that I'd printed
my special image into the fabric of the Worm a while back.

If I'd had eyes to close, to shut those images out, maybe I could
have avoided having to travel the psylink to Eeden as the cat's paw
of the Worm. Maybe I could have become one of the ordinary river-
dead, reliving my own life and other lives.

But I couldn't, so I didn't.

How to convey those images? They were shapes of power, if I can
put it that way. They weren't pictures. Yet they conveyed knowledge, and this knowledge seemed to pop into my mind as if from
nowhere. It was just as if the Worm knew exactly how my own

thoughts were woven together, so it presented suitable patterns—and these immediately became garments of thought which I was wearing within me.

Stolen garments! The Worm had filched these from the line where they hung: that line linking Sons of Adam (now deceased) with the Godmind far away.

I began to understand the psylink. Somewhat. Perhaps "understand" is too ambitious a term. Say rather that I knew how I would be using it in rather the same way that I knew how to talk, but couldn't for the life of me have said what went on in my mouth when I spoke.

I was aware, as if the knowledge had been born with me, of how the Godmind had sent out ships with seeds of life on board. When our parent ship arrived here, its seeds were adapted to our world. Out of the substance of the ship, bodies were bred, and minds were printed upon these bodies: minds which the Godmind could fish back to Eeden when the bodies died. The Godmind could fish back all natural descendants of those first "artificial" colonists and replant their minds in artificial bodies, to live a second life back in Eeden; all, with the exception of those who were filtered out into the *Ka*-store of the Worm. And so the Godmind populated the universe with people, and brought back the knowledge thereof.

This was slightly at odds with what the Sons thought in their cruel and jumbled way. Andri had once told me that all of us were Eeden minds in puppet flesh. Not so! Only the first generation possessed manufactured bodies. Later generations were all genuine persons of *our* world. However, the psylink survived, and was passed down from generation to generation just like blue eyes or red hair.

Eeden must be getting kind of crowded by now, I remarked.

Ah, but those second-lives will also end, as soon as the bodies wear out.

What happens to their Ka*s after that? Do they just dissolve? Evaporate, what?*

Maybe, the Worm said in jolly vein, *the Godmind eats them. But I'll get you back, I promise, then you can tell me what the Godmind really is—and why it bothers with human beings at all.*

Why it bothers: what do you mean?

Consider: the Godmind uses people as its tools on distant planets; as its eyes and ears. Why bother, when it can send out machines so clever that they can build people? What's the plan? Where do people come into it? Who dreamed up the plan in the first place? And what about me? I was put here ages ago to stop intelligent life from blooming. Who put me here? Why? Okay, off you go, then!

Hey, I'm not ready! There are a zillion things I don't know.

Me neither. In at the deep end, say I.

Ho ho. That ought to have been *my* line. (With the caveat: "Just so long as there aren't any stingers in the water!")

By now the shapes of power had melted back into the blue. I received the *Ka* equivalent of a pat on the back. Needless to say, the gentlest of touches on a spinning top will send it skittering wildly away. . . .

I skittered; dizzyingly, a flutterbye blown by a storm.

A storm: oh yes, there *was* a storm in the vicinity. This was no storm of clouds and rain, of thunder and lightning. This was a turmoil in the blue nothingness; and thanks to those power-images, I knew the cause.

The psylink stretched away to Eeden like a long hawser mooring our world. Vibrations sped along this hawser. Where the hawser tethered our world, it splayed into a million separate fibres. A fair number of these hung loose. Tendrils of the black current, feelers of the Worm, blocked and parried many of these questing loose ends; there in what I now thought of as *Ka*-space. Others the Worm hung on to, knotting round them. This dance of thrust and riposte in *Ka*-space constituted the "storm". It caused a turbulence which hid any sight of far Eeden. I felt buffeted and battered.

What was the nature of these tendrils? Emptiness, nothingness. It seemed as if knots could be tied in nothingness; as though emptiness could be braided; as though strings could be formed by winding the void around itself—invisible strings as lengthy as thought itself.

Suddenly I was clear of the storm-front. I was a vibration travelling along the hawser. Actually, I felt I was two things at once. I was a wave; and I was a mote bobbing upon that wave. My bobbing (no, my *spin)* produced the wave whereon I travelled. Equally, what propelled me towards my destination was the twitching of the hawser, the fluid rhythm of the psylink.

A slim tendril of the black current had attached itself to me. This stretched out and out in my wake. By means of this I would find my way back to the *Ka*-store of the Worm . . . eventually, somehow, perhaps.

I wondered what Doctor Edrick was doing. Was he breaking open my bedroom door? Kidnapping Narya? Burning the house down in pique?

I would never know the answer. Not for a very long time, at least.

Eventually I might re-live a life which could tell me, if I ever got back to the Ka-store. Eventually: that might as well be never.

Was Edrick doing any of these things *now,* at this moment? It might only be a short while since I'd died; equally it could be hours or days. No units of time meant anything any longer. In the blue void of death, with no sun shining nor stars, there was no way to tell the time or measure distance.

I sped. I wasn't cold, I wasn't hot. I wasn't hungry, or even lonely. I was just me.

I tried to recapture the sense of completeness I'd known once before in the Ka-store, when I'd taken passage aboard other finished lives. I tried to enjoy the luminosity that floods a life when it's over. But this balm wouldn't come. For although I was dead, things weren't over yet. I couldn't re-live my life. I could only remember my life ordinarily; which is to say: not very well.

I sped through the nothing. If nothing happened soon, how much longer could I go on being me?

I really ought to have borne in mind what Andri told me about all those *babies'* bodies lying in cold caverns under Eeden waiting for dead Kas to return from the stars to occupy them. A full-blown artificial body awaiting me at journey's end wouldn't have been a bad exchange; but what happened next was downright humiliating.

The Worm had known what I was heading into. Obviously! And damn it, *I'd* known too, deep down. Yet I'd made believe that in my case things might be different, special. I was the secret agent of a junior god, wasn't I? A secret agent is a bold adventurer. She's competent. She's always on the move. She's able to look after herself.

All of a sudden I was in some other place. Bright lights were blinding me. *Things* were interfering with me. And I was feeble. And I was tiny.

I screamed.

Don't babies always scream?

Part Two
CHERUBS

I was racing through redwood forest as fast as my little girl's legs would carry me. The ground was scant of undergrowth, naked of boltholes or brakes where I could hide. Between each massive trunk was so much open space that it was easy to spot my fleeing shape from way behind. Even the lowest branches were far too high up for a little girl to leap and scramble into.

A metallic macaw watched me from a high perch.

"Help, they'll kill me!" I called to it raggedly.

The mech-bird bobbed its head, as much as to say, "Message acknowledged!" but it did no more. Or, if the bird did speak to the Godmind, it didn't bother telling me so. I pounded on, although my legs were turning rapidly to jelly.

If only I could get out of line of sight! Then maybe I could slip behind a trunk and slide around it while the bloody-minded boys— Sons of the Truesoil, all of them—raced past . . . Well, *that* wouldn't work.

I glanced back.

The hunting pack of little boys had strung out, but that didn't mean I was outdistancing them. They were running relays now. As soon as those in the lead tired a bit, they dropped back to a quick trot, letting the former laggards sprint ahead. Me, I had no choice but to *race,* fit to burst my heart.

My glance excited them.

"Witchette!" taunted a voice. "Wormy wormy witchette!"

Witchette, indeed! Not even a full-blown witch. They were really playing the part of small boys now. Maybe they thought if they kept up a pretence of fun and games, the Godmind would condone their antics. But in those young bodies nestled evil, squalid, adult minds, bent on tearing me to pieces.

The Godmind couldn't be so dumb, even if this bunch of cherubs *were* Flawed Ones, from our own notoriously disadvantaged world. Maybe the Godmind wanted me ripped to shreds.

"River-bitch!"

"Water-witch!"

In another minute my heart would crack. My lungs would burst. My legs would flop. How far did this fucking forest stretch? Right the way across California? Where was the next service-hatch?

At least those squalid little boys couldn't possibly rape me before killing me—not unless they raped me with a stick.

Hey, wait a bit! If they did start in on torturing me instead of killing me straight off, and if they took their time over it, and if the Godmind did decide to butt in, then I could probably be patched together again. I simply couldn't let them kill me. I didn't know enough yet, to die.

Come to think of it, what better way to goad these Sons into tormenting me than by sneering at their prepubescent impotence? By taunting their lost manhood, their vanished virility? That ought to rankle.

Well, *I'd* been the one to think of rape; with a stick. . . .

I saw a fallen stick, the size of my arm. (Which wasn't very large.) A cudgel, no less! Skidding to a halt, I hoisted the stick. I needed both hands to hold it. Stumbling to the nearest trunk, I backed up against the bark and waited for the boys to come, ready to swing my weapon.

A fair bit of wood was lying around hereabouts. Enough for a bonfire? Suppose I could incite them to burn me, the way they burned witches back home? That should set off a fire-alarm and bring the Godmind's bits and pieces rushing to the rescue.

Oh hell and shit. Rape or the fire; or both.

One puzzle remained: *how* had they rumbled me? Or had I been set up?

The boys straggled to a halt in a half-circle. They were panting heavily.

* * *

"The Flawed Ones": that was how cherubs from our world were known, here in Eeden upon the planet Earth.

Earth was the name for this world of our origin; I knew that now. Eeden was merely the name of the reception area set aside for us millions on millions of reborn cherubs: roughly speaking, half of the North American land-mass (which is considerable).

In choosing the name Eeden, the Godmind had been "mobilizing a precognitive myth". So I'd been told by my Cyclopedia.

Precog myths were tales dreamed up by our primitive ancestors on Earth which forecast the far future—in other words the present time, the now—and which were used as guidelines to bring it into being.

One such myth concerned a God who would be born of flesh. And lo, the Godmind had evolved out of the thinking-machines conceived by human brains, built by human hands.

Another myth concerned Eeden: the paradise which lay ahead in time. The ancient spinners of precog myth back in the past were exiled from paradise by the span of years yawning between then and now. Yet one day, they dreamed, paradise would become a reality on Earth; and now it was so.

Precog myth also foresaw how the spirits of the dead would take up residence in another world, as cherubs. And so it came to pass, with the slight difference that it was the star-dead from other worlds in the galaxy who flocked home along the psylink to Eeden to be born again.

"Unless ye become as little children," declared the myth. Also: "And in the resurrection they shall neither marry nor bear babies." Our growth from babyhood was enormously speeded up compared with normal development, but our bodies quit growing short of puberty. We born-again cherubs all retained children's bodies life-long, till we died our second deaths. Such was the nature of this new flesh given us by the Godmind.

Outside of Eeden in the rest of Earth, people grew up normally to womanhood and manhood. Yet it was we cherubs who brought those ordinary mortals wisdom—by going out amongst them as the little aliens in their midst, the harvest of the galaxy, the perpetual children of the stars. "Out of the mouths of babes. . . ." There in the outside world we cherubs were adored, protected, cherished.

In another week's time I too was due to go outside. So this was the Sons' last chance to clobber me.

Maybe the Godmind had been watching me all this while, wondering what my plan was; and now it had decided to have me snuffed. Again, maybe not.

But I'm running ahead of myself—would that I could have equally outstripped my pursuers!

I'm running way ahead. . . .

When I first came out of *Ka*-space and became a baby, I was pretty confused. I was lying flappy, floppy and feeble on soft fabric in a low glass cradle. I was blinded by bright lights, I was assaulted by machines.

And these machines were most unlike any we had back home. These ones had as many soft parts as hard parts. What's more, they acted of their own accord, like living creatures.

I soon calmed down. A machine saw to that. It squirted a blue fog at me, and panic went away.

"Rejoice!" proclaimed a voice. "You are safe in the bosom of Eeden, as promised. Your new brain is programmed with Panglos, in which I'm speaking to you. You'll need to exercise your voice for fluency. For the present kindly blink thrice to signify yes, twice for no. Do you understand me?"

I blinked three times.

"Ex-cellent. Now: are you fully aware of your situation?"

Ah. They didn't know who I was, or where I came from!

This was a ticklish moment—and I don't just mean because of the tubes and other things tickling me, or the peculiar squirmy in-sucking sensation down in my crotch region. What sort of new arrivals *wouldn't* be fully aware of their situation? Presumably those from a world such as mine. How would the machines go about disposing of undesirable babies? Would knives descend? I felt like a fish hauled ashore, flopping helplessly, about to be gutted. But I had to chance my hand; I needed information.

So I blinked twice, for no.

"Acknowledged." This was a new voice. A crisper voice, as though there was a different type of mind behind it. "It's highly probable that you're from a flawed world where the Satan-Snake foretold by precog myth has confused or corrupted my people, correct?"

Deciding to go along with the voice, I blinked: yes.

"Since you agree with that analysis, I can assume that my heritage still remains intact on your world. So: do you struggle to defeat the Snake?"

Yes, I lied. (Well, that was true of half of my world. The nasty half.)

"Are you from a waterworld of islands?"

No.

"Are you from the western shore of a long river bounded by wild ocean, precipice and desert?"

Yes.

I wasn't born in the west, but surely I could pass for a westerner. . . .

"Identified: World 37."

The next question really caught me off balance. (In so far as any baby lying supine can be caught off balance!)

"Nearest large town?" And the voice started to reel off a list of western towns. The Godmind knew more about our world than I'd expected. Yet of course that figured: it had been receiving new arrivals for centuries. Luckily for me the string of names began in the north. This gave me a few seconds to decide which foul hole in the south (which I knew at first hand) to plump for.

". . . Adamopolis?"

". . . Dominy?"

"Pleasegod?"

I blinked yes.

"Acknowledged." And at once a different voice commenced my orientation. This last voice belonged to my Cyclopedia.

Cyclopedia! Once again I'm running ahead!

At this point I think I'd be well advised to capsule the set-up on Earth quickly so that I can get on with my story. (By the end of *The Book of the River* I flatter myself that I'd learned a few of what the Ajelobo critics call "narrative techniques".)

So I'll allow a couple of pages for *your* orientation, gentle reader; then it's right on to my meeting with Yorp the Exotic and his gang. And if you think I'm being stingy about facts you might need to know if you go to Eeden when you die, believe me, by the time I've finished gabbing on you'll know all you need to know, for what the information's worth. If Eeden's where you're headed—and of course you might not be—you'll arrive so wised-up compared with the majority of cherubs that you might be well advised to act dumb; otherwise the Godmind may just grow suspicious of your motives.

* * *

We aliens were all reborn in baby bodies at one or other of numerous crèches scattered throughout Eeden. The host bodies were continuously being produced in underground bio-vats by machines of the Godmind, like pie crusts in a giant bakery awaiting the filling to be popped into them. After manufacture, these bodies "lived" in a state of "ego-suspension", awaiting our influx down the psylinks from wherever. On being "activated" the new bodies grew greedily and rapidly—such was the nature of our new flesh—till within about eight weeks we were toddling competently and within a couple of years we were fully-fledged boys and girls of apparent age eight or nine years. At that apparent age we would stay.

We all spoke Panglos, the polyglot world tongue of Earth designed by the Godmind long ago before the seedship that settled our world even set off. Even today our own native language isn't too different from Panglos. Panglos isn't a language that drifts easily, and our own speech certainly hasn't drifted far at all compared with the home languages of the Exotics.

(Exotics: there I go again. Getting ahead of myself.)

As soon as we grew into toddlers, we were shunted out of the ever-busy crèches to one of many minivilles. These were miniature towns, under weather domes, all built to toddler size and copied from various ancient cities of Earth. (Cities which themselves had been rebuilt by the Godmind, life-size, on their original sites for the ordinary Earth folk to live in.) I myself spent this period of adjustment in Little Italia, first in Classical Roma, then in adjacent Renaissance Roma. All this time I was accompanied by my personal Cyclopedia, a mobile fact-machine and nursemaid on which I could ride, a-saddle, whenever my sprouting young limbs grew weary.

Then it was goodbye to the minivilles, and out into Nature: a nature which was wild yet benign and well supervised. No Cyclopedia accompanied me now. Scattered across the surface of Eeden, instead, were large numbers of service-hatches providing nourishment and knowledge and most anything we wanted, including transport through underground tubes to any other part of Eeden. Assorted beasts and birds, which were actually machines (called Graces, Loving Graces) kept an eye on the land and on us.

Out in Nature, roaming, we young aliens got to know the smell and touch of the Earth—and oh, the marvel (for me) of the waxing and waning of the giant Moon in the sky! We also got to know each other better; and got to know ourselves, discovering what sort of little boy or girl we were each growing up to be.

Our host bodies were made in vats, as I say, by bio-machines. But they were all different. Thus I was the only one in my particular crèche group with almond eyes, and on my head grew straight, jet-black hair. (Though no darkling hair would ever grace the rest of my anatomy.) My skin was cinnamon in hue, and I was inclined to be plump if I didn't watch my diet. On the other hand I was fairly tall for a child, which compensated for this. Though I would never be a woman, at least I was female.

I suppose we cherubs could as easily have been sexless. But the Godmind liked the idea of us being little boys and girls, just as it liked the idea of the ancient cities of Earth. On first arrival in Eeden our *Ka* triggered the host body's anatomy into a male or female shape—which was the reason for that uncomfortable squirming sensation I'd felt early on. Obviously this permitted us cherubs a certain limited amount of eroticism, between friends, if we felt so inclined. But not very much. The mind might be willing; the body wasn't quite up to it. Especially not in the case of boys.

I'd *liked* my old body; I'd been at home in it! Yet I didn't feel that this new body of mine was unbearably strange. Definitely it was the same sort as we had back home. However, for some of us cherubs—the Exotics—a body of this kind was weird. Which brings me to Yorp and his gang, whom I met while I was wandering through California.

I'd spent the previous night on a beach, unable to tear myself away from my first sight of the moonlit Pacific Ocean. How much calmer and warmer a sea this seemed than our own wild northerly waters back home! When I had laid me down to sleep on a raised bar of that wide soft strand—edged by sculpted turrets and jagged crests of rock—the ocean had lain, too, flat as a silken sheet.

When I woke to the half-light before dawn, I was soaking wet and spluttering. A flood of water was pouring around my sandy hammock, trying to drown me. A breeze had sprung up. Waves were rolling in. Worse, most of the beach had vanished. It was just as if the world had tilted, sloshing the water towards me. All of a sudden I was in the midst of the sea. How could a breeze push the water so? Maybe great monsters of the deep could reach me now! Big brothers to the little scuttling crabs I'd been watching a few hours earlier. . . .

Plodging and stumbling, I fled to what was left of the beach and found shelter by a spur of rock. I stripped off my shorts and blouse and hung them up. At least the wind was warm.

I was pacing about waiting for my clothes to dry and for the light to brighten a bit; my stomach was starting to grumble and I was wondering which way it was to the nearest service-hatch for breakfast—when I noticed this shape approaching along the strip of sand. It moved through the half-light in quick darts and dashes and crouches. It looked like a giant crab, carrying its home on its back.

"Hey!" I called, alarmed, and the crab tossed back a hood.

Visualize a seven-year-old boy. He was on the skinny side, with blue eyes and a cotton-top of blond hair. The boy wore a flappy brown burnous, so that the hood enclosed his head in a dark cave, and his sandalled feet stuck out of the bottom of the cloak like scrawny claws.

The boy scuttled closer. He hunkered down, pulled in his head, drew up his feet and disappeared inside the hooded cloak entirely.

"Hullo. Been for a swim?" said his voice from within.

"Not likely! I was sleeping, and the wind shoved the sea right up the sand."

"It did what? Oh, I get it! You're from a world without a moon. Without a big one, anyhow."

"We didn't have any moon at all back home."

Somewhere inside his big hood he chuckled. His chuckle sounded like one of our croakers around the Bayou back home, vibrating its throat pouch. "A big moon drags a bulge of ocean round the world with it. It's called a tide. That's why you got wet."

"Tide." I recognized the word. Of course; my brain knew it. Alas, I hadn't thought of applying this knowledge when I lay down on that dry and mellow beach with the sea decently distant. "Damn." I felt stupid.

"I'm Yorp," said the boy. He poked his head out.

"Yaleen," said I.

We got on fine together. I soon told him I was a Flawed One. "I've met a few of those," he said. "But not *nice* ones, like you . . ."

Maybe that was why we got on so well. I was crippled and flawed on arrival in Eeden because the Worm had scrambled up our heritage. I did my best to act deprived, which gave me a good excuse to quiz my Cyclopedia about things I might otherwise have been expected to know in advance; though I never pushed my luck.

Yorp, on the other hand, had always expected to wind up here. His people possessed the heritage of Earth unbrokenly, and here was his goal. But I could fit into my new body without any undue awkwardness. The heritage of Earth—the foreknowledge—hadn't helped *Yorp* any, when it came to donning an earthly form so very different from his former body. He was hamstrung.

Yorp had run into other cherubs from his world, but they had all adjusted far more easily. This only made matters worse and more poignant for Yorp; he felt doubly a stranger. Perhaps the root trouble was that those others from his world had always been humans at heart. Yorp hadn't; he had been truly Other.

Till now Yorp had been hanging out entirely with Exotics from various worlds, who felt the same way. So I was a sort of psychological bridge for him; I was an abnormal normal.

This all spilled out as we talked.

"Mine was a heavy world," sighed Yorp. "Here I feel just like a puff of dandelion-down about to float away.

"Mine was a darkly cloudy world, with the thickest storming gases. Here, there just doesn't seem to be anything to breathe! Though of course I do breathe easily. . . .

"And now I've only two legs! I feel as if at any moment I'll fall over!"

We were making our way together to the service-hatch. And a crab-like sideways way it was too! The sun was up in the sky by now, shining from the same inland direction as we were heading. To my eyes there seemed nothing unduly bright about the sun of Earth. But Yorp flinched from it. His cherub eyes were adapted to it, just like mine. He never acted as if they were. He was a crepuscular person, a person of the dusk and the pre-dawn—happiest then. If his new eyes could have seen in the dark, he might have lived nocturnally. But they couldn't; so he didn't.

On Yorp's world, the parent seedship made huge changes in those multi-million-letter words of life, the genes. The resulting bodies were squat, bulky and armoured with two arms and four legs; the tough hide was beautifully marbled in distinctive pastel shades. The leathery bellows-lungs breathed poison gases under pressure. The crystalline eyes saw heat as well as light. The genitals were hidden in a horny slot. Oh yes, Yorp was exotic. Now he was just a shadow of his former self, a crab robbed of its shell, with two legs broken off. (I hadn't at this stage seen the animal called a "tortoise", which could pull its head right inside its shell!)

When we got to the service-hatch I met his gang: Marl and Ambroz, Leehallee and Sweets. All of them felt equally out of step in different ways.

Leehallee and Sweets had been merpeople of a shallow water world. Now, as though the plug had been pulled on them, they were exiled on dry land. They grieved that they could no longer breathe water and swim with the fish, like fishes. The swimming ability of the human body seemed a joke to them; and the need to keep an earthly body dry for comfort went against their basic instincts. Nor could they now echo-locate, and see (quite literally) through each other. Now they could only see surfaces. When they spoke they heard no echoes from within. For them a screen had come down, isolating them inside their new bodies. (In this respect their sadness was the opposite of Yorp's; *he* felt terribly exposed.) These two girls went naked. Even bare flesh was too much clothing of the inner person.

Marl, on the other hand, was *grounded* on the Earth. He and his kind had been fliers: hollow-boned, hugely airy-chested, with great wings sprouting above their skinny arms.

They lived in eyries in honeycombed mountains high above a wind-whipped marshy world whose surface was plagued by vicious little beasties swarming and slaughtering each other.

To the tune of the winds blowing through the organ pipes of porous cliffs they warbled songs. On the treasured bone-flutes of the dead they piped the music of their ancestors. From one cliffy minaret to the next they whistled messages.

And now Marl the airy flier was a heavy little runt. He'd been condensed. His voice had sunk way down the scale. Highpitched back home, his name had been a bird's mewing cry. These days it sounded more like a clod of soil. Yet Marl still clad himself in a coat of bright feathers: borrowed plumes.

And Ambroz? Ambroz was the most exotic of all.

His world was as flat as a platter. Only huge, deep-rooting vegetables broke the monotony; and in the atmosphere of his world there existed a curious form of energy-life—which was attracted, devastatingly, to any motion faster than a snail's pace or the growth of a plant. Ambroz's people surmised that the surface of the planet itself, over millions of years, had been rubbed down by the action of these energy-beasts. They surmised, too, that this energy life was somehow related to the giant local vegetables, or even generated by them. If a cabbage can have a free-ranging *Ka!* Perhaps the energies had been born aeons earlier as a defence against grazing animals. Of which none now remained. This wasn't proven, nor was there any communication with these energies, if indeed they were alive at all.

A world where there was no way to move without being blasted —and not much point in moving, since everywhere was just as flat! The decision to colonize such a place with plant-people—who would stay rooted and immobile most of their lives, only occasionally uprooting and waddling very slowly indeed—might have seemed a cruel joke on the part of the Godmind. Yet the inner lives of Ambroz and his kin had been vastly rich and contemplative. Besides, there was always the promise of an afterlife when they would all be able, at last, to move freely about . . . The plant-people communicated with each other by means of "radio waves", a sort of heliograph signal employing not light but other invisible vibrations.

Now that he was in Eeden Ambroz could walk wherever he wished, through a world full of ups and downs, and ins and outs; and he was disenchanted. For no journey brought him any closer to himself. Ambroz's cherub body was tubby and brownskinned, his hair was curly black, the pupils of his eyes were chips of coal; and he wore a grubby blue dhoti.

Over the next few weeks we all wandered about together, mostly on foot, occasionally taking capsules through the tubes from one service-hatch to another chosen at random. Generally we avoided other cherubs. We visited mountain and seacoast, desert and forest.

And we talked, of course. I told them about my world, though without betraying myself. They told me more about theirs. Marl and Yorp and the two mergirls talked most. Ambroz was inclined to be taciturn, verging on surly. Besides, there wasn't much to tell about a flat platter of vegetables; and his inner life and musings remained his own.

I did manage to coax Yorp out of his shell once or twice. He even skinny-dipped with me in a lonely lake.

I learned from him (what I could have asked my Cyclopedia or any service-hatch, if I'd been a bolder spy) that the Godmind didn't have any precise location. The Godmind was a whole set of communicating systems buried all over the planet. There was no single centre, no headquarters. So much for one half-baked idea, of breaking into its den clutching a hammer. (But why should I try to smash it? The Godmind didn't seem particularly malign, in the way the Worm had pictured it. Did it?)

I also learned from Yorp that the whole colonization programme had been—and possibly *still* was being—launched not from the Earth itself but from the huge Moon out in space. Thereafter I used to stare up at the Moon even more avidly, when it was in the sky and when the sky was clear, hoping to see some fire or flash of light; but I never did.

"How do you get to visit the Moon?" I asked Yorp.

He cringed. "Visit it? There isn't any air on the Moon! The Moon isn't heavy enough to hold air—it's even worse than here!" He retreated inside his burnous; I'd undone my good work.

One afternoon we were camping on the edge of redwood forest when Ambroz broke a broody silence which had lasted for the best part of two days.

"There doesn't seem very much *direction*," he groused. I assumed he was grumbling about our aimless wanderings. But no.

He went on: "What a huge purposive *thrust* there has to be behind this colonization project! Yet what's it all for, Yaleen? So that we cherubs can eat lotuses a while in Eeden, then dispense our alien wisdom out among the Earthfolk—who are all living in a huge *museum!* Is that the only way to unify and conquer the cosmos? By turning people into toys on strings?"

"Conquer?" I asked. "Who's conquering?" This was getting interesting.

"The Governor. The Godmind. It's using people as von Neumann machines to fill as many worlds as it can."

"As what?"

He bulled right on. "Why doesn't it use machines pure and simple?"

This was something that the Worm had wondered.

"What's the point in cluttering up the universe with junk?" asked Yorp.

"I suppose we shouldn't complain," said Sweets. "If there hadn't been any colonies, we wouldn't have been alive!"

Ambroz was really worked up after his long silence. He was like a constipated hen, nerving itself to lay an egg.

"The clue is *Ka*-space," he said. "People die. And people have *Ka*s. *Ka*s can come back here very quickly to spill the beans on how it's all going out there. Radio messages would take hundreds of years. Thousands! *Ka*-space is a way of keeping in touch."

"One-way only," said Marl. "The Godmind doesn't talk back to its family of worlds."

"I've thought about this a lot," said Ambroz. "Half my life, it seems! So have a group of us on my world. Perhaps it's because we couldn't move about, and because of the way we communicated . . . but we suspect that when *we* were made, we were made as a sort of model of the colonies. Each of us a separate world unto ourselves, but able to project ourselves—and thus try to plumb all sorts of philosophical depths. Old Harvaz the Cognizer came up with this theory, and I was working on it till I died. Some of us swore we would keep this secret till we could walk about freely and find an answer."

"Go on," said I. "You can walk about now."

"Well, the colony programme seems like . . . like the building of a very big radio telescope—made of *minds!* Like a giant array with an enormous base-line spanning hundreds of light years."

"What's a radio telescope?" Leehallee wanted to know.

"It's a machine for listening to things very far away and very long ago. If you have two of those a good distance apart but slaved to each other, you get much sharper reception. Suppose you had a hundred of them whole star-distances apart . . . they'd be too far apart to keep in touch or act in concert using radio waves. But suppose you could build your machine of *minds* linked through *Ka*-space, and then switch it on—"

"Wouldn't you have to kill everybody on all the worlds, to do that? So that they'd all be dead?" asked Sweets.

"Would you?" cried Ambroz. "Would you indeed? A star which explodes lights up the whole galaxy for a day. Does a species dwelling on a hundred worlds, all of whose minds explode at once, light *something else?* Something far vaster? Universal?"

"Go on," I encouraged him.

"Well, I suspect—in fact I'm sure—that when the Godmind has all its colony pieces in place, when it has *enough* of them—"

We were interrupted by the noisy arrival of a party of boys. Six or seven boys rushed out of the forest towards our impromptu camp, whooping and shouting. They were naked to the waist, above buckskin breeches, and their chests and cheeks were daubed with slashes of pigment. They wore sweatbands with feathers stuck in them round their foreheads.

The leader ran directly up to Marl, tore a plume loose from his bird costume and jammed the trophy into his headband. He pranced around us, stamping his feet and hollering in triumph. His followers capered after him.

"Hey!" cried Marl, springing up as if to take flight into the sky.

Leehallee shrieked a little. Yorp shrunk into his burnous. Ambroz went rigid.

I jumped up. "What's with you guys? Cut it out!"

The boys straggled to a halt. Their leader squared up to me. He had fair hair, keen blue eyes in a thin pinched face. Those eyes looked rather mad. He was tall and gangly but I thought I could take him if I had to, given the edge on weight.

Of course I couldn't take all of them, and most of Yorp's gang weren't going to be much help in a fight. Though why the hell should it come to a fight? We cherubs were all grown-ups. This was the first sign of trouble I'd come across in Eeden.

"Okay," the leader said evenly, "just a bit of *fun*. By way of saying hullo." I didn't care for the way he said "fun"; he fairly snarled the word.

He gazed at me hard. "Should we not all enjoy bliss in Eeden? The bliss that the Godmind promised us! How better to bless the Godmind than by being perfectly the children He has made us? Until our serious mission of sainthood starts!"

Oh dear. He *was* nuts.

He returned the stolen feather to Marl, with a sardonic bow and a sneer on his face. Marl managed to grasp the feather, but only just. The other lads applauded and hooted until their leader clapped his hands for silence; which he got.

"Eeden is the promised Truesoil!" the boy shouted. And my heart sank further. I knew all too well what sort of people talked about Truesoil. None other than my old friends, the obsessed and vicious Sons of Adam!

"Are we not the Godmind's best beloveds?" the boy harangued his team. "Those who struggled, while most other worlds dwelled easy in his bosom?"

There was, I decided, something horribly familiar about this *particular* boy. . . .

. . . whipping up fervour, to win followers—and thus win approval of the Godmind? Or to persuade himself that Eeden really matched his zealous expectations, when in fact he had suddenly become a minnow in an ocean?

"If I was as heavy as I *used* to be," I heard Yorp growl from his burnous. His head emerged. "And if I had my armour on, and all four legs to bear me. . . ." He adopted a crouching stance. *"You!"* he bellowed. "How dare you talk about other worlds having it easy!

How dare you burst in on us! What do you know, you painted savage?" He was really incensed. This was a new side to him; but believe me, did I welcome it!

The leader of the boys pursed his lips. "Savages? Ah, I see. Here we have a sophisticate. So what if we're savages?" he snarled. "We'll wear our savagery with pride in the service of the Godmind! As His true soldiers!"

"What does the Godmind need soldiers for?" asked Sweets.

"Why don't you just go away?" sighed Ambroz.

"Are we not all true Sons and Daughters of the Godmind here?" the boy demanded, staring at each of us in turn.

I was beginning to wonder whether it was pure chance that this band of Sons had turned up at our camp. I fervently hoped that none of Yorp's gang would utter my name. . . .

"I wasn't aware," drawled Ambroz, "that the Godmind is greatly bothered what we think of it. Unless you lot happen to be its special buddies, and can advise me otherwise?"

"You: what's your name?"

Don't anybody say my *name!*

"Not that it's any of your business, but I'm called Ambroz." Weak, weak! You should never answer the questions of a bully. "Go fry your face" is the best reply. Maybe Ambroz realized this, a little late, since he added, "What's *yours?*"

Proudly the boy said, "Edrick." His followers all nodded, as though that name said everything.

Which to me, it did.

If Edrick was here, then he hadn't survived my murder by too long; which was nice news. Less nice, to run across him again light years away from home. Since there were millions of us cherubs bumming around Eeden, this roused my deepest suspicions. Still, coincidences happen. Sometimes our lives are chockful of that delightful ingredient. I kept a pan-face.

"And you? What's *your* name?" Edrick was addressing me now.

My heart thumped. (Never mind, he couldn't hear it thumping.) "Go fry your face," said I.

Yorp glanced at me oddly; and I realized that I'd spoken deeper and rougher than usual. I'd altered my voice in case Edrick somehow recognized it.

For a moment I thought Edrick was going to assault me then and there; or order his troops to thrash me. Instead, he sucked in his breath.

"Not very friendly, are we? The Godmind wishes us all to live together as little brothers and sisters, doesn't He? Let's try again."

"How do you know what it wants?" I retorted. "Did it tell you to come here and proclaim all over us?"

"Yeah, how do *you* know?" Sweets sang out; and from the speed with which Edrick swung to confront her, I decided a few things.

I'd told the Cyclopedia my real name. And why not? As far as Cyclopedia or Godmind were concerned I hailed from Pleasegod in the west. The only way Edrick could have come hunting for me personally was if he'd told his own Cyclopedia a hell of a lot about me and how I was such an agent of evil, and if the Godmind's bits and pieces had done some checking, and sent him. In that case, he should have known what I looked like, right off. *My* Cyclopedia had always been able to recognize me without any bother. Probably I was safe. Edrick's arrival was an unfortunate coincidence. Edrick just wanted to browbeat anyone; Sweets would fit the bill.

Yet . . . could Edrick and I possibly have some sort of affinity for one another? Not a pleasant kind of affinity, I hasten to add! Maybe this sort of thing happens when you murder someone, or when you think long enough and hard enough about killing them. This perverse affinity had guided him here, without his being aware of it.

Edrick glared at Swets, but he didn't answer her. I'm sure he would have done so, if he'd had some special commission from the Godmind to fulfil. His troops would expect it of him—all six of them. (How were the mighty fallen!)

At this point one of the other boys chipped in.

"I've figured it out, Ed . . . I bet they're Exotics, right? They think they're better than us. That's why they won't tell you their exotic names—'cept for fatso in the blue sheet there. Bet you can't get a human tongue around their names." He spat a gob of saliva on the soil.

Edrick looked pained at the coarseness of his follower. Or did he? Spitting their juices at the Truesoil seemed to be a bit of a habit with Sons. Edrick knit his brows. Was he trying to connect something, remember something? Slowly he turned back towards me.

I chose my words carefully in the hope that my companions would realize I was giving them a message, about *me.* "That's true, we're *all* Exotics here. All of us, aren't we, Gang? And proud of it."

Alas, things went downhill from there.

Yorp had said how his people grew body-armour on their heavy world. He hadn't said why exactly . . . I'd associated these two facts as though one explained the other. Heavy worlds, heavy bodies.

Yet if everything weighed heavier, armour was the last thing you would want to haul around. You would only do that if you *needed* to, because of vicious beasts you might have to fight. You would only wear armour if rough-houses tended to happen. . . .

And Yorp was a true native of his world.

He gave vent to the sort of battlecry a giant male croaker might utter if in dispute over a lady monstrosity of that ilk. "Yup! Yup! Yup!" Lowering his head, and almost running on all fours, Yorp charged at Edrick.

Edrick was taken by surprise. Yorp knocked the wind right out of him and bowled him over.

But Yorp was of slight build here on Earth. The next boy he rushed at was forewarned, and easily clinched with him. A third boy began to thump Yorp viciously.

With a cry of, "Come on, Gang!" I jumped to Yorp's rescue. A few flurrying moments later the whole lot of us were tangling with Edrick's troops, with greater or lesser success. Ambroz surprised me with his speed and vigour. In the midst of tripping someone, he flashed me a grin: "Here's a *reason* for moving!"

But Leehallee was squirming on the ground, nursing a bloody nose; and Marl wasn't doing much except flap his arms frantically. Perhaps he feared they might snap in half if he actually hit anyone.

Edrick was up, recovering his wind.

He jabbed a finger across the mêlée. "That one! Catch her, hold her! She's from *our* world! She's a witch!"

I took off as fast as I could for the woods. This wasn't an act of cowardice. The odds on our gang winning the fight were lousy. At least this way—I told myself—I would lead trouble away from Leehallee and the others. Maybe they would be able to summon help.

Supposing Edrick's arrival *was* a coincidence, how on Earth had he rumbled me?

I sprinted.

Backed up against the tree, I swung my club slowly to and fro.

"So who's first?" I sang out to the surrounding Sons. "Come along, little boys! Can't kiss me, so you'd better kick me, eh? Truesoil is, you can't do nothing that *real* men can do. Can't shove your precious squirters anywhere, no more. 'Cos they're soft as worms, for ever and ever. You must be *burning* with frustration!"

Enraged, one Son rushed me. I swung. Rather to my surprise my club caught him full in the mouth. Wailing and clasping his face, dribbling blood and bits of tooth (I think), he stumbled back.

I jeered: "Ya! Ya!"

"*Ya*leen, you mean!" snapped Edrick. "That's who you are! Why don't you use your full name as your warcry, Yaleen?"

"Who's she?" I retorted.

"She's you. Knew you were of our world, soon as you sneered at me *proclaiming.*" Edrick was still panting. "Nobody else would have used that word. Only in a *Ka*-theodral does one proclaim." (So that was it! Me and my mouth.) "Why pretend you're an Exotic, unless you're really a witch of the east? And who's the witch of the east most likely not to want me to know her?"

"Why would you be chasing after witches, whatever they are?" I swished my cudgel. Another Son had tensed up to spring—he untensed again. "Is the Godmind holding a witch-hunt?"

If so, I'd be well advised to get myself killed as quickly as possible; and goodbye to any fancy notions of being nursed back to health by Loving Graces . . . At least then I'd be on my way back home along the psylink to the *Ka*-store. Perhaps, maybe.

"I said, is the Godmind shitting bricks about witches?"

"Blasphemer! Why should the Godmind worry about the mildew on a single leaf? Yet His dutiful gardeners will strip that leaf for Him!" (Ah, so the Godmind wasn't behind this. Back to Plan A, alas: slow torture.) "I know verily which witch you are, to speak so vilely! The Godmind will reward us, Brothers. She was an agent of the Satan-Snake until I stopped her tricks! But she evaded my questioning; and maybe those questions are still worth asking!"

Edrick couldn't possibly suspect that I was here on Earth as an agent of the Worm. Would I be likely to babble that under torture?

"Reward you?" I hooted. "The Godmind doesn't care a shit about you. Or about the rest of the human race!"

Edrick spread his hands wide in appeal. "How can you call all this we see about us here in Eeden, *not caring?* This fulfilment of the Godmind's promises! This blessed land!"

If only these wretched boys hadn't burst in on our brainstorming session. Ambroz had spent half his life arriving at his conclusion: the telescope theory, the construction of a *Ka*-lens of galactic size.

But could he ever prove it? Perhaps only the black current was equal to that task. . . .

Where were my friends, anyway? Where was help?

"How *can* you?" Edrick cried again and again. He seemed genuinely dismayed. Maybe he was just being rhetorical, to work himself up. "What do you mean, the Godmind doesn't *care?*"

Maybe I shouldn't have mentioned the matter.

"Oh, Eeden's *tidy,*" I said quickly, putting a sneer into my voice. "It's a lot tidier than your *minds,* you bunch of. . . ." And I said a rude word.

They rushed me.

They got on with their fun. Pretty soon I was screaming and finding how very difficult it is to faint when you really want to.

The fact that this was only a host body they were wrecking was, believe me, no consolation. All nerve endings functioned very nicely, thank you. Nor was it of much comfort that on this occasion Edrick lacked equipment such as a fingerscrew. I won't go into what they did to me. I've no wish to relive it. Suffice it to say that what seemed like a week later ingenious new pains stopped happening, leaving only the ones already in residence to carry on. But I hadn't spoken—I'd only screeched. When the symphony of pain changed key, I thought maybe it was bonfire time. I rather hoped it was.

A hawser squeals and groans when a boat tries to snap it in a gale. Then the gale drops and the hawser goes slack. So it was with my mind. With the decrease in the force of agony, my mind went slack at last. I faded out.

To awaken in a bath of fire!

No actual flames were dancing about me. The fire was inside. The fire was me, my body. The slightest movement hurt me so much I tried not to breathe; but that was impossible.

Above: tiers of branches and blue sky. Then something bulky got in the way. A bristly muzzle dipped. Crystal mech-eyes looked into mine. A mech-deer? A mech-bear? A Loving Grace, at any rate!

"They've gone," it said. "I sent them away. It is over. You will be well."

A puff of green smoke issued from its nostrils. This time I actually felt pleasant as I conked out.

* * *

I spent the next three or four weeks—I wasn't sure exactly how long —lying in a tub of jelly in some underground service-chamber being repaired. Soft machines attended me. Latterly one of these asked me questions about the assault. These questions seemed aimed more at working out the hang-ups of the Sons, than in trying to uncover perfidy in me. I lied through my teeth.

They were still the same teeth as before. I vaguely recalled that Edrick had left my mouth intact so that he could question me; the Sons had concentrated on other targets.

Towards the end of my convalescence, Yorp and gang visited me. With the mother-hen machines present, I couldn't say much of importance. But I managed a bit, as if in private code.

"Shame they interrupted," I said. "It was getting interesting. Telescopes, eh?"

Ambroz, bless him, understood. "To light the darkness."

"And see *what?*"

"To the end, and start, of everything. Why it all *is*. People are a way of seeing things. If you stare at the sun, you burn your eyes out; though you *do* see, for a little while. What if you stare at a billion billion suns at once? It's said on my world that a moment of illumination outweighs an eternity of blind ignorance. It's also said that people are the eyes of God." Ambroz grinned crookedly. "We're His pupils. Yet we taught Him to exist in the first place."

"Excuse me," interrupted a machine. "Please clarify."

Ambroz shrugged. "Enough said. Time to go. Mustn't tire the invalid. But first, a kiss seems to be the custom hereabouts. Oh these soft and sloppy lips!" He bent over my jelly-tub and his mouth brushed my cheek. Quickly, very quietly, he whispered, "Forget it. It doesn't matter. If our friend needs the whole galaxy as its eye, it'll take a thousand centuries yet."

He straightened up. "Let's go," he said to Yorp.

The cotton-head Exotic wrapped his burnous about him. "Come along, Gang." I didn't see them again.

A week later I was hale and hearty, up and about.

A machine told me that I should take a tube to a certain service-hatch down south, to be sped from there to commence my cherubic duties. To be a starchild apostle, a focus of adoration. As many had been before me; so very many. I was to be routed by deep-tube under continent and ocean, to Venezia in Italia.

* * *

A few months later, like any good espionage agent, I was in deep with the rebel "Underground".

Such as it was.

Venezia is a city built in the sea. The city had drowned a millennium or more ago, but the Godmind had raised and rebuilt it. Indeed, so long ago had this happened that once again, where the tideline lapped, the city's stones were worn away like diseased teeth. Palace walls, balconies and turrets were fretted by brine spray. Before long, from the looks of it, the city would fall to pieces and sink for the second time. Though meanwhile, this vein of rot running through the fabric of Venezia seemed to make the place not moribund, but somehow more alive—like some ancient beast whose senses have sharpened amidst infirmity, who has grown subtle and tricky, and even entered on a second childhood of playfulness. And always within Venezia's sloshing foamy veins—reviving even as it destroyed—flowed the living sea.

At least that's what I *thought,* to start with! It took me a while to discover the truth about all this decadent decay: which was that the Godmind had rebuilt and embalmed the whole city in exactly this latterday condition—the way some people bore phony worm-holes in a piece of new furniture. Most other ancient cities had been rebuilt pristine and brand-new; not Venezia. It was rebuilt with worm-holes; with a skin disease grafted on to its walls.

It was one windswept early evening on the Zattere when I met Bernardino. Spray was whipping up on to that quay-road, slicking the worn stones. Clouds like enormous purple fists were punching each other landwards, over the sombre choppy waters. Blue lightning flickered out to sea. A skinny scruffy cat slunk for shelter.

(The Zattere: I shall mention the place-names of quays and canals, arching bridges and alleys and piazzas just as though you know as much about Venezia as you know of Aladalia or Guineamoy. Venezia *exists,* upon the planet Earth; be assured of that.)

Thunder growled. The Zattere was deserted . . . until a man came sneaking out of shadows. He was wearing soft shoes called sneakers, slacks, a blue jersey, a beret. Perhaps he was one of those who rowed the gondola canal-boats, stirring the water with a single oar from the stern, like a cook mixing a pudding. He had a ruddy jolly face.

I wasn't too worried about his furtive manner. What harm could come to us starchildren? Old black-shawled women called us "little angels". Gondoliers gave us free rides to wherever, whenever we wanted. Restaurant proprietors rushed to serve us the pick of their menus. All because our eyes had seen the sunlight of another star.

In return, we cherubs talked of our home worlds in the many "churches" of the Godmind: ornate buildings, these, full of paintings of cherubs and visions of *Ka*s flying to and fro in the heavens, and other stuff from precog myth. We had lodgings in grand hotels, and mingled and mixed as we chose.

In Venezia when a starchild died, he or she always received a fine send-off to the Isle of the Dead reserved for us out in the lagoon, San Michele by name. And his or her *Ka* flew away to the bosom of the Godmind, so it was said.

When a starchild died—of old age, after twenty or twenty-five years of extended childhood. . . .

That's right. Our new bodies weren't very long-lasting. The Godmind hadn't bothered to include that piece of information in the heritage of Earth; I only found this out from another cherub in the hotel where I was staying, *à propos* a death and a funeral. But said cherub wasn't bothered about it. "We go home to the Godmind."

I didn't believe it.

Oh, the twenty years bit I believed all right! But not the other.

"Excuse, Starchild," said the man. "May I speak? I heard *you* speak of your world in La Salute today."

"Oh did you? Have you been following me?"

He grinned. "But of course! How else do we meet? Don't worry, though."

"Why should I worry?"

He waved an idle hand. "Oh, it's such a dingy evening! Nobody about, not even an eye of the Godmind. A storm rises. A small body might be swept off this quay."

"Thanks a lot! I feel totally reassured."

My curiosity was teased; and surely that was his intention. The man wasn't behaving in an unfriendly manner, but he certainly wasn't adoring me, either.

"As a former sailor-woman," he said, "you must find life in our city very compatible, hmm? All these waterways!"

"Oh yes, wouldn't I make a fine gondolier? Lazing around the lagoon, ferrying artichokes and whatnot. Pity about my size."

"Yes, what a shame you can't sail boats here . . . But you never were a sailor-woman, *were* you? You lived on the west bank of your river. You kept well away from the water because of that thing in it which is the enemy of the Godmind, hmm? That's what you told us in church. We all know that old habits die hard—so naturally here you are hugging the waterfront!"

Oh hell and damn it.

The fellow chuckled. "You described your star-home in too paltry a way, you see. Not because you are poor at describing; oh no! The real reason is, you don't know *quite* enough about that west bank. And frankly you were more elegant in your account, poor as it was, than I could account for coming from a woman reared in such a sanctimonious pigsty. Then when you mentioned that river and the boats far away across it, your eyes lit up; though you pretended ignorance. So I followed you out of La Salute and saw you watch our boats plying the Grand Canal. You watched with delight—yet with a certain air of superiority, as though you had seen better boats; and sailed better boats yourself. Don't worry: no one but me would have noticed."

"What do you want?"

"That's easy. I'd love to know the real tale of your world. I'd love to know of *your* side of the river; the side where you actually lived. Here in Venezia over the years we have hosted several boy-cherubs from your eastern shores. Yet they don't know any river secrets. Never once has a river-woman come here as a cherub—not till now —which is odd."

No, it wasn't odd. When river-women died, they all went to the *Ka*-store of the black current. I said nothing, just looked at the man.

He said, "My friends and I follow these things with care. We take notes. Allow me to surmise, admittedly on insufficient evidence, but—" and he tapped his nose—"on superlative instinct, that perhaps you are the first riverwoman ever to reach the Earth?"

"You're assuming a lot, Mister."

"Bernardino is the name."

Had he heard about our war back home? Undoubtedly not! It was too recent. Cherubs were routed to destinations all over the Earth; and the Earth was a big place, with a million times more land than our own riverbank.

"I'm betting," said Bernardino, "that you're a riverwoman who is concealing this fact. Now why should that be? My friends and I would be most intrigued to learn more of this current, which fights the Godmind."

"Why would you be interested in something that's hostile to the Godmind?"

"Ah, I place myself in your hands! Perhaps, perhaps that's because my friends and I are opposed to the Godmind too? We've heard of the flaw in your world. We're hungry to learn more."

"Haven't you ever . . . ?" 'Met anyone from a flawed world before?' was what I was going to say. I checked myself. Probably they would have seen a few flawed cherubs in church now and then; but could they ever have accosted one with any confidence? Hardly! Cherubs who arrived on Earth from flawed worlds wouldn't be very proud of the flaws back home; and probably would be pretty ignorant of the cause—they certainly wouldn't be intimate with it.

How many worlds had the Worm said were flawed (according to the Godmind)? Half a dozen, wasn't it? Myself, I hadn't run into Flawed Ones from any world other than mine—on that single unforgettable occasion! Six worlds (plus mine) wasn't a large number. Proportionately there must be fewer *Ka*s reaching Earth from such worlds than from unflawed ones. I hadn't exactly gone searching for such flawed folk in Eeden; maybe I should have done . . . Oh yes indeed. Score one black mark against this secret agent, who had been a bit too secret! Now here I was in Venezia, where cherubs weren't nearly as thick on the ground. I could hardly buttonhole all my fellow cherubs at the hotel and ask each in turn, "Psst, are you a Flawed One?" The only way to root one out would be to spend all my spare time in churches listening to others speak, waiting for the odds to pan out eventually. But as a rule we cherubs never attended each other's "services". Eeden had been the place to get to know each other. In Venezia sensible cherubs got on enjoying their earthly afterlife.

Hmm. I'd been deficient.

Don't blame me. Look what happened when I didn't run into some Flawed Ones, from my own world. Flawed Ones from other places might have been even worse.

"I'm hungry," repeated Bernardino. "Are you perhaps hungry too? May I invite you to dinner?"

"I can get a meal anywhere, any time I want."

He kissed the tips of his fingers. "Yet not such a meal as this! Nor such conversation, either." His eyes twinkled. "Come and discover a conspiracy."

Without openly committing myself, I went with Bernardino. The promised conspiracy might give me a chance to stick my oar in and stir things.

We hurried through alleys across the narrow spit of land to the Accademia bridge; thence to the Piazza San Marco. Only a few old ladies were about in the Piazza, feeding flocks of pigeon-birds. A hundred or so pigeons clattered into the air at our approach. The majority of the birds wheeled around steeply to land again but a few peeled off and flapped up to perch on the Basilica where four galloping bronze horses pawed the sky. (A horse: imagine a goat as big as a cow. It's used for riding or racing.) Maybe one or two of those pigeons up there were eyes of the Godmind, mech-birds. . . .

Some preliminary stinging raindrops overtook us as we sped along the Riva degli Schiavoni. Way out over the water, rain was already sheeting down upon the Lido.

"Not much further, little lady!" Bernardino assured me.

We turned up the Calle delle Rasse between the twin buildings of the Royal Danieli. The narrow lane took us to Giacomo Square. Down some other Calle we hurried, and just as the clouds really opened we dodged inside the Doge's Tavern. We puffed and shook ourselves, then Bernardino led me upstairs to a private room.

The window overlooking the narrow Calle was shuttered tight. Illumination came from glass bulbs in sconces, each with a tiny bright fork of lightning captive inside. A table was set with glasses and cutlery, the starched tablecloth white as snow. Above a sideboard hung a tapestry featuring an antique war fought by men wearing suits of metal, many on horseback. I recalled the tapestry in the cabin of that schooner at Spanglestream, far away and long ago. Three men and two women stood chattering by the sideboard; they hushed as we entered. Here was another sort of conclave entirely. The five regarded me.

Bernardino beamed. "It's okay. I was right."

He was right about the meal too. A smiling though silent waiter rushed in and out discreetly, dishing it up. Mounds of tasty seafood, lobster, clam, octopus, sprats in batter. The works.

He was also right about the conversation—just as soon as I had a bit of wine inside my young frame and decided that I *would* converse.

Thumbnail sketches of those present:

Tessa, otherwise known as "The Contessa". She was elderly, with lively sparkling eyes and a habit of darting her head to agree with something, like a pigeon-bird pecking seed. She wore jewels and rings galore.

Prof, "The Professore", a dapper fellow in his forties; what he professed was science, though there wasn't much demand for this since machines of the Godmind did most of it.

Then there was Cesare, a burly fellow, a baritone singer at the Teatro della Fenice.

Luigi, an art restorer; he seemed sly.

And finally: Patrizia, young, dark and fiery. She described herself as their theoretician.

I soon gathered that there were several dozen others of like heart in Venezia, organized into separate self-contained "cells". Elsewhere too, in cities all across Europa, similar cells existed. This particular one was the "Doge's Tavern cell". (Oh, and a "doge" is the name for a chief magistrate of old, a city boss; no connection with four-legged barking beasts.)

Presently Luigi said to me, "Not everyone is so sure that you cherubs are aliens at all."

"That's dumb."

"Is it? It's a minority view—I don't hold it personally. I'm sure no one here does. I merely mention it. But consider: maybe the Godmind manufactures you all in its private province over in America, and fills your heads with false memories?"

I gaped at him. "Whatever for?"

"Why, to give us tame idiots the illusion that human history is still happening—if not here, then somewhere in the galaxy! Thus we won't lose heart and die out from lack of stimulus. Lack of events; lack of *change.*"

"Huh. Nothing much changed on my world for long enough. When something big did happen, I don't know that it was such a boon!"

Bernardino said, "You must tell us how your world changed, hmm? And what part *you* played in that momentous event?"

"Did I say I did?" I clammed up; and ate a few clams.

"No, you didn't say." He chuckled. "But you showed it. Whatever Luigi says, *I* believe in you, my little visiting alien."

"And I too!" exclaimed Tessa.

A little later Prof began to profess.

He said this: "The Godmind is well known to be the end product of intelligent intuitive self-directing machines built by our ancestors. But alas, our ancestors themselves weren't too bright when it came to organizing the world. They brawled like brats, and they were on the verge of destroying this planet with incredible weapons.

It's small wonder that the Godmind decrees a quiet static world. Small wonder, either, that it ranks children above us."

"Children in appearance only," I reminded him.

"Yet appearances *count,* Yaleen! Centuries of admiring you starchildren has bred in us a certain humility, a meekness. Which suits the Godmind perfectly. In the beginning—before it got its own act together—the Godmind must have inherited some inbuilt directives, though; just as people have behavioural instincts wired into them by evolution. Now what would its directives be? I've done research amongst the data still on access, from which I conclude that our Godmind's 'instincts' were twofold: to preserve humanity, and to enhance it. Yet there's a huge difference between preserving—and enhancing."

"There's practically a contradiction," chipped in Patrizia. "You can't simply preserve a living system in stasis, or else it dies out. Look at us: refugees in our own world, dispossessed of our initiative!"

"Hence," said Prof, "the role of you starchildren: continually to top up the psychic energy pool of a time-locked Earth. It's you who do the enhancing, by returning from the stars. If you didn't return, humanity would wither. The discovery of *Ka*-space and the psylink allowed the Godmind to enhance and to preserve, at once; but at a cost to us. We consider that cost too high."

I shovelled some Fritto Misto dell Adriatico into my mouth and chewed the crispy lovelies. "Is life on Earth so bad?" I asked, still munching.

"It's a question of dignity," replied Tessa.

"Of liberty," Patrizia corrected her. "We wish to decide our own destinies. And we don't. We can't even make our own mistakes. We built a God for ourselves, and now we have to carry out its oh-so-benign will."

"A God as foretold by precog myth?" I mumbled.

"Pah!" snapped Cesare. "There's no such thing as 'precog'. I don't believe that our ancestors in the deep past intuited all this stuff happening. I say the Godmind just used a lot of myths and symbols to play a tune on us."

"Long ago," said Prof, "an age of religion gave way to an age of science. Yet the psychic forces of the previous age remained extremely powerful. We aren't particularly rational creatures, Yaleen— and as an aside, if the Godmind was *obliged* to preserve us, it would need to preserve our irrationalities too! So it kept the form, but it dumped the earlier content. Deep down, as Cesare says, humans think symbolically. Now we are just the living symbols of the past. Nothing new occurs here. Whatever is new comes from the stars, where at least you aren't ruled directly by the Godmind on account of the sheer distance. But it can still haul you home through *Ka*-space, like fish in a net; then serve you up for our mental feast."

"From which we depart," concluded Patrizia, "with our bellies forever empty. Those of us who still care deeply enough about human independence."

"So you see," said Bernardino, "it excites us to meet somebody who is hiding important knowledge about an enemy of the Godmind. Any enemy of the Godmind's is a friend of ours."

They all looked at me expectantly.

It must have been the wine. Or else a need for allies.

I told them: of our river and our way of life. Of the black current, and the war against the Sons. Of the Worm's head and how I had ridden it. And of how I had died.

The only major thing I held back was that I was supposed to be here on Earth as an agent of the Worm.

This narrative took some while, and it was interrupted as much by crashes of thunder as by questions. By the time I'd finished, the Doge's Tavern was closed for the night; the waiter and proprietor both joined us. My throat was as rough as an old boot in spite of many cups of capuccino coffee and glasses of aqua minerale.

"That's all," I growled at last.

"Bravo, well sung!" Cesare applauded.

"Dear child," exclaimed Tessa. "Dear cherub, a thousand blessings!"

Bernardino grinned. "That's all? Apart from the one little secret that you're keeping to yourself?"

"What secret?"

"I'd hazard a guess that it has to do with your presence here on Earth. Hmm?"

"No comment."

Prof rubbed his hands gleefully. "Ah, this is excellent. Far better than I hoped! So this Worm of yours was placed on a number of worlds long ago, as a destroyer of intelligence? An aborter of native life which might evolve? That would be very much in keeping with a mission to enhance the human race out amongst the stars. How better to pursue this mission than by strangling the competition in advance, before it even got going? Think of the destroyers that way, rather than as a set of ambushes laid for the Godmind's seedships! Maybe worms were planted on *all* suitable worlds—but most duly expired when their work was done!

"This would certainly explain something which has always rather puzzled me: namely why no intelligent life evolved on any of the colony worlds.

"But if this is true, two startling facts emerge. Fact number one: the Godmind is a master of time, able to send those worm creations back into the distant past of our galaxy. And fact number two: the Godmind doesn't know this."

"Eh?" said I. "How could it be a master of time and not know it?"

"Easily. Either it has *not yet* done this deed, nor even foreseen the doing of it . . . that's one possibility. Or else the Godmind isn't as united as we thought. Parts of it operate independently, unknown to the rest of it—just as the workings of our own subconscious mind are mostly hidden from our waking consciousness. If so, potentially it is a house divided against itself.

"That," I said, "is like adding two and two together and getting twenty-two."

"Sometimes twenty-two might be the right answer. You have to learn to see things from a new perspective. A new perspective sometimes reveals the *true* picture, as Luigi can tell you."

"Can I?" said Luigi.

"Yes, yes, that painting of the skull and the carpet you told me of! Look at it ordinarily, and you just see a carpet. But if you tilt the picture and look at it askance the carpet becomes a human skull."

"Oh, Holbein's *Ambassadors*. Right."

The worms could have been sent *backwards in time* by the Godmind? But the Godmind didn't even know this? And most worms had done their duty, nipping competition in the bud then faithfully expiring? But a few had survived and awoken when the seedships arrived? My brain buzzed. It made a crazy kind of sense, if the end result of colonization was to be as Ambroz and his mentor Harvaz the Cognizer suspected. Death at the starting line, death at the finish!

I hadn't mentioned to my new friends what Ambroz had said. I'd been busy talking about my own world and the war and the Worm. Now I told them hoarsely of Ambroz the Exotic and of the telescope the size of the whole galaxy.

When I'd done, Prof got so excited that he knocked a glass of

water over. It's remarkable how much liquid a glass holds . . .
when you knock it over. A pool spread. "So, so, so," he exclaimed,
thumping his fist into the palm. Everyone ignored the spillage.

Bernardino frowned. "What, kill everyone just to use their *Ka*s for
a few moments? That makes as much sense as burning down a
pigsty to get a plate of pork."

"No, it does make sense," said Prof. "The Godmind can cast its
fishing net in *Ka*-space, but essentially, it's a thing of the physical
universe, our Godmind. It doesn't control *Ka*-space; it doesn't understand it. It just uses it. I'll wager it can't have a *Ka*-store like Yaleen's
Worm. Our Godmind's bosom is empty."

"Perhaps," said Cesare, "that's what it wants to see with its telescope; if indeed it *does* have its eye set on building this lens, whatever the cost. It wants to see how to own *Ka*-space."

"Well, it *would,*" said Prof, "If *Ka*-space is the clue to what the
universe is, and why there's one. *Ka*-space certainly seems to be the
domain of the dead. Maybe the dead are like a sort of . . . subconscious of the cosmos? Life evolves in the universe through the aeons. *Ka*-space fills with more and more dead souls. So does the subconscious grow richer and deeper? If so, the real key to action may
lie with the dead. Yet how can the dead ever act?"

"You're becoming metaphysical," Patrizia chided him. "Fascinat-
ingly so, perhaps! But I say we should discuss possible action in the
here and now. Yaleen has given us a lovely tool to subvert the Godmind and seize our freedom again: this threat that the Godmind
means to snuff us all one day."

"One day," agreed Luigi. "One day a thousand centuries hence.
How many people care about such a time-span?"

"They ought to!"

"Ought to. But do they? Do revellers worry about the hangover
the next day? Or the state of their liver in twenty years' time?"

"We needn't *mention* the time-span. If we spread this rumour, and
alert our contacts throughout Europa to spread it too, and then if a
starchild should publicly denounce the Godmind—"

"Don't look at me." But of course Patrizia already was.

"Who was it who said they could shift the Earth if they had a
lever long enough?" she asked.

"And somewhere to stand," Prof reminded her. "Archimedes said
that."

"Maybe we have such a lever here—a lever as long as the distance
from the Sun to Yaleen's star!"

"What about the Godmind controlling time?" I objected hastily. "If what Prof says about the origin of my Worm is true—"

"*Your* Worm?" Bernardino seized on this avidly. "Why not come completely clean with us, Yaleen?"

"Because, well . . ." (His grin broadened.) I tried to recoup. "If the Godmind controls *time,* damn it, what hope is there?"

"Look at it this way," said Prof. "A new perspective! If you introduce things into the past, albeit far away in space, maybe something has to vanish from the present—or change—to compensate. To preserve cause and effect. That something may well be the *knowledge* of what you have done. Anyway, dear cherub, you too have tricked time already. So have all starchildren who have died and been reborn here."

"How do you work that out?"

"You arrive here through *Ka*-space much faster than the ordinary universe permits anyone to travel. So the dead travel through time."

I yawned. I just couldn't stop myself. I was dead beat. After all, I was only a little girl.

"You shall have a room tonight here in the tavern," Bernardino said amiably. "Tomorrow, we'll all have lunch together, hmm? You can come as clean as this tablecloth—*was,* before we began." (The pool had soaked in. Crumbs were scattered about, and a couple of purple rings marked where wine glasses had stood.) "We shall decide; and act. That's why you came to Earth, isn't it?"

"Do you read minds?" I grumbled at him.

"No, only faces. And the language of the body. Right now I read that if you don't soon go to bed, you'll fall asleep in that chair."

So over lunch next day (fish soup and liver risotto) I did come clean about the Worm and me, much to my new friends' delight. Tessa even presented me with her favourite chased-gold ring—she *said* it was her favourite, anyway. For had I not worn a fine ring when I triumphed, Worm-wise, once before? I accepted it as a fair substitute for my lovely diamond ring, lost forever.

Over the next few weeks the conspiracy thickened. The Underground contacted cells of comrades all around Europa, in Paris, Berlin, London, Petersburg, by "phone"—the lightning speaking tube. Journals began to pick the rumour up. According to Prof, there used to be much quicker ways of spreading news around: by radio (which Ambroz had mentioned) and even by picture-radio. However, the governing Godmind had phased these methods out, as inappropriate to its design for order, calm and joy on planet Earth.

During those weeks I learned quite a bit of this-and-that: things which my Cyclopedia hadn't bothered to fill me in on. (Not that I'd asked. I hadn't *known* what to ask. And I hadn't wanted to alert it by too many leading questions.)

What particularly caught my attention was the system of justice on Earth—since I presumed that I would (to say the least) be committing an antisocial act by foul-mouthing the Godmind.

Patrizia explained all this to me. The name of the system was Social Grace; and its ultimate sanction against anyone who oppressed anybody else was permanent banishment to some distant place of exile, which was generally assumed to be an icecap or a desert. (Though *how*, Patrizia insisted, could my proposed misdeed be regarded as "oppressive" of anyone, when it was clearly liberatory?) In contrast to directly-administered Eeden—God's own half-billion acres—law enforcers on the rest of the Earth were humans: Paxmen. These Paxmen advised and arbitrated, and soothed and smoothed out disputes and difficulties. Sometimes they were assisted by machines: a mech-bird or mech-hound.

Now, nobody knew of any family whose son had ever entered the Paxman Corps. Besides which, all Paxmen had a striking similarity of countenance which bespoke body-engineering. Either they were specially bred to their role, in vats; or else, as one whisper went, they were actually recruited from the ranks of ornery people who fell foul of the Paxmen: murderers, rapists, vandals, arsonists, insane devotees of weird imaginary gods, or whatever. According to the whisper, these criminals were made over in a body-vat, and had their minds changed too; *this* was their exile—an exile from themselves, poetic justice.

Patrizia thought this whisper unlikely to be true, since on Earth nowadays there was precious little murdering, raping, vandalizing or whatever. Luigi, who restored pictures, knew that things had been otherwise in the bad old days, back when "life was Hell". Many ancient paintings showed atrocities: burnings, lootings, butchery, rapes, people nailed up on wooden crossbars.

The pacifying hand of justice was, according to a saying, "both light and dark". It rested *lightly* on the world the majority of the time, caressing and gentling, barely even felt; but it could grip tightly and suddenly. And it was *dark:* hidden away until the moment when it popped into sight.

I myself hadn't even seen any Paxmen. I hadn't come across any of the "fingers" of the Godmind. My schedule of talks in various churches—hardly a very punishing schedule—had been arranged by the hotel management.

According to Patrizia, Paxmen had never bothered very much with the Underground in the past. Why should they? So far as I could see, the Underground hadn't *done* very much till now, beyond gourmandizing and theorizing—and circulating leaflets which most decent citizens promptly tossed away, as nonsense. For did not the Godmind genuinely resurrect its starchildren to the glory of Humankind? Had it not brought Heaven to Earth? It delivered the goods (as foretold by precog myth).

So the Underground assumed that they could carry on playing treason games, and maybe play them so well that one day the Godmind would suddenly, to its surprise, find itself defeated.

I wasn't so sure. Maybe the activities of the Underground simply amused the Godmind—to the extent that they were wide of the mark, and ineffectual.

After several weeks of preparation, the Doge's Tavern cell decided that the time had come. I was due to appear in the Basilica of San Marco, the grandest church in Venezia. It was there that I should denounce the Godmind.

Came the day, I felt damn glad to be wearing that ring of Tessa's. It was *something* to set against the glittering splendour of that "Church of Gold". Oh the sensual glory of that Basilica, crusted with scintillant mosaics inside and out—and its golden altarpiece studded with two and a half thousand jewels! Oh the glory of the Godmind, dwarfing the rebel cherub: me.

When I arrived, a machine was playing a symphony from the gallery by way of warm-up. Long golden chord progressions soared and soared. The Pastor took me into an antechamber and supplied me with a white soutane and a square white biretta hat to wear for the occasion. Thus attired, I was escorted down the nave by the Pastor, a doting old codger dressed in the usual belted red frock. The symphony faded when I arrived at the altar-rail. I turned and stood near the speaking-tube, which would make my voice resound around the Basilica.

"Earth-mortals of Venezia," the Pastor cried out through the tube. "On this blessed morning we mass together to hear from the cherub

Yaleen, daughter of an alien sun, starchild of the Godmind. Let us praise her!"

The audience did so by clapping loudly and calling "Bravo!" The Basilica was packed, and for a moment I thought that none of my friends were in the congregation. Then I spotted Bernardino near the front. He winked. With fingers crossed I rubbed my ring, and kissed it for good measure.

The Pastor departed back up the nave; silence fell. To me, this silence descended like a ton of feathers, suffocatingly. What the hell was I going to say? I'd made my mind up to speak simply and clearly, as in previous churches, but this building was so *ornate*. How could I match it? I licked my lips. Then I recalled the old fragment, *Julius Czar.*

"Mortals, Venezians, Earthfolk, lend me your ears," I sang out. "And keep them open please! Don't stick your fingers in them. I come here to bury the Godmind, not to praise it. I come to bury it under a pile of accusations which are all too true! Why? Because it intends to bury us all, starfolk and Earthfolk alike. It means to light a bonfire with our minds, burning our brains out so that it can see to the end of the universe in one big flash—"

This was *awful!* Burials, bonfires, big flashes. I glanced at Bernardino; he grimaced. A rustling mutter of perplexity spread amongst my audience, like a scuttling rat. Or six rats.

"Look here," I said, and proceeded much more simply.

Things went better from then on, for the next five or ten minutes. The rats of murmur didn't quit their scampering but now they mostly scurried to my tune. Or so I thought.

I was helped by my claque in the audience. At one point Tessa rose, dressed in black weeds—I hardly recognized her at first till I noticed all her rings. Wringing her hands, she wailed, "It's true! The Godmind is a Devil. A Satan rules the Earth! The Demon of precog myth!" Quickly she subsided back into her seat.

Cesare and Patrizia and Bernardino also joined in briefly from seats far apart. What's more, members of other cells seemed to be scattered about in the congregation. Then Luigi spoiled the effect by appearing in the gallery and showering down leaflets. He hadn't said he was going to do this; Patrizia glared angrily. (Or *was* she angry? Her expression was weird.)

The Pastor, after flapping his hands at me for quite a while from the back, arrived at some decision and left.

I spoke on. Presently a drab little man leapt up. "You insult us!" he cried. "You insult our Basilica. You insult those robes you wear."

"You insult us!" parroted the woman next to him.

"You aren't a real starchild!" another woman shrieked. "You're an imposter!"

"No she isn't!" someone else shouted back. A member of the Underground? "No normal child could speak that way. So she must be a cherub."

"Nobody normal would talk that way!"

"Shut up! This may be true!"

And so on.

"Yes, hear me," I called. I had the advantage of the speaking tube. "Hear me—for the sake of the future! Listen, for the sake of life on all the worlds!"

At this point the speaking tube went dead. And just then two pigeons flew into the Basilica. They flapped up together to perch on the gallery.

"Here comes the proof," I shouted, in my child's unaided voice. "The Eyes of the Godmind! No doubt the Fingers will follow. But am I oppressing anybody? No! So why should I be silenced?"

Sure enough, two tall strapping men hove in sight. Both wore identical sky-blue uniforms. They could have been twins. Neither of their broad bland faces bore any hint of personality.

I crossed my arms and awaited them there at the altar-rail. The congregation had hushed; and so had I. I had no intention of being dragged shrilling from my podium. There was, as Tessa had observed, such a thing as dignity.

The pair of Paxmen halted a few spans away from me. And then, from the machine-mouths which had made music up in the gallery, spoke a voice: a rich, sonorous, sombre voice.

A voice which could only be the Godmind's own. (And in the audience: muted gasps, wide eyes. Somebody keeled over in a faint.)

The pigeons cocked their heads, and the Paxmen stood blankly before me.

"In precog myth," said the voice, "a child went into the Temple to argue with the Wise; and ended up nailed to a tree. . . ."

"Really?" I croaked. I cleared my throat. "Is that so?" I said, more boldly. "There aren't too many trees in Venezia! So will you nail me up on the bell-tower? Nice view from up there."

"Do not mock me, cherub."

"Why don't you tell all these people the truth about what you're actually up to?"

"Why, cherub, the truth is that I am filling this galaxy of stars with human souls. Did you not know that?"

"Did *you* know that you sent black destroyers *back through time* to all sorts of worlds—so that you could stroll in later on and set up shop? But the scheme didn't pan out properly everywhere!"

Luigi raised a ragged solitary cheer. Which I suppose was quite brave, or stupid.

"Silence! You refer, cherub, to the precog myth of Satan-spirits expelled from God's bosom before the Earth was peopled? Why? That did not come to pass."

"Oh didn't it? Where else do you think you got the idea for the black destroyers—on World 37 and elsewhere? You've cocked-up, and you don't even know it. If you mess around with time, you change what happened—and that includes knowing that you did it! You made your own enemy on seven worlds at least."

"Interesting hypothesis," said the voice, after a while. "I shall think about this."

"Of course," I ploughed on, "it's also possible that *part* of you knows this—and is hiding it from the rest of you!"

"Now you're trying to be *too* clever, cherub. You've had one bright idea. Yes indeed, I shall know the answer. . . ."

"When? When you've filled the galaxy with human minds? And then set light to them, to see to the end of the universe through the biggest lens you can build?"

There was no reply to this. None. Soon the congregation began to whisper.

So I called out, "It's the dead who will know the answer, God-mind—not you!"

"Then should not everyone die?" came the soft reply.

Now there was shock and consternation on many faces.

"If a God is immortal—" began the voice.

I interrupted. "Oh, so that's it! You want to preserve your own existence for ever, even though you're only a created thing, made by people? Let me tell you, you'll get goddamn bored with no people around to occupy your idle aeons. Everyone will have vanished into furthest *Ka*-space."

"Be quiet, cherub. This is a holy moment. A moment of illumination. I see now that if an immortal God comes into existence at a particular point in space and time—it must become preexistent too. Otherwise how could it be immortal?"

"Eh?"

"The God must be able to reach back into the past; and in the process it will cause precog myths of itself to be born. Yet the knowledge of how this can come to pass . . . may vanish in the very instant of its happening. . . ."

The voice suddenly grew harsh. "If Satan is the blindness of a God," spake the Godmind, "that blindness may yet be burnt out in a flash! You: I will put you somewhere safe while I think on these things."

The pigeons took wing. The Paxmen advanced a step farther.

It was at this point that a riot broke out in the Basilica of San Marco.

Part Three

THE ROSE SHOW ON THE MOON

*B*LACK smoke billowed above the Basilica. Fountains had begun to blossom from the Piazza. Motor boats of the fire brigade clustered at the nearby quay like flies busy at a cowpat.

We were fleeing—not very fast—in a commandeered vaporetto, Bernardino at the helm.

Maybe we'd have done better to escape into the alleys of the city. But Paxmen had begun popping up all over. By the time we did decamp, slumbering bodies already littered the Piazza San Marco. The Paxmen were gassing everyone with their mercycans.

There may not have been any riot in Venezia for centuries; or anywhere else for that matter. But the ability to riot obviously hadn't been lost . . .

I wasn't too clear about the exact sequence of events, though I guess that's in the nature of riots, especially when they're being deliberately fomented. But anyway, the sudden eruption of brawling throughout the Basilica caught the two Paxmen off balance. Interrupted in their attempt to arrest me, they tried first to quell the congregation. Tough as those two servants of peace were, they were quickly overwhelmed and beaten senseless. Oh it was chaos in there; not least from the point of view of a little girl. All those big adult bodies crashing about. Then Bernardino appeared, picked me up bodily and forged through to the exit. When we got out into the Piazza, *that* was in turmoil too. But the fires of violence had already

been lit out there. What spilled out of the Basilica was only extra oil
to add to the flames.

Just as Bernardino set me down, Prof and Luigi happened by.
"They're ruffians!" Prof was shouting at Luigi. "You've hired ruffians!"

"Hired? They're volunteers of the Underground, that's who! Well,
most of them. So maybe some people have had a few drinks. But
use your eyes, man! It's the normals who are berserking. The sheep
have got their dander up at last." Luigi danced aside to shove somebody into someone else. This someone-else swung round and
punched his supposed attacker.

Prof grabbed Luigi by the arm to stop him from slipping away.
"There'll be a dire come-back for this!"

"It's worth it." Even thus impeded, Luigi stuck out a foot to trip a
careering youth, who cannoned into the two brawlers. "Paxmen
can't arrest a thousand people. Won't! This thousand will remember.
Think of the news value. Journals pick this up all over Europa. After
we phone 'em." Shaking loose, Luigi kicked a stout matron in the
butt. She plunged screaming and flailing, claws out. Bernardino
sheltered me.

Luigi cried, "It's a huge spontaneous explosion of protest at
Yaleen's revelations! Needn't have happened if those Paxmen hadn't
tried to shut her up. That's what angered everyone."

"They'll find our *leaflets* in there, you idiot!"

"Will they? Will they? Don't count on it! Anyway, we've drawn
the Godmind into the open. We've called its bluff!"

Just then Patrizia, fiery and radiant, came wading through the
mêlée with Tessa in tow. A woman was lying on the ground, bleeding and moaning, and feet were trampling her heedlessly. A fat man
was stamping around, grunting like an angry pig as he nursed a
broken finger. Tessa was cackling with glee, and for a moment it
seemed to me that these people were totally childish. They were the
children, not me. They knew *nothing*. They'd never been in a real
conflict, or seen Verrino trashed. They didn't even understand pain
—till they got hurt. (But did that mean it was *mature* to go through a
war?)

That was when three crackling bangs came from within the Basilica one after another. Heat gusted out.

"What in the name of—!"

"Firebombs, Prof," bragged Patrizia—as the congregation began flooding out, everyone fighting to be first. "Come on, Lui, *action!* But always from the rear."

"Don't I know it!"

"Down with the Godmind!" she shouted. The two of them melted away into the mob.

I grabbed at Bernardino. "You set me up! You really fooled me!"

"Not me. I'm as astonished as you are. Oh, we had a plan to save you from the Paxmen; to spirit you away safely. But not all *this!* Pat and Lui must have cooked it up between them."

"If you're so damn clever at reading people's faces, how come you never suspected?"

"I didn't read Pat's intentions—because I already *knew* her so well. I never thought to!"

Smoke began drifting out of the Basilica. Some hideous cries still came from inside.

Bernardino looked sick. "I didn't know her!" It was hard to say what anguished him more: the agony inside the burning building, or his own failure of insight.

Tessa directed a ringed finger towards the south end of the Piazza. "The Paxman cometh," she said whimsically. Me, I couldn't see a thing, down where I was.

"He's not the only Paxman," Prof cried. "Look, look."

Rioting may not have been in fashion for ages, but the Godmind's response time was speedy enough; its officers were armed with mercy-cans, as used by medics. They mowed the rioters down with smoke.

Looking back on it, Bernardino didn't quite have his wits about him. Or else he was determined to prove his own good faith to me, in recklessly chivalrous style.

For him, Prof, and Tessa the obvious way out would have been to let themselves get gassed in amongst the milling crowd and take their chances. I, of course, would have been arrested. I was far more identifiable: a child in a white soutane.

Instead of letting the confusion be his cloak, Bernardino acted on one of those impulses which seem like a good idea at the time. He hustled us down to the waterfront ahead of the advancing Paxmen. Bellowing something about evacuating victims—as though that was *his* job—he boarded a waiting vaporetto. The pilot didn't argue too much at the change of command; not after Bernardino pitched him into the water. Then Bernardino ordered panicked refugees on to the boat—enough refugees to confuse things—and we promptly took off, while more people were still trying to board. A couple of men joined the pilot in the water. We headed out and away, on the regular route towards the Lido. Like any ordinary bus-boat.

Naturally, this way of escape isolated us conspicuously on a huge expanse of water where any mech-gull could spot us.

Even so, we almost got away.

From somewhere along the Lido, an absurd contraption arose. It tilted, and headed in our direction.

It was a balloon the size of a sloop, striped in red and white, with a basket dangling below. This basket was being hauled through the air by a flight of four great white birds in harness. The birds had necks as long as snakes. Their wide wings beat lazily but firmly, towing the wicker carriage, and the air-bag that held it aloft, towards us apace. Two Paxmen in sky-blue clutched the ropes of the basket, staring our way.

I couldn't help wondering if this crazy form of transport was meant to *say* something to me. Was this some precog myth, specially staged for my benefit?

"Oh, the swans! The swans!" exclaimed Tessa. She sounded more enchanted than scared.

"They're mech-swans," Prof told me. "They—and that balloon—were at the festival of the marriage of Venezia with the sea."

"Yes, when a ring is thrown overboard to wed the city to the ocean!" Tessa promptly stripped off a ring (the one with her family seal embossed) and tossed the ring far out. "A signet for a swan, sirs!" she cried. Obviously she had gone bananas. She laughed gaily. Then she leapt overboard.

I shouted, "Bernardino, stop the boat!" But we had already left Tessa behind. "No, *don't* stop! Circle round!"

Tessa was bobbing in our wake, supported by her outspread skirts. She appeared to be wearing several white petticoats under the black weeds. She was making no effort to stay afloat, yet the air trapped in the layers of her garments prevented her from submerging. Angrily she began punching at her costume to beat it down; to no avail.

Prof clapped his hands. "She would rather drown than be exiled from Venezia! How romantic."

"Don't be stupid. We can't let her drown!"

Our boat's engine was roaring at full thrust, though oddly we didn't seem to be moving so fast. "Bernardino, I told you to circle!"

"I just reversed the engine!" Bernardino shouted back at me. "We'll be going backwards in a moment." (And meanwhile our passengers milled and pointed and protested.)

"Oh . . . So who's going to jump in?"

"Alas," confessed Prof, "I cannot swim. But why should anyone jump in? This is the Contessa's own free choice—to preserve her honour and dignity."

I jerked my thumb towards the wallowing, flapping woman. "You call *that* dignified?"

It was all an academic question. The swans were already upon us. The *swish-swish* of their wings beat overhead. Both Paxmen leaned out, to drop green glass globes resembling fishing floats. Several of these burst on our deck, disgorging clouds of green smoke. . . .

For a brief moment after I awoke I thought that I'd died and was back in *Ka*-space without a body; I simply had no weight at all. Then I opened my eyes and discovered that I was strapped to a seat inside a travel-capsule of some sort. Slouching figures lolled in other seats. Arms floated in mid-air. Hair stood up like waterweed.

No windows, no sense of motion, *no weight*. I let my hand lift itself with hardly any impulse of the will. Where the hell was I?

Ah: I spied Prof slumbering open-mouthed two seats away.

I squirmed round, though the straps clung tight. Tessa slept in the seat just behind. Her clothes were bone dry; so time had passed by, but how much? All the other faces I could see so far were unfamiliar, and some looked quite exotic, for Venezia. Black, brown, yellow. Were we anywhere near Venezia at all?

Then a door slid open. A Paxman stood . . . No he didn't. He floated. His feet were half a span off the floor.

As soon as everyone was awake, the Paxman made an announcement. We were all criminals who had seriously violated Social Grace. Therefore we were being sent into exile.

On the Moon.

On the Moon: Tessa had a feeble fit of hysterics at this; but she calmed down quickly, and thereafter sniffed superciliously at everything the Paxman said.

Concerning how to unfasten our seat-belts.

And how to move around the "shuttle" without bashing ourselves.

How to use the toilet in back. How to vomit without filling the air with a cloud of spew. (But anti-nausea medicine had been pumped into us while we were asleep, he assured me.) How to eat our food-blocks and drink our squeezy-juice. Concerning the pills we should take to avoid farting.

Give me *Ka*-travel any time!

Our journey would take three days. During this time we were sternly warned against brawling, riot, mutiny, vandalism, or spitting at the crew. Any of that, and we would all be gassed again; and this would cancel the effect of the anti-farting pills. So saying, the Paxman departed. He ignored all anxious queries about the Moon.

Out of the twenty criminals on board, only four of us were former members of the Venezia Underground: me, Prof, Tessa, and Bernardino. I hadn't spotted Bernardino when I first woke up. He looked wretched. Prof, on the other hand, appeared chirpy and alert; he busied himself with little experiments in weightlessness.

No sign of Luigi or Patrizia. Or any of the real stirrers of the riot. How damned unfair.

Most of the other criminals weren't even from Italia, and no one knew where our ship had sailed up into the sky from; we'd all been asleep.

In our group were two brown-skinned Indians from India, woman and man; a black African, an Arab, a Chinese . . . there were people from all over Earth. Amongst our crimes we numbered: murder, banditry, fanatic worship of "Allah", drug peddling, not to mention vandalism and arson. This all emerged courtesy of the Indian bandit-woman, Kalima, who floated about demanding answers and getting them. (A "bandit", by the way, is an armed robber who way-lays wayfarers and attacks lonely farms; they're not unknown on the west bank of our own world.) But it was Tessa who averted what might have become a schism between the ordinary criminals and us members of the Underground. Since we were in the minority, such a schism wouldn't have been a good idea.

Loosening her seat-belt, she rose up, holding on to the back of the seat with one hand, and declared penetratingly, "No matter why we are here, we must all now support each other in adversity. The Earth is gone from us forever. So are our former lives. The past is erased." She floated across the aisle and held out her hand to the Chinese "opium-man"; who clasped it. Kalima regarded Tessa sharply, then nodded and smiled faintly.

The Bandit-woman drifted over to me. Her hair was a long black braided rope. "Why is a child here?"

"I'm a starchild," said I. "The Godmind decided I wasn't its favourite cherub."

"*I* kidnapped a starchild for ransom," announced Kalima. "I did so because a bandit is courageous! And because you cherubs are set above us like little rajahs and princesses."

"Don't pick on her," said Tessa. "We must all support each other."

"Don't presume *too* much, old lady!" our bandit warned.

"Nor you," growled our black African. "We want no leaders."

Kalima swung around, as a result of which she floated away from me. "You may not *want,*" she told the African, "but you will get."

On that score, alas, Kalima was to prove perfectly correct.

By the time we landed, three days later, inevitably hierarchies and alliances had formed amongst us; whatever use, or otherwise, these might prove at journey's end. Kalima emerged as top card of the pack, with Tessa playing a grandmotherly role in the background.

What had prompted Kalima to become a bandit, of all things, back on the peaceful orderly Earth? Despite Tessa's dismissal of the past, curiosity finally overcame her and she asked Kalima this. The answer snapped back:

"My ancestress was a bandit, long ago. I am her, come round again on the Wheel of Years. Perhaps!"

Later, Kalima added, "My family hoped I might become a *pandit.* That's our name for a wise person. I must have misheard them! Who needs pandits on the Godmind's Earth?"

"*I* was a pandit," said Prof. "Not," he hastened to add, when Tessa frowned, "that I'm bragging about it."

Kalima laughed. "Being a bandit was more fun! I earned my ride to the Moon."

Other vignettes from the journey:

Muhammed Ibrahim, the worshipper of Allah (which was an ancient name for a God) kneeling and bowing in weightlessness, facing the rear door that led to the toilet on the assumption that the Earth lay in that direction.

Chu Po's mockery: "Where there's no religion, opium's what the people need!"

Max the murderer looming over me: "I killed two starbrats. Two!" He dragged a finger across his throat. "Me! I killed. . . ." He sounded dim-witted. But was he scary! Kalima swam through the air: "Do you want both arms broken, or your back?" "Uh? Do I want . . . ?" Max's brain tussled with the choice. "Never mind!" snapped Kalima. "Get back in your seat. Strap in and stay there."

On the whole, though, we all got on together and sorted ourselves out. Eventually the Paxman came to tell us to strap in for landing. Shortly after that our weight returned in surges, accompanied by a roaring which went on and on. I felt crushingly heavy. When the roaring died I was left feeling much lighter than I ought to be.

We didn't see the surface of the Moon. Nor did we even see the outside of the ship. A long metal corridor led directly from the door through which we disembarked. The shipside end was linked to the shuttle by massive rubber seals; and the corridor, lit by glowing strips, terminated in a largish metal chamber some way away. We had to walk carefully in case we bounded off the floor.

Once we were inside that chamber, a thick door sighed shut behind us. Bright violet light pulsed from glass tubes on the ceiling. Stinging misty vapour filled the air, then was quickly sucked away. At the same time I could feel the entire chamber starting to sink slowly. Down it travelled for several hundred heartbeats before the door slid open again, and a harsh but more natural light flooded in. Out we all filed gingerly, into the belly of the Moon.

Imagine a vast pit roofed with rock. Up on the ceiling, lights too bright to look at burned like little suns. The pit was a coneshape, with the apex at the bottom.

Imagine this; and now carve a road spiralling round and round, descending. Then hack out one grand staircase, for speedier descent. Quarry caves and galleries, grottos, cells and tunnel-mouths so that the rockface becomes a stony honeycomb, with people as the bees. Let there be terraces for green crops, and irrigation ditches, as well as a long cascade of water feeding these ditches, before emptying into a lake at the very bottom of the cone.

"Why, here is Hell," exclaimed Prof, enthralled. "We've been sent to Hell." The metal door clanged shut behind us.

We were on a broad platform up near the roof of the pit. Because we were close to the suns, it was very hot. Six or eight scruffy, burly fellows lounged about awaiting us. They were stripped to the waist, well-tanned and bearded. A bushel of beards! Black. Ginger. Shaggy. Bunchy.

The neatest of the Beards produced a notebook.

"Names?" he demanded.

We told our names one by one. When Kalima gave hers, she added, "I'm the leader of this group. We remain together—except for him." She jerked a thumb at Max. "Him, we expel. The rest of us are to be housed together."

The man laughed nastily for a while.

"Ah yes, madame? In a suite of luxury apartments? Now you listen to me. All new arrivals are assigned billets where *I* choose, and wherever's convenient. Don't expect to sit around sunbathing and dabbling your toes in the streams, either. You'll work. At cultivating, tunnelling—"

"Are you trying to escape?" broke in Muhammed Ibrahim eagerly. "In which direction? Which way is the Earth?"

"Are we trying to escape? Did you hear that, boys? Shall we dig a tunnel through hard vacuum? And if the vacuum's hard enough, crawl through it? Brilliant idea!" He rounded on Kalima. "Every new intake needs to be taught a damn lesson, one way or another. Right! So you spoke of expelling that one, did you?" He indicated Max, who stood lumpishly. "Obviously he deserves it. So be it. You shall see someone expelled. It's a while since we've expelled anybody. High time we did! Couple of hundred metres along this way is the exit tube for rubbish, with an inspection screen showing pretty pictures so you can check it's clear. It's our vacuum cleaner, you might say. Bring him!" he told his men. "You lot follow me."

Two Beards glided smoothly forward and pinioned Max with some sort of thumb-lock. They shifted him by the simple expedient of lifting him bodily off his feet. He didn't weigh much here. Max protested feebly, grunting and shaking his head.

Tight-lipped, Kalima stepped in the way. "Wait! This is unnecessary."

"You just expelled him from your group, remember? Any trouble, and you're next. I can call on forty men for assistance. Don't try to play the saint suddenly."

Fury in her eyes, Kalima yielded.

"Follow!"

They went. We followed.

A straggly line of scantily-clad, sweaty men and women was portering wicker baskets up the grand stairway, towards our destination, which was a cave mouth. Some baskets contained dead chopped vegetation. Others had broken stone in them. Porters carried their burdens into the cave. Others emerged with empty baskets and rubbed sweat from their eyes before descending the stairway.

"But how inefficient!" complained Prof. "Where are the machines?"

"Keeps people busy, don't it?" said one of the Beards. "Toughens 'em up."

"For what? Toughens them for what?"

There was no reply. We had reached the cave by now. Our host shouted for the work to cease. All the ascending porters unhitched their baskets and sat down. One woman, whose basket had already been emptied, sat down too. Our host promptly kicked her in the butt, knocking her down several stairs. The woman might have tumbled all the way if she hadn't fetched up against another porter sitting on a basket of rocks. The basket toppled over, tipping its contents a long, slow way down the stairs. Cursing, the man laid into the woman, who scrabbled to pick up his debris. Our host laughed.

The cave was as big as the main hold of a schooner. Within we found the contrivance which got rid of rubbish. This was an enormous metal cauldron resting in a deep hole cut in the cave floor. The cauldron was attached to rails running up at a steep angle through an open hatch in the roof. It was about a quarter full.

The two Beards threw Max unceremoniously over the side into this cauldron. Our host stepped smartly to a panel set in the wall and pressed a button. Immediately a see-through lid sprang up and closed the cauldron, imprisoning Max. Next to the panel there hung a large glass picture. This showed the cauldron in miniature, with us all standing about. It was a picture that moved and represented real life as it was happening.

Max had gathered his wits by now, and decided that something was amiss. He scrambled up on the rubble and other refuse and thrust in vain at the lid. He hoisted a hunk of stone and began to batter. With no result; obviously the lid wasn't made of glass.

Our host pressed another button and the cauldron began to rise smoothly up the rails. Max's efforts redoubled. The cauldron was above us now, but we could still see Max inside it on the picture-screen; its vantage point was changing to match the progress of the cauldron. Once the cauldron had cleared the roof, a metal door sighed shut above.

Now, side by side, the picture-screen was showing two separate scenes. One was of cauldron and contents rising up the rails, as seen from above. The other was of the empty rails ahead of it. The rails seemed to lead to a blank metal wall, but then another door slid aside. We saw points of light, stars. None of them were winking.

Then there was only one picture again: of a dead, harshly sunlit landscape—grey hummocks, craters, boulders casting jetblack shadows. A ramp towered up, supported by struts and pillars. A mobile machine with a scoop on the front was shifting debris away from underneath. Then the cauldron emerged from a hole in the ground and slid up the ramp.

When the cauldron reached the top, the lid sprang back into the metal body. The whole container tipped, dumping its load—and Max.

He fell. So did the stones and other scruff. But that wasn't what killed Max. He leapt when he hit the ground, missing most of the avalanche. He took two giant steps. Then he seemed to shrivel up. He hunched. At the same time he threw his arms out, fingers clawing. His mouth gaped so wide he could have dislocated his jaw. Blood bubbled. His eyes bulged. He fell over. He writhed a while, scratching the dust. Soon he was still.

Above, the cauldron righted itself. It slid back down into the Moon.

"Doesn't the Godmind *care* if you kill?" cried our other Indian. "Why don't the Paxmen stop you?"

"Because," bellowed our host, "the Moon is not your soft and pampered Earth! That's lesson number one. The Godmind has other ambitions here. Lesson number two is that I've just done your ex-companion a favour by freeing him from this hole."

"In that case," murmured Tessa, "spare me your kind favours, sir."

The ceiling hatch re-opened. The cauldron slid down the rails into its previous berth. We regarded its empty belly warily. It seemed to catch my breath away.

"The third lesson is that we only have so much space, and so much air and food. We get some rations from Earth, but space we have to hack out for ourselves."

"I'm surprised," said Bernardino lightly, "that you don't just kill everyone new who arrives." In the circumstances I thought he was taking an almighty risk. But he looked relaxed. He must have read something on our host's face that reassured him. Perhaps we had all passed over some emotional hump. Or maybe Bernardino was so sick at heart, he didn't care.

"The Godmind wouldn't like *that,* friend! It makes use of us; and it likes a lot of variety. Your next lesson is: when the Paxmen call on you to serve, you go with them tame as a lamb."

"Serve?" I asked. "How?"

"By donating part of yourself for the seedships. The Godmind builds 'em in another cavern—it uses tissue samples from us. The scum of the Earth are here on the Moon, girl, and that scum is a powerful brew. Strong and ornery and bold. That's how new colonies got going on Earth in the old days, I'm told. Our Godmind's got a long memory. Now *you* tell me what a little girl's doing here."

"That's simple," said I. "I'm a starchild, and I think the Godmind sucks. I said so in the biggest church in Venezia, then we burnt it to the ground." (Not quite true, but never mind.) "I'm fairly ornery too! But I don't need to toss people out with the trash to prove it! That isn't very bold. Real boldness would be messing up the Godmind's shipbuilding plan."

"Oh, would it? You listen to me, tiny tot. We're stuck in a stinking hole on a dead world. No way can we upset the Paxmen or the Godmind. And why should we? This way at least a bit of us escapes and gets back to Earth eventually, transfigured. Here's where *your* stock came from originally: the bowels of the Moon. So don't be smug."

"A bit of you gets back to Earth eventually: that's your consolation prize?"

He swooped and open-handed me across the mouth. The blow knocked me right off my feet. I didn't crash too heavily, though. Through tears I saw Kalima square up to our host.

"So you hit children too?" (Kalima was a fine one to talk. She kidnapped children.)

"Lady, I was hitting an *adult.* That's what she is." (Still, he sounded . . . distressed.)

"What you just hit is your so-called salvation: starchildren."

"Shut up!"

I thought he was going to hit Kalima too—which could have ended up with her in the cauldron. I struggled up. Wiped some blood from my lips.

"Sod all starchildren!" I said. "Do you know what the colonies are

all about? They're about the murder of the whole human race—
everywhere."

"What do you mean by that? Explain!"

I explained as briefly as I could. Even so, he soon interrupted.
"Rubbish. I don't believe a word of it."

"He can't believe it," said Bernardino. "He *daren't*. Therefore he
won't."

Surprisingly our host let this pass. "Okay," he said grimly, "if
we've all *quite* got over our teething troubles, play time is ended.
Unless you want me to vacuum someone else. My name's Jean-Paul,
and I'm your boss—"

And.

And.

One of the poets of Earth was once of the opinion that "The best
lack all conviction, while the worst are full of passionate intensity."
Chu Po, our drug peddler, told me that. I suppose the poet must
have been Chinese.

The Best were all on Earth. They were the sheep whose only
conviction was a dumb faith in the glory of the Godmind and the
wonder of its cherubs. Here in this hell below the surface of the
Moon, the Worst had their abode. Here the offenders against Social
Grace were simmering away in a nasty stew; this was being spooned
out by the Godmind into its seedships.

And the stew had to be stirred and kept on the boil. Hence the
hardships. Hence the rock-hewing and toilsome agriculture. Hence
the arbitrary punishments and random acts of violence. All these
added savour and spice to the stew.

Prof poured scorn on this idea that human tissue-samples could
be tempered and toughened through the struggles and suffering of
those who owned the flesh in question. But obviously the Godmind
found life in this pit poetically appealing. The Moon-Hell was fulfilment of yet another precog myth, was it not? Heaven on Earth,
Hell on the Moon. And here in Hell the Godmind used the wicked
to bring about eventual Good: namely the winging homeward to
Eeden of starchildren.

Generally the Paxmen kept out of our way. They let us exiles
bully and harass each other and fight to be top dog or run with the
pack in charge.

Generally. But if Hell showed signs of becoming too comfortable,
the Paxmen would reduce the quality of life for a while by switch-

ing off the water-cascade or raising or lowering the temperature so
that the exiles cooked or froze. They'd done this before; they would
do it again, if we ever looked to be having it easy.

Now, once you got used to the assorted rigours and cruelties, life
was rather better than it *appeared* to be—to those who weren't themselves living it, namely the Paxmen whose abode was way off in
another cavern. So after a while I realized that Jean-Paul's regime
was almost benevolent. He'd been boss for half a dozen years, and
he was a more complex tyrant than at first he seemed. Looking back,
the sudden arbitrary murder of Max had been done to prove how
savagely Jean-Paul ran the shop, but without actually killing anyone's dear friend in the process. Likewise, his other outbursts of
violence. Booting that porteress. Slapping me so hard.

We were allocated billets around the various circles of this spiral
Hell. Tessa and I were assigned to a nook close to Jean-Paul's own
king-pin cave. Only later did I cotton on that this was so that Jean-
Paul could keep a semi-kindly eye on the two of us: the old woman
and the child. To begin with, I would never have believed it. My
mouth was still stinging from his blow and my teeth felt loose
(though they weren't), so I hated him.

Ours was a tiny little cave. A tatty curtain hung over the entrance,
and inside there was barely room enough for two sleeping pallets.
("Farewell, my lost palazzo!" mourned Tessa when she first saw
inside.) On the other hand, we had no possessions to clutter the
cave with. All hygiene and cooking was communal, carried out
nearby. Unlike some other new arrivals, we were well away from
the worst heat of the suns.

The suns: these dimmed but did not die by night, which was
twilit throughout. Someone told Tessa that not once during Jean-
Paul's reign had the Paxmen quenched the lamps of Hell to chasten
its inhabitants. On several prior occasions the whole Hell-pit had
been plunged into darkness for days on end. People had fallen to
their deaths. A few had gone mad.

Tessa was set to work as a cook; and indeed she showed such an
ingenious flair for improving the cuisine that one day Jean-Paul felt
obliged to stop by specially to kick over one of her best creations.
Tessa took this in her stride as a compliment to the chef. She had
cottoned on to his real motives a bit ahead of me.

I was set to work as her assistant peeler and washer-up. Shades of
my stay with Doctor Edrick!

Of Bernardino and Prof we saw little. They were labouring over on the other side of Hell. Of Kalima we saw a lot more, since Jean-Paul had ordered her to his own billet, beaten her a bit, and taken her as mistress. Personally I wouldn't have trusted Kalima in bed with me in case I got knifed in the ribs while I was snoring. But obviously I'm not always a brilliant judge of character. She seemed to acquiesce happily in her new role. She put on queenly airs. Now she was Jean-Paul's "secretary".

There were no kids, except for me. Apparently the water contained a drug very like our own Safe back home. An exile's only offspring was whatever they contributed to the Godmind's seedships.

Thus life proceeded, after a fashion.

For me, this was a routine of peel, peel, fetch and carry, scrub, scrub. Now and then the monotony was interrupted by the spectacle of fights or beatings administered by the swaggering Beards. As punctuation we heard the occasional muffled bang as new galleries were blasted in the rock. I began to appreciate another reason for the arduous chores hereabouts: there was nothing else to while away the years.

Nothing at all?

Oh, with one exception! Every now and then a couple of Paxmen would appear, locate somebody and lead them off in the direction of the great enterprise, to donate of themselves. The donors departed from a distant cave housing a transport tube. They always returned, none the worse for wear.

The Paxmen had no difficulty in locating whoever they wanted, because we were all under surveillance in the pit. Powerful glass eyes watched us from the roof, hidden amongst the suns. So when Jean-Paul had kicked Tessa's vegetarian lasagne over, he'd expected this to be noted on high with approval.

One day a couple of Paxmen came for me.

"Accompany us," said one of them.

"I'm not donating so much as a flake of dandruff to your wretched seedships!" said I.

"No," he agreed blandly, "you aren't. The Godmind wishes to converse with you privately in His garden."

"In its *what?*" Incredulous, I took in the terraces of cabbages, beansprouts, watercress, whatever.

"Not here. Elsewhere. Hurry up."

* * *

The Paxmen escorted me to the cave I've mentioned. This was bare, apart from several glass eyes scanning the interior. The travel-tube itself was sealed off by a metal door, to which one of the Paxmen had a key. He only used this when a green light glowed to show that a capsule was waiting on the other side.

We boarded. With the exception of a number of seats bolted to the floor, the capsule was almost entirely blank metal inside. No windows at all. A fan-machine purred behind a grille, creating a draught.

One Paxman sat in the nose where there was a tiny control panel. The capsule door shut. We sighed away.

The other Paxman sat opposite me, watching, barely blinking.

"Hey, you guys," I said, "when you're off duty what do you do for fun?"

"A Paxman is never off duty," my escort replied. Ah, here was progress indeed! No one had ever got very far trying to chat up a Paxman. If the Godmind had decided to talk to me, maybe their tongues were loosened too.

"Don't you have desires, ambitions?"

"We desire to do our duty; that's our ambition."

Hmm. Did I say progress? Maybe not.

I tried: "Were you born, or made?"

"Which were you?" he countered.

"Born, of course!"

"Wrong. Your body was vat-made in Eeden."

"Oh, I know that! But *I* was born: the original me. How about you?"

"Made to measure. To suit the Godmind."

"Hey, are you trying to be witty? Well gosh, witty folk like you must do something to amuse themselves!"

The Paxman regarded me levelly, then said, "I garden."

"You do *what?*"

"I garden roses."

Roses: you know the name? "The Queen of Flowers", so-called. You'll never have seen any roses, of course. To us, they're just a myth.

I first saw roses in palazzo gardens in Venezia. Roses come in different colours and styles. Some are big, some are tiny. Some are flat and simple, others densely petalled. Some are climbers, others bushes. Many are perfumed. Roses have nasty thorns to prick your flesh.

So where, inside the rocky Moon, did my Paxman garden roses? Or was that just a conversation stopper? It certainly put a stop to my chatter!

Our capsule soon soughed to a halt. The door opened upon an empty, well-lit platform with a wall mosaic announcing: *Rosaluna Station.* The other Paxman stayed inside when we two stepped out. Behind us, the capsule itself was hidden by a second wall, of metal.

A corridor curved away. We went along this, passing through a couple of metal doors intended to keep the air in, in case of moon-quakes.

The third door opened upon. . . .

. . . masses of foliage and blooms under a sunlit, cloud-dappled blue sky! There were beds and thickets and mazes of roses. There were arbours, pergolas and archways all clad with leaf and flower. There were trellises, screens, tubs, hedges, brick walls a-blossom! Extending how far? Three thousand spans in length, and as much in breadth? I don't know which sight was the more amazing; the garden or the view of the sky above!

About one hundred spans above. I could tell that the sky was artificial. The real sun shone down through it from beyond, but the white clouds floating about were flat. They were squeezed between two giant panes of glass the size of the garden itself; and were adrift in some blue liquid. Since the clouds changed shape slowly as they drifted, they must be like blobs of oil in water: of a different substance from the blue medium they floated in. The false sky filtered and diffused the sunlight which would otherwise, perhaps, be too fierce—as there was no air between the Moon and the Sun.

The sky surely couldn't be made of ordinary glass, else it would have snapped under its own weight, not to mention the weight of the liquid sandwiched between. Anyway, didn't little rocks rain down on the Moon all the time, according to what I'd heard? That was why Hell was underground.

Yet here was a sky! So why couldn't Hell have a sky? Presumably because Hell was Hell. . . .

A number of Paxmen were browsing, here and there, snipping off overblown blooms and wiring up stray new growth.

We descended a broad brick stairway between trusses of fluffy white blossoms, on to an earthen avenue. This avenue was flanked by large bushes bearing vermilion and creamy-buff flowers alternately, and led towards a metal gazebo set upon a low mound in the very centre of the garden; the gazebo roof was ringed with glass eyes.

We were only part of the way towards that gazebo, which I guessed was our destination, when my Paxman turned aside to lead me around by pebbled paths on a guided detour.

He stopped by a trellis tangled with branches bearing pinky carmine blooms. "This is *Zepherine Drouhin*. Uniquely, as you'll see, it has no thorns. It's a climbing Bourbon rose, with semidouble blooms. Please smell the fragrance."

To oblige him, I sniffed. "Nice," I said.

"We have to watch out for spindly growth. That's on account of the lower gravity. Equally, there's the plus of bigger blossoms and a longer flowering season."

"Oh really?"

"And here we have *Picasso*, the first Floribunda rose to be described as 'hand-painted'—though of course we don't literally paint it by hand."

Next he pointed out a blood-red specimen. "Ah, *Parkdirektor Riggers*. It's vulnerable to mildew and blackspot, but of course we don't have any of that on the Moon."

He pinched off a couple of flowers which were nearly finished. It occurred to me that Edrick would have felt beautifully at home here, stripping off mildewed leaves to the glory of the Godmind, though of course there weren't any such diseased leaves, said my guide.

"Now here's *Pink Grootendorst*, a rugosa shrub. Observe the frilled petals. The bush itself isn't much to look at. But the flowers are excellent for displaying at our annual rose show."

A rose show? And practically next door we had to grub around in our wretched pit painfully growing vegetables!

"Are you mad?" I said.

Ignoring my jibe, he indicated a bush of silvery lilac flowers which looked like thin porcelain. "Here's *Blue Moon*. It's as close as you can ever breed to a true blue rose. Why? Because the rose family doesn't anywhere include the blue pigment Delphinine."

"I shouldn't have thought the Godmind would have too much trouble making a blue rose! Not when it can turn people into alien birds and merfolk at long distance."

"Ah, but that would be cheating."

"I give up."

I oughtn't to give up, though. Not if the Godmind cared so much about this crazy lovely garden. How, I wondered, did one go about introducing mildew and black spot into it? Was that why we had been sprayed when we first landed on the Moon?

Why the hell did the garden *exist*? What did it all *mean*? Could the Godmind's glass eyes really perceive beauty? Could these robotic Paxmen?

Aha. If the Godmind tried its hand (a mech-hand) at painting or pottery to prove to itself what an artist it was—just like real human beings!—it might have made a fool of itself. But flowers were safe. Flowers were already dipped in beauty.

Our route led us back presently to the metal gazebo.

"You go on up, Yaleen. I'll be dead-heading nearby." My Paxman gave me a little push in the right direction.

I mounted the metal steps and entered. "I'm here, Godmind," I said to the air. "Why roses?"

After a wee pause the same rich sombre voice as I'd heard in the Basilica spoke from the roof. (If I remember aright. It was a catchy little verse):

> *"Gather ye rosebuds while ye may,*
> *"Time is still a-flying:*
> *"This same flower that smiles today*
> *"Tomorrow will be dying. . . ."*

"You're lucky to be here while so many are coming into bloom, Yaleen. Roses are transitory. Humans too."

"So you *do* admit it!"

Pause. "Admit what?"

"Admit that you plan to burn the brains of everyone alive in another thousand centuries or so!"

Pause. "Well, aren't you going to answer?" I demanded.

"Please note that our conversation will inevitably suffer from brief delays. That's because I am on the Earth, which is some distance away. You can see it, if you look at the sky above the entrance."

I hastened to look, and spotted a swirly blue and white ghost of a disc beyond the blue of the false sky . . .

"I shall say 'finish' when I finish speaking," the voice went on. "You will kindly do the same, otherwise we may get tangled up. I've been considering in depth your idea that I have had, or have, or will have mastery of time. I've been mulling your theory that I myself planted—or will plant—the black destroyers, yet do not know this. Alternatively, that such creatures exist as a result of my past or future effort to reach back through time. You sparked an interesting speculation, and I'd be interested to learn exactly how you arrived at it. Finish."

I was just about to say that I was a whole lot more interested in the fate of the whole human race, finish, goddam finish. But then I had an inspiration.

"Don't get me wrong!" I assured the voice, in a tone which I hoped sounded fervent and sincere. "I've changed my mind a lot recently. I think your plan to build a lens is a super, fabulous one. It's a stroke of Godly genius. It's far beyond the sort of thing that *people* could dream up, which is how I had trouble adjusting to it." My brain was zipping along nineteen to the dozen. "I want in on your plan. I want to know what the universe is all about. I want to know what time is, and what *Ka*-space is, and why anything exists. That's what I really want. But *you* need someone on your side who understands you, and who isn't just a puppet. I'm sure you do, or you wouldn't be talking to me now! . . . er, finish," I concluded breathlessly.

Pause.

"You've changed your tune, Yaleen. It isn't long since you abused me bitterly. And set fire to my Basilica."

"Oh *that!* I had to draw attention to myself. In any case, I didn't personally burn the Basilica."

". . . a spell in Hell is salutary, perhaps? Please don't interrupt."

"Sorry! Oops."

". . . but how can I know if this is a true seeing-of-the-light upon the Damask road, as in precog myth? Finish."

Whatever was the Damask Road? I visualized a bolt of rose-red silk rolling out along a highway.

"Oh precog, tree-frog!" said I. But this hardly squared with my new demeanour. "No, wait! What I mean is: precog myths mightn't be precog at all. They might be the proof that you influenced time past—that's how they got planted there in the past. But anyway: about my change of heart. People often oppose things because they secretly want in on them! Didn't you know that? The closer folk come to seeing the light, the more bitterly and blindly they oppose it. Till all of a sudden, flip. That's human nature. Finish."

One thing stood out for sure. The Godmind didn't really know me. The Worm had strolled around my mind nonchalantly, whether

I liked it or not. The Worm really knew the *Ka*s in its *Ka*-store. But the Godmind could only use the psylink to shift *Ka*s around: back to Eeden to inhabit new bodies.

Maybe it could build a lens with the *Ka*s of all the dead, but they certainly wouldn't inhabit its bosom afterwards. Not unless the view through its lens showed it how.

Whatever its limitations, the Worm had *insight*. The Godmind didn't. Yet. So the Worm was like the blind spot in its eye: an entry point to awareness, where nothing could actually be seen by it.

"Conversion is a behavioural jump, as in Catastrophe Theory?" The voice seemed to be asking itself, not me. "Perhaps—" and this definitely was addressed to me—"you're just fed up with peeling carrots and washing dishes? Finish."

"Oh no, that isn't it! It's all on account of this fabulous garden. Here's my damask rose. Road, I mean. I'm overwhelmed. I've fallen in love with it. I mean, just look around! Here in this garden you're searching for order and beauty—for the roots of existence! And the blossoms. Anyone who can fix up a garden like this just *has* to be on the ball. Finish."

The Godmind was obviously proud (as Hell) of its garden. Maybe, when it had solved the secret of existence and wiped out the human race in the process, here it could walk in the afternoon warmth of the lunar sun, alone and content.

"Walk"? If the Paxmen all went "poof" at the same time as everyone else, it could always jolly up some mech-gardeners with glass eyes. . . .

"Ah yes indeed. This is probably the leading rose collection anywhere in the universe. It far outrivals the Empress Josephine's Malmaison. It can definitely hold a candle to the Parc de la tête d'Or, the Westfalenpark or the Hershey Rose Garden. You still haven't said how you arrived at your other conclusions. Finish."

"I *intuited* them, Godmind. Because . . . because I guess I must have been born with a freak gene for intuition! I can guess right, and I usually do." (What a lovely lie. If only it were true!) "Here's an example. This is just on account, as a goodwill gesture. I'll tell you how you'll be able to zap your enemy the black current, and any others of its ilk that are lurking about. I'll tell you how to wipe that cataract from your vision, that blot from your plan, that warp from the lens of your telescope!" Nice rhetoric, huh? "When your lens is ready," I said, "why should it only receive? Why shouldn't it also transmit? And focus? and. . . ." I left my clue dangling.

A tasty bait for my prospective partner, if I say so myself! I'd thought of it on the spur of the moment.

Even though I hadn't said "finish", the voice purred at me: "And *burn*. Oh yes. Destroy the snake which partly masks your world from me! And so I shall connect you all to me without exception in that climactic moment when I carry out so many billion operations!"

Aye, while many billion patients die.

The Godmind was definitely going a bit over the top, I thought. Though maybe when you've hatched such a mega-scheme you're entitled to go over the top? and who was I to criticize—me, who had just claimed impeccable intuition?

"I shall tell you a secret, Yaleen. My plan doesn't require as great a time as you thought. By no means do I need a whole galaxy to build my lens. I only need part of the galaxy, quite a small part. Finish."

I felt such a chill in me as though the sky had cracked and space rushed in.

"You're still building new seedships and launching them, though? Finish." (Spoken casually.)

"The second-last seedship is approaching completion right now. It will fly away within twelve Earth-weeks. Only one more to go after that." (I'll skip the finishes from now on. You've got the idea.)

"Maybe they'll both get an attack of the Worms at journey's end!"

"I doubt it, statistically. Besides, that direction has been safe so far."

Obviously the new-style Yaleen had to pretend massive commitment. "Oh dear! When they arrive, it'll take lots more years to establish colonies!"

"Not really. A few years will ensure a size that's adequate for the purpose. A presence is what counts. It's more a question of the topology of connexions in *Ka*-space."

"Oh. But it'll still take those last two ships simply *thousands* of years to get to the far frontiers. I'll never live to see the outcome!"

Something resembling a chuckle issued from the gazebo roof. "When I plan, Yaleen, I plan ahead. The earliest seedships travelled to the far frontiers. These last two ships are heading for the *nearest* stars with usable worlds. They'll arrive quite soon. It'll seem ever sooner to anyone on board. Accommodation can be added for a passenger."

"What do you mean?"

"You wish to be in on the, ahem, *kill?* If you stay here, you may miss out. But if you travel as a passenger on this ship that's about to depart, you'll enjoy the boon of time-squeeze. You'll arrive in good time to be around when the final colony blossoms. You'll live to see the light. This shall be my gift to you, on account of all you have suggested. My ship will be programmed to amuse you *en route.*"

Oh no. No, no and no.

"Meanwhile, as an immediate reward you shall judge the rose show this year."

"I'll *what?*"

"From amongst my new varieties, plus the older established specimens, you will select the Supreme Rose; and award it a gold medal."

"Er, just where do I find a gold medal?"

"You're wearing a gold ring on your finger. That will do excellently. You can slip it on to a stem of the victorious rose."

"I don't know how to judge roses! There weren't any roses on my home world."

"That's because I didn't send roses anywhere else." *(That* figured. In alien soil, under alien light, we aliens might have built up better rose gardens!) "My Paxman will bring you here often, to instruct you on the relevant criteria. Fear not: you'll have time enough to learn. Then after the show your ship will fly to a nearby star. *Paxman to the gazebo!*" the voice blared out.

My escort came running.

"So what happened?" asked Tessa when I got back to our Hell's kitchen. (Incidentally, it took the capsule at least twice as long to return, as to go to Rosaluna Station.)

"I'm going to judge a flower show," I told her. "Then I'm going to zoom off to another star. What else did you expect?"

"Dear child, once I have swallowed the elephant of Hell, should I strain at a gnat? Tell me all."

I did; and as she listened, her head pecked away like a pigeon's at every grain of detail. At the end she said firmly, "You must speak to Jean-Paul."

"What for? What's he got to do with it?"

"Ask yourself this, child: what will the Godmind do about Hell, and about us who live here, when the final ship flies away? Maybe it'll still require a Hell for its exiles. But what if it doesn't? It won't need tissue samples any more. What if it just turns off the heat and light and water?"

"I hadn't thought of that."

"No. You will be going; so you didn't think. Such is human nature. But *we* will all be staying."

"Oh Tessa!"

"Ah, I tell the truth—and I hurt your feelings."

"No, it's you who's hurt! Isn't it? Because I'll be giving your favourite ring away, to a rose! And I'll be leaving you with all the washing up."

She laughed; and I laughed too. Then she said, "Do go and see Jean-Paul. If he kicks you, that's the fate of messengers who bring bad news. No, wait! The eyes in the roof will see you going to his cave. No doubt they're keeping a special eye on you. I'll go instead."

"And get kicked?"

"I'll take him some cannelloni."

"Don't make it too tasty, then."

At breakfast time next morning Kalima came to see me, ostensibly to grouse about the rubbish we'd been dishing up. She slapped me about, smashed a plate or two, then hauled me roughly into the nook where we stored the victuals which the boss's men doled out.

"Tell me, but speak softly," she whispered.

I told.

Afterwards, she brooded.

"So you will learn how to judge roses," she decided. "And you'll keep your eyes and ears open for me."

"For you, or for Jean-Paul?"

She smiled, twistedly. "You'll report to me, when I collect meals. Confide in no one else."

"Maybe," I suggested, "you should bring Prof into this? Remember the pandit from Venezia? He knows science, and he was a member of the Underground."

"We're all underground here, little girl."

"Do tell Prof—and Bernardino. Please."

"Are you seeking privileges for your friends? Beware you don't double their burdens."

Carefully I said, "They're good at . . . organizing."

"So," snapped Kalima, "was *I.*"

Soon after, my Paxman collected me to return to Rosaluna Station and the rose garden.

During the next several weeks I began to get the hang of roses. Assiduously I studied the difference between Hybrid Teas, Floribundas and Polyanthas; between Rugosas and Hybrid Musks. I mastered the distinction between flowers that were high-centred, open-cupped and pompon. I learnt all the criteria for showing at exhibition: blooms should be pointed, without a split centre, not blown, free from blemish . . . I memorized strings of strange names, such as *Napoleon's Hat, Little Buckaroo,* and *Thrilled Nymph's Thigh.*

Meanwhile the ghostly Earth went through phases in the false sky, but the Sun sank out of sight. In its place sun-lamps blazed from the four corners of the enormous skylight. I wondered why I hadn't seen this huge lighted window on the Moon when I was watching from California, but maybe it didn't look so big and bright from Earth.

I also asked my Paxman questions such as, "Don't the roses get too much light with the Sun shining non-stop for two weeks?" (The sky, it turned out, could be dimmed to imitate night.) "Oh, how's that? What's the sky made of? What happens if a rock from space smashes into it?" (Not to worry, Yaleen. "Radar-controlled laser-zappers" were watching out for any stray rocks zooming in from the void.)

And most importantly: "How many Paxmen will be at the rose show? What, all of you? Gosh, how many's that?"

One day the Godmind summoned me to the gazebo.

"How's it going, Yaleen?"

"Well, it's absolutely fascinating. Intoxicating! Gosh, am I grateful to you!" (In fact, it *was* quite interesting. Definitely a lot more interesting than scrubbing dishes.)

"Good. Now, on the topic of time . . . it seems to me that when my lens is complete, and when I annihilate the black current through *Ka*-space, that will also be the moment when I discover how to send those destroyers back through time to reserve habitable worlds for my seedships. I shall tear the blindfold off, and hurl it into the past; as it were. The circle will be complete, and causally closed. I shall proceed onwards."

"That's really neat, Godmind! Could I see the ship I'll fly in? Please?"

"Does your intuition tell you that I'm right, Yaleen?"

"Oh absolutely. Well, that's to say: *almost* absolutely. I'm a bit fuzzy about this because, because . . . because if you foresee something *too* clearly, then it can't happen exactly so. It'll happen, but in a slightly different way. If you follow me." (*I* certainly didn't!) "But getting back to my ship . . . what a huge explosive force it must take to chuck a ship at the stars! Could I take a peek at it? Please."

"I have to plumb time itself, Yaleen! *Ka*-space is non-spatial. Yet it is analogous with actual spatial locations existing in the here-and-now. Maybe an implosive event such as the sudden death of all conscious beings can deform *Ka*-space along a time-axis, thus opening a paradox channel into the distant past of the universe. . . .

"The ship? Ah, the ship. Yes, you may see it provided you can answer a couple of questions successfully."

Questions about *Ka*-space, paradox channels to the past, and my intuition? I suppressed a groan.

"Ask away."

"My first question is: Which was the first serious challenger to *Allgold* for the crown of top yellow Floribunda?"

I did groan. "Er . . . *Sunsprite.*"

"Correct. And now a harder one: What is the pedigree of *Pink Perpetuity?*"

"Um, by *Danse de Feu* . . . out of *New Dawn.*"

"Well done. Your Paxman will take you to view your seedship."

So my Paxman and I returned to Rosaluna Station earlier than usual that day. Once there, I discovered that I hadn't taken off my gardening pinafore as I usually did before quitting the garden for the day. Such is the interruption of routine.

I'd decided a while since that the tube line must run in a large circle, with traffic travelling in one direction only; but on no previous return journey to Hell had the capsule stopped at any other intermediate station, and unless it did, and the door opened, there was no way to see out.

"From Hell to Rosaluna, from Rosaluna to where?" I quizzed my guide.

"To our Pax barracks. Then to the Navy yard. Then to Hell."

Four stops in all.

"So the Navy yard is quite close to Hell?"

He nodded.

"And the ship I came in landed between the two?"

"Correct."

"Do you know?" I said, "in all this time you've been my teacher, you've never once told me your name. Do you have a name?"

"Of course. I'm Pedro Dot."

Pedro Dot: he had been one of the great rose breeders of the distant past, from the part of the Earth called Spain, home of the fabled Parque de Oeste rose gardens . . . Well, well.

Just then a green light lit, announcing that our capsule had arrived.

This isn't a discourse on how to build seedships. That would fill a whole tome by itself, and I'm certainly not the one to write it. Most of what I saw in the huge crammed hall of the Navy yard, I couldn't fathom. Still less could I plumb the workshops and flesh-vats adjacent. Nor, since most of the work was being done by soft machines, with only a handful of Paxman technicians in attendance, was it always easy to distinguish the makers from what was being made.

What I *did* understand well enough, and what curdled me, was my proposed accommodation aboard the seedship.

To reach this we rode up a gantry. Up top within the hull the "pod"—to use Pedro's word—lay open for inspection. Air-and-water-machines were being fitted round it.

It wouldn't be quite fair to call the pod a tomb. It was a bit bigger than that, with a window-dome on top, for journey's end; but much of the space inside was taken up with exercise machinery including a treadmill—so that I could march to infinity, getting nowhere, on magnetized shoes. Pedro showed how.

After this, in there, we tried out a snack of food-bars produced by a machine which, Pedro assured me, would turn my shit back into food with added goodness. Great, delightful. *Go eat shit yourself, Godmind,* I thought.

So much for my bodily comfort. How about my mind?

I had a library of machine-music and another library of thousands of picture-radio stories from the ancient days which I could summon up on a screen. I flipped through a few of these: men in funny hats rode horses and shot each other with pistols; men drove four-wheeled metal machines which crashed and burned; a man in a loincloth swung from tree to tree . . . Thus would I while away my idle hours when I wasn't busy treading, rowing, pulling and pushing.

Just *how many* idle hours?

And lo, it transpired that whereas I would be First Lady of the world I arrived on, I wouldn't—couldn't—myself be modified to fit the alien planet. I would have to stay indefinitely inside my pod, which would be deposited on some hilltop with a nice scenic view from the dome if I was lucky. Or if I wasn't, maybe it would be deep in some swamp or jungle.

That was the bad news.

The good news was that when the colony came to life I could set up—still stuck in my pod—as a wise oracle and source of advice. I would be the repository of the heritage of Earth; until such time as the whole colony and every other colony in the galaxy had its mind blown out.

Shit, with knobs on.

So much for the pod. Of rather more urgent concern to me was the matter of how the ship was powered.

Pedro had already satisfied my seemingly innocent curiosity on this point. On our way to the gantry he had indicated a hopper which was excreting orange "fuel-balls" on to a moving belt. Each fuel-ball was the size of a marble. I had no idea what sort of fuel this was, but it surely had to pack a lot of power. Farther along the belt a machine was inspecting the balls and plucking out the occasional one with a suction tentacle, to toss down a chute.

As I say, I was still wearing my gardening pinny with a pair of secateurs in the pouch. This, over my soutane, with its generous sleeves which were practically pockets in their own right. When we were coming out of the pod on to the gantry again, I tugged Tessa's ring off my finger and dropped it into my pinny. Rings can be quite useful sometimes.

As soon as the hoist-platform was descending I jerked my hand up. "My ring!" I babbled. "It's gone! I've lost it! I knew something felt queer—it must have slipped off. The Godmind will be so upset! He wants me to present that ring to the champion rose, you know. We'll have to find it, Pedro!"

The platform reached the ground. "Inside the pod: is that where you dropped it?" he asked.

"I must have. Yet I'm not sure! I think I may have lost it earlier. It might be up there, though! Will you go and look? I'll search around down here. We have to find it, or the rose show will be ruined!"

He nodded. "I'll go back up and look. You stay here. You can search around a bit, but don't get in the way of any machines—they wouldn't notice you." (That was nice to know.)

While he was riding up again I made a show of hunting about in the immediate vicinity for my mislaid treasure. As soon as he was out of sight I took the ring from my pinny and hid it under one of several crates which were standing about. Then I sprinted tippy-toe back to the hopper. Snitching several fuel-balls, I hid them in my sleeves. I returned just a few seconds before Pedro emerged, on high. "Not inside!" he called down.

"Oh dear!" I wrung my hands. (I'd always wanted to wring my hands ever since I read *The Cabin Girl and the Cannibal.)*

Once he'd returned to the ground I made a big and frantic show of casting around—then finding the ring. Actually, this *was* quite a frantic show, since I couldn't find the damn thing when I did descend on the crate in question. At last I spotted it and hooked it out. "Phew!"

When we got back to Hell station later, I had the bright idea of insisting that Pedro return my pinny with its nice big pouch to its rightful place in the garden. Should any machine count balls and come up short, *that* ought to allay suspicion.

I asked Tessa to go immediately to Jean-Paul to arrange a meeting between him and me. And never mind about his supposed orders to the contrary, as relayed by Kalima! I sent one fuel-ball to Jean-Paul, care of Tessa, and kept the rest up my sleeve.

A couple of hours later the man himself hove in sight.

He jabbed a finger at me. "Hey, you! Yes, you, what's your name! We have a sneaky swine of a crack that needs widening. You're just the right size to place the charge."

Grabbing my arm, he hustled me away down the grand staircase then along a spiral path past a procession of rockporters. We came to a narrow crevice which ran back a dozen spans or so. Jean-Paul stuffed me inside then rammed his body into the gap behind me, plugging it. I managed to squirm round but couldn't see his face too clearly, what with the way he was corking the entrance, blocking most of the light. But I saw his raised fist. He opened his fist; in his palm nestled the fuel-ball.

"How many more have you got?" he murmured.

"Five. Know how they work?"

"No."

"Prof might be able to tell you."

"Who?"

"Prof. He arrived on the same shuttle as me. He knows science; he was in the Underground. Didn't Kalima *tell* you?"

"No."

"Didn't think she would. I told her you ought to have a talk with Prof. And you must!"

"Must I?"

"Yes! The last two seedships will fly soon. No more need for Hell after that, eh?"

"What? The Godmind wouldn't trash us!"

"Want to bet on it? Well, do you?"

"No."

"Listen, there are one hundred and fifty-three Paxmen on the Moon, and they'll all be at the rose show. All standing tamely underneath a sky that isn't solid rock. Suppose they all happen to meet with an accident, do you think you could run the Moon yourself?"

"Go on."

"With them out of the way, you can seize the Pax barracks and the Navy yard. You'll have much more space. You'll have machines and food. I've seen one machine that'll turn any old crap into meals. Build more of those, and you're laughing. You've got yourself a treasure cave next door. You'll survive. And you'll be *free*. You won't have any more people cramming in, either, not unless you ungimmick the water supply and start having kids yourself."

Jean-Paul licked his lips. I could see his face more clearly now. He was sweating.

"Who knows how to build more food machines?"

"Prof could work it out." (Could he? Maybe, maybe not.)

"The Godmind wouldn't like it."

"The Godmind's planning to murder everybody sooner or later. It told me so! If the last two ships can't fly, maybe it'll have to think twice."

"It'll send more shuttles full of Paxmen to the Moon to quell us."

"So then you can burn them out of the sky. There are laser-zappers for shooting down stray rocks. Prof can fix them so that they'll shoot shuttles too. He'll have time enough. The Godmind will be in a right old state of shock and sorrow when all its lovely blooms get blown away." (Would it be? Maybe.)

"Just what are you proposing, Yaleen?"

I told him, and he whistled long and low.

"You do understand what'll happen to you?"

"All too well. I saw Max vacuumed, remember?"

"Okay. Rather you than me." Jean-Paul pocketed the fuel-ball. In its place he produced a thin stick resembling a pencil. "You came here to blast rock supposedly, so you'd better blast some. Crawl in as deep as you can, stick this in some crack then snap it where the wire's wrapped round. You'll have three minutes to get clear. If you're stuck I'll haul you out by the heels. Oh . . . but first of all hand over those other fuel-balls."

"Right." I surrendered them promptly.

A few minutes later we were both safely outside the crevice. I'd got out without having to be hauled. The blasting stick went *krump,* and dust gushed out.

"So!"

I was grabbed by the hair. I dropped a plate, which smashed on the rock. My head was twisted round—to face Kalima.

I gritted my teeth. "Shut up!" I hissed. "Or you'll spoil things. If you do, Jean-Paul'll expel you."

"You got me into trouble, over your precious Prof." Kalima did look a bit bruised. "Me, his secretary!"

"He'll get over it. Play your cards sensibly and you'll be queen— of a lot more space."

"Do leave her be," said Tessa. "Surely there's no reason to be *jealous* of Yaleen? Bit on the small side, isn't she?"

"You caused me a spot of unpleasantness." Kalima touched a purple patch on the dark skin of her cheek. But her other hand did relax its grip.

"A beating a day keeps the Paxmen at bay," said I. "Jean-Paul will change, afterwards. He'll become gentler."

"He'd better not!"

"Oh, you like that sort of thing, do you? How screwed up can you get! You ought to be thanking me, then!"

"What I *meant,* Yaleen, is that if all goes well—with the venture— people will wish to relax, and that would be dangerous. Jean-Paul will have to carry on bossing them. But how?"

"He'll need a subtle diplomat at his side. You, Kalima, eh? Better start being subtle. Get some practice in now."

She looked daggers, only for a moment. She controlled herself. She even managed a smile. "Yes, you're right. Jean-Paul admires you, Yaleen. I mustn't resent that, must I? Because you're no competition."

"Exactly what I said," muttered Tessa.

"Especially not afterwards."

Tessa raised a quizzical eyebrow. I hadn't told Tessa the plan. Kalima obviously knew it, though.

"Afterwards?" said Tessa. "After *what?*"

"After Yaleen here—"

"Be quiet," I snapped. "Be quiet."

And Kalima indeed was quiet. She nodded thoughtfully. Before departing she actually stroked my hair, smoothing the yanked strands back into place.

Prof turned up to work nearby with light duties only. Bernardino, also. Jean-Paul was discreetly assembling his team for the aftermath of the Plan. Just as I'd recommended.

Meanwhile I continued to be escorted to Rosaluna by Pedro Dot, to learn how to judge the finest rose show in the universe.

I felt quite jolly about the way things were proceeding, so I fairly threw myself into rose appreciation, much to Pedro's satisfaction.

One day I had another interview with the Godmind, who was suddenly bothered as to whether my famous intuition mightn't prejudice me when it came to deciding upon the champion rose. I mustn't on any account try to foreguess the winner. That would be a lazy short cut. I must put my wild talent on one side—that wouldn't be difficult!—and abide solely by the rules of the game of roses.

I promised faithfully so to abide.

One thing which amused me almightily was that two new varieties of rose recently bred by the Godmind and for which it had high hopes had been given the names of *Bombe Glacée* and *Bombe Surprise*. Both of these were fine white roses, with *Iceberg* somewhere in their parentage. Both boasted high-centred inner cones and the insides of the petals were neatly striped: nearly blue in the case of *Glacée*, crimson in the case of *Surprise*. These two "bombe" roses were named after ice cream puddings. "Surprise Bomb": there's my baby! I thought.

Prof dropped by one evening, to confirm in a whisper that he had put together what he insisted on calling an "infernal device", using the rock-blasting pencils as detonators for the fuel-balls.

That was a relief. I hadn't been entirely sure that he could make a bomb even if he put his mind to it. Unlike Luigi.

"It should work okay," he said. "I scraped a tiny flake off one ball and got it to flare wildly. It's just a matter of concentrating and maximizing the bang." He pulled a flat can of fish—sardines—out of his pocket. "A present for you. Same size, same weight. Try it out."

"Shall I toss it high in the air, as if in glee?"

"Better not. The Paxmen might think you were trying to knock out one of their glass eyes. Just get used to it. Imagine chucking it."

I passed the can from hand to hand a few times, weighing it.

"Even with a kid's strength behind it, it'll hurl high enough here on the Moon," he murmured. "It'll go the distance. I'll stick a tuna label round the real thing, so you won't get your cans mixed up." (A tuna is another kind of Earth fish.) "Before you throw the real one, you should shake it roughly. The instant it stops going up and starts descending, it'll explode."

"We hope."

"We shouldn't have any trouble hot-wiring the tube trains. But we won't be able to recover any, um, bodies. From that garden, I mean."

"That doesn't bother me. This is only my second-best body."

"I'll deliver the tuna the day before the show."

"Oh no you won't. What if they change the day? I want my *bombe* with me up my sleeve the whole time from now on. And will you get me some more sardine cans too? I'll take one to work with me from time to time. I'll produce it out of my sleeve, rip the tab off and eat the fish for lunch. Pedro'll get used to seeing me with a can of fish. Just now and then, though. So he doesn't wonder if I've cornered the market."

"I'll ask Jean-Paul."

"No. You'll *tell* him."

The day of the show was drawing closer when something new cropped up. Another spaceship-load of exiles arrived.

Pedro was late collecting me that morning, so I had time to spot Jean-Paul and his bearded brigade toiling up the grand staircase. Shortly after, Kalima stopped by and murmured, "Paxman told the boss to get upstairs. There's a new batch due in an hour or three."

"Don't they know the exact time a ship's due?"

"Paxmen do, but if they told Jean-Paul that would be convenient, wouldn't it?"

"Oh, and he wouldn't be in such a bad mood by the time the new lot arrive."

"He isn't in a very jovial mood right now." And she told me how the impending arrival had thrown Jean-Paul's resolve somewhat. True, one last seedship was still scheduled to be built and stocked with snipped, sliced rebel-flesh. But surely there was enough rebel-flesh on the Moon already? Why continue sending people into exile if the idea was to close down Hell in another two or three years? Maybe the status quo was safer, after all? Maybe it would be better to wait.

"I shall work on him," she promised. "I'll keep him staunch and courageous, never fear! There's only one golden opportunity: yours." She reached out and stroked my head. "Yet who am I to tell *you* not to fear?" She was really behaving far more nicely.

"So long as my little plan works," I reminded her. "Don't count too many chickens."

"If it does work, then you'll go to the bosom of the Godmind, won't you? The Godmind isn't going to be very fond of you. Maybe this Hell will be nothing compared with a Hell in the Godmind's heart."

"I'll go *where?*"

"If it's true about the bosom of the Godmind. . . ."

Of course! She didn't know that I had a lifeline (or rather death-line) stretching way back to the *Ka*-store of the black current . . . Assuming that I *did* still have.

"That's just a rumour, Kalima. I don't believe it. In fact I'm sure it's a lie."

"Let's hope you're right, for your sake."

Oh, I was right, and no mistaking. Final proof: if the Godmind could operate a *Ka*-store it wouldn't have needed to reincarnate us all as cherubs, to keep tabs on the fortunes of its colonies. Though admittedly cherubs were a neat way of keeping old Earth from dying of boredom . . .

"I assure you, Kalima, *anything's* better than spending the rest of my days locked up in a pod eating shit!"

"Which reminds me, I'd better rush. I have to tidy *our* pod. Jean-Paul messed it up a bit this morning."

"Wait: ask him if there's anyone called Luigi among the new arrivals. Luigi, or Patrizia. They understand . . . you-know-what."

"Will do."

I watched her go, then for a while I stared across this disgusting slave-pit buried in the Moon. I realized that I was becoming very homesick: for Pecawar and Spanglestream, for Aladalia and Verrino. Then I saw Pedro striding my way and hurried to meet him.

Neither Luigi nor Patrizia were amongst the new intake. Tessa passed the message on that evening after I got "home" from a hard day's rose appreciation.

Tessa told me that Jean-Paul had spent hours up at the top of Hell with his men before the new people stepped through the door. When he came back down to his cave he looked boiling and furious. But Kalima must have worked on him (or under him) well. The next time Tessa saw Jean-Paul outside the cave, he looked loose and easy. Kalima had stopped by later on, unbruised, to pass the news: no Luigi, no Patrizia.

Why did I want them, anyway? Luigi had only been involved in making fire-bombs, which might just have been wine bottles refilled with oil with a wick stuck in them. Or something of the sort. Besides, both he and Patrizia had acted irresponsibly without regard for the innocent or even for old comrades. We could do without them. Anyway it was too late to involve confused new Moon-virgins in the plan. The Event was nigh. Event with a big "E": for explosion, which I hoped would also be big.

On the great day of the rose show Pedro Dot collected me as ever, and we rode to Rosaluna. By now I was so accustomed to carrying that phony tuna can up my sleeve that for one ghastly moment on the tube-train I thought the *bombe* wasn't there! A quick squeeze reassured me.

When we arrived at the garden, Pedro stuck close by; much closer than usual. When I tried to hang back at the top of the brick stairway, where I was closest to the sky, he draped a comforting arm around me. This effectively scuppered any chance of tossing the can then and there at the very outset.

He couldn't imagine, could he, that the prospect of being supreme rose judge of the cosmos awed me? Or that I was daunted by the massed phalanx of Paxmen awaiting me below? Oh yes: all one hundred and fifty-two of them (minus Pedro)—or what looked like that many—were drawn up to attention in two long columns lining the avenue between the foot of the stairs and the Godmind's gazebo. The rose show was the event of the lunar year: the big treat, not to be missed. Attendance compulsory. Every twenty spans or so on either side stood a Paxman. Faced with such an assembly, how could I possibly haul out a can of tuna for a supposed quick tuck-in?

"It's *okay*," I muttered. But Pedro officiously led me all the way down the stairs betwixt white trusses into the dappled sunlight. (It was daytime again on the Moon.) Never mind—maybe the false sky was more vulnerable in the *middle* than round the edges. Maybe it was thinner there.

Each Paxman I passed wore a tiny vermilion rose in the button-hole of his sky-blue tunic; and I had no difficulty in identifying this as *Starina*, queen of the miniatures. I felt tawdry beside these immaculate troopers. I was wearing the same old soutane as ever; and as we advanced at a slow and stately pace through their ranks I panicked a bit in case I might be asked to slip into something more elegant. Something without big sleeves.

Sensing my flutter, Pedro hugged me even closer.

"It's *okay!*" I shook myself brusquely to disengage him. He finally got the message and I stepped out ahead, leaving Pedro a pace behind. Meanwhile the Paxmen fell in behind two by two, as escort.

The entire area around the gazebo was crowded with benches loaded with vases, bowls and boxes of cut blooms. I halted, and tried to look snooty.

"Welcome!" the Godmind's voice boomed out. "Welcome to the annual universal rose show. As judge this year we are privileged to welcome the cherub Yaleen. . . ."

The Paxmen crowding the end of the avenue applauded.

". . . who will open our show officially, then select the category winners, and finally choose the supreme champion rose!"

"So what do I do now?" I muttered to Pedro, who was breathing down my neck.

"You should make a little speech from the gazebo steps. A few words will do. Then declare the show open."

"Right. I can handle it. You stay here." He did.

I mounted the steps. I turned and confronted my audience: of Paxman faces and of roses. I was on my own at last.

This, of course, was the right time. There mightn't be another.

I swallowed. I nudged the can in my sleeve.

Why not make a little speech? I wouldn't want the Godmind to think I'd rather blow myself up than say a few words.

"Godmind . . . and Gentlemen," I called out. "And when I say 'gentlemen', what gentle men you are indeed! Such preservers of peace—and of course *Peace* is a beautiful rose, is it not? And what a mind our Godmind has, to breed such beauty amidst all his other cosmic duties!"

More applause. This was going down quite well.

I held my hand up modestly for silence. "I have here a golden ring to present to the grand champion rose of my choice: the prime rose of the Earth and the Moon, the best rose in all the galaxy.

"But first, by way of appreciation of the honour done me, here's a little personal trophy of my own."

I yanked out the can of tuna, shook it violently, flexed my knees, and leapt—sending the can soaring skywards.

"Sucks to you, Godmind!" I shouted.

I had a few seconds left in which to reflect that vandalism was getting to be a way of life. First the Basilica of San Marco; now the premier rose garden in the galaxy.

I didn't look up to follow the progress of the can. Most of my audience did.

Then the bomb exploded.

Oh indeed. Shock and heat beat down, sending me sprawling back inside the pergola, though the roof had sheltered me from the worst of the blast.

Tough as they were, many of the Paxmen sagged. A lot of them were clutching their eyes. Petals rained off roses by the thousand. The show tables were particularly devastated.

I rolled to where I could peek out and up. Globs of cloud-ichor were oozing from a shattered sky.

With a ripping thunderous crack, the upper layer of the sky also parted.

It seemed then, when all the air howled out into the void, that the garden itself screamed. Leaves, flowers, branches from all over, all the cut blooms and even small bushes flew upward.

Along with the air from my lungs. Along with the heat from my body. Along with sound itself. Oh the lancing pain of my eardrums bursting! (But that was the least of it.) Oh the sudden empty silence!

For a while—which seemed too long to me—my body was flopping and clawing for life where there was nothing to sustain life. Like Max, when Jean-Paul had ejected him, I was hollowed out inside; and the hollow collapsed into itself, all my inner surfaces sticking together.

Stars burst behind my eyes. I tasted blood which froze.

Okay, Worm! I screamed within me—no other place left to scream than in my bursting skull. *Do your stuff! I'm counting on you!*

Part Four

NARYA'S NARRATIVE

THANK goodness, I was dead!

Once more I was in the blue void. Once more I was spinning, bodiless. With a difference this time: no storm was disturbing the weather of *Ka*-space.

I quickly became aware of a huge number of cords, of hawsers, converging from all over upon some place nearby. Upon Eeden, centre of the web of the psylink.

Myself, I felt no urge to fly there. Indeed I felt that I couldn't even if I wanted to. I wasn't riding back to Earth from a far world like a bead on a string; on the contrary a thin string stretched away from me to some far elsewhere. And besides, I was twice-dead.

If it weren't for my deathline, where would I go? I searched for clues.

The psylink extended through *Ka*-space; but did *Ka*-space itself have any pattern or texture? Any directions, any destinations?

I concentrated on this. After a while—which might have been a short while, or quite a long while—I began to grasp something of the essence of the blue void which was *Ka*-space.

My first impression was of timelessness. There seemed to be no way to measure any activity. Maybe a moment lasted for an aeon. Or maybe an aeon of events could be packed into a moment.

Yet that wasn't quite it.

Rather, it seemed as though time was bubbling up within this timelessness. The void *simmered.* Pockets of time occurred, expanded, vanished again. Bubbles fluctuated in and out of eternity, as if the void was breathing them in and out. Each of these bubbles could be an age, or no time at all; or both.

I strained to understand this.

Here was nothing; here was no-time. Yet something was occurring. Here in *Ka*-space, as in a river, floated the keel of the universe —of that I felt sure. And what shaped the keel, what caused its existence, what measured its progress was this bubbling up of time, this flow of the current of the void.

But how? Why?

Could the answer be: for no reason at all? Could the answer be: that the universe simply occurred, like a bubble containing whole aeons? Yet eventually it was nothing? Just a bubble?

There was only one of me. If I were many, would I see better? For a moment—or an age—I felt that I was on the brink of . . . some transformation, which would allow me to see.

Then I felt a tug on my line. Faint, feeble, insistent. I started to move through *Ka*-space. And as I moved, I lost touch with my source of inspiration.

I was soon aware of something else: namely that my Worm wasn't a particularly good angler! (How could you expect it of a worm? That's like expecting a sheep to herd dogs.) I speeded up crazily. Soon I was lurching and bumping along, fit to snap the line. This made me slip off my proper course. I started sliding sideways. And here's where things started to go wrong.

Think of a ball on the end of a long string. Imagine this ball being hauled at breakneck speed, quite without finesse, through an obstacle course consisting of, say, a number of logs. They're all just floating nowhere in particular; in a fluid with eddies in it.

The ball bumps and bounces. The string gets bent against one log. When the ball gets there, it doesn't zoom past the log. It wraps around it, clings a while—before unwrapping and flying free. And now though the final goal is still the same the ball is even further off course. Another log gets in the way. The ball wraps and clings; unwraps. And so on.

The ball was me. The string was my link to the *Ka*-store of the Worm. Those logs were: other worlds, full of *Ka*s.

It was only after the second such collision that I worked this out. And you'll have to bear in mind that this is simply a *picture* of what happened. I think I saw it this way because of my nightmare flight through the Californian redwoods. Of which I'd had dreams which were similar in style! Dreams of the trees reduced to stumps, of myself as a ball that the boys intended to kick about.

To begin with I was pretty confused. I thought everything had messed up.

Suddenly I was in a body.

When I say I was *in* a body, I don't mean this was like being reborn into a new body in Eeden. I'd *been* the body, then; the body had been me. Now was different. I was only along for the ride.

And that ride was through the air.

It was through gusting air high over blue and bile-green swamp bristly with tufted weeds and wafting sedges. Denser brakes of tangled podvines sprawled across sand-bars and isles of silt. My eyes were intent for signs of movement. Whenever these eyes of mine fastened upon something interesting, the whole central portion of my vision magnified it.

Down below, a dank pool suddenly erupted with a squirming mêlée of furry bodies, red eyes, teeth and claws. Strings of blood coiled in the water like purple toadspawn or thin sausages, so quickly did it coagulate. It was as if I were holding a lens over the landscape.

This wasn't what I wanted. I glanced briefly behind me—and in that glance I discovered great broad-feathered wings, which were silver-blue, barred with ochre and gold. Skimpy arms were tucked up tight under these. A bony claw of a hand clutched the corpse of some finned snake-creature. I also caught a glimpse—a foggy one since I wasn't focusing there—of distant castellated cliffs soaring upward in tiers and towers. The sky above was streaked with high hairy dazzling clouds. My eyes wouldn't look at the sun.

And I knew where I was.

Why, it's Marl's World! I exclaimed to me.

In surprise my hand dropped the snake. Immediately my body veered, plummeted—and I had caught my prey again.

What are you? What are you doing in me?

Oops, pardon the intrusion. I'm just a Ka on my way to another star. I'm trying to get back home.

A Ka? The dead do not return.

No, but I tend to. Listen: I was good friends with one of you birdmen, back in Eeden. Name of Marl. He can't have died more than three or four years ago. If he and I got on, so can you and I.

Marl?

I rose a few octaves in pitch in my thoughts, to repeat the name. My bird-host caught on. *Ah, Maaayyrrl! No, I never knew such a person. If you've really been to Eeden, stray spirit, sing me a song of Eeden! Sing it in my bones.*

A song? Well, I'll give it a go. . . .

I was just about to—after which we might have got down to business, such as how to live together—when I was rudely torn away. Back to the blue void.

In the next world I collided with I was back on my own two feet again. Or rather I was on someone else's feet. Those feet were toiling up a steep stony track between tumbles of boulders and wiry bushes tipped with saffron fluff. It was hot. Mostly I stared down my bare, duskily-tanned legs at my ropy sandals. I seemed to be a woman. Black beetles with horns scuttled over the pebbles of the path; I trod indifferently on a few.

When exhaustion overcame me and I started staggering, I offloaded the burden I'd been toiling under. This was a huge block of yellow wood, slung in a cradle of rope. I subsided beside it, to rest.

Dully my eyes noted the distance I'd come—up amidst savage slopes of scree and scrub. Finding some sprigs of bitter herb in a pocket, I chewed, and stared at my toes. The nails were coarse and horny. Maybe they were meant to be. My hand strayed aside to the wood, which resembled a churnful of very stiff butter, and stroked it idly.

Excuse me, I thought, *but what's the wood for?*

My body jerked to a crouch. In my hand a bone-handled knife with short bronze blade had suddenly appeared. I stared about wildly, spying only harsh slopes, angles of stone, mauve sky. Drooling herb-spittle, my mouth cried out, "Who speaks? Does the dead tree speak? Is that what a lurker wants me to think? To confuse me and steal?"

She surely believed in voicing her thoughts aloud! (Yes, I was sure I was a woman.)

"Aiieee!" cried my host. "Aiieee! Aiieee!" I cocked my head to listen to the echoes. "Aiieee!"

Was this to summon help from further up the track? Or to deafen the "lurker" which didn't like loud noises? (But which could throw its voice in whispers?) It had been so very silent before. When the echoes faded it was still totally silent.

Please calm down, I thought. *I'm inside your head, sharing it. If you'll just listen, I'll explain—*

"The dead tree has entered me!" she howled. "Through my backbone it has bored a hole!"

No it hasn't. Don't be hysterical.

"I only port heartwood to the Sculptor! The tree is bled dead! No offence!" (No offence to whom? To the tree? To the Sculptor? To the lurker amongst the rocks?)

No need to get upset! I don't think I'm going to stay here too long.

Never a truer word. Before I could work out what was going on, I was wrenched on my way.

Only to collide, next off, with a farming wench. She was wading knee-deep in a paddy field, with her skirts hitched bunchily up around her waist. Several large snails with opal shells were crawling on her thighs. In the distance a tall lizard-thing stood bolt upright. Her pet? Her guard? The creature looked totally dull and in a stupor. Two suns shone in the sky, one of them tiny but blinding bright.

Presently the wench that was me paused in my work. I plucked one of the snails from my wet flesh, cracked its shell and munched the contents. . . .

Next I was gutting long black fish on a white marble worktop. I was an old crone blind in one eye. The fish-shed was lit by flaring torchlight. I spilled the guts into drums. I slid the flesh along to another crone, for her to chop into slices with a hatchet. I chanted over and over to myself an idiot ditty:

> "Eelfish,
> "Peel fish,
> "Make a wish!"

These brief encounters were quite confusing. Not to mention the vertigo of plunging in and out of them. Even so I was almost beginning to relish these dips into other lives. Quite like being in the *Ka*-store of the Worm, it was! I might already be at journey's end, bouncing from one dead life to another . . . except that back home we had never lived such lives as these.

I was starting to feel like a child swopping seats on a wheeling carousel. Maybe I would carry on around the whole sphere of star colonies in similar style, bopping back into the void between whiles!

But then, en route from my eel-wife, the void bubbled up more bubbly than ever.

Ever?

Ever-never? ¿ɹǝʌǝ-ɹǝʌǝN I moved sharply otherwise, otherways. How can I put it? No words come close!

What happened now was to a moon as is the colour of blood in a pitch-dark room by night. It was to a fish as is the smell of a rose-bush in space. To a diamond as is the timelost instant of orgasm.

You see? No you don't.

All those things I've just mentioned connect, if you try hard enough. A diamond is an eternal kernel of light, outside of time. So also is ecstasy, the bright inner light. They can be related and make sense. Poetic sense. Ultimately in a poem almost anything can be related to anything else.

But if this happened ordinarily we would be drowning in a sea of chaos.

What was happening to me was a *relating*—a relating and a re-ordering along an unfamiliar axis: the name of which, for me, was "never-ever".

It was *ever*, and always. Yet also it was *never* because no happenings are unalterable. Nothing that happens in the universe is locked like an insect in amber. All is a shifting fluid—and this is as true of the past as of the future! What-had-been and what-might-be were both "never-ever". I felt very strongly that this was so.

Here was an answer to that old riddle which occurs in the *Alice* fragments supposedly written ages ago by the Artful Dodger's Son. I'd seen this discussed at length by savants in an Ajelobo newspaper.

The riddle: "Why is a raven like a writing desk?"

(For those who don't read Ajelobo newspapers, a raven is an ancient flying creature with feathers, a sort of black chicken that likes to steal bright objects such as rings.)

I knew the answer now. And the right answer was: "Why *shouldn't* it be?"

Please bear with me. Words divide things from other things. They box things into categories and classes. And so words make the world. They build reality. But words are also gluey, melty things. They leak. (If you say the same word a hundred times over, it leaks all over the place.) So eventually any word can stick to any other word; and I guess poetry is all about the glueyness of words rather than their usual role as solid boxes.

In exceptional circumstances, reality can be leaky too. It can get glued together in a different way.

Or maybe I should say that there isn't just one single reality. There are many possible realities, out of which only one exists. Whilst it does so, it excludes the others.

Okay. Call one reality "the raven". Call the other "the writing desk". They're as far apart as any two things can be. Thus good old familiar reality exists. A raven is. A writing desk also is. Has been, and will be.

But glue *can* join them together. And when this happens in *Ka*-space, where the keel of the universe sails, things can change.

I was sure now that the void "imagines" the shape of the universe which is sailing upon it. Yet the void is unaware of what it dreams. Awareness only exists inside the universe dreamt by the void.

Admittedly people possess imagination too, in a weaker form. But people keep ravens well clear of writing desks, because words say that ravens and writing desks are far apart. Only poets, madmen and riddlers ever say otherwise, and they're in a minority of one, besides being stuck in a universe where one individual can't alter things.

I sensed two forces at work upon the universe. There was a dividing force, which was strong, which kept all classes and categories of things neatly organized. There was also a glueing force, which was weak and which could alter the way things were arranged in their various boxes. In the never-ever of *Ka*-space, where an aeon could be a moment, the weak force could beat the strong.

You might suppose that my own "reality" was weird enough to start with! Here was I, zipping through *Ka*-space and bouncing off alien lives on other worlds. That was *nothing* compared with when the void bubbled; when I dived into ever-neverland, when I lost all familiar connexions.

One connexion which I lost right away was my deathline. The fibres parted; it snapped. Perhaps it was the snapping of my deathline which caused the bubbling of the never-ever? So thoroughly did the order of events collapse that I couldn't say for sure. Now and then, before and after: all melted.

And in this moment it seemed to me as if the void was bubbling out of itself a private time and private place for me alone, a tiny universe of mine own which would shrink back again into the void, with me contained inside it.

I wasn't having that.

That's when I cried out to my mother-world. I cried out to my home; to Pecawar; to the house where I was born and raised and murdered. And to my mother too. Oh yes, even though a mother can do nothing you still cry out to her!

That was when the never-ever twisted.

That was when the raven became the writing desk. When I cried.

Cried and cried.

I stopped crying.

I was feeble. I was tiny.

I knew what I was, and no mistake. It wasn't all that long since I'd been a baby back in Eeden. This was altogether a wetter, stickier, messier experience. My hips hurt like a wash-leather wrung out by strong hands. My face felt squashed out of shape, clogged-up and mucky. Someone else's upside-down face swam before my eyes. Presently this other face flipped upright and stabilized. Hands held me firmly but gently. Arms cradled my body. My eyes were dabbed clean, my nostrils too.

And because I'd been in this selfsame predicament within recent memory I had the wit to shut up and not scream out in my baby voice . . .

. . . the name of Chataly, my mother's cousin who choked on some food in her sleep and died, yet who was now tending at my delivery into the world . . .

. . . from out of a woman who lay on a bed, sweaty, hairslicked and weary, her legs still wide apart, leaking some blood and the long white cord which was my birth-string.

I didn't recognize my mother immediately; not looking like that.

When I did, I didn't want to. This may seem ungrateful in the circumstances, since she had just given birth to me, but the mother I knew wasn't this drenched exhausted naked suffering animal lying on the bed. Mother was cooler and neater.

Chataly set me down for a while, to cope with the cord sprouting from the midst of me.

That was what the string connecting me to the *Ka*-store of the Worm had become, when connexions changed! And the blue void had changed into the waters of the womb! Way back home, where I'd cried to be.

But I wasn't a baby *Yaleen*. I wasn't back at the time of my own original birth two decades earlier. I didn't make the mistake of supposing that! Mother was so bedraggled by the effort of giving birth

that I couldn't have said what age she was. But I remembered full
well what Chataly had looked like in her later years; and these
definitely were Chataly's later years.

Taking me up, she laid me under my mother's breast. Mother's
hands held me. Her heart thumped under me. She crooned. My lips
tasted sweet milk bubbling. I squirmed my floppy head aside but
then thought twice about refusal and suckled a bit. Obviously I
would have to feed.

Chataly must have been tidying the afterbirth away into a pan,
meanwhile; rearranging sheets and so forth. Next I heard her call to
my father. A door opened. I heard Dad's voice, close by:

"She's lovely! Oh isn't she wonderful! Our own little Narya—oh
doesn't she suit the name!" *(Do I, Dad?)*

I kept quiet while he fussed in my vicinity. Truth to tell, quite
soon I fell asleep. That little body of mine was tired.

As you can perhaps appreciate, this was a difficult period in my
lives!

Unlike in Eeden, here at home I wouldn't be growing up at high
speed. I would be advancing at the same slow pace as any other
baby born of woman. I would be suckling and pissing myself for
ages. I'd be unable to walk, unable to do most anything till my body
decided it was the right time to perform. I'd be a floppy doll. The
prospect frustrated the hell out of me.

I think I could have managed to talk within a few days. It was
entirely up to me what sort of noises I set my vocal chords to work
on. But I didn't dare talk. I didn't dare be anything other than a
baby. (Crying was a total waste of time; why bother?) I had to
think, think, *think.* Ahead. Behind me, and all around.

I'd done what the Godmind couldn't do. Or couldn't yet do. I'd
gone back in time. Right now, at this very moment, Yaleen—that's
to say, *me*—was somewhere off along the river, up to her adventures.
Those adventures were only about to happen, or in process of happening. And they must. Happen.

I'd lost any link with the Worm, of course. How could I be its
bosom-buddy when I hadn't yet died into the *Ka*-store? Let alone
boarded the Worm at Tambimatu, with diamond ring held high? Let
alone dived headlong into the black current for the first time?

But *why* "must" my adventures happen as before?

What if I spoke to Mum and Dad instead (shocking them silly)?
What if they spoke to the Guild? What if the Guild knew in ad-

vance that there would be a war, and chaos, if Yaleen crossed the
river? The Guild would surely believe me once one or two things
started coming true.

Lying first in my crib, and latterly in a cot, I played endless variations upon the theme of "What If?" Yet all variations seemed to
come up with the same answer.

If I spilled the beans, then I wouldn't be murdered by Doctor
Edrick. I wouldn't zoom off through *Ka*-space. I wouldn't return
home again, reborn as the new baby me. In other words I wouldn't,
couldn't, be here.

I remembered what Prof had said in Venezia (far away, but *not yet)*
about how something might vanish from the present if the past was
altered. I called to mind what I'd sensed in *Ka*-space about reality.
And I nursed a dire suspicion that if I was indiscreet, then something might indeed vanish from the present. Namely *me*—plus
chunks of history which were yet to happen. Yaleen's life would
surely change as a consequence, and couldn't lead to me now.

Meanwhile oceans of time slopped slowly by: oceans which had
flowed by once already.

I tried counting the nights (they're more distinctive than days) but
I soon lost count.

And I still couldn't come to any conclusion other than: *keep silent!*
Keep mum. Whilst Mum kept me.

One day she lifted me on to a rug to practise rolling and crawling
and holding my head up. Other highlights: I started to eat mash and
hash and broth and custards. Presently I was given rusks to suck and
grind my gums on.

Oh but wasn't I just a cute child! Hardly any bother at all. And oh
shit, wasn't I bored! But I sure as hell wasn't going to liven things up
prematurely.

After goodness knows how long, the stairs got carpeted in my
honour.

One night I seemed fretful. I was, too. So Mum carried me out
into the garden to see the stars. "Look, Narya: little lights all over!
They're called *stars*. Can you say stars? Stars, darling, stars." She was
worried because I wasn't yet babbling or lisping. I stayed mute. I
knew what my first word had to be.

Swaddled in her arms I gazed straight up, wondering which of
those little lights I had visited personally. Which was the sun of the
world where the birdpeople flew? Which, the suns that shone on the
wench with snails on her legs? Oh the ludicrous indignity of it,

when I'd been to those goddamn stars myself! I definitely deserved a star—a gold one—for patience.

Fearing a chill, Mum took me back inside and tucked me in, to dream sweet dreams.

Hi there, Yaleen: where have you got to by now? My older, younger sister; my self. As far as Edrick's house at Manhome South, is it? Or as far as the conclave at Spanglestream?

Edrick! Well, at least I wouldn't have to bother with that sod ever again; he was dead.

Oh *no* he wasn't. Must keep events in their proper order, mustn't I? Edrick would have to pop up in my life once again like a bad fincoin.

I was losing touch with the order of events. I had to go back over everything; just as if I were rewriting *The Book of the River* entire, from memory, having lost the manuscript. Which I had. Since it hadn't been written yet.

I was finding it increasingly hard to figure on Yaleen as a real person, or as the same person as myself. When she finally arrived, wouldn't she seem like some sort of living *fiction?* There she would be, saying her piece and doing her thing just as if she were the author of those words and deeds (which she was), yet with a few choice words of my own I could edit her life savagely and alter the whole story line!

If I did that, perhaps I would simply vanish out of her life, and her story. Then she would indeed be the free author of her destiny, and I would be . . . a blank. A page unwritten. Try as I might, I couldn't imagine what it would be like to vanish. But I surely wasn't going to take any chances on it!

About this time I realized that it wasn't sufficient for Yaleen just to turn up and get herself killed a bit later on. Before I could speak out, *The Book of the River* would have to be published, otherwise my words mightn't have the same impact. They wouldn't carry as much weight; so I told myself. (Weight to do what? Aha! If only I'd known the answer to that.)

Besides, what with Yaleen seeming so unreal, I felt that I needed the tangible reality of the book before I could become Yaleen again. It was as though her life was stored in there and could only become available to me when the book was issued. Ordinary memories grow fuzzy and mixed-up. Ordinary memories aren't the same as the experience of reliving a life in the *Ka*-store. Yaleen was a part of me which had fallen into the pool of time-past. She could only be hauled to the surface and regained, in the shape of her book.

Her reality had become the pages she would write. Meanwhile my own reality had shrunk to even less than book-size—down to matchbox-size. And all this while the whole cosmos was crashing silently and ever so slowly about me. Oh how the aeons flowed downstream, with me no more than a dayfly on a ripple.

Frankly, I'd say I deserve a bit of credit for not going crazy during this long waiting period. I merely seemed quite odd to my parents; rather out of step. (I'd started to take a few lurching steps.)

One day it rained. It poured, it bucketed. This was most unlike the usual Pecawar weather.

So I said, "Wain."

My parents were delighted. They were over the moon. (Ah, but we had no moon here, did we?)

So I obliged them with a few more ill-uttered words. But then I shut up again. I had to, hadn't I? Otherwise I might have spoiled everything. Still, Mum and Dad seemed satisfied with small mercies. For the time being they appeared relieved.

Whom did I pity more: them, or me? Them, I suppose. Myself, I was almost beyond self-pity. At times this whole charade even struck me as weirdly amusing. Yet how cruel of me—how cruel to Mum and Dad—to feel amused by it. What's more, if I let myself become too amused I might go mad, I feared.

So I soldiered on (as people would say, once the not-yet war was over). I spent my days wrapped in memories. I devoted less time to trying to chart unchartable options and alternatives, which in any case I didn't dare opt for.

"Wain." Big deal.

Oh, but I'll make up for my silence by and by, Mum and Dad, I promise. Yet will that make you any happier?

Problem: I knew how Yaleen had reacted to Narya. I remembered, albeit fuzzily. But how had Narya reacted to Yaleen?

And what had happened in the house after Edrick murdered Yaleen? I had no idea. If only I knew! If only Edrick had dropped some hint when we were in Eeden.

But no, no, no! Here yawned a trap into which I mustn't fall—and now I realized that I'd been sliding into this trap for months. The name of the trap was foreknowledge—the paralyser of initiative. It was *me* who was in peril of becoming a puppet, by following the story line exactly. Not Yaleen, but me! No wonder my parents often looked concerned, as though their Narya were missing some spark or other essential element of life: wilfulness, originality, whatever.

I made an effort to be more spontaneous and affectionate. I laughed and clowned a bit. Dad took me out for rides around town on his shoulders; I chirped appreciatively. I was sleeping in Capsi's old room by now. Dad added giant baby animals to Capsi's panorama of the west bank and coloured them in. I cooed and chortled.

Time sludged by.

We celebrated my second New Year's Eve with caraway cake and candles and gifts. Amongst other presents received by me—with wordless cries of delight—was a toy pussy-cat, which I could pull after me on a string. The cat wore a collar of tinkly silver bells.

Shortly after that party, Mum and Dad were discussing in hushed tones the amazing withdrawal upriver of the black current. Soon invasion was on their lips—and war. . . .

Mum's other cousin Halba came to town on business at this time, when Pecawar was a-buzz with fearful rumours. She owned a spice farm up-country, and had never been especially close to Mum; though Halba did pay us a number of visits over the years, and when I was twelve years old Capsi and I spent several weeks' holiday with her—a vacation which I wasn't likely to forget in a hurry, since Halba had fed us growing kids quite meanly and had made us toil for our keep.

Take the spice mace. Nutmeg balls, so sweetly smelling, come from little trees with yellowy blossoms. The blossoms are followed by a fruity "droop" the length of your little finger—inside which is a stone, the kernel of which is nutmeg. But an outgrowth from the base covers the nut with a crimson network called the "aril"—like a sort of thread fungus—which has to be picked off by hand, oh so carefully and painstakingly. And that's mace. Little fingers can get quite weary and knotted, unpicking the aril for a good few hours.

Take cloves. Cloves are simply the dried, unopened flower buds of a tree related to the nutmeg. Halba had a little plantation of these, and every bloody one of the blood-red buds had to be picked by hand, up ladders, double quick, before they could open.

Luckily, while Capsi and I were visiting, the vanilla orchids were still in bloom and hadn't yet set pods, or we might have been in for the treat of burying them in hot ashes and subsequently digging the shrivelled brown fingers up to rub them individually with olive oil. The corner of Halba's farm, where the vanilla orchids grew, did intrigue me, though. Hot water bubbled up from underground into rocky pools, so that the climate in that one particular spot was uniquely moist and steamy, unlike anywhere else for leagues and leagues. It was ideal for vanilla; Halba was the only local supplier of this spice.

Oh, and I'm forgetting the gentle art of peeling cinnamon, supposing that we had any spare time from unthreading aril and plucking clove buds. Capsi and I really needed those hot orchid-ringed pools to soak our feet in after a few happy hours spent rubbing the bark from the young cinnamon shoots with the soles of our feet, Halba's preferred method of unpeeling.

Halba was a stout, bustling woman who seemed jolly and was actually downright mean; and on those occasions when she visited us she brought nothing by way of a visiting gift yet always heartily ate her fill and generally contrived to carry something off with her—an ornament, a bag of fruit, some dried fish, a book, anything which she fixed upon and decided was surplus to our requirements. The time when she bore Capsi and me off was, of course, designed to save wages at harvest time. And did she resent the waste of a day to bring us home again to Pecawar afterwards, with a bag of her best dried brittle quills of cinnamon which we had "earned"! (We had, needless to say, eaten her out of house and home; as I recall my mother felt obliged to press some expensive candied blue-pears on Halba, which she accepted as her right.)

Anyway, Halba turned up in the midst of all the pother about the war—mainly to pump Dad about the likely long-term effect on prices and exports, a topic which he had no wish to discuss. (More about this anon.) After feeding herself generously at our house, and having commandeered a bed for the night, she then took herself off for the evening to visit "her friends" (which presumably we weren't).

Mum immediately buttonholed Dad.

"How lucky that Halba's come!"

"Is it?"

"Yes, don't you see? You and me and Narya should be ready to quit Pecawar at a moment's notice—in case those savages invade here next. This new local militia of ours mightn't be able to cope. We could go and stay with Halba, where we'd be safe. *Nothing* must harm Narya! That would kill me."

Dad sighed. I could see him weighing which argument was best, to pit against this folly. If he pointed out the truth about our "friendship" with Halba—and how little she would want us roosting on her in the country—this might make my mother stubborn. It might stir her to prove that nobody could *not* want Narya and her. Likely she would accuse Dad of a failure of love; of not wanting to bother disrupting domestic routine even to save his family from peril.

Dad hummed and hawed for a while—till Mum grew quite peeved—before he found the right tack.

"Look, if there's an invasion, the riskiest thing would be to take to the roads. Supposing there's trouble—I don't say there will be, but supposing—if we stay indoors here at home, villains would have to make a deliberate decision to break in and harm us. But if they caught us out in the open, harming us would be the most casual thing. In fact, if you're an invader that sort of behaviour makes sense. It spreads fear and disorder. Don't you see? We'd be mad to flee up-country."

"Maybe we should go right now, before those brutes have a chance to invade. Narya and I could leave with Halba tomorrow. You could sort out some leave and follow on."

"I really don't advise isolating ourselves out there. Look at it statistically. In a place as big as Pecawar there's no reason why we especially should be harmed. But on a lonely farm, with fewer people thereabouts, it's more dangerous. Not less! Don't you see? If the enemy turns up there, you'll be in real peril. . . ."

The argument rambled on for a while, without any direct references to Halba herself, and in the end Dad won. No request for sanctuary was put to the woman.

Yaleen was also mentioned that evening; speculatively, not too fretfully. Never once did I hear my parents refer to Capsi. Maybe they spoke of him in private.

No invasion came, of course. But came the day when Dad bore me out, shoulder-high, to see the rump of the junglejack army trudge into town.

Hitherto Mum had refused to let him take me to watch boats unload weapons or to view the advance guard of the army—the river-virgins, the first arrivals—performing their drill. She thought that the sight might scare me and upset my peace of mind. I, who was responsible for half of this! When it came to greeting the 'jacks who had tramped such a long way to our aid, Dad put his foot down. Both feet, in fact: one in front of the other, and me on his shoulders.

We took up station on Molakker Road—our southern approach—amidst quite a crowd, and Dad gave me a bright red kerchief to wave. Presently the troops tramped into view and did their best to put on a show for us. Oh, the glamorous, smelly, travel-stained warriors twirling their swords and axes, pikes and spears.

"Soldiers," said Dad. "Those are soldiers."

"So-jers," I repeated. I cried the word over and over as we watched the rather weary parade. How delighted he was with me.

Alas, there was an accident. As the rearguard made their way by, a 'jack with the build of a bull whose black hair was curled into horns by sweat tossed an axe right up in the air, to catch it by the handle. At that moment an older man in front, who must have been exhausted, stumbled. In an effort to recover step and poise, he pranced backwards. The two men collided. The toppling axe caught the older man on the side of the head. He screamed, fell, writhed in the dust clutching at his injury. Blood pumped from the ruin of his ear, bright as the kerchief I was waving.

Dad hastily reached up and clapped a hand over my face. With a groan, he whirled me away. When he set me down and let me see again, we were behind the high brick wall of a builder's yard hidden from the commotion in the road.

"See so-jers," I said cheerfully, and flapped my red flag.

"Yes, soldiers. But we'll have to get on home now. Your mother will be wondering where we are. It was good seeing the soldiers, wasn't it?"

"Mmm. Mmm!"

There were other outings in addition, though never by way of the quayside itself. On this score Dad heeded Mum's wishes. Maybe he didn't want another daughter of his to be prematurely intoxicated by river life. Or maybe he was worried in case I might lisp some indiscretion when we got back home. Not that I had betrayed him regarding the soldier's mutilation; but he may have believed he had acted so promptly that slow, strange Narya noticed nothing horrid.

These were outings to Dad's place of work; and if I've never before mentioned the fact that Dad worked, or at what, there's a good reason—though I've only become aware of it now!

The truth is that during all the years while Capsi and I were growing up at home, we knew in the abstract that our Dad worked as a spice clerk, yet never once did we get close to his actual work; neither physically close nor mentally close.

Dad's job certainly left its aroma on his clothes and on his skin. However, this was no more and no less than the aroma of Pecawar town itself, fainter or stronger depending on wind direction, but always pervasive. Thus Dad seemed like a distillate of Pecawar, the centre of things, the origin. The spice warehouses, the drying and crushing and blending sheds and whatnot, were relegated to the edge of our mental horizon, as an effect rather than a cause.

Dad always held his work at arm's length, well away from our home life. Presumably he and Mum discussed work and money matters together; but we kids heard nothing of it. Nor did Dad hobnob in his spare time with any colleagues from work; we kids saw nothing of them or of their kids. We didn't mix. As a result there was simply no sense of connexion between our home and the place to which Dad went during the day. The work side of Dad's life was a blank. It was something carefully screened away. Yet the screen hid no vital secret or romantic mystery. It just concealed something boring, something which didn't involve us.

Nor was the episode of our hardship holiday at Halba's farm an exception to this general rule. Dad neither escorted us to the farm nor brought us back. He worked in town, at the merchanting end of the spice business, and though he must have known all about arils and droops, when Capsi and I had recounted our harvesting experiences Dad had merely raised an eyebrow and soon changed the subject. I only remember him tousling our heads and saying, "Well, you're home again; that's the main thing."

Looking back, I believe this is one of the main reasons why I was so keen to sign on a river boat as soon as possible. And I guess this is what made Capsi scan the further shore in an effort to fill in its much more interesting blanks. Dad's workaday life didn't exist for us. By extension the workaday world of Pecawar wasn't for us either (a prejudice amply confirmed by our visit to Halba). It had no meaning.

Do you know, I'm not even sure whether Mum, in her youth, had brought Dad home from Sarjoy itself or from somewhere smaller on the way to Aladalia! No doubt we kids enquired, at the age when kids ask such things. No doubt Dad told us. Yet the notion of him being from somewhere else made very little impression. He went nowhere, to work. He must have come from nowhere too. Capsi and

I had no desire to devalue those other magical exotic towns by overly identifying Dad with one of them.

As Capsi grew up, he of course came to understand that he could only ever visit foreign towns once in his lifetime—in the same manner that Dad had once voyaged to Pecawar as a young man to wed Mum. To do what thereafter? To tot up accounts or inventories or whatever. This realization turned Capsi against all of our shore, in favour of the other.

But then—so much for youthful rebellion!—what did Capsi do but run away to the Observers? To those who spent all their time totting up the account and compiling the inventory of the blank west bank, filling in the ledger of our ignorance. Capsi may have been rebellious, yet in a fateful way he was still the son of his father! Had it not been for me he might have spent the rest of his days up that Spire in Verrino, as a clerk of a different stripe.

I didn't consider that I was the daughter of either Mum or Dad in quite the same repetitive fashion. Except that by now I was their daughter *twice over*. Which was certainly a repetition!

In a surprise reversal of times past, Dad now took me several times to his place of employ. This, during a war! Yet here perhaps lay the key to this change of heart—rather than in any suspicion of his that he had lost his other children through a lack of workaday connexions. I'm sure Dad wanted to prove that he too was doing something significant, and that soldiers weren't the only ones who served. He wanted to show me this (as though I would understand, or even remember, at such a tender age!), and by so doing persuade himself that he was proud of what he did, and hadn't wasted his life.

Mum demurred at these trips to work, but Dad insisted. Now was a time when men were putting their feet down. Tramp, tramp. Quick march. About turn!

Since Dad was senior in his job these days, there was no bother about my turning up at work. He always chose routes to and fro which kept us away from the waterfront, but once at the counting house I had the run of the place and of the adjacent warehouses and processing sheds, some of which were seductively close to the river.

Generally the janitor, old one-eyed Ballow, kept his eye on me. Well, he wasn't really one-eyed; a milky cataract eclipsed his left pupil, and he wore a grey patch to cover it. Early on in our acquaintance he revealed his disfiguration, to warn me about the pair of ginger cats which slunk around the buildings (keeping these clear of shrew-bugs and of any intruding Golden Spritsail flutterbyes which would lay their eggs on spice sacks). Years ago Ballow found a hurt cat. Foolishly he picked it up, increasing its pain so that the animal struck out, puncturing his eyeball, letting in a disease. So he said.

"I often dream," he told me confidentially, "that I'm a cat—with the eyes of a cat. It's as though they owe me an eye, and repay me. When I'm awake, like now, I see everything flat. When I'm asleep, I see things deep as can be, the way they used to look. That's why I'm kind to the cats here, since it wasn't that sick one's fault. But don't you ever put your lovely little peepers anywhere near a pussy's claws, or your Dad would never forgive me."

He pointed at one of our hunters, which had actually spotted a shrew-bug clinging on to a coriander sack—a fairly rare encounter. Ginger was arse-squirming towards its prey, taking his time, teasing the tip of his tail to twitches of delicious frustration. Eventually he launched, patted the shrew-bug to the floor, played with it till it was broken, then ate it.

"There's an old tale, you know," observed Ballow, "concerning three friends who only had one eye between them to see with. And one tooth between them to eat with. And one long fingernail to scratch with, and stir the porridge and pick your nose. When it came time to swap the eye and the tooth and the fingernail around, you might suppose as you couldn't trust the friend with the eye since he could see where the tooth and the nail were, so he might grab them and run off. But no. All three friends could see through that one eye at the same time, no matter whose head it was in, no matter if the three were leagues apart. Not that they ever were leagues apart, since without a tooth you can't eat, and without a nail you can't scratch; and they were always awful itchy, these friends, and they often had colds as blocked their noses up. But finally one day the friend who had the eye at the time—let's call him Inkum—he did seize the tooth and the nail by guile. He stuck the tooth in his gob, and the nail on his finger's end, and he took off at a run. His friends —whom we'll call Binkum and Bod—could see where he was running to, from his point of view, so they raced after him to keep up."

Ballow sat himself down on the coriander sack. He slapped his hands on his knees and squinted at me. "So what do you suppose happened next?" And he waited.

Now, I wasn't in the habit of answering anyone; and Ballow was really being quite a disgusting old buffer at the moment, though maybe he thought he was entertaining me or even educating me.

But he just carried on sitting there on the sack, and every now and then he asked me again, "So what happened?"

I could of course have walked away, and maybe I should have done, but I was thinking that Yaleen was my absent eye and I wouldn't be able to see or do anything effective till she turned up and surrendered her viewpoint to me.

I had an inspiration, and stuck my tongue out at Ballow.

He chortled and slapped his knees again.

"So you'd trade a tongue for an eye, would you, little girl? You'd trade a tongue for an eye! But it's you as needs a tongue, eh? Tell you what: if you'll give Ballow one of your eyes, Ballow'll give you his tongue to talk with. How's that?"

I revised my opinion sharply. Ballow wasn't daft or disgusting at all. What a perceptive old codger he was, to be sure. I wondered whether my Dad had put him up to this, having known Ballow for years; whether this was the real why and wherefore of my outing. But no, no, I doubted that. Dad, who had clapped a hand over precious Narya's eyes so that she wouldn't behold a wounded ear, would have clapped his hands over her ears if he had heard half of Ballow's banter.

I had to play this just right.

I flexed my fingers like claws. Said, "Miaow!"—and hissed.

"Okay, okay," said Ballow. "So you're hurting inside, like that pussy I mentioned. No need to scratch my other peeper out. What I see in you—with one peeper, which is better than most folks with two—I won't say to a soul. There, that's a bargain, eh? We're friends now."

He stuck his hand out. It was big and tough as a cow's hoof and dirty. I wrinkled up my nose, but laid my little hand in his.

And we were friends from then on. Firm friends. One of us half-blind, the other one mostly dumb.

"I'll show you a game you can play with peppercorns," he said. "You have to build a pyramid. . . ."

These excursions turned out to be the pleasantest hours of my phony infancy. What with the war and so many boats being used as a navy, the export trade was at a virtual standstill; though the clerks still had work enough on hand, analysing and accounting. Nevertheless, Dad always spared some time to walk me round the warehouses and processing sheds. I showed my appreciation by smiling and crowing, and touching and sniffing: the spices, and Dad. Connecting, connecting the two.

He too made a connexion one day—between time past and time present. I was in his little office, boxed off by a bamboo trellis from the rest of the spice-musty counting house. I was hanging on to the edge of his desk which was piled with open ledgers, crammed with figures in his neat hand, some fresh, some old and faded.

"Now supposing we'd fled to Halba's for refuge," he remarked, more to his ledgers than to me, "we'd have had to rely on her for charity, and repay her with labour, hoeing and pruning and hauling, wouldn't we? As our Yaleen had to, once, at harvest time. Instead of relying on ourselves alone. But maybe if you rely on yourself entirely, that's what you become: alone. Then one day you break your leg, and who's there to help? Who's there?"

I drummed my fingertips on the desk top, as much as to say, "I'm here."

Dad laughed, and drummed his fingers too.

"Ah, what would we do without you, Narya? And what would we do without those brave 'jacks?"

Even after the war was won Dad continued, jauntily, with these treats. Yes, jauntily. For men of the east had marched far from their homes and gained a victory; and he was a man. So his heart quickened to the distant drumbeat. Thus maybe the Sons, in defeat, had gained one small, nasty victory; for what woman in her right mind would ever thrill to the clash of swords and the excitement of busting heads? To the looseness, violence and anarchy of it all? Oh yes, Dad had groaned when that 'jack lost his ear to the axe; but he groaned because his little girl might have noticed—and perhaps, perhaps, because that was the real outcome of wielding weapons, and he didn't wish to know.

Long ago, Yaleen had told that brother of Dario's that she sympathized with the frustrations of men. That was before she had been tortured in Cherubland by frustrated Sons who bated women. True, those Sons were exceptions . . . mad dogs. Nor had the 'jacks who fought in our campaign exactly changed into crowing cockerels as a result. But there did seem to be an insidious equation between violence and the sporters of penises, when men were able to rule the roost. It had been so on the Moon, whatever Jean-Paul's secret intentions to preserve and protect his flock. (Though who had murdered umpteen Paxmen with a bomb? None other but the cherub Yaleen. . . .)

And yet, and yet, men were diminished by our way of life. That was true, too.

Or had been true, till now. The war had loosened certain inveterate restraints. Should those be bound up again tightly—or not? Maybe no debate was needed. The black current already stretched as far as Aladalia. Restless men could always walk to beyond Aladalia—where indeed they might be useful as soldiers, guardians of our freedom.

Meanwhile relations between man and woman were subject to a degree of flux, and Dad stepped out defiantly, perhaps unaware why there was a different spring in his step.

Then one day as he was bearing me along dusty crowded Zanzyba Road, just as we were drawing close to the Café of the Seasons, a voice cried, "Dad!"

I saw Yaleen sitting there.

Dad broke into a gallop. I giggled with relief and nerves.

It was like a reverse of that time when I returned to war-wrecked Verrino and hastened up to the top of the Spire, only to find emptiness and nobody there (until Hasso turned up). Here was Yaleen at last, in exactly the right place. I felt hysterical. Hilarity welled up in me. The charade would soon be over. I could start being myself again, just as soon as there wasn't another self bumming around in competition. I could stop being Narya—and become . . . Naryaleen?

A tricky moment, this! Trickiest of all when I winked at Yaleen. She gave me such a peculiar look; but I couldn't resist the wink. Besides, I had already seen myself wink at me, a few years earlier at this very moment. I was grinning stupidly when I todded over to the table, but I composed myself.

"Hallo, Narya," said Yaleen. "My name's Yaleen. I'm your sister."

Supposing I said: "Oh no you aren't"? Supposing I said: "You and me are the same person"?

I didn't. I wasn't going to throw away two years' drudge on a wild whim. Would you?

Since I merely stood there mute, Dad and Yaleen got on discussing my supposed problems, over my head.

"Ah, she's my big darling, aren't you?" said Dad after a bit. He hoisted me aloft. "Let's step on home, Yaleen."

I steered Dad home by tufts of hair as though I were steering worlds. Or suns around the galaxy; keeping reality from colliding with itself by a hairsbreadth.

You already know the events of the next two weeks. During that time I was an arrow notched on a taut string, ready to fly to its target: namely that night when my parents would be away at Chataly's; and when I would lock Doctor Edrick and Yaleen in the bedroom together. But beyond that point I would be shooting blind.

Do you know, I'd been passive for so long that it even seemed possible to me during those last days that I might simply continue thereafter in the same vein? That this might be preferable?

I could start to talk more freely. I could grow up ordinarily. I could make believe that I was just like any other child. Ultimately I might even persuade myself that during my infancy I had been insane. Them, having duly grown up, I could steer well clear of Worms and rivers for the rest of my days, and nobody would be any the wiser. . . .

During that same fortnight, Yaleen too had been going through similar mood shifts. She also had been thinking about opting out. She had nursed fantasies of marriage, or of becoming a hermit or a poet; now hadn't she?

Taut as I was—stretched like a banjo string—was I resonating in tune with Yaleen? Was I echoing her? Or had she perhaps been echoing *me* unawares? Had vibrations been passing up and down the same *Ka*-tree, on which we both were leaves, travelling through the ever-never?

It's odd: I only grasped this aspect of that last fortnight just now when I set it down on paper. Obviously there's some use in writing books; you discover things you didn't know before! Or do you perhaps invent them? Then convince yourself that they are and always were the truth, because they explain events more neatly than the confusion—the shooting in the dark—of the actual time?

To act or not to act? If I didn't act, I would forever just be the kid sister of Yaleen of Pecawar, author of *The Book of the River*. That wouldn't do at all, now would it?

So was my pride more of a spur to action than the threat posed by the Godmind and its burning lens? Perhaps! The Godmind and its concerns seemed far away from our little family home in Pecawar; from the smell of cinnamon coffee, from the gaudy barrel-gourds in the garden. My universe had diminished drastically, but at least I had my pride to see me through.

*   *   *

Chataly choked to death. Mum and Dad departed. Yaleen cooked a pudding, brewed cocoa, read to me and saw me off to bed with a kiss.

Before story-time I sneaked into the kitchen and unbolted the back door. Yaleen never did get round to wondering how Doctor Edrick had managed to enter the house without smashing and crashing. When he popped up, that was that. Busy! And after she was murdered, Yaleen had other things on her mind. Unbolting the door may seem a somewhat shitty thing for me to do. Hardly fair exchange for a pudding, a bedtime tale and a kiss? Well, if I can put it this way, it seemed a *likely* thing for me to do. When I locked the bedroom door upstairs I would close a trap; so presumably it was up to me to open the trap in the first place. It balanced out.

As soon as I estimated that Yaleen had settled down with the poems of Gimmo the Tramper, downstairs from my bed I crept. Yaleen would doze off before Edrick arrived, and I didn't know how long she would snooze. Hunkering down in the dark outside the door, I waited.

Not long, as I discovered.

Then everything happened very suddenly—just as it had happened once already. (Though this was the first, and only time.)

When Yaleen noticed me skulking there, I scrammed. I hid behind the urn in our entry hall. No sooner was I concealed than Yaleen came crashing through the door and scrambled upstairs pursued by Edrick. I counted slowly to ten and followed them. Opened the bedroom door, got the key, closed and locked it.

When I turned that key I locked another door as well: the door of foreknowledge. Suddenly the future was a blank, unwritten. Now the burden was gone; I was free. I felt as though I'd spent these last two years gaga in a trance. . . .

Action, now! I hastened into my own room, to drag a chair against the open window. I climbed on to the sill. That was when I heard the bang of the pistol, muffled by Yaleen's mattress and a couple of intervening doors. *(Bye, Yaleen! Fly away!)* On the wall outside was a rickety trellis supporting a creeper which bore hosts of tiny flame-blooms every spring. The creeper pretty well hid the spars of the trellis, as well as holding them together. If the trellis had been easier to spot—and bear in mind—Dad would probably have torn it down to prevent precisely such an escapade as followed.

I edged out, latched on, and climbed slowly, feeling my way up to the flat of the roof. It was a good thing it was night. Apart from some escaping lamplight, the only light came from the stars. Just enough illumination, not too much. Any brighter, and I might have been *scared*—what with the cliff of wall above me and the gulf below and me only being little. One rotten spar snapped but I didn't lose my grip. The trellis sagged but didn't collapse. I soon humped myself over the guttering and lay a while, panting. Then I stood up on the roof and screamed my lungs out to the neighbourhood.

It's amazing how much noise a small child can make. And I made it all. I didn't bother with words at first, just noise. Then I decided to switch to some words in case the neighbours thought I was merely a tom-cat with its dander up.

"Help! Murder! Enemy! Enemy! Help!" I shrieked.

By now Edrick had probably discovered that the door was locked, and kicked it loose. He'd be able to hear my shrieks, though since the noise was coming from overhead maybe this would confuse him. If he did dash into my bedroom and try to climb the trellis I was sure the structure would collapse; though come to think of it, Edrick only needed to stand on the windowsill to chin himself up to the roof. But why should he bother? Why should Yaleen's little sister matter to him now? He'd be best advised to cut and run.

Lanterns and lamps lit up in the nearby houses.

"Help! Help!" Raggedly; my throat was giving out.

People soon came pounding along the lane to our front door. I heard cries of "Stop!" and half of the people rushed on by; so Edrick must have decamped. Pursuit receded into the distance. Very public-spirited, but hardly sensible! Why run after a killer?

Lantern light spilled into our garden from downstairs, supplementing the faint glow cast by Yaleen's reading lamp, so neighbours were inside the house by now; Edrick must have left the front door open in his haste.

In the distance I heard the crack of a shot.

I squatted on the edge of the roof to await rescue, while above me blinked the stars. My stars.

Death never makes things simpler. Oh what a fuss there was with Yaleen found dead! And Doctor Edrick also dead, as it transpired.

Needless to say, in the eyes of my saviours I was simply a shocked little child, so I had a bit of difficulty working out exactly what had happened to Edrick. By and by I pieced it together. I gathered that his pursuers caught up with him in a blind alley, where Edrick fired his pistol, smashing someone's shoulder. Then the pistol must have jammed, or maybe it could only fire two shots before reloading; so our local heroes rushed him, and Doctor Edrick collected a knife in the guts.

No doubt this was a sign of the times in once peaceful Pecawar. Our local newssheet had published details of "war atrocities" in Verrino. My parents had discussed these hushedly, other people not so hushedly, it seemed. Though the people of Pecawar hadn't themselves been injured by the war, this seemed to make them the more virtuously incensed on behalf of Verrino and its victims. It was noteworthy to me that the people of Verrino itself hadn't flooded out en masse to the prison-pens to try to massacre their former tormenters. They were numb with their sufferings. But Pecawar people had the energy to feel aggrieved. Thus a presumed absconding murderous Son armed with a gun and an offbeat accent deserved a quick reprisal, rather than citizen's arrest and investigation. (An investigation, just in case he was indeed a junglejack deserter, some poor wretch desperate to get home to Jangali.) When our citizens knifed Edrick, they didn't even know he had murdered anyone; not for sure. Such a thing wouldn't have happened before the war; but at least nobody openly boasted of planting the knife.

That was the least of the fuss; and I'm anticipating things, rather. That's because I want to tidy Edrick away quickly, since he has no further role to play in my story. So we'll put a speedy full stop to him right now, just as one of our good and kindly neighbours did that night with a blade. As the Godmind would say: "Finish!"

Back to myself awaiting rescue. This was accomplished by one of the neighbours, Axal, husband of Merri. He fetched a ladder, brought me down to the ground and took me round to the kitchen, there to fix a hot spiced milk to distract my innocent mind; whilst upstairs the floor of my slaughtered sister's bedroom creaked underfoot. Merri also soon arrived, wrapped in a nightrobe.

Every now and then concerned faces appeared in the kitchen doorway, calling Merri or Axal (mainly Axal) into the living room to confer; there where Gimmo's *Songs of a Tramp* still lay on the floor. Bustle, bustle.

"Did you raise the alarm, Narya?" Axal knelt to enquire of me between whiles. I stared at him dumbly, clutching my cup for comfort.

Sadly Merri shook her head. "It must have been Yaleen."

"How did Narya get on the roof?" Axal asked his wife. This was a leading question.

"Yaleen," I whimpered plaintively. "Yaleen!"

"Hush, darling," Merri soothed me. "Your sister's gone away for a while."

Oh yes indeed. Too true. Gone away for a while. *(Fly away, Yaleen!)*

"You can sleep at our house tonight, darling."

I scrambled to clutch the edge of the sink. "Home!" I insisted.

"No, no, it's a *good* idea to visit our house till your Mum and Dad get back."

"Home!"

"The poor dear's had an awful shock."

"Those sodding Sons," Axal swore. "Serves the swine right."

"Shhh . . . ! Do you think there are any more about?"

"Militia'll be here soon. Carlo's gone to rouse the 'jack captain and the quaymistress."

"At least," whispered Merri, "Narya's too young to understand. That's a blessing. But we must get her over to our place. And you're coming as well! I should think so, with runaway Sons around."

"Of course, of course." So what did Axal do but rush off into the living room to talk to someone instead? Excitement, danger, action! It was quite some time before we left the house; and Merri had more trouble prising Axal away than me.

Mum and Dad arrived back late the following day. The neighbours knew where they'd gone to. (Just try to keep your business private in Pecawar! Well, Dad had always done his best, till recently. . . .) The riverguild had sent a messenger. Chataly's funeral rites had to be somewhat rudely abridged; Mum and Dad returned hastily to tuck me back under their wings, and to grieve and bury anew.

To grieve; and not let me see how deeply they were grieving— blessing me the while with smiles and hugs and stray touches. But I saw. Oh all the grief!

I'd minimized this aspect of Yaleen's murder. I'd hardly given it a thought, in fact! Because Yaleen *had* to die; and I was her, anyway. But Mum and Dad didn't know.

I didn't—or rather, *couldn't*—console them. What a selfish shit I felt.

Not least when they took me into Yaleen's room a few hours before the funeral to say goodbye to her. The body was lying on bedding in an open box laid across trestles. A blanket was pulled up to Yaleen's chin. A crown of green leaves, pulled from the same creeper that grew on the wall outside my bedroom, was bound round her brow. I was supposed to cover her mouth for a few moments with my fingers. I was to hide her closed eyes with my hands. (The eyeballs had sunk in; the lids were flaps.)

Yaleen's bare arms were holding the blanket in place, her hands crossed above her breast. On her right hand, was my diamond ring. What a nerve! They were going to bury it with her.

After I'd covered her mouth and her eyes—rather perfunctorily—I seized her cold and waxen hand.

"I want this ring," I said. "It's mine. It belongs to me." I started to haul the ring off; or to try to.

What a brat, what a brat.

Though goodness, I was *talking!* And in real sentences! Consequently the pain I caused by this misbehaviour was shot through with surprise and delight, judging by the glances Mum and Dad exchanged.

"No, Narya," Mum said gently, "you can't have it."

"Oh but I must. Yaleen wanted me to have it. She was going to give it to me. She promised."

Mum thought a moment. "You wouldn't be telling us a little fib, would you?"

A *little* fib? Gosh no. I'd only been lying my arse off every day for the last two years; by omission if not by commission.

"Yaleen said so, when you went away. When you left us." That should make them feel guilty. Insert one thorn of self-recrimination. How nice of me. But hell, I wanted that ring back. When all is explained, I told myself, all shall be forgiven.

"I don't *think* she'd make such a thing up," murmured Dad.

"Darling," said Mum, "Yaleen probably meant it for you when you were grown up, and when she was an old woman."

"A promise is an oath," I said. (Dad raised an eyebrow.)

"A diamond ring isn't suitable for a young child," Mum insisted.

"You can keep it safe for me," I said. "In trust."

This time they really did exchange glances.

"Where did you hear that word?" asked Dad.

"Yaleen said it. She said 'in twust'."

"It must be true." Dad twisted the ring off Yaleen's finger. "We'll keep this somewhere very safe till you're a little older, Narya. But it's yours, I promise."

Mum began to snivel, then turned to hug me. "Now there's only you! But you're talking to us! It's like a little miracle. It's as if we've lost Yaleen but. . . ." She choked.

Sure. But gained a real little girl; fitted with a voice and vocabulary.

"Perhaps," said Dad, "the shock has, well, made her bloom?"

"You *will* go on talking to us, won't you?" begged Mum.

What a question. I tried to look gaga and wide-eyed, and merely nodded.

"Say you will! Please!"

"My dear," said Dad imploringly.

Maybe I ought to have let them bury the damn ring after all.

"She might be able to say what happened on that terrible night!"

Definitely it was high time for a bit of acting. "Oh, night!" I cried. "Bad man! Oh! Oh!"

Dad shook his head sternly at Mum. "You shouldn't remind her of that. Let her think of the ring. The ring replaces Yaleen. Children are like that." He held up my diamond. "We'll put this somewhere safe, Narya. And soon we'll put your sister somewhere safe too, where she can sleep and dream of you."

Sleep and dream, eh? Yaleen had told them a bit about the *Ka*-store of the Worm, but obviously it hadn't quite sunk in . . . as yet.

"Nice sister ring," said I. "Keep safe."

So then it was time for the funeral; and quite a cortège hummed its way through the dusty streets. A lot of neighbours joined the procession. The local militia, led by their 'jack captain, paid their respects by carrying the death-box and by escorting it. The quaymistress—successor to the woman who had arranged my initiation—led a crew of riverwomen. Nice to know that I was missed!

Out to the graveyard we hummed our way wordlessly, for death was a time when the talking stopped; when no more could be spoken. Of death itself, whatever personal fantasies or preferences one might have, nothing of value could be said in public. Or so these people all thought, for a wee while yet. Till *The Book of the River* came out; till they learned of the *Ka*-store of the Worm. . . .

Meanwhile they hummed. They made a voiceless music to express love and sorrow; and by virtue of that hum, issuing from lungs which still breathed, the town breathed on, and everyone in it.

As ever, no one knew how the hum would develop; whether it would be soft, or loud; what sort of tune if any it would carry. No one in particular began it or led it. It arose. It gathered. It *was*. Grief and painful thoughts would die away in the living hum. Then after the death-box had been dumped in a shallow hole inside our sandy, walled cemetery, and after the "Rods" had filled in the hole, the humming would die away. (Of course deaths are viewed a little differently nowadays; but you still have to dispose of the corpse!)

The death-hum at my funeral was a rich, loud plainsong. Presently it began to sound like the tune *Under the Bright Blue Sun*, no doubt thanks to the choir of riverwomen. I hummed along with glee till we arrived at our destination.

It was years since I'd visited the graveyard, but it hadn't changed. Worn stone windbreak walls wandered around the perimeter in a series of silted bays. Despite these walls the wind when it blew carved dunes and troughs. A fire-blackened fused patch at the far end marked where the Rods burnt whichever old death-boxes worked their way back to the surface, or were uncovered by the breezes. . . .

For the benefit of readers leagues away from Pecawar, with somewhat different customs, I should explain that the Rods took their name from the way they probed the sand to find space for new death-boxes. Maybe a corpse would lie in the ground for a hundred years, or only a couple of years, but sooner or later it would surface in its box. The Rods would haul it away, and up it would go in smoke. That day, as ever in the cemetery, a few wooden edges and corners were poking up here and there like sunken vessels. This arrangement would hardly have worked in steamy, reeky Tambimatu! But it suited us in Pecawar. The dryness of the air and the sand soon turned bodies into leathery mummies. There was no smell.

So when Yaleen had been sunk in the sand and covered, the humming ceased. The militia marched off. Neighbours shuffled away homeward—increasing their pace as soon as they were out of sight, I don't doubt. The riverwomen departed, all except for the quaymistress. She lingered around the stone archway of the graveyard, and as we three family mourners emerged she approached my parents.

"Did Yaleen tell you that she left a memorial?"

"What do you mean?" asked Mum. "A memorial? I don't follow you."

"Yaleen wrote a book."

"She never said!"

"It'll soon be published in Ajelobo."

"How soon?" I butted in. "My sister book, how soon?"

The quaymistress smiled down ruefully at me. "Maybe twenty weeks." She ruffled my hair. "A long time for a little girl!"

Not really. I had an actual deadline now; a schedule for coming fully alive, as me.

"What sort of book is this?" asked Dad. "What's in it?"

"Her life is in it. All of her life. I haven't read the manuscript myself, but that's the word on it."

"And she never said!" exclaimed Mum. "Never!" She glanced back towards the grave as though a hand might break surface, waving the book at us.

"Maybe when we read it," said Dad, "then we'll *really* know her."

"Aye, when it's too late! First Capsi, now Yaleen. We're plagued." Mum clutched me close.

"The Guild will see to it that you receive the very first copies." The quaymistress went on more crisply, "There'll likely be some income, too. Maybe a fair amount. Yaleen wrote the book for the Guild, but in the circumstances we'll remit you fifty per cent of any royalties accruing."

This was really *crass*. And what a cheek: there would "likely" be "some" income!

"We don't need money," Dad said coldly.

Oh, great!

"Take money, Dad," I lisped. "Fish are for catching."

He stared at me oddly. "We'll think about it," he said with dignity.

"Do! Do! When you decide, just get in touch." The quaymistress beamed. Mentally I consigned this particular specimen to a deep pool cram-packed with stingers. Then I hauled her out again, because in due course I would have to do business with her.

So we returned home. As soon as I reasonably could, and before Mum and Dad could nerve themselves to sort through Yaleen's few possessions, I slipped upstairs and into her room. I quickly found where I'd put my private afterword to *The Book of the River* and smuggled this into my own bedroom. Folding the papers up small, I stuffed them into a hole which I poked in the belly of my cat on wheels.

My afterword. Yes, mine. Now that Yaleen was safely sunk in sand, my two "I"s had flowed back together. The two streams of my life had rejoined.

Two years down, twenty weeks to go.

The weeks went. Not without strain, not without problems. Now that I'd begun to talk I couldn't very well stop as if struck dumb; but I had to watch every word I said.

What's more, Mum *treasured* me. Now more than ever. She acted as though I might suddenly succumb to ague, fever, paralysis, food-poisoning, night-chills, simultaneously or in any combination thereof. And whilst treasuring, she grieved, nobly and tight-lipped.

At last came the day when an advance copy of the book arrived by special messenger from the quaymistress's office. Mum didn't tell me what it was. She set it by in a safe place till Dad came home from work; she needed his company before she could tackle it. But I did catch a glimpse of the volume. It was bound in stiffened cloth, with a zigzag black and blue pattern suggesting waves, rivers, black currents. My name and the title were printed in silver lettering. The book looked handsome indeed. The Guild had taken pains.

That evening I was packed off early to bed so that Mum could settle to read the story aloud to Dad—all evening along and what seemed like half the night.

Upstairs, I stayed awake in the dark, latterly by pinching and slapping myself. Every so often I sneaked downstairs to check on progress. At long last I was in the belly of the Worm (in bookland). Mum's voice was sore and cracked. No doubt her eyes were giving out too. I settled silently on the stairs.

Finally Mum read out, *"That's what choices are for. To savour them while you can, and then to seize one. Or the other. . . .* That's it: the end," she said.

Before she could begin to weep, and soothe her eyes with tears, I ambled into the lamplit room.

"Pretty good, eh?" I said. "Hullo, Mum, Dad. I wrote all that. I'm Yaleen. That's who I really am."

What happened next wasn't quite what I'd expected.

Dad spanked me.

He delivered four thwacks across my backside—and though I can't pretend that this hurt me worse than being tortured by Edrick and his boys, it had, um, impact. Whilst he was spanking me, Mum turned her head away, her hands still fondling *my* book.

Then Dad hauled me unceremoniously upstairs, stuck me back in bed and slammed the door.

Bloody hell.

At breakfast next morning I tried again. (Breakfast was spiced oats, nuts, bran and milk; the latest health fad for me.) Mum immediately looked fraught and remote.

Dad quickly interrupted.

"Narya! Last night you caused us a lot of sorrow, at a most precious moment. I realize you don't understand *why*, but I should have thought you learnt a lesson last night—much as I loathed having to teach you it. I'll do the same again if I have to."

"Hang on, Dad! How do you explain I can suddenly talk like a grown-up?"

"I know you've become wonderfully precocious of late, Narya. And we're delighted. Truly! It's marvellous. You were such a slow starter. But I must draw the line at this . . . this unkind pretence."

"There *is* no Narya, Dad! There never was. I've been Yaleen all along—I had to make believe till now."

"Make believe," he repeated tightly. "Exactly! Just so. Children often make believe. But children don't think things through. You could hardly be Yaleen, when Yaleen was in the same house as you. So let's have no more of it, understand?"

Mum clasped Dad's hand. This at least stopped me from being thumped immediately. "Might this be more serious?" she whispered. "The shock of that night, do you think?"

"I was Yaleen all the time," I insisted, "because after I was shot by that sod Edrick—yes, that's who it was!—"

Dad shook his head at my foul language. Another symptom of my infantile brain-fever?

"—after that, the black current sent me down the psylink to Eeden, and I was reborn as a baby there. Later on I died in an explosion and started to come back here. But things went wrong and I twisted backwards through time. . . ."

They listened. I think they were both trying to decide how ill I was.

"Enough, enough!" Dad broke in as soon as I began to fill in more details. "Can it be that Yaleen's spirit has, well, taken possession?"

Mum shuddered. "So where did our Narya go?"

"Nowhere," I told her. "You must realize: *she never was*. She was me, pretending. I'm sorry, but I had no choice. Why do you think I

THE BOOKS OF THE BLACK CURRENT

wanted my ring? Look, Mum, there's more to *The Book of the River;* more upstairs. I wrote an afterword to it. I hid it in that toy cat. . . ."

Mention of something as comically banal and homely as the toy cat had a curious effect on Dad. He rose.

"I . . . I have to go to work. Or I'll be late."

"That's true," agreed Mum. Oh the comforts of the familiar, the balm of routine.

"You can't go to work today!" I protested. "You have to take me to the quaymistress's office. Though I guess I could find my own way there. There has to be a conclave of the riverguild. And I need to contact the black current again. Because unless we can avoid it somehow, our world's going to come to an end!"

Dad stared at me bleakly. "I think our world already came to an end."

"No, no, don't you see? I'm back with you. This is a whole new start."

"Of what? Of the end? What end? What are you talking about?"

"Oh, I'll have to write another whole book to explain! And I need to drink of the black current again. I'll have to . . . oh, there are oodles of things! But I must talk to the Guild in conclave first."

"I suppose," allowed Dad, "I *could* stay off work today." He sat down again, wearily, confused.

Mum and Dad didn't suddenly accept me as Yaleen, in the way I'd naively expected. There was no overwhelming revelation, no abrupt and wild embrace. There was no single moment of truth, joy and discovery. Instead: a gradual shift, a slow slide in their attitude, away from me-as-Narya, towards me-as-Yaleen. This went on for a number of days, accompanied by occasional forgettings, temporary lapses on their part. Perhaps this was a better way to cope with the shock than the sort of dramatic climax I'd pictured to myself.

Curiously, by the time that my parents *had* come to accept me fully as Yaleen, the real and only, it was me who felt most keenly the absent "ghost" of Narya. It was me who heard the footfalls of a shadow person next to me. Narya had only ever been an invention —a character in a fiction (of my own devising). Yet she had lived in this very house alongside me, and I had fully believed in her, and in her selfish little wiles. She had been real; now she wasn't. She had never existed; yet indubitably she had. So therefore somehow she still did exist—invisibly in some mirror world of my mind, inhabiting some echo existence. She was a different me, who might have been born if I hadn't been born instead. Yet she genuinely had been born. And now was unborn, once again. Thinking of her, I thought a lot about the riddle of the raven and the writing desk. . . .

Later that same morning—subsequent to my confession over breakfast, and whilst our family relationship was still in flux—Mum, Dad and I did set out together, nonetheless, for the water-front; there to beard that mercenary, calculating quaymistress in her den.

That particular woman's disbelief I finally dispelled by revealing a certain kinky little initiation ritual of our guild which I *had* kept quiet about when I wrote *The Book of the River,* and which I intend to keep hush about here as well. (Always keep a card up your sleeve, eh?)

She believed. She set in motion the summoning of a conclave. Signals flashed up and down stream.

Four weeks later, in front of a conclave, I told all—just as it's set down here. I told of *Ka*-space and Eeden and Earth and the Moon; of Exotics and Flawed Ones and alien stars; of the Godmind's scheme to build a lens of burning minds to pierce the dark mystery of existence. I told of seedships and rose shows. Of Venezia and California. "Out of the mouth of a babe"—as precog myth put it!

And on board that schooner, *Oopsadaisy,* where the conclave was being held, I demanded and was given a slug of the black current to put me in tune with my old friend the Worm again.

I drank my slug on the third day of the conclave. That night, like the previous nights, I spent at home; and before falling asleep I fixed my mind on what I would like to dream. If you concentrate hard enough you can carry this trick off; though there'll always be changes which try to take you by surprise so that you're dumped into a different dream, not of your intention, where you'll forget yourself and just float along with the phantasmagorias.

I dreamed, as I'd intended, of a schooner sailing proudly on the river out near the black current. A conclave was taking place on board—since this was also uppermost in my mind—though alas, and unaccountably, this was happening in the open air on deck and consisted not of women but of beasts. Sows, bitches, ewes, turkey-hens and whatnot. Never mind! I paid no attention to the assorted bleating, yapping and oinking which might have tricked me into a farmyard fantasy; and presently from the water the Worm's head rose. The Worm had found me in my dream—to its considerable surprise!

Yaleen? It's you! But how? You aren't here. You can't be. She's—

The schooner's deck had emptied; all the animals had faded. The dream was of a different quality now: Worm and me, mind to mind.

Listen, Worm! Whatever you do, don't break the psylink with dead Yaleen! Don't lose your grip or you'll spoil everything! Got it?

Yes. But—

Just listen! I've carried out your little mission. I've been to Eeden and now I'm back again, but not in the way you expected. . . .

I was getting rather tired of repeating all this! To Mum and Dad; to the Guild; now to the Worm. Obviously I would have to write a book. Then I could just hand out copies.

My account took a while, but at least I didn't have to worry about the dream fading out midway. By now the Worm was clinging on tight.

Worm, you still there?

Hmm? Oh yes.

Like the pillow talk of lovers, yet!

A fin for your thoughts?

Oh . . . You've flooded me, Yaleen . . . I'll have to think about all this. But well done, don't you know! Well, well done! Can you sail out to me so I can get all this directly from you in the Ka-store? I promise I'll return you safe and sound. You're so important to me!

Thanks. I'm flattered. Another swim in you: is that what you want?

It would be friendlier if you visited my head.

Off Aladalia? What, and wake up poor old Raf again?

I could come and collect you off Pecawar.

Withdraw yourself to Pecawar? That wouldn't make me very popular with people!

Do come to Aladalia! I'll reorganize my body. I'll provide excellent accommodation. You could stay a while.

I'd heard that kind of offer before. How about spending the rest of my life in a seedship pod?

We'll have to think about it, I said. *These one-night stands are sweet, but I wasn't exactly thinking of moving in with you.*

Oddly enough, to my amusement I found that in a weird sort of way I'd missed the Worm during my absence!

And maybe I'm a bit young for you yet? I said. *A bit tiny to go jumping into black currents, and down Worms' throats?*

If you came inside me, Yaleen, I could grow your body up—while your mind romped in the Ka-store.

How long would it take to grow me up?

I don't have vats and soft machines, I only have me. It would take as long as normal growth. Another twelve, thirteen years or so would see you all set up. You certainly wouldn't feel bored in the meantime.

Thirteen years? That's hardly fair on my Mum and Dad. No, I couldn't possibly.

Do try to take a swim in me at least.

Sure. Why not? Just so long as you'll promise to tell me what it's all about. What Ka-space is. How the psylink works. How we can stop the Godmind. And where you came from. And how time got twisted.

And why a raven is like a writing desk?

That too.

I may have enough clues. It could take a while to fit them all together.

So start trying, will you! There has to be a way to stop the Godmind from burning us all up.

Has there? What if there isn't?

Then I shall be quite annoyed with you, Worm.

Oh dear.

Mad, in fact.

Hmm, I think I'd best be going. . . .

In that case . . . goodnight, Worm. Be with me in my dreams again.

I will be. 'Night, Yaleen.

The next morning Mum walked me down to the waterfront again to board the *Oopsadaisy* for the final session of conclave.

There, in a cabin panelled in expensive ivorybone wood and hung with a remarkable collection of fish-masks, I told the assembled mistresses of my night-time chat with the Worm, concluding thus: "How about me having a swim? A black sort of swim?"

Which is when, as ever, things started to go wrong.

I don't know whether I'd been putting these good ladies' backs up during the past several days. Had I been acting too pert by far? Truly I hadn't intended to. I thought I'd become a whole lot more considerate, subtle and persuasive recently. (Besides, in memory at least, my bum still ached from Dad's smacks!) On the other hand, why had I dreamt of these 'mistresses as a gang of honking geese and bleating ewes?

"A swim? Not yet," said one 'mistress.

"No, we can't have you running off and disappearing," agreed another.

The quaymistress of Pecawar, Chanoose by name, was particularly adamant. (I'd already crossed swords with her previously on the topic of my literary earnings.) "When all's said and done, you belong to the Guild, remember!" She waved at the fish-masks on the wall to remind me.

Another 'mistress whom I knew from way back—two lives earlier, at that other conclave held in Spanglestream—was dusky old Marti of Guineamoy. She challenged me with, "How do we know you're telling the truth?"

"The Worm can back me up any time!"

"Oh, I'm not disputing that you're the same Yaleen as I met before. Or that something truly remarkable happened to you. You were murdered; then reborn. But when did you *really* come back to life? Can I credit that you waited whole years to reveal yourself? Maybe your spirit has possessed Narya, after all? And what actually did happen in between your death and resurrection? You may have dreamt all this business of your trip to Eeden in the *Ka*-store. Or even made it all up. Can you prove otherwise? *The Book of the River* is a somewhat inventive document in places, I suspect. I've read it, and I don't entirely believe in that giant croaker which tried to squash you in the jungle."

"Oh don't you? Well it did!"

"Maybe you were hallucinating, from starvation and exhaustion. And maybe you weren't. But to my mind that part of your story *does* verge on romance, of the Ajelobo brand. Likewise I have my doubt about the dead man of Opal Island. Strange and marvellous things certainly happened, yet perhaps at times you also let your imagination run away with you? Which allows you to be as rude as you please, under the guise of honesty and frankness. I'm thinking now of your remarks *à propos* our other conclave at Spanglestream. 'Mistress Nelliam, with the face of a prune, indeed!'"

"I didn't say anything rude about *you*, Marti."

"No, but you blithely and impertinently made me an 'ally' of Nelliam's. And whether or not I agree with your character assessments of Tamath and Sharla in *some* respects, you hardly do justice to the other fine qualities which deservedly made them Guildmistresses."

"That's a matter of opinion."

"True. And we're very tolerant of your opinions, are we not? But mightn't all your revelations about Earth and Eeden simply be . . . matters of opinion, too?"

"The Worm—"

"The black current believes what you told it. Or at least you tell us so. I suppose, since you rode the current all the way from Tambimatu to Aladalia, we must allow a large degree of credence to this. . . ."

What *was* Marti getting at? I felt perplexed. That other meeting of a conclave at Spanglestream had taken me on trust; they hadn't cast sly doubts. The present conclave seemed to be up to something. They were hunting around for justifications—but for what?

"Myself, I look around and I see our world; and the black current, yes indeed. We know what you say it is; and we accept this, basically. We know that originally we came from a distant star. But I don't see any concrete *evidence* of Eeden or Venezia or that huge moon."

"What did you expect? That I'd bring back a rose, clutched in my soul's teeth?"

Marti pursed her lips. "That might have helped. The problem for us is this: the happy balance of our world and the prestige of our guild have suffered upsets lately. I think we need a breathing space. Quite a long one, too. Approximately as long as it takes a little girl to grow up. Yet some things can't be gainsaid. Such as the *Ka*-store of souls. Such as the fact that a dead person can be reborn. Or the fact that the black current watches over us and knows us; as our Guild chapbook, handed down from forever, tells."

"It's hardly handed down from *forever*. If you don't mind my saying so, 'Mistress Marti, you seemed a lot more analytical in Spanglestream."

"Dear child, I *am* being very analytical—of the situation. Incidentally, your book is published now. Consignments arrived here yesterday in bulk."

"Well, thanks for telling me!"

"You can collect your copies afterwards, from my office," said Chanoose.

"It's already being read with the greatest excitement upriver," Marti went on. "You're becoming a heroine to people. Yes, a heroine, from the ranks of our Guild! We did worry whether people might assess your chaos-causing career uncharitably. Wonder of wonders, not so; from the reports we have already. A heroine," she repeated softly, "and a martyr too. What better way to speed a book to dizzy heights than the murder of its author? We're encouraging newssheets up and down stream to gossip."

"Publicity pays," said Chanoose. "Expect to be famous in your home town presently."

"A heroine," Marti enthused, "who has now been reborn out of the black current—as its, and as our, *infant priestess*. Reborn as she who proves that when we die into the bosom of the current, we live."

"Oh no. Look: most people don't die into the Worm's bosom. Weren't you listening at all? Most people go to Eeden. To Godmind territory."

"Against that, may the black current defend us . . . If your account should be real, and not fantastic! Yet doubtless with an intermediary of your calibre on tap, and given enough time, we may be able to offer the hope that everyone—woman and man alike—will benefit equally from the *Ka*-store—one day in the future. If everyone supports us." Marti smiled. Wryly? No, slyly! "The *Ka*-store sounds much more convenient than a trip to Eeden. So much closer to home. So much more convincing. Why, news of this may even convert those Sons across the river; it could make them see sense, and change sides.

"And *if* what you say about the Godmind is true, what better way to thwart it than to rob it of this world? How better can we save ourselves from this universal doom you speak of—should there be any such thing!—than by detaching ourselves from that Godmind? How better than by forging a compact with the black current on behalf of all our people? A compact to which our own guild holds the key—in the person of your own good self, Yaleen? Our own priestess.

"If you did indeed sabotage the colony programme on that giant Moon and set it back—or rather, if you will do so in future—surely we have ample time. If doom there be a-waiting. And if doom there isn't, and it's all a fantasy of yours, no matter!"

"Oh," said I. What Marti had just said made a crazy sort of sense. For this priestess scheme to work, it needn't even be based on truth.

I can't say I cared for it! What sort of life would an infant "priestess" live? How could anybody who read *The Book of the River* be daft enough to imagine me as a priestess? And besides, outside of the pages of a few old fables hardly anybody knew what a priestess *was*.

Maybe that would make things easier. Maybe people would be daft enough. Suddenly the Worm's offer seemed almost attractive.

"Okay," said I, "I was lying all along. I admit it. I'm not Yaleen. I'm just Narya."

Marti laughed. "Too late for that! You've been far too persuasive. May you persuade many other people too!"

"This is the judgement of the river guild sitting in solemn conclave aboard the *Oopsadaisy*," said Chanoose formally. "May the black current show us our true course. Through you, dear river-daughter, Yaleen of Pecawar."

"You might at least make me a guildmistress," I grumbled.

"What, a little girl a 'mistress?" asked Chanoose incredulously.

"Tush, this is much more important than being a 'mistress." Marti favoured me with a dusky smile. End of conclave.

By the time Dad got home from work the evening after, a few townsfolk were hanging about outside our door, looking somewhat embarrassed and sheepish.

By the following evening, numbers had swelled. The hopeful spectators seemed more sure of themselves now, more ardent. They wanted to see us, touch us, hear us, just for a moment please. For this was the family home of Yaleen, heroine and martyr. On Dad's advice, which was sensible, we all stayed indoors. Some people kept up their vigil till quite late that night.

And on the evening after that, Dad fairly had to force his way home through a crowd packing out our lane. Mum and I were upstairs watching from behind a curtain. A lot of copies of my book were being brandished, clutched to bosoms, or still being feverishly read. A fair number of newssheets were flapping like flags. I recognized some neighbours in the crowd, amongst them Axal and Merri. Their faces looked different, changed.

"So this is what it's like being a successful author!" I quipped to Mum.

"Fame at last," said Mum, trying to match my mood.

"How awful," said I.

"How scary," she agreed. "Still, it's a great thing, isn't it?"

I only had myself to blame—plus the Guild, who had set up a fair old rumour factory, now working overtime. The day before yesterday, the newssheet had simply boosted my book. Yesterday, it went on about how I'd been murdered recently, and dropped hints of more amazing revelations to follow. Mum had folded those two newssheets away (after almost learning them by heart) as though they were printed on gold leaf. I don't know that she was looking forward quite so avidly to this evening's news.

But maybe she was.

Dad finally barged his way through and got safely indoors, shutting out folks with difficulty. He tossed the newssheet on the table and headed for the kitchen. I hung on to the table top on tiptoe while Mum spread the sheet out. I never knew that such large type existed as I saw bannered across the top. Maybe it had been specially made for the occasion. My resurrection was officially announced.

Dad returned with a bottle of ginger spirit and poured himself a stiff drink; which wasn't like him at all.

"Oh, I can't tell you what it was like at work after this came out! Didn't get a thing done for the last hour or so. I should have quit and come straight home." He drank half the strong liquor in one gulp.

I shan't go into the *details* of the news story. Basically they were all perfectly true. Merely—how shall I put it?—angled somewhat.

Outside, we heard a rising murmur, which presently became a chant.

"*Ka . . . Ka . . . Ka*, Yaleen!" After a while this blurred into "*Ka*leen!" as though my name had altered, from Yaleen to Kaleen. Maybe that would be my holy name; my priestess title.

Our front door began to rattle, and a few rude bold enthusiasts scaled our garden wall to perch there. *We* retreated upstairs. Even so, things were getting hectic when, at roughly the critical moment for us, and for the mob as well, through the curtains we spied the militia come marching along, forcing their way to our door. In their van was quaymistress Chanoose. Not the 'jack captain, no. The jungle guild weren't in on this power play.

The area before our house was cleared. Trespassers on our wall were hauled down and hustled back through the ranks.

We went downstairs again; Dad answered a rap on the knocker.

In strolled Chanoose. She bowed her head to me—I hoped *that* wasn't going to be catching. "Good evening, river-daughter! You need protection from admirers. So here it is." She glanced round. "This house isn't suitable."

"What's wrong with it?" growled Dad, invigorated by the ginger spirit.

"It's too small. Too modest. Too vulnerable. The Guild will build you a temple somewhere downtown."

"A what?" I cried.

"A temple—dedicated to the black current. A *Ka*-temple. Your very own temple, Yaleen."

"Oh I *see:* imitating the *Ka*-theodrals of the Sons? Except that we'll have the temples of the Daughter instead?"

"Something like that. We might as well call the place a temple. What would you rather we called it: a palace? I don't think our finances quite stretch to a palace. There's a war to pay for; and future defence."

"Oh so the Guild is hard up for a few fish? How sad. How amazing. My heart bleeds. Better get the worshippers to bring offerings!"

"Obviously this is all rather unfamiliar," Chanoose carried on, clearly enjoying herself. "So we must extemporize. Your parents can live in the temple with you, if you like; and you'll have a permanent honour guard of attendants from our guild to look after the practical details, the daily routine. Right? You can also have some, um," and here she had to jog her memory, "yes, some acolytes—of your own choice. That should be nice and cosy. Maybe some of the friends you made on the river, as detailed in your book, hmm? Or even some of your enemies!"

"Will you take a drink, 'Mistress?" offered Dad.

"Why not indeed? How charmingly hospitable."

Dad poured a glass for Chanoose, and a few more fingers for himself.

"Can I have a drink too?" I said. "I've almost forgotten the taste, it's been so long."

Chanoose's look reproved me. "What, a little girl tippling strong liquor? I hardly think so! You'd make your stomach bleed. Or you'd faint."

Dad didn't pour me any. Just as well, probably.

Chanoose raised her glass. "To our reborn priestess! To Yaleen of Pecawar, intermediary of the black current, annunciator of the *Ka*, living proof of afterlives, star-traveller—"

"Oh stow it! I don't want a string of daft titles."

"I'm just improvising, as I said. So: simply to you, Yaleen. May you show us the way."

I pointed. "The door's that way."

"How witty. You know, Yaleen, you mustn't imagine that with all your funny little traits you're unsuitable to be a priestess. On the contrary! You're someone with whom ordinary folk can identify."

"I want to write another book," I said.

"Pen and paper will be provided. And even ink."

"I want to bring my story up to date."

"So write it! People will adore it. They'll believe everything in it that they wish to believe. But they won't stop believing in you. In fact, we want you to write another book. Say whatever you wish. Even about this part of it. Feel free to treat me as another Tamath—though frankly I flatter myself that I'm a bit more precise than her. Writing a holy book is just what you should be doing whilst you're a priestess. Everyone will be agog. Call it *The Book of the Stars.*"

"I certainly *shan't.*" Though the title did have a certain ring to it. . . .

"That reminds me," I said to Dad, "I need my ring. I want to wear it."

"Ah, so you still have your famous ring?" Chanoose crowed with delight. "How excellent. Visitors to the temple could kiss it."

"I'm not having people slobbering all over my hand!"

"Oh, I shouldn't think they would. Not slobber, surely? We're all civilized people. Ceremonials are always so nice, though, don't you think? I noticed you glancing at those fish-masks in the cabin. Bring back thrilling memories, eh? But let's not forget, Yaleen, that this isn't play-acting. If what you tell us about the Godmind is true, well, here's the way to defeat it. By mobilizing our world. By unifying. By setting ourselves apart from Eeden forever. That's what you wished for, right?"

Alas, I had to agree.

"As priestess, you will commune with the black current—"

"And I'll try to persuade it to take everyone into its *Ka*-store—male and female alike—if we all drink slugs of it? Served up by me in a silver chalice?"

Chanoose frowned. Her look became distant. "Everyone? We'll have to think about that."

"Why? Oh, I see. That would muck your monopoly up! If men could drink of the current, they could sail forbidden waters whenever they wanted to."

"We don't know that men can drink it—not yet. Anyway, we have to consider the Sons—"

"Not to mention their poor womenfolk!"

"Ah yes indeed. But the conversion of the Sons could take ages. It would be equivalent to a declaration of war. We can do without another war, don't you think?"

"You aren't by any chance thinking of doling out entry tickets to the *Ka*-store only to your *friends?* That wouldn't thwart the Godmind much! And once the shorelubbers over here who weren't your special favourites figured this out . . . well, there'd be riots. A bloody rebellion! Have you no imagination?"

"As I say, we'll have to think about this carefully. Softly softly, catchee fish. First of all we'll install you in your temple. We'll take things from there."

And all of a sudden I put two and two together in my own head— and oh, but Chanoose did have imagination, all right!

When the Godmind created its lens, it wouldn't be setting fire to worlds themselves; merely to the minds of people on those worlds, all the people who were in psylink with it, all those whose *Ka*s flew home to Eeden.

No riverwoman's *Ka* ever flew to Eeden; nor any *Ka* which the black current claimed. So therefore, when the Godmind finally made its move, everyone would be snuffed out with the exception of those protected by the Worm. All those pesky Sons and their ratbag population would be dead. Problem over; without us having to pick up a single sword.

Meanwhile at a stroke the followers of the black current would become the total human population of the galaxy.

Plainly Chanoose wasn't planning on riverwomen *alone* surviving (plus assorted men-friends and supporters). That would be both vicious and idiotic. If the Guild tried to play that game there would be a civil war. Besides, think of all that useful new land left lying fallow over in the west after the demise of the Sons and all their kin. No, we would need the whole mass of our own population alive and kicking.

But by playing a waiting game—by not opposing the Godmind outright, merely recruiting our own people to the black current cult —we of the east would inherit the whole world. That was why the Guild were going to think carefully; I knew it in my waters!

Yet that was all beside the point. The point, to me at least, was: what about the rest of the galaxy? What about all the other colonies with their millions on millions of people?

The trouble, here, was that nobody but me had bounced around the stars. Nobody but me had been to Earth or to any other planet. As far as the folks here at home were concerned, that world where the wench chewed snails or that colony where the crone crooned her eel-song might as well be fictions. If those worlds were all snuffed out, what did it matter? (But it mattered to me!)

The Book of the Stars, indeed! What a nerve Chanoose had to suggest such a title.

Now I was *determined* to call my next book just that. And I resolved that I would make the book as real as could be, so that readers would get the message that genuine people lived on lots of other planets.

But would the guild print the whole of it, once I'd written it in my temple in downtown Pecawar, surrounded by an honour guard? Whatever fair promises Chanoose made to softsoap me now, might they only print part? The part that suited them? There was only one way to find out.

"Right?" said Chanoose. She liked saying that word, since that's what she was in her own mind: right.

"Right," said I. But what I meant, was: Write!

"It'll take us a few weeks to organize suitable premises. Might take longer, depending on the degree of grandeur. Till then, what with all this wild excitement I think the three of you would be better off on board a boat at anchor—"

"Hey, my Dad's a man!"

Chanoose peered at me. "Fathers usually are."

"So he can't board a boat. He already sailed once in his life."

"Oh, I *see*. Couldn't you intercede with the current on his behalf? As a special exception? Then he could drink a slug and—"

"Chanoose! If you think I'm going to gamble with my own Dad's life and sanity, to test whether the current will allow men to—! I swear I'll kill myself; then you won't have any priestess."

"What a fuss you do make! In that case your father can bunk down in my office. You and your mother will come on board the *Oopsadaisy.* I'll post guards here tonight to keep the curious at bay. Tomorrow they'll escort you down to the quay in suitable style." Chanoose turned to Dad. "Don't worry about this house; we'll caretake it properly. And if you want to keep your job for a while, naturally we'll provide an escort to the spice houses."

"Keep my job," said Dad thickly. "Not much point in that, is there?" He looked shrunken and drained, as though instead of having swigged the liquor, it had swigged him.

But Mom looked excited. Proud.

* * *

That night in the midst of a dream of Port Firsthome the Worm surfaced. Like an ordinary soil-worm, but much huger, it burst up through the turf beside the Obelisk of the Ship. Its foundations disturbed, the Obelisk tottered and crashed down upon some picnickers: a capering old man, a kissing couple, two naked children, flattening them all.

Mud dripped from the Worm's dream-jaws. *Listen, Yaleen: you're going to blow up all the Paxmen on the Moon in another couple of years, approx? The prisoners of Hell will rebel and seize control?*

That's the general idea.

So then the Godmind won't be able to launch its last two seedships?

Not unless it can recapture the Moon. Against those laser-zappers.

But what if it over-budgeted the number of colonies it needs, just to be on the safe side? What if it already has enough people spread around? What if the lens mightn't be quite perfect—but nevertheless could be good enough? What if the Godmind doesn't need to recapture the Moon? What if it decides to go ahead with Project Lens right away? Directly, in a couple of years' time?

Gobbets of soil dribbled from its mouth.

One of the crushed, trapped children was still alive. A girl: she squealed piteously, like the voice of all the human worlds crying out for help.

A clammy feeling crept over me. *Are you implying . . . that I've buggered everything up again? Instead of slowing the Godmind's plan down, I've speeded it up?*

Could be.

There must still be a few ships en route.

Heading for stars close by. Maybe they're nearly there.

Shut up! I covered my ears. But the Worm's voice droned on inside my dreaming head:

There's another point I'd like to raise. What if you were right about the Godmind being able to zap me with its lens?

You mean, what I told it in the garden? Oh, that was all hogwash!

I know it was. But what if it's possible? What if you gave the Godmind a bright idea?

Oh.

What if you get it all fired up about that in a couple of years' time, and it sees how to do it?

If the Godmind could zap the black current, then obviously Chanoose's plan wouldn't work. Nor could any plan of mine. The *Ka-*

store itself would be burnt out . . . Surely the Worm couldn't be serious! Surely I couldn't have planted the seeds of *that!*

You're joking, Worm.

Just think about it, eh? And down its mucky wormhole in my dream my old friend withdrew.

Hey! I shouted after it. *If that's true, you've got one big vested interest in helping to save everyone!*

But the Worm had gone.

I thought. Hell, *how* I thought—even in my sleep. I seemed to be floating just below the surface of sleep for hours, my mind churning over and over while the rest of me got precious little repose.

I woke next morning with a thunderous headache, as though the Godmind had already tried to set fire to my brains and everyone else's.

After breakfast (for which I insisted on a greasy spicy omelette with a splash of ginger spirit on top) Mum and Dad packed a couple of bags.

Presently, came a polite rap on the door.

And before long we three set off on the first stage of my latest journey, which wouldn't be nearly as long as any of my previous travels: this time merely to a schooner anchored offshore, and from there a few weeks hence to a temple. To become the lady high (infant) priestess of the Worm.

As we proceeded through town, flanked by our escort of militia, a clamouring procession just grew and grew in our wake till I felt I was wearing a tail of people as long as the black current itself.

THE BOOK

OF

BEING

Contents

Part One
TAM'S POTS

So it was as a child just a quarter short of my third year that I was installed in the temple of the black current in downtown Pecawar. I'd be public proof of how we could all be saved by the grace of the Worm, courtesy of its *Ka*-store. Whilst in actual fact the whole human cosmos was about to come to a sticky end, maybe no longer than two years hence!

I soon called in the promise which Quaymistress Chanoose had rashly made; namely that in addition to my honour guard of guildswomen I might gather a few friends about me. I asked for Tam to come.

It may have been cruel to wrench Tam away from fair artistic Aladalia to dusty Pecawar. It might have been inconsiderate to ask him to squander his one-go on the river so that he could squire a mere child, in whom happened to have been reborn the young woman he had loved besottedly. Nevertheless I wanted him. I knew I would need the services of a loyal soul or two.

"Tam's a potter," I told Chanoose. "Doesn't Pecawar, baked by the sun, and the colour of clay already, need a potter to give it some bright glaze? Doesn't my temple need ornaments—such as vases for the flowers my pilgrims will bring? And splendid faience plates for them to pour coins into?"

I also requested the presence of Peli, the songful water-wife. Peli originally hailed from Aladalia too.

"It might be better," replied Chanoose, "if you chose your companions from different directions—not both from the same place! Can't you think of someone from Jangali or Tambimatu? That way you'd be forging symbolic ties. Two from Aladalia seems like favouritism."

"I want Peli." Her, I could trust. "Besides, then Tam won't feel so lonely." It almost sounded as if I was trying to fix up a marriage between Peli and Tam.

"Oh, as you please! I don't suppose it matters; if it'll make you happy."

We were talking in the audience chamber—alias throne room—of my temple. Let me describe the edifice.

It had been a disused spice warehouse, which was swiftly but quite elegantly converted by masons, carpenters and furnishers hired by the guild. The rear backed directly on to the river; a new covered verandah overlooked the water. The front faced Pemba Avenue, which converges on Zanzyba Road close to the Café of the Seasons. The claybrick frontage was dolled up with outriding sandstone columns to provide a roofed arcade, where food hawkers and lemonade lads soon took up residence along with various licensed souvenir vendors; chief amongst whom was the bookstall proprietor who held the temple franchise to sell copies of *The Book of the River*. (This was shortly going to be reprinted with my private afterword included, according to Chanoose.)

A grand flight of steps bridged the arcade, running up to an entry porch above. These steps were clad with thin flags of purple Melonby marble to prevent the feet of countless pilgrims from wearing them away too soon. There hadn't been enough stock within easy reach of Pecawar to build the steps of solid marble. In any case, think of the expense. And the effect was the same.

In this manner the entrance was relocated one storey upward—so as to convey a sense of ascendance. Yet the steps mustn't be too steep; nor must they commence in the middle of Pemba Avenue. Consequently the entry porch had to be recessed well behind the original wall. This meant that busy teams of craftsmen had their work cut out reconstructing a lot of the interior to accommodate stairway, upper-floor porch and foyer. They laboured overtime and even through the nights by lamplight at double rates.

My audience chamber, which led off the foyer, was mostly panelled with rich gildenwood. A couple of tapestries covered stretches of cheaper old wood. One of these tapestries was a rather abstract representation of desert dunes; it flowed nicely into the gildenwood.

The other tapestry pictured a fishmask regatta at a fanciful Gangee. I was assured that weavers would soon set to work upon thoroughly relevant new tapestries depicting scenes from my past life—such as how I had ridden in the mouth of the Worm with the sun's rays shining forth from my ring. Or how I had confronted a giant croaker in the jungle, me armed only with a sharpened wand (the weavers would need me to be holding something, for the composition). Or even how I had been martyred (but surely not cowering under a bed?).

And in my audience chamber upon a dais, I had a tiny tot-size throne of rubyvein with a fat tasselled cushion for my bum.

The honour guard—who doubled as temple officials—occupied the remainder of that upper storey. My own private living quarters were down below; as were those of my parents, various empty rooms destined for my personal retinue, and the temple treasury—which, when I moved in, was also empty. Short of jumping into the river off the verandah I could only leave my new home by mounting and using the main entrance, which immediately involved an escort; this kept me conveniently in my place.

It had been decided not to include a kitchen in the temple. A tad undignified, perhaps, to have smells of stew wafting over my waiting worshippers? Thus meals were ordered in from outside; and mine were generally cool by the time they reached me. This was a fatuous strategem, since the whole place reeked of spices. All of the surviving fabric was imbued; and doubtless there was a carpet of spice dust a thumbnail deep beneath the ground floor. A thorough scrub-out with soap didn't make one whit of difference.

When eventually there was enough money in the coffers, the idea was to erect a really stately temple mostly of Melonby marble, with a large courtyard, somewhere out in the suburbs. Meanwhile I must make do with this converted warehouse, which looked sumptuous enough so long as you didn't try to prise off the veneer, and made believe that the powerful odour was some kind of incense as in old tales.

And why not make believe? In spite of new gildenwood panelling and those tapestries which blanketed the surviving old wood, for some reason the smell of spice seemed particularly noticeable in my throne room. This set me to wondering whether visitors from other towns might imagine that it emanated from my presence, diffusing hence to spread throughout the town! Just so had I once imagined that Dad, in his working clothes, was the source and origin of Pecawar's native aroma.

Which brings me to the matter of Dad himself. His was a slightly tragic case, which I was truly sorry to see—albeit that I was to blame. Me; and Chanoose's machinations in making me a priestess.

Mum was up; Dad down. Mum revelled in the glory. She was proud and committed. Dad, on the other hand, was out of a job—since he could hardly continue counting spice sacks and totting up ledgers now that his daughter was a high priestess. Worse, he was out of a job inside a former warehouse where every sniff reminded him of his previous independence. He who had ever held his job at arm's length, far from family matters—save for those excursions with Narya during the war—now had his nose rubbed in empty reminders of the past; with wife and "false" daughter always close at hand. However, he put a brave face on necessity. Mum and Dad occupied a decent suite adjacent to my own; and whilst Mum found much to busy herself with in improving the accoutrements of the temple, Dad gravitated inevitably (though a little grimly) towards the counting house. Soon he was totting up donated fish-coins with wry perseverance and improving the bookkeeping.

By now our family house had become a museum. Mum happily countenanced this and acted as advisor in the matter. Dad refused to go back there or have anything to do with this conversion of his former home into a tramping place for curious strangers.

So now we had two prongs of pilgrimage: the temple, and our house along the dusty lane. A third holy place could obviously be the cemetery where Yaleen's murdered body lay—Must keep pilgrims busy! Give them a full itinerary!—and about this, debate grew a little heated, with me entering the fray.

It was a lamplit evening in my throne room, and Chanoose had a pronouncement to make. Present to hear it were myself, Mum and Dad—and Donnah, captain of the guard and major-domo of the temple.

Donnah was a tall busty redhead, with noteworthy muscles and strapping shoulders, whose attitude to me—the holy brat—I still hadn't quite figured out. By her accent Donnah was from further north. Sarjoy or somewhere. She managed to be both extremely protective, to which end she always wore a four-shot Guineamoy pistol, and quite offhand in her duties as major-domo; which was how Mum found an easy entrée into temple management. To be sure, the temple was Donnah's command; but it wasn't exactly a boat, to be kept spick and span. I suspected that Donnah was the restless sort and may have felt miffed to be made captain of a re-vamped warehouse—never mind that she was performing sterling service for her guild: its prestige, its revenues. In Donnah, I fancied, Chanoose had appointed someone who wouldn't become a kind of rival quaymistress in town. Yet Donnah's inner person remained opaque to me; far more so than dear conniving Chanoose. Of one thing I was certain: Donnah wouldn't allow me to manipulate her, or gain the upper hand.

I perched on my throne. The others squatted on quilted floor-cushions, Jay-Jay guildhall-style, except for Chanoose who stood.

"We must decide about the cemetery," she declared. Donnah im-mediately nodded agreement. "Yaleen's grave ought to be visited."

"That could be difficult," I pointed out, "seeing as I'm sunk in sand in an unmarked spot."

"We must mark it, then."

"And how would you find it, to mark it?"

Mum spoke up. "I'm sure *I* haven't forgotten the spot." Chanoose smiled brightly at her.

"Maybe my death-box already broke surface and got burnt," I said.

"Oh no." Chanoose shook her head. "Impossible. Far too soon. Now as to a memorial—"

"But the sands shift," said Dad. "The memorial would lean. It might fall over. That isn't very dignified."

"In that case," suggested Donnah, "maybe we should retrieve the body and build a proper marble tomb nearby? With the corpse em-balmed within?"

Dad twisted his hands about. "I doubt if the people of Pecawar would consider a tomb all that proper! You should leave her poor body be. She was my daughter—I do have a right to say this!"

"I still am your daughter, Dad."

Dad looked bewildered for a moment. He sighed; subsided.

"It seems to me," I went on, "speaking as your priestess, that the whole idea's nonsense. It defeats the purpose of why I'm here in this temple. What we're concerned with is *Kas*, not bodies. Not that I'm disparaging bodies! But damn it, I've had three of them by now."

"You are the three-in-one," said Chanoose, amiably toying with this new phrase. "Three bodies! Surely you can spare one of them for cult purposes?"

"No, no, no. It's stupid."

We argued a while; and to my surprise I won. The guild would not, after all, exhume my semi-mummified remains from the sands. Instead they would merely affix a plaque to the stone archway of the graveyard. Then of course eager pilgrims could always hope that a fierce gale might blow up on the night before their visit. The corpse of Yaleen might possibly surface in its death-box specially for them. The Rods could rake in some spare cash, if they were ingenious. They could try to sell relics. Splinters. Ashes. Hanks of hair.

Visits! By pilgrims! Now we come to the meat of my role as priestess (as opposed to the bones in the sand).

The idea was *not* that I should actually proclaim to visitors, even though I'd had a fair amount of practice at this while I was a cherub in Venezia. Visitors were expected to buy my book, to receive my message. They practically had to flash a copy to gain admission. And by now Chanoose and I (and Dad) had sorted out the vexed question of royalties, not wholly to my satisfaction. . . .

A word about this. The guild had invested heavily in me; so the cost must be amortized. One source of revenue was straight donations to the temple. Another was entrance fees to our house—cash which seemed to be swallowed up in the cost of caretaking! A third source was profit from my book, less the six per cent which I could keep as my private purse. This was a far cry from the fifty-fifty split which Chanoose had brashly offered at my graveside; but then circumstances had altered radically, hadn't they? As financial consultant to myself and the temple, Dad actually concurred in this arrangement, though he insisted on a fatter split in a few years' time. Meanwhile he and Mum were living free. As was I. And what could I possibly spend money on? If I did set my heart on something, said he, far better to soak the temple for expenses and keep my purse intact. (True, temple expenses would have to be met from the same sources—and I later discovered that such expenses included the cost of Tam's fare to Pecawar; the guild wasn't picking up the tab.)

Enough of fins and fish! As I say, the guild were wary of any proclamations I might make; but I must needs be present twice a day in my throne room for audiences, with Donnah and a couple of guards standing by.

Goodness, did some visitors try my patience—no matter how goodly a store of that commodity I'd garnered during the two years while I was pretending to be a normal infant! A stooped old lady would approach, clutching her copy of the book. She would cast a handful of fins into the offering bowl, then address me as if I was some fortune teller.

"My eldest daughter—Shinova, you know—she died of a fever in Port Barbra these nineteen years since. Did you meet her in yon *Ka*-store? Is she well and happy? Will I join her when I die? And it won't be long now, not the way I felt in my heart this Winter. . . . I shouldn't want to go to yon Eeden, and never see my flesh again. If Shinny's in your *Ka*-store, give me to drink, child wonder, tiny joy!"

"Have you ever drunk of the black current before, Mother?"

"Never."

"Drink now."

One of my attendants would present this old biddy with a slug of darkness in a little glass cup. Exit another satisfied customer, wiping her lips. Her name and address would be registered for temple records; she was enrolled.

Other petitioners were sharper-brained. Indeed I suppose the majority were, so I shouldn't be too anecdotal. But I had to pack a lot of people into these sessions, and she was the sort who stood out.

Soon a flood of local landlubber women were joining the new cult; and Chanoose reported delightedly that much the same was happening in other towns, where proxies of mine administered the dose. For some reason Guineamoy seemed a tough nut to crack—while north of Aladalis progress was hampered somewhat by an absence of the black stuff locally. Barrels of black current had to be boated to Port Firsthome and beyond.

"I do hope," I remarked to Chanoose one day, "that the black current can replenish itself quickly enough!"

"How do you mean?"

"At this rate we might drink it dry."

"You can't be serious. We're only taking a tiny portion. And it's allowing us. No boat sailing out to the midstream for fresh supplies has met any bother. Besides—"

"Okay, just a joke."

"This isn't a joking matter."

"Sorry."

"Our volunteers are working double-time at Aladalia to supply the northernmost towns."

"Ah, the brave black current bucket brigade." I wondered who was paying them. Me, probably.

"Yes, brave indeed! But we aren't rushing recklessly."

"I didn't suppose you would be."

"Still, we'll have to start enrolling men before too long; or we might lose impetus. That reminds me: this fellow of yours, Tam, is starting upstream soon. He's booked passage."

"Glad to hear it. But *not* so glad that the one thing reminds you of the other! I recall you fancying how my father's might be a convenient toe to dip in the water, to see if he got stung. So it's to be Tam's toe now: is that your idea?"

"It'll have to be *some* man's toe, sooner or later. Will the current accept men? Thereby hangs our whole enterprise in the long run. Obviously the man in question should be somebody you're close to, so that the current can share your concern. Speaking of which: have there been any intimations lately, which you've neglected to mention? Any messages, contacts?"

"I've been a little busy of late, Chanoose. Or hadn't you noticed?"

"Not when you're asleep, you haven't. I don't think you're trying. It's a priestess's duty to mediate with . . . whatever she's priestess of."

"So maybe the Worm's still mulling over all I told it."

"You could enquire."

"I'm bloody tired when I get to bed. I probably sleep too deeply. I'm only going on three years old, remember? And maybe our Worm has its work cut out with all these *Ka*s pouring in."

"Rubbish. Women aren't dropping dead just because they drink the current."

"Okay, okay. Yawn, yawn. So when's Tam due to sail? Not, I hasten to add, so that he can become the first male toe in the water!"

"In a week or so."

It was Peli who arrived in Pecawar first; and what a reunion that was.

The last time we'd seen each other was when the nameless ketch, renamed *Yaleen*, sailed me out to the Worm's head up beyond Tambimatu. But naturally I wasn't the same Yaleen as Peli had bidden adieu to back then. My face was another's. And I had shrunk considerably! So when Peli bustled into my quarters late one afternoon, shown the way by Lana, one of the guards, my friend halted as if aghast at what she beheld—she was hamming it up a bit—then she burst out into joyful laughter.

"Oh I *knew!*" she whooped. "But it's one thing knowing, and another thing seeing!" She snatched me up into the air and spun round, hugging me; which almost made Lana have a fit.

"Hey, *hey!*" I protested. "I'm fragile. I break easy."

"What: *you?*"

"Okay, so I'm not particularly."

"Only when you had a hangover!"

"But I have me, um, dignity to think about." And I winked full in her big red burly face, loving the sight of it.

"You may depart," I told Lana; who did.

"Quite the princess!" Peli declared.

"You mean priestess. You don't mind, do you, Peli?"

"What, mind you being a priestess?"

"No, you noddle. Mind being dragged all the way here. Being hauled off the river. I need friends, Peli."

She had sobered. "I guessed as much. What for?" she whispered.

"I'm hemmed in. I'm smothered with attention. Watched. Just yet I don't know what's best to do—"

"But when you do, I'll be here to help." Peli looked round my quarters, noting the child-size bed, the profusion of flockity rugs to cushion any falls, the doors to the river verandah with their great bolts set out of reach, my bookcase crammed with Ajelobo romances, my antique ivorybone scritoire with a pile of blank paper and a pot of ink in it. . . .

"Wondering where I keep my toys?"

She grinned. "Wondering where you keep the booze."

"Aha." I headed for the brass bell mounted over my bed and clanged it. Lana reappeared speedily. "What'll it be, then?" I asked Peli.

"A drop of ginger spirit wouldn't come amiss."

"A bottle of," I told Lana. "Plus a spiced ale for myself."

"A small one?"

"But of course."

Lana nodded, and soon returned with the drinks on a copper tray. Peli and I settled to talk the rest of the afternoon away; and the evening too till dinner time.

Peli had of course noted the pile of paper waiting to be inked. "Another book?" she enquired eventually. I thought it had taken her rather a long while to ask. "Mmm. This time I think it would be wise to make *two* copies."

"Why's that?"

"One to smuggle out. Somehow or other."

"Oh, the guard frisked me on the way in—looking for hidden

hatchets or bludgeons, I thought. Do you mean it's the same when you leave? Hey, I do *get out,* don't I? I mean, I'm allowed into town?"

"You're allowed. No problem. But they'll be leery of what you might take out *with* you. Nobody could slip a whole wad of paper past the guard, and page by page'll take ages. Still, a page at a time is how the copy'll have to be made if prying eyes aren't to see."

"Sounds difficult." Peli glanced at the verandah door.

"They keep an eye on the water. No rowboat could sneak up."

"Sounds downright impossible."

"Oh, come off it. Is this Peli talking? There's bound to be a way. But the first stage is to get the copy made—whilst I'm busy writing the damn book."

She looked unaccountably troubled. "Is this new book of yours really so important?"

"Oh, merely to untold millions of people on lots of other worlds, whose brains the Godmind means to fry. Just *that* important."

"Hmm. Important enough."

"Right now we're only intent on saving ourselves. No one but me has any concept of other worlds."

"Yes I know that, but do you honestly think a book could alter anything? That's what I wonder." Peli poured herself more ginger spirit, a bit urgently. Myself, I'd long since quaffed my spiced ale. Any more booze at the moment would send a little girl to sleep; though with dinner to soak it up I might manage another small ale later. "I mean, for starters there's the whole problem of how to get our own *men* into the *Ka*-store! Not to mention that mob on the west bank. Aren't you being too ambitious. I honestly don't see what any of us could *do* for a hundred other worlds." (That was two "honestly"s in the span of a minute. So what was Peli being *dis*honest about?)

"Neither do I! Not yet. But you surely aren't saying you don't even *want* to try to help save hundreds of millions of people? I don't know how—but *somehow!* For a start, by making everyone aware."

Peli looked downright miserable. "Yaleen, what I'm saying . . . as regards copying your book . . . is that I just don't write too well. Or read, for that matter. In fact, I just *don't.* Read and write. Can't," she mumbled.

"Oh grief." I didn't know what to say. I hadn't for one moment suspected. And I don't suppose that anybody else ever had; for I could see how much this confession cost her. "Oh Peli, I'm sorry."

"I go cross-eyed when I see words written down. The letters jump around and do dances." She wouldn't meet my eyes.

"And you from Aladalia, Peli."

"Where everyone is so brilliant! Don't I know it? That's why I became a riverwoman. But at least, if I can't read, I can sing."

I had to smother a chuckle. "Of course you can."

"But I'm still ruddy useless to you. It was a waste of time asking me here."

"No! Don't say so! I haven't been able to confide in anyone till now. I need you, Peli."

"Can't copy your book, though."

No, and I couldn't copy it either. I already had enough other duties on my plate. Once I actually started writing, my spare time would be gobbled up.

"We'll think of something. You and I," I assured her. "Don't fret; I really do need you here."

Didn't I just! It seemed to me a fair bet that the guild wouldn't publish this next book uncensored. They might be selective, or they might simply sit on the book. I could be wrong, but I wasn't going to risk it. So: how to smuggle a copy out, supposing one could be made?

How could it reach a printing press? And how could copies get distributed—with the guild in charge of all cargoes? Peli was going to have to be a smuggler, and a courier, and more. Ah yes: I would pretend to quarrel with Peli. I would send her away with a flea in her ear, and my book in her duffle bag. Somehow.

Peli brightened. She drained her glass and refilled it with the last from the bottle. "Let's sing a song for old times' sake, eh?"

"Why not?" said I. So we carolled our way through till it was time for dinner, which luckily for the ears of anyone musical in the neighbourhood wasn't too long a-coming.

Dinner was served in Mum's and Dad's suite, and consisted of pig's kidney and tomato kebabs on a bed of saffron rice; all of which no doubt had been hot enough when it set out from the café. Peli switched to ale, and I got my hands on a second small mug too.

I could see that Dad took to Peli, though the booze made her distinctly brash and chortly—I guess she was rebuilding her self-esteem after the confession of illiteracy. Oh what, I wondered, would Dad—who could read a whole page pf spidery writing and crabbed numbers in two flicks of a lamb's tail—have thought of *that?*

Oddly enough, I didn't think he would have minded. Mum, on the other hand, merely tolerated Peli. Mum put up with her.

It was only during dessert (of sorbet blancmange) that I realised that Peli couldn't possibly have read *The Book of the River.* She surely wouldn't have asked any riversister to read it aloud to her! This meant there must be great gaps in her knowledge of my adventures, ones which she hadn't enquired into while we were chewing the fat earlier on; so as not to betray herself. *I'd* mainly been bringing her up to date on what had happened since Edrick murdered me.

I determined to puzzle out what these gaps must be and try to plug them as diplomatically as possible during the course of the next few weeks.

The very next day, in between my stints in the throne room, I began to write *The Book of the Stars.*

It wasn't easy at first. I admit to a few false starts. For here was I, writing about how Tam suddenly hove into sight in Aladalia whilst I was busy writing *The Book of the River;* and lo, Tam was about to sail into view once again, this time ex Aladalia and at my own behest! So events seemed curiously overlaid, as if I were suffering from double vision. Also, I was writing about happenings which seemed fairly remote to me, who had spent two 'extra' years in between on Earth and its Moon; but to Tam and Peli and everyone else these same happenings were much more recent. I'd looped back through time; they hadn't.

Soon I was quite intoxicated with my reconstruction of the past. It came as something of a shock when Chanoose announced one day, "Your Tam's due tomorrow noon, aboard the *Merry Mandolin.*"

Peli, I hasten to add, had been allowed to turn up at the temple without prior advertisement. So no doubt Chanoose said this to get in my good books. Literally! Plain to see that I'd begun writing something. Chanoose and Donnah were well aware that I intended to; so if I had tried to conceal what I was up to, I'm sure this would have roused suspicions. (The copy was what I intended to conceal; howsoever it got done.) Consequently I tackled the job in a spirit of brazen privacy. The privacy component was that I kept my finished copy locked up safely in my scritoire, and made no bones about not letting people kibitz on my work in progress. The brazen part was that I tore up numerous sheets of spoiled paper, cursing roundly in my kiddy voice. This display of artistic temperament deterred en-quiries, but more importantly I noted how all such torn scraps disappeared from the straw trash bucket with an efficiency which I ascribed not so much to impassioned tidiness on the part of Lana and company, as to a desire to oversee all of my abortive scribblings. Once I got into my stride—and was in fact writing smoothly—I catered to this appetite by scrawling a few extra irrelevant lines especially to tear up.

The basket squatted beside my scritoire like a big hairy ear hoping to eavesdrop; but I wasn't worried that eyes would pry into the scritoire itself whilst I was otherwise engaged being priestess. Peli mightn't be able to write but she could certainly perform other neat marvels with her fingers. In town she had purchased a complicated lock, cunningly crafted in Guineamoy. This, she substituted skilfully for the lock in the scritoire lid as supplied, to which I assumed Donnah would have kept a spare key. I always wore the new key round my neck.

If Chanoose was hoping to ingratiate herself, that was her mistake. Forewarned, I insisted on going to meet Tam when he docked the next day. And why not, indeed? I was sick of sitting on my backside in the temple. Sitting at my scritoire. (I'd found that I genuinely *had* to turf Peli out while I was composing my narrative, by the way, so maybe my temperaments weren't all pretence.) Sitting on my throne. Sitting at the dinner table. And occasionally sitting out on the verandah, either playing cards with Peli and Dad, or else with my nose in a romance; before tossing it aside—the romance, that is!—to get on writing my own romance. I had to get out!

Halfway through the next morning's audience, I rose and quit; went down to my quarters to pace the verandah.

Presently a brig schooner drifted into view, angling in towards the shore. At that distance I couldn't quite read the words painted on the side, but a flag hung over the stern from the ensign staff with a design stitched on it which was either a semitone sign or else the outline of a mandolin. I ran indoors and clanged my bell.

Donnah had decreed that I should be escorted through the streets to the docks with all due dignity; namely, perched shoulder-high in a padded chair strapped to poles. So much did my litter rock and bob and undulate upon that journey that for a while I, who had never been water-sick but once—aboard the *Sally Argent,* and then not because of waves—feared that I might turn up at the quayside green and puking. However, I gritted my teeth and even managed to grin and wave my free hand to passers-by who stopped to applaud and blow kisses and fall in behind us; with my other hand I had to clutch the chair-arm.

Still, at least by this method we proceeded apace. Once we were within sight of the quay, with the *Merry Mandolin* yet to heave its mooring ropes ashore, I cried, "Set me down! I'll walk from here!" And so I did, with my guards cordoning me from the wake of townsfolk.

When Tam appeared at the head of the gangplank—a huge bag in each hand—he just stood there for upward of a minute blocking the way. I was waiting at the bottom, with Donnah and her gang. Behind, a fair throng of spectators loomed. Yet Tam didn't seem to notice any of us. He was only seeing—well, he told me this subsequently when we were walking back to the temple together; with his bags riding in my chair rather than me, to Donnah's chagrin—he was only seeing that gangplank which led from water on to land. He was seeing the fact that whilst he stayed aboard the *Merry Mandolin,* he could still sail anywhere—even all the way back home to Aladalia. But once he crossed that bridge, he would be marooned ashore. Tam was sure he had left something in his cabin; and indeed he had. It wasn't anything tangible, though. What he had left was the way back home. That was why he hesitated for so long.

He descended. We shook hands—quaintly, his big lumpy hand making mine disappear. I argued with Donnah a bit. The guards hoisted his bags; we set off.

I soon heard his confession. "But it's so wonderful to be here with you!" he insisted. He was stooping over me from what now seemed to me a hugely gangly height. "That you should have asked for me out of everyone—well, well!" His voice sank softly so that only I should hear. "I have the fleuradieu you sent me, pressed and dried in my luggage—and I have a surprise as well. A present. I never thought I'd actually deliver it. I hoped you might come across its like in some far town one day, and realize that it was for you."

"That sounds delightfully mysterious."

"The mystery is *you,* Yaleen."

He seemed genuinely happy when he said these things. I decided that this was because he had at last found a way of fulfilling his impossible love for me. He could be near me, adoring me to his heart's content and even touching me, as a big brother a sister; our relationship had suddenly been blessed with innocence. Now he was exempt from any ordinary expectations a lover might have had of him, where he might have fallen short. Equally, no one else could ever win me from him, since I was physically unwinnable. No need for jealousy. He was cured, redeemed, his aching ecstatic heart's wound salved.

Or so I told myself while he escorted me, nudging my guards into the background merely by the way he walked. At first I had felt qualms about that business at the gangplank, as he explained it; yet now I congratulated myself somewhat.

Till Tam sniffed the air anxiously. "It's so dry here," he said, more to himself than to me.

"Yes? Pecawar's near the desert."

Tam's feet scuffed the dust. His eyes assessed a warehouse built of sandstone blocks which we were passing.

"Dry. Even the river was dusty."

"What's wrong, Tam? It's a different place, that's all. Aladalia isn't the whole world. If you'd wedded, you'd have had to—"

"I wedded my art."

"Which you can practise here as easily as. . . ." I faltered. For in that moment I had seen what he was seeing.

"Clay," he murmured. "A potter needs clay. And not just any sort of mud, either! I need kaolin clay and petuntse clay. Kaolin is decomposed granite, and petuntse is decayed feldspar which melts into glass. That's if I want to craft real porcelain. . . . For soft pasteware I'd only need chalk, white clay and frit. But frit's made up of gypsum, salt, soda and quartz sand. Anyhow, pasteware scratches easy and picks up grease marks. . . . And if I just wanted to craft faience or majolica, I'd still need the right sort of soft earth, wouldn't I? It's so arid here. All dust and sand. I hadn't realized."

"Whatever you need, the guild will get."

Tam laughed. "What, tubs of the right kinds of clay all the way from Aladalia?"

"Why not?"

"They'd probably dry out. Anyway, it isn't the sort of stuff you buy in any old quayside shop. It has to be sought. A potter should know his clay like his own flesh, or else he botches. He turns out second-best that cracks and crazes."

"Can't you write to friends in Aladalia, saying exactly what you need?"

"And wait weeks and weeks, and meantime change my plans? No, a potter should work with the local clay that he's in touch with." His shoe grooved the surface of the street. "Dust and sand all around me. Oh well, I guess I can try my hand at brickwork. Why not? I'll be a big fish in a pond that's otherwise empty." He grinned lamely.

But of course I didn't yet know the half of it; and it was Peli who got Tam to explain fully over dinner, which we three ate privately that evening in my own chamber.

Just before the meal was served, he presented me with his gift: a bundle of straw tied with twine. Within was a mass of chicken feathers. And nestling inside those . . . a fragile translucent white bowl.

A bowl about the size of Tam's hand. The sort of bowl that ought only to hold clear water with a single green leaf afloat. Or only air. There was already something floating at the bottom of the bowl beneath the glaze: a dark violet fleuradieu, last flower of deepening winter. For a moment I thought this was the very bloom which I had sent to Tam by way of goodbye. But no; it was painted exquisitely on the porcelain.

"Why, Tam! It's beautiful. No, it's *more* than beautiful. Did you really craft this?"

"Who else? It's part of a series showing all the hues of the farewell flower from summer's powder-blue to the midnight blue of year's end."

"How did you manage it?"

He shuffled his big feet and twisted his knobbly hands about. Lana had finished setting out some lacquer food boxes for us. She said, "Better fetch a brush and pan for the feathers, hadn't I?"

"No. Just leave us, will you?"

When she'd gone, Tam said, "How indeed? Well, when you sent that flower, Yaleen, something altered in me. This emblem . . . purified my art; enhanced it. It's only a little while since; it's a big change, I'd say."

"A breakthrough?" queried Peli.

"Hardly the word a potter would use!" Tam chuckled and pinged the bowl with his fingernail.

"Don't!" cried Peli in alarm.

"It won't shatter unless you chuck it across the room. It's frail but strong, as an eggshell is. A fat hen could sit on it. Talking of chickens and eggs, let's eat. I'm starving."

We took the lids off the food boxes only to find that we'd been served with raw fish, Spanglestream-style. Obviously this was a new experience for Tam. The fish of the northern reaches are coarse and indelicate compared with those of the south. Northerly fish need frying, boiling or barbecueing. True, we didn't have such delicacies as hoke or pollfish or ajil in Pecawar waters, either. But a few species made passable substitutes. What's more, the new Spangle-stream-style restaurant whose fare we were sampling that evening had begun to experiment with importing the yellow pollfish and madder hoke alive in nets towed behind boats—though frankly these fish didn't seem to travel too happily; their flesh became a tad lacklustre en route.

Needless to say, I hadn't asked Donnah to order in a raw fish banquet for us; and I feared this was a bitter jest aimed at discomfiting the newly-arrived Tam who had never eaten such a thing in his life before. Maybe Chanoose had suggested our evening's menu to Donnah! Though raw fish was to my own taste—with reservations—I felt bound to apologize for the strange cuisine and assure Tam that it had nothing to do with regular Pecawar cuisine. I knew that he preferred spiced sausages, lamb pasties, faggots, blood pudding and such. If I'd had any sense, I should have foreseen something of the sort. I resolved to have a firm word with Donnah the next day.

But Tam claimed to enjoy all this raw fish, dipped in pepper and mustard sauces, as a novelty; and Peli pressed questions on her compatriot to make him feel very much the honoured guest; and perhaps distract him from what he was munching.

As she quizzed Tam, so the true—shall I say *enormity?*—of what I'd done in summoning him to Pecawar became more apparent.

Soon curious words and phrases were flying about, such as "saggars" (which are fire-clay boxes) and "biscuits" (which are what you call fired pots before they get glazed), and "overglazing in a muffle fire" and "burners who watch the kiln".

"Burners?" I interrupted.

"People have to watch a fire to keep it constant."

"How long do they do that for?"

"Sixty hours or thereabouts."

"Oh. And your clay has to be crushed and churned first of all under a millstone?"

"Right; that's to render it soft and fine enough. Oh, I could fix up a grinding wheel sufficient to my needs, though I doubt I'll need one."

"Why not?"

"No suitable clay. I'll have to turn my hand to brickware—or lustre and majolica. I reckon I can design a small kiln which won't need constant attention."

"I'll pitch in," said Peli. "It'll give me something to do with my paws. Who knows, you setting up shop here could be quite like, well, the new Spanglestream restaurant opening!"

Tam surveyed a few slivers of fish remaining on his plate. "Perhaps," he sighed.

"Tam," I said, "I'll find you the clay you need—the clay to make fleuradieu porcelain! I promise I will."

"But . . . how?"

"Tell me exactly what these kaolin and petuntse clays look like and smell like, and anything else about them."

So he told me, though it isn't too easy to detail the hue and the feel of types of clay. I don't suppose he believed my promise, and I didn't explain further in case nothing did come of my plan.

That night I dreamed up a river for myself. That night I dreamed up a Worm. And the Worm rose from the depths of the waters; from the depths within me.

Hullo, Worm. Solved any riddles lately?

Hullo yourself. It isn't easy. Why is there a universe? Why is there a me? *There's nothing to compare me with. Now if only I could contact another of my ilk. . . .*

Just what are you getting at?

'Tis but an idle notion.

Well, we don't have time for idle notions. What are we going to do about the Godmind, eh?

Aren't people doing it already, by booking tickets for my Ka-store? *Pity there's an upper limit to the number of Kas I can swallow.*

Say that again!

There's still room for you, if you get bored with being my priestess. Just jump in the river and I'll see to the rest.

You're having me on, Worm. You're trying to panic me. Admit it!

You can hardly expect me to swallow an infinite number of persons. Obviously there's an upper limit.

And it's large enough for everyone, I'll bet!

I do wish you would join me.

Sorry. Other duties call. And here's one of those duties, right off: I need clay.

Clay?

I need certain types of clay. Otherwise I'll have done the dirty on my friend Tam.

Explain.

So I did. *Will you search the memories in your Ka-store? Someone may know where to find kaolin and petuntse locally.*

No problem. I already know.

You do?

It's underwater, on the bed of my river. The stuff you call kaolin is about a league south of here. You'll find petuntse half a league beyond.

On the river bed? Sequestered by water and stingers, and by madness for any man. . . .

The stuff's just offshore. A person could wade out and dig, if they held their breath.

Worm, it's time to talk about men.

Need some advice?

Don't be daft. I want you to promise that if Tam drinks of you you'll let him enter the river.

And my Ka-store too? I don't much care for the taste of the several dead Sons I swallowed.

Tam's different. He's gentle. Most of our men are, over here in the east. They've learned to flow with the world.

Hmm, I seem to recall they weren't so gentle recently—during a certain war.

And whose fault is that? You provoked the war!

Oh. So I did. And now you're asking for all men to drink of me and enter the Ka-store? That's what this request of yours implies.

Anything to get Tam his clay! *Okay, so that's what I'm asking.*

Hmm, but that would put an end to the female monopoly of the river. Which would turn your own world upside-down and *my Ka-store too. My whole inner landscape would alter. I don't think I like that.*

If all our men get burnt up by the Godmind, and there are no more fathers, your inner landscape isn't going to get much more input from anyone!

My dear, I already contain multitudes of experience; so many are the Kas that I have swallowed.

Look: the Godmind wants to zap you. It'll find that a damn sight easier if it has access to crowds of dead men's Kas hereabouts.

True. . . . I must survive. Therefore you must all survive in me, man and woman alike. You're right. Together we stand; together we'll unriddle the universe too, who knows?

Couldn't you accept men into the Ka-store but somehow forbid them access to the river? Except as now, for the one-go?

In that case how could Tam go plodging in the water to dig clay?

Oh. Um.

It's more of a problem than that, Yaleen . . . though I believe I spy a solution.

Let me explain how it is at present that men are able to sail once and once only; and why twice brings madness and death. Down Tambimatu way, deep in the jungle, there's a little plant which catches insects to eat. This plant resembles toothy green jaws, yawning wide. If you touch the jaws once, nothing happens. A falling leaf might touch them once, or a drop of water. But if you touch them twice in the same manner, the jaws snap shut and devour. You see, something which touches twice is alive and active. I'm like that plant. I have arranged myself so as to ignore the first touch of a man—his first journey on my river.

And if the same fellow touches you twice, you seize him?

Just so. I could re-arrange myself so that a man's first brush with me kills him. That way men could drink of me, and gain the Ka-store, but they couldn't ever stray off shore. Alternatively I could re-arrange myself so that men always have free access to the river.

Wait a minute! Are you saying that you could have fixed things during the war to give our whole army safe passage downstream? You could have kept your jaws shut?

Dear me. Those Sons might have sent reinforcements over.

Fat chance, with you back in position blocking the way across! You just wanted to spin things out.

Might I remind you, Yaleen, that you never asked any such favour of me?

True. Too damn true. Right then I could have curled up inside with embarrassment and grief. All that extra needless suffering; now I knew it for a fact. I wished I hadn't mentioned the matter.

Smug bug, I snarled.

Tem-per! You do want some clay for your boyfriend, don't you?

Yes. Sorry.

To resume: what I propose is that I shall turn out my lamp of death, which burns the moths of men. I shall extinguish it for a while. Your Tam will gain access to his clay. During this time you should build dikes in the shallows where the clay is, to hold the water back. You could drive in stakes to fix a wicker fence to, then pile bags of sand and heaps of stone along this fence. After that, bail out all the river-water. That part of the river bed will become land. Once that's done, thereafter I'll kill any man who ventures on the water at all. But all men shall drink of me and enter me at death—of the wisdom of that, I'm thoroughly persuaded. And only women shall sail.

Hang on. If men can't sail at all, how will they get wedded? How can they follow their fiancées to distant towns—hundreds of leagues in some cases? Lovers would have to aim their arrows much closer to home. What fun would a girl's wanderweeks be? How could our towns be meshed by marriage, and the gene-pool stirred?

Just last week I gathered in the Ka of a woman who fell from the sky at Guineamoy.

What?

And from her I gather that some people have started experimenting with transport by steerable balloon. Excellent! Such balloons can carry lovers on honeymoon flights—how enchanting! A once in a lifetime experience. I think that solves the problem.

Balloons! There'd been some talk of military balloons, but I thought nothing had come of it. . . .

Well I never did, I said.

Somebody else did. But she fell out—from a few hundred spans high. It's a really neat death. Elegant and graceful; bar the final splat. *At the time she rather spoiled the effect by being so scared but in retrospect she can appreciate it better. If you want to die and join me and don't fancy drowning yourself, I'd seriously recommend leaping from a balloon. I assure you the last instant, when you get broken, is hardly noticeable.*

Thanks for the tip. I was planning on surviving a while longer. In fact, I was planning on everybody, everywhere, surviving.

Thus totally trouncing the Godmind?

That's the general idea.

I need a fresh perspective on that, Yaleen. I've been trying to feel my way along the psylink to Earth, then out again in another direction. I need to find another Worm like me. Strength in numbers! Two eyes see deeper than one! Frankly I'm not having much luck on my own, so if you'd care to jump out of a balloon. . . .

So that was it. The Worm wanted to project me through *Ka*-space once again.

Since I didn't answer, the Worm continued. *Meanwhile, that's the offer. Your men gain access to my Ka-store—and lose the river entirely.*

All for a few barrels of clay. . . .

No, not just for that. For the sake of every man alive. Actually, the Worm's offer ought to delight the river guild. They would continue to control the waterway.

Does my priestess so pledge, for her people?

Okay, agreed.

So be it. Now you carry on dreaming, and I'll show you the precise sites of those clay deposits.

At first Chanoose was incensed.

"You want to make mud pies? What is this, a complete reversion to childhood?"

"I intend to help my friend and companion get the materials he needs for his art. I *insist*. You yourself said we could do with some decent plates and vases in the temple."

"I did?"

"Didn't you?" I asked innocently.

"So now you want a gang of riverwomen to dam and drain two stretches of river!"

"Ah, there's more to this, Quaymistress. And if I don't get my way, you won't get yours. What I've arranged with the Worm is as follows. . . ." And I explained.

When I'd done, Chanoose said quietly, "You impulsive imbecile. You really are incredible." She spoke for form's sake only; I could see that her brain was pumping away nineteen to the dozen.

All of a sudden her eyes shone and she almost did a dance, there before my throne. "Got it! Oh yes, I've got it! We time the work on these wretched dikes just long enough to *sail* all the captured Sons up north and ferry them over. That way, we shan't need half a 'jack army to escort them. We can keep the Sons chained up. We can take on local militia guards at each town. And while *that's* going on, we'll sail the whole 'jack army back home to Jangali—before they get too accustomed to foreign parts, or too restive.

"All those repatriated captives ought to mess up the west bank nicely. I shouldn't be surprised if half of them turn bandit, or try to overthrow their government. Then when everyone's well and truly back where they belong, hey presto, the dikes get finished. Your Worm opens its jaws again. Immediate embargo on the river! Brilliant, brilliant." You'd think she had thought of it herself.

"Yes indeed! And we'll start putting men on the temple rolls. They'll accept the new set-up. We'll say it was the only way we could negotiate them a safe conduct into the *Ka*-store. By the way, the Worm's spot-on about balloon experiments. I think I'll slip news of those to the *Pecawar Publicizer*—"

"Including how you can fall out of them?"

"We'll have to tighten our grip on balloons. Invest in them; that's best. Hmm, which leaves us with one little problem: the black current only stretching just north of Aladalia. . . . Never mind, never mind! You can have your dikes, Yaleen; rest easy. And *I* have signals to send."

Departure of one satisfied customer. Or so I thought; she was back within a minute.

"Entirely forgot! This all drove it right out of my head. Double benefit, though, Yaleen! Recently a savant in Ajelobo approached the Guild. He's done a couple of services for us before. Sees things our way, he does. Well, he's been trying to analyse the nature of the current and the Godmind, based on what's been published already. So, what with the river being open to everyone for a while, we can sail him down here—"

"I'm not having anyone kibitzing over my shoulder!"

"Of course not, dear girl. He won't bother you. But if he's on hand when you finish *The Book of the Stars*—which I shan't even enquire about, so as not to irk you—how utterly convenient! Meantime, you could possibly bring yourself to iron out a few earlier points which puzzle him."

"Such as how he's going to travel home afterwards? It's nigh on four hundred leagues to Ajelobo."

"Not *quite.*"

"He won't be able to sail home."

"Nor could the army, till now—and look how that problem's been solved. This fellow will probably return by balloon. Mind *you*—" and Chanoose smartly changed the subject—"if the Sons mount another invasion while the river's open, we could be in a mess— supposing the current let them plough through it on rafts. Which I doubt! Rafts haven't the draught of a boat, and the current's substance isn't ordinary. But even so! We'd better send all prisoners north securely battened under hatches in their chains, so that no westerners spy what's going on. We'll ferry them across at the last possible moment."

"If the Sons wanted to invade, they could do it now—up north of Aladalia."

"And doesn't every last jill and 'jack from Firsthome to Umdala know that, Yaleen, thanks to you! But really, that's way beyond the other enemy capital at Manhome North; so presumably the logistics forbid. That *was* your reasoning in leaving the far north unprotected, I take it?" (To which I said nothing.) Chanoose rubbed her hands. "Fine, that's settled then."

Off she went again. Five minutes later she was back, whistling *Masts High! Breezes Fly!*

"While the river's open to everyone, we'll hold a Grand Regatta here, that's what. We'll bring the date forward from the autumn. We'll invite men from Verrino and Gangee. There'll be a grand initiation ceremony, with flags and bunting and masquerades and dances aboard the boats. It'll be a sort of official opening of the *Ka-*

store to men—though obviously Pecawar men can join in earlier, and the 'jack army will be passing through beforehand."

"Hang on! Aren't all our boats going to be full up with prisoners and armies?"

"I'm sure we can spare a few more vessels—if we suspend ordinary trade for a while, and cram those prisoners in tight."

"Poor sods."

"You don't mean that."

"Maybe not."

"That's how we'll do it."

"Yes, but we're sending the Sons north under hatches for security reasons. Now we're going to have men dancing on deck—not to mention a whole 'jack army on the water."

"Ah, but the command in the west will assume we've made a compact with the current. They won't know what sort, so long as they don't see their own men benefiting. *Actually*, it would be really neat if we could fool them into launching rafts across the current. Maybe we ought to feed some half-truths to the captives? Stuff they could blab when they got back home?"

"Some people can be too clever for their own good, Chanoose."

"I thought that was *your* speciality, Yaleen." Oh, she was indefatigable.

"So," I said, "We'll recruit lots of fellows from nearby towns by offering free trips to the Pecawar regatta."

Chanoose looked amazed. "Free? Who said anything about *free*? Does it cost nothing to build your dikes? Or to lay on a regatta? Plus a balloon—we'd better get hold of a balloon to accustom young lovers to the idea. Free indeed! What an impractical child you are."

"Not quite! Maybe we ought to discuss the royalties for my next book here and now!" Here I was feeding *her* a half-truth; for I was pinning my hopes on the copy, not on the original.

She ignored this feint. "I'm grateful for your comments. You point up the need for tight logistics." And off she went, humming her tune.

After this I put on a spurt in my writing, other duties notwithstanding.

Time flowed.

I made one trip out of town, suitably escorted and on a day set by Chanoose, to point out to Tam and herself exactly where his clays were supposed to lie bedded underwater.

Naturally, the night before setting out, I had reminded the Worm of its promise to shut its man-trap down. Even so, my heart was in my throat when Tam waded out into the water, wearing anti-stinger gear, carrying a scoop-trowel and with a safety line around his waist. Breathing deep and ducking under, he brought up samples from the bottom, carried them ashore, dissected them with his gloves off, kneaded them, sniffed them, and even tasted them with the tip of his tongue before pronouncing them pukka. Probably; he wouldn't be absolutely sure till he had ground and fired the clay.

That evening Chanoose sent the signal for the 'jack army to set sail from Verrino; and for the prisoners to be freighted north, in the opposite direction. The 'jacks' voyage would span twice as many leagues as the captives covered, so the captives would be carried more slowly. Nobody wanted to erect temporary prison pens in the pastures by Aladalia.

Work commenced on the two dikes, and proceeded at a leisurely pace as ordained by Chanoose. Tam wasn't idle meanwhile; nor had he been so before that day when we sought out the clay. Already, with Peli's assistance, he had rigged up a grinding wheel and a potter's kick-wheel and had built a kiln to his own design.

The kiln was housed in a hut in a small yard abutting the north end of the temple, the only access to which was through the temple itself. A high claybrick wall tipped with jagged glass surrounded the yard, so I wouldn't be able to smuggle anything out by that route. Since the said area wasn't enormous, Tam stored finished wares in his own room, and a good number of items spilled into my own quarters. He wasn't producing porcelain (yet), but I liked his handiwork to be around.

To fuel the kiln he relied on quite costly nuts of coal imported by the sack from Guineamoy. Not for him the oil of Gangee which most people in Pecawar used for cooking and lighting and occasionally to take the chill off midwinter days. Occasionally; by no means everyone went in for such luxury. A Pecawar winter was never especially bitter. We preferred to shiver a bit (as I had shivered during the first week or so in the temple) and don a few more clothes. Wood, of course, was scanty in the region; imported timber was reserved for building and furnishing, not for fires.

So while I was turning out pages to lock in my trusty scritoire, Tam was creating nicely glazed brickware—painted with fleur-adieus, to keep his hand in, he said. Soon he was selling his wares through one of the stalls along the arcade. And Peli, sweating at the kiln, seemed happy as a flutterbye which has found a saucer of syrup.

Obviously I couldn't ask Tam to take time off to copy my pages. He wrote a neat hand, but that wasn't what his hands were for. I certainly wouldn't impose on him for something slavishly routine.

The problem of how to get a copy made resolved itself in an unexpected way with the arrival of the savant from Ajelobo. Aye, resolved itself, and led to an awful outcome. . . .

But I anticipate.

Already a fleet had conveyed our victorious army homeward, southward, through Pecawar. During the few days of the stop-over the scene was quite like the promised regatta, what with all those boats tied up at quays or anchored offshore, and the streets thronged with 'jacks in much gayer mood than when I'd spent time with them in Verrino.

My temple was also thronged; and many were the slugs of black current dispensed to ex-soldiers.

True, a certain stink of crowded travel hung about the 'jacks. (The guild was economizing on boats as much as possible, to meet all its commitments.) At least they weren't footsore, with holes in their boots and blisters and bunions. Their gait was sprightly. You'll recall my nagging sense of guilt in the matter. At least now I'd put things right—albeit I'd principally been thinking of how to supply Tam with petuntse and kaolin.

Thou shalt not congratulate thyself. Reality reared its head when I discovered that the hale and hearty 'jacks who strode jauntily along Pemba Avenue and crowded into my throne room were not the whole complement. A number of disabled 'jacks hadn't disembarked. Those sad fellows were lying in bunks on various vessels, tucked away out of sight. Still, this way they would get home alive, even though they might never shin up a jungle-giant again.

Given all this influx of visitors, it wasn't surprising that some old acquaintances turned up at the temple. One such was Captain Martan, the officer with whom I had conducted interrogations of prisoners—in another body, during another life.

As soon as I saw him, I wanted to grant him a private audience; but Donnah wouldn't allow it. With so many fighters infesting the place, my guards were in a high state of alert. During those days of the fleet's lay-over, a pile of weaponry often lay in the entry porch atop the purple stairway, confiscated from the 'jacks before they could enter my presence. Donnah ever kept her hand close to her pistol during audiences, while the other guards dangled best Guineamoy machetes behind their backs in addition to the daggers they wore in their belts. My women had little enough experience in wielding such—compared with the visiting soldiery! Maybe that was why the visitors regarded my armed guards so nonchalantly, by and large, and didn't take offence.

I had to hold my tettytet with Martan in public.

"You witnessed an important moment in my lives, Captain," I said to him.

"You are She who has several lives." Martan gave a practical kind of a nod, as though by the law of averages important moments were bound to crop up more often during the course of several lives, then during one; irrespective of how short they were. He sounded as though he was bestowing a title: She Who Has Several Lives.

"Do you recall that brute of a Son we questioned? The one who berserked?"

"How could I forget, little lady?" Oh, wasn't he the one for fine labels of a sudden! Or was he teasing? There seemed to be a twinkle in his eye. The Martan whom I remembered had been an honest, wholesome, realistic fellow, doing a dirty job as decently as possible. He hadn't been one for airs and graces, or hypocrisy.

So I grinned at him, and he grinned back.

"If we'd gone ahead and tormented that Son," I said, "we would have learned about Edrick for sure. He likely wouldn't have killed me. So none of what has happened would have happened."

"Just as well we didn't torture him, eh?" Torture: he used the true word.

"It was you who tipped the balance, Martan."

He looked surprised. "Oh, I don't think so."

"You told me you wouldn't want to be tortured yourself. That was a crossroads in my life. And even though Edrick got to torture *me* on the planet Earth—"

"Where? He did *what?"*

I lowered my voice. "You'll have to wait for my next book, *The Book of the Stars*. And though he tortured me, I say, I still believe we made the right choice that day. I learnt a lesson from that. If we on this world wouldn't like our brains burnt out by the Godmind of Earth, neither would anybody else wherever they are, whether they're Sons of Adam or fishpeople of a far star. We've no right to save ourselves at their expense."

He spoke softly too. "What's this about burning people's brains?"

"Hush for now, Martan. Keep your ears open."

He gazed at me a while, then nodded.

Among soldiers who have risked their lives together I suppose there's a comradeship beyond even that of a guild. I hadn't fought alongside Martan and his 'jacks, but we'd spent several weeks together at the prison pens; and thanks to that rabid Son's assault on us, I believe I shared a bond of comradeship. When Martan was departing, Donnah buttonholed him. I heard her demand to know what I'd whispered. "Just giving me her private blessing, that's all," came Captain Martan's reply. He spoke loudly so that I would hear, and looked calmly across at me.

Another visitor whom I received later that same day was the acerbic "Moustache", last encountered in the Jay-Jay Hall at Jangali.

This fellow wanted neither to bless me nor to receive my blessing. (Not that I'd been especially obsessed with "blessing" people, until Martan came up with this excuse! I'd stoutly resisted having my hand slobbered on by ancient grannies, who were looking forward to reliving their gay young days in the *Ka*-store.)

Moustache's attitude to me hadn't changed. He sketched a parody of a bow.

"Thanks for the ride home, Trouble. Though no thanks for the walk to the war."

"Welcome into the *Ka*-store," I said. "And may you not enter it too soon by tumbling out of a hoganny."

"Never say that to a junglejack!" he growled back. "It's ill luck."

As with Martan, I lowered my voice. "Don't you know yet? There's no such thing as ill luck for us any longer. There's only ill luck for everyone else in the galaxy."

"Eh?"

"Talk to Captain Martan. Keep your ears open."

Moustache had argued strenuously in council that the 'jacks should let Verrino go to rack and ruin just so long as Jangali, cordoned by jungles, was okay. "What's Guineamoy to us?" he had said. He had been proved wrong.

"What's Earth to us, when we have our fortress of a *Ka*-store? What does Marl's world matter?" The same principle applied.

When my news of the stars broke, I hoped Moustache would make the connexion and be conscious of why I'd spoken. He was influential. He was my enemy (though maybe that's too strong a term). And I was apparently impregnable. So why had I chosen to confide in him? This should make him wonder if all was quite as it seemed.

But I was about to relate the unexpected solution to my problem. . . .

The 'jacks had already departed Pecawar a while since when the promised (or threatened) savant sailed in ex Ajelobo. Chanoose took time out to present him formally in my throne room.

Would he turn out to be a grim pedant? A smart pretentious spark, or what? I had no inkling—and didn't much care, either way. All I foresaw from him was nuisance; and who wants to brood on varieties of nuisance? (Well, some people do. . . . I once knew one such aboard the *Speedy Snail*. Nuisance possessed that particular lady to the virtual exclusion of all else. Everything was a source of nuisance to her; including most of her riversisters, turn by turn. She squandered half of her life by inflaming herself at *this* nuisance, and railing at *that* nuisance. She provided an object lesson; and I hadn't allowed the prospect of our savant's arrival to sour one moment of my writing.)

His name was Stamno. He was of medium height and build, with receding fawn hair which was wispy and greasy (when I first met him). An unfortunate centre parting made it look as though someone had tried to saw his skull open. The surviving thatch, he wore longer than suited him; fraying oily curls lapped the nape of his neck. He must have been in his forties, yet his face was a very young one—so long as you ignored some deep criss-cross creases around his eyes. His manner was extremely courteous and attentive; unctuously so.

To anticipate somewhat: by that same evening he had washed his hair, which had been soiled by travel, and during the course of his stay in the temple he must have repeated the treatment at least once every two days. He was a sort of sensual prude, if I can put it that way. He was the kind of person who would flirt but never actually fondle, as if he was holding himself in reserve . . . but for what? Perhaps in pursuit of some ideal. One day he would wake up and his life would have passed him by; meanwhile he wore a velvety maroon doublet and green hose, washed his locks obsessively, and spoke in consciously well-turned phrases.

"I'm delighted to acquaint myself with you, priestess!"

"And hullo to you."

"Of any service I can be to you, only let me know." Sometimes he tried to speak too cleverly. His phrases were so well turned that they turned head over heels. They tripped themselves up, instead of tripping off his tongue.

"I'll be sure to, Stamno."

"Certain problems present themselves to me, which I hope you may be able to clarify. For instance. . . ."

I listened to a string of *for instances* with mounting exasperation, though I didn't let this show.

"An exegesis is called for," he concluded.

"A what?"

"An interpretation of your book; a commentary. Exposition. Or should we say—" and he smirked ingratiatingly—"of your books in the plural, since I understand that most happily you are busy upon—"

"Who's calling for a commentary?" I interrupted.

"Why, *The Book of the River* itself calls out; surely."

Feel free! Comment away till you're blue in the face. And meantime, the Godmind gets ready to burn brains.

"Oh, piss off," I muttered under my breath.

I think Stamno heard me; and this was the strangest thing, for his eyes seemed to light up gleefully. Pleased at being able to interfere with me? I thought not. Pleased, for some other reason. . . .

"We do hope you'll co-operate with Savant Stamno," said Chanoose.

"Who could resist it?" I said. "But I'm sure Stamno wants to settle in right now."

And Stamno smoothed his wayward, failing hair.

In the event Stamno didn't make himself too much of a nuisance, though he did keep on dropping convoluted hints about my work in progress. I tossed him a few sprats of information to chew on. He couldn't tell the guild anything they didn't already know.

Work on the dikes proceeded. I carried on writing, at speed, and was nearly at the end of the book. Tam continued crafting pots and bowls to be sold outside. Pilgrims persisted in calling; and preparations for the Grand Regatta came to a head. Once the regatta had seemed weeks away; all of a sudden the quays were crowded with vessels once more, and men from Verrino, Gangee and even Gate of the South were wandering around town. Not too many from Verrino. In the wake of looting and other ravages of war, maybe they couldn't scrape up the fare. The weather was hotting up.

Oh what a fine regatta it was, to be sure! Masts high, scraping the sky—flags and bright rags of bunting—a small orchestra on one deck, a flute and drum band on another! More fish-masks than I'd ever seen being sported by riversisters; it seemed as though the contents of the deep had hopped ashore. A conga-dance wormed along Pemba Avenue then all around town. Races were run up rigging to release bladders painted silver and red, inflated with watergas. And there was the marvel, as promised by Chanoose, of an enormous passenger balloon.

This balloon was a sphere, open at the bottom, buoyed up by hot air rising from a gas flame in the basket beneath. The basket was big enough to hold half a dozen people including the operator, with a fair-sized telescope for them to peer through. The flame was turned low every ten minutes and the balloon guided back down by its tether rope to allow as many brave spirits as possible to ascend. I need hardly add that the tether was essential, else the balloon would have departed on the breezes; which made me puzzle about the reliability of honeymoon flights. Apparently means of steering were under investigation.

And there was a parade—and a multitude of tasty snacks—and tipple a-plenty, not forgetting slugs of the black current which I doled out for hours from a tented pavilion erected on the waterfront. This was a bit of a bore. On the other hand I couldn't manage much real tippling on my own account. Spirit willing; body too young.

Nor could I participate in the other amusements except as spectator, for reasons of dignity, safety, short legs and such. I did at one stage beg childishly to be allowed to go up in the observation balloon; *not,* I hasten to add, out of any sudden urge to heed the Worm's suggestion and leap to my death. Donnah, ever nearby, put her foot down.

"If a lunatic slashed the rope, you'd drift away. We could lose you."

Dad, who was sitting at a portable table noting names and addresses and keeping a tally of newly-enrolled devotees, nodded his entire agreement.

Round about the middle of the afternoon, Tam sidled up to me.

"Popped back to the temple," he murmured. "Found Stamno rifling your scritoire, reading what you've written. He'd picked Peli's lock." In his hand he disclosed a strong wire with a little hook on the end.

"Chanoose put him up to it! While we're busy here! I bet she did."

"No, no. That's where you're wrong. Guards didn't even try to delay me on the way in. Just nods and smiles from them. *They didn't know.* Stamno seemed scared I'd kick up an almighty barney, and they'd find out. Practically begged me to shut up."

"That's odd. Are my papers safe?"

"Made him lock them up again."

"Tonight, Tam, you and I will have a few words with Master Savant Stamno!"

We did indeed. And be damned how tired I was feeling after my day's activities. (Or inactivities.)

Peli was also present when Tam hustled Stamno into my chambers late that night. A single oil lamp burned. We seated Stamno near this so that his face was brightly lit, while ours were in the shadow. I noticed how Stamno had taken time out to wash his hair yet again.

"Well?" I said. "Explain yourself, snooper."

Stamno worried at a fingernail; though more as if he was manicuring it.

"With pleasure," he said. "I'm delighted to tell you. For you are not quite as you seem, any more than I am."

"Aren't I, indeed?"

"You wish to save other worlds from the Godmind, not just ourselves. *How* this could be accomplished, you don't know. Nor do I. But you wish it."

I nodded. "Carry on."

"Whereas the river guild want to sew this one world of ours up tight—irrespective of the Sons, irrespective of any other humans in the galaxy. Even irrespective of whether the Godmind might attain reality and truth, though the price be high."

"You aren't rooting for the Godmind, surely!"

"No; I belong to the Guild of the Seekers of Truth."

"Never heard of it."

Stamno shrugged. "If truth be hidden, let its seekers also be concealed."

"Cutely put," said Peli. "Doesn't that boil down to your belonging to some nutty little cult consisting of about three members?"

Our savant pursed his lips. "We have connexions with wise women in the Port Barbra hinterland."

"You mean those sex fiends who orgasm for hours on a fungus drug?" I chipped in.

"Your information is distorted, Yaleen. That is only an aspect." It was his first use of my name; hitherto he had only called me "priestess". Suddenly his voice was full of wonder, as though here at last was the ideal—the climax—for which he had preened and prepared himself, and withheld himself waiting, all his born days. "To halt time itself, Yaleen! To perceive the Real beneath the flow of Phenomena! Why, *you* actually turned time back upon itself."

"Sure I did. Which gives us a wee breathing space before most of the human race gets snuffed."

"That too is important," he acknowledged.

"You don't say."

"Your new book won't be printed—not entire. Yet it *must* be. I'll tell you how. A copy has to be smuggled out."

"Tell us something new," said Peli. "Those guards watch what goes out like snapperfish."

"Merely a practical detail! First, we need a good copy. I shall make it. I pen quickly. Once my copy is clear away from here—"

"You'll send it straight to your crackpot Guild of Seekers," Tam said suspiciously. "And that'll be that."

"No! Everybody must read it. Obviously it can't be printed here in Pecawar. It should be printed in Port Barbra."

"Uh?" said Tam. "No books are ever printed there. They don't know how."

"Hear me out! That's an excellent reason for sending the copy there."

"What, where it can't be printed?"

"Listen to me. All the type for Ajelobo's printing presses is made in Guineamoy. Likewise the type for newssheet presses everywhere. En route here, I stopped over at Guineamoy and made enquiries. I seek truth everywhere, you see! I assess all options. I discussed with a metalsmith the crafting of a special new fount of type—and the cost plus a price for discretion. We agreed; I commissioned the making of the fount."

"You hadn't seen Yaleen's new book then," said Peli. "You're lying."

"We Seekers, in Ajelobo and 'Barbra, wish to print pamphlets privately. Truth is about to blossom. Such changes recently!"

"Yon bunch of Seekers must have plenty of spare fish to toss around," said Tam.

"In the past—how shall I put this without sounding coarse?—several prosperous patrons have appreciated the erotic aspect of our investigations."

"And burned themselves up in the process, I'll be bound!" I said. "I know about that drug. You're old by thirty if you overdo it. So your Seekers are content to hook rich fools on early death, and buy printing type with the proceeds!"

Stamno's eyes gleamed. "Never mind about that. The whole galaxy might die before its time. In any case I must dissociate the Seekers of Truth from some of the more carnal activities of our own associates—which are best regarded, mind you, as a mask, a guise, a Special Path."

"Path where? To the graveyard?"

"You don't understand. Hear me out. The new type fount will be consigned to Port Barbra. Our associates have great influence over the newssheet in 'Barbra. Necessarily so! They don't want slanderous rumours published about them. *The Book of the Stars* will be printed in that newly minted typeface—untraceable! It will appear in the form of a flat newssheet of many pages. It won't be elegant and it won't be bound. The paper will be raggier. But it will be shipped everywhere covertly in that disguise—then released simultaneously. After which, you will publicly confirm your authorship."

"If I'm allowed."

"If you aren't, savants in Ajelobo will soon prove by exegesis that it is no forgery."

The confrontation had got completely turned around; and in short order. I began to appreciate the cunning style in which Stamno must have inveigled his way into the good graces of the river guild over a number of years without any 'mistresses suspecting deceitful intent; all for the sake of his ideal. There was a lot about this set-up which I didn't like. But nevertheless . . . and nevertheless, again!

"Okay," I said, "we'll do it."

"That's all very well," said Peli, "but how do we smuggle *Stamno's* copy out? I can't very well stuff the pages up my whatnot." She nudged Stamno, embarrassing him.

"In pots!" exclaimed Tam. "We'll smuggle it out a part at a time in pots with false bottoms. They're used to seeing me shift pots around, and take them out to the stall."

"Where I'll ensure that they're snapped up promptly," said Stamno. "I'll employ an agent."

"They're used to looking in my pots, too. That's where the false bottom comes in."

"Forgive me if this is a dumb question," said Peli, "but won't the papers burn to a frazzle if you're baking a false bottom over them?"

"No. I'll put them in pots I've already made. I'll fold the sheets tight, wrap them in waxed paper, then tamp clay down on top. I'll just dry the false bottom by hanging the pot over a lamp; and I'll brush paint on to look like a glaze. The guards can peer inside to their heart's content. I'll make the necks of the pots too narrow to get their hands down."

Two mornings later, there was a bustle on the river. All the regatta visitors were being packed off home again. (Incidentally, I'd hoped that Hasso might avail himself of the temporary liberty of the waterway to pay me a visit. No such luck; maybe he couldn't afford the fare.) In the midst of these manoeuvres, hoping that they provided a pretty distraction, I sought Donnah and requested a lot more paper.

"Why? Is the book turning out long?"

"Oh yes. Besides, I spoiled oodles of sheets."

"That many? I hadn't noticed."

"I threw them in the river, didn't I? I made paper boats."

Donnah provided paper.

Stamno set to at his scribing task, working in his own cubby-hole of a room which he kept locked without causing comment, since he of course was a friend of the guild. Tam for his part began producing pitchers with narrow necks so that the guards would get used to seeing them. And I rushed to finish my writing.

Quite soon came the day when Chanoose called by to announce that work on the dikes would be completed the following Tauday. The 'jacks were almost home. The prisoners were safely beyond Aladalia, battened down, ready to be freighted over. Another few days, and the water could be pumped out of the dikes.

"What a fine success our regatta was," she cooed at me.

"I couldn't agree more." That was when we had uncovered Stamno and hatched our scheme.

"The number of visits here is falling off, though."

"Yes, I'd noticed." Thank goodness; I'd needed the extra hours.

"It's only to be expected. Price of success, eh? Do you know, we've enrolled almost the whole of Pecawar? Therefore the guild has decided that shortly you should go on a grand progress lasting

half a year or so—down south to Tambimatu, first, then all the way
north at least to Aladalia."

"But . . . but Tam just came from Aladalia to be with me!"

"Not to worry! With all that expensively gotten clay in his hands,
he ought to be as happy as a mud-hopper. You see, people *are* joining us in the other towns—but your presence on the spot will attract
many more. We do want the maximum number safely in the fold
before the Godmind attacks, don't we?"

"Yes," I mumbled weakly.

"Good, that's all settled. You can set off on Rhoday next. Women
only on the river by then!"

"Rhoday next, eh?" Stamno smoothed the hair lapping his nape.
"I've nearly caught up in my copying."

"There's only a tiny bit more," I said. "I'm nearly done."

"We'd better start smuggling tomorrow. Right, Tam?"

Tam was staring at me slack-jawed.

"Half a year or so! What does 'or so' mean? Maybe they'll decide
you ought to tour the river permanently. In which case, why did I
ever come here?"

"To make pitchers, that's why," replied Stamno. "Pitchers in
which to hide paper."

Tam bunched those bony fists of his; for once in his life he looked
on the point of striking someone.

"I'll stick by your side," Peli promised me. "You can count on it."

This only made matters worse; Tam smashed his fists together. He
pounded his knuckles.

"Stow it!" snapped Stamno. "I don't see this as an ultimate tragedy. If need be, you can always walk home."

"After all this effort they've put into getting the right clay for me,
who says as I'll be allowed?"

Stamno disregarded this. "If Yaleen's well away from here when
The Book of the Stars appears, and if the river guild get vengeful, and if
she happens to be in the general area of Ajelobo or Port Barbra—we
Seekers can offer sanctuary."

"I can hide in the forests and be the pet of your cult? Lovely,
charming! Just what do you think the guild would do for revenge?
Cut my head off?"

Stamno laughed in a dry, rattly way. "We're wasting time in idle
speculation. Fact number one: Yaleen is going on a trip. Fact number
two: we have work to finish."

"Just a mo," said Peli. "What are you going to be doing after Rhoday next, Stamno?"

"Me? I'll remain here in all innocence and study the writings which Yaleen leaves behind. What else? Thus Tam shall not be entirely bereft of congenial company." Was this some essay at humour?

Tam, bless him, grinned crookedly. "With Peli gone off sailing, I could use another pair of hands at the kiln!"

"Oh dear me," said Stamno.

"I hear you're going away," said Mum. "I think I shall come with you."

"What? How about Dad? He can't sail. He's stuck here, same as Tam."

"I'm not stuck."

For a brief moment I almost hated my mother.

"Your father will be happy with his facts and figures," she continued lightly. "Temple statistics matter more than his spice accounts of old. Though of course those were also important; in their way." Her voice hardened. "I don't have a home any more, except with you, Yaleen. Do you suggest I remain as caretaker of an empty temple? A sort of human dust-sheet?"

"This temple won't be a ghost when I'm gone! If you think so, what price Dad's facts and figures—not to mention his happiness?"

She shrugged. "This trip is different from your other trips, daughter dear. This time you won't be a young woman well able to look after yourself. You're only three years old."

"Peli will be going."

"Is Peli your *mother?*"

"She's a riverwoman! Um, maybe you and Dad ought to move back to our house while I'm away?"

"And caretake there, for a change? No, Yaleen, I want more. I have a right. Didn't I endure childbirth twice for you?"

"Yes, yes. But look, I really don't see how you can do this to Dad."

"What am I doing?"

"Abandoning him, damn it!"

"Yet it's all right for me to be abandoned?"

"You wouldn't be. You'd be together."

"Since I moved in here, Yaleen, I've become a person of some import. That's a new sensation for me. Your father and I spent years cosseted together. Narya's birth reaffirmed our ties—but it was a false reaffirmation, wasn't it?"

"Have you spoken to Dad about this?"

She shook her head. "Not yet. I thought I'd tell you first. It's my decision, mine alone."

"Mum, this trip mightn't be plain sailing."

"Why ever not? Are we boarding a leaky boat?"

"Life's uncertain. Anything might happen."

"Equally, anything might *not* happen. We'll just be away half a year, you and I."

"Really made your mind up, haven't you?"

"High time, too! Others have been arranging my life for long enough. You, Chanoose, the guild. Yes, it's time to assert myself—just as you have always done. The mother learns from the daughter." Mum smiled benevolently; it was such a smile as I had seen on Chanoose's face.

"Assert? I don't know that I've been in much of a position to do that lately."

"Opinions might vary on that score. People seem to be forever running errands for you. All the way from Aladalia and Ajelobo. Building dikes, goodness knows what else. Now let's do something for *my* benefit, shall we? In turn I can help you assert yourself more effectively."

This business has all gone to your head, I thought to myself. *You've become a dowager, from out of a story book. . . .*

Again, that smile. "Do you know, daughter, I haven't travelled anywhere significant since my wanderweeks all those years ago. *Now* I shall."

"But. . . ." *But I don't want you on that boat. I'm not really a child. Your presence will make me into one! You'll diminish me. You'll elbow out Peli who's my true ally.*

I couldn't bring myself to say any of this. She was my mother, after all. My mum twice over.

It was early on a Newday morning. In just twenty-four hours we were due to sail—me, Mum, Peli, Donnah, and assorted guards—aboard a schooner, the *Crackerjill,* which had been placed entirely at our disposal. First port of call: Gangee.

Almost the whole of Stamno's copy of *The Book of the Stars* had already been smuggled out of the temple at the bottom of various pitchers. The previous evening, I had finished the last few pages—

for Stamno to copy, and Tam to encase in clay. The job would have been completed overnight.

I was sitting on the top step of the marble stairway which led down to Pemba Avenue. I was hugging my knees as I watched the world go by to work. Quite a few people waved to me; I smiled and ducked my head at them. Guardswoman Bartha loitered a few paces behind, keeping an eye.

I heard voices from the entry hall: Tam's—and Mela's. Mela was another guard.

"Let's have a look, then," she was saying.

"Oh, you've seen the like of these before." Tam sounded perfectly casual.

I looked round. He had one pitcher in his hand and another tucked under his arm.

"Just so," said Mela. "I've been thinking how that style's rather ugly for a hot-shot potter—specially now that you have the super clay to make true porcelain."

"I've had to keep my hand in."

"You couldn't even get a hand in one of those. How do you clean it? I wouldn't buy a jug I couldn't clean."

"It isn't a jug. It's a pitcher. You just swill it out."

"Yet most days lately I've seen you take a couple of those down to yon stall; where they certainly don't gather dust. They're grabbed almost before you can say *Ka*-store."

"That's gratifying to hear."

"Oh, didn't you *know?*"

I didn't dare continue watching, in case I seemed anxious. Perhaps it was time to arrange a little diversion? Such as Yaleen tumbling downstairs?

"Let's take a closer look at these much-desired items, shall we?"

I heard fumbling, stamping—then a splintering crash. "Oh *shit!*" cried Tam.

I jerked round. The pitcher from under his arm lay shattered.

"Look what you've gone and done!" he bellowed. But he didn't sound panicked.

"That's exactly what I'm doing: looking." Mela toed the fragments with her boot, sorting them about.

Ah. The broken pitcher had been a decoy. Tam had dropped it deliberately.

I jumped up. "Hey, you! Mela!"

Bartha clamped a hand on my shoulder, suppressing me.

"Now let's break the *other* one," suggested Mela silkily.

"Oh come on," growled Tam. "What do you think you're playing at?" But his cheeks had flushed.

"Guild security," said Mela. She snatched at the pitcher in his hand. Tam jerked it away. She grabbed again. He swung it high out of reach.

Then the incredible happened. To extend her reach, Mela unsheathed her machete and slashed at the pitcher. The target clove in half, leaving Tam clutching the neck. The base flew away in my direction, smashing on the floor. Potsherds lay scattered—and amidst them a slab of uncooked clay, with an edge of waxed paper sticking out. Bartha's hand became a vice on my shoulder.

"What's *that?*" exulted Mela.

Tam lost his cool. Discarding the top of the pitcher he dived to secure the waxed package. Mela also dived. The machete, which was still in her hand, was a part of her hand. It was the reach she lacked. As Tam's fingers closed around the clay-wadded paper, Mela's hand descended fiercely. The machete blade chopped Tam's wrist and stuck in the floor.

Pulsing squirts of blood spouted—over a hand which lay severed. Tam's blood was pumping from a stump. Mela's machete had sliced right through flesh, muscle and bone.

Tam didn't howl. Maybe he couldn't feel any pain yet. Maybe the pain was blotted out by the sight before his eyes. He lay sprawled, staring madly at his potter's right hand—and his wrist-stump spurting life-blood.

Mela sprawled too. She still held her weapon, with the edge buried like a cleaver in a butcher's block. Her teeth were chattering crazily.

No, Tam didn't howl. But I did. And what I was howling was, "Current! Current! Madden Mela! Kill her! Send her to the Earth!"

No such thing happened. The Worm didn't rear itself in Mela's mind. (And maybe this was just as well. Who wants a priestess who can frenzy you and slay you when she fancies, with a chant of hatred?) Nor did my frantic wrenching release me from Bartha's grasp. But my cries alerted the temple. Feet came running.

Donnah took in the scene in a trice. "Tourniquet!" she screamed. Tearing her own belt free, she ripped Tam's sleeve away and began binding the belt above his elbow. "Another one! Wads! Bandage!" Within moments Donnah was tightening somebody else's belt just below Tam's shoulder. I'd run out of breath to howl by now—and he, I think, had fainted. "Salve! And clay! Wet clay to plaster on!"

Presently Donnah rose. Mela hovered nearby, brandishing the waxed package. Her blade stayed stuck in the floor. She thrust her discovery at Donnah.

"Here! He was trying to sneak this out. It was buried in clay at the bottom of the jug. When the jug got smashed he tried to snatch it. He would have run off with it. So I had to . . . . It was an accident, Donnah: his hand. I swear it."

Donnah accepted the package. She ripped it open, unfolded the sheets written in Stamno's hand and scanned them. "So," she said.

"It was an accident." Mela's voice pleaded. "That thing's important, isn't it?"

"Yes. But you . . . exceeded all bounds. And in front of _her!_ Get out of my sight, Mela!"

Mela fled.

A wide board from a trestle table was brought. Tam was eased on to this. By now he was moaning and shivering. Tremors racked his body. Two guards bore him away, within.

Donnah approached me slowly, and knelt to be on a level with me. "I think we've saved him, Yaleen."

"Saved him?" I cried in her face. "You've destroyed him! He's a potter without a hand! You might as well kill him, and be done. Let him go to the _Ka_-store. That's the only place where he can be a potter now—the potter of his memories!"

"With good care, he'll be well." Her face twisted. "He'd better be. I have questions to ask—him, and Savant Stamno. I shan't bother you with such questions, my priestess. You have much to occupy your mind, with the _Crackerjill_ due to sail." She was controlling herself only with difficulty. She was trembling. She was scared. Of Chanoose's reaction to the news of this obscene mutilation? Or of her rage at _why_ it had occurred?

"I'm not sailing anywhere, you stupid sow! You pissing stinger!"

"Tam will be most courteously looked after. I swear by _The Book!_ I do realize what he means to you, Yaleen. We may even be able to fit him with some sort of spatula on the end of his wrist."

"A spatula? Why not just nail a shovel-head on him!"

"Reports of his progress will be flashed to you faithfully. Mela will be punished. She'll be kicked out of the temple. Right out of the guild! I promise you she'll never sail again. But *you* must sail, Yaleen —for everybody's sake."

To my astonishment I saw that she was weeping. She put an arm around my shoulder and hugged me tenderly. Her salt tears were on my cheeks. I was so surprised that I didn't spit or hiss or bite her.

I felt my own eyes watering, and a moment later I was sobbing— just like the kid I looked to be. Peli wasn't there to comfort me. But I knew that I couldn't have surrendered to Peli in the way that I now surrendered to Donnah—because Peli was my comrade. Nor with my mum could I have broken down. Yet with Donnah suddenly it was possible. Why so? Was it because I had betrayed Donnah; and now found myself comforting her just as much as she was comforting me?

"I'm still not going," I sniffled into her red hair.

"If you don't want to, little one," she murmured, "your boat can wait. We can wait. The whole world can wait."

Which, of course, meant that I would have to sail as planned. No world can wait. Neither ours, nor all the others.

"Yaleen!" It was Dad's voice.

"Donnah," I whispered, "I only did what I did for the best, without malice." Gently I detached myself from her embrace; gently she let me do so.

"Of course you did," she murmured back. Sad? Scared? I no longer knew.

"Yaleen." Dad strode across the hall, skirting the blood-puddles and the machete. "I just heard about Tam. It's terrible. Awful. The poor lad! I promise I'll care for him. I shan't let him despair. I'll help him be whole again—in spirit at least."

"Thanks, Dad. But I *am* sailing tomorrow. You needn't worry on that score."

His look showed that I had wounded him. But he merely said, "Look after your mother for me, will you? Whilst I'm looking after Tam?"

"If I can, Dad. If I can. It isn't always easy to look after people— when they have the wind in their sails."

"Don't I know it," I heard Donnah say softly.

We were all being very delicate and tender with each other. We were all hurt equally, and we had enough strength to wallow in our hurt. Unlike Tam, whose wound was the worst. The most unendurable.

* * *

Tam's condition was stable by the evening. He wasn't going to die. He wasn't going to lose the rest of his arm to gangrene. The tourniquets had been removed.

Stamno had vanished. Nobody could find him—and no one had seen him go out that morning. So presumably he hadn't been lurking along Pemba Avenue waiting for his agent to acquire the last pitcher from the arcade. He must have heard the commotion—and somehow decamped, over the yard wall, though I would have thought that impossible, and him not much of an athlete to look at. Clearly the threat to his quest had driven him to some desperate exertion.

Or had he contrived to slip out earlier on? Had he been intending to decamp in any case—contrary to what he had told me—just as soon as he laid hands on the last sheets? I didn't know.

I certainly didn't volunteer any information about Stamno, to a most displeased Chanoose. I didn't breathe a word about the typemakers of Guineamoy, or the Seekers of Truth, or the Port Barbra cult women.

Chanoose walked off with my own original copy of *The Book of the Stars.* Actually, I presented this to her before she could confiscate it. The book had ruined Tam; *I* didn't want it any more. Not that particular manuscript. And the copy, wherever it was, was only missing a few last pages of no great moment; in retrospect, of very little moment indeed.

The next morning I bade an awkward farewell to Tam. He lay in his room looking ashen—and so alone, though my father sat by him.

He did bring himself to say, "I always had too many bones, Yaleen. Always, didn't I?" I didn't know whether he spoke bravely, or dementedly. Nor did I want to decide. I kissed him on the brow and fled upstairs—whence I was conveyed ceremonially to the quayside, perched in my seat strapped to poles.

We boarded: guards and Peli and Mum and me. Donnah too—my travelling major-domo now. Donnah looked mightily relieved to be sailing forth again. Yet until we actually cast off, she often glanced ashore as though Chanoose might decide at this last and cruellest moment to replace her.

It was bright and breezy that Rhoday morn, though the sun would blaze hard by noon. Out on the waters the air smelled hopeful and healthy. Presently I spied the first of Tam's dikes. At that distance from shore I could barely make it out: just a thin line fringing the river, with a rude hut nearby for the watchman to occupy.

I imagined water being allowed to seep back to cover the exposed clay during the long weeks to come.

I hurried to find Donnah. I told her to send a signal back to Chanoose insisting that both dikes should be kept drained even if Tam looked like never crafting another pot in his life. Even if Tam *demanded* that they flood the beds of clay. Even if he quit Pecawar to walk home.

But nobody else should ever use that clay.

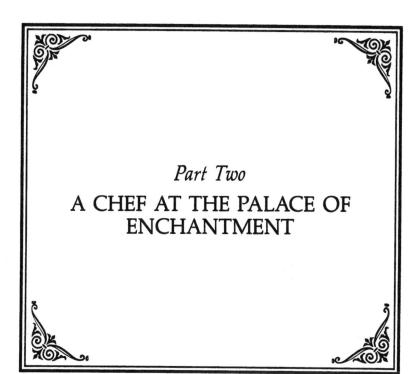

Part Two

A CHEF AT THE PALACE OF ENCHANTMENT

WHEN we arrived in Guineamoy the town seemed even dirtier and smellier than last time I'd visited the place. The war had stimulated industry and with the coming of peace the host of manufacturers pursued the old avenue of profit with renewed vigour and capital, meanwhile searching out new ones too, for their rejigged workshops to supply.

Fresh advances in forging and metallurgy had occurred. New chemicals had been cooked up, and mixed in novel combinations (original object: combustion, explosions). Gases were being extracted from coals and other sorts of rock. Experiments were afoot.

More especially experiments were in the air—that was where you could sniff them. And spy them, too. Guineamoy was the home of the balloon which had graced our grand regatta. During our stay another hot-air balloon was undergoing trials. This specimen had wooden "fans" jutting from its passenger basket. Powered by compressed air, these fans swished round to steer the balloon—slowly, by and large—against the breeze. Yet this method of steering couldn't have been too reliable. One day I saw the balloon drifting through the smoky sky without fans turning, heading towards the river. All of a sudden the flicker of fire and shimmer of air above the basket disappeared and the balloon was dropping fast. Before the craft could crash into the ground, the flame leapt briefly alive to buoy it up—and a rope with an anchor on the end was tossed out, its hooks snagging on a roof below.

However, the kind of industry I was interested in was typefounding. Whilst I was presiding over what had come to be called "communion" with the Worm—the solemn drinking of swigs of the black current—Peli was busy in town doing a spot of investigating. (I suppose I was in town too. But only just. Since men couldn't board the *Crackerjill,* a pavilion had been erected for me on the quayside; just as at Gangee and Gate of the South.)

I'd tried without success to deter Peli from aping a Port Barbra accent—the quiet murmur, the softly hooded consonants—as subterfuge. If she got excited she couldn't keep this up; and besides it was Stamno who had commissioned the new type fount, not some woman of 'Barbra. (Or so, at least, Stamno had told us.) But Peli liked the idea of disguising herself. She went equipped with a long scarf to wind round her head as a 'Barbra-style hood and mouthmask while she was prowling the streets of Guineamoy. I'm sure this must have made her stick out like a sore thumb. It was high summer by the time we arrived. The heat wasn't so fierce or the air as humid as in the deep south, but the atmosphere was still pretty stifling. The sun was hazed with an overcast of smoke which pressed the hot exhalations of smelters back down to earth to add to the season's natural warmth.

True, a few of the locals had taken to wearing thin muslin masks to keep the smuts out of their nostrils; and coifs or snoods, besides, to protect their hair. Yet these eccentrics were strictly a minority. Judging by glances directed askance at such, not everybody in Guineamoy admired this new fashion. *Proper* Guineamoy folk should obviously suck the dirty air in with relish. They should stick a finger up their snouts and lick the grime. Undeterred, Peli sallied forth with six spans of wool to wrap about her countenance.

Wool was also wrapped around the whereabouts of the metalsmith with whom Stamno claimed he had struck his secret deal. I had no special reason to think that Stamno had been lying, but in view of our savant's disappearance it seemed as wise to check up; and for a whole week Peli drew a blank.

She slipped into my cabin on the evening of that day when I saw the balloon make its emergency descent. She was muffled up to the gills.

"Peli, you nitwit! Do you want the whole boat to see you sneaking round like that?"

A chuckle issued from the scarf as she unwound it. She was grinning mischievously. "Never fear: I just bundled up right outside the door. Figured a dramatic entry might be in order. Because . . . I found out!"

"You did?"

"Absolutely. Today I went over to Ferramy Ward. That's out towards the lake of filth. Town's expanding that way apace, Worm knows why, though I reckon some bright sparks must have found a way to use the liquid spoils. I spotted big barges with bucket chains tethered to buoys on the lake; not that I got right up to it, seeing as Ferramy Ward's already enough of a jungle of workshops and whatnots—"

"Yes, yes, but what *happened?*"

"Well, I used diligent guile. I didn't make myself conspicuous by asking leading questions. I found the fellow by a process of elimination. His name's Harrup, and his little factory was thumping away like a heart in love, stamping out this and that in hot metals, with balls of steam puffing out of the ventilators as if it was breathing. . . .

"Anyway, I made out I was from 'Barbra, taking passage home aboard this *Crackerjill* of ours. That's just in case Harrup turns up here for his slug of darkness and spots me on board and wonders. I pretended Stamno was acting as our agent—us being the 'Barbra mob—and how we were concerned in case he'd run off with our funds, seeing as we hadn't heard from him since. This was to winkle out whether Harrup has heard from him lately; and he hasn't. So anyhow, Harrup protested that he'd already consigned the new fount of type to 'Barbra a fortnight ago. This was a bit of an awkward moment, since it turns out that Stamno only paid Harrup half of the price in advance, and now Harrup wanted the rest—from *me.* But I said we'd only pay up when delivery was confirmed. Do you know how Stamno paid?"

"Cash?"

"No, diamonds. Lots of little sparklers from Tambimatu. Well, they don't really sparkle much, that sort, but it seems they've a use for them here on the tips of drills. So as diamonds go, they're poor specimens. But they aren't exactly cheap. Nor was the job."

"So it's all true. That's a relief. Now we just have to hope that Stamno got the copy off safely."

"He'd have been wise to walk to Gangee or Verrino first. The guild could have been searching all cargoes ex Pecawar."

"I'm sure he'd have thought of that. But listen, Peli: you say he paid in Tambimatu diamonds. How did he get them?"

"From the cult women? He said they batten on rich patrons."

"Yes, but wealth in 'Barbra means costly woods."

"He could hardly carry a couple of cords of rubyvein around with him."

"Hmm, and I doubt you need diamonds to drill holes in ivorybone. So why and whence the sparklers? *I* think there must be cultists, or at least Seekers for Truth, in Tambimatu too."

"That figures. I prised a name out of Harrup, without him suspecting as I didn't know it. It's the name of the woman he sent the fount to in 'Barbra. She's called Peera-pa."

"So?"

"So it's a Tambimatu name. When I was hunting round Tambimatu town for that bangle of mine—the coiled one, remember?—I noticed a name just like hers painted up over a lapidary's. Peera-sto; that was it. Odd name; stuck in me mind."

"It could equally be a 'Barbra name."

"So it could. But there's an obvious connexion. Funny things fester in deep-south jungles, Yaleen, and spread like sprintweed."

Just then we heard a cursory knock on the door, and before either of us could react Donnah strode in. She held a letter in her hand.

"For you, Yaleen. Compliments of the quaymistress. It's from your father. There's one for your mother too."

Ah, the post had caught up with us. Hitherto I'd had to rely on signals from Chanoose, attesting to Tam's well-being; whether true or false.

Donnah waited. So did I, till she went. Then I tore the letter open.

Dad confirmed that Tam was okay in body, and reasonably so in spirit too. He had declined Chanoose's fatuous offer to fix a wooden spatula on his stump, so that he could shape clay. One night Tam had wept in Dad's arms; though I wasn't ever to let Tam know that I knew this. The tears seemed to have flushed the poison from his soul. On the very next day he had gone to the dikes, with Dad accompanying him. As I read this letter I realized that Tam was fast becoming the son whom Dad had lost in Capsi. Together they brought back tubs of clay on a cart.

Tam, the one-handed potter, set to work again. However, he was no longer working with his kick-wheel. Instead—slowly and patiently, often cursing humorously—he was modelling porcelain *hands*. Hands reaching up. Hands holding fleuradieu blooms. Hitherto all of Tam's hands had proved to be abortions. Yet he insisted that he was going to craft the perfect porcelain hand, one which would blush like flesh and seem to come alive at night by lamplight.

Dad thought this was a healthy, creative response. I wasn't so sure, though I tried to believe it.

I mustn't have succeeded. That night I dreamed of the noon when Tam had arrived in Pecawar. In the dream I was waiting to meet him fresh off the *Merry Mandolin*. But when he strode down the gangplank towards me (minus any bags) the hand which he held out in greeting was a porcelain one, fused to his wrist of flesh and bone. The moment I clasped his hand, it cracked into a dozen pieces which fell tinkling to the flagstones of the quay.

We tarried four full weeks in Guineamoy. The reason was that in Guineamoy people seemed generally less eager to partake of the current and gain their ticket to the *Ka*-store than had been the case in Gangee or Gate of the South. A fair number did, to be sure. But the majority ignored us. And that would be their folly.

The Guineamoy quaymistress ascribed this reluctance to the prevailing ethic of practical utility, self-help, faith in tangible things. For instance, most metal equipment used on boats—such as anchors, rope-rings, winches, pumps—was manufactured in Guineamoy. Now in reality Guineamoy depended upon the river for its exports, but local wisdom held it that all river business hinged on Guineamoy skills. Thus men of Guineamoy weren't going to drink from the "oil-pipe" of the current (as some local wits described it) any more than they would consider lapping bilge water.

This worried the river guild, on account of all the skills which would be lost if most smiths had their minds fried; which is why we lingered till visitors fell off to a mere dribble. Then we cried quits.

We stopped over at Spanglestream a single week; likewise at the Bayou. In both places our reception was everything we'd hoped for.

So, not long after, we were tying up at the massive natural stone quays of Jangali.

Of our stay in Jangali, the outstanding feature which I must mention is the conduct of my mum; and of that acid old acquaintance whom hitherto I have called "Moustache"—but who naturally had a name of his own, to wit Petrovy.

The catalyst between Mum and Petrovy ("catalyst" being a term I had picked up in Guineamoy) was none other than dusky Lalo. You may recall Lalo—and her fiancé Kish—as the two who took passage home to Jangali aboard the *Spry Goose*, and who raised the alarm while I was rescuing the drugged Marcialla from her perch. Then a year later I had found myself pitying Kish because Lalo's mum was so thoroughly overbearing.

On our second morning in Jangali Lalo turned up in our reception marquee on the quayside. She was hanging on the arm of Moustache (whom I shall call Petrovy from now on), and at first I must admit I didn't recognize her, though I noticed Petrovy soon enough.

I was doing the honours, while Lana kept me supplied with constant refills of the current and Mum established some order among the throng of applicants.

A throng it was!—and Petrovy, with that young woman on his arm, didn't press forward right away but hung back for ages observing me. As the crowd thinned, Mum tried to usher them forward. Instead of heeding Mum's urgings, the young woman began chatting to her. Petrovy joined in, grumpily at first—so it looked to me—but soon with an increasing show of chivalry.

Now, that young woman was slim, wiry, taut and muscular. *I* would have expected Lalo to flesh out in the period which had elapsed since last I saw her. She'd become a mother. She had settled down, and under the aegis of a stoutly complacent parent who wished her to have at least three children in quick succession. I also recalled Lalo's crack about how the fungus drug didn't make sex any more thrilling. At the time she had spoken chirpily and innocently enough, but I remember suspecting a certain—shall we say?—undertone to her remark. If that note had become dominant, I shouldn't have been surprised if Lalo's initial interest in exciting Kish might not have gone to seed; along with the tone of her body.

Anyway, in the end Mum did bring Petrovy and the woman forward. Almost everyone else had gone by now, and no new arrivals were being admitted; it was almost lunchtime.

"I believe you know these two of old," said Mum. "I present Petrovy—and Lalo."

"Lalo!" I cried, connecting at last.

"Why yes." The lithe dusky woman executed a full turn—as if to show off a fine costume. Actually she was wearing a faded, stained scarlet blouse and baggy breeches tucked into fork-toed boots.

And then I made the full connexion and realized that she was indeed showing off her duds—her *work* clothes—as well as her new tougher leaner self inside them.

"You've become a junglejack! During the war, while the men were away—of course!"

"And after the war; and for a long while yet. I'm enjoying it. It's fun. I might possibly quit in ten years' time." She squeezed Petrovy's arm. He uttered a *hrumph.*

"We always did have a few women junglejacks," she added. "Now we have a lot more."

Hrumph again. Petrovy sounded resigned. "We lost a fair number of guildsmen in the fighting. Lalo here has become quite an organizer. She's on the Council. She's shot up to the top of the hoganny tree faster than a cowchuck ball."

"Amazing," I said. "And how about Kish?"

"Oh, he's happy enough looking after our kid." Kid, singular. Obviously the grandmotherly ambitions of Lalo's mum hadn't come to fruition quite so quickly. Even so, Kish seemed to be a loser either way—unless he truly didn't mind.

"Nothing wrong here," said Lalo, perhaps reading my look. "Me, I'm jungle born and bred. Be cruel to send Kish up a tree. Remember how we joshed him about it? Kish and I discussed this, of course."

No doubt they did. Presumably, though, Kish didn't need to feel jealous of Petrovy into the bargain. By hanging on the older junglejack's arm Lalo was mainly emphasizing a professional relationship—rubbing and squeezing it home, no less. Presumably.

Just then Petrovy did detach himself from Lalo, gently but firmly. Turning to Mum he said, with a bob of his head, "Madam, I should be delighted if you would accept my hospitality in town. Here in Jangali we have a fine local watering-hole, by name—"

"The Jingle-Jangle," Mum nodded. "I've read of it."

"May I assure you that it isn't too rowdy during the day?"

Mum's eyes gleamed; and in that gleam I saw that she was determined to recapitulate my own adventures. "I'd be delighted," she said.

"Perhaps Lalo and Yaleen would prefer to mull over old times," suggested Petrovy.

"Whilst *we* mull something else! Ah, but you don't mull junglejack. I'm mixing my drinks!"

Petrovy grinned. "Mustn't do that."

"Oh I can't stop," breezed Lalo, "much as I'd like to. I have trees to shin up this afternoon. And as to booze, a shot of the black current will suit me fine for now."

This was duly provided. Whereupon Lalo departed, giving me a cheery smile—followed in short order by Mum, who had taken

Lalo's place on Petrovy's arm. Which left me to wonder: *What is Petrovy up to?*

As soon as I got back on board I had an urgent word with Peli. "Peli dear, would you mind going to the Jingle-Jangle right away?"

"Just try to stop me!"

"Mum's gone off there with that 'jack I told you about: the one with the moustaches."

"The big-shot you hinted things to?"

"The same. His name's Petrovy. I want to know what his game is. Can you keep an eye on them both from a distance?"

"I'll wear my scarf. They won't spot me."

Peli didn't report back till nightfall, which was a good while after Mum herself had returned on board.

"Well?"

"That's exactly how they got on! Well indeed. Your mum and Petrovy spent two solid hours in the Jingle-Jangle. They didn't drink immoderately, but by the time they left they were into quite a tettytet. Oh they were brushing against each other every few minutes accidentally on purpose in the way of two people who have every intention of, well. . . ."

"I get the picture."

"So then Petrovy escorted your mum back to his own house. Leastways I'm assuming it was his, and not just borrowed for the occasion. To get there you head past the Jay-Jay Hall then turn right down Whittlers Alley, then—"

"I'm not planning a visit, Peli. What happened?"

"They stayed together around three hours. Then your mum left, on her own; and I hung around to see whether Petrovy would rush off anywhere. But he didn't; and that's why I'm back late. It wasn't the sort of place you could sneak up and peep into. It's the second storey up a jacktree, so I don't actually know what went on inside."

"But we assume they went to bed."

Peli scratched her head. "They must have done, I'd say. Your mum's hair was astray when she came out, and she had a certain look on her face. Cat and cream, cat and cream."

"You must have watched for ages."

"Oh, I've stood watch on a boat. It's no different on dry land, except you have to watch out for people spotting you. Bit tiresome, that's all."

"Hmm. I wonder how tired Mum's feeling?"

"She didn't look the least bit tired."

Next morning I arranged to have breakfast with Mum, just the two of us alone together.

"So what did you make of Petrovy?" I asked over a waffle. "He's a vigorous sparring partner. Er, in debate, I mean."

She looked me right in the eye. "Whereas your dad has always been so gentle, eh? That's what's nice about your father. But one man isn't all men, Yaleen. And of course I'm no-one's fool, either— so whenever my new friend ventured queries about a certain surprise which priestess Yaleen might have in store, I found more interesting business to occupy us. If he was keeping his ears open, I plugged them with my tongue. Figuratively, of course."

"Of course, Mum."

"Not that I have any inkling what this certain surprise might be! Nor how Petrovy has any inkling of it—though I must say he seemed sympathetic. To it; and to me. Thankfully, my inevitable reticence on this point," and here she chose her words very carefully, "did not put a strain on his courtesy. Had it done so, I should have felt rather disappointed in him. I might have suspected that he was paying court to the daughter through the mother. That would have been quite galling, don't you think?"

"I'm glad to hear you enjoyed yourself."

"Oh I did. I enjoyed being with him. Though since there was apparently a hidden motive, I think I shall not repeat the experience. That might prove boring."

Oh dear. Mum had had time to mull over the events of the previous afternoon and see those in a new light—one to which, despite her insistence, she had perhaps been blind at the time. And she blamed me. I had robbed her tryst with Petrovy of a certain precious spontaneity.

"Incidentally," she added, "I did notice your Peli lurking in the Jingle-Jangle. She isn't always enormously subtle."

Oh double dear. "Look on the bright side, Mum. If Petrovy *hadn't* wanted something—"

"Then he wouldn't have wanted me? Charming."

"No, what I mean is. . . ." I trailed off. I was only putting my foot further in my mouth.

Mum patted my hand. "Never mind, Yaleen. A mature woman can set aside a smidgeon of subterfuge, from the meat of the affair."

"Oh. Good."

"How fascinating if I knew what your little surprise might be! I imagine Peli knows."

"Uh," I grunted, and concentrated on waffle.

I related all this to Peli to caution her. Thus it was with great glee that she in turn related to me, two nights later, how Petrovy had just happened to bump into her in town that day, and how he had whisked her off to the Jingle-Jangle. Obviously Petrovy hadn't spotted Peli spying on his courtship of Mum.

"So I says to myself," said Peli, "if your mum can enjoy herself, why shouldn't *I*? Not that I'd ever dream of putting her nose out of joint by letting on! Anyhow, I did bear in mind that I wasn't supposed to know the way to that house of his. Wouldn't have done if I'd charged hot-foot ahead through every twist and turn, would it now?"

I giggled. Yet in fact—would you believe?—I was starting to experience a twinge of jealousy at these amusements in which I couldn't participate. Truth to tell, I was feeling a tad frustrated. Not that I could have imagined amusing myself with Petrovy, of all people! On the other hand, Peli with her bluff red face and her hair like a haystook, wasn't as, well, attractive as I'd once been. . . . (Unworthy thoughts! That's what a pang of jealousy does to people.)

"So when we got back to his house up the tree, we pleased ourselves; and I shan't go into that. But while I was feeling, um, relaxed he started hinting on about the little surprise. 'I don't want to tease you, Pet,' I said to him. He didn't seem to mind me calling him Pet. 'I'll tell you the truth,' said I. Seeing as your mum said he appeared to be sympathetic—"

"Hey, Mum might just have said that so that if Petrovy found out, he'd tell her; and she could tell Donnah!"

"Your mum said she wasn't going to see him again. But that's by the by. I'm no one's fool, either. What I told him was this: 'There's a surprise all right, Pet, but it'll have to stay hush for the moment. If the river guild hears about it . . . you follow?'

" '*I'm* not river guild,' says he.

" 'Ah, but you don't always know who you're talking to,' I said.

"He seemed a bit offended. 'Don't I just?'

" 'No,' I answered him. 'For instance you've been talking to Yaleen's mum—and *she* doesn't necessarily see eye to eye with

Yaleen.' That took the wind out of his sails, all right—as well as serving to caution him.

" 'You wily old fox,' he calls me. But I gave him a cuddle to make up. 'Foxes are legends,' I said, 'but there'll be real foxes somewhere else in the galaxy—and lots of other people, who are just as real as you and me. Be a shame to lose them all forever, now wouldn't it be? All those deaths would diminish us—and the river guild would be the one big fish forever after, monopolizing *Ka*-store and everything.'

" 'That's not on,' he says, 'not after all we've fought for. Though mind you, I do believe in the *Ka*-store.'

" 'But you don't want to pay *too* high a price for the privilege,' I put it bluntly.

"He frowns at me. 'Look, Peli, our different towns and guilds have always had a lot of independence. Happen we've had to rely on one particular guild to link us all up, but still the river guild couldn't rule us. That's what bothers us here in Jangali—aye, even while we're swilling back the black stuff for the sake of our souls, to keep us out of that Godmind's clutches after we're dead!' And he promises me that he'll hang on for our surprise. And he'll help if he humanly can—so long as it suits the junglejacks. 'Can't commit us, sight unseen!'

" 'Fair enough, Pet,' I told him. 'I'm sure you'll find it suits you. What's at stake is *big.*'

" 'And Yaleen isn't her own mistress?'

" 'No more than I'm yours,' said I.

" 'Oho,' says he, 'we'll see about that!'

"So we did."

All in all—a whiff of jealousy aside—I judged that Peli had done rather adroitly; and enjoyed herself into the bargain. Though Petrovy's comment didn't amount to an absolute promise, it was a whole lot better than a poke in the eye. The 'jacks had all flooded back to their patch of forest, but they were a proud mob. Once military—twice militant?

It was at Port Barbra that things really happened.

The Worm's priestess was highly popular in that town. Umpteen spectators turned out to see the *Crackerjill* tie up. Such was the throng that several women and girls got pushed into the water and almost came to grief squeezed between our boat and the jetty. They either swam clear or were fished out in time, unstung, and fortunately no men had ventured as close to the riverside as those who got a ducking.

As I've said before, Port Barbra is a tawdry, muddy slum of a place where the locals pay little heed to the graces of life such as clean streets or elegant housing. They wrap themselves up in hoods, scarves, veils, kerchiefs; as well as in their own inwardness.

On the afternoon of our arrival the people of 'Barbra were definitely more forthcoming. They didn't actually cheer, but they did croon and sigh as if their voices were a wind in a great chimney.

Another sort of crowd also greeted us: a host of tiny midges. We on board were soon muffled up like the folk on shore, and were practising talking with our lips shut and squinting through half-closed eyelids.

"The worst it's ever been!" Peli groused.

"Mmm," I agreed. "Glad I'm titchy now. Less of me to bother."

I observed that 'Barbrans didn't waste time and energy on slapping these pests or trying to waft them away from the areas of flesh left exposed. They just ignored this inconvenience—in the same style that they spurned the conveniences of life.

When the horde of welcomers at last dispersed, so too did the clouds of flies. Perhaps it was the people themselves who had attracted the pests, by congregating in such a mass. We weren't persecuted as badly again.

For me the next few days were busy, busy. A marquee had been erected near the quaymistress's shack—this was Port Barbra, remember, and the guild didn't wish to be ostentatiously at odds with local building codes. The entrance to the marquee was hung with curtains of muslin, to exclude unwelcome miniature visitors whom I, for one, had no wish to take to the *Ka*-store with us; should flies have *Ka*s and fall into the waiting jugs of current and be drunk, so that you had to share your afterlife with a zizzing midge. No, I'm joking. Fly-curtains were standard fittings on 'Barbra doors and windows to keep winged pests out of homes. This much comfort the locals allowed themselves, otherwise they would have gone mad; and such curtains increased their privacy. Alas, out of respect for a visiting priestess the local contractors rather outdid themselves on muslin drapes. As a result the tent grew stuffy and headachy. The year was dipping towards its finale by this time, thus the weather wasn't as hot as it might otherwise have been. Even so, we were deep in the tropics. I had to ask Lana to fan me with a huge leaf;

which must have made me look positively pampered to 'Barbra eyes. Or perhaps this enhanced my image as exotic emissary of the Worm?

Anyway, I was busy; and Peli was busy too. She visited the local newssheet printer and enquired about Peera-pa, saying that she had an important message to deliver. The printer-*cum*-editor fellow was reticent (weren't they all, hereabouts?), but he assured Peli that he would ask around.

Peli brought back with her a copy of his weekly product, *Barbra's Bugle.* For the most part the contents seemed to consist of aimless gossip—aimless, because most of the names were concealed by initials, though maybe everyone in Port Barbra knew who was referred to. Actual news from the rest of the river was condensed into short snippets, run together and crammed into a box. What a contrast with the sophisticated repartee and tidbits of wisdom to be found in the flourishing Ajelobo rags only forty leagues downstream! Nor was the printing any too choice.

"He ought to have called it *Barbra's Bungle,"* joked Peli.

The headline story, about my own impending arrival at such and such a time aboard the *Crackerjill,* struck me as distinctly odd. It read less like news than like editorial, practically instructing readers to present themselves for a dose of the current (if they hadn't already enrolled via the quaymistress). Half way through, the column turned into a downright homily upon the *Ka*-store, which was described as *"the place where time stops and the plant of life becomes the death-seed, with all contained within alive for ever and ever",* or some such.

According to Stamno the 'Barbra newssheet was under the wing of cult sympathizers. So maybe this *Bugle* was written partly in code? Maybe what I took for aimless gossip really consisted of secret messages and parables with quite other meanings, crystal clear to those who were in the know. Scanning the *Bugle* I began to get an even ickier feeling about Port Barbra than I'd had on previous visits; and about my book being printed here in the guise of a newssheet. The place was creepy. The lives of the locals were a strange charade.

Then two mornings later a little girl delivered a sealed envelope to Peli.

Inside was this message: *The one you are interested in will meet you and your little riversister outside the Bugle office when dusk is night. Both of you; but no one else.* The note was unsigned.

Peli got a chance to show me the note privately back on board just before lunch. It had been a hectic morning in the marquee and it looked like being an equally hectic afternoon. We might well have to extend our stay in Port Barbra from one to two weeks, thanks to popular demand; which was an improvement on extending our stay thanks to indifference, as at Guineamoy. Who would have thought so many people inhabited the environs—and were able to decode their local paper?

" 'Little riversister' has to mean you, Yaleen."

"No doubt."

"So whoever sent this knows that you and me are as thick as thieves."

"Right. So we're getting somewhere. How do I sneak ashore?"

"Eh? You can't possibly risk—"

"I can. I'm fed up with temples and tents and cabins and guards. Don't you worry about Donnah."

"It's you I'm worried about, you chit."

"Well, I'm *going.* The question is how. Could you carry me ashore wrapped in a rug?"

"Don't be daft. What would I be carting rugs ashore for? At dusk?"

"Okay, it'll be dusk. Still possible to see, but not too sharply. You disembark ordinarily, Peli. Pile some rubbish near the marquee—there's always plenty lying around there. Remember to take a bottle of oil with you. Soak the rubbish, stick a couple of tapers in and light 'em. Then you nip back along the quayside. Meanwhile I'll have crept along to the stern. *Whoosh* goes the bonfire. Immediate distraction! Guards and boatwomen rush to the bows. I'll jump. Just make sure you catch me."

Peli groaned, but didn't argue further.

Suddenly she grabbed hold of me, and with an almighty heave tossed me several spans in the air.

"Hey!"

And caught me.

"Checking your weight," she explained with a grin.

I suppose that also explained the groan. One of anticipation: weight-lifter style.

Dusk found me crouched behind a coil of rope astern, having second thoughts about this escapade. The drop from afterdeck rail to jetty looked a *long* way down.

But then flames flared beside the marquee. A voice cried, "Fire!"

Figures rushed towards the bows. And the figure of Peli loomed below. I scrambled. I threw myself.

"Oof." Peli staggered back with me clutched tight, but she didn't fall over. Still clutching me, she trotted off through shadows, only setting me down—crushed breathless—when we gained the wooden walkway of Treegold Mall (which might better have been named Muck Street). Gazing back, we saw flames writhing high.

"Some bonfire," I gasped.

"Um, maybe I piled stuff too close to the canvas. Good cover there, though."

"Looks like you've torched the whole tent."

The leaping flames soon died and the orange glow faded. Well, any idiot could quench a blaze with a whole river on tap. We went on our way through the darkling dirty thoroughfares.

The *Bugle* office on Bluecloud Boulevard was nothing grand. It was a low clapboard building with a few poky windows fronting the messy roadway. By the time we arrived there, stars were brightening in the gloom. I couldn't imagine that daylight would have improved the looks of the place, though Peli had described the office as running back a way, with good skylights.

I didn't get to enter. Waiting for us outside in deep shadow were two hooded and scarved shapes. One of them was burly, the other slight. The burly shape uncovered a lantern, producing a pool of light. The slight figure stepped forward.

"What was that fire?" The voice was hushed and soft, though far from diffident.

"Our little trick," I said, "to get away unnoticed. Are you Peera-pa?"

"Yes." Peera-pa gestured at her henchmate. "I believe you know my friend."

The big person threw back her hood and loosened her scarf. Chopped-off pigtails, framing a large girlish face . . . it was Credence. The same Credence who had been boatswain of the *Spry Goose!* Who had tried to steal samples of the black current for the cult women. Who had marooned Marcialla up a tree, drugged and in danger of her life. Credence who had deserted in Jangali, after I foiled her scheme.

None of which inspired much confidence, even granted that she'd been manipulated by the Worm.

"Hullo, little one," said Credence. "I forgive you, on account of all you have become."

"That's nice of you. Forgive me for what?"

"For ruining my life as a riverwoman."

"There might be two ways of looking at that! Marcialla's career wouldn't have been improved much by falling out of a tree and breaking her neck."

"Ah, that was unfortunate. If only she'd seen sense."

"Let's hope I don't have to be persuaded to see sense likewise."

Peli drew me aside. "Something wrong?" she murmured.

Peera-pa, used to conversing in murmurs, heard her clearly. "Nothing is wrong. Just old history. Yaleen is safe with us."

"She's safe with *me*, you mean," asserted Peli. Peera-pa's eyes looked amused.

I said to Credence, "I suppose you don't have as much trouble laying your hands on doses of black current these days?"

The former boatswain began wrapping up again. "Hmm, it isn't as easy as all that. The guild make people drink it on the spot. They register names." She didn't, mark you, say that it was impossible.

"Shall we go?" enquired Peera-pa.

"Go? Where? I thought we met here to discuss my book and Stamno's whereabouts."

"We know where he is, Yaleen. He's with friends in Gangee. Your manuscript is safely in our hands. It will be printed."

"Soon, I hope! You do realize that the Godmind is getting ready to zap everybody in the known universe?"

"For the sake of awful knowledge. Yes, so I understand. If that is what must be done to acquire such knowledge—"

"Then we're better off without it," Peli said bluntly.

"I was going to say that, in that case, we are a mere span—to the Godmind's league. But still!"

"Still what?" growled Peli.

Peera-pa's voice was silky. "Still, we have a priestess with us now. We can contact the black current directly. We can set foot upon the true path of time and being. In return, we shall publish a certain book right speedily."

"So that's the deal?" I said. "Stamno never mentioned any deal."

Beyond the yellow pool of Credence's lantern it was black by now. Only a few distant windows down Bluecloud Boulevard showed smudges of illumination, while the stars above twinkled to themselves alone. I felt disadvantaged.

Peera-pa spoke gently. "If anything effective can be done to save our cousins in the sky, you must know in your heart that the lever to achieve this cannot simply be some spontaneous outcry by your readers. Most people aren't interested in great truths."

"They've been interested enough so far," said Peli. "In their tens of thousands! That's what Yaleen's first book achieved."

"So her second book will have a similar effect? Pah! If you think that, you're a fool. People wish to save their *own* souls. Once that ambition is achieved, why strive further?"

"We've had some guarantees," Peli said. "Though I'm not naming names."

Peera-pa chuckled. "Political promises? Perhaps they'll be ful-filled—if it suits those involved. Really, what difference can that make? I'll speak more plainly. What possible difference—other than to salve your own conscience? Other than to exonerate Yaleen from any personal guilt in the cosmic massacre?"

Peli said, "I don't see how she's to blame. Any more than me!"

"Quite. But anyone is to blame for something awful if they know about it and don't exert themselves to the utmost to stop it. Or if they adopt the wrong strategy—a strategy which *appears* to be bold, but which is really a lesser strategy—likewise they are blamewor-thy. So let's consider strategies, greater and lesser. To defeat the Godmind means to lock it up everywhere, not just to check it on one piddling little planet. The only way to do that is to discover the key which the Godmind searches for; *before* the Godmind finds it. You must search for the key to the Real—the truth-key. That's why you really sought me out; or else if not, it ought to be. If Yaleen hadn't sought me out, we should have sought her out soon."

"You certainly fancy yourself!" said Peli. "What do you know about any of this, compared with her?"

"We know how to look for the key, and where." Peera-pa slid two fingers under her scarf and whistled into the night. Hand-lan-terns appeared ahead of us, and behind. Hooded shapes approached. Peli flinched, but since there were at least half a dozen newcomers she subsided.

"We shall go into the hinterland," Peera-pa told us. "We will go to our private place."

"What, by night?" I tried to keep a light tone to my voice. "Isn't that carrying discretion a bit far?"

"We know our way, Yaleen. And at our private place there's a person you should meet. As to carrying, why, Credence will carry you. You can sleep in her arms. She's tireless."

"What if I prefer being carried by Peli?" I said this, not so as to burden Peli, but simply to check that Peera-pa's plans included her.

Apparently they did. "Peli might stumble on a root. We don't want you hurt. Or tired out by a bumpy journey."

"I guess riding Credence is a change from her telling me to swab the decks. . . . Say, how long is this journey going to take?"

"We shall arrive by dawn."

"And get back when?" demanded Peli. "Donnah's guards are going to take this town apart."

"With teeth and claws. What a delightful notion. Alas, they won't learn much. That's why we need to go inland—and quickly. Your silly bonfire may already have alerted them. Come!"

"There doesn't seem a lot of choice," I said. There wasn't, either. And maybe, maybe, Peera-pa's plan was the right one.

Credence scooped me up in her arms. She arranged me so that my head rested on her shoulder.

At quite an early stage during our subsequent journey—down some winding track through pitch-dark forests—lulled by her surprisingly smooth motion, I nodded off.

What woke me hours later was the noise of Peli falling asleep. The ingredients were a thump, a crash, and loud confused moans.

A black army of tree-masts and a dark crowded canvas of foliage sailed overhead against a livid sky. Dawn was almost upon us. Where was I? What was going on? Moans were going on.

"Whazzit?" I groaned, blinking and stiff. "Peli!" I cried.

Black figures milled around the source of the noise—which became ripe, weary curses. A shape was hauled out of coaly shadows.

"S'nothing." Credence yawned in my face. "No crisis."

"Peli!"

The shape blundered in our direction, shaking off the arms which tried to guide it, or restrain it.

"Where are you, Yaleen? You cried—" Peli stopped short, just near me, and clutched at her nose. "Oof!" It was too dark to see if she was bleeding.

"I'm here, Peli. I'm okay. What happened?"

Peera-pa's voice: "She fell asleep on her feet, that's what."

Peli mumbled, "We must have tramped a hundred leagues this night."

"Hardly!"

"I was dreaming. Then: *wham."*

"She walked into a tree."

"I feel half-dead."

"That's a pessimist's view. Try to feel half-*alive,* instead. We'll arrive soon. Once we're there, we can all get some shut-eye."

As full dawn crept closer, progressively more light soaked down through the trees. In consequence the contrast between brightening sky overhead and the dark forest of our journey diminished. Soon the sky was no longer obvious. The visible canopy of foliage now hid it.

The track which we were following led through a medley of coarsewoods interspersed with occasional ashen groves of ivory-bone. The path hugged a meandering stream. In places where undergrowth was dense and scratchy, the path *was* the stream. We quit the guidance of this brook at a bend where a fallen jacktree sprawled rotting across the water.

Soon we came upon a huge boulder splotched with lichen. Behind, as if emerging from an invisible door in the rock, a pavement commenced: an actual pathway of flagstones. Our party fairly trotted along this pavement for a third of a league, winding between the trees. Then ahead the forest parted, opened up.

The pavement led into a long glade. Close at hand, a low stone bridge crossed the narrowest point of a marshy mere; above the sedges the air was fuzzy with gnats. Beyond stretched a great sward of voluptuous velvety moss, purple and violet as eggplant skin. That dark moss defied the light blue of the open sky above. It seemed to blot up the shafts of low sunshine lancing through the treetops—so that it still might have been night throughout the glade, except that you could see everything plain as day. Here was midnight magically made visible, as some nocturnal rodent might see it.

The sward rose up towards . . . a little palace! A palace which stood out against the moss like a precious Aladalia ornament upon a pad of velvet.

The palace had two storeys and looked to be octagonal. Hat-like, it wore a superimposed tile roof with eaves upswooping. Long leaden beaks jutted far out to spill rainwater clear of the curtain walls of gildenwood, polished and gleaming. Orange marble columns divided each wall from the next. Numerous tiny windows, set at random, were outlined by frames of bloodthread rubyvein. Each little window appeared to be of opaque wax-paper rather than glass.

What a splendid, enchanting, rich palace this was! That it should be found out here deep in the forests was an astonishment to me— though such an edifice, in tatty Port Barbra, might have been even more amazing.

"Our private place," said Peera-pa.

Credence set me down at last.

I was too stunned to comment. Peli likewise. Or maybe she was still stunned from her encounter with that tree.

The stone pavement cut through the moss to the palace, which it encircled. As we were drawing close, I found my voice.

"But *why?* Why such a building?"

"All the usual reasons," said Peera-pa. "Keeps the rain out. Wild-life too."

"No, but why so beautiful?"

"The path of truth is beautiful, Yaleen. If an answer isn't beautiful, how can it be right?"

"Oh. Is this the path of truth we're walking now?"

She chuckled. "Commencing in the midst of nowhere; yet arriving at a marvellous destination? Perhaps!" She tossed back her hood. She lowered her black gauze scarf. For the first time I could scrutinize her features.

She was at once old, and young. By which I mean that her face was the face of a young woman, yet at the same time it was wizened. Her hazel eyes were lively, youthful—yet webbed around with wrinkles. Her hair was part auburn, part ashen grey. Her teeth were white and untarnished; the mouth which held them was puckered.

Here was somebody who had over-used the fungus drug. Were her limbs lithe and smooth, I wondered, or shrivelled?

Obviously she read my thoughts. She smiled enigmatically. "It doesn't matter, this. You see, I have lived as long as anybody else has lived; namely, the whole of my life." She slid a door aside on runners and called, "We're here!"

The entry was hung about with muslin drapes, one behind another. A strong smell of herbs and spices drew my attention to little bags of popery dangling on strings; or is the word "peppery"? Peera-pa held the first veil aside. Peli and I slipped through the various layers—she sneezing thunderously mid-way.

Within, the lower floor of the palace seemed to be all one huge room; with eight, yes eight, sides to it. Various lacquered cabinets, red and black, hugged the walls. The floor mostly consisted of springy straw matting of the tight sort, pack-woven inside large cloth-edged frames which fitted neatly side by side. However, there were also several sunken pits containing piles of cushions, in all shades of red. In the pastel light diffusing through the paper windows, these pits looked like storm-tossed pools of blood. A broad brass stairway circled around upon itself, to gain the upper storey. Descending those stairs, carefully, came a bald fat man.

The man wasn't just fat. He was a pyramid of flesh. He wore a pink silk blouse of considerable volume, embroidered with flutterbyes, and matching trousers of even greater girth with a mauve sash tied around his equator. The blouse and trousers clung sweatily to breasts and paunch; though it was still early in the morning. When finally he achieved the floor, he waddled beaming towards us. His smile was a twisting mass of blubber.

"Peepy!" he panted.

"Papa," said Peera-pa affectionately.

"Uh?" said I. "Is this your dad?"

"No, Mardoluc is an honoured friend. And a wise one. That's why I call him Papa."

The man squinted at me from amidst pouches of fat.

"Blessings, Yaleen!" he wheezed. "I cannot easily kneel or bow. Blessings, none the less! Oh no I cannot easily bend myself to you. As soon fold a world in half." A snorting noise commenced deep within him. This increased in volume as it penetrated through the layers to the outside. He wobbled violently as if massaged by hidden hands. Tears squeezed from his eyes. I decided that he was laughing.

Presently the convulsion subsided. Clutching his belly with both hands—as if otherwise he might burst apart—the gross figure headed for the floor-pit closest by. He entered this like a boat launched down a slipway, displacing a wave; in this case, of cushions. Somehow he managed to rotate as he sank so that he came to rest upon his back, facing us.

He thumped cushions. "Bless us, that you're here! Yaleen: come and talk to Papa Mardoluc!"

At this point Peli yawned; none too quietly. That yawn gave Peera-pa her excuse.

"Sleepy time," she announced, "for all but those who have slept already." Linking with Peli, Peera-pa started to hustle her off in the direction of the stairway. Peli blundered along, confused. The rest of our troupe crowded in behind. So did I. Credence promptly picked me up and turned me around, while my legs were still busy walking. I felt like a wind-up toy automaton such as I'd seen kids playing with in Venezia. Pointing me back towards the pit, Credence gave me a push.

Unlike a toy, I turned again.

"No, no," said Credence. "You heard the lady. You've had your snooze. Stay and amuse Papa. Play with him. You might learn a few new tricks."

"Hey! I'm not some fat ogre's plaything!"

Looming over me, she smiled nastily. "He isn't going to *bother* you, dearie. What a grotesque notion. Whatever put such a fancy in your head?"

"You just did," I muttered. Her smile became a smirk. "Oh I get it!" I hissed. "You've nobly forgiven me for ruining your life—but you don't mind a spot of venom on the side."

"Dear me, and after I carried you all this way! I'm sure I don't know what you're on about, little priestess."

"Don't you just."

"Yaleen!" bleated recumbent Mardoluc.

"Is something amiss?" Peera-pa called from the stairway.

"No!" I bawled back. "Everything's lovely!" So as not to afford Credence further cause for petty satisfaction, I headed for the fat man's pit under my own sails.

"Amiss!" cried Mardoluc. "Amiss, is food. We'll need food, Peepy. Food for our guest, food for me. In proportion! The pot's on the hob upstairs." He licked blubbery lips and flexed podgy fingers: a display which I decided wasn't aimed at me personally. Even so, I perched on the edge of the pit well out of reach.

So he'd been cooking; hence the sweat. . . . As he wallowed expectantly, I found to my surprise that his gross conduct was actually whetting my appetite. There was a kind of, yes, blatant innocence about it, which I almost found endearing. Almost.

Cancel that "almost". Before long I found myself really regretting that I'd ever called him a fat ogre. (Put it down to nerves!) We got on like a house on fire.

The catalyst, the spark, was the meal.

Mardoluc wasn't any old cook. He was a master chef. What came down on trays to our pit was a dream: bowls of thick peppery bean and potato soup, vine leaves packed with minced lamb, broiled land-snails, sour curd with pollfish fritters (eccentric but yummy), sweetbread buns spread with lime jelly. Confronted with such foods one could only become the Complete Gourmand: both glutton and gourmet at once! Which Mardoluc certainly was, gluttony-wise; for this was just breakfast time. Yet he managed to combine the gutsiest exuberance with appreciative finesse in an infectiously persuasive blend.

He munched. He sucked his fingers. "You need to slacken up, Yaleen. Relax."

"Do I?" I nibbled and licked.

"Yes indeed. You're like a coiled spring. That's why you snap at people." He seized a soup bowl. "Glub-glub-glub-glub." He actually said this as he drank; I kid you not. "Slurp the stuff down, but savour it too."

"Likewise, gobble your famous fungus?" I'd been picking at my food on the lookout for any fungi, whether whole or minced. Which was simply a waste of time. As I recalled, the cultists were supposed to use the fungus in powder form. The meal could have been laced with it, and me none the wiser. Maybe the fungus possessed a distinctive tang. Never having tasted any, how should I know?

"There you go again!" He emptied a last dollop of soup down his throat, and then his tongue was out questing into the bowl, lapping up the smears. "That comes later, not now. So dig in; don't be shy. *That's* better!" He cheered me on as I began to do more justice to the stuffed vine leaves. He thrust a snail at me, expertly cracking the shell. "Try one of these!"

Eventually I had to cry quits. There are limits.

By the time that stage arrived I felt sleek and sensual; and I'd joined Mardoluc lolling amidst the cushions. (Somehow, he'd managed to avoid spilling anything.) He had awoken a buried fire in me which so far had only peeked out in the form of flashes of jealousy at Mum and Peli; and he'd done so without anything overtly erotic occurring. (Else, I'm sure I would have screamed the palace down.)

How can I put it? Touch had transmuted into taste; and now I wanted to taste more experiences, and wilder, but in some different mode than usual. I'm aware that frustrated people often console themselves with food, but that wasn't the case here. Mardoluc was flesh supreme. Flesh-plus. Consequently he was more than flesh. His presence made me bigger and fleshier. He freed the woman hidden in the child. He expanded me. This made me want to expand further still, into some new sphere.

"You are one fine cook," I said.

He looked comically pained. "Just *one?* Not two? Or three? Or a whole kitchen of cooks all rolled into one?" A tear rolled down his cheek (with difficulty).

"Sorry, chef!"

"Apology accepted! Ah me, but I'm still famished."

"You can't be serious."

"Oh I am. I'm starving. I have a hefty appetite for truth, too."

So saying, we got down to business.

Truth. The truth about Mardoluc was that he had inherited a modest family fortune when he was barely out of his teens. The money came, of course, from trade in precious woods. Mardoluc's parents had been married ten years, with still no sign of an heir, when at his mother's persuasions they finally consulted a wise woman of the hinterland. She solved the problem—of sterility or impotence—with a potion. After Mardoluc's birth, however, his mother's womb had sickened, so that the boy would remain their only offspring ever; no daughter would inherit. When Mardoluc was ten, his mum had died. Heart trouble killed his dad a decade later.

Mardoluc only discovered the secret history of his conception upon opening his dad's death-letter. Presumably his dad spilled the beans in the hope of filling his heir with a new sense of responsibility. For had not Mum and Dad risked their health and mutual happiness to bring their son into the world? Whether accurately or no, his dad traced the genesis of his own heart condition back to that trip up-country and to the wise woman's medicine; not to mention the sickness of the womb which made his wife ail. Mardoluc, by his teens, had become something of a sensualist and epicure—hardly the sort of young fellow to hand over to with a light heart, unless he was first thoroughly dunked in cold water.

Mardoluc read the death-letter differently. To him it was clear that the wise woman in question had been a cultist; and that his mum and dad had conceived him by rutting whilst drugged. This accounted for the sensuality of his nature; and now his sensuality was pointed in a certain direction, namely the hinterland. Hitherto his epicurism had been cramped by the general squalor of Port Barbra; which is why he had lavished so much energy upon superb cuisine. Mardoluc was a creature of good taste, but only one sort of good taste—of the food variety—seemed possible in 'Barbra itself. Now he decided to search out his real home and extend the realm of his pleasures.

Yet the concept of a "real home" begged a number of questions. Such questions as: "Could I ever build a real home for myself anywhere in this world?" He knew that he might have fulfilled himself better in Ajelobo or far Aladalia. To be sure of this he would have had to sail to Ajelobo or Aladalia as a lonely passenger, unable to sail back again if he discovered he had made the wrong choice.

Questions such as this: "My parents risked a lot to bring me into the world; okay, point taken. But where did they bring me *from?* What was I, before I was? Am I even the same person as I was yesterday?"

In Mardoluc's case good taste wasn't confined to the sensual domain but was a general cast of mind: composed of savour and discrimination. So whilst he fed his flesh excellently—increasing his already hefty anchor-hold on the world—he also asked himself some deep questions.

In the course of our tettytet he said, "How much do you remember of your own first origin, Yaleen?" And he answered himself, thus: "Why, nothing! At first your mind wasn't capable of knowing that it existed. It had to learn existence little by little. When it had learnt, and when you'd become a person with an identity, everything which went before became hidden in a timeless mist. You had congealed out of that mist, like a roux stiffening a milky sauce, but never at any single definable moment.

"Perhaps something akin happens throughout life. Identity isn't born of communion with the past. It's caused by *loss* of the past. Forgetfulness forges the person; not memory."

"Till we enter the *Ka*-store, Papa!" I'd taken to calling him that. "When we die, our whole life is ever-present to us."

"Ah yes. We're only fully present after we die. Not before. Do you know, I suspect that we might have been looking at existence the wrong way round? Could it be that our *Ka*s originate not at birth, but at death? Could it be that they give us our being in retrospect? Could it be that from out of the illuminated *Ka*-state after death we project a cone of awareness backwards through our whole lives like the beam of a lanthorn—a beam which fades out, the further that it pierces into the past? You have twisted back into the past, Yaleen. Thus it is written in *The Book of the Stars.* What say you?"

"Gosh, I dunno. So you've read Stamno's copy?"

"But of course. The copy's back in 'Barbra now." He waved a hand dismissively. "What say you?"

"One thing I do know: the *Ka*-store can't last forever. If our sun ever blazes up and burns the world, or if its fires die and our world freezes, I guess the Worm will die too. Where *Ka*s go to *afterwards*, seems a good question."

"Maybe they don't go, but come. If only we could solve this teaser! The moment flees; we cannot stop it—only slow it with a drug. You twisted back into the past, Yaleen. If only you could halt the flow of time—without having to die! We might learn what time is, and existence too. Then we could really fight the Godmind."

"So that's what you want from me. Do you know what the Worm wants, Papa? It wants me to contact worms on other worlds. It thinks I ought to jump out of a balloon and kill myself."

"A balloon? I don't follow."

"I should go up in a hot-air balloon and leap out of the sky. Splat. Then it can scoop me up and send me through *Ka*-space on my travels."

"My proposal seems rather less drastic, don't you think?"

"I wonder. I do wonder."

"Are you worrying that you might end up like Peepy, prematurely aged? Or like me, a monstrous mountain of lard, a tun of tummy? Oh I fully admit that this fullness of fat can't all come from eating!" He grinned. "How could mere eating have done this to me?"

"A complete mystery," I said.

"I'm thirty-two years old. Soon I'll have a heart attack, just like my own dear Papa. The circle of my existence will be complete. Pretty big circle, though, stretching all the way around me! Big enough, maybe, to bend time itself? If you could but show me how. . . . Time might stop and I might live forever inside a single moment. Ah dreams, ah just desserts, ah extraordinary dinners!" I couldn't tell how much was joke and how much in deadly earnest; but if plea this was, he didn't stoop to beg or wheedle.

"One use of the drug won't warp you," he promised.

Well, one use of it hadn't warped Marcialla; just screwed her up for a while.

"Maybe," I said, "you can't actually stop time entirely. If you get close to doing so, maybe time shifts you—to some other time?"

"Ah! Now, why's that?"

"Perhaps if time did stop completely, everything would have to stop existing?"

"We would only find non-existence: is that what you're saying?"

I shook my head. That didn't seem right. I'd spent time—no, not time exactly; I'd spent a period of "never-ever"—in the void. In the void there was nothing. But the void itself wasn't nothing. The void was bubbling and simmering with—

"Not non-existence," I said. "Pre-existence is what you'd find. The potential to exist."

As we talked, it became increasingly obvious to me that probably that very same day I was going to sample some fungus powder, no doubt in a black current cocktail. Papa Mardoluc had gained some curious insights by use of the drug; and the same drug had acted as a *catalyst* upon the Worm too. (New words: use 'em, or lose 'em!)

Later, half a dozen more women arrived accompanied by a couple of men. They bore baskets of provisions. Mardoluc explained how a thriving little farm had been set up nearby especially to supply the palace. This farm even had its own miniature river, according to him. A stream had been deepened, widened and diverted round in an ox-bow shape for part of its length. A bucket-chain, worked by a windmill, quickened the flow by transferring water from the tip of the downstream "horn" across to the upstream horn; hence the presence of pollfish on the breakfast menu.

Presently Mardoluc heaved his way upstairs to see to lunch. Since he declined my offer of culinary assistance, I was left to my own devices and I went outside on to the moss-sward so as to be alone of my own free choice rather than by default.

In full daylight the moss appeared darker than ever. The living velvet had become a black mirror, a lustrous hummocky expanse of polished jet. It reminded me of a certain lava-field near Firelight. Here, however, the surface might *look* as hard as could be—stiff, slippery—yet really it was soft and yielding. My eyes told me lies about it. Only touch told the truth. Earlier on I'd been leery of touch. Now I sank my fingers into springy vegetable flesh.

Flies seemed to shun the moss. Maybe they could smell something which I couldn't smell. More likely the darkness of the sward confused their simple senses. The sward confused me too, but I adored it.

No, that was *why* I liked it! It upset my balance—in a way which made me feel more agile within myself.

Meanwhile, what of the *Crackerjill?* My absence would be a certainty by now. Peli's, too. The possible consequences bothered me a bit. The river guild could hardly cut off one of my feet in reprisal, the way they had cut off Tam's hand. Even so, they might send Peli away from me as punishment. They might beach her in 'Barbra as tit for tat for her part in my misdemeanour. I would have ruined her life; and I could hardly see Peli becoming a bosom-buddy of Credence's.

While I was brooding about this, and trying to imagine agile solutions, sprightly outcomes, Peli herself emerged from the doorway. She looked more edgy than refreshed.

I scrambled up and was just starting to reassure her that we were in safe hands—when Peera-pa followed her through the veils, wrinkling her nose.

"You can relax," I was saying.

"Shut up, will you?" muttered Peli. "I just farted in there, that's what. I didn't think anyone would notice. But it smelt like a kitchen-full of fried poppadums."

"Oh dear."

"I was amazed."

"That's quite a nice smell, poppadums."

"Not when it comes out of someone's arse." Peli shifted away, stared at the sky, whistled innocently.

"Ahem," said Peera-pa.

"Oh hullo," said Peli. I giggled helplessly.

Peli made a bluff lunge at conversation. "Er, why does that fat fellow call you Peepy, then?" she asked.

Peera-pa pulled up her hood and half-veiled her face.

"Perhaps because I only peep at the Truth instead of peering steadily." She sounded hurt. "A glimpse is better than being blind!" Aye, and perhaps her name hinted how strangers *peeped* at Peera-pa's young-and-ancient face?

"Dum-di-dum-di-dum," hummed Peli.

A whole kitchen-full of big thin crinkly flour-biscuits, sweaty with boiling oil! *Papa*-dums! I sniggered and hastily slapped myself across the cheek.

"Sorry," I said.

"For what?" asked Peera-pa, staying veiled.

"Thought a fly bit me. Forget it, forget it. It's nothing."

Perhaps Peera-pa had come out with the intention of confiding in me, as Papa Mardoluc had done. (Unless she had simply popped out for some fresh air!) Alas, if so, Peli's fart and its aftermath had blown that tender chance away.

"Hmm," said Peera-pa. "We should have lunch now. Empty bellies, empty brains; empty bowels and gasbags!"

"I'm still stuffed tight from breakfast," I said. "Papa's such a *splendid* cook." Might honest flattery retrieve the situation?

"You'll be starving later on. It's better to fill up beforehand."

"Before I take the timestop drug?"

She nodded, as though this was taken for granted. Perhaps Papa had already tipped her the wink, that I would.

"Incidentally, Yaleen, I ought to advise you that some participants may be more interested in the erotic aspects."

"We're not prudish. Are we, Peli?"

"Dum-di-dum. Oh no."

"That's their chosen path. You two won't be involved." Peera-pa turned back to the doorway. Over her shoulder she added, "Peli can be, if she wishes. Assuming that she hasn't put everyone off." She disappeared through the veils.

"Oh sod," mourned Peli. *"How* can I go back inside?"

"Um, sweet as roses?"

"Sweet as what?"

"Roses. The Godmind's favourite flowers. Never exported to the colonies."

"Oh, those."

And so to lunch: of snakemeat in aspic, galantines, salads, quiches, stuffed bluepears. I don't know how Mardoluc managed, either in the preparation or in the consumption. Trays sat everywhere and people moved from one to another, continually changing places— except for Papa in his pit, to whom mighty tidbits were brought whenever anyone shifted. The meal was like a weird change-your-partners dance, or a kids' game of musical cushions. I didn't notice anyone conspicuously avoiding Peli; though with everyone, us included, bobbing up and sitting down elsewhere, you never knew where you were.

I did notice Credence staring fixedly at me, at one point, like a cat intent on a flutterbye. She hastily adopted a sweet smile. Peera-pa, unveiled once more, dipped into our orbit amiably enough then out again. I exchanged pleasantries with many of the cultists, and they with me. In the midst of all, conducting the food-dance, reposed Mardoluc.

Finally, Peera-pa clapped her hands. The trays were all whisked back upstairs—whither Peli and I and others all repaired briefly to visit the privies.

Once we had all reassembled in the big room, Peera-pa unlocked one of the lacquered cabinets. Within, were bottles of an oily yellow liquid with several fingers of sediment in the bottoms; numerous glasses; and a few phials full of darkness which I had no difficulty in identifying as the substance of the Worm.

Peera-pa unstoppered the phials, emptied these into one of the yellow bottles and shook vigorously so that sediment and oil and blackness were mixed into a turbid cocktail. She agitated a couple of other yellow bottles too, without adding anything.

"Today," she said to the assembly, "Papa and I will pierce the veil of fleeting phenomena in company with the priestess of the current, blessed be she. We three shall follow the black way. Monitors will be Credence and Zelya and Shooshi. Everyone else will follow the usual amber path."

"Excuse me, but what are these paths?" I asked.

Peera-pa indicated the different bottles.

"Oh. And what are monitors?"

"Monitors don't take any drug. They stay in ordinary time, to watch over you. When you speed up afterwards, they ensure that no harm comes."

"And they see to our nourishment!" Mardoluc had hauled himself out of his pit by now and joined the rest of us. "The drug takes about ten minutes to act," he told me. "The slowing effect can last for a good five hours, though it's strongest earlier on. Then the speed-up takes over—"

"And we gobble all the left-overs. I've seen the drug in action."

"Left-overs! Tut, you insult me. There's a whole new feast awaiting."

"Those who wish to take partners may now disrobe," announced Peera-pa.

Both men from the farm and four women undressed. They jogged up and down for a while, showing off.

Peera-pa distributed glasses of the amber liquid first of all; and Peli wound up with one in her hand.

"Wait a mo," she said. "Why shouldn't I be a monitor?"

Credence answered, "You've no experience. Drink up, now!"

"I ought to keep an eye on Yaleen."

"You'd find it very boring."

"What, me, as can keep watch for hours without fidgeting?"

A chuckle rumbled from deep within Mardoluc. "In that case you're an ideal subject for the drug." Other people were already downing their amber drinks.

Credence gave a negligent shrug. "It's up to you. We can hardly pour the stuff down your neck. But you might easily misinterpret what you see, seeing as you know fart all about it."

Peli flushed redder than usual.

"Which might make you interfere inappropriately," agreed Mardoluc. "You might do something we'd all regret."

"It's okay, Peli," I murmured. "Honest, Papa knows best."

"Fart all," repeated Credence. "Be a good big sister, hmm? Show an example."

"Damn it," swore Peli, and swallowed her drink.

Credence patted her on the arm. "Take my advice: pick a quiet spot, sit down and calm down. Here, I'll find you one—where you can watch the love-making, if you like. That's always nice to meditate on."

Indeed, those who had taken their clothes off were already occupying one of the pits and engaging in gentle preliminaries.

"It's all a question of timing," I heard Credence remark, as she drew Peli away.

Of the cultists who were still clad, one woman had lain supine on the matting. Another was kneeling. A third sat hunched over her knees. Several still stood, and looked like staying that way. It was then that I cottoned on to the reason why the numerous windows were tiny and opaque. This must be to stop participants from being blinded should the sun stare in their eyes while they were slowed, and no monitor happen to notice.

Peera-pa handed Papa and me our dark drinks. She raised her own.

"We three will hold hands. That way, I hope we may commune. It's quite possible in timestop. You being priestess makes this highly probable."

"Does it? I shan't have much of a view round Papa's belly."

"The view you seek is within," she said.

"Okay. Cheers." I drank. So did they. Shooshi relieved us of our glasses. Peera-pa, Papa and I linked hands.

The first thing I noticed about being drugged was that I'd been like this for an immensely long time. Yet the experience had only just begun; I was aware of that too. There was simply no borderline to mark the change. Once crossed—as soon as I realized the alteration —the borderline itself receded infinitely; vanished. The immediate past fled away. My memories were of a timelessness to come.

I knew now where Papa had got his idea about how we emerge as full persons from out of a fog which, thereafter, hides the nature of what we were *before-we-were.* My own sensations were similar. I had gained Time—some sort of absolute time—by losing touch with ordinary time. Here was the same kind of "never-ever" as I'd experienced in *Ka*-space during my crazy homeward flight from Earth.

Indeed, for a moment (but a moment of what magnitude?) *then* and *now* connected up seamlessly. Past event and present event were one. Whatever had occurred during ordinary time between whiles became an ox-bow lake of happenings—something pinched off from the stream of never-ever.

For a moment (but a moment of what order?) I thought I understood the means by which I had twisted back through time. I hadn't slid down a ladder of years, which everyone else must needs climb upward. I had simply floated from the outflow of the ox-bow of events, back into the inflow; for both lay side by side in the never-ever.

When that had happened, I'd been dead; detached from the world. Now, however, the world confronted me—in the shape of Mardoluc's belly mainly, but also including his podgy hand holding Peera-pa's (I could see that), a patch of golden wall, a distant wax-paper window outlined in bloodwood.

As I stared fixedly, belly and wall and window began to blank out.

After an immeasurable while, the world came back, glowing with the message of its existence!

I had *blinked;* that's what. I had blinked my eyes. The blink had lasted for dark ages.

It came to me now that the whole world was actually winking in and out of existence constantly; yet we never noticed, because of the pace of time. Yes, the world forever came and went, just as it had done in that eyeblink!

For an age the world glowed and vanished and glowed again. Why should it remain the same, each time it returned? Why should it not be different?

Presently the answer became clear: the world remained constant because it was only a shadow. It was the shadow of the void. The shadow of nothing is something. The shadow of blackness is light. The shadow of a *Ka* is a person. The shadow of Potential is objects, things, events.

You can't change shadows by grasping them. You have to grasp the original. But how can you grasp a void?

I'd gone back through time, but I hadn't changed anything. I'd been scared to try—in case I vanished. Everything had to happen exactly as before.

I was breathing ever so slowly, in and out. His hand and hers grasped mine. Increasingly I became aware of the pressure of palms and fingers. My nerves had taken so long to pass the message on that when it finally arrived, it wasn't a whisper but a shout. Hearing this message of touch coming in so slowly, my brain opened its ears wide to hear it. Was it thus with those lovers rubbing against each other in the pit? Every feathery touch became a huge caressing wave? And orgasm itself, a volcano?

Aha, little priestess! Ho there, Peepy, we've done it! This way. Over here! Join in, do!

Not only possible, I told you, but probable! Rejoice!

Whilst simultaneously. . . .

Yaleen!

Worm?

It's me, all right. But you're so quick.

Quick?

Compared with sluggish old me. You're time-slowed, aren't you? I've done that too. Part of me can match you for a while; the rest can catch up later. How's tricks? Given any more thought to my proposal?

About jumping out of a balloon?

Either that, or some other method. 'Tisn't as though you lack the knack of dying.

I wasn't planning on becoming an expert.

I'm one, and it hasn't done me any harm.

Come off it, Worm. You've never died.

Ah, but thousands have died into me. I know ten thousand deaths, and more. Things are getting critical, Yaleen. Your first incarnation has been dead about a year and a quarter. She'll be blowing up the Moon in a few more weeks.

Quite a few. Two score or so.

Time flies.

Not at the moment!

Why are you hanging back? What is it that scares you?

Being killed, old pal. Being tossed willy-nilly halfway to nowhere. You lost me last time, in case you've forgotten.

I have a stronger grasp now. I've analysed your last flight, in as much depth as I'm able, and I do believe I've figured out how to steer you to a worm-world.

Ho hum.

Worm of the River: is that you? This was Peera-pa, sounding somewhat awed.

Mardoluc was less abashed. *Excuse me: is this a private quarrel, or can anyone join in?*

We aren't quarrelling, said the Worm, *we're merely discussing tactics.*

Can you slow time at will? asked Peera-pa. *And can you dream the True which lies behind phenomena?*

Can you stop time completely? Mardoluc asked.

Me? Er . . . not quite yet. Look, folks, I really can't hang around much longer. I'm losing touch with myself. I'll see you all when you die. Bye!

Hang on! I cried. But the Worm departed, with what seemed to me like suspicious haste.

Mardoluc sighed. *Oh dear. So near, yet so far. Shall we show Yaleen the five rites of contemplation?*

Yes, that might bring a breakthrough.

What are those? I asked.

Techniques of ours, he said. *There's the rite of duration and the periodic rite. Then there's the ephemeral rite and the instantaneous rite and the synchronous rite, which is what the time-slowed lovers are busy at. . . .*

What kind of breakthrough?

Why, to being! exclaimed Peera-pa.

Oh, you mean to those shapes that cast the shadows?

You can actually see those? Peera-pa sounded a bit awed once again.

She already glimpsed them in Ka-space, Peepy. She says so in her book. Remember the riddle of the raven and the writing desk? Remember how she guessed that the void dreams the shape of our universe, unawares? She already knows more than the River-Worm knows. But she doesn't know what *she knows.*

I'll say I don't, I said.

That's because you haven't disciplined yourself, Yaleen. You've gobbled knowledge like a cat let loose on a finger-kissingly cooked bouillabaisse of butterfish. The cat doesn't know *the soup; it just feeds. In its haste, it doesn't really taste. Next moment it will catch and scrunch a fly.*

How do you know a cat doesn't appreciate good cooking? Maybe a crunchfly for afters tastes as good as a crouton? (I didn't really believe it!)

There you go, off at a tangent.

Huh. You mentioned cats. I was talking about shapes that cast shadows—which I happened to glimpse just a bit ago, before you two joined me!

Really? There's hope for you yet! Let's instruct you in the first rite, of duration.

Okay, if it'll pass the time.

No, you mustn't pass time. Time must pass you. Start by observing what you see. Next, try to observe what you can't *see. Look in the gaps! Catch the breath of Being on the hop, between in and out. Usually the world is breathed too fast for us to notice. . . .*

Immeasurable intervals passed by.

I didn't become too adept at this breath-of-Being business. Nor did my two instructors seem unduly adept; though I guess they had to be a long way ahead of anyone else I'd ever met. Maybe the Cognizers of Ambroz's world could have given Papa and Peepy a tip or two, but again maybe not.

Anyway, whilst I was busy observing and not-observing, something sinister started to happen. Credence loomed slowly into view, close by Papa. With what seemed immense patience she began prising Peepy's hand out of Papa's grasp—and suddenly I lost touch with the two of them!

At a snail's pace Credence slid her leg in front of Papa, as a pivot. Sluggishly she heaved.

I had all the time in the world to work out her intention. I even managed to loosen my own hand slightly from Peepy's. I even succeeded in shifting ever so slightly aside.

By now the something-sinister had become something very nasty indeed. How I tried to escape! And how useless it was to try!

Slowly Papa toppled. His bulk bore down on me, while Credence slid from sight. His huge belly began to push me over backwards. Slowly I fell—and the mountain of Mardoluc followed me down.

Oh yes, I had plenty of time to observe what was going on. And what was going on was a "tragic accident", during which poor little Yaleen would be crushed to death by the enormous chef who had alas lost his balance. Crushed, suffocated—one, or both.

Where the shit were Shooshi and Zelya?

Upstairs, no doubt! Sent up there on some pretext by Credence, who would now doubtless be up there too. She would distract and delay the two monitors—establishing her alibi in the process—then after a suitable interval she would pop back to the head of the stairs, spy the horrid mishap, and shriek.

Under normal conditions I don't suppose that Credence could possibly have thrown Mardoluc. He had to be time-slowed, unable to readjust his balance. So who would credit that she *had* thrown him? Not Papa or Peepy, I feared. Credence had stationed herself quite astutely before interfering.

I hit the matting, slowly-o. And he crushed down on me, oh so slowly-o.

Damn the Credence bitch!

No, wait. When Credence had acted treacherously before—that time when she suspended the drugged Marcialla high up a jungle-giant—it had really been the Worm who was responsible! My old pal had admitted as much. The Worm had played on Credence's dreams; had steered and manoeuvred her without her knowing it.

The Worm had just bragged that it *knew ten thousand deaths.* Ten thousand ways of dying. And it wanted me dead. In Credence's mind it could soon find anti-Yaleen grievances to bring to the boil. It had taken a quick look at the set-up here, and broken contact with indecent haste. . . .

Mardoluc's mass pressed down fiercely.

The mat beneath and the belly above soon lost any bounce or sponginess. They were twin slabs of granite, squashing together—with me sandwiched in the middle. I was buried alive, and a mountain was being piled on me pound by pound, tun by tun.

Oh yes, the Worm had manipulated Credence. I was sure of it. Credence was just a dupe. And Mardoluc? Oh he was the fall-guy, for sure.

The Worm might know ten thousand deaths, but I bet it never knew a death such as this one.

Being shot by Edrick had been quick. Shrivelling, freezing and bursting in the wreck of the rose garden on the Moon had taken a while longer; it hadn't been interminable. This was.

Now my ribs were giving way. Slowly. But slowly.

I was nailed to the bottom of a lake, with half a league of water overhead, trying to drag a bucket of air down from the sky for my lungs; in vain. I was impaled by slow rods of blazing pain. I was torn apart inside. I was squashed as flat as a fleuradieu under a pile of books. Ever so slowly.

How I begged to die. Permission denied. Denied. I could repeat it for a hundred pages. For this went on. And on. And on.

After the hundredth, or thousandth, stage of my death: that was when my mind snapped and I went mad.

Part Three

ALL THE TAPESTRIES OF TIME

*I*т's a weird old business, going mad. Going mad isn't something which just happens to you. It isn't like getting trapped in a thunderstorm, or catching a chill. It's something which you *help to happen*.

You know that you're beginning to go mad. So you experiment with the madness. You give it a nudge here and a shove there. That's because you have to escape. When you're trapped in a vice that's squeezing you intolerably, and when this just goes on and on; when you can't die, or even faint—madness is the only way out, make no mistake.

Your mind-paths start to go astray. They bend. They deform. So you help them bend more. Your mental links start to snap, to dangle down into depths where you can hide. You follow them down gladly.

Your self splits up. You become separate selves, part-selves. Nobody knows these new persons, thus nobody can capture them and hurt them; not easily! Not even *you* knew they were inside you. No more than you paid attention to the workings of your womb and spleen and heart.

Imagine a body splitting up into independent heart, and spleen, and womb. Imagine each organ going its own way, toddling off on tiny legs. Now the organs of your mind do likewise.

The funny thing is that each mind-organ on its own seems more complete—more fully furnished, competent, consistent—than *you* ever did before, with all your ragged edges and loose ends!

These mind-organs, these part-selves are as the different cabins in an enormous boat.

This is the biggest boat you have ever sailed in. It isn't a mere *boat.* It's a legendary galleon—and argosy, and more! A river is too small to float it. It needs a whole sea.

You've grown not lesser by splitting, but larger.

A few cabins are bare and austere; a single oil lamp lights those. But for the most part, oh the furnishings! The panels of gildenwood and rubyvein, the ivorybone shelving, the chairs of hoganny, the ebon scritoires inlaid with pearly shell, the voluptuous bedding, the handbasins of mottled marble, the silver sconces, the bluecrystal candeliers and chandelabra ablaze with candles which never burn low or drip wax . . . !

Most of all, the tapestries.

A tapestry adorns one wall of each cabin. Portholes are clamped tight, wearing thick brass lids; it is the tapestry which weaves the view instead.

So here's a view of dusty Pecawar when you were a little girl (before you became a little girl again). Here, of broad Aladalia when you dallied innocently with Tam. There, of the spinach purée jungles by Tambimatu. . . .

Of the storm-lashed Zattere in Venezia.

Of the star-dunes of the eastern desert when you were dead, a stowaway in Lalia's memories. . . .

Those cabins which are bare of luxury are set so deep beneath the waterline that if you did undog their brass port-covers the water outside would be as black and solid as a coal seam. Even though you don't go near the portholes you're aware of this.

Why should you go near them? Those shuttered portholes are your protection. As are the cabin doors, which all stay locked.

To move from one cabin to another you don't use doors and dart along corridors and up and down companion ways. Oh no.

Bend of hull, contour of deck and bulkhead, make the space of each cabin unique to itself. And each cabin is a separate person, a part of yourself. In order to reach another cabin you need only *fit yourself* to the right shape. That's the knack. You shift there immediately.

That's why the invading pirate enemy can't catch you. As soon as pain lays its hand on a doorknob you're off somewhere else.

But beware: if your madness isn't clever enough you might lose the knack. You might end up fastened away for your own safety in the most sunken cabin of all, so deep that no enemy could reach it by diving, so well concealed in the keel that your foe could spend the whole voyage forcing entry on the upper decks without ever scenting you. Your madness might swallow you—and then it might *swallow itself.*

So therefore: flow with the madness. Keep shifting. Dart from cabin to cabin, and from self to self.

Your madness is many things.

And you are many.

Where does this fine argosy sail to? Where's its destination? Why, anywhere in any tapestry! Your madness steers the vessel by shifting you from side to side like cargo.

In the eyes of the foe your galleon may seem like a bumboat or a wherry, something paltry. Your foe only glimpses a bit at a time. You alone know your vessel's true many-chambered immensity.

Shifting, shifting, you die. You can't avoid dying. And your galleon becomes a *ship of* Ka-*space. . . .*

Spinning-top in a blue void. Bodiless in empty sky-space. Nothing visible but azure light. . . .

Nothing at all?

Faintly you still sense cabins and tapestries.

Concentrate!

One tapestry takes on hue and texture. The rooftops of up-and-down Verrino. Plus river. Here's a tapestry such as poor dead Capsi might have woven high atop the Spire, had he crafted panoramas with needle and silk instead of pen and ink.

Sunshine shimmers on wet roofs; rain must have showered recently. Sunlight also sparkles on the river, showing how it flows. Clouds shadow-dapple the riverscape and shore. Their shadows slowly drift across the fabric like grey bruises.

An inky ribbon swims into sight from the south. It speeds along the midstream. Suddenly it ripples free of the river. Rising, it flaps bannerlike upward towards you.

The Worm's ugly head dwarfs buildings. Its body eclipses the whole river. But it doesn't dwarf you. Framed within the tapestry, the Worm is a huge *miniature.*

The head wavers. It quests about. You know you can't play hide-and-seek with the Worm the way you could to escape the torture-foe. But maybe you can fool it.

The Worm's head pops right out of the tapestry.

Gotcha! My, that was quick work, getting yourself killed so soon. Glad you saw sense. Well done, Yaleen.

Did you say quick? I was pressed to death for a year and a day!

Nonsense! You and I were chatting, oh, not an hour ago. So what happened?

You know very well.

Don't!

So take a look. Who's the master of ten thousand deaths? You are! Try another one on for size.

Um, I'm trying. . . . Can't quite seem to find. . . . Odd! Something's clouding it. In fact, you seem a bit odd yourself—as though you aren't all there.

(Do you hear a footfall in one of the dark corridors of your galleon?)

Damn it, Worm! Credence tripped Mardoluc. She threw the fat bugger. And he squashed me to death ever so slowly.

I'm really cut up to hear that.

Hypocrite, you arranged it! You used Credence the way you used her against Marcialla that other time. That's why you scrammed in such haste—to get busy burrowing in her brain, urging and prompting.

Gosh, Yaleen, but you're my friend.

So you'd do anything to ensure the pleasure of my company, including crushing me to death?

Gosh, I'm sorry. If only you'd taken my advice.

Hmph!

Please don't be bitter.

Bitter? Why should I be bitter? Off on my travels, aren't I? So let the shapes of power dance! Let's see how I'm going to find the worms of other worlds. Oh, do get on with it!

You're in such a rush, all of a sudden. Something's wrong.

(Hidden cabins, hidden tapestries, hidey holes, alternatives . . . and footsteps, creeping too close for comfort.)

Maybe that's because I'm the wrong shape. Such as: flat as a pancake? And who was whining about time, not so long ago? Just a few weeks left till the end of the world, nag, nag!

(The footsteps pause.) *That's possible, Yaleen.*

I'll say! The Godmind'll be mindburning everyone before you can sing out "Jawgee Pawgee made 'em cry". Oh, it'll clap the telescope of time to its eye. It'll spy out the key to existence in a trice. And zap you with it. So let's get busy, hey?

(Sound of footsteps retreating in panic.)

Very well. Pay attention. Last time, you followed the psylink back to Eeden and became a cherub. This time I'll give you an extra shove. What's more, I'll armour your Ka against being reborn. Assuming that I've got it right you'll swing around

Earth and fly off along another psylink. You'll follow a psylink that's ravelled or tainted to a world where there's a worm in residence. . . .

(Shapes of power begin feeding you your sailing orders, setting the canvas of your *Ka*-ship. The tapestry has vanished.)

. . . You won't be reborn. You'll simply share people's heads, the way you did with that heartwood porter and that eelwife.

How do you know about them?

I've been reading your record while we talked. Mind you, your record's strangely patchy. Can't figure out why. . . .

(Faint tread of an intruder once again?)

Don't bother! What happens then?

I'll be keeping a tighter rein on you. Once you've contacted another worm and wised it up to the situation I'll yank you straight back here—thus providing a direct link with my new ally—then I'll pump you outward again to hook another worm.

(The shapes of power continue priming you whether you pay attention or not.)

It'll just be two or three worlds—against hundreds!

What's up with you? One moment you're keen as mustard. The next, you're pussyfooting.

What's wrong is that I haven't any choice in the matter!

(And you need choice. Lots of choice. Many cabins, many tapestries, many alternatives! Last time when you were in *Ka*-space on your way back home you saw how choices could be made. How a raven could be a writing desk. Yet you chose to be a baby girl in Pecawar, marking time and repeating yourself. Ah, but *then* you weren't mad—and many!)

All in a good cause, Yaleen!

If you say so.

That's my girl!

(The shapes of power fade. . . .)

Hang on! What about afterwards? When the great victory is won; when I'm back here for good?

Afterwards, welcome to the Ka-store. Where you can relive any life you choose.

Relive—aye, and not change a single detail.

You'd rather be alive again? Hmm. Do you suppose your mother might be carrying Petrovy's child?

No thanks! I've no wish to be anyone's little baby again.

You are hard to please.

What about all the loose ends I've left behind? What about Tam, stranded in Pecawar? What about the loose end of his arm? What about you—stopped short at Aladalia? What about men never being able to sail again? What about—?

You can't be responsible for everything.

(Why not, if there are enough of you?)

That's Godmind megalomania, Yaleen. Are you sure you're quite in your right mind?

(Footfall on a companion way. . . .)

(Right mind, port mind; south mind, north mind. Aft mind, for'ard mind, 'tween-decks mind.)

I feel super. Never better. I'll settle for the Ka-*store. Let's get on with the job. Right!*

This time, no gentle pat on the back sends you zipping through Ka-space. You're picked up and hurled through the storm-front, through the blue void. Surely the Worm must have noticed that it was heaving not a cockle-shell but an argosy? No. The weight of a Ka stays the same: zero. Onward your Ka-ship sails, through a nothingness simmering with potential. . . .

If you were many, would you see better? That's what you wondered once before.

That's the Godmind's project: to set fire to minds on a hundred worlds, to make a many-fold Ka-lens—and in that moment to try to master time, and Being.

The void bubbles. The void breathes.

You once felt that you were on the brink of a transformation. Then the Worm yanked you home. You chickened out.

The void dreams the universe. But the void is unconscious. The universe has consciousness, but it can't control the breath of Being. A strong force, the inertia of normality, rules the universe. So the universe always chooses the same state as before. It sustains itself; limits itself.

In Ka-space, the weak force rules. The force of choice. Yet no one chooses.

It's said in old myths that wizards could change men into toads, stones into bread. Those wizards must have tapped the weak force. Never for long, always on a tiny scale—because they lived in a universe ruled by the strong force.

The universe is dreamed by the void. It is made out of . . . grains of choice. Grains of virtual existence.

(Yes, *now* you're beginning to see.)

These basic grains are . . . *electons.* They elect their state of being.

Now look closer. Electons are really tiny dots, consisting of a circle of Ka-space rolled up compactly. Forever they unroll back into the void. Forever other bits of void roll up to replace them exactly. Roll up, roll up! Thanks to the pressure of public opinion in the neighbourhood, the new electons choose to be just the same as the old ones.

All these electons roll-up compactly in the same direction. Thus time flows in one direction, in the universe. In *Ka*-space the electons aren't rolled up. So there in the never-ever all time is one, and timeless.

A mind, a *Ka*, must be a mesh of electons which are only partly rolled-up. Thus minds delve into time-past, into memory. Minds resist the flow of time.

That must be why old folk say that time speeds up as you grow older. The more you know and remember, the more your *Ka* resists. A fish washed along by a stream hardly seems—from the fish's point of view—to be moving at all. A fish swimming against the stream sees the water rush by on all sides. . . .

Each death, each disappearance into *Ka*-space, removes a fraction of resistance. The forces balance again quickly. New *Ka*s come into existence.

What sort of shock would the death of almost all the minds in the galaxy deal to reality?

Enough to cause a lurch, a melting, a possible re-ordering of things?

Enough to bring about mastery of time—and mastery of Being— locally, for a few crucial moments?

The Godmind must think so.

Meanwhile your ship of *Ka*-space sails the void.

Could it explore many routes at once? Routes which would be real for a while; and then, not real? Many routes—which would later collapse into the one-and-only?

En route from Earth's Moon, once upon a time, the void bubbled and almost trapped you. You leapt out of that trap, into Narya's new-born body. Now you can escape any trap by shifting cabins within your many-chambered *Ka*-ship.

Find the place where that happened before!

Though it isn't one place. It's everywhere, anywhere.

Summon up a tapestry! And shift!

Yaleen! (A distraught cry in the distance.)

You goofed, Worm!

Summon another! Shift again.

Cross leagues of river
By balloon
Beneath a Californian moon
In darkness
At the height of noon!

This waterworld of isles
And seas
Where Crackerjill
Flags down a breeze
And deserts into icecaps
freeze!

Worm-	*Papa's*	*Worm-*	*Cognizers*
Stranger	*Weight*	*Friend*	*Brood*
Tell of	*Will soon*	*To Ocean's*	*Where you*
Danger. . . .	*Abate.* . . .	*End.* . . .	*Intrude.* . . .

Suddenly you're in a body. As before it isn't yours to operate; you're only along for the ride . . .

. . . aboard a boat! Spray flies blindingly. Sails boom and clap. The deck pitches and rears. Through the yowling squall voices scream:

"Get to the lee of Rokka!"

"No, outrun! If them round north, them'll cut us!"

"Us could double."

"Into *this?* You're mad. Outrun, I say!"

The mainmast creaks and groans as it leans this way, that way. Halyards crackle like whips. Figures in leathern cloaks haul themselves along the handrails.

And you? You're hunched in a wooden cage. One of your ankles is shackled with rusty iron to a bar. You're barefoot. Your torn linen gown is sodden. The cage is roped to belaying cleats, yet it still lurches to and fro on the slippery planking.

More figures loom. "It's she as them want. Toss she overboard, cage an' all!"

"Naw. Them want we too."

"Them might drop sails, try an' pick she up."

"Cage 'ud break in that swell. Them never see."

"God's mind! Try it, man!"

"Naw. Soon be in clean water. Just think how wor vicars shall smile when us turn up with a blackmind infanta. En't been a good torment on Soltrey since last all-eclipse. Them shall forgive us wor fines, eh?"

Bloody damn. You've been dumped in deep dung. This must be the waterworld of islands, all right, where the Godmind's good folk struggle against an evil worm. And no doubt it was predictable that you'd end up sharing minds with someone belonging to worm territory. Did she *have* to be a prisoner, caged, in the teeth of a storm, bound for torment?

Probably. Probably that put the worm uppermost in her mind. Probably her mind was naked to terror and desperate hope.

You're watching through her eyes. You're hearing through her ears. At least you aren't feeling the sting of the spray or the soak of her clothes.

So if she *is* tossed overboard, you personally won't have to endure choking. Or if she's delivered into the hands of their "vicars" you yourself won't have to be cooked alive, or stretched, or whatever's planned. Presumably.

Why complain? Quite the home from home, all things considered! Here's a boat, right? (Though on what wild wide water, in what vile weather!) Here are more sodding swinish Sons, or the local equivalent.

Hey, *men* are sailing this vessel. Men.

Don't assume that everything's the same!

Make contact with your hostess. Find out what's what.

Hullo there.

Sweet Lordevil! Tis you! Save your servant! Oh Lordevil, you've come.

Sorry, but I'm not what's-his-name. My name's Yaleen. Is Lord of Evil what you call your worm?

Worm? What's this?

Is that what you call your sea-worm? Your black current?

Lordevil, don't mock when I need you so.

Hmm, this'll take a bit of explaining. I'm Yaleen, right? What's your name?

You know me, Lordevil!

I don't—honest. I'm just visiting. But I do have an urgent message for Lordevil, if Lordevil's who I think it is.

My black name's known only to you, Lordevil! Why do you not know it? Are you 'rasing me early, before the pains? Please call me by my black name.

Sorry, I don't know what a black name is. How about telling me your, um, white name?

Tisn't my blame they took me!

Of course not. They probably wanted lessons in elocution. Look, let's start again?

A wave breaks from starboard and sloshes right through the cage, battering it about. The ropes wrench but they hold.

Take me, Lordevil! Set me free! Or begging your pardon, it shall be too late. Turmoil's easing.

You could have fooled me.

No! Tisn't even tempest, this. Sky's breaking clear.

She could be right. There's a definite distinction between sea and sky ahead.

There's still the last wave, Lord! Tis skerry moil, this. There shall be the Mountain, yet.

If the storm's easing, your friends might catch us. They're chasing, right?

They shall quit at the edge of empty sea! You know that! And if they do overhaul before and these vicars' lice barter me, in their eyes mine's the blame; though it shan't cost my skin flayed cruel on Soltrey, only my having to be . . . but you know.

I keep telling you I don't.

You shall make me tell, still hoping for your help?

Yes, tell.

Why, I shall be anyone's bugger-butt, shan't I be?

Sounds disgusting. Say no more. Er, just how do you expect me to help? If I'm Lordevil, what form do I take on this planet?

You ask that? You can't be my Lord! You're personating!

I did just tell you my name's Yaleen, not Lordevil.

You're from the vicars' Godmind!

I'm bloody not. I'm from another planet. I'm waging war on the Godmind—and I want an alliance with your Lordevil!

Tis coming.

Lordevil's coming?

The Mountain comes!

As my hostess stares between the bars, the boat leans over and slides downhill into a sea-valley. A hill of water looms. Mountains on this world can't be enormous—not a patch on the Far Precipices —but the onrushing mass is still noteworthy.

" 'Ware! 'Ware tall water!"

Sailors in their leathern cloaks cling tight to any handyhold; but your hostess hurls herself wildly from side to side, adding impetus to the slitherings of the cage. The mighty wave heaves the boat up high, askew. The spray-whipped cage slews violently. Tethers wrench at wooden bars. One bar snaps jaggedly. Rope snakes away. Cage spins, ripping free of other tethers. It's loose! It skids down the slanting deck; crashes into a rail. More bars splinter. Rail lurches outward.

Already the deck is righting itself; the cage hasn't managed to fall overboard. Your hostess wrestles frantically. Your shackle is free! You claw and heave, careless of any hurt. You ram your body through broken bars.

" 'Ware, captive!"

"Stop she!"

As the boat swings back, the hull becomes a steep and soaking hillside. Boulders of water pile at the bottom, crashing and splitting. There's no waiting! You slide headfirst down the timbers into the avalanching sea.

And under, and away.

You're upside-down. Twisted about. Rocks of water crush and pummel. Spew you up, drag you down. If the whole boat rolled over on you, you'd hardly know the difference.

Now and then your head breaks surface. You grab air. Air and water are so much churned together that hard knobs of sea burn in your sinuses, lodge in your lungs like stones.

Amazingly a barrel bobs by. With hoops of rope attached. Your spray-blind eyes nearly miss it. Blink, blink to see! Your fingers catch hold. You clutch tight—and wretch liquid fire-stones from your chest and skull.

A rope drags across the clashing waves. A high hull grinds by, darkly. But from which boat does this life-rope hang? Is it from Bark's, or Soltrey's?

Abandon barrel. Catch rope. Hang on.

Papa's	"Hea-----ve-------ho!"
Weight	Slow voice, slurred and blurred.
Will soon	Gradually the crushing weight lessens.
Abate	Air can enter. Light, and life.
	The mountain rolls aside.

Revealing Shooshi! And—"Looks like we're in time!"—Zelya; hovering over you in the palace of the time rites. The mountain is, of course, Mardoluc.

You're sitting up, gasping, grabbing air. How can you manage to sit up, or grab anything? It's far too sudden. Credence is nowhere in sight. "Where is she? Where's Credence?" Shooshi and Zelya flutter hands in consternation. (". . . only *pretending* timestop?" "Impossible, Shoo-shoo!") Everyone else who was in a trance is still in a trance. Frozen lovers in the cushion pits, kneelers, hunchers. Peli down on her butt watching time-slowed ecstasy. Peera-pa just next to you, holding nobody's hands in hers. Not you: You're up. You're dancing with impatience. Shooshi and Zelya are gabbling and darting around.

"Stop it!" you shriek.

And still you speed up. Not just you—*everything else* as well! This isn't how it was when Marcialla speeded up. It's the whole world that's racing now. You can't follow what you're doing, you're doing things so fast. So who's doing them? You can't follow what the monitors are doing. You can't follow what they're saying, in their high-pitched squeaky voices. You can't follow what you're saying, yourself. So who's speaking?

Oh the wild onward rush of light and sound and action!

Weren't you supposed to be dead? Weren't you meant to be somewhere else? Wasn't there something about cabins in a ghostly galleon?

Ghostly is the world. Life is a fleeting wraith. Shadow and sun, places and people flicker wildly by. . . .

Worm-   It was the boat from your home
Stranger   isle of Bark which rescued you.
Tell of   That's weeks gone by, and now
Danger   you and your hostess know each
          other rather better. . . .

Her name is Infanta Farsi-podwy-fey, though you call her Pod for short. That's her "sunshine name", the name by which she's known to family and acquaintances. Actually the "farsi" and "fey" bits of her name are titles, descriptions. Pod sees fleeting glimpses of events happening far away on her waterworld; that's *farsi.* She has an instinct for when people are about to die; that's *fey.* The "infanta" part means that she's an unwed talent of Bark.

Pod also possesses a "black name". A person keeps their black name private, telling no one. The black name is a talent's powername: the name which summons their power. If a stranger learnt it he might gain power over her. Or so they fancy, on Bark! The black name comes to a talented person in their dreams; and those dreams are sent by the worm of their world to all talents who inhabit isles in the great "blackwaters" region—sent by Lordevil.

Some talents on Bark can envision far-scenes more vividly than Pod. Some can heal the sick, or sicken the healthy. Others can pick up lightweight objects with the force of their minds—or even project convincing illusions of simple objects such as chairs or vases. Pod's talents aren't outstanding; though at least she has them, which makes her an infanta.

Alas, the isle of Bark is right on the very periphery of Lordevil's influence. His ink stains the waters only thinly in this region. Five hundred sea-miles further west, in the heart of Lordevil's Dark, talents are much more powerful and dramatic. You find wizards and sorcerers.

It's true that such talents remain a minority of the total population throughout Lordevil's Dark. But where the seas are darkest—glossiest with Lordevil's presence—there's more power. A wizard who sails out from one of the central isles to somewhere like Bark loses some of his power; though he would still be a more potent wizard than any of the Barkish.

Obviously these talents are genetic—whatever Pod supposes about them being linked to eclipses of the various suns and moons. Just as obviously it was the urgent screaming need in her which drew you to share with her mind, rather than with some major sorceress of the inner Dark; with whom you might have been far better placed to contact Lordevil.

So here you are on Bark, instead. The isle is shaped like the skull of a hound: jaws agape, skerries for teeth, two freshwater lakes filling the eye sockets. Here you are in rocky Bark town, built on the steep brow frowning over the lake called Stare. (Of *stairs,* carved in rock, there are enough in this town to trump Verrino twice over in up-and-downness.)

More specifically, here you are ensconced in the Infantry of the Duenna; whence Pod slipped away, up and over the brow and down to the sea-shore on a mischievous cockle picnic—only to be waylaid and kidnapped by those uncouth pirates of Soltrey.

Luckily she jumped bravely overboard; so the Duenna frowns, but she hasn't decreed Pod's public humiliation. Whether Pod will now be traded westward, deeper into Lordevil's Dark, well-dowered by Barkish standards and in exchange for a dowerless maid of stronger talent who can breed Wizz-brats on Bark, remains a moot point.

(This whole business of trading maids is something to which *you* take considerable exception! Pod can't understand what you're rabbiting on about; so you've rather given up on the propaganda. As Pod sees it, how else could talent be improved out on the fringes? How else could powers best be stirred, so as to flow in a current, in and out?

(Why not trade stud-boys instead, say you!)

Here you are, looking from a stone casement down over roofs and stairs—and over Lake Stare—on a morn when Bigmoon is eclipsing Blindspot, sending temporary shadow across the town.

Blindspot is the sun which you don't even *glance* at if you value your eyesight. It's tiny and intensely bright—though its light isn't steady, more like a mirror flashing, flashing fast. There's also the giant sun Redfog, which is currently approaching hidden Blindspot; and elsewhere in the sky is the more sensible, yellow Homesun.

Moons also come in three sizes: Bigmoon, Midmoon and Baberock.

So Lordevil is spread throughout the blackwaters region, eh Pod? But he can clump together and rise up anywhere? In the sea off Bark, for instance?

He never has. That was desperate wishful thinking on my part—hoping he might somehow save me from the louts' ship. There isn't enough of him here at his edge.

Hmm. And Lordevil gathers in the Kas of the dead? So that they can relive their lives in the Lord for ever after?

Oh no. I hardly think so! When people of the dark waters die, Lordevil sucks back the powers he gave them—and he sends those powers forth to young new talents. Now do you understand?

Yes. Lordevil is kin to the black current of my own world. Obviously Lordevil stores Kas, the way those 'lectric batteries on Earth store power. He must have been dumped here once to soak up any native talent that emerged. Now he's gone his own way. He can make certain people in his domain powerful. And the goodfolk of the clean water hate him deadly. Does Lordevil understand what he is? Do you, Pod? Does anyone?

Some of the Wizzes of Omphalos may. I once farsaw a Wizz communing with Lordevil. It was just a glimpse, quick as a Blindspot flash.

You must get yourself traded to Omphalos!

I thought you were opposed to that sort of thing?

I am. But you must.

What, me? A half-baked farsi-fey from a jewel-less isle on the very verge?

"Look, they're coming," she says aloud.

Way below, four men who are wearing great white bone-combs in their oiled black hair are escorting a bald young woman, whose face is painted orange, up Plunge Stair. Those are the talent-traders from Tusk, a hundred sea-miles inward, accompanying their merchandise.

If only you could demonstrate a new talent, Pod!

I can't even show much farsi. As for fey, why fair enough if one of them's about to die! Which should make him very happy, I'm sure! The seer amongst them shall hear my Duenna's affidavit and shall peep me, and that shall be it. That's supposing I didn't throw all my chances away when those Vicars' lice took me.

Your Duenna said you were brave and adroit to get away into the waves.

Oh to save face she said it.
What if you could astonish the seer?
They should re-trade me further inward. Fat chance!
I'm with you, Pod. Maybe he could peep me.
You aren't talent, Yaleen. You're only a visitor squatting in me.
All the things I could tell you, to tell him!
So? He should have to peep them for himself.

(So . . . sew. *Sew* tapestries! You'd almost forgotten about those other cabins! Is it possible to show their tapestries?)

Listen, Pod: I'm many persons. Each of me weaves her own vision. I want you to try as hard as you can to farsee my other selves. Your talents spring from Ka-*space —that's the key to my other cabins.*

I don't understand.

Let the seer peep tapestries of other worlds. You'll be the farsi who sees furthest of all! Try it! Together we'll get to Omphalos.

A distant bell begins to dong, summoning Pod and other infantas to the deep-hewn rock-room called Cave of Scales, where fates are weighed and talents are traded.

The walls of the Cave of Scales are scalloped by the chisels of long-dead stonemasons. The main body of the rock-room is a dome. Four subsidiary cupolas sprawl like paws. Two rock-shafts are the eye sockets of the room. By now Bigmoon has shifted aside from Brightspot, and Redfog is starting to eclipse the white dazzle; the light admitted down those shafts grows golden, amber. You're inside the shell of some great armoured beast eaten hollow by ants; only its corset of scales remaining.

Beneath one of the cupolas is a stone block whereon stand weighing pans of copper—a more obvious kind of Scales. (As so often on Bark, there are two levels of meaning. One is insufficient.) Both pans are piled with Barkish treasure—since you could hardly fit a talented maid into either of those pans, and if you did, it would likely bankrupt Bark to balance her weight. A relatively humble dowry is on show, though displayed to best effect. There are well-sheened nacre shells, goblets of volcano-glass, jars of seacumber salve, a conch-trumpet with silver clasps.

Candidate infantas occupy benches beneath the second cupola. Under the third cupola, alone on a low stool, sits the young woman with shaved head and orange face. She looks disdainfully amused by her out-isle cousins. The fourth cupola shelters her escort of talent-traders. Centre stage—the dome itself—is occupied by the Duenna, her face and figure enveloped in black fish-net garb.

"Farsi-podwy-fey," creaks her voice. Now it's Pod's turn to show off her wares.

As Pod rises and advances, the seer from Tusk adopts a poised, intent stance.

Now, Pod!

Pod whispers her black name to herself in an undervoice which you cannot hear.

Shift! Shift cabins in your ship of *Ka*-space. Linger. And while you linger, a sister of yours shares Pod's mind.

Shift back.

Yes?

Oh yes.

Pod farsaw a tapestry of bile-green swamp and silt isles. A honeycombed cliff reared high. She hung frozen on a breeze: birdwoman. Suddenly the woven threads had writhed into reality. She plummeted, to snatch a swimming snake. . . . It was Marl's world.

Shift! Linger. Shift back.

This time Pod farsaw a world of yellow clay, flat as a platter. Several great globular vegetables, crowned with horny leaves, broke the monotony; also a pear-shaped plant, its midriff plated with stiff leaves. From the top of this pear rose a thin erect stalk like a root tapping the air. In the crown of the pear three hauntingly human eyes stared fixedly ahead. Energy crackled in a cloudless eggshell sky. Stabs of lightning slashed at one another. . . .

The seer, astonished, kneels before Pod.

With a lurch, the flickering lights and shadows slow abruptly. . . .

Oh wasn't Donnah furious when you and Peli got back aboard the *Crackerjill* after your truant trip to the temple! That's when she muttered darkly, "Just you wait, little priestess. Just you wait."

Wait for what?

Wait for weeks. Weeks while your priestess's progress took you onward to Tambimatu. Weeks more while *Crackerjill* sailed back north again.

On the return voyage *Crackerjill* only called in quickly at the towns en route: barely half a day in port to stock up on fresh fruit and veg, and no stopover whatever at Port Barbra. Presently you docked at smoky Guineamoy.

Fortunately it's wintertime, so you don't have to open the port for ventilation; the outside air is none too sweet. (To the people of Guineamoy, does the air of other towns smell wild and raw, uncivilized?) Through the glass port, in the grey sky over the town, you can watch a huge balloon blundering through its paces. . . .

You can. You.

This is the weirdest thing. Many weeks have flown by at utmost speed, far too fast for you to notice anything beyond the rushing and the flickering, the tick-tock rhythm of day and night. You can't say you've "lived" through those weeks. Yet now that time has suddenly resumed its normal pace, you can recall everything that happened in the interval, just as though you'd been a conscious part of everything that occurred.

You've been part of a living tapestry. One which alters and evolves. One which shows you what will happen if you start from such and such a point, and move in a certain direction. Why, after a while you must reach Guineamoy.

"Yal-eeeen!" Boots bash along the corridor. The cabin door wrenches open. Donnah bursts in.

"Why, you little—!" She's livid with anger. She brandishes papers, pages of newssheet.

"This is on sale all over town!" She thrusts what she's clutching under your nose.

It's *The Book of the Stars* by Yaleen of Pecawar, printed in neat columns on big smudgy sheets of newsprint. Of course. What else?

"Right here in Guineamoy, where we've had the most trouble persuading people to take their medicine!"

"Good. Maybe this'll do the job better."

"Will it really? Well I'll have you know that I've sent urgent signals north and south."

"What for?"

"To search all cargoes, dear girl! To intercept the rest of these."

Should you tell her the truth about the way your book has been published? Should you keep mum about it? Which?

The entire boat trembles. The cabin and Donnah are suddenly double before your eyes. Two Donnahs, two cabins occupy the same space, superimposed. In one of these cabins you tell Donnah. In the other you don't tell. Whole tableaus of ghost events weave forth from this moment, till whenever.

Donnah steps back and sneers. "That'll settle you, my child. Don't think we can't manage to contain this. Difficult, I admit! But possible. Possible indeed."

"You could have saved yourself the bother of signalling, Donnah."

"Oh really? This certainly wasn't on sale in Spanglestream a few days back. And we haven't received any signals from Gate of the South, have we? I presume it appealed to your sense of vanity to have this thing published just as you arrived in town."

"Wrong. It's on sale everywhere from Tambimatu to Umdala. Simultaneous release, today." (At least you hope so.) "It's a fate accomplished, Donnah, that's what it is. A fate accomplished. But don't *worry*. The book won't do any harm. Only good. If good can be done."

"I see." There's great restraint in her voice. But not in her hands. She hurls the sheets of the book at you; though since these are loose they simply unfurl and flutter variously to the floor. *"Yours,* I believe. May a drunken spider have misprinted everything."

You recover a sheet. "Looks okay to me."

"Oh, *by* the way." Donnah pauses at the door. "I believe the guild will now wish to shift the current further north—before anyone hatches fancy ideas of exporting your words to the Sons, for their salvation."

"But . . . but what about all that land that'll be left vacant over there? After the Sons get brainburnt? I thought your plan was. . . . I mean, if you completely block passage over the river. . . ."

"Look out that port. Balloons are coming along famously here. On a calm day it shouldn't take much power to push really big passenger balloons across the river, nice and high above the current. Balloons crammed with colonists, eh?"

"Oh."

"Ever had a hankering to sail the wild ocean, in a Worm's wide mouth?"

"I shan't do it."

"I wouldn't force you. That's the honest truth. You know how much it appalled me when your boyfriend Tam lost one of his hands. But I'm not in Pecawar, where Tam is. Where your dad is. Both of them within a stone's throw of Quaymistress Chanoose! Chanoose is a ruthless character; be warned."

"That's how things stand, is it?"

"I wouldn't say they stand this way; or that way. I'm simply speculating."

"That's a pretty poisonous speculation."

"Blame the Sons for poisoning us."

"It's foul! Don't ever bother washing, Donnah. You can't cleanse yourself. You smell—*inside.*"

"Ho, ho; now the little innocent speaks of cleanliness, after spreading that document across the land without permission."

"I only needed my *own* permission."

"Did you? Why, in that case maybe anything is permitted to anybody to achieve what they want. Sauce for the goose, Yaleen!"

"Um . . . how would I get back from the ocean?"

"Nothing simpler. The Worm gulps you down, and wriggles you back through its body—to some agreed pick-up point, hmm? Fate accomplished, Yaleen! Yours. Most likely."

Everything rushes into a blur.

It's been a good few bigmonths, many midmonths and lots of babemonths since you and Pod set out from Bark, escorted by those Turkish traders with the bone-combs in their hair. Everything has taken far too long.

At last you're on the isle of Omphalos. This island is a ring of hills lapped by the black sea. Set on the tips of the crags are the keeps of the Wizzes. In the broad bowl of valley within, are farms, forests, lakes of flying fowl—and a town called Tomf. The name Tomf sounds like the dull throb of a giant kettledrum. Imagine vellum stretched from crag to crag across the fertile cauldron of the valley. Consider the homes of the Wizzes as drum-screws. Sometimes the most powerful Wizzes play strange music upon Tomf from their heights.

How soon will Yaleen destroy the Godmind's rose garden on the Moon?

How soon will the Godmind decide that Project Mindburner might just as well commence?

Soon, perhaps.

"Infanta Farsi! Redfog eclipses Blindspot! Tis time to leave the inn!"

Check your orange-painted face one last time in the brass-framed mirror. Make haste. Unlatch the door. Your talent-trader, Seer Makko, awaits.

His hair is freshly oiled and his comb poised jauntily. He sketches a quick bow, casual, almost affectionate. This man of Tusk respects you, wonders at you. During the long voyage of many landfalls you have, what's more, become his friend.

His strongman, Innocence, lingers further along the buckled

wooden corridor; knife tucked in his belt, sack slung over his shoulder containing your portion of the treasure dowry of Bark. Pod, who farsees distant worlds, is her own treasure by now. She is a veritable Princess of Talents. So perhaps her dowry has come to seem excessive, albeit no jewels are included. Half a dozen gingerworms wrapped in a leaf might be more suitable. Yet since the traders set out with that sack, deliver it they must.

"We must hasten, 'Fanta!"

Along the corridor. Down squeaking stairs. Into the flaking whitewashed vestibule betwixt boozery and kitchen where Mistress Umdik presides—"Mild days, Mistress!" "Mild days, Sirs and 'Fanta!"—and out on to the cobbled thoroughfare.

Already, as Blindspot shines through the fringe of Redfog, the street of timbered houses is gilded. By the time you reach the marriage mart the daylight will be full orange. *No one gets hoodwinked when Blindspot hides;* so goes the saying. During Blindspot's eclipse a person can look everywhere, consider all aspects of a bargain. Indeed you could even glance directly at Blindspot, masked as it is by Redfog, transfiguring Redfog into a huge glowing fruit in the sky; though no one would dream of such rashness.

Up Stargazy Road you go. Across the Avenue of Heartchoke, and you're there.

The marriage mart itself is a white dome set on pillars in the midst of Omblik Square. Omblik Square is where the blackfish vendors usually sell the fruits of the sea, kept fresh in all manner of tanks: tanks made of glass, of stone, of caulked wood, of canvas. Today only the permanent tanks are present, some brimful, some empty; some pure, some rank. No vendors; not of fish, at least.

Soon you're moving amongst infantas of other isles accompanied by their traders. Some wear silken saris—of purple, pink and patchwork—far more elegant than Pod's kirtle, shirt and plaid. Nobles and humbles of Omphalos circulate and chatter and assess; any of whom is more richly robed than the most princely person on Bark. Already dowries are set out on tables; Innocence hastens to set out Pod's. Some dowries are splendid indeed; perhaps the infantas in question are poor in talent. Perhaps where these infantas come from such a heap of riches is considered a humble dowry fit for a powerful talent.

Redfog burns orange in the sky. The burly marriage mistress claps her hands; she wears a full black weed-veil set with sparklers, dropping down from the crown of her head to her toes.

"Because of extraordinary claims, I call first upon the Infanta Farsi-podwy, all the way from far Bark."

"Claims!" mutters Makko. "She insults you."

"She left out the last part of my title!"

"If the Infanta hides as huge a talent as we've heard," continues the veiled woman, "why does she not bless the outer isles with herself? So that we can balance and build our abilities throughout all of Lordevil's Dark?"

"I'm she," Pod calls out, "and I shall only wed a Wizz. None less. Together we shall speak to the stars. Tis why I'm here."

"Your traders have voiced it about that you shall only wed a Wizz —but has any Wizz heard this?"

"Yes indeed," calls a tall slim handsome fellow. A cloak, clasped at his throat with a golden buckle, swirls about him as he forges through the crowd. On his head he wears a slouch hat with tail feathers of fowls sticking out behind like the rudder on a windmill.

"You, sir?" The veiled woman's tone is hesitant, shy.

The tall man doffs his hat and bows. For a moment or two, while his hat is off, he flickers and is someone else: someone old and small and chubby with a mischievous smile. As soon as he resumes his hat, he appears as he was before.

"Ah!" Makko murmurs into Pod's ear, "It's a master of illusions! If he takes to you, he shall pay me well for my work."

The man's eyes bore into Pod's, piercing any illusions she herself may have.

Farsee, Pod! Farsee!

(Shift! Shift!)

Briefly puzzlement is writ on the master's face. Soon, fascination —and bewitchment.

With a jolt, the world slows. Other fiercer jolts continue. The Worm has left Umdala far behind; Umdala with its geometric rows of blockhouses, Umdala with its estuarine marshes. Onward, north-ward, the Worm courses, smashing through ever more swelling waves which are whipped by wind and ocean width and by the torque of the world, as the estuary widens out into the wild dire salty seas where no one ever dare sail.

Spray drenches you, girl, as you crouch in the Worm's maw, wretched, on the point of puking.

And you remember: how long it took you to arrive here. How long, since Guineamoy. How the tapestry has evolved meanwhile.

The waves jog other knowledge too: knowledge of a wild storm on a waterworld of islands many "months" ago.

Where does this knowledge come from?

Worm?

What?

I'm some place else, as well as here! I'm in many places! You tried to kill me in the time temple. No, that's wrong! You did kill me. What's happening now is what would have happened, if you hadn't killed me. It's what-was-possible. It's happening just as if it's real.

Oh what a potent potentiality this is! It could become real indeed. You're sure of it. But then, what price your other selves? Would they be lost? Would you be lost?

Are you feeling okay, Yaleen?

Of course I'm not! I feel like spewing my guts all over you.

Not much of a sailor, are we?

This isn't sailing. This is lunacy. How much further?

Just till I reach where I was formerly. Soon, soon.

The Worm's head rolls through a hill of water. Spray smashes into the open jaws.

Of a sudden, the onward motion ceases. The Worm lolls.

Have we arrived?

Yaleen! It's starting! Mindburner's starting! Oh the light, intolerable light! Oh the dying! The lens of Kas is forming. Oh the power—it's sweeping all the stars. I can't shelter, can't protect—!

Worm?

A scream in the mind.

Escape! Track back. Shift, shift!

Mount Mardoluc, in falling upon you, broke your leg. You stayed on at the temple, scoffing gourmet meals while your bone mended. Peli also stayed. Credence made her peace with you.

Then you stayed on some more, really getting yourself involved in the synchronous rite and the periodic rite. By the time *The Book of the Stars* was in print everywhere, you were too deep into the rites of Being to tear yourself away. Besides, the river guild would dearly have loved to lay their hands on you.

Some tens of weeks later, while you're en-tranced in the synchronous rite, Mindburner strikes. . . .

Shooshi and Zelya saved you from suffocation; and Credence fled. She jogged back to 'Barbra. To win her way into the favours of the river guild, she not only told where you were—she betrayed the whole scheme to distribute *The Book of the Stars* secretly everywhere from Tambimatu to Umdala.

A runner arrived with a warning, not far ahead of Donnah's guards. You fled the temple, with Peli and Peera-pa. Papa, of course, couldn't flee. By forest and jungle ways you fled, ending up at last with friends of the 'Barbra cultists in Ajelobo.

Donnah burnt down the glorious secret temple; so an Ajelobo newssheet reports. The story doesn't say whether Papa Mardoluc was inside at the time. . . .

You didn't open your big mouth to boast, aboard the *Crackerjill* docked at Guineamoy. You blamed Stamno the renegade for the publication. You blamed the river guild for bringing him to Pecawar to corrupt you. You were shocked. You bitterly regretted. Donnah believed you.

In the end Mindburner comes. When the Worm is quenched and wrenched through time and space, your shield is gone.

And the Godmind slays you impersonally. Not even in revenge for blighted roses. More like piranha-mice on the rampage, hungry for every last living morsel. . . .

You stand atop the Spire at Verrino, looking down upon town and river, remembering your first view of this vista.

Suddenly, there appears below you the bowl of a valley instead. Farms, forests, lakes of flying fowl, and a strange town (yet not so strange)—all enclosed by a great rim of crags.

One tiny fierce sun glares through a second foggy red sun, like a life-seed incandescent in the yolk of an egg. The seed is near the edge of the yolk. There's also a third sun, mellow yellow. A moon of bone shares the sky.

An inner light blinds the universe. A worm writhes and withers. Mindburner!

"And as my wedding gift to you, dear Podwy," the small chubby old man promises, "I shall weave the grandest of all illusions!"

You're on the topmost platform of Master Aldino's tower. Flagstones spiral outward from an open stairwell, each flag painted with a different faint and flaking but still potent symbol, work of the previous owner. The circuit wall is a shade too low for comfort. It's barely waist-high. Immediately below, there's turf. Then jagged crags drop away. On the north side of the tower these dive down to the black sea. Southward, they tumble into the valley. To east and west the chain of hills strides away. This keep is poised on the sharpest ridge of all, as if balanced on an axe blade.

A path winds steeply down the south face; none down the north face. Omphalos harbour lies far away, beyond the softer southern crags.

As hat, the tower wears a cone of wood on stilts. A system of gutters pipes rainwater down into tanks on the floor below. One of these tanks is heated—spasmodically, clouds permitting—by a mirror contraption jutting from the wall, which by means of clockwork follows the path of Homesun to concentrate its rays. Thus there is hot and cold running water in the living quarters, gravity-fed from overhead. This is only one of the ingenious comforts. As a home, the keep isn't to be sniffed at; though admittedly it's a strenuous climb down to the valley and back to fetch groceries. If the crags were a bit nearer vertical, a bucket on the end of a rope mightn't be a bad idea. Two other wives already reside in the keep, along with a number of servant lads—potential Wizzes. So there's company, besides Aldino's.

He gestures grandly across the valley, almost overbalancing. "This afternoon, yon vale of Omphalos shall wear any guise you choose. Um, within reason."

And tonight, in the bedchamber, shall he don his best illusory body in Pod's honour?

So long as old Aldy isn't too drunk to concentrate (said senior wife Lotja, teasing—or bitching).

"Choose, my dear! Choose one of those other worlds which you farsee! We shall let the good folk of Tomf wend their way for an hour or so bemused through alien thoroughfares. Um, I hope no other Big Wizz gets annoyed. Still, why should they? We're all friends, after a fashion. It's my third wedding day. Licence is allowed."

"Shall other Wizzes be coming as guests?"

"Perhaps some shall peep in, from far." Aldino's finger wavers about till he locates the fretted bump of another keep away to the east. "Perhaps Master Airshoe shall float over. Let's hope he doesn't bother. Has an eye for my Lotja, does Master Airshoe; and this evening I shall have my attention diverted, eh Podwy?"

Time to prompt Pod.

"Do tell me, Master, how do you manage to weave such wonderful illusions for all to see?"

"Um. Well, let me see. Waves of energy are forever rebounding off the world. Some of these waves—only a few, mark you, out of many—pass through the windows of your eyes. Right? So already you're gathering in just one aspect of a reflection. What's more, your eyes don't actually see. They simply gather the waves. When those waves wash against the back of the eye, echoes are made. And those echoes of an aspect of a reflection travel onward into your head."

He taps his balding pate. "In here your brain dreams up images which it believes to correspond to those echoes. By now you're at four removes from reality. Count them: image, echo, aspect, reflection. What I do is reverse this process. I imagine that I'm seeing something quite different, something I wish to see. I send out echoes of stronger, more potent aspects. Other folk in the neighbourhood reflect those echoes—and they dream that they see what I'm imagining."

With that mischievous grin of his, he adds, "Leastways, that's what I *feel* that I'm doing, my dearest. That's the way I have to feel to accomplish illusions. Yet mayhap I'm really doing something entirely different! Mayhap what I've described is only the emblem which I show to myself, wherewith to unlock my magic." He stabs a demonstrative finger at various symbols on the stone flags. "An emblem such as those ones; though my own emblem is inscribed inside my head, out of sight. Of course, while doing all this I need to bless the name of Lordevil who empowers me."

You confer with your hostess.

Pod says, "Master Aldino, I've decided which world I wish to see spread across this vale."

"Dino to you, dearest girl." He pats and tweaks Pod's shoulder, where some flesh is exposed. "Would you care to give me a teasing glimpse?"

Wedding hour. Homesun beams down. Blindspot burns through Redfog. Bigmoon is a faint white bone aloft.

Below in the living quarters a feast awaits: of spit-roast fowl, gingerworms baked in sweetcrust, pickled cumber, decapod claws, wrack cake, rasperry pud, ricewine.

Up atop the tower here, Lotja plays airs on her xithar whilst midwife Polloo chats to Master Airshoe who did indeed float over. He arrived on a fluffy little cloud of his own conjuring. When Airshoe walks on air, he prefers not to see too much empty space yawning beneath. He's a well-built fellow with a neatly jutting beard and a big tuberous nose. His lips are fat and juicy. Studiously ignoring Lotja for the nonce, he occupies himself with Polloo.

Plus several more guests; no doubt including some uninvited ones who aren't present in person, only in the mind's eye. However, the guest list shall shortly include every soul in Tomf, and in Omphalos valley too. Hand in hand with Pod, Aldino poses at the parapet. He looks outward. He breathes deeply. He looks inward.

Now, Pod! Farsee!

And shift!

Shift back.

Appears Verrino. . . .

You're high atop the Spire (of course). Below in the vale is Verrino town, just as it was before the Sons trashed the place. No ash heaps or rubble. No broken windows; no smashed terracotta urns.

You can see all these details clearly, for Verrino town is magnified, enlarged. Verrino fills up half of Omphalos valley—surely Aldino got things out of proportion! Verrino isn't superimposed on Tomf, one to one. Tomf is totally submerged by the visionary city. Maybe a single Verrino plaza or wine-arbour holds the real Tomf hidden within. Far from having to blunder through the alien alleys of another world, the good folk of Tomf can only stare amazed at this city of giants which has suddenly sprung up, swallowing and dwarfing their mini-ville.

Where are the giant inhabitants? No one is about in Verrino. It must be very early morning.

Beyond Verrino, bends the river.

Ah, now you understand the workings of this vision. The whole vista is as if seen through the eye of a fish. Consequently the heart of Verrino town is enlarged, and fills up the foreground. At the outskirts it bends away, shrinking fast. The river also bends away, curving beside increasingly distorted shores. The whole illusion seems wrapped around a globe of air, or a balloon, which nestles in Omphalos vale.

The vision is how you imagine one of those goose eggs which Dario's brother said he painted; if instead of men's nude bodies curving around the shell you had a whole town and river, with the vale as the eggcup.

It's a circle of *Ka*-space, wrapped compactly around itself—writ large. It's an electon, hugely magnified.

The electon encloses a whole town. It could easily enclose an entire world. It's only a conjured illusion. *Or is it?*

"Bravo!" applauds Master Airshoe. Lotja riffs her xithar, repeating the same phrase a dozen times over.

"Your wedding gift, my dear," puffs the proud conjuror.

"Oh Dino," breathes Pod, "for sure, you're the Wizz of Wizzes."

And of course this vision of Verrino—and of the river bending away in the background—comes complete with a worm, thin as a thread upon the shrunken water, yet blackly visible.

"One more boon, husband-to-be! You bring me this vision through your skill—but also through the power of Lordevil, isn't that so? Shall you summon Lordevil himself? Shall you make our black lord manifest in some guise or other? If only as a voice in our midst! Let Lordevil bless our union personally."

"Humph. Is that all? Perhaps you should also like Blindspot as a brooch?"

"Oh Dino, do you mean you can't contact Lordevil?"

"Course you can," chips in Master Airshoe. "Big Wizz like you."

"I shall tire myself. This is a conspiracy!"

"Nonsense, old friend. Shall I help? Shall we join forces? Do permit. Let this be my wedding gift to yourself and your beautiful bride."

"Ach, you already have your eyes on her too! One of my wives isn't sufficient to seduce!"

Verrino flickers and wavers; then holds firm again.

"No such thing, old friend! Curb your wild suspicions."

"Hrumph."

"If that's what you suspect, shouldn't you prefer me to exhaust some of my—ha, ha—over-abundant energy?"

"That," remarks Polloo, "might be a good idea." She eyes Lotja, who looks somewhat crestfallen and strums a discord.

"Oh very well. The two of us in concert. You take the lead, Airshoe. I shall sustain my vision. Though mayhap I should let it pop? Dear Podwy has already admired one marvel. Now she cries for stronger music and for madder wine."

"No, no!" protests Pod. "Sustain it. Please! It contains. . . ."

"Contains what?"

"It contains an alien Lordevil, in that river there."

"Does it indeed? Whatever makes you think so?"

"I, er. . . ."

"Tell me, wife-to-be!"

"I'm, er, I'm carrying a passenger within me."

"You're *pregnant?* Already? This wretched Airshoe only met you a moment ago!" Aldino's eyes widen. Again Verrino ripples. "Was it your escort? That grasping talent-trader whom I paid so handsomely? Did he enjoy you on shipboard?"

"No, no, Dino, you misunderstand. I'm an honest virgin. My passenger is in my mind, not in my womb. She's from that city there below."

I'm from Pecawar, Pod. But let's not split hairs.

"Podwy! Do you mean to tell me—*now,* five minutes into our nuptials—that you've been farseeing these alien worlds of yours not by virtue of your own talent, but courtesy of some infestatious visitor? One who might fly away again? Leaving you bereft of your farsi? Ach, I've been cheated!"

Pod is on the verge of weeping; you buoy her up. Pride flares; honour burns bright. "Master Aldino, *sir,* I am the Infanta *Farsipodwy-fey,* of Bark Isle! See within me what I am, and who is within me! See how great her mission is!"

"Farsi . . . courtesy of another! That's what I see. Oh what a blind old fool I've been. I'm gulled and flummoxed. What price your feyness? Is that a cheat too? Go on: fey something! I'll tell you what to fey. Fey yourself falling from these battlements, right soon!"

"That, I shan't permit," declares Airshoe. "I should hold her up."

Lotja sniggers. Other guests studiously scrutinize the sky.

"Podwy! You shall fey *Airshoe* colliding with cliffs—when my illusions warp his knowing where he is!" Oh, Aldino is working himself up into a right old petulant lather. Verrino looks sadly tatty and wispy.

"Fey! Fey away! I'll bet you can't fey the death of a fly."

Furious, Pod cries, "I shall fey in truth! I feel the talent rising. I shall fey your own fate, sir, contemptuous husband."

No, Pod. We're diving into deep manure. This is awful. I absolutely must contact Lordevil—while Verrino's still here, with my Worm. Cool it, will you?

However, Pod rises on tiptoe. "I fey—!"

She screams.

Horror twists her face.

"I fey death! Death everywhere! The death of everyone! All the vicars of whitewater and all their Godmind flock, across the world—

burnt up! Lordevil destroyed and changed a moment later! Every soul I've known on Bark. Everyone who's harboured in Lordevil's Dark. All the Wizzes and all the commons of Omphalos— brainburnt! And me, me too. A faggot to fuel a blaze."

She sinks down, devastated. "Oh I fey, I fey indeed. Never did I fey like this. I farsee-fey: death everywhere in all the stars. The finish of life. Lordevil's end. The stop of the whole world, and all worlds. All at once."

How soon, Pod? How soon?

"As soon as Blindspot leaves Redfog. When Blindspot burns bright, we burn!"

"What's this?" a shocked Aldino asks.

Beg him to raise Lordevil, Pod. Quickly, do it quickly.

"Dino—husband—if you don't summon Lordevil, we're doomed. Even if you do, we're doomed—since I fey it so. I'm so scared. But do it, do it!"

Already the orange hue is lessening. Day is whitening again.

"What do you make of this. Airshoe?"

"I think, old friend, mayhap we should err on the side of credulity."

"Believe her?"

"Exactly."

Hurry, hurry!

Aldino and Airshoe link hands. They begin to leap up and down, jumping as they do so from one flagstone emblem to the next, panting rapidly, deliberately.

Day whitens.

An inner light dawns, such as no other light that ever was. The light blazes up in Pod's mind. The whole universe burns with it. The light is a vortex of brilliance, tearing her loose from herself, sucking her up towards. . . .

. . . a pattern, a bright web which spans the shadows of the stars, the ghosts of all the worlds.

Recognize the pattern? How could you not? You've been well trained in the appreciation of it! It is a pattern of a hundred petals, unfolding across the galaxy, blooming fiercely. It is a cosmic rose. Each world is a petal. Each cell in each petal is a *Ka*. And all of those petals focus *Ka*-light through the heart of the rose.

Yaleen has blasted the garden in the Moon. The Godmind has struck out. This is Mindburner.

But you're *already* dead.

Cognizers
Brood
Where you
Intrude

The world's as flat as a pancake. Shabby yellow. Colour of clay. Sometimes energies discharge across the streaky sapphire sky. That's about it, by way of action. Otherwise night follows day follows night.

In fact it's hardly a world at all. It's just a flat surface, with length in one direction and breadth in the other. Life's hardly turbulent. Your hostess Hovarzu has stood in this same spot for the last five years. No doubt she could stand here for the next five.

Yet within her there is such richness and such depth. Abstract tapestries—models of the cosmos—beckon and glisten inside her. Many of these are strange and fanciful; others are rigorous and austere. It's these models that she strolls around in. She's good practice for if you ever break your back and have to spend the next ten years in bed.

Hovarzu used to be a friend of Ambroz, whom you met in Eeden. When he was alive they often talked by "radio". From her point of view he hasn't been dead and withered long at all. Ambroz was a disciple of old Harvaz the Cognizer; so too is plantlady Hovarzu. During your stay in her mind (which seems *interminable)* you've enriched her quite a lot. She has made new cosmic models and beamed these to other kindred cognoscenti amongst Cognizers.

Not all plant-people are Cognizers. Some make music in their minds. Some chant epic poems full of Earthmyth and anticipations of an afterlife when they will all stride freely forth, alien Aeneas and Achilles in the Champs Elysées. Others ponder the varieties of infinity from the aspect of beauty. They classify the orders of magnitude aesthetically: the infinitesimal, the purely infinite, the set of sets, the alephs and omegas, the satori series. Still other plant-people tell the beads of the genes.

Not all Cognizers concern themselves with the methods and motives of the Godmind. But Ambroz did; and so does Hovarzu. That's why you vectored in on her; on account of the echoes you both share. So she tells you.

Hovarzu doesn't find it a weird experience to host you. She's used to radio-voices in her brain; to whole tapestries of thought being transmitted into her from a distance.

Lodger-within, let us consider Kas!
Yes, let's.
And dimensions; and electons.

Right!

After all this time you have a pretty good idea what Hovarzu looks like to an outsider; though it wasn't too easy to find out.

True, she keeps her three eyes open during the day. But that isn't so that she can admire the view—or keep tabs on her personal appearance. Her eyes, in common with her leaf-plates, are designed to drink light and turn it into energy. (If they weren't so designed, maybe she would shut her eyes and never bother to open them again, given the monotonous poverty of the view. Might this be the real reason why her eyes sup light? To keep her at least somewhat connected with the world around?)

A few other huge native vegetables break the uniformity of the plain. Some look like leeks carved of wood. Others resemble artichoke heads. But no other plant-person is in sight. That's why it took a while to work out Hovarzu's own design—a topic of little interest to her.

She resembles a very tough pear. Below her waist she's skirted by leaf-plates which she can open and close. She's rooted by a trifork of toothed spade-roots, and a retractable tap-pipe runs down to the water table. (How you had to nag to garner this item!) It's upon those spades that she can waddle away, if she ever wishes to. A stalk rising from her head is her radio antenna. Her inner workings are a mystery.

So the universe is composed of electons, which are infinitesimal circles of Ka-space rolled up very compactly. That's so, Yaleen?

That's how it seemed.

And electons usually choose to be what they have always been. So reality recreates itself from moment to moment, from amidst a flux of options. This process is the breath of Being. But the world doesn't wink in and out of existence all together, on-off like a signal lamp. No! All of reality is forever winking in and out simultaneously. Thus reality sustains itself. There's always a familiar neighbourhood.

Makes sense!

Yet I believe that there are minor cycles within the breath of Being. By breathing in tune with these, the wizards of old Earth must have worked their temporary alterations of reality—if legend can be trusted. In addition there is also a Grand Rhythm, a Climacteric Rhythm—whereby large zones of reality eclipse in and out, restoring themselves exactly as before, unconsciously.

Could be. So where do Kas come into this?

Kas, Yaleen, must be dimension-fields of electons where the field itself is conscious. What happens, then, when true death arrives? Supposing that a Ka is not bound by a worm? Supposing that it is not drawn back into flesh by the Godmind?

This is the great mystery. Perhaps the Kas of all those who are truly dead diffuse into the infinitude of Ka-space—where each contributes one more iota of will and awareness. Then one day in the distant future Ka-space will become fully conscious. It will be able consciously to project forth the universe that it chooses; not just the universe which happens to exist already.

Unless the Godmind gets there first.

The Godmind is a creation. It is not the Creating. Nevertheless its schemes are clever. If it succeeds in marshalling this cosmic lens of electons, it may discover how to control reality; how to become the guiding overseer. It may achieve this feat long before Ka-space evolves the capacity on its own account—from out of the stored will and awareness of all the dead. Then the Godmind will be a God indeed. Perhaps only the God of a single galaxy out of many million; but a God, even so.

But it'll have killed off everyone. What's the point in ruling a graveyard?

It may gain the power to recreate people! To restore their Kas to the flesh! As well as the power to twist the black currents back through time as destroyers of potential rivals! Consider the proposed act of mass murder further, Yaleen. The transfer of so many dimension-fields will send a shock through Ka-space and through the universe which it projects. Locally, at least, in this galaxy of ours. The breath of Being will break rhythm. Minor cycles will culminate. A Grand Climacteric will quake forth. This will—

Hovarzu?

The dazzling inner light! The deadly radiance!

Shift out! Shift out!

When you all shift at once, you all collide.

You, overlooking Omphalos, belly-button of Lordevil's Dark.

You, planted on a plain that's flat as a platter.

You, who've probed the secrets of the heartwood porter.

You, on another worm-world: one of volcanoes, rivers of fire, pools of liquid tin.

You, you, and you.

You, probably at Verrino.

You, potentially aboard the Worm's gob out in the wild ocean.

You, possibly engaged in the synchronous rite during timestop in the palace of enchantment.

You, you.

Cabins tumble into one another. Tapestries interweave. You

U-nite!

I. . . .

I span the ghosts of stars. I grasp the rose. . . .

. . . as the souls of the colonies, and of Earth and Luna too, are all sucked into *Ka*-space, shaking the ever-never fabric of the void. . . .

. . . as the Godmind turns its lens of death upon Deeptime, upon distances so great that they aren't to be measured in millions of millions of leagues but only in aeons of aeons. . . .

. . . all at once.

Ineffably swift, the lightflood pulses. Oh let me timestop it. Let me catch it on the hop. Oh yes.

The heart and lungs of Being beat and bellow. Let me lay my finger on that heart, let me collapse those lungs then kiss life into them again. Yes, oh!

I am here, I am everywhere, I am never-ever. I am the raven and the writing desk. I am she who was born and born again. I am she who twisted time. The radiance shines through me. I've captured the rose dynamic. I am the lens; I am the rose.

The Grand Climacteric is here, my darlings. The college of electons is in session, all of one accord at once.

Down there in the worlds of death, reality crackles like ice. It melts, it flows. So many streams, so many branches! So infinite a pool of possibles. So many actuals, woven in my memories. Taught in timestop (thanks, Peepy!), taught in farsee (thanks, Pod!), taught in the mastery of illusions (thanks, Dino!), taught in the record of memory and in the shapes of power (thanks, Worm!), taught in the guile of shifting cabins (thanks, Credence!), taught in cognizing (thanks, Hovarzu!), taught many other precious things (thanks, whoever you are!); even so I cannot choose by thought and will. I can only let myself be chosen. I can only let my heartself, my wish-self, be the new pattern. Melting, flowing; and in the moment of *I am*, refreezing. . . .

. . . I am drawn down, descending with the rose.

Part Four

THE ROSE BALLOON

*B*LOOD streamed through the sky over Manhome South. Scarlet gore flowed above Brotherhood Donjon and Kirque and prayerhouse, where proclaimers would rant every Firstday.

Peli examined the sunset critically. The fussy second storey window, with its many tiny panes of thick glass, was wide open; this window at least had hinges!

"Must be a ton of dust up there," she said.

"Dust?" Yaleen looked up from her packing, which was almost done.

"Why, to make such sunsets as we've seen! It isn't at all cloudy. So the reason must be dust."

Yaleen joined her friend at the window. True enough, only the faintest muslin brushstrokes of cloud hung aloft. Yet most of the sky-dome was dyed garishly.

Peli waved a hand westward. "I'll warrant there's been a huge sandstorm in the desert. What price this madcap scheme of yours if the balloon runs into a sandstorm? That's if it ever gets off the ground!"

"Balloons generally get off the ground, Peli dear."

"Ah, but will the scheme? What will the river temple say? You need their blessing."

"Hmm," said Yaleen. "We'll see."

"So what *do* you do, supposing there's a sandstorm?"

"We'll be floating high, Peli. That's where the winds are that'll take us eastward."

"Eastward forever, never to return."

"You old doom-monger!" Yaleen ran a fingertip along the windowsill, held it up stained grey. "It's just ordinary dirt, not desert dust." By way of cleaning her finger she printed the tip on the cracked tawdry plaster of the wall.

"How I hate this dump," growled Peli. "Just look at that street down there. Hounds nuzzling turds—human, I'll be bound. And this is the posh part of town. Can't wait to get back to civilization!"

"Bit grimy in Guineamoy, too."

"That's for a reason—industry!—not from sheer sluttishness. At least in Guineamoy men never look daggers at a girl for going about her own business."

Yaleen chuckled. "Should we give the Sons a lesson in spit 'n' polish? Scrub the building from stem to stern? Spend all night at it, leaving it gleaming in the morn? You'll be a boatswain yet, Peli."

"Not likely. When a permanent mission gets here, *they* can set to with their scrubbing brushes." She still stared at the sky. "Superstitious dogs, these Sons! I wonder if they're taking all that blood up there as an omen? Started when we arrived here, fortnight ago; been the same ever since. Let's hope our team have been able to scare them with the slyblaze. Or the Sons might just think it's a sign to take knives to our throats on the way home."

"Hey, you're kidding."

"I dunno. We aren't in on the negotiations."

"Oh come on: Tamath and Marti have told us a fair bit."

"Yes, to wise us up to the local taboos. I do hope our bosses aren't contemplating *us* as future embassy cooks and bottlewashers."

"They'd better not be. I have my own plans."

"Of sailing upon a sandstorm; don't I know it. Let's hope the local shitheads see all that red stuff as the blood of birth." And Peli mimicked Tamath's stance and style. "The birth of a new and productive relationship between our two great riverbanks, blah blah. Rather than the blood of death. Been enough of that."

"Birthblood? Looks more like a massive haemorrhage to me."

"So it's a big birth. Of a new way of life: west and east seeing eye to eye, sort of. Them treating their women a bit more decent. Less of them imposing their riverphobia on the ladies. Their women might even take up boating."

"I don't believe," said Yaleen suddenly, "that these sunsets have anything to do with the desert. I think something else shook up all that dust." She shivered as she spoke. "I think it was the Pause, Peli."

Peli was silent for a while. Then she snorted.

"Of course, don't blame the desert for anything!"

"It was the Pause," Yaleen repeated.

"Just you shut up about that. There was no Pause, or whatever you call it. That's all in your imagination. I don't know what gives you such ideas."

"You felt it, too—when the whole world paused for a moment. Why not admit it?"

"Okay, maybe there was an earthquake. A little one."

"Was there? Everyone skipped a heartbeat, all at once? That wasn't any earthquake."

"Was. It stirred up stacks of dust out in the desert; because that's where it happened. What do you know about earthquakes? They don't happen once in a blue sun. Stands to reason, everyone's heart would skip a beat."

"The sun *is* blue, Peli."

"Clever you. You won't fluster me that way. 'Once in a blue sun' is just a word-fossil. Obviously we all once hailed from a world where the sun wasn't even a bit blue."

Yaleen inspected her fingerprint upon the wall. "Something else happened. I'm sure!"

"Didn't."

"Oh have it your own way. At least you'll agree we don't have to bother about sandstorms."

"We? Who's *we?*"

"Tam. Hasso. Me. Anyone else who's coming with us."

"Tam and Hasso, indeed! You'll have your work cut out."

"I can balance them. I can handle it."

"Now get this straight: *I'm* not coming along. Specially not to occupy Hasso while you're busy with Tam, and vice versa. That's why you really want me along, isn't it? Come on, confess."

"Oh, you."

"Hey, here come our diplomats." Peli hauled the window shut.

The sun had sunk by now. The blood was draining from the sky. From the Kirque a bell tolled lugubriously; and it occurred to Yaleen that during that strange moment a fortnight ago the whole world had seemed to ring like a bell. She fingered up more dust from the inside sill and placed the tip of her finger back upon the print on the plaster. When she took her hand away she could detect no smudging, no overlapping of the intricate whorls of skin-lines. She'd achieved a perfect fit. For some reason she found the lack of change in the print both gratifying and alarming.

"What are you playing at now?" said Peli. "They'll be famished and parched!"

As indeed they were. They, being senior Guildmistress Marti, her junior Tamath, Truthseeker Stamno, and Captain Martan of the 'jack army. The four 'jack soldiers who acted as escort and porters (and perhaps as a covert jungleguild caucus?) took themselves off to their own quarters.

In the dining room, Peli poured local mild ale for the diplomats while Yaleen unwrapped the buffet dinner of cold mutton and pickles.

"Do join us," invited Marti.

"Honoured, I'm sure," said Peli. "Thanks, 'Mistress." She poured ale for herself and Yaleen, but ignored plates; the two of them had eaten earlier.

"Though first, you might light something."

The dining room, with its stained saggy ceiling, its great creaky floorboards which old varnish and the dirt of years conspired to blacken, and its single window which didn't open, was growing gloomier by the moment. This was a lunky old house which the western Brotherhood had assigned to the mission from the recently victorious east; though at least it was close to the other governmental edifices, and spacious. Maybe for Manhome South it was the height of elegance. Peli hastened to flame an oil lamp.

"Reason why I asked you to stop," said Marti a while later, as she battled a slice of boiled sheep, "is that a couple of Sons are joining us after dinner. This pair'll be sent as ambassadors to us, so I want as many eyes as possible to look them over. They aren't true bigwigs yet, but they *were* close associates of a certain Doctor Edrick who died in the war. He was one of the biggest wigs of all."

"Do the most important Sons really wear wigs when they're in council?" asked Yaleen.

Marti smiled. "Of course. That's to hide the horns on their heads."

Peli cleared her throat circumspectly. "But 'Mistress, I thought the idea was for them to send women representatives? You know, to improve the status and dignity of women over here?"

Tamath laughed sourly. "Oh yes. We wanted their best women sent. There's a remarkable lack of candidates."

"Are the Sons putting obstacles in the way?"

"Not exactly, Peli," said Marti. "There just *aren't* any best women —as yet. I'm sure there will be, after a few years of witnessing our embassy at work in Manhome. Things will change. But not over-night! Meanwhile, these two particular Sons seem the best of a bad bunch. At least they're comparatively sympathetic. And they're bright; more flexible than the prime bigwigs. We need to know this pair, um, informally. Maybe get them drunk. That's why I asked you to stay, Peli."

"Oh thank you, 'Mistress. Glad to hear that this old tosspot has her uses."

Marti laughed. "Okay, unfortunately phrased!" Noticing Yaleen staring at her, she added, "Oh yes, and you too, Yaleen. You're only a *gairl,* as they say over here. But you've won your ticket. You risked death by stingers to save Marcialla from drowning, that time she fell from the main yard; didn't you? You're already a good boatwoman, if wayward and flighty. You're proof of our way of life. So if those two Sons have a few drinks with us, they'll see—"

"How can I hold my tipple?"

The guildmistress sighed. "I was going to say, that we can all relax on equal terms."

"Pardon me, 'Mistress," said the 'jack Captain, Martan. "I'm not planning to relax too much. I want to winkle out of these two fellows how they're set up regarding the fungus drug. We never got very satisfactory answers to that, did we?"

"While for my part," declared Stamno, that unprepossessing Truthseeker with the mincing turn of phrase, "I should dearly like to explore the possible relationship between *their* drug, which suppresses riverphobia—and *our* drug, which allows us to glimpse the ineffable. Thus, to pierce those veils of obfuscation with which the world, and the people in it, wrap themselves!"

Peli hoisted an eyebrow. "He's obfused me, all right," she murmured at Yaleen.

"You be a good Seeker and don't get too soaked," said Tamath. "See if you can detect when they're telling the truth."

"I should *never* contemplate blunting my faculties with excess alcohol!"

"Jolly party this'll be," remarked Peli to no one in particular.

"Oh I'll certainly make a show of drinking," Martan said. He turned to Stamno. "Tamath's just teasing you. Let's you and me try to find why they really ran out of their new drug, hmm?"

"And whether we can ever produce it for ourselves! And control the supply!" Yaleen exclaimed, though no one had asked her opinion.

Yaleen's intervention provoked a furious scowl from Tamath. Martan, on the other hand, looked thoughtful. Marti adopted an expression of nonchalant disinterest.

"Aha." Stamno's eyes crossed—this was one of his less endearing traits—as he focused upon the hidden truth of this moment. "Do I detect a naive young person happening to pierce one of those very veils to which I have just alluded? Let me see . . . We men, whether of west or of east, are all inhibited—are we not? The western Sons feel a huge instinctive revulsion against the river and its mighty flow. Whereas we in the east can sail the river once in our lives, and only once, to get wed. Now along comes a certain drug, discovered here in the west, whereby the western soldiery can overcome their inhibition temporarily—"

"We know all that." Tamath tried to shut him up.

"So they invade the east. Yet subsequently their supply of anti-inhibitor drug dries up. Consequently they can't reinforce—and we win the war. In so doing we capture a small remaining stock of the drug, courtesy of which I am here today together with my good colleague Captain Martan.

"How do our 'pothecaries fare in their analysis of this drug? Not well, I hear. And maybe it is all for the best that they fare poorly? Maybe success on their part would turn our society topsy-turvy! And maybe, too, control of the *source* of the drug—namely the fungus, supposing that it grows in our own jungles—will set the political pattern of the future.

"This pattern might be envisaged in one style by the river guild— but in quite another style by our other guilds! From the point of view of the river guild the ideal situation might well be a useful *trickle* of the drug, but not a flood. Is it then coincidence that our two impending guests—those whom the guild prefers as ambassadors— are also reputedly the original discoverers of the fungus drug?"

"Reef your sails!" snapped Tamath. "You're racing headlong into Precipices."

"Oh gosh," said Yaleen, dismayed at what her guileless contribution had provoked.

Stamno swung round. He trapped her in his cross-eyed stare. His eyes focused on a point just before his own nose, in such a way that his gaze seemed to divide, bend around, and drill a hole through the back of Yaleen's skull.

Stamno mightn't booze, but suddenly he was intoxicated—with himself. "I perceive a thin black barrier hundreds of leagues long running down the whole midstream of our river! This barrier is one which only *men* heed; and then, not with their eyes. It is inscribed only in the brain. For men to dare this barrier, is to risk madness, sickness, and death. Who inscribed it, but our distant ancestors? Those who were ancestors of our ancestors? Yet a drug erases its black ink for a while. What is written, can be unwritten. Then written again otherwise!"

"Control yourself!" Marti pitched her voice like a slap on the cheek. "Our guests will be here soon. You're babbling balderdash."

"Quite," said Martan. Martan was a practical man, to whom a tree was a tree. Far from stimulating his train of thought, Stamno's outburst had knocked it on the head. Repelled, he drew his chair noticeably away from the Truthseeker. Stamno refocused, and looked crestfallen.

A moment later the door-gong boomed.

The names of the two Sons were Jothan and Andri. Jothan was a red-head; Andri's hair was jet black. Both men wore beards which had recently seen scissor-work. Their drink was strong ale. Therefore jugs of this were poured, and replenished, and no one retired till nearly midnight.

Later, as Yaleen was about to bed down with a whirlpooling head, she recalled a sozzled Captain Martan blinking at her in a puzzled way at one stage, and muttering, "I shouldn't be here. Shouldn't at all. Dear me, what am I saying? I've no idea!" He covered his flagon with his palm. "Enough. Obviously I've had enough. Damn this ale. What *am* I doing here?"

'Mistress Marti patted his arm. "Whenever we're feeling confused, Captain, we should be guided by tradition."

"Exactly!" said he. "Exactly. But our guests are guided by their own traditions. That's the whole bother of it."

The Son called Andri grinned like a hound about to bite. "We're all of us guided by the words of life; that's a fact. What guides us is words a million million letters long, written in our flesh. *Our* words here in the west are spelt a bit different from yourn in the east. And our words say 'no' to the river, while our women's words say summat contrary. Your men's words say 'no—except once'; and your women's words say the same as our women's. Who's to say which spelling is the right 'un? Happen yourn's a prettier way to spell. Happen indeed." Andri regarded Yaleen across the table for rather too long a time, till with a creepy feeling Yaleen thought that the man fancied himself as owning her, using her for his amusement.

"You'll benefit by a spell in the east," she said to him. "Men know how to behave like human beings there."

"I never had no truck with incinerating women, let me tell you! And we've stopped that now. Part of our peace agreement, right? Now we'll receive fine wines and gems and oh, all sorts."

"The goods we'll trade aren't bribes to ensure good conduct, sir!" said Marti.

"Didn't say as they was. Though happen we'll pay for 'em sometimes in conduct rather than coin." Dismissing Marti from his attention, Andri returned his gaze to Yaleen.

Marti would not be so easily dismissed. "Plus a decent road to the riverside, sir, built by you. And a proper quayside there, with your women in charge of it."

"Yes, yes." Andri continued his scrutiny of Yaleen. "Have you thought," he said to her, "you so slim and fresh, with the nutbrown hair and that beautyspot on your neck all unveiled!—have you thought that mayhap the agency as wrote those words in our flesh intended all of us to act humanely, by *limiting* what us men can do? 'Cause we're descended from beasts with a taste for territory and flesh, and a yearning to shove our squirter into any woman as looks good; and when our dander rises we snarl and hack and rampage.

"Only, that agency limited us wrong—by making us men madly fear big stretches of water. We said a flat no to the river—and to our women, too, who like the waves. We didn't let women take the lead, as you did. We specialized ourselves, like piranha-mice as can only ravage whatever's in their way; then fall asleep oblivious. Truesoil, I'm saying now, sweet maid." He leered.

Eat dirt, thought Yaleen. But she buttoned her lip.

"In my opinion," said Marti, "our origins must needs remain a mystery—at least till such time in the far future when perhaps we can sail the sky, and find out. Right now, the shape of that future's up to us. We shall change what was written in the past. Bit by bit."

"Change what was written!" echoed Martan drunkenly. He hadn't done too well at only making a show of drinking.

Andri gazed at Marti. "Happen a person *can* wash out the dye he's first dipped in. Or leastways change the hue. Happen I need one of your fine gentle ladies to rub myself up against, to teach me graces? Get to know her really well." He took a swig of ale then tilted his flagon in Yaleen's direction. "As a human being."

Yaleen decided it was high time to knock her own ale-pot over. Or maybe the pot knocked itself over; she wasn't sure.

"Oops!"

Yaleen dreamt a peculiar dream. For as long as the dream endured—and who can say how long that is?—she was convinced that she was wide awake; until some backyard cockerel crowed, and the dream fled from her awareness. . . .

She was standing in the Kirque of Manhome South, a building she had never been inside. Even so, she knew that it was the Kirque.

The interior was blue and cavernous. Ribbed and buttressed walls curved upward to a vaulted roof. The floor was of bumpy turquoise cobbles, which felt strangely soft underfoot. Mauve-fronded ferns sprayed out from terracotta pots; the air smelled of dead fish.

In the midst of the Kirque stood a hillock of white marble, with steps mounting one side. Chiselled into the front of the hillock was a word, *Ka-theodral,* which meant nothing to her. From the apex rose a tall marble reading-stand carved in the shape of a flutterbye. The open wings held a heavy volume.

A man popped up behind the reading-stand. He was nude and totally bald of any hair. His whole body was as blanched and soft and sickly-looking as a war casualty's whose bandages have just been taken off. His flesh was poached egg-white. He looked like a giant jungle-grub. Yet from the man's cross-eyed expression Yaleen knew that he must be Truthseeker Stamno.

Gripping the open book, Stamno proclaimed at her:

"What you write, so let it be! But do you remember when the void bubbled up about you in the never-ever? You might have dived into a private time and place. Into a personal universe! Thus everything happening to you thereafter—"

"Voids?" cried Yaleen. "Bubbles? What are you talking about?"

"I don't say that you *did* do so. I only say that you may have done. Alternatively, when you died into the *Ka*-store—"

"The what?"

"—of the Worm—"

"*Who?*"

"—when you died with your mind split in madness, then also you might have woven a world-for-one. Or on the other hand the Worm might have woven it for you."

"I don't understand a word of this! Shut up!"

"Then again, maybe we should consider the effects of the time-stop drug? Unusual effects, in your case. Exceptional effects. While time halted, during the Pause a whole skein of private events might unwind."

"Pause? What do you know about the Pause?"

"I don't say that such suppositions are true. Merely, that they might be true."

"Who are you?"

The grub-man gurgled out a laugh. "Who am I, indeed? A Seeker of Truth? A ghost of a Worm? The voice of the void? Or of the assembly of the dead? Or of all the worlds which might have been?" The naked man stabbed an accusing finger at her. "Or am I simply *you*, Yaleen? Maybe everyone is you!"

Although Yaleen didn't understand this, she felt terrified. She fled from the Kirque out into the open air.

Where a cockerel crowed.

Whereupon she awoke.

And awaking, forgot.

As she lay abed, calmed by dawn light, listening to the doodle-do of the bird and the soft snores issuing from Peli in the neighbouring bed, to her astonishment Yaleen discovered that she was wearing a ring. A diamond ring! Scrambling from the covers, she darted to the window, the better to examine her discovery.

The ring must have cost upward of sixty fish!

She had never owned a ring before. Yet for some odd reason this particular ring seemed to belong on her finger—as though it had always been there, but invisibly and intangibly.

Quickly she roused her friend.

"Oh thank you, Peli dear! It's lovely. It's too much. What a surprise."

"Eh? Uh? What?" Peli struggled blearily to focus on the hand held before her face.

"Does this mean that you'll come along in the balloon, Peli? Does it? Or, oh dear, is it your way of saying sorry, no, adieu?"

"What are you talking 'bout?"

"This! Your gift. The ring you slipped on my finger while I was zonked out!"

Abruptly Peli sat up. "I did *not*. No such thing!" She seized Yaleen's hand. "You're joking. Where did you get that?"

"Do you swear by the river you didn't put this on my finger?"

"Honest. May I puke if I lie."

"But if *you* didn't. . . ." Yaleen's hand leapt to her mouth. "That man Andri! He was giving me the eye last night."

"An eye's one thing; a diamond ring's another."

"He must have come back in the wee hours! *They* chose the house for us—maybe there's a tunnel from outside leading to the cellar. He must have crept up here and done this without waking me."

"How romantic."

"I don't think it's romantic. He's put his mark on me, Peli, like a farmer tagging a cow. Probably thinks he owns me now. Or that I owe him something. Or whatever rogue thoughts infest their heads over here. I'm going to throw this away. I reject it. I'll leave it on the pillow."

"Don't be daft, a lovely ring like that."

Yaleen tugged tentatively at her finger. On second thoughts she settled the ring back. "I, um, I don't want to take it off."

"Don't! Wear it. Enjoy it. We'll be shot of this dump before you can say hickity-pickity. Why not write a rude message to him on the window pane? Then if he comes snooping once we're gone. . . . No, better not. He's s'posed to be one of the decent Sons, eh? I still can't credit he sneaked in here. But the nerve of it, if he did!" Peli inspected her own hands. Comically downcast, she said, "Don't I rate a ring, too?"

"You can have it, Peli! Take it. I mean that, honest. I'll likely just lose it, up in one of your sandstorms in the sky."

"Don't be silly. It's yours. And my fingers are all too big. Tell you what: scratch your name on the window with it. That'll mean it's yours for ever and ever."

"Okay. I will, too."

So therefore, in spidery style, Yaleen cut her name upon one of the crude little greenish panes. Close up, the glass distorted the view of the Kirque beyond. Each tiny motion of her head, as she worked, either compressed or stretched the building.

"Vandalizing embassies, eh!" Peli chortled. "What'll it come to next?"

"Huh. Small beer, this, compared with how they vandalized Verrino."

"That's all water down the river now. But their beer isn't water. Nor all that small! Oof, my head. What a way to wake up."

Yaleen stepped back to admire her efforts. The pane looked as if it had been signed by a shaking, arthritic grandmother.

A few hours after that, the party of ten easterners departed on their return trek towards the river, where a vessel stood at anchor waiting to convey them back to Guineamoy.

No one waylaid them en route, to try to murder them; so the mission must definitely be accounted a success.

Whilst tramping along, Yaleen started rehearsing excuses just in case the river guild asked her to return to Manhome South as part of the permanent embassy. Or in case they wished her to tarry in Guineamoy, there to receive the embassy from the west, help Andri feel at home, and gentle him. *Her* personal sights were set on the sky, on the desert, and on what lay beyond. Maybe she would be obliged to sign off the river entirely, instead of just taking leave?

On the other hand, the river temple still needed to give its blessing to the proposed expedition. Lacking that, the balloon venture would be taboo.

If the worst comes to the worst, thought Yaleen, *maybe I can live with a taboo? Supposing that Tam and Hasso and their sponsors can.*

Next, she thought to herself: *Is that the real reason why they invited me along? Not because they really love me—but because I'm of the river, a member of its guild? Thus they propitiate the river temple?*

No! They do love me.

And I love them. I love Tam. Hasso. Tam. One of them; I don't know which. I'm sure I do.

Trouble is, I don't know what it is to be in love! That's because I've never been in love before.

But I shall be in love. That's a promise.

What is this thing called love? Maybe I'm in love already? Without realizing? In love with Tam.

Yes, with Tam. Him.

While the *Blue Guitar* sailed away from the western shore, Yaleen concentrated upon this concept of love—realizing that by so doing she would indeed truly fall in love, presently.

Was that the real purpose of this ring she wore? So that she could present her ring as a love-pledge to Tam?

Hardly! Tam's fingers were so big and knobbly (though not clumsy, not in the least). In which case, was the ring mocking her?

Absolutely not. The diamond was brightness, light, purity of purpose, truth. It sparkled, like sunlight on the wave tops where the water was chopped by the passage of the *Blue Guitar.*

The initiative for the balloon expedition had originally come from Hasso, one of those Observers who spied on the west bank by telescope from Verrino Spire. Much good their vigilance had done Verrino town when the western soldiery invaded, drugged to resist riverphobia! But at least the Spire had held out; though now that the war was over and the west bank was less of a mystery, the Observers' role might have fallen into abeyance—were there not still outstanding the even greater mystery of what lay beyond the inland desert, which had swallowed several parties of explorers in the past.

What better way to observe vast new vistas than from the newly invented balloons which Guineamoy's artisans had crafted under the stimulus of war?

But of course this mode of transport was still in its infancy. Whether it would remain just a novelty or would develop into something grander and life-changing depended largely on the say-so of the river guild and river temples. In Manhome South, Guildmistress Marti had stated, "Whenever we feel confused, we should be guided by tradition." Even Yaleen allowed that this was a sensible axiom. When it came to the possibilities raised by balloon flight, many factors were involved.

Rampant balloons might upset the traditional female monopoly over trade and communications. They might weaken, or wipe out, the taboo against men travelling more than once, a taboo which for the most part had served eastern society well. The taboo was backed by sound medical sense, since a mental and bodily crisis afflicted any man who broke the prohibition against repeated river travel, and could easily kill him. But if men were able to float high above the river, and so become mobile and taboo-free (disregarding for the moment the problem of the anti-inhibitor drug), men might conceivably try to dominate affairs, as a cockerel treads its hens—something which the Sons in the west had so signally shown might happen. The Sons had turned their own more stringent river-taboo on its head, and forbidden their women to go near the water at all, fighting liquid with fire. Such men in power had proved themselves oppressive, thrusting, warlike.

Westerners needed to mend their ways and learn the womanly, flowing touch. Their own women, emerging from the dark cloud of ignorant centuries, must learn the way to show them; and learn how to sail the river. Yet would that happen, if balloons could carry men hither and thither untrammelled?

Thus balloon travel should only be introduced cautiously, in tandem with social improvements in the west; many 'mistresses said so. Any balloon must be strictly licensed and approved. Otherwise the world might plunge into another such calamity as the Sons' discovery of the fungus "anti-inhibitor" had unleashed. (It was fortunate that the Sons had so ignorantly exploited the fungus, virtually wiping it out in its jungle haunts! Or so they claimed; a claim lent credence by the abrupt collapse of their war effort.)

On the other hand, the jungle guild were rooting for balloons. Ridiculous to conceive of ever shifting timber by balloon, needless to say! But it was the men of the jungle guild who had made the long march from Jangali to Verrino to win the war. They deserved some recompense for all their suffering and sacrifice; such as a guarantee that *next time*—though pray river there wasn't a next time!—they should fly to war, not walk. So when the trans-desert balloon expedition was mooted by the Observers, the 'jacks supported this. Support also came from certain important industrialists of Guineamoy, purveyors of the weapons used in the war, who saw balloons as a future source of profit.

The prevailing winds mainly blew north or south along the river. However, the weather patterns of the highfleece clouds showed that further up in the atmosphere, and in particular over the area where the desert pressed closest to the river, in the Gangee-Pecawar region, air-streams often blew due eastward. Hence the site selected for assembly and launching: namely Pecawar. To begin with the balloon would drift south as it arose, but then it would enter the east-bound sky-stream. (A hundred leagues further south, high winds often blew in from across the desert towards the west; so there was a fair chance of returning, depending upon the kind of country encountered beyond the eastern desert. Assuming that the desert eventually gave way to hospitable terrain.)

"Let them go!" argued some voices in the river guild. "Let them equip! Let them launch their balloon! They'll never come back from beyond the desert. Probably there's just desert, and nothing else beyond it. We'll lose our adventurers—bravely, tragically, and foolishly. Balloons will dip in esteem."

Work on the big balloon began, and continued, but the river temple had still not pronounced the final word of consent. Yet privately guild and temple were sure of one item. If the balloon *were* to fly, young Yaleen of Pecawar should be part of the crew. Her wayward wish should certainly receive the blessing of her guild.

Yaleen herself was determined to be part of the expedition—even if she was compelled to take "drench leave" as she said fancifully of anyone quitting a boat in mid-passage (to fall foul, no doubt, of stingers). Her friend, Observer Hasso, had promised her. So also had her other friend, Tam the Potter. Tam had used up his one-go on the river to sail to Pecawar to experiment with the unique clays found locally (as well, perhaps, as making a romantic, quixotic gesture in pursuit of Yaleen). On the boat ex Verrino he had fallen in with Hasso, and these two men were soon as close as two slices of bread, glued together by the butter of Yaleen; perhaps foolishly so, should the butter melt one way or the other.

What Yaleen did not know was that though her guild might well favour her dreams of desert flight—even to the extent of publicly nominating her—this was because she was totally dispensable. In fact, therein lay her value. Already her brief career had been marked by various embarrassing scrapes; such as the time when she made a fool of herself at the Junglejack Festival—or that other occasion at Port Firsthome when she teamed up with a party of treasure hunters who were convinced that something rich and rare lay buried under the Obelisk of the Ship, and by burrowing almost toppled the Obelisk. True, she was bold and energetic and even diligent, but such incidents practically guaranteed that at some stage—either literally or metaphorically—she would poke a hole in the balloon. If the guild's rumour-mongers reported accurately, Yaleen bid fair to set two of the expedition men at jealous loggerheads.

This was why the guild had despatched Yaleen on the brief preliminary mission to Manhome South as a jill-of-all and general bottlewasher. Fingers crossed, she was unlikely to provoke any serious contretemps. She went along in a strictly minor capacity—to a place where mere "gairls" were held in contempt. (And if she did get into hot water, well, she was an example of an independently minded female.) By sending her, the guild promoted her to sufficient prominence to be worth nominating, and subsequently losing. . . .

A few days after the *Blue Guitar* docked in grimy Guineamoy, Yaleen was summoned to the river temple. By this time the leaders of the mission had had opportunity to debate their findings in conclave.

Yaleen reported to the temple, ready to spill out her excuses. She felt somewhat cocky; somewhat apprehensive.

Her cockiness proceeded simply from the fine diamond she wore. Quite why this should be, she wasn't sure. The ring had rapidly come to seem like a personal talisman. Spirited on to her finger by a lecherous Son, that lucky find had now become her luck; and why not?

Her apprehension came from a different quarter. The very same day that the *Blue Guitar* arrived, Yaleen had been interviewed by a man from the local newssheet, the *Guineamoy Gazette.*

This interview was arranged through the quaymistress's good offices; and it took place in a back room of her office, though the quaymistress showed no desire to eavesdrop or supervise. The newsman was seeking what he called a "human interest angle" on the trip to the Sons' southerly stronghold.

"I'm hoping this story will be syndicated up and down the river," the fellow confided to Yaleen. His name was Mulge; but that was his misfortune. The name matched him, though.

He was a grey, stout young man. Grey of skin, as though the sun had never shone on him. Grey of demeanour: stolid, serious, lacklustre, untouched by much imagination. Pencil-grey, smoke-grey.

"You'll be famous," he said in a flat tone of voice, as though the notion of such exposure worried him, though equally it was his stock in trade.

Duly, the very next day the following column had appeared in the *Guineamoy Gazette;* and perhaps this ought to be quoted, rather than a blow by blow reprise of the interview itself, since the following is what emerged for public scrutiny and is what was uppermost in Yaleen's mind when she paid her visit to the temple.

Her attempts to enthuse Mulge on the subject of the desert expedition had, it transpired, been so much water off a duck's back. Maybe he thought she was indulging in a different sort of flight— one of fancy. Maybe he wrote to the limits of his understanding— maliciously, so it seemed to Yaleen when she first scanned his column. How he had garbled and idiotized everything. His account read as though he hadn't harked at all. Mulge could as easily have stayed at home and made the whole thing up.

GANGEE "GAIRL" IN SONS' LAIR

Crewwoman Yaleen of the *Blue Guitar*
said yesterday how glad she is to be back

> in civilization after acting as "cabin girl"
> for the momentous peace mission to
> Manhome South.
>
> "I felt scared all the time," she con-
> fessed. "But I didn't show it. Those Sons
> call all young women 'gairls', with a
> sneer in their voice, as if we're kids. But
> now because of us they've stopped burn-
> ing women. One of the Sons even fancied
> me! I didn't fancy him.
>
> "But yes, I'd go back again—into the
> wild dogs' liar—to show what we're
> made of over here."

(This was the bit which worried Yaleen most of all.)

> Of her ordeal, Yaleen said . . .

There was more, in similar vein; and the piece ended off thus:

> Yaleen's deputy mission commander,
> Tamath, commented: "Yaleen's too mod-
> est. She behaved as a fine representative
> of our way of life. She's young but she
> already distinguished herself on several
> occasions. She's our finest."

True, typeface and layout were excellent—though "lair" was mis-
spelled as "liar", which seemed appropriate—but on the whole
Yaleen had felt like curling up in a dark corner. Alternatively: like
coming out with fists flailing.

And why had Tamath said those things? Simply to counteract the
impression of breathless naïvety conveyed by the rest of the piece?

Mixed in with her cocktail of embarrassment and defiance, Yaleen
also detected a third, odd flavour. This was the sense that, with her
interview in print, somehow she was "emerging"—from anonymous
obscurity back into the light, not unlike some death-box buried in
Pecawar cemetery being disinterred by the breezes of time.

What became of death-boxes when *that* occurred? Why, they
were soon burnt up and destroyed!

Yet Yaleen had always been obscure and anonymous; nobody special, save to friends and family and three or four lovers, and herself.

Whence came this sense of familiarity at being mentioned in print? Which was this light she was emerging into? She didn't relish the sensation. It felt wrong, even dangerous.

After mulling the matter over for a while, she decided that basically she was a proud creature. Mulge's column constituted a satire on that pride, a caricature.

So as she approached the river temple that morning along Bezma Boulevard, she felt apprehensive. But she also blew on her ring and polished it and felt proud.

The river temple was a sprawling ancient structure constructed of rusty orange ironstone. Recently the stones had been repointed with yellow mortar, but in years past the walls had bent and bellied and been corseted with metal bands and rings, which were now picked out in black paint. The whole edifice resembled a strongchest for storing treasure; a somewhat grimy and eroded one, despite its refurbishments, due to the pollution in the air.

Indeed the temple did contain treasure. It enshrined the spirit of a way of life—along with the political and moral embodiment of that way of life, the river priestess. Additionally the temple cellar guarded the guild treasury (Guineamoy account). While on the ground floor at the rear this particular temple housed the Mint, which stamped and milled all scales and fins and fish for distribution up and down stream.

By tradition a triumvirate supervised the Mint; this trio consisting of a 'mistress of the river guild, plus a Guineamoy metalmaster, plus a "witness woman" from as far away as possible. Once every two years a new witness was elected, alternately by the towns of Tambimatu and Umdala. For manufacturing reasons the Mint must needs be sited at Guineamoy. For historic reasons the river guild gave it a roof. The witness ensured that new coins all duly entered circulation, and did not slip "through chinks in the floorboards" down into the river guild treasury in the cellar below.

Yaleen entered by the arched doorway, gave her name to the clerk-acolyte on duty, and was led to priestess Kaski's parlour for her audience.

When she was shown in, the parlour was empty. Cushions lay scattered on the polished hoganny floor before a low throne. A single mullioned window gave sight of the river, where a brig was sailing by. Old tapestries showing ancient boats cloaked the walls.

These tapestries caused Yaleen a momentary sense of terrible unease. Instead of admiring them, she focused her gaze upon the genuine vessel sailing the waters.

A rustle. A swirl of fabric. And Kaski appeared—stepping directly out of one of the tapestries! The tapestry was actually in two separate parts, though they had hung as one. Behind, a door was concealed.

Supporting herself with a silver-tipped cane, Kaski hobbled slowly in the direction of her throne. Yaleen almost darted to assist; but this might have been impertinent. Besides, the shrivelled old woman had paid no heed to her yet. Yaleen shuffled uncertainly.

Then the crone did reach her throne—and swung round, sitting smoothly and swiftly, not at all like somebody suffering from crippled joints. Her eyes took in Yaleen, with piercing familiarity.

"River bless you, child of the flow!" The priestess's voice was clear, purposeful, precise.

Yaleen realized that Kaski must have been watching her for a while through a crack in the divided tapestry before emerging. And that slow walk of hers had been hoo-ha, designed to put Yaleen off stride. Maybe Kaski could fence with that cane of hers in as sprightly a style as any 'jack soldier. Perhaps she could tap-dance rings around Yaleen.

"River lave you, 'Mistress Priestess."

"Hmm. Read that story about you in the paper, I did!" said Kaski without more ado.

"Oh dear. Honestly, I've never seen such a jumble of drivel in a newssheet—not even at 'Barbra! It makes me out such a silly chit."

Kaski, however, rapped her cane on the floor. "Yaleen, you should realize that *all* reports are garbled to a greater or lesser degree. Even the best newssheets are always a sort of fiction concocted out of what's real. This is simply the first time you have encountered the phenomenon from both sides: as reader and as originator of the news."

"He even got my home-town wrong."

"Gangee's nearer to here than Pecawar," said Kaski airily. "And 'Gangee girl' has a better ring to it, wouldn't you say?"

"Nor did I describe myself as a cabin girl!"

"Not to worry. It's the spirit that counts."

"I certainly didn't say I was panting to go back west."

"Aha, here we have the nub. You want to go on that mad balloon expedition instead."

The suspicion dawned on Yaleen that Mulge might have been

manipulated by Tamath in what he wrote. How could she avoid going back west, should the guild ask her to—when thousands of people had been informed that Yaleen was their junior champion?

Alternatively: how could she avoid lingering in Guineamoy to be hospitable to visiting Sons? Thus to make up for her rude remarks about them (which she hadn't uttered quite so)? If *that* was what the guild preferred.

Which way did the rudder point?

"Oh," she said.

But again old Kaski surprised her. The priestess chuckled. "Never fear, child! We intend to give our benediction to the balloon scheme. *And,* what's more, to your participation in it. In fact, you will become our official representative. There, how's that?"

What a shift of the wind to an unexpected quarter!

"Eh?" said Yaleen.

"I believe you heard me well enough."

"Ah. Yes. Um. Can Peli be part of the expedition too?"

Now Kaski frowned. "What's this? Your friend Peli?"

"She's very competent."

"I'm aware of it. Is she asking to go?"

"Not *quite.* I could persuade her, with your blessing."

"You'll do no such thing. It would be wholly unethical to pressure such a competent crew member into quitting the river."

"Who's quitting? We'll be back."

"Mind your manners! You presume too much. The guild does not give its blessing to Peli going, especially when she has no wish to do so." As if to soften the severity of this, Kaski added, "To be sure, you'll be back. . . ."

"My apologies."

"Accepted. It's good that you've had this exposure in the newssheets."

"Is it?"

"This establishes you as a personality, expedition-wise. You're up front, as *our* person. I'm sure you won't let us down. Nor for that matter, the balloon." Wreathed in wrinkled smiles, Kaski arose nimbly from her throne.

Ro-ses are bloo-ming in Pecawar—!

Yaleen whistled this old tune to herself as she trod the dust of her home town on her way to visit the expedition headquarters.

Capiz Street stretched out eastward towards open country, accompanied by its aqueduct along which a rill of water purled.

At this distance from the riverside and the Wheelhouse, the aqueduct had descended nearly to ground level. Its piers were only three bricks high. Its gutter had narrowed to concentrate what was left of the flow. Entry to the walled gardens of houses on that side of the road was by little bridges which stepped up over the 'duct; whereas closer to the town centre the piers were high enough to walk beneath.

This whole network of 'ducts which carried water to homes and irrigated gardens still enchanted and intrigued Yaleen almost as much as it had when she was a child. Truly, the system was one of the wonders of Pecawar. (The second wonder being the many rose gardens, both public and private, which availed themselves of the moisture.) The flow commenced high and huge at the Wheelhouse by the river. There, giant archimedean screws forever quarried water; themselves powered by great wooden waterwheels which a headrace flume kept in constant motion. The prime source soon branched into a number of different, slowly descending, circuitous aqueducts, which branched and branched in turn—till out by the edge of town where she now walked, a 'duct would be diminuendo, about to peter out.

The elevated 'duct system had been in place a hundred years and more. Its designer of genius, architect Margeegold of Aladalia, had paid close attention to another, and complementary, sort of flow: to wit, the smooth passage of people and goods through the Pecawar streets. Hence the many convolutions of the network, even downtown where the 'ducts marched high. Moving further from the source, the branching 'ducts as they descended often compelled lesser streets to tunnel underneath, or bridge up and over with ramps or flights of steps. In the past this had proved a cause of complaint to the elderly who could remember a flat, no-fuss Pecawar. To Yaleen's way of thinking all these ups and downs brought some of the charm of Verrino to an otherwise level town. Maybe she had even elected to become a riverwoman in the first place thanks to Margeegold's aqueducts; for riverwater continually bubbled through her home town, along red brick veins, like lifeblood.

Without a map it was hard to say which branches led where. Whether the Pemba Avenue 'duct ultimately watered her home neighbourhood—or the Zanzyba Road one! As a child, oblivious to the likely existence of an official plan (or rather, disdaining this type of adult approach to something enchanting), she and her friends had formed a gang pledged to solve the riddle of the waterways. This, they had set out to achieve by perilously scaling downtown piers and launching paper boats with identification marks on them. Then they had raced off to try to catch these, much further down 'duct. In a papery way she was already becoming a boatwoman.

One day her brother Capsi tried to spoil this fine sport by presenting his own pen and ink diagram of the network—the true layout, so he claimed, arrived at by observation and deduction.

Yaleen and friends had snatched his work. In furious petulance at Capsi's blindness to the unwritten magic rules of their boat-chasing game, they had torn the map up and floated the pieces away.

But thereafter the magic perished. The gang didn't scale any more piers. Besides, they had already been hauled down on two separate occasions and harangued by an aquaguild worker. Capsi, for his part, became alienated after that. He concentrated his attention upon the further shore, which was then still taboo. . . .

As Yaleen walked along, whistling repetitively, her mind had wandered back into past. Now the tune suddenly restored her to herself.

Roses were blossoming indeed. Climbers sprawled over garden walls. Here, *Zéphirine Drouhin* the thornless rose bloomed carmine-pink, its rich scent strongly assailing the passer-by. There, *Felicity and Perpetuity* rambled its red-flecked ivory rosettes.

Ahead, a grey globe loomed over walls and rooftops: the "first stage" of the balloon! It had been just the beginnings of a framework of split bamboo the last time she saw it. Yaleen quickened her step and presently she arrived at the workyard from which balloon and gondola would rise one day soon.

At once she caught sight of Tam and Hasso labouring together on the gondola. *That* hadn't even existed when she sailed from Pecawar. A true boat on the sky, it now rested in a supporting cradle underneath the tethered globe.

Other men were working, too—she recognized Observer Tork, and Farge from Guineamoy—but it was Hasso and Tam for whom she had eyes.

Tam most of all. Tam.

Yes, she *did* love him. She knew that now. She had rehearsed loving him times enough on the voyage back from Guineamoy. In so doing she had found that a person could indeed teach herself to believe in love by concentrating; by invoking the image of that love a sufficient number of times—like a piece of music much practised till playing it became second nature. Oh yes, there was an art to love, akin to complex music. This art was distinct from the skill of sexual pleasure, which was a simpler tune that the body played. Just a tune. Love was (could be, should be) a symphony, a heart-chorale.

And now the actual music-drama of this love could get under way; though Hasso, her other former partner in the tune of sexual amusement, must of course remain a sweet friend.

She broke into a run across the yard. "Tam! Hasso! Tam!"

The men turned. Hasso started towards her. But Tam stepped past him, for she had called Tam's name twice; and it was into his arms that Yaleen jumped. Tam hugged her, released her. She spun; and touched Hasso's hand, but only touched it.

She laughed. "I'm back!"

"From the wild dogs' lair, eh?" Hasso gave a wicked grin.

"Oh, *that!* Listen you two: the river temples have given their blessing. And what's more, *I'm* my guild's chosen nominee—to fly! They haven't just said okay; they've made me their official representative."

"What marvellous news," said Tam.

Hasso nodded. "It's all in the latest newssheet, of course."

"Really? I haven't been home yet. Left my kit in town; rushed straight out here."

"To your future home-from-home." Tam stretched his right hand invitingly towards the light wooden gondola. This gesture tugged his sleeve up, exposing the queer thin red birthmark which ran full circle round his wrist.

"Definitely worth a fortnight in Manhome South, to prove your mettle," said Hasso. "Seriously, I mean it."

The two men were competing subtly. But did not Hasso already sound just a tad resigned? Perhaps even cynical, with a hint of bitterness? She certainly hoped not; that would be a shame.

Though if Hasso read the signs aright—of her plunge into Tam's arms—was he not obliged to withdraw somewhat?

Not really!

At this point one of the motives behind her decision to prefer Tam became crystal clear to Yaleen. Maybe it was a kindly motive; maybe it was selfish. The fact was that Hasso was sufficiently experienced in the ways of the world to play second fiddle; whereas Tam could have been deeply, heartachingly hurt.

Damn it, why should there *be* any need for a choice between them?

Ah but there had to be, if she was to explore the full symphony of love, all the obsessive ache of it (as opposed to convivial amorousness).

Tam seized up Yaleen's hand. He held it, stroking her fingers. "Hey, what's this?"

"Oh, my ring?"

"Noticed it right away," commented Hasso. "Ve-ry pretty. Gift from an admirer?"

"You could say so."

"How's that?" asked Tam, letting go her hand in panic; at which Hasso smiled and looked serene.

"Long story! Tell you all about it later. Look, don't I rate a drink? I'm parched."

Hasso jerked a thumb at the smaller of the two substantial storage sheds. "I've a bottle of decent vintage stowed over there."

"I think I'd prefer ale if there's any." Yaleen waited a moment before turning to Tam, so as not to seem to snub Hasso.

"I could easily run and fetch a jugful," Tam offered. "It isn't far."

"Shouldn't take him more than half an hour," said Hasso.

"Oh Tam, you mustn't bother! That's ridiculous. How about coffee? Or lemonade?"

Tam brightened. "Lemonade, it is!"

So the three friends headed for the shed.

Part of the shed was stacked with dried food, preserves, blankets, empty demijills for water, and such. Yaleen spotted an unmade bed.

"Is one of you sleeping out here?"

"Somebody has to, to guard the balloon and basket," said Hasso.

"Gondola," Tam corrected him. "It's much bigger than a basket."

"Like a little boat," agreed Yaleen.

Tam fetched a flagon of lemonade to a table spread with charts. These charts were mainly blank. A couple of Tam's pots with sprays of *Pink Parfait* roses glowing through the glaze weighed them down. Tam poured a couple of glassfuls, glanced at Hasso, poured a third.

"We've decided on a name," he said.

"A name?"

"For the balloon, of course! Boats have names. A boat of the air deserves one—we're going to call it *Rose.*"

"Because we hope it'll rise," joked Hasso. "Myself, I thought we should call it *Dough*. But I got outvoted."

"Ho ho," said Tam. "I'm going to paint a huge pink hybrid tea rose on the globe. *Gavotte* or *Stella;* haven't made my mind up yet."

Yaleen caressed the flowers painted on one of the pots. *'Rose:* I like it. Good choice. Emblem of Pecawar, eh? I'd have voted that way myself."

It was more diplomatic, she thought, to describe the rose as symbol of Pecawar rather than as Tam's own adopted motif. He had begun to decorate his pots with roses back in Aladalia soon after he had got to know Yaleen and had first gone to bed with her. Before that, his pots had usually sported fleuradieus in various shades from light blue to dark purple, depending on his mood.

They drank lemonade, they talked. They visited the other shed, where she admired the waxed silken bags of the balloon's "second stage" folded up neatly in three white mounds.

The balloon needed two stages if it was to rise high enough to catch the easterlies. The globe alone could not do the job. Buoyed up by hot air rising through a chimney from a heater in the gondola, the globe would only hoist its burden eight thousand spans into the sky at most; and that was going at full blast, which would burn up too much oil too soon. To enter the highfleece region required more altitude: twice that height. Thus a cluster of three great gasbags would tower above the globe, quite dwarfing it. These would be inflated with the lightest of all gases, watergas. Supplies of bottled watergas came from Guineamoy, where it was obtained by destructively distilling coal in closed iron retorts to produce coalgas, from which the fire-damp was later removed. The globe would hoist the gondola. The gasbags in turn would hoist the globe; and the hot air rising up around the globe would magnify the natural lift of the watergas.

What's more, much of the watergas could be pumped back down through condenser valves into the bottles mounted around the crown of the globe. Thus the gasbags would flop sufficiently for the whole ensemble to descend at journey's end without any need to vent and waste the irreplaceable watergas. (Given time, and being so light, watergas could waste itself well enough by breathing out through the skin of the bags.) By this means the balloon ought to be able to ascend a second time, perhaps even a third. By this means they might return home.

It was Tam, with his knowledge of furnaces and clays, who had cooked up the strong lightweight ceramics for use in the hot-air breeder, gas-jars, pumps and such; thus solving a problem which had foxed the factories of Guineamoy with their prejudice in favour of heavy lumps of metal.

Of steering, the balloon had none. As yet, steering—by means of wooden fans turned by compressed air—was inefficient and exacted a toll in added burden. Consequently it had been sacrificed in return for extra altitude and payload. They would sail where the high winds willed, and would hope that they could pace their eventual descent so as to choose a safe, hospitable landing spot. (Still, some time in the future Tam's ceramics would likely lead to the production of powerful lightweight "engines", which could direct the course of a balloon no matter which quarter the winds blew from.)

Next, they visited the gondola and climbed inside. Tam and Hasso competed in showing her the fittings: canvas hammocks, tiny galley, privy cubicle (with a large hole venting down). Yaleen imagined herself floating through the sky, peeking out of the little window of the privy, and peeing rain—after which a wind wiped her bare bum dry.

Tam displayed the hot-air breeder.

"We *can* convert it to work on charcoal, which we can make out of any wood we find. That won't be as efficient as oil, but it'll still do the job. We'll be glad of the hot air when we're up on the heights of the sky."

"Why's that? We'll be nearer the sun."

"Ah, but where do you suppose hailstones drop from? Up there! So the higher you go, the colder it must get."

She corrected herself: a wind *freezing* her bare bum, while she peed yellow ice.

Hasso explained how partitions and lockers could be dismantled, and reassembled so as to form a big cart—or, depending on terrain, a sledge. After landing they might have to haul the *Rose* some way southward by hand to gain the westerly returning highfleece winds, should the low winds prove unfavourable. The gondola (with its privy stool duly plugged and dogged) would even double as a clumsy boat, using silk for a sail. Should there be water beyond the sands, and the water not provoke a phobia.

For the first time the possibility occurred to Yaleen that they might not be coming back; might not be able to. But she shrugged this prospect off.

After a couple of hours spent at the expedition headquarters

Yaleen departed homeward along Capiz Street with a shopping list in her pocket. Of spices, yet! So that they could pep up their "wooden rations" and also whatever fodder they found at journey's end, if any. Drench the cooking; kill the taste—said Hasso. She forgave him for his cavalier attitude to meals. He had endured the belt-tightening siege of Verrino Spire, and had learned to despise good food.

Caraway, oregano, chilli powder, pepper, paprika, cloves! She also forgave Hasso for his blithe—and mean—presumption that she had some intimate and cut-price relationship with spice sacks, courtesy of the fact that her dad worked for the industry. Perhaps Hasso just wanted to make her feel, now that the expedition was almost ready, that she was contributing something vital? Well, she was! She was contributing *herself*. She forgave him; but of course when you forgive somebody, that forgiveness comes between you. It separates you by an invisible barrier, where you are the forgiving one, and he is the forgiven; a picture frame, with you as the painter, and him as the painted, coloured a certain hue for ever more . . . or at least for a while.

"Mum! Dad! Is anybody home?"

Yaleen's mother appeared at the head of the stairs. She smiled and held out her arms and descended, her sandals clopping on the waxed treads. She trod the stairs slowly, with a cautious grace.

"Don't hug hard, darling! I'm pregnant."

"What?"

Yaleen's mum laughed. "You needn't look so surprised. It's possible, you know."

"Where's Dad?"

"I didn't become pregnant this very moment, daughter dear! Your dad's at work. Where else? I imagine he's busy counting peppercorns."

"Oh. Of course." Where *else* would her father be?

Mother appraised her. "We read of your exploits in the newssheet. And just yesterday we read how you're going to leave us—by balloon. Maybe it's best that we're having another child, your father and I."

"How do you mean?"

"If your heart's set on this venture I shouldn't try to dissuade you. I imagine that it's a brave thing to do—braver even than going to that vile place in the west. Besides, your guild is honouring you. But who has ever come back from the desert? *Who?"*

"Look, Mum, those earlier expeditions all failed because explorers tried to foot it over the sands. We'll float over fast, and in comfort. It'll be a picnic."

Besides, thought Yaleen, *I'm in love. At last. Am I not?*

I'm almost in love with love itself! And Tam is my emblem of love; just as surely as love's own emblem is the rose. So obviously I must help him (and the others too; don't forget the others!) to sail our rose of love through the sky to another land, somewhere or wherever.

Then back home again. Back home; goes without saying.

My love is a brave rose balloon. Let nothing blight it. Let no thorn prick it.

Yet why, oh why, should I feel this whelming need to love? This urge to surrender myself—not so much to a particular man (absurd idea!) as to love itself? This need to submerge myself (that's it, submerge!) in an ecstasy of the emotions?

Perhaps a Creator might have felt such an urge, once she had crafted her universe. This desire to submerge Herself in the stream of Being! To surrender Herself to the flow of feeling—so that thus her worlds should be truly alive, free to live as they choose.

(Supposing that there is *a Creator! Or ever was. That's an unsatisfactory proposition without much meat on it. A dry bone for Ajelobo savants to chew over.)*

Let's look at this another way, hmm? I've spent years crafting my own self. I've crafted my life. Now I must dive into that life headlong—to become who I really am.

Just so, does my mum become a mother again. She does so instinctively, irrationally, capriciously—whatever she says about reasons, after the event! Yet perhaps she does so wisely too, with the wisdom of the heart, not of the head.

Such strange heady thoughts are brewed by love! Such an intoxicating ferment!

All things outside of me—a ring, a rose, a gondola, the sky, those dunes which I have yet to glimpse—all of these connect up with the feelings which are inside me; expressing them, voicing them, illuminating them. That's why love matters: it makes the world bloom with new meaning.

Gently Yaleen embraced her mother. "Don't worry. I'll be back to play with my new sister!"

"Sister? It might be a brother. Or twins."

"Oh, I suppose so! Dunno why I said that. You'll come to the launching, won't you, to wave us on our way?"

"I imagine we will."

"Don't imagine. *Do!"*

Mother laughed. "Very well!" Only then did she spy the diamond ring on Yaleen's finger. "That's beautiful. If you fall among savages, you can buy food with it."

"Maybe we'll fall amongst *aliens!* Among natives of this world who were here before ever our people came. There they'll be on the other side of the sands, hiding in their burrows beneath ruined palaces. Harking to us with their huge ears, or in their dreams."

"And pigs might fly."

"If a rose can fly, a pig might fly too."

"Tonight's won't. We're having fried pork for dinner."

Dad came home late that evening; though not so late that the pork was spoilt. (Mother had commenced frying, irrespective.) Naturally, Dad was chagrined to be late on this day of days, of his daughter's surprise return. Mother appeared richly amused at his chagrin— though she was amused in a composed, controlled, almost artificial way which struck Yaleen as most peculiar. Mum obviously *relished* something, yet she wasn't going to split her sides laughing. In case she split the sprig of baby loose inside her? Yaleen was quite puzzled.

The truth came out over dinner.

Dad had just dished out an extra dollop of nutmeggy apple sauce on to Yaleen's plate, and he was quizzing her as to whether those Sons used spices much at Manhome South; and if so, what kinds, and how (which in itself was odd, since Dad had never been one to bring work home with him, save for the tang of it on his clothes); when Mum remarked casually, "By the way, your father's having a love affair."

"What?" Yaleen was flabbergasted. First a baby; now an affair? Had she heard aright? Had Mum really meant what she seemed to mean?

"We're also having a baby, your mother and I," said Dad. He didn't sound too discomposed, though perhaps he laid undue stress on the "we".

"I know you are. Mum said."

Mum smiled. "Quite ingenious of your dad, I'd say. He can have an affair *and* a baby. An affair with one woman, a baby with another." She didn't sound sarcastic; but maybe she was playing a deeper game than simple sarcasm. "Usually it's the other way about, isn't it? You should know that, Yaleen. A riverwoman has her affairs —and her husband stays home with baby. How the world's changing since the war! All that marching by, and the distant clash of weapons, must have fired ambitions in your dad."

"Oh." Yaleen examined the grain of the wood in the kitchen table —a black knot seemed to be coming loose.

"How was she this evening, then?" enquired Mum.

"Fine, thanks. Fine," said Dad.

"I'm glad to hear it. I'd say we owe her a debt of gratitude. Perhaps we should even ask her to be guidemother to our baby when it's born! You'd imagine that a love affair would, well, dilute the passion of the loins. Divert the seed; water it down. But no. Provenly not." Mum patted her tummy. "A lover has to make bigger, fiercer efforts; and this spills over, doesn't it? The lover has to prove how he's big enough for two women. And prove it he does."

Dad grinned lopsidedly. "I certainly seem to have done."

They didn't *seem* to mind discussing this business; though for sure a strand of tension twanged beneath the amiable veneer.

"Do describe your friend, hmm? Tell Yaleen what she looks like."

"Oh, who cares what she looks like?" said Dad, sounding ever so reasonable. "Looks, indeed! It's her person that's important. It's what she is, that counts."

"To be sure! And she's strong. Independent. Assertive. And subtle; but then all women are subtle."

"Er, what's her name?" Yaleen asked cautiously.

"Her name's Chanoose," replied Mum. "She's the quaymistress."

"Her!"

"Oh yes, I was forgetting you must know her."

"Well, not intimately."

"Unlike your father. And despite her strength and independence, this same Chanoose has fallen under your father's spell—as if enchanted. It quite makes me proud."

Yaleen turned to her dad. "Was that why you were asking me about the spice-trading prospects over in the west?"

"I don't follow."

"Has your Chanoose set her eye on exporting best Pecawar spices to the west bank? Those Sons don't need hotting up, you know. They need cooling down. They need blanding, not peppering."

"No, no, I just asked out of curiosity."

And so the meal continued, in amiable enough vein, with bluepears in syrup for afters followed by cups of cinnamon coffee.

Later on, when she was in her room, Yaleen tried to assess more calmly her mother's attitude to the recently conceived foetus. Of whose love was it really the product? Why, of Mum's and Dad's, obviously! But wasn't the enigmatic Chanoose in a sense the mother too, even though she didn't bear the child? Didn't Chanoose provide the *catalyst*, as they said of chemicals in Guineamoy? Barren herself, presumably "safe" from conception, hadn't she nevertheless caused the event to occur? So had Dad given Mum the baby to prove his continuing fidelity, despite the affair? Had Mum insisted upon this, as her price for condoning it? Or had the affair itself transformed Dad in his middle years, compelling him to create new life like a fountain bursting forth in a desert?

And how had he captivated and besotted Chanoose, who had always seemed—from a distance—so aloof and powerful? How had the 'mistress become a mistress, in this strange triple relationship?

Yaleen found herself feeling deeply glad and thankful on her dad's behalf. But what preoccupied her most was the queer way that this affair of her dad's, coupled with his role as sire of a new baby, seemed to reflect her own love-dilemma. What a peculiar model of her own experience! Might she also manage to maintain a similar balance—between herself and Hasso and Tam? Could she? Ought she to try?

Somehow she suspected that the situation involving Mum and Dad and Chanoose was inherently unstable. It was indeed unlike the rompings of a riverwoman in a distant port, reaping wild oats far from her shore-husband's ken. Yet with taboos perhaps about to fray under the pressure of a certain fungus-drug and cross-river intercourse—and with balloons in the offing—might not everyone's current way of life become unstable presently? Might not drug chemistry and balloon technology cause changes which the war itself had failed to cause (though the war might have been the initial catalyst)?

Maybe, maybe not. The river guild and river temples were subtle, old, and unlikely to spring leaks too large to caulk.

She considered recent events again: the mooting of the desert expedition, preparations for this, Chanoose's affair with her father, the pregnancy, her own mission ex Pecawar to Guineamoy thence to Manhome South culminating in her official secondment as guild representative aboard the *Rose*.

Wasn't there something odd about the sequence? Something more than coincidental? Chanoose must have become intimate with her dad at about the time the guild must have seriously started to consider the advantages, and the possible threat, posed by the expedition. . . .

No, no, this was nonsense. The day had been long. Yaleen was tired out—by delight at the balloon; by the energy she had poured into her love for Tam, and into the *decision* to prefer him; and finally by her astonishment at her parents' capers.

Chanoose had fallen in love irrationally. "Enchanted" had been the word Mum used. Even if Chanoose was also "subtle", she surely hadn't *chosen* to fall in love—or pretend she was in love. What possible advantage could she gain? Some form of leverage over Yaleen, through her father? Hardly!—unless Chanoose was thinking in terms of when the balloon returned; and even so, she carried more clout in her official capacity than she could bring to bear as a sort of erotic "stepmother". . . .

There remained the possibility that Chanoose was deliberately presenting a pattern—an unstable one—which she knew would find an echo in Yaleen's behaviour. . . .

No. Chanoose must have been emotionally snared at about the time that Yaleen landed on the west bank; when the world shook slightly and all hearts paused, as though in tribute to the peace mission.

Yaleen climbed into bed; and slept too deep for dreams, or for dreams to survive the dawn undrowned.

Just three weeks later, of a Tauday morning, a crowd gathered out at the big workyard at the eastern end of Capiz Street.

The majority of people present were sightseers pure and simple, for the *Pecawar Publicizer* had done as its name implied in honour of the launch. Others were more directly involved, including men of the aquaguild. One of the duties of the aquaguild was, of course, to douse any serious fires which accident might spark off in Pecawar, fires too fierce for neighbours to quench; and the aquaguild boss—having done some homework—was dubious of the wisdom of lighting a hot-air breeder anywhere near three bags full of watergas.

"If your *Rose* does conflagrate on take-off," the aquaboss was saying to Hasso, "it'll drag a torch right across those houses there."

The trio of gasbags already bobbed slackly overhead, straining slightly southward in a gentle breeze. The day was sunny, almost cloudless. The *Gavotte* rose which Tam had painted on the first stage —the hot-air globe—was the height of a tall man. *Gavotte* was a high-centred bloom of warm pink, renowned for keeping its shape for ages. Might the balloon likewise keep in shape.

'Mistress Chanoose intervened. "Don't worry about it, Aquaboss. I doubt if these adventurers would intentionally fly a bonfire through the sky! And if that happens—which it won't—I'm sure your fellows are up to soaking any wreckage; even out here where your 'ducts drip the last drops of river-juice."

A sly put-down, this, implying a contrast between the authentic river, plied by women, and this model river running tamely around town in brick courses. The aquaboss shrugged and turned away.

Yes, Chanoose was present. How could she fail to be, when Yaleen represented her guild? This was the first occasion since Yaleen's return to Pecawar that she had been in close proximity to her dad's mistress; and Yaleen really scrutinized the woman, limning her in her mind.

Undoubtedly Chanoose was a handsome woman. She was tall, with short curly flaxen hair, an oval face of clear skin, and sapphire eyes of the first water. Her nose was slender, though her lips were large and fleshy in sensual counterpoint. Her fingernails were long and well-manicured, as if to emphasize that whenever *she* worked at something physical, she never worked clumsily; nor need anyone else. Yaleen tried to imagine those nails teasing her father's buttocks, urging him; but she couldn't quite succeed.

Chanoose stared clear over other heads, to where Mum and Dad were lurking near the back of the crowd. Mum, hiding in her belly the jewel of a new life, wouldn't stray any closer to the *Rose,* whose dangerous gasbags even now towered high as a hoganny.

"Excuse me," Chanoose said, "I should pay my respects to friends." She departed, Dad-wards.

"And excuse *me!*" said a gnome of a man. "I'm from the *Publicizer.*"

Yaleen wasn't inclined to give any more dumb interviews; and besides—"All aboard!" shouted Tam from the gondola door—the balloon was about to depart.

The hot-air breeder was lit; which made the crew swelter somewhat and long for the cool of the sky-heights. The gasbags were swollen full of watergas, straining erect. Tethers were cast off—and the *Rose* climbed swiftly away from the eastern suburb.

Since the south-by-south-east drift was gradual by comparison, the crew had many minutes to admire the spread of the whole town.

"Oh this is the way to make maps!" crowed Hasso. "If only there was some means of fixing quickly what we're seeing." But there wasn't any such way. He dug Tam in the ribs. "If only you could glaze this spectacle on to the window-glass."

"Then we shouldn't be able to see where we're going, the rest of the time," Tam pointed out.

Yaleen mainly had eyes for the thin red veins of the aqueduct system. These seemed to print upon the town a single complicated, curlicued letter from some unknown alphabet of signs. Or maybe it was a whole word in such a sign system. A name. A signature, which she wasn't able to decipher. The higher they ascended, the less visible this word became. It soon disappeared into the shrinking tapestry of the town, one set of threads lost in a bigger pattern which diminished quickly. Spice farms below were tiny patchworks. Away to the west, the river was but a glossy road.

"How does it feel to be a heroine?" Tam asked Yaleen.

"I think," she said, "I already was one."

"Uh?"

"I feel as if I already did something splendid and awesome! But I've no idea what! I can't ever know what it is—because, because it surrounds me on all sides. It's the air I breathe. It's everything. There's nothing else apart from it."

"That's a psychological condition known as *dayjar view,*" remarked the woman Melza from Jangali. "When you tipple too much in the heat of the day, suddenly it seems as if things that are taking place, have already taken place before. This can occur in your dreams, too. You're convinced you're revisiting the dream—not viewing it for the first time. It happens to everyone at least once in their lives. *Dayjar view.*"

"Oh," said Yaleen.

Presently they were high enough to enter the airstream blowing from the west. With a lurch and a bump and a twist about, the *Rose* changed course and picked up speed.

A panic breathlessness assailed Yaleen. However, she stood still and breathed slowly and pretended to herself that the *Rose* was merely afloat upon preternaturally clear water—and that a solitary cauliflower cloud down below was only a reflection of itself.

Before long they were crossing a featureless light brown plain. Beyond that plain long ridges of dunes, toothed with arrow-heads of sand, webbed the surface.

The invisible living current of air swept them onward, eastward.

Afterword

THUS it was in the time of Yaleen of Pecawar—perhaps!

Nowadays, of course, the whole of our planet has long since been thoroughly explored and thoroughly settled. We have launched machines and a handful of people into orbit around our world. There's serious talk of sending ships of space out to visit the moons of great distant gaseous Hepseba which shares this sun-space with us; though such a voyage would last for many years. Hepseba is so far away that it went unheeded by our ancestors. Some day in the distant future we might even go further, inconceivably further, to the stars to plumb the mystery of our origins.

Meanwhile we confront the mystery of these three texts discovered inside a fallen obelisk—twin to the so-called Obelisk of the Ship, buried by sand near the eastern edge of the Oriental Erg.

The Book of the River is an ancient printed volume. *The Book of the Stars* is a roll of antique newsprint tied with twine. *The Book of Being* is a bundle of manuscript papers written in three distinct and separate hands. Whereas most other ancient paper has perished over the centuries, down the millennia, these three examples were preserved by the dryness of the desert—and by their hiding place within mortared stones, which themselves were hidden inside a dune.

To say that we question the veracity of these texts is the wildest understatement. We well know that our ancestors were great romancers. (Admittedly, so are we; though nowadays we at least strive to be self-consistent in our flights of fancy!) And we know how they lived in an age of taboo and superstition—not forgetting the fungus-spore amnesiplague, which we have eradicated.

Yet why should these three documents in particular have been considered valuable enough to pack inside that obelisk? And considered so, by whom?

Had the erectors of that stone finger in this quixotic location simply found themselves one block short? Thus one of the construction crew, who happened to be a devotee of romances, used a book and a roll of newsprint and a manuscript continuation of those first two tales, as wadding to stuff into the vacant central space. And perhaps all the masons involved were romancers, since it's a romantic endeavour to rear a column of stones in a desert where it can only serve as a landmark to itself alone! Besides, as I say, at least three hands were involved in composing the third volume.

But now consider: if the first two printed books are "true", then the third book cannot possibly be true. And vice versa. Yet if the third book alone were true, how could it have been written? Most of it would have lacked foundations (much like the obelisk!).

Only the final section of *The Book of Being* strikes us as familiar in its portrayal of our world. On the other hand, all of the persons in this last part—barring one or two minor figures—are already established in the first two books.

And what of the section written in the second hand (and second person), entitled "All the Tapestries of Time"? Perhaps here we have a curious and cavalier attempt to connect the first two volumes with the reality of "The Rose Balloon". Perhaps this part was scribbled by one bored, though ingenious, stone mason whilst the construction crew sheltered in their tents during freak sandstorms. Let us imagine this author comparing notes constantly with a rival mason and would-be romancer who was busily scribbling the final part during those same storms. Both of them took as their starting point two genuine romances of the period. The first had been printed as a proper book. The second had been issued more cheaply—or more popularly?—on newsprint. And of course a partial continuation already existed in manuscript alone; which they happened to have with them in their tents. From which fact, do we deduce that a *third* mason was the original author—but he had run out of steam, and cared so little for the final product that it was left abandoned inside the obelisk as makeweight? Or that the masons feared they would die in the desert, and felt so proud of their collaboration that they sealed it inside the stones for safety?

Perhaps this is the explanation of *The Book of Being.**

As to the content of the first two volumes, what can one say? Except, to begin with, that in many respects our ancestors viewed the world upside-down! Thus the Tambidala River flows "down" to the north. Knowing only one river, they didn't feel the need to give it a special name; but being the only one, it was the norm. Now that we're acquainted with the other major rivers on our planet—all of which flow otherwise, from north to south—we would phrase this differently.

Secondly (and more important) through no fault of their own our ancestors were taboo-stricken; and being great romancers into the bargain they often thought mythically and metaphorically when treating taboo topics.

Thus the "black current" is a picturesque metaphor—a myth—used to express certain inhibitions which were programmed into us originally; which were built into our two core societies (on the east and west banks of the Tambidala) when this world was first colonized, as a way of ensuring our survival along lines presumably different from those of our mysterious mother world.

Likewise the "Godmind" is a myth representing our designers.

Likewise the epidemic of forgetting when Godmind and "Worm" first battled (an earthquake of the mind which is echoed later on by the final scribe's "Pause") reflects the spore-derived amnesiplagues which caused chaos at widely separated epochs in our consequently tattered and fragmented history.

Such examples could be multiplied.

Yet curiously, as myth these texts aren't as heroic in sum as one might expect of ancient days. They also mock themselves, especially when the final "stone-mason scribe"—in the process of purging the story of false infinities—chooses to make Yaleen marginal and submerged, rather than some hidden ruler of the world cloaked in disguise. Perhaps what we witness here (and elsewhere) is transitional

---

*In recent avant-garde numerology I believe there is a trick called "renormalization", whereby so-called "false infinities"—essential to the manipulation of esoteric theories of the universe—are subsequently got rid of, *purged,* so that an equation collapses back like a babel-house of cards into a single expression, presenting a single world, a single order. Temporarily an equation possesses an infinite solution—then suddenly a finite, graspable one emerges. I fancy that my (admittedly imaginary) masons may have been the precursors of such tricks, in words rather than in algebra. How they must have adored a concrete solution—to have set that stone finger amidst a shifting sea of sand!

myth: the withering of myth into ironic fancy in face of early indus-trialization and science.

Finally, "*Ka*-space" is a myth for some hyper-reality or dimen-sion, as yet unforeseeable by us—through which the original star-ship must have flown.

Might not "*Ka*-space", as envisaged by the Yaleen author, seem a dangerous myth today? One which might bring superstition back into the popular mind, to oust our rational sciences? How can we contemplate *Ka*-space when our greatest dream is to launch a puny ship, our best, to the world next door—on a journey of *many years?* *Ka*-space would dwarf our efforts.

Yet the imagination needs uplifting. Joy is not to be sniffed at. So therefore let these three books be printed out of our own resources, and enjoyed.

—*'Mistress Charmy-Chateline,*
Guild of Boats & Spaceships
(advised by Savant Perse-Kirsto)